TUESDAY'S

HIDE'N GO SEEK

MADDY'S FLOOR

Book #1–3 of Psychic Visions

Dale Mayer

Books in This Series:

Tuesday's Child
Hide'n Go Seek
Maddy's Floor
Garden of Sorrow
Knock, Knock…
Rare Find
Eyes to the Soul
Now You See Her
Shattered
Into the Night…
Psychic Visions 3in1
Psychic Visions Set 4–6
Psychic Visions Set 7–9

PSYCHIC VISIONS BOOKS 1–3
Dale Mayer
Valley Publishing

ISBN-13: 978-1-988315-72-0
Print Edition

Back Cover

Tuesday's Child

What she doesn't want…is exactly what he needs.

Shunned and ridiculed all her life for something she can't control, Samantha Blair has learned to hide her psychic abilities, forcing her to live on the fringes of society where she can only ever be a lonely outsider. Whether she wants this gift or not has never been in her power to choose. When she inadvertently taps into one killer's prey, she finds herself taking unwilling possession of another woman's body as she's being violently murdered. Only when death claims the victim is Sam released back to her own body. Her mind ravaged by the horror she's experienced each time, Sam has no choice but to seek out the only ones who can stop this atrocity. Getting the rugged, no-nonsense detective in charge of tracking down the serial murderer to believe her is her first obstacle.

Detective Brandt Sutherland only trusts hard evidence yet even he can't deny that Sam's visions offer him the very clues he could use to catch this elusive killer. Unfortunately, the more he learns about her incredible abilities, the more he realizes he's falling hard for this woman of profound grace and the clearer it becomes that her visions are putting her directly in the line of fire. How can't Brandt save her from something he can neither see nor understand…something she can't stop even if she desperately wants it to?

As danger and desire collide, the stakes are raised so high, they don't dare lose.

Hide'n Go Seek

Celebrated search-and-rescue worker Kali Jordon hides her psychic abilities by crediting her canine partner, Shiloh, with the miraculous recoveries made over the course of her career. The Sight Kali inherited from her grandmother allows her to unerringly track dark waves of energy back to victims of violence. She's managed to keep her secret safe…until a maniacal killer challenges her to a game of extreme Hide 'n Go-Seek that threatens the lives of those closest to her.

Pragmatic FBI Special Agent Grant Summers has sworn to protect her, but Grant's own honed skill of sensing what's beneath the surface goes haywire each time he's around Kali and Shiloh. He's certain there's more to both of them than meets the eye.

As the killer cinches a tighter and tighter web around Kali, there's no longer any place for them to hide. As she has so many times before, can Kali's visions allow her to trace the latest victim's whereabouts before it's too late, or will this diabolical game of Hide-and-Seek cost her everything?

Maddy's Floor

Are some souls not meant to be saved?

Psychic medical intuitive and licensed physician Madeleine Wagner thought she'd seen every way possible to heal a diseased body. But, when her patients begin dying from mysterious causes, Maddy realizes she might be dealing with an evil force that may be outside her ability to cure.

Maddy's medical facility, Maddy's Floor, has helped countless terminally-ill patients to miraculously live. Now something malevolent has taken up residence on the ward. Not sure how to deal with this on her own, she calls on her psychic friend and mentor, Stefan. Together, they delve beyond the physical plane into the metaphysical…and find utter terror.

With two family members in Maddy's care, Detective Drew McNeil finds himself wondering frequently during his visits about the woman and not just the miracle worker. Who takes care of this selfless soul who gives everything she has to save every single patient? When does she ever allow herself to rest, relax, and *live*? The more time he spends with her, the more he wants to get to know her privately.

Bizarre events in Maddy's facility draw Drew's professional curiosity. Several intersect with one of his cold cases, causing him to wonder if an old killer has been resurrected…literally. If so, Maddy's directly in the path of danger. Drew wonders, How can anyone stop a force of nature – whether good or evil – that no one else can see, feel, or, frankly, *believe*…unless Maddy has the ability to do all those things and more?

Sign up to be notified of all Dale's releases here!

http://dalemayer.com/category/blog/

Your Free Book Awaits!

KILL OR BE KILLED

Part of an elite SEAL team, Mason takes on the dangerous jobs no one else wants to do – or can do. When he's on a mission, he's focused and dedicated. When he's not, he plays as hard as he fights.

Until he meets a woman he can't have but can't forget. Software developer, Tesla lost her brother in combat and has no intention of getting close to someone else in the military. Determined to save other US soldiers from a similar fate, she's created a program that could save lives. But other countries know about the program, and they won't stop until they get it – and get her.

Time is running out … For her … For him … For them …

DOWNLOAD a ***complimentary*** copy of MASON? Just tell me where to send it!

http://dalemayer.com/sealsmason/

TUESDAY'S CHILD

Book #1 of Psychic Visions

Dale Mayer

CHAPTER 1

2:35 am, March 15th

SAMANTHA BLAIR STRUGGLED against phantom restraints. *No, not again.*

This wasn't her room or her bed, and it sure as hell wasn't her body. Tears welled and trickled slowly from eyes not her own. Then the pain started. Still, she couldn't move. She could only endure. Terror clawed at her soul while dying nerves screamed.

The attack became a frenzy of stabs and slices, snatching all thought away. Her body jerked and arched in a macabre dance. Black spots blurred her vision, and still the slaughter continued.

Sam screamed. The terror was hers, but the cracked, broken voice was not.

Confusion reigned as her mind grappled with reality. What was going on?

Understanding crashed in on her. With it came despair and horror.

She'd become a visitor in someone else's nightmare. Locked inside a horrifying energy warp, she'd linked to this poor woman whose life dripped away from multiple gashes.

Another psychic vision.

The knife slashed down, impaling the woman's abdomen, splitting her wide from ribcage to pelvis. Her agonized scream echoed on forever in Sam's mind. She cringed.

The other woman slipped into unconsciousness. Sam wasn't offered the same gift. Now, the pain was Sam's alone. The stab wounds and broken bones became Sam's to experience even though they weren't hers.

The woman's head cocked to one side, her cheek resting on the blood-soaked bedding. From the new vantage point, Sam's horrified gaze locked on a bloody knife held high by a man dressed in black from the top of his head down. Only his eyes showed, glowing with feverish delight. She shuddered. Please, dear God, let it end soon.

The attacker's fury died suddenly. A fine tremor shook his arm as fatigue set in. "Shit." He removed his glove and scratched beneath the fabric.

In the waning moonlight, from the corner of her eye, Sam caught the metallic glint of a ring on his hand. It mattered. She knew it did. She struggled to imprint the image before the opportunity was lost. Her eyes drifted closed. In the darkness of her mind, the wait was endless.

Sam's soul wept. Oh, God, she hated this. Why? Why was she here? She couldn't help the woman. She couldn't even help herself.

She welcomed the next blow – so light only a minor flinch undulated through the dreadfully damaged woman. Her tortured spirit stirred deep within the rolling waves of blackness, struggling for freedom from this nightmare. With one last surge of energy, the woman opened her eyes, and locked onto the white rings of the mask staring back. In ever-slowing heartbeats, her circle of vision narrowed until the two soulless orbs blended into one small band before it blinked out altogether. The silence, when it came, was absolute.

Gratefully, Sam relaxed into death.

Twenty minutes later, she bolted upright in her own bed. Survival instincts screamed at her to run. White agony dropped her in place.

"Ohh," she cried out. Fearing more pain, she slid her hands over her belly. Her fingers slipped along the raw edges of a deep slash. Searing pain made her gasp and twist away. Hot tears poured. Warm, sticky liquid coated her fingers. "Oh. God. Oh God, oh God," she chanted.

Staring in confusion around her, fear, panic, and finally, recognition seeped into her dazed mind. Early morning rays highlighted the water stains shining through the slap-dash coat of whitewash on the ceiling and the banged up suitcases, open on the floor. An empty room – an empty life. A remnant of a foster-care childhood.

She was home.

Memories swamped her, flooding her senses with yet more hurt. Sam broke down. Like an animal, she tried to curl into a tiny ball only to scream again as pain jackknifed through her. Torn edges of muscle tissue and flesh rubbed against each other, and broken ribs creaked with her slightest movement. Blood slipped over her torn breasts to soak the sheets below.

The smell. Wet wool fought with the unique and unforgettable smell of fresh blood.

Sam caught her breath and froze, her face hot, tight with agony. "Shit, shit, and shit!" She swore under her breath like a mantra.

Tremors wracked her tiny frame, keeping the pain alive as she morphed through realities. Transition time. What a joke. That always brought images of new age mumbo jumbo to mind. Nothing light and airy could describe this. Each blow leveled at the victim had manifested in her own body. This was hard-core healing – time when bones knitted, sliced ligaments and muscle tissue grew back together, and time for skin to stitch itself closed.

Sam understood her injuries had something to do with her imperfect control, paired with her inability to accept her gifts. Apparently, if she could surmount the latter the first would diminish. She didn't quite understand how or why. Or what to do about it. Her body somehow always healed, the physical and mental scars always remained. She was a mess.

The physical process usually took anywhere from ten to twenty minutes – depending on the injuries. The mental confusion, disconnectedness, sense of isolation took longer to disappear. She paid a high price for moving too soon. Shuddering, Sam reached for the frayed edges of her control. It wouldn't be much longer. She hoped.

Nothing could stop the hot tears leaking from her closed eyelids.

This session had been bad. Apart from the broken ribs, there were so many stab wounds. She'd never experienced one so physically damaging. Nervously, she wondered at the extent of her blood loss. If she didn't learn how to disconnect, these visions could be the end of her – literally.

Just like that poor woman.

Sam hated that these episodes were changing, growing, developing. So powerful and so ugly, they made her sick to her soul.

Several minutes later, Sam raised her head to survey the bed. The pain was manageable, although she wouldn't be able to move her limbs yet. Blood had soaked the top of the many Thrift Store blankets piled high on the bed. Her hollowed belly had become a vessel for the cooling puddle of blood. Shit. The stuff was everywhere.

The metallic taste clung to her lips and teeth. She rolled the disgusting spit around the inside of her mouth, waiting. She wanted to run away – from the memories, the visions, her life. But knowing that pain simmered beneath the surface, waiting to rip her apart, stopped her. Weary, ageless patience added to the bleakness in her heart.

Ten more minutes passed. Now, she should be good to go. Lifting her head, she spat the bloody gob onto the waiting wad of tissue and noted the time.

Transition had taken fifteen minutes this morning.

She was improving.

Oh God. Sam broke into sobs again. When would this end? Other psychics found things or heard things. Many of them saw events before they happened. She saw violence – not only saw, but experienced it too.

Occasional shudders wracked her frame from the coldness that seemed destined to live in her veins. The odd straggling sniffle escaped. She couldn't remember when she'd last been warm. Dropping the top blood-soaked blanket to the floor, Sam tugged the motley collection of covers tighter around her skinny frame. Warmth was a comfort that belonged to others.

She wasn't so lucky. She walked with one foot on the dark side – whether she liked it or not. And that was the problem. She'd been running for a long time. Then she'd landed at this cabin and had been hiding ever since. That was no answer either.

Her resolve firmed. Enough was enough. It was time to gain control. Time to do something. This monster had to be stopped. Now.

Christ, she was tired of waking up dead.

CHAPTER 2

10:23 am, 16th May

THE POLICE STATION, a huge stonework building, towered above Sam, blending into the gray skies above. Or maybe she just felt small. Insignificant. She couldn't imagine choosing to spend time in this depressing place. It only needed gargoyles hanging from the dormers to complete the picture of doom.

The entire idea of what these people did defeated her. She understood the necessity, yet given her insider knowledge, this whole human viciousness thing was too much. She wouldn't be here now except another woman had been murdered.

Given her past interactions with the police, even that wouldn't have been enough to make her sign up for more. The last cop she'd dealt with had been one bad-assed bastard.

No. The ring had brought her here.

This morning's killer had worn a similar ring to the one Sam had seen several months ago in another vision. She'd caught only a brief glimpse of it then, with the memory surviving transition to burn an indelible mark on her heart. Even the mask and gloves had looked similar. The biggest nail in this guy's coffin had been the energy. Like DNA, energy was unique, a personalized signature so to speak. Both killers had the same energy, the same variations in wavelengths and ripples. Even the same type of vibration. But that was hardly police evidence.

Knowing that some asshole had killed again, filled her heart with sorrow and slowed her steps. Several fat raindrops splattered her face – the joys of living along coastal Oregon.

The weather didn't bother her; the crowds and noise did. And the smell. Exhaust, sweat, and perfumes mixed to become something only a city dweller could love. No, the outlying community of Parksville suited her perfectly. The trip into

Portland was only twenty minutes on a good day.

Strangers with umbrellas shouldered past her. Would any of them believe her if she told them about the murders she'd witnessed, experienced? She'd faced distrust and skepticism with every foster family. As a precocious six-year-old, she'd told her foster mother's coworker to look after her son better. She'd been punished at the time. But when the boy had drowned in his backyard pool, Sam had really suffered. She'd been dumped back into the system and the label 'odd' had been added to her file. Her *gift* scared people.

Today, she had no choice. She had to come here. She couldn't stand by and let this guy kill again. Still, it was a long shot to ask the police to believe her when she couldn't supply a time frame, a name, or even the location of victim or killer. She just didn't know.

She squared her shoulders. Hitched up her faded jeans. No more. Disbelief or not, she had to do this. She ran up the last few steps.

The interior of the station felt no less imposing. Twenty-foot ceilings lined with dark wood created a doomsday atmosphere. Great. She lined up and waited. When her turn arrived, she stepped to the counter.

The officer glanced at her. "Can I help you, miss?"

Wiping her damp palms on the front of her jeans, she took a deep breath and muttered, "Yes." She paused, eyeing him carefully. How could she tell the good cops from the bad ones?

The older-looking officer, his expression encouraging and steadfast, helped calm her nerves. Except her ability to judge people had never been good. Sam hesitated a moment longer before the words blurted out on their own accord. "I need to talk to someone about a murder."

He raised his eyebrows.

"Two murders." Even she recognized the apology in her voice.

His eyes widened.

Okay, she sounded like she had one screw loose. Still there wasn't any delicate way to approach this. She dropped her gaze to her tattered sneakers, almost hidden beneath her overly long pants.

"What murders, miss?" His voice, so kind and gentle, contrasted with the sharpness of his gaze.

Shifting, she glanced around. She didn't want to talk about this out in the open. The line of people started several feet behind her. Still… She leaned closer. "Please, I need to speak with someone in private."

She twisted the ribbing of her forest green sweater around her fingers – a response to the intensity of his gaze. Catching herself, she stilled, as if locked in space and time. Not so her stomach, which roiled in defiance. This had to happen now, or she'd never be able to force herself back again.

When he nodded, she breathed a deep sigh of relief. "Thank you," she whispered.

"Go take a seat. I'll contact someone."

Sam spun away and stumbled into the next person in the line behind her. Flushing with embarrassment, she apologized and retreated to a chair against the far wall. She closed her eyes and rubbed her face as she tried to calm her breathing. She'd made it this far. The rest...well...she could only hope it would be just as easy.

It wasn't.

"Okay. Let's go over this one more time." The no-nonsense officer sat across from her in the small office. His crew cut had just enough silver at the tips to make him distinguished-looking, accenting what she suspected would be a black and white attitude.

He scratched on the paper pad for a moment and frowned. He tossed his pen and opened a drawer to search for another one. "*Two* women have been murdered? You just don't know *who*?" He glanced from his notes to her, in inquiry.

She shook her head. "No, I don't."

"Right," he continued, staring at her. "You don't know by *whom*? You say one man killed both women, but you don't know that for *sure*? And you don't know *where* these women could be. Is that correct?"

Sam nodded again. Her fingers clenched together on her lap.

"Therefore these women, *if* they existed and *if* they were murdered, could have lived *anywhere* in the world – *right*?" He quirked an eyebrow at her.

"Right, but..."

"Just answer the question. Could these women and their supposed killer be, for example, in England?"

Her shoulders sagged. Why couldn't anything be easy? "Theoretically, yes. But I'm not—"

"I have enough dead women right here in Portland to go after. Why would I waste time working on a 'possible two more' that could have happened anywhere? Not only that...you're saying that one woman was strangled and then stabbed and the other one was just stabbed. That's not normal. Killers tend to stick to the same method for all their kills." His annoyance pinned her in place. "Prove that a crime has happened."

The detective tilted his head back, his arms gestured widely. "Show me a body, either here or somewhere else, and I'll be happy to contact law enforcement for that area. Until then…if you don't have anything else, why don't we call it a day?" He waved in the direction of the door.

Sam stared at the irate officer, her initial optimism long gone. The problem was, everything he'd said was true. She didn't have anything concrete to tell him. She'd hoped the description of the ring would help validate her story. Frustration fueled her irritation. Both boiled over.

"It's because of my abilities that I know these murders occurred close-by." Sam poked her finger toward the floor. "I'm not strong enough to pick up images from so far away. These *are* your cases – you just need to identify them."

"How?" he snarled. "You've given me no physical descriptions, no names, and no location markers. How can I identify them?"

All the fight slipped down her back and drained out her toes. She studied him for a long moment. How could she get through to him? "The first woman will be in your case files and for this morning's victim…chances are it hasn't been called in yet. I'd hoped that knowing there was more than one victim would make you take notice." She paused. "Can't you use the ring to track the killer down?" She leaned closer. "He *will* kill again, you know. You *will* remember this conversation later."

He shrugged, his eyes darting to the open doorway. He was obviously wishing she'd disappear, preferably forever.

Sam assessed his face and found only disbelief. Her shoulders sagged. It wasn't his fault. He'd reacted as she'd expected. Skeptical and derisive. Sam flipped her braid over her back and rose. She'd tried. There'd be no help here.

"Fine. I don't have any proof, and I didn't think you'd believe me, but…well, I had to try."

She straightened her back, thanked the glowering officer, and escaped into the hallway. Ahead, the front glass wall glinted with bouncing sunlight. Freedom beckoned. Her pace quickened. By the time she'd rounded the corner and caught sight of the front entrance, she'd broken into a half run.

11:10 am

DETECTIVE BRANDT SUTHERLAND smiled at the young rookie. "Thanks, Jennie, I appreciate this."

Pink bloomed across her features, accenting her age, as did the ponytail high on the back of her head. Did they still wear those in school? As a new recruit, her arrival last week had caused quite a stir, her fresh innocence a joy to the department full of jaded detectives.

"Sure, any time." She gave him a shy tilt of her lips at first, which then turned into a real grin before she hurried back to her desk. Still in the hallway, Brandt opened the file and glanced at the photos. His stomach dropped. His mood plummeted further as he checked out the other pictures in the stack. Another one. Damn it.

A commotion down the hall caught his attention. Glancing up, he frowned. What was that? A small bundle of moving clothing and flying hair bolted toward him. Brandt jumped out of the way. His open file smashed against his chest, only to end up in her path anyway as the tiny woman dodged sideways in a last-ditch attempt to miss him.

"Easy does it. Watch where you're going." He reached out to steady her as she stumbled. His hand never quite connected as she slipped away like thin air.

Huge chocolate eyes, framed by long velvet lashes, flashed. "Excuse me," muttered the waif before she continued her sprint to the front door, her long braid streaming behind her.

"Wait," he shouted, but she'd gone, leaving Brandt with an impression of soft doe eyes – evocatively large, yet filled with unfathomable pain. Brandt felt like he'd just been kicked in the stomach – or lower. Mixed impressions from those eyes, flooded his mind. Frustration. Defeat. Pleading for help, but no longer expecting to receive any. Yet, he could have sworn he sensed steel running through her spine. Somewhere along the line, life had knocked her down, but not out. Never out.

He took several steps after her, only to watch her bolt out the front door.

Who the hell was she? He shook his head in bemusement. Two seconds and he'd felt enough for a psychological profile. Yeah, right. Still, how could anyone have that much torment going on and still function? Staring after her, he wished she hadn't escaped quite so fast. He didn't know what she needed or why, but surely he could have helped somehow.

His curiosity aroused, he walked into the office at the end of the hall, and studied the lone occupant. "Kevin, were you just talking to that young lady?"

"What young lady?" Detective Kevin Bresson looked up from his keyboard, his gray eyes confused and disoriented. Reaching up, he jerked on the knot of his tie.

"The tiny one that's all eyes."

Kevin's brows beetled together and then comprehension hit. "Oh, the skinny one." He shook his head and grimaced. "Jesus, I'd stay away from her, if I were you."

Brandt stared toward the front entrance, unable to forget her haunting image. Or his inclination to follow her. A compulsion he had trouble explaining even to himself. "Why?"

"The moon must be full or close to it – the wackos are coming out of the woodwork."

"She's nuts?" Brandt pulled back slightly, jarred by Kevin's comment. "No way."

"Yup, crazy as a bedbug." Kevin checked his desk calendar, pointed on today's date. "Look at that. I'm right. It is a full moon tonight."

Brandt readily admitted he didn't know much about the cosmos, still he'd have bet his last dollar there'd been sanity in those eyes. There'd also been a hint of desperation, as if she'd hit the end of her rope maybe, but at least she'd known it.

"So what did she want?" Brandt worked to keep the interest out of his voice.

Kevin tossed his pen down on the desk and leaned back. "She tried to tell me this crazy-ass story about waking up inside another woman while she was being murdered." Kevin snorted. "I've heard a lot of stories over the years, but that one topped my list."

Brandt straightened, stepped closer. "She's a psychic?" He didn't quite know how he felt about that.

Kevin shot him a disgusted frown. "If she is, she's not a very good one."

Brandt frowned. "Why? What did she have to say?"

"Something about a killer murdering *two* women. *Both* times, she says she witnessed the murders as they happened, from *inside* the dead women's bodies." Kevin shrugged as if to say *People, what can you do*? "Even odder, she says this killer used a different MO each time."

That was unusual, yet not unheard of. He only had to think of the animal he was hunting. If he was right about him, this guy constantly changed his methods.

"Did she offer any proof? Some way to identify the killer? Did she know who the women were?" At Kevin's shaking head, Brandt felt pity for the woman. He hadn't been here at this station for long and he didn't hold a position that invited confidences – only, detectives were the same across the country. Some were good cops with limited imagination, some had too much imagination and had a hard time playing by the rules. Kevin appeared to be squarely on the side of the disbelievers and rule makers.

Brandt, well, he'd admittedly done more rule breaking than was probably good for him. Old-fashioned detective work did the job most times, but not always. And he didn't give a damn where the help came from, as long as it came. He couldn't resist asking, "Anything concrete?"

"Nope," Kevin answered with a superior half-smile. "I told you – lots of nothing."

Brandt stared out the hallway teeming with people. It had to be lunchtime. "Damn." Just before walking through the doorway, he turned back one last time. "Nothing useful?"

"Nope, nada."

Disgusted, Brandt walked away. At least that partly explained the panic in her eyes.

"Except the ring," Kevin called out, snickering.

Brandt spun around. "Ring? What ring?" He walked over and put his palms on the desk. "You didn't mention a ring."

Kevin leaned back in surprise, his hand stalled in midair. "Hey, easy. I didn't think anything she said mattered."

"Fair enough." Grappling for patience, Brandt threw himself down in the chair. "What *did* she say?"

"Fine." Kevin shifted to the side and reached for his notebook. He flipped through the pages until he found what he wanted. "She didn't say much," he said, frowning at his notes. "She woke up twice 'inside' different women while they were being murdered. She sees what the women see and when they die, she snaps back into her own body."

Brandt frowned, puzzled. "Odd ability to have. Where does the ring fit in?"

"She said that when staring out of the women's eyes..." Kevin rolled his eyes at that. "She couldn't see much of the attacker because he wore a full ski mask, like a balaclava. You know the ones with only eye holes and a mouth hole. She remembers his eyes being black and dead looking. And..." he paused for effect.

Brandt glared at him in annoyance. "Come on...come on. Stop the melodrama."

"Jeez, you're a pain in the ass today. What gives?"

Brandt rolled his eyes. Camaraderie was slowly developing with Kevin. Brandt had joined the East Precinct four weeks ago, but on a temporary basis. His boss had arranged for Brandt to have an office and access to all files, current and cold, as he searched for information on a potential serial killer, before heading up a task force if his findings warranted one.

He'd come into contact with this killer years ago and had run him to ground in Portland a year ago. Then nothing. A year. He couldn't believe they still didn't have a lead. This killer had become his nemesis. His Waterloo.

Most of the guys here had accepted him. It would take time to develop more than that. Time he didn't have.

"Fine then." Quirking one eyebrow, Kevin continued to read. "She mentioned seeing a ring during the one murder, and then she thought she recognized it again during the second one," he said in an exaggerated voice.

"Did she describe it?"

Kevin nodded and glanced down at his notes. "Some sort of four-leaf-clover pattern with a diamond in each of the leaves. A snake, or something similar, coils between them. According to her, one of the stones was missing."

Brandt sharpened his gaze. "Color? Size? Gold? Silver?"

Kevin searched again through his notes and shook his head. Casting an eye at Brandt, he said, "She didn't say and...honestly, I didn't ask. I thought she was off her rocker." He scrunched his shoulder. "Jesus, her cases aren't even related, yet she says it 'feels' like the same killer. Something about having the same energy signature. Whatever the hell that means." He dropped his gaze, a frown furrowing his brow as he doodled on the corner of his notepad. "I gather you're not dismissing her story?"

Brandt considered that. He'd used psychics before. In fact, he'd been friends with Stefan Kronos for a long time. The reclusive psychic was a difficult person to get close to. And even more difficult to be close with. The man was painfully honest. Brandt knew what valuable information they could give, but also knew using them could be a crapshoot.

"I don't know what to think. The changing MO thing is unusual, but it happens. That's why I'm here, after all. Still, if she had concrete information, it would have been easy enough to check out against our cases. But she didn't though, did she?"

Kevin shook his head. "Not really. The last murder happened this morning, which could mean that we haven't found the victim yet, or it happened in a different country and we'll never hear anything about her. Oh yeah, this morning's victim had a tiled ceiling with deep crown moldings and frilly pink bedding. That is, if any of this can be counted on." He waited a heartbeat. "Here. Go for it. I'll log it in, but you can have this." He ripped off several pages from his notebook. "Personally, I think it's all bullshit."

Brandt half nodded and walked back to his office. Bullshit or not, he'd still check it out.

An hour later, Brandt slumped back in his computer chair, stumped. Killers were normally predictable in their methods. They stayed with what worked and few killers changed that. Those that did had been in business for a long time. They'd evolved. This made them incredibly difficult to hunt – as he well knew.

He checked Kevin's notes again. With only a comment or two on the women's hair and the way they'd died – it would be hard to identify the victims. He had too many possibles to sort through. In a busy metropolis like Portland, murder was an everyday affair.

Speaking into empty air, he said, "This is ridiculous. I need details, damn it."

He needed a time frame or details of the victims themselves. How could Kevin not have asked for more? Not that he could blame Kevin. The city was overrun with nutcases. Who could tell them from the *normal* people these days?

He scratched down a couple more questions before returning to his screen. This particular nut had a name – Samantha Blair. He tried to fit the name to the image of the skinny, panicked woman from the hallway.

Back at his screen, he brought up all the information the database had to offer, which was scant at best. She was twenty-eight years old with no priors, no outstanding warrants, and no tickets or parking violations.

The phone rang, interrupting his search.

"Hello."

"Hi, sweetie. How are you today?"

Brandt leaned back with a grimace. "Mom, I'm fine. I told you yesterday, the headache was gone when I got home. Nothing to worry about."

"Yes, dear. I just wanted to call and make sure you're feeling better."

"I am. How are you? Are you ready to leave that place yet?" Brandt pivoted in his chair to stare out the window. The sun had managed to streak through a few of the gray rain clouds, lighting the sky with colored swaths.

His mom should be sitting out on her little deck in the assisted living center a few miles out of town. She'd been happy there – too happy. This was supposed to be a temporary situation. Somehow, every time he mentioned her leaving, her lung condition or diabetes acted up or she came up with some other excuse to stay a little longer. The center didn't mind. They were in the process of adding a new wing to accommodate more seniors. His mom had money and paid her way. It was to be closer to her that he'd requested the switch in location to this particular station.

"I'm not that good. My hip has mostly healed, but it still feels weak." She sniffled slightly.

Brandt grinned. What her hip had to do with a fake cold was anyone's guess, still she pulled out a sniffle every time.

Her voice almost back to normal, she asked, "Do you have time for lunch today?"

"No. Today's not good."

"Oh dear. Well, how about tomorrow then?"

"Mom, I'd love to if it's just the two of us. No more prospective girlfriends, okay?"

"Now honey, I wouldn't do that. You explained how you felt about my 'interfering,' as you called it. But, still," the raspy voice dropped to a sad whisper, "I do want to see you settled before I die."

"Oh, hell," Brandt muttered. The sweet long-suffering tones somehow managed to convey lost hopes and dire endings soon to come. "Mom, you aren't dying. And I am in the hands of a good woman. Many good women in fact." Her shocked gasp made him grin.

"Don't say that. You need a wife, not those…those," she spluttered.

He couldn't help but chuckle at her outrage. She deserved it for her constant interfering in his private life. Her persistence came closer to smothering than loving.

Brandt groaned under his breath. He straightened, stretching his back. "Enough about my girlfriends. Mom is there anything else you need, because I've got work to do."

"No, I'll save it for lunch tomorrow at the Rock Cafe. Be there at one o'clock like you promised."

Brandt's chair snapped forward, his feet hitting the floor hard. "What? What's this?" She'd hung up on him. "Damn it."

Irritated, he stared at the phone in his hand. His mother's machinations were legendary, and though he hated being outmaneuvered, it was his fault. He'd been letting her get away with this for thirty-four years, so there'd be no changing the status quo now.

Good humor restored, he turned back to his computer screen. According to Kevin, Samantha lived in the nearby community of Parksville where she worked at a local vet's office part-time. The sparse facts didn't begin to explain the haunted weariness that had so touched him. He'd seen a similar look in the families of victims and those at the bottom of their world.

He forced his attention back to Kevin's notes. It appeared Samantha had said something about both women having long hair. The one from several months ago had been a blonde who'd been strangled. So, how many unsolved cases could he find with long-haired murdered victims?

His fingers flew across the keyboard. Three cases listed for the last year. One of them flagged as possible prey of the Bastard, the serial killer he'd followed to Portland. A killer that had been active for decades, possibly all over the States, with no one connecting the dots – until Brandt.

This killer's victims were always young, beautiful women that were either happily married or in strong, committed relationships. All had been raped. And that's where the similarities ended. Some women were strangled in their beds, some stabbed in their living rooms, others tortured for hours. Portland was the geographical center of the most recent attacks.

The police had an old DNA sample that had degraded over the years and a couple of hairs from very early cases – and no one to check them against. This asshole had started his career before the labs became so sophisticated. He'd adapted and learned well. To date, they had no fingerprints and no hits on any databases.

That's why Brandt had trouble convincing his boss that they

had a serial killer. Hence his job, pulling together everything he could find to get the backing for the task force to hunt down this asshole.

A knock sounded on the door. "Move it, Brandt. We've got another one."

CHAPTER 3

11:27 am

SAM SAT IN her dilapidated Nissan truck at the stop light. Who was that man she'd mowed down in the hallway? It might have been a fleeting contact, but he'd left a hell of an impression. Strong, determined, surprised and even concerned. Sam wrapped her arms around her chest. Not likely.

A honk from behind catapulted her forward. She drove down Main Street before pulling into the almost empty parking lot at the vet's office, her insides finally unfurling and relaxing after the tough morning. The animals always helped. It's not that she didn't like people, because she did. But the foster home mill hadn't given her much opportunity to understand close relationships.

Whenever she'd tried to get close to another child, either they or she'd ended up shipped out within a few months. Sam had grown up watching the various dynamics around her in bewilderment. From loving kindness, to sibling fighting, to lovers breaking up and making up, everyone appeared to understand some secret rules to making relationships work.

Everyone but her.

She'd tried several relationships, even had several short-lived affairs. In the last few years, they'd been nonexistent.

Sam locked her car and walked through the rear door of the vet hospital – her kind of place. She had a kinship with animals. They'd become her saving grace in an increasingly dismal and lonely world. She stashed her purse in the furthest back cupboard, peeled off her sweater, and tossed it on top. Then she tucked in her t-shirt and got to work.

Moving through the cages, Sam grinned at Casper, a tabby cat who'd lost his leg in a car accident. "Hey buddy, how're you doing?" She opened the door and reached inside. Instantly, the cat's heavy guttural engine kicked in. She pulled the big softy out of the cage, careful for his new stump. The bandage had stayed dry at least. That had to be a good sign. She gave him a quick cuddle. "Okay, Casper, back you go. I'll get you fresh water. And how about a clean blanket?"

Sam bustled about taking comfort in the mundane and in the service of others – animal others. She hummed along until she came to the last cage. Inside, a heavily bandaged German shepherd glared at her. She halted at the hideous warning growl.

She stretched out a hand to snag the chart hanging from the front of the cage.

The growls increased in volume.

Sam stepped back to give the injured animal more space. She'd intruded in his comfort zone, something she could respect. Bending to his level, she spoke in a soft voice. Without his trust, taking care of him wouldn't be pleasant for either of them. And this guy looked like he'd seen the worst humanity had to offer.

The growl deepened, but stayed low key – a warning without heat.

Sam could respect that, too. She sat cross-legged at the edge of his space and continued to talk to him until he calmed down.

"Hey, Sam. I didn't hear you come in." Lucy, the gregarious vet assistant's voice boomed throughout the furthest corners of the room, giving Sam no opportunity to ignore it. She hunched her shoulders at the intrusion, keeping her eyes locked on the dog.

"I came in the back," she called out in a low voice.

The dog stared at her.

Sam shifted slightly and narrowed her gaze. The shepherd's gaze followed every movement. She grimaced. Strange, but she could almost sense his interest.

"There you are. What are you doing sitting on the bare floor like that? You're going to catch a cold." Lucy's voice sounded behind Sam's shoulder.

Sam jerked then twisted around to greet the large older woman, and for a startling moment saw another Lucy instead – Sam's murdered best friend Lucy, from a decade ago. The long familiar brown hair appeared braided off to one side, with her sweet smile spread across her face. The image was old and faded and yet still heart wrenchingly clear.

Pangs of guilt wiggled in Sam's belly. The dog's low growl tore through the image. Sam shook herself, concentrating on the office manager and not her old friend. "Hi, Lucy."

The older woman fisted her hands on ample hips. "Come on out front and have a warm cup of tea."

Sam glanced at the dog. His black gaze locked on the two women.

Lucy reached down a beefy hand to help Sam get to her feet. Sam winced. This morning's vision had left her stiff and sore. Her police disaster had left her aching.

With slow careful movements, Sam brushed off her clothes and hung the chart back on the dog's crate.

"Jesus girl, you're freezing. Lord, this child can't even take care of herself, let alone no animals."

Sam shook her head at Lucy's habit of directing comments to the almighty above. Still, she had a point. Cold, Sam's constant companion, had settled deeper in her bones. She found herself propelled to the front offices and the small cozy lunchroom. There, a hearty nudge pushed her to the closest chair. Within minutes, a hot cup of strong tea with a gentle serving of cream arrived before her.

Lucy, with a second cup of tea, took the chair opposite Sam.

Unable – and unwilling – to stop them, Sam confronted memories of the other Lucy. That Lucy had loved her tea too. The two of them had shared many cups. During one such moment, Sam had broken her own rule and had trusted her enough to tell her about her 'gift.' Poor Lucy. She'd thought it had been so cool. Then one night after drinking too many B52s, she'd told everyone, once again making Sam an oddity – an outsider. And reminding Sam of a sad truth – even friends couldn't be trusted. A lesson she hadn't forgotten since. Her friend had died an ugly death. And Sam hadn't been able to help her. More guilt.

Sam sighed.

"Heavy thoughts," said Lucy gently. "Care to share?"

Sam's mouth kicked up at the corners. "Nothing worth sharing," she murmured.

Lucy leaned back with an unsurprised nod. "Just so you know I'm always here if you ever want to talk." After a moment, she continued in a bright cheerful voice. "Here, try one." A plate of cookies appeared beside the hot mug.

"Thanks." And Sam meant it. Choosing a peanut butter cookie, she bit into it. She closed her eyes, a tiny moan escaping. In the darkness, the rich, buttery peanut taste filled her mouth. Delicate yet robust and sooo good.

"Not bad, huh?"

Sam nodded, wasting no time in popping the rest of the morsel into her mouth. Lucy nudged the plate closer. Sam grinned, and snatched up a second cookie. Lucy gave her a fat smile of pleasure.

Her mouth full, Sam considered the woman beside her. This Lucy gave from the heart, freely offering acceptance and reserving judgment. Sam understood the value of the gift. At the same time, all that emotion made her nervous.

"Thanks for the tea and cookies." She took her cup to the sink.

"What do you think of our new patient?"

"The German shepherd." Sam spun around. "What happened to him?"

Lucy rose and brought her cup to the sink. "Sarah found him." Lucy turned around, "You remember my daughter, Sarah? She works at the seniors' facility…" Without waiting for a response, she continued talking. "She called in to say a resident had found the dog injured in the parking lot. Dr. Walcott drove over and picked him up."

Sam watched as Lucy turned on the hot water and dribbled a little dish soap over the cup in her hand. Sarah, she vaguely remembered was activity coordinator at a home between here and Portland.

Lucy gazed at Sam. "He was in tough shape. And since he woke up after surgery, well…" She placed the clean cup upside down on the drying rack. "He won't let any of us near him unless he's sedated."

Sam chewed on her bottom lip. "Is he eating? Drinking?"

"Through his IV," Lucy said with a small grim smile. "We'll see what he's like when it comes time to check his wounds. Don't get too attached. His prognosis isn't good."

Already halfway through the doorway leading to the back of the hospital, Sam stilled and glanced back, seeing only concern in the other woman's eyes. Resolutely, Sam headed back her charges.

The shepherd's low growl warned her halfway.

"It's okay, boy. It's just me. I'll be taking care of you. Give you food, fresh water, and friendship. The things that help us get along in life." Although she kept her voice quiet, warm, and even toned, the growl remained the same.

She couldn't blame him.

He might be able to get along without friendships, but she wanted them. Except for her friendship with Lucy, she'd never had that elusive relationship that others took for granted.

Sam approached the dog's cage with care. According to his chart, he'd had surgery to repair internal bleeding and to set a shattered leg. On top of that, he'd suffered several broken ribs, a dislocated collarbone and was missing a huge patch of skin on both hindquarters. Written in red and circled were the words: aggressive and dangerous. The growling stopped.

Sam squatted down to stare into his eyes. The dog should have a name. He didn't give a damn. But a name gave the dog a presence, an existence...an identity.

"How about..." she thought for a long moment. "I know, how about we call you Major?"

The dog exploded into snarls and hideous barking, his ears flattened, and absolute hate filled his eyes.

"Jesus!" Sam skittered to the far corner of the room – her hand to her chest – sure her heart would break free of its rib cage.

"Is everything okay back here?"

Sam turned in surprise to see one of the vets standing behind her, frowning. "Sorry," she yelled over the din of the other animals that had picked up the shepherd's fear. She waited for the animals to calm down before continuing. "I'd thought of a brilliant name for the shepherd, but from his reaction, I think he hates it."

The vet walked over and bent down to assess his patient. "It could have been your tone of voice or the inflection in the way you said the name. He'd been abused, even before this accident." After a thoughtful pause, he added, "I'm not sure, but it might have been kinder to have put him down."

"No." Sam stared at him in horror. "Don't say that. He'll come around." At his doubtful look, she continued, "I know he will. Give him a chance."

That she seemed to be asking the vet to give her a chance hung heavy in the room, yet she didn't think he understood that.

He stared at her, shrewdness, and wisdom in his eyes.

Then again, maybe she'd misjudged him. She shifted, uneasy under the intense gaze.

"We'll see. We'll have lots of opportunity to assess his progress as he recuperates."

Sam had to be satisfied with that. She knew the dog was worth saving and so, damn it, was she. Her salvation and that of the dog's were tied together in some unfathomable way. She could sense it. She'd fight tooth and nail to keep him safe.

In so doing, maybe she could save herself.

11:45 am

THE BASTARD HAD been busy.

Brandt grimly surveyed the room. The woman lay sprawled across the bed, killed by multiple stab wounds if the massive blood loss was anything to go by. Any number of perps could have done this, but Brandt knew the scene would be clean. Squeaky clean, just like every other one he blamed on this asshole.

And the woman would have drugs in her bloodstream, just enough so she wouldn't have been able to struggle – at least not much. A signature obvious from the more recent cases. Brandt frowned. This case would move to the head of Brandt's list. Ammunition for a task force to put this asshole behind bars.

His fists clenched and unclenched. Christ, he wanted to kill the Bastard himself.

Blood spattered the walls, carpet, the trashed bedding…a few drops even going so far as to hit the ceiling. A large pool of black blood had congealed on the floor beside the night table. This woman hadn't been murdered – she'd been butchered. She had to have been in a drugged sleep at the time of the attack. The only signs of struggle were on the bed, and not many of them, at that.

She also had long brown hair with a hint of a curl in it at the ends. Or would have had if the stands weren't flattened by the weight of the dried blood. The bedding was some kind of ruffled rose paisley thing. Two points to Samantha Blair. Deep crown moldings on the ceiling gave her a third.

"Brandt, the young man who called this in is waiting out back."

Adam was the youngest member of the team, with only six months' experience behind him. Always pale, today his red hair and freckles stood out more than ever, giving his face a clownish appearance. He tried to look anywhere but at the body on the bed. "Kevin said you can take the lead. He'll be here soon."

Another test. Fine with him.

"Then, let's go have a talk with the guy out back." Brandt headed outside of the brick house to question the waiting man.

Tall, slim, and overwrought, the mid-twenties man sat on the brick step, his hair was brush-cut and his head cradled by his folded arms. His blue shirt was soaked with tears and his shoulders heaved and shuddered even as Brandt watched.

Brandt waited to give the young man a moment. "Jason Dean?"

The younger man snapped to his feet, nodding in between the tears. "Yes, that's me. Is…is she being taken away now?" He wiped his eyes with his sleeve, like a young child.

Brandt glanced back inside the small dwelling swollen with law enforcement and CSI. "Soon. The coroner isn't quite done yet."

The man's face paled even further, and his bottom lip trembled. He took several deep, bracing breaths and nodded.

With gentle coaxing, Brandt managed to get the whole story out of him.

They both worked for the same company and had been going out for close to a year now. They'd gone out for dinner and drinks last night before returning to her place. He'd stayed for several hours, leaving around one-thirty in the morning. When she hadn't shown up at work, he'd called numerous times and then had slipped over to check on her.

After finishing with Jason, Brandt walked back inside to wait. Within minutes, Kevin arrived with the other two homicide detectives on the team, Daniel and Seth. Brandt paced back and forth in the hallway, chewing on the information in his mind while he filled them in on what he knew.

"It's him, isn't it? The one you're always talking about?" Daniel, the second youngest member on the team asked, a frown wrapped around his forehead. He tucked his thumb into his pant pockets. Daniel's paunch matched his wife's five-months-pregnant belly – a fact the team teased him about mercilessly.

Each team member in the East Precinct pulled long hours. Brandt respected that. He wasn't here to rock the boat. But any cases that could be the Bastard's, he wanted in on. Simple. And so far, nothing. Except more bodies.

Grimly, Brandt watched as the gurney was wheeled into the bedroom.

"Chances are good it's him. Toxicology should confirm it." Brandt leaned against the bedroom wall and tried to assess the scene – a difficult task with his emotions still unsettled. He'd have to wait for the tests to come back to know for sure.

She'd been deliberately arranged with her legs splayed wide apart, her arms above her head. Open display, mocking and degrading her for maximum humiliation. Another similarity between the killer's victims, posed…yet not always in the same way.

Irrational rage from a rational mind.

"Okay, we're ready to move the body." One of the CSI team spoke to them.

Brandt nodded. "Thanks. How's the scene? Are you going to be able to get much?"

The investigator shook his head. "Not much. The scene is clean. We might find something when we run our tests, but I'm not counting on it."

"Her name was Mandy Saxon," said Brandt abruptly. Her purse sat on the kitchen table, unopened and undisturbed, along with a briefcase of work she'd brought home. She'd been an accountant, a thirty-year-old junior member of a successful firm here in Portland, with her whole life ahead of her.

Now it was all behind her.

Stone-faced, the detectives watched two men bag and load the body onto the gurney before wheeling it out the door. Brandt would catch up with her at the morgue tomorrow.

Turning back, he caught sight of the coroner leaving.

"James, have you got a time of death?"

The grizzled coroner answered, "The best I can do at the moment, is between two and five." James shook his head. "I'll have more after the autopsy." The coroner walked out after smacking Adam's shoulder.

Turning back to the crime scene, Brandt watched as one of the CSI officers picked a tiny object off the carpet with tweezers. He waited until the item had been bagged and tagged.

"Stanley, what did you find?"

The man stood, holding the bag aloft for Brandt to see. "It appears to be a diamond or a zirconium. Have to wait until I get it back to the lab to know for sure."

Brandt stared at the tiny twinkling object. "Earring?" It could be the right size. He turned toward the open doorway. The stretcher had long gone. He'd have to wait to check what jewelry the victim wore.

He walked over to the open jewelry box on the dresser to

rummage through the few quality items inside. All the settings appeared intact. None matched the stone.

Stanley, who'd worked alongside Kevin and his team for over a decade, joined him. "I'll run it through some tests. It's pretty small, probably part of a design."

Like a four leaf-clover design? Brandt couldn't remember the exact details of Ms. Blair's statement. Had the ring always been missing one jewel or only the last time she'd seen it? Had she even mentioned that detail? He'd have to wait until he got back to the office to be sure – but it felt right.

That waif's story sounded beyond wild, but that look in her eye had been real. Whatever demon drove her, she believed in it. Staring down at the tiny jewel, Brandt realized he couldn't discount it either.

"Okay, keep me posted."

Stanley nodded and headed back to his kit with the evidence bag.

It took another hour before the room emptied, leaving only the brutal evidence of death behind. Bloodstains perpetuated the smell of death. Vestiges of violence remained behind. Brandt swore he could almost see and hear the play-by-play of her death from the scene laid out before him.

He didn't have psychic abilities in the normal sense, still, like many of his coworkers, he had a strong intuition. Whether it had developed through his years of police work or through his long friendship with Stefan, didn't matter. He'd learned a long time ago to listen to it.

And right now, it was screaming at him.

2:20 pm

KEVIN BRESSON PULLED into the station parking lot. Lunch was over and the place was packed as usual. Around the back of the building, he found a spot and parked. "Home sweet home," he said to Adam, who was sitting in the passenger seat beside him.

"If you say so."

Kevin glanced over at him. "Can't be cynical at your age. Come on, you haven't been on the force long enough for that. Give it a decade or two like me – then you've earned the right to be sour."

Adam got out and closed the door of the black SUV. He waited while Kevin grabbed his bag before walking to the rear entrance.

"I'm not being cynical, exactly. But it's a little hard to stay positive when you come from scenes like that one."

Kevin's normally stern face darkened. "I know what you mean."

Adam held the door open for him. "Do you think Brandt is right? That there's a serial killer working here?"

Kevin's pace never slowed as he headed for the elevator that would take them to their third floor offices. "I don't know. I've only seen some of the evidence. It would take more to convince me fully. Still, he has got a couple of valid arguments. Too many to discount his theory."

"He thinks this is another one."

"And that's possible. We'll work on it the same as every other case, and either he'll pull it for his list or he won't. We have enough work to do without keeping tabs on what he's up to."

"Right."

Kevin entered the waiting elevator with Adam on his heels. He was tired and fed up. The last thing he wanted was for Brandt to be correct and that a serial killer had been operating under their noses for decades. Just as the door was about to shut, a yell went up.

Kevin stopped the doors from closing long enough for Dillon Hathaway to get on.

"Thanks Kevin."

Dillon grinned that affable smile that always pissed Kevin right off.

"I hear you caught another bad one this morning. Let me know if you need any of my expertise to close this for you."

Kevin stiffened. Just because the 'kid' had a couple of college degrees didn't make him better than the veterans on the force. Now if Dillon had some experience to go with that piece of paper then people might be more inclined to listen. As it was, Dillon, in his late twenties, had only about six months of experience. Kevin wondered why he hadn't gone into business. He had that wheeling dealing kind of attitude and dressed the part too. He'd have done well.

Covertly, he studied Dillon's designer suit and lavender shirt. No wonder the guys in the department laughed at him. Although, it was his insufferable know-it-all attitude that made everyone want to kick his ass.

Adam wouldn't stay quiet. Kevin shot him a warning look, but it was too late.

"I think we can handle it. Other people, beside you, know how to do their jobs, you know."

Grinning, Dillon put his hands out in front of him in exaggerated supplication. "Hey, no problem, Adam. Just wanted to let you know that you can call on me any time. But I understand pride. So just trundle along in your usual way."

Kevin clenched his jaw and rolled his eyes. He did take pride in the number of cases he'd closed over the years. But no matter how many he solved or how many assholes he put behind bars, there were always a dozen more ready to take their place. If Brandt was right, they were in trouble. A serial killer with the skills to stay undetected for decades was just bad news – for everyone.

But working with Brandt was a different story than asking this young upstart for help. Brandt might be new to the department, but Kevin respected the man – unlike Dillon. Brandt was a straight up kind of guy who you could count on in a tight spot. What made working with him hard was his special assignment status. Not that he played the maverick card, but he worked with his own agenda.

Kevin wasn't sure what Brandt did all day exactly, only that he showed up for their meetings and any crime scenes that fit the parameters he was searching for. Cushy job if you could get it. As long as he stayed out of Kevin's way then he could work on all the task force preparations he wanted to – no harm done.

The elevator opened. Kevin, already focused on his job at hand, pushed all worries of Detective Brandt Sutherland from his mind.

CHAPTER 4

3:45 pm

SAM HIT THE next rut hard, bouncing across it before she had a chance to maneuver her truck to the left. Her driveway had more potholes and grooves than drivable surface – a free bonus with the cheap rent. Her little pickup shook hard with the next hit and never had a chance to stop trembling before it bounced again.

Sam grimaced. She'd soon be black and blue just from the trip home. Great, more bruises. As if she needed more pain. Turning the last corner, she leaned forward to see her favorite view.

The tree line opened to the full valley and lake. Glittering water glistened for miles. She lived for this moment. The hills and mountains in the horizon bled into wonderful shades of blue and the trees…the greens and yellows, an oil canvas of joy. She smiled. This vista sustained her soul as food never could.

Parking the truck, Sam hopped out. Off to the left she could see her small cabin nestled just far enough back from the shore to give a front yard. She realized once again how blessed she was to have been given a chance to live there. A perfect place to stop running.

When she'd found it, the owners – an older couple – hadn't wanted to rent it out. She'd been in dire straits and once they'd sensed that, their attitude had changed.

Sam appreciated their change of heart. Life had dished out a couple of bad months. She winced. Who could talk in terms of months? Her life had been a cesspool for years.

The sun twinkled overhead. She smiled at the sky. Opening the driver's door, she started to hop back in when pain lashed through her. Black tentacles reached inside her skull and clutched her brain, dropping her to her knees.

She cried out, her hands cradling her temple. She doubled

over, rocking back and forth, as darkness filled her mind. Her chest constricted. She struggled to breathe. Then she started to panic.

Just before she lost control, the curtain of blackness ripped aside. Sam breathed hard, struggling with the new images. They weren't of her truck or of the woods around her.

She stood outside a coffee shop in an area she didn't recognize. The only familiar thing came from behind her. A feeling, a gaze, an energy. Comprehension hit her slowly. "No," she cried, her hands covering her eyes. Pain seared her heart as her mind finally understood. Nothing could stop the tears from welling up and tumbling down her cheeks.

The killer had just found another victim.

3:55 pm

BRANDT PREFERRED TO gain information in a less formal way, yet his badge did loosen tongues. Or it had until Parksville. The rotund postal clerk hadn't recognized Sam's name until Brandt gave her a description. She'd clammed up immediately, to stare at him suspiciously. When he brought out his badge, she became even more belligerent – if possible.

"You can ask your questions over at the vet hospital as she works there part-time." She turned away to speak with another customer.

Dismissed, Brandt left – his curiosity aroused. He walked across the street to the Parksville Veterinarian Hospital and asked his questions there.

"Sorry, we don't give out personal information on our staff." The older woman was striking in her own way, except for the waves of protectiveness rolling off her. Odd, she too saw him as the enemy. Not an unusual reaction from the drug runners and hookers on the streets, but from someone who looked more at home dishing out apple pie and lemonade – very strange.

Brandt turned his badge her way.

She raised one eyebrow, yet didn't relax. Instead, she held out her hand. Brandt passed over his badge and watched as she wrote down the information before passing it back.

"Now, can you provide me with her address, please?" he said in his most official voice.

She appeared to consider his words. What required consideration he couldn't begin to understand. "Excuse me," he snapped. "Does she work here or not?"

"Yes, that's true. She does." The dragon smiled as if happy to be able to answer him.

"Good. I *need* her address and her phone number." Using his well-honed eagle eye, he stared her down.

To no effect.

"I don't think she has a phone." She assessed him again, with that same calculating look of his grandmother. "Why the interest?"

"It's personal, ma'am." Brandt had been thinking to save Samantha unnecessary questions about the police looking for her. Then he saw her knowing glance and groaned. Heat flooded his face.

The older woman smiled.

Brandt shuffled his feet as if still in high school himself.

Her smile widened.

Shit. Brandt couldn't believe it. He shook his head to clear his thoughts and tried to regain control of the wayward conversation.

"Police business," he clarified, hoping to get this conversation back on the right direction.

After another long look, the dragon, as if realizing he couldn't be put off, walked toward the desk, wrote something on a small scratch pad, and held it out to him. "Here you go – her address. Now, if you'll excuse us, we have to take care of our customers." She motioned to several people waiting behind him. "Hello Mrs. Caruthers. What's the problem with Prissy?"

Brandt snatched up the paper and strode through the front glass doors. Once outside, he glanced down at the address.

"Shit." She'd given him the same PO Box address he already had. Technically, she'd done what he'd asked, while avoiding giving him what he needed.

"Is there a problem, sir?" A competent-looking older man approached him. "I'm Dr. Wascott. This is my office. Maybe I can help you?"

Brandt smiled, happy to find someone normal in the town. "I'm Detective Sutherland." Brandt once again reached into his pocket and pulled out his badge. "I'm looking for directions to Samantha Blair's place."

"Oh." The older man smiled, his bushy brows giving him a Rip Van Winkle look. "That's easy. She's at the old Coulson homestead." He turned and pointed out the direction. "Head up the highway to the large gingerbread-looking house. Turn right onto the dirt road past the house and follow it all the way down to the lake. She's pretty isolated down there, but seems to enjoy it." He opened the front door of his office. "There's no problem, I hope?" He paused and looked back at Brandt, one eyebrow raised.

Brandt shook his head, tucking the slip of paper into his shirt pocket. "Not at all, I'm just checking on some information she gave us."

"Didn't think so. She's not the type." Smiling, the vet walked inside, the glass door shutting behind him.

Brant stared up the road. A gingerbread house – that should be easy.

4:09 pm

SAM DRAGGED HER sorry ass out of the truck and up the wooden stairs. The vision had left her feeling as if she'd gained a hundred pounds. Every shuffling step had become an effort. That insight into a killer's mind had been downright unpleasant. Knowing he'd found another woman, hurt her. That she'd had the vision at all terrified her. It was yet another sign her 'talent' was changing. And she didn't like it one bit. Her head throbbed from the remnants of sensory overload.

Moses barked excitedly, his madcap tail waving in the wind. He shoved his wet nose into her hand.

"Hey boy. Sorry to be so long today." She scratched the big dog's head. The golden haired Heinz 57 mix easily came to her mid-thigh. She smiled at the oversized black paws. Moses had been the main man in her life for a long time.

Shifting her library books, picked up over her lunch break, she strode up the front steps. On psychic phenomena, these books might hold the answers to her perpetual problem. At one time, she'd asked experts for help. Unfortunately, she'd chosen the wrong kind of expert.

Images of padded walls and needles slammed into her mind. Ruthless, and with more experience than she'd like to admit, she slammed them right back out again.

Moses slumped to the deck in his usual jumble of muscle and sinew, thumped his tail once, and fell back asleep.

"Good companion you are, Moses."

His tail thumped again, but he couldn't be bothered raising his head. Sam bent down to stroke his back. Her fingers slipped in and out of the thick golden pelt, enjoying the silky contact. A great sigh erupted from him, and he relaxed even further.

Sam laughed at his total exit from the world. He had the right idea. She needed sleep, too.

Exhaustion from her vision had caught up to her. Even running a hand over her forehead brought a tremor to her spine. After putting on the teakettle, she walked into the bathroom, dampened a washcloth, and wiped her face. The cool wetness helped refresh her.

Catching sight of her face, she winced. Her porcelain skin – always translucent – now seemed paper thin, transparent even. She looked friggin' awful. She closed her eyes, shocked at how far her health had sunk. If she didn't find answers soon, her 'gifts' would kill her.

She was halfway there now.

While she walked through the tiny cabin, loneliness crept in. She stared at the plain walls, her hip propped against the counter and a hot cup of tea warming her hands. The support walls were old logs and the floorboards had been cut from hewn wood. They'd worn down in places and would have some incredible stories to tell if they could talk. Unfortunately, in her case, they could. Depending on the day and the strength of her energy as to what signals she picked up, the stories went from unsettling to downright nervy.

Moses raised his bushy head and growled. Sam glanced around, puzzled. "What's the matter, Moses?"

He growled again, staring at the place where the driveway drove out of the evergreens at the top of the ridge.

Sam gazed out the living room window, but couldn't see anything. Living out here, wildlife often shared her space. She loved watching the deer make their way to the river for a drink. Thus far she'd also seen raccoons, coyotes, and once, in the evening, a bear. If the animals left her in peace then she'd be happy to return the courtesy.

A faint rumbling told her what she needed to know. A vehicle. She retreated into the house, a leery eye on the driveway. It didn't take long before a black pickup bounced into view and rolled to a stop at the porch stairs.

A tall, rugged man got out, removed his sunglasses, and tossed them on the dash. He appeared vaguely familiar, yet she couldn't place him. Using the one gift that she'd come to accept, Sam assessed the waves of determination pouring from his shoulders. This man was nobody's fool. And he wanted something from her.

Moses growled again.

That face. The lock of brown hair falling down on one side, piercing eyes and a 'take no prisoner' attitude, dressed in denim. He was a cop. Recognition flickered. He was the man she'd almost run into at the police station. Curiosity and fear mingled. What could he want? Her stomach acid bubbled as tension knotted her spine. She chewed her fingernail as his six-foot frame climbed the stairs.

The heavy pounding on the other side of her head startled her. She cursed silently, but with full force, letting it bounce around inside her mind. She wiped her moist palms on her jeans, and opened the door.

"Yes?"

His brow furrowed. "Samantha Blair?

She frowned. "Maybe. Who's asking?"

An odd light shone deep in his Lake Tahoe blue eyes. "Detective Brandt Sutherland, at your service, ma'am."

"Your badge, please," she said.

His eyebrow quirked, still he didn't say anything. He reached into a back pocket and withdrew it for her.

Sam plucked it from his fingers. She read the number on it several times, committing it to memory.

He reached for the badge. "Satisfied?"

Sam handed it back to him. "Maybe. What can I do for you?"

Tucking his badge away, he stared at her, an odd glint in his eye. "You spoke with Detective Kevin Bresson at the station this morning, correct?"

Nerves knotted her stomach tighter, pulling down the corner of her mouth. Sam frowned at him. What was he up to? "Yes. You saw me there." Her stomach heaved. "What's this about?"

He shifted his weight. Why? He didn't seem the type to feel discomfort about much in life.

"May I come in?"

She considered his request for a long moment before opening the door wide.

Moses followed, staying close to her side, and nudged her leg. She dropped her hand to his head, reassured by his warm presence. "Good boy, Moses."

Big brown eyes laughed up at her, his tongue lolling to one side.

"Moses, is that his name?"

Sam nodded slowly, studying this lean muscular male, hands fisted on his hips, as he watched her. Raw sex appeal oozed naturally from his very presence. She frowned. He was too damn appealing. She didn't like that. Cops were not her favorite people. Sexy ones definitely didn't make her list.

Glancing around the small living space, she realized she didn't know what to do. She'd never had any company here before. Did a police visit count as company? Did she sit down with him? Offer him a cup of tea or what? Awkward – and hating the uncertainty – she repeated abruptly, "What do you want?"

He surveyed the simple living room, walked over to an old sofa, and stopped. "May I sit down?"

With a new perspective, Sam saw the threadbare furniture for what it was – shabby signs of dire poverty. It wouldn't have mattered any other time – after all, she lived it. She didn't understand why it mattered now. "Sure."

She sat on the couch opposite, trying to understand why he intrigued her. He glowed – with life, with health. He had so much vitality that everything around him paled by comparison. His energy was a beacon she couldn't help but find attractive – the lure of warmth and strength, something she'd experienced little in life. He dwarfed everything in the small open room. Sam felt tiny, insignificant against his more dynamic presence.

He reached across and placed his huge hand over hers.

Sam froze. His touch burned into her icy hands. Heat flared. So did confusion. Attraction. Hatred. Pain. Heat. Everything rolled together. Her gaze flew up to meet his.

He squeezed her fingers. Only then did she notice she'd been twisting her fingers around and around in a nervous pattern. A habit she'd tried to break for years. She yanked both hands back and tucked them under her thighs, leaning back. Heat still pulsed inside her veins. Heat she wanted to nestle closer to, yet couldn't explain why. Or didn't dare try. Nervous energy bubbled up. She clamped down hard and forced her errant muscles into stillness. Sam waited for him to speak.

"Are you okay?"

She jerked her head up and down.

"Good. Then let's go over the statement you gave Detective

Bresson."

"Why? He didn't believe me."

"But maybe I will," he countered. "So, please, from the beginning."

The beginning. She cast a careful eye over him.

He prompted. "You said you woke up inside a woman's body as she was being murdered?"

Oh, that beginning. Relief blossomed, and she settled back into the couch. Slowly, succinctly, she explained her story again.

"Any idea if his ring had real diamonds in it?"

She glanced at him in surprise. "No. I wouldn't know the difference."

"Could you see the woman's hair?"

"This one had long brown hair. I think it had a slight curl to it."

He raised an eyebrow at her and pursed his lips. "Curly?"

Sam swallowed hard several times, overwhelmed with the memory. Soft and feathery, the dead woman's beautiful curls had stroked against her neck with every twist and turn of her head as she fought for her life.

Locking down her grief and stiffening her spine, Sam explained. "I could feel it curling around my neck."

The look on his face eased.

Sam had no idea if he believed her or not.

"Can you tell me anything about his height, the clothes he wore, the type of mask he had on…anything?"

His mask. Shivers raced down her spine. The madness in those eyes – those glowing orbs still made her nightmares hell. Green neon had shone with joy at the pain he had inflicted.

Sam could hardly speak. Her voice hoarse from unshed tears, she explained what little she'd seen, and the impression the killer had left on her. She hunched her shoulders against the lingering horror, hating the power the memories held over her.

He asked a few more questions. She slid into monosyllabic answers, wishing he'd finish and leave.

Finally, he snapped his notebook closed and tucked it into his shirt pocket. "Thanks." He stood and walked to the door, and turned back to face her, pulling out a business card.

"I don't know if I believe you or if what you've given us even helps, but I appreciate you having come in to share your information. If you think of anything else, please let me know." He nodded politely and walked out.

Now that he appeared ready to leave, Sam's emotions scattered. She didn't know what to make of him. His presence confused her. Interested her. Intrigued her. Memories dictated that she should be angry, scared even. But she was none of those.

Sam trailed him onto the porch. The detective hopped into his truck and drove off. He never looked back.

Sam stayed, bemused, until his truck bounced and shuddered out of sight. For the first time in years, a faint hope came into being. Maybe something could be done after all.

"And just what the hell was that all about, Moses?"

His heavy tail brushed over the wooden planks. Not much of an answer, still it was the only one she was going to get. She headed back inside, Moses at her heels. A chill settled into the room – or maybe it was into her soul.

She wandered around the now seemingly overlarge, empty space...lonely space. The ancient floors creaked under every step in a rhythm that was almost comforting.

The detective probably considered her a suspect by now and if not he would soon. That's how they worked. The police were suspicious of anyone odd. She knew that. She'd come under their scrutiny more than once. But especially from one detective.

Her thoughts blackened at the reminder. That man had been out to get her, and she'd only been trying to help. Damn him.

Even if this detective did put her on his suspect list, she had no one to blame but herself. She'd known it was likely to happen. Still, she'd had to do something. Those women had no one else.

A shiver of apprehension raised goose bumps on her arms. The last thing Sam wanted was to have her life examined under a microscope. She avoided people because she couldn't stand their questions. And sooner or later, everyone asked questions.

5:19 pm

BRANDT GRINNED AT his mother's antics. He'd stopped in at her self-contained unit in the seniors' complex, for coffee and to apologize for canceling out on lunch tomorrow. It didn't take more than a few minutes to realize that some things never change.

A beautiful young woman, Lisa, knocked on the door not five minutes after he arrived. Maisy wasted no time inviting her in to meet Brandt.

An obvious setup, yet no different from what his mother put him through on a regular basis in her quest to see him married. Not that old age had crept into her bones, nor had her health deteriorated. Still, she sought grandkids in the worst way. And she had no compunction about using underhanded methods in achieving these goals.

Studying Lisa more closely, he could see the classical beauty his mother would think appropriate. Baby blue eyes with a guileless innocence, long straight blond hair and a slim, but curvy shape. And none of it mattered to him.

All he could see were Sam's haunting eyes. He had no idea if Sam's body curved or bumped. He knew she had a slight build and that she didn't eat enough. With her oversized sweater on, not much else showed. He didn't quite know how he felt about this interest, but was willing to see where it went.

He understood that his 'type' was fluid and fluctuated on impulse. He considered that normal. That didn't mean he chose to go out with all of the women who appeared on his radar.

"Brandt. *Brandt*?"

Brandt focused on his mother and smiled sheepishly. Her knowing smirk immediately put him on his guard. With a sinking feeling, he realized he'd been staring at Lisa too long. He groaned softly. Maisy's smirk widened.

"Now Brandt, I know she's adorable. Do try to concentrate, dear."

He rolled his eyes and stood up. "I'm sorry, ladies. You'll have to excuse me. It's time for me to head out."

"Oh, no," Maisy cried out. "You never stay for a real visit. Won't you stay for dinner at least?"

Trust her to ignore the fact that he'd been here for dinner just a couple days ago. Today, he'd come straight from Samantha's hideaway, needing a touch of normalcy after seeing her. Only to realize that he preferred Sam to the Lisas of the world. How contrary could he be?

He excused himself from dinner and said his good-byes. The sky had clouded over giving an unusual darkness to the horizon. Once in his truck, his mind immediately returned to the tiny woman with a huge impact. Sam and that overgrown mutt, Moses, had chosen a singular existence out in the middle of nowhere. The dog had been protective when Brandt first arrived. After a once-over he'd gone and lain down. A guard dog would never have done that.

Pulling off to the side of the road, he called into the office for updates. Then he tried calling Stefan, his difficult, contrary, and incredibly gifted psychic friend. And left another message.

Given the lateness of the hour, he decided to go home and mull over the contrariness of human attraction.

CHAPTER 5

11:05 pm

LYING IN BED that night, Sam couldn't sleep. Her overwrought mind refused to let up. The tantalizing possibility that she was meant to do something with this gift worried at the frayed edges of her mind. Depressed and unsettled, she fell into a fitful sleep, her dreams dark and disjointed pieces of past visions.

Screams jarred her from a deep sleep. Confusion turned to fear when Sam realized the horrific sounds were coming from her own mouth. Even worse, she had no idea where she was.

Terror overwhelmed her. Her fingers spasmed in a death grip around a strange steering wheel as the car she drove careened further out of control. Still trying to toss off the remnants of sleep, Sam yanked hard on the wheel in a futile attempt to turn it. The mid-sized car plowed through a steel barricade to hang suspended in midair before plummeting to the rocks below. Screams ripped from her throat and she reefed again on the useless steering wheel, helpless to stop the deadly impact. Her foot pounded on worthless brakes. The front grill of the car crumpled and metal buckled upward. The car slammed into the first of the rocks below, snapping her forward into the windshield.

Agonizing pain radiated off her shattered spine. Grinding metal, exploding glass, and continuous crunching sounds filled the air as first the bumper flew off, then the rear window shattered outward. The car tumbled, smashed on a huge rock, careened to the left and flipped end over end before coming to a hard landing on its wheels, right side up at the bottom of the cliff.

Then utter silence.

Sam trembled. Shock and pain pulsed through her veins even as her blood dripped out one beat at a time onto the shredded seat beside her. God, she didn't want to die.

She wanted to live. Please, dear God.

Someone help!

Blood streamed over her face, her spine…where a shearing heat set off continuous stabbing pain. The steering wheel jammed into her ribs. The front dash had crumpled into a mess of twisted steel and plastic. The famous Mercedes emblem now hung drunk in midair over the remains of the once beautiful cream leather seats.

Sam couldn't feel her right arm. And wished she couldn't feel her left. She closed her eyes, willing away the image of bone shards that had sliced through her sweater, a few loose strands of wool clinging to the ends. Heart wrenching sobs poured from her throat, tears coated her cheeks. She was alone. And dying.

A brilliant flash of light engulfed the car as the fuel from the pierced gas line flashed into flames. Heat seared her lungs and scorched her hair, the strands melting against the inside of her car window. Panicked, she screamed as flames licked at her feet, burning, and cooking the flesh right off her bones.

Agony. Pain. Terror.

A voice whispered through the blackness of her mind, so odd, so different it caught her attention. She strained to hear the words.

"Let go. It's time to let go."

Sam stared through the flames, stunned. *Let go of what?* She couldn't hear over the roaring fire and could barely see, but knowing that someone was there stirred her survival instinct and she started fighting against the seatbelt jammed at her side. She was saved. Just another minute and they'd open the door to pull her free. She'd be fine.

"Please hurry," she cried out.

"Let go. You don't need to be in there. Let it all go, and come with me."

She peered through the golden orange windshield to see a strange male face peering at her through the flames.

He smiled.

"Come with me."

"I want to, damn it. Can't you see I'm trapped?" she screamed, her vocals crisping in the heat.

"Release yourself. Come with me. Say yes."

The pain hit a crescendo. She twisted against it, hearing her spine splinter. The car seat melted into her skin. So much pain, she couldn't breathe. Blackness crowded into her mind, blessed quiet, soothing darkness. She reached for it.

"Let go. You don't need to go through this. Hurry."

She started. Why wasn't he opening the door or getting others to help? He should be trying to save her. Shouldn't he? Sam, so confused and so tired she could barely feel the pain overtaking her body. Where had he gone? She tried to concentrate. His face was now only a vague outline that rippled with the heat waves. A soft smile played at the corner of his mouth. The flames burned around him, weird as they centered him in the warm glow. She wanted to be with him. To live.

"Here, take my hand."

Dazed and on the brink of death, Sam focused on the hand reaching for her. She struggled to raise the charred piece of flesh that had been her arm and reached out to grasp his.

She was free.

Overwhelmed, cries of relief escaped. She turned to hug her savior, her head just reaching his shoulder. He stood beside her, the same radiant beaming look on his face. His blond hair glowed, and he had the brightest teeth.

She sighed. This beautiful man pointed to her right arm. Confused, Sam glanced down at her burned arm, realizing she could feel none of her injuries. Just like her other one, her broken arm had miraculously healed – whole, smooth, and soft. Her skin hadn't looked this good in ten years.

Realization hit.

She spun around to find a massive fireball below. What the hell? She had to be dead. But instead of the horror or shock, she expected to feel, she felt good. In fact, she felt great. She turned to the ever-smiling stranger.

"Let's go, sweetheart."

Sam didn't know why he'd called her that, but she bloomed under his loving gaze. Honestly, she was so damned grateful to be out of the car, she let him get away with it.

Holding hands, they floated higher into the cloudless blue sky. Then when the crash site below had become a tiny speck, Sam felt a hard flick on her arm and the words, "Thanks. I can take it from here."

And she woke up.

6:05 am, June 16th

STUNNED AND DISORIENTED, Sam lay rigid in bed. The sense of loss overwhelmed her. *He* was gone. She needed his gentle warmth. He made her feel loved and cared for. Bereft, hot tears welled at the corners of her eyes. She didn't want to be back here in her own body. She wanted to be that other woman. That lucky woman.

Sam stopped in shock. That woman was dead! How lucky could that woman be? She'd be fine now, happy and at peace…with that man at her side. Lucky to be so loved.

And who the hell was he?

Sam couldn't believe her vision. Even now, instead of being overwhelmed with shock and pain, she felt uplifted.

Mystified, she questioned the difference this time. Not the death itself, that part unfortunately, had been normal, right down to the excruciating pain. But afterwards…? She didn't know who the man had been or what he might have been to the victim, but he'd cared about her. She wished she'd had her wits about her to talk to him at the time. Now it was too late.

There'd been one other major difference in this vision.

Always before, Sam had been forced to endure the horror of what one human being could inflict on another. This had been her first accident. Or was it?

What's the chance someone killed the woman to make it appear like an accident?

Sam narrowed her eyes, thinking. Given her relationship to violence – and there's no doubt the woman had died a violent death, had foul play been involved? Sam replayed the video locked into her psyche. The brakes hadn't responded, neither had her steering wheel – then they weren't built for flying. Suspicion remained. Intuitively, she felt more was involved. But could she prove it? No. She did know the woman had not been sleeping at the wheel or drunk. Living her last moments had given Sam clarity into the woman's mental state. There hadn't been any drugged or hallucination type of sensation.

Her car had to have been sabotaged. Sam snorted and threw back the blankets. So what? Just because she 'thought' foul play had been involved didn't mean it had been. Or that she could convince the police of it.

Grabbing up her journal, she wrote down as many details from this vision as she could. A process she went through every time. The impressions about the man were so clear, so poignant she had to write them down. Finally, she was done. Closing the book, she put it beside her bed, ready for the next time. She stared at it for a long moment. If anyone found her journals…she glanced over at the box beside her suitcase…they'd be used as evidence against her.

She had to question what her role was this time. She hadn't been able to help the poor woman. If she had a 'gift' then she wanted – no *needed* – to use it to make a difference. And had yet to do so. The idea, the concept…to help the victim find justice tantalized her. And then again, attempting to help these women meant working with the police. Bile immediately bubbled up in her stomach.

Sam leaned over, reaching for clean jeans and a t-shirt – dressing while deep in thought. Making a quick decision, she reached for the card and punched the number on her cell phone before she had a chance to change her mind.

"Hello?"

Fear caught her sideways. Words refused to come out.

"Hello. Who is this?"

The sharp demanding tone made her wince. She glanced at the clock on the stove and grimaced. He'd been asleep.

"God damn it, answer me." Anger reached through the phone to squeeze her vocal cords.

Samantha rushed into speech. "It's me. Huh, hmmm, Samantha Blair."

"Samantha," he said, enunciating the words slow and clear as if trying to place her.

"You came out to my place at the lake to ask me some questions yesterday," Sam started to explain.

"Oh. That Samantha." The anger shifted down to a growl.

She could almost see him shift into gear.

"What can I do for you?"

"Umm." Now that she had him on the phone, she didn't quite know what to say. "I know that some of the stuff that I told you might have been a little difficult to believe." She paused, not quite knowing where to go from here.

"Maybe," he answered, huskiness clouding his voice as if he was still groggy from sleep. It did funny things to her stomach.

She focused on his answer, his wariness. Determinedly, she forged ahead. "I saw an accident happen this morning. I thought if you could verify these details, you might have more faith in the other information I gave you."

Dead silence.

Oh God, why had she called him? She chewed on her bottom lip. What madness possessed her to call? She glanced out the window. It was just starting to get light outside.

"What kind of car accident?" His voice sounded brisker, more alert.

"A woman drove over the cliff and crashed onto the rocks below." She hesitated for a moment then rushed into speech. "The thing is…this time I recognized the spot. She drove off at Emerson Point."

"Emerson Point?" Now she had his attention. He was all business.

Feeling reassured, she continued. "Yes. She went through the guardrail. The car landed on its wheels before exploding."

"Hmmm. Time frame?" He cleared his throat.

That husky sound made her stomach do a slow tumble. Sam struggled to consider his question. But images of him leaning against the head of his bed, running a hand through his ruffled hair, the blankets resting low on his hips made her swallow and close her eyes. What had he asked? Oh yeah, it had been something about time frame. Had the accident been in real time? She cleared her throat. "About thirty, maybe forty minutes ago."

"You think?"

She hated the apologetic tone in her voice. "I woke as it happened. All I can say is that I think it played out in real time."

More digestive silence.

"Right. Make of car, color, and license plate? Anything specific that you can tell me."

"I experienced her death the same as always. So, I couldn't see the license plate because I was, in effect, driving the car. She drove a dark colored Mercedes. I don't know the model."

"How did you know the type of car then?"

"Because I could see the logo inside the car."

Sam could hear the scratching of pen on paper. She waited.

"Right. Anything else?"

"Her name was Louise." Sam's voice hitched and stopped, surprised. Where had that come from? The name danced through her head. It felt right.

She took a deep breath, knowing this could be the point where he suspended belief. "And I think she was murdered."

6:30 am

BRANDT RUBBED THE sleep from his eyes. Jesus, what a way to wake up. Every time he spoke with this woman, he couldn't get a grip on her. Was she for real?

He threw back his duvet and headed for a shower. At least this time, she'd given him something concrete. If it checked out.

Two hours later, at the station, he stood frowning down at an accident report in his hands. Incomplete as yet, just chicken scratch as the cop on the scene hadn't had a chance to finish the paperwork.

"Jackson, any sign of foul play?" Brandt glanced up from the paper, his piercing gaze nailing the young traffic cop.

"No, sir," Jackson said shifting his large weight from one foot to the other. "Not that I could see."

The younger man rubbed his face, fatigue pulling on his skin, giving him a much older appearance. The job did that to everyone after a while. "There isn't much left. The fire burned everything to ash."

"There weren't any secondary vehicle marks on the highway indicating she might have been forced off the road?"

"No, nothing like that. Her car headed straight for the guard rail, went through and over."

Brandt shot him a hard look. "Suicide?"

Jackson shrugged. "No idea."

He looked like he didn't give a damn. It must have been a long night. Brandt nodded and handed back the report. "We'd better find out." He turned away, heading down the hallway.

"Uh, Brandt, sir?"

Brandt stopped before slowly turning around. "What?"

"Do you know something about this woman? Something that pertains to the case? Because this seems straightforward. Open and shut type of thing."

You mean, 'you don't want to be bothered' type of a thing, Brandt thought, his cynicism rising to the surface. Too often, it was more a case of working in the areas where progress could be made and leaving the time-wasting for others. Still, his placement here put him in an awkward position.

"Maybe," Brandt answered. "Then again, maybe not." He turned and walked away. He needed to talk to Samantha again.

The hot July sun shimmered between the leaves to bounce off the hood of his truck as he drove past the gingerbread house. The place was a remarkable landmark. Further down, fir growth grew thick on the left and several poplar groves dotted the fields on the right. Signs of improvement done over the years blended into the natural habitats. Drainage ditches ran along the side of the well-maintained road. Generations had put their heart and soul into developing this place.

Brandt could only wish he had something as nice to pass on to his kids.

Kids. He grimaced. He didn't dare go there. It led to his mother and all her machinations. The truth was, at thirty-five he'd given it a whole lot more thought than he wanted to admit. Especially to his mother. He saw the worst that people could do to each other, and at other times, events were so poignant they made his heart hurt. It was at those times, he gave serious thought to his future. Thankfully, these lapses were short-lived. The divorce rate in his profession was out of this world. He'd be willing to try, but honestly, he'd never met anyone he couldn't live without.

Besides, it would take a unique woman to accept his work.

He rounded the last corner. The old homestead sprawled off to one side, lazy and serene. Except for the dog barking on the porch, the cabin appeared deserted.

Braking, Brandt brought the truck to a gentle stop beside her red one. Was that rust or paint that gave the vehicle its color? He studied it closer as he opened his door and hopped out. It didn't look road safe. He frowned. She needed a better set of wheels.

The screen door banged shut.

Brandt turned quickly. Sam stood, arms akimbo, apparently surprised to see him.

"Louise Enderby drove her Mercedes off the highway between 5:45 and 6:15 this morning," he said as way of greeting. Alarmed, he watched the color drain from her face. Brandt reached out to steady her, except she pulled back before he had a chance to make contact. His left hand still in midair, Brandt blinked at the speed she'd moved to avoid him.

In general, women liked him. He couldn't remember a time when one had avoided his touch. He didn't know if he should be amused or insulted. Instead, he felt oddly hurt.

"Why did you come?" she asked.

He glanced at her in surprise. "I thought you'd like to know."

She frowned. "You could have called me."

"But then I wouldn't be able to see you in person. By the way, was this morning's call an emergency?" He raised his eyebrows.

Samantha frowned. "I couldn't leave her alone in the car."

Interesting wording. Alone. He had to know. "Why?"

Her solemn gaze studied him for a long moment. She sidestepped the answer. "The bastard needs to be caught."

Brandt's heart stalled before starting again – double time. "The bastard?" Did she know about the serial killer he'd been chasing this last year? How could she know anything? Unless she was for real? God, could she help? Hope flared deep within.

"The killer."

Oh, that bastard. Damn. His heart rate returned to normal. "I'd like to ask you a few more questions. May I come in?"

She took a step back, paused, then stepped off to the side giving him room to pass.

Brandt walked inside. It seemed as bleak as he remembered. The threadbare furniture, plank floors – everything clean yet old. Bare kitchen counters...only one mug stood by the sink full of water.

He stopped in the middle of the room and turned to stare at her.

She hadn't moved.

What was wrong? He opened his mouth to ask, when she walked to the stove and put on a teakettle. As usual, she had on a sweater several sizes too big that hung almost to her knees, only this one was a brown cable type of thing. Threadbare jeans and white cotton socks completed the picture. And the perpetual braid down her back. He eyed her outfit. She barely made five feet and her clothes accented her thin frame, but there were hints of curves in all the right places.

"Do you want a cup of tea?"

He'd rather have a coffee, yet with no coffeemaker in sight, there didn't appear to be much choice. And her offer could be deemed a definite step forward in the social game. Even for a prickly female like her.

"Thank you. I'd appreciate that."

He watched as she pulled out a teapot and teabags from the cupboard. She never made idle chitchat or unnecessary movements. Economical all the way. She fascinated him. He couldn't think of another person like her. He walked over and sat on the same sofa as last time. "This is a nice place."

"I like it."

"Have you been here long?"

She shot him a suspicious look. "You mean you don't know already?"

His lips quirked. "I'd like you to tell me."

Samantha shrugged. "I've been here close to six months now."

"And before that."

She rolled her eyes. "Before that, I was somewhere else."

"Of course you were," he murmured. Her full history had been on his desk half an hour after he'd learned the details of the car accident she'd 'seen.' It hadn't taken long as there'd been little to add to what he already knew. Today's accident had opened doors for him. He wanted to learn the extent she was willing to fill in the missing details.

"Did you sabotage her car?"

She froze in the act of pouring water into the teapot. Her back went rigid. Fury visibly radiated through her bunched shoulders, rage-like waves he could almost touch. Ever so slowly, she finished filling the pot and replaced the kettle on the stove. Just as slowly, she turned around.

Brandt prepared to be blasted and found himself stunned at the pain evident in her eyes. Anger, yes, but he'd also hurt her. He grimaced. Damn, he'd judged that badly. He couldn't figure her out and had automatically tried to shock her out of her silence. Instead, it appeared he'd locked her deeper inside.

"I'm sorry. I had to ask."

She stared down at the kitchen floor, the muscles in her jaw twitching. She walked to the small fridge and pulled out a carton of milk. After a long moment, she shuddered once before answering, "When I have these visions, I'm not on the outside looking in. I'm inside these people staring out." She shot him a look. "Believe me, it would be much easier if it were the other way around."

That was understandable. If what she said were true, she must experience what they experience. He didn't think that included the pain – no one could stand that. Still, being inside must forge a personal connection. And how hard would that be given the eventual outcome?

He waited until she'd brought his tea. "Can you do this at will?"

"No."

Did that make it better or worse? Brandt stayed silent. She didn't offer any more information. "What about controlling it?"

"I wish."

"So, what can you do?"

"Endure." She bit her lip afterward, but it was too late. The word had slipped out.

God. Brandt paused, cup midway to the table. So softly spoken, the word said so much. He stared at her. She didn't like her gift. She hadn't learned to live with it yet. Or to control it. It controlled her. A rush of sympathy washed through him. Gifts like these, if real, were very unforgiving.

Few people had strong psychic abilities. Of those, some went insane. Some survived – barely, and a select few learned to control them and lived quite well. From what he'd seen, she could be one of the stronger ones. Except without the control, she was dangerous. Very dangerous.

Stefan had often extolled the dangers of psychic power without training. Brandt narrowed his eyes. Maybe Stefan could help her. If she'd accept any help. He stared at her in consideration.

Uncontrollable power was a disaster waiting to happen.

He should get the hell out and not come back. Even as he thought it, he knew he wouldn't. He couldn't. He needed to learn more about her. To understand her. After confirming the details of this morning's accident, he was willing to buy into her story as a psychic. But his personal interest bothered him. Especially when his better judgment told him to leave her alone.

She sipped her tea, apparently comfortable under the intensity of his gaze. She didn't fidget, move around, or make artificial conversation.

"Well," she asked. "Did you make up your mind?"

He lowered his cup. "About what?"

"Whether to believe me or not."

"I'm willing to believe up to this point. Your information checked out on the car accident and until I find out otherwise, I'll give you the benefit of the doubt."

"Gee, thanks." She peered over the rim of her teacup, derision in her voice.

Exasperated, he said, "You can't expect me to jump for joy over all of this. I'm a cop. I like things to be cut, dried, and clear. I also know that it rarely happens. So if there is information that can help, then I will listen and say thank you."

She stared at him, a frown between her brows.

He had no idea what she was thinking. Samantha had the odd distinction of being the only person to throw him off balance every time he saw her.

She shrugged. "What questions did you come to ask me?"

Damned if he could remember.

He took another drink of tea while he racked his brain. Oh yeah. "I'm hunting a particular killer. I wondered..." He leaned forward. "Can you find people?"

She cocked her head to one side and narrowed her gaze. "I don't know. I've never tried." Almost apologetically, she added, "I don't have any formal training in this."

He nodded. Stefan would have a heyday with her. He thought about it for a half second, then grabbed his notebook from his pocket and wrote down Stefan's phone number. He continued to ask several general questions about her abilities and the things she'd seen.

Ripping the note off, he placed it on the coffee table between them. She could contact Stefan on her own if she wanted to. He asked one last question. "Is there any particular trigger for the visions?"

That caught her off guard. She stared at him, her eyes flat. "Yes."

"And that is?" he asked.

"Violence."

CHAPTER 6

10:19 am

"YOU CAN'T PUT him to sleep. He's been doing great. I don't understand." Samantha blocked the cage containing Soldier, the name she'd settled on for the injured German shepherd. The rest of the staff faced her as one group.

"Samantha, we warned you about his lack of progress. He isn't adapting to people. No one will be able to handle him. The shelter won't take him now."

"Then why did you save his life?" Damn, she hated to beg, but someone needed to stick up for the dog. "If he was worth saving then, he's worth saving now."

Lucy stepped forward, placing a comforting arm around Sam's shoulder. "Honey, we tried to warn you. We hoped he'd get better, but he hasn't."

"He just needs a little more time." Samantha didn't know what tactic to try next. Her hand clenched again, fingernails sliding into half-moon impressions already there. She knew she had to keep trying. She hated the compassionate looks from her co-workers, hated their detachment. No one had taken the time to get close to Soldier like she had. It wasn't fair.

Just this once, she'd broken her own cardinal rule and gotten close. Too close. Her heart ached. She couldn't stand the thought of something happening to him.

That made it an easy decision.

"I'll take him," she said abruptly.

The room exploded.

"No Samantha, you can't do that. He could be dangerous."

"Sam, that's a bad idea."

"I wouldn't recommend that."

Sam refused to listen. They didn't understand. She *had* to give

Soldier a chance.

"I have to try. He's not comfortable here. If I take him home, he'll have an easier time of it. He needs to learn to trust again. He can't do that here."

"And then what?" Casey, the only female veterinarian on staff, spoke the collective voice of reason. "What if he attacks you?"

"He won't." Sam answered with more confidence than she felt. Stubbornly, she repeated, "I have to try."

Dr. Wascott walked over and squatted down before the German shepherd's cage. Dangerous growls filled the room.

"Sam, I can't let you do that." He sighed. "He's dangerous. I can't have that on my conscience."

"Well, I don't think he is. But, if you give us a chance and it turns out he doesn't improve or gets worse then…then you can put him down."

Standing up, the vet snorted, his hands on his hips, staring at her in concern. "At that point, no one will be able to get close enough and we'll have to shoot him."

Some truth existed in his words, but Sam wouldn't be swayed. Not now that she'd sensed a sign of weakening. "I'll need to borrow a cage to transport him." She double-checked the size of the dog. "And a hand to load him."

"The only way I'll agree is if you keep him in his cage for at least another week." He reached out, placing a hand on her shoulder. "I'll come and see him then and re-evaluate. He's too dangerous to be free right now. He could hurt himself and anyone in the vicinity."

Sam interrupted him. "Which is why my place works. There's no one around for miles." Tossing him a smile of thanks, Sam headed out to her pickup to make room in the box.

Moving Soldier went well, with everyone's help. Once Sam made it on the road, she kept checking the rearview mirror to make sure the cage hadn't shifted.

Driving gave her time to think. Like about the name and phone number Detective Sutherland had left behind, with a casual comment. "He's a strong psychic whom I've worked with in the past. Call him if you need someone to talk to."

Then he'd left, seemingly not realizing what a bombshell he'd left behind. Sam had snatched up the paper, read the name *Stefan*, then tucked the information away in her purse. She'd wanted to grab the cell phone and call right away, but hadn't a clue what to say. Now, excitement bubbled in the back of her mind. Terrifying her with the possibilities. She hadn't been able to call yet. In truth, she'd rather have Brandt with her when she made contact. Less awkward that way.

Sad to say, but this had gone a long way to improving her opinion of this particular detective. She wrinkled up her face at another truth. To have the handsome detective believe her would be great. To earn his respect, now that would be a bonus. There was just something about that look in his eyes. As if he cared. As if he cared about *her*.

How sexy was that? To actually know that someone was listening, paying attention. Just his focus on her with such intensity made shivers go up her spine. His dynamic features, so alive and always shifting, intrigued her. But then so did his lean muscles cording his neck and forearms.

Goose bumps raised on her arms, even though she drove in the heat of the melting sun. For the first time that she could remember, she'd found a man that intrigued her. She grimaced. That a cop had been the one to bring her dormant sexuality back to life was beyond ironic. Women had been attracted to men in uniform since time began. Just not her. Too many bad memories.

The trip had to be hurting the dog in the back, yet she hadn't heard him complain once. The cabin came into view, surprising her at the speed of today's trip. Once home, she backed the truck up to the porch.

Moses waited, wagging his golden plume of a tail. She hopped out, gave him a swift hug, and went to open the tailgate. It stuck, as usual. She pounded it a couple times before it finally dropped. Moses bounded into the truck box, eager to check out the new arrival.

He loved other dogs. Most of the time, they loved him. Soldier curled a lip, but other than that showed no reaction. Sam watched their interaction carefully. Except for a low warning, Soldier ignored the other dog.

Sam, hands on her hips, spoke to the dogs. "Now would be a good time for the detective to show up. We could use his help – or rather his muscles." The cage rested on an old blanket. She'd had plenty of help loading him, now she'd have to tug on the blanket to drag him off.

Despite working alone, the blanket system worked well. Although, by the time Soldier had been safely moved to the porch and under the overhanging roof, Sam's limbs were shaking from the effort. Soldier never made a sound.

Even now, he lay there and regarded her with his huge eyes blackened with pain. They locked on her as if he understood. Her heart melted a little more.

Sam collapsed beside his cage, her breathing ragged. "There you go, boy. Life will be much nicer here." Using the bottom of her t-shirt, she wiped the rivers of moisture from her forehead.

Moses and Soldier sniffed each other through the steel mesh as Sam rested and watched. The patient needed fresh water, clean blankets, medicine, and food. Lord, she needed food. And a shower.

With full bowls of food and water, Sam returned to see Moses stretched out against the side of the cage, staring at her reproachfully.

"Don't look at me like that. I can't let him free. He might take off." Placing the bowl down, she unclipped the front door.

"Hi, Soldier." Soldier's dark pain-filled gaze locked on hers. He slumped lower.

"Shit. Are you hurt? Damn it. I knew we shouldn't have moved you. I'm so sorry, Soldier. I had to. They were determined to put you down."

He closed his eyes, his mouth growing slack.

Fear clutched her heart. She struggled to open the tight clasp on the cage door. The closure snapped open and she stretched a hand toward him.

He didn't growl and only opened one eye. Pain clouded his gaze, but a much less heated warning remained.

"What's the matter, no more fight left inside? Or are you prepared to give me the benefit of the doubt after rescuing you from there?" She stroked the thick, lush fur. Dried blood decorated his dark coat. As her fingers worked deeper and deeper, she found sand and grime worked in to skin level. "Poor guy. It's been a long time since anyone cared about you, hasn't it?"

Sam's knees and back ached from the cramped position. She scrubbed his back and neck for another moment. While she worked, she told him about his new life, using a quiet calm voice. She didn't know if it helped or not, yet knew it was what she'd like done if she were in the similar situation.

Stupid. It's not as if she'd ever be huddling in a cage. She stopped, her fingers deep in his thick fur, stunned by the correlation. She might not have been in a cage, yet she'd been living as if she were an injured animal anyway. Wary, hiding from the next blow that life would deal her.

She laughed. "Enough for both of us, huh?"

The cage door clipped her as she backed out, making her curse. Moses whined. Soldier even lifted his head. With both dogs' gazes on her, Sam managed to extricate herself from the wire. She stayed on her knees for a long moment, considering the door. If she disliked it, imagine how the dog liked it?

But if she left it open, would he run away? Or worse, get hurt? The cage offered safety for him. But what kind of life did he have without freedom? As he'd still be in the cage, she wouldn't be going against her word to her boss. Not that he'd see it that way.

Moses stuck his nose on her neck, reminding her she'd been motionless for too long.

Wrapping her arms around his neck, she gave him a warm hug, burying her face in the thick ruff. "Oh, Moses. Tell me this is going to work out for the best."

She reached down to shut the cage door, and stopped. Both dogs stared at her, ears up. Soldier couldn't go anywhere right now. His injuries would stop him from running away. But what about her agreement with the vet? She made a gut decision.

"Fine. We'll try it your way."

Sam walked into the cabin, the cage door wide open behind her.

7:22 pm

WHISTLING CHEERFULLY, THE tall, heavily built man tugged on the lead he awkwardly held in his left hand along with one of the two dog crates. He should have made two trips, but he'd had enough for today. It was time to head home. Past time.

He'd held his temper all he could this day. He was quite proud of himself. It took inner strength to remain calm when inside he despised being here, despised the people, and particularly despised the women.

He should get an Oscar for that alone.

No one appreciated how hard it was for him here. No one. He was capable of so much more. Still, it was their loss and his gain. He knew he could do more. In fact, he *was* doing more – they just didn't know about it. A malicious joy seeped through him.

"Hey, Bill."

Jack, one of the organizers, had chased after him and almost reached him. He sighed, took the last few steps to his van, and put down the crates. Damn, these dogs were getting heavier every time he had to take them anywhere.

"Good class today. Thanks, buddy. Did Dolly Seymour ask you about fitting in a new session next week? This would be another private session."

Bill opened the back door to the van. "She mentioned something about it. I haven't confirmed availability yet. I'll have to call her in the morning."

"No problem. This is the same group from last week. They want to work on individual training, so maybe you can see your way into accepting this one."

Bill had a grin plastered on his face. On the inside, though, he was tired of smiling. He was tired of being nice all day, and he was fucking tired of the whole mess. Surely, his luck would change soon and he could split. "No problem. If I can, I will."

"Good enough. We'll see you later then."

Jack headed back into the clubhouse. As he opened the door, a slinky brunette in tight-ass capri pants and a shorty midriff top walked toward him, a tiny white Lhasa Apso sporting a big pink bow, in her arms.

Bill grinned at the beautiful woman walking toward him and stopped loading his stuff into the back of the van to talk with her. "Hi, Caroline."

A bright smile broke across her face. "Thanks for today's class, Bill. I'm just sorry Jared couldn't be here today. He'd have really enjoyed it."

Bill smiled as expected. In truth, if he heard one more thing about her husband, Jared, he was liable to scream. If there was one thing he couldn't stand – it was gushing females, particularly when they were gushing about their males.

Still, he managed to keep an eye on her nicely rounded ass as she walked past to her black Porsche several vehicles down.

He just might have to do something about that…and her.

2:30 am, June 17th

SCREAMS ECHOED IN the darkness. Sam twisted and pulled, struggling to get away from whatever held her fast. She couldn't get free. In a blind panic, she realized her body no longer answered to her commands. Her eyes opened. She shuddered. Shearing pain melded with terror as she took in the blood dripping to the floor. It ran down the folds of the floral bedspread to soak into the cream carpet waiting below.

"Please don't…no more." A voice not her own spoke the words in her head. A blow shattered her breastbone. Her screams poured into the small room. Sam barely flinched. Her attacker laughed.

"Like I'm going to listen to you, bitch. You like this. You must. You let that useless husband of yours beat you all the time." His hideous laughter added to her horror. God, how could he laugh at her? He was an animal. She died a little more at his unexpected pleasure. Monster.

Maybe it had something to do with his unseemly pleasure, or maybe it came from her absolute fury at yet another murder, but somewhere deep inside, Sam's consciousness attempted to reassert itself. In a weird way, she became aware of both worlds at once. Her awareness built, a small step at a time, allowing her to put a slight distance between her and the dying woman. Fog grew between the two realities, buffering her from the poor woman's pain and fear.

Groggy and disoriented, Sam tried to snap out of the psychic episode fully, only to slam back inside the injured woman. Her body lurched uncontrollably. Sam tried to ward off the oncoming blow, but couldn't make the right arm move.

"Stupid woman. What good are those looks of yours now? It's far too late to run away." The fists lashed out, once, twice and then yet again. Muscles tore and internal organs bled under cracked bones. The poor woman arched her back, lifting high off the bed. Both women screamed. Cries echoed inside and outside of Sam's mind, building, and blending into a crescendo of terror.

"Why are you doing this?" Blood trickled down the corner of her mouth. Sam didn't know who spoke – her or the victim. It didn't matter, the words were the same.

"Because I can, bitch." Mocking laughter echoed through the small room.

"But…?" She gasped, fighting the vomit in the back of her

throat. "Why me?"

"You're weak. You deserve killing. Staying with an asshole like that. Besides, I hate him. Maybe the cops will think he's good for this one."

"No," she gasped. "Please, don't."

"Too late."

He raised his fist and landed a blow below her eye socket. Bone shattered, making little scrunching noises. There'd be no white knight coming to the rescue. Ever. There was only Sam and she didn't know how to help.

Through the bloody haze, Sam, desperate to take something useful back with her, struggled to open her good eye. Swollen and bloody and not her own, made the job damn near impossible. Light slid painfully under her sore eyelids. She struggled to bring the scene in focus. The bastard was getting off her bed. Blood splatter covered his shirt and jeans. He wore unrelenting black with the blood standing out in dark wet spots. He wore gloves and a ski mask. Same height and same build.

Same energy pattern. Damn, him again. At least she thought it was him.

Only one eye could see. Sam couldn't even tell if this man wore a ring or not. The light in the room started to fade, as if the sun were setting at rapid speed. Except the curtains were closed and it was the middle of the night.

Her vision narrowed, locked on her killer's face. The circle grew smaller and smaller. Sam knew her time was almost over. She could only watch with painful understanding as the circle of light reduced to a pinpoint before finally, thankfully, blinking out. Forever.

It was over.

Sam woke in her own room, minutes later. For the first time, grief didn't overwhelm her. She was angry. She hurt for the victim and her family. But even more, a deep pulsing fury permeated her soul. That asshole had way too much fun doing what he was doing. He had to be stopped.

When she could, she shifted upright. Pain still coursed through her body, but the anger provided a dense barrier, letting her cut through the pain. Inner excitement grabbed hold. This time she'd had some kind of conscious awareness. She'd kept a part of herself intact while living what that poor woman had experienced.

Poor soul. Sam sniffled. Why was this guy doing this? Surely, he had a reason – more than just for entertainment.

Lying back down, she thought about the details from the vision. Once again, the killer had been fully hidden, so no face or ring showed. There'd been light-colored walls, a plain white ceiling, and a cheap floral bedspread. Again, nothing helpful.

It was six in the morning now. Surely, someone would find the woman today? Depression set in.

Tucking the blankets around her, she reached for the phone. There was no answer at Detective Brandt's number. She hung up. Then changing her mind, she redialed and this time left a message. Afterward, she sat, undecided, before dialing the station.

Five minutes later, she was sorely regretting that action.

"I'm sorry, ma'am, could you repeat that?"

"Could you please have Detective Sutherland call me? I know this sounds bizarre, but I can't give you any more information. A woman has been murdered." Samantha tried to keep her voice from showing her frustration. Just going over the details hurt. Damn it, why wouldn't anyone listen to her?

She cleared her throat from the confused emotions clogging it. "Excuse me, could you just pass the message on, please?" She shifted the phone to the other ear.

"I'll see that he gets your message," replied the cold voice on the other end of the phone.

"Thank you," she answered, and hung up. There was nothing else to do.

It took twenty-five minutes to hear from him.

"Samantha?"

"Yes," she answered, relief rushing through her. "It's me."

"And?" he asked, concern in his voice.

Sam took a deep breath, snuffling back tears. "He's killed again," she whispered.

Dead silence.

She scowled into the phone. She could almost hear the gears in his mind churning at lightning speed.

"Did you see him?"

"I saw him, not the ring. He kept his gloves on the whole time." She shivered at the memory, still fresh in her mind. "He wore all black, including the ski mask."

"Can you identity him in any way?"

Sam shook her head then realized he couldn't see her. "No.

Not really. I might recognize him by size, carriage, maybe his way of moving. His gaze…" Sam closed her eyes and swallowed hard, hating the fear clinging to her skin. Some belonged to the various victims and to a certain extent – some of it was hers. The killer breathed evil. She got a grip again. "It won't stand up in court, but I would recognize his energy if I ever saw him again – at least I think so."

"What does that mean?" His sharp voice cut through the lines.

She stiffened. "When he kills he lets himself enjoy it. Energy has its own individual pattern and changes with moods, etc." She paused for a moment. "I think I might recognize it again, but I can't say for sure."

"Hmm."

Sam waited in edgy silence.

"Is there anything you can tell me about the victim?"

"Like what?" She relaxed slightly. With it, fatigue set in. She was so tired.

"Like where she lives, a house, an apartment…something to help us find her faster."

Samantha sighed. "When you're being attacked, you don't think, 'I'm so and so and live at 146 Pine Street.' Women think about being rescued, and why them, and toward the end…" Sam caught back a hiccup of a sob. "Toward the end," she continued, her voice a hint above a whisper, "they only think of those they're leaving behind – their loved ones." Sam could barely hear him through the chaos of her emotions, yet, she could sense his sympathy. She could hear him scratching down notes. "He beat her to death."

"He beat her? No knives?"

"No. He hated her husband. The husband beat her so he took her away from him. If that makes any sense."

"Nothing a killer does, makes any sense."

Sam hesitated. "Another thing. Her eyes were damaged. It was hard to see clearly." Sam stared bitterly out the large bedroom window, where raindrops started to ping against the panes of glass. She would see another sunny day, but the poor women wouldn't.

"Can you tell me anything else? Her name? You got the name of the car victim."

"That was different." Violent imagery coursed through her mind. Was there gold to be mined in there somewhere? "Just a minute." Sam closed her eyes, trying to let the images she'd been forcing back, flood her mind. Maybe, there was something useful there. Fists. Blows. Blood. Screams. Red. Pain. Grief. Sam doubled over, gasping at the emotional onslaught. She fought to stay conscious, scared all over again as the pain and images took her back into the horror. *There.* What was that?

A name. Sam fought to leash the demons in her mind, scrambling for the safety of her physical reality, desperately wanting to return to her small cabin by the lake. She shuddered and opened her eyes.

A whitewashed ceiling stared back at her.

She shivered. How could anything so bizarre happen in such a calm and normal setting?

"Sam, damn it, answer me." Brandt's voice screamed through her phone, dragging her attention back to the task at hand. "Are you there? God damn it!"

"Brandt." Sam's vocal cords sounded wrong to her own ears, hoarse and rough. She tried again. "It's okay. I'm here."

"What the hell happened? Jesus, you said just a minute. I thought you'd gone to get something."

Sam frowned. "How long was I gone?"

"At least two or three fucking minutes." His voice calmer now. "I almost hopped into my truck to drive out to your place. Jesus, don't scare me like that again."

Sam shook her head. That long? No, surely not. She stared uncertainly at the small plastic clock on the milk crate that passed for a nightstand.

"So what the hell was that all about?" Brandt blasted her, obviously pissed now that she'd returned.

"Sorry, I didn't mean to worry you. Her husband's name was Alex."

"Husband? Was he the killer?"

"No." She rushed to explain. "That's what the killer wants you to believe."

"So, the husband was a wife beater?"

"I think so."

Silence through the phone as he digested that information. When he spoke again, he was all business. "I've got to take another call. I'll need you to come to the station and give a statement. How about eleven? I'll see you then."

Sam stared down at the dead phone. "Shit. That was so *not* what I wanted to happen."

CHAPTER 7

8:55 am

APPROACHING THE SAME imposing building for a second time was no easier. She glanced at her cheap watch. Right on time. The station had called just over an hour ago asking her to come in for nine instead. Two hours earlier meant two hours she didn't have to wait and worry. Taking a deep breath, she straightened her shoulders and walked in.

Her reception, this time, was quite different. After letting the front desk know she was there for her appointment, she was taken to a small room and left alone. Sam shivered as she took in the square table and two chairs. No windows, no couch, nothing to indicate comfort. This appeared more like an interrogation room. Silently, she walked to the far side of the table and sat down. Sam didn't need any other cues to understand she could be in serious trouble.

She just didn't know why.

The door opened, admitting an older grizzled cop. "Miss Blair, thanks for coming in. I'm Detective Stan Robertson."

Sam grimaced. Warily, she watched as the man pulled out the other chair and sat down, dropping a file folder on the table.

"So you're a psychic, are you?"

She replied, "Somewhat."

He glanced over at her, his bristly eyebrows slightly raised. "Explain."

"Sometimes I get visions, but I can't read tarot cards or anything like that."

He opened his folder and started writing notes on his pad of paper. She tried to read his chicken scratch. It proved impossible. She waited until he'd finished writing before asking a question of her own.

"Why did you call me in?"

"You reported a murder." Calm, quiet, he gave no inkling of his reaction to her report. He could be writing out a grocery list for all the emotion he showed. Sourly, she realized he'd probably been on the force so long nothing fazed him.

"Where's Detective Sutherland?"

"He's off duty right now. He'll be in soon."

"I'd prefer to speak with him." Actually, she wanted to speak with only him, suddenly realizing she might not have the chance. What the hell was going on?

"We'll have him call you to follow up." His demeanor suddenly changed. "So where were you when this murder happened?"

"In bed, sleeping."

His disbelief should have been an early warning. It wasn't.

"The same bed as this woman?"

Blindsided, she slumped in her chair. So, that was it. She was a suspect. Wait a minute. She sat straight up. "Did you find her?" she asked.

"Why don't you tell me?" He smirked at her and returned to note-taking.

Sam didn't know what to think. Every time she stepped forward to help, she became a suspect. But stupid her, she kept coming back for more. When would she ever learn?

"So where were you at…" the officer stopped to look at his notes, "between midnight and four this morning?"

"At home," Sam answered, her shoulders slumping. "And yes, I was alone."

"So you have no alibi." He jotted something down.

"If I'd known ahead of time that I'd need one, then I'd have made an effort to be with someone. But I didn't." Sam glared at the man sitting opposite her. She didn't want to be here. She should have told Brandt that she couldn't come.

"I'd like to talk to Detective Sutherland," she repeated.

"Yeah, we'll get on that right away."

He never moved.

Sam snorted before subsiding into silence. She was past helping him.

"Let's get back to exactly what you were doing the evening leading up to the death of your friend."

"She wasn't my friend. I didn't know her. I don't even know where she lives." It took effort to keep the wobble from her voice.

She didn't think she'd ever get used to the accusations or the mockery that often accompanied the disbelief. She eyed the officer writing extensive notes. What the hell could he write to fill two full pages?

Without a word or a glance her way, he got up and left the room.

Sam waited with mounting frustration, and when an hour later, she was still sitting there, the frustration morphed into an insidious fear. She couldn't stop trembling. She interlocked her fingers and sat on them. *Focus, you idiot. Don't let them get to you. You can do this. There's no reason for them to hold you here much longer.* Using a mantra that had helped her in the past, she mentally repeated: All will be well. Everything happens for a reason. All will be well.

Shit happens. That was the other mantra of her life. And it sure as hell had.

All will be well. All will be well. All will be well.

The door opened suddenly.

She forgot to breathe.

The same detective she'd seen at the very first meeting walked in.

She sighed in disgust.

"I'm Detective Bresson. I need to ask you some questions."

"Why? You didn't believe me when I walked in here the first time. What's changed?"

He ignored her.

Sam listened in disbelief as the questioning started all over.

An hour and a half later, Sam was shown the front door, the officer's words echoing in her head. *Don't leave town.*

Go where? Bitterness overwhelmed her. She had nowhere to go.

10:50 am

BRANDT CHECKED HIS watch as he pulled the pickup into the side parking lot and hopped out. With any luck, he'd have time to grab a mug of coffee before Sam arrived. He'd tried contacting the police artist last night without success. He'd left a message. Hopefully, she'd gotten it and had shown up, too.

Sam had too much valuable information locked inside her

head not to take advantage of it. Their police artist had an eerie interpretation of people and events as well. Maybe together, the two of them could produce a little bit of useable magic.

He pushed open the side door and nodded at Jensen, just leaving. Walking straight to the lunchroom, he snagged a mug, filled it with coffee, added cream, and headed to his desk. So focused on his time frame, it took him a minute to notice the unusual silence in the station.

Glancing around, he frowned. People weren't smiling at him. No one said hello or good morning. What the hell?

"Hey Adam, what's up?" The younger man was hunched over his keyboard, staring at his monitor as if it held the answer to life on it. He started; red flushed over his face and neck. He mumbled and refused to face Brandt.

"What?" Brandt walked over until he stood directly in front. "Adam, talk to me."

Adam's shoulders slumped. "I think you'd better talk to the captain."

Brandt stiffened. "The captain? Okay, how about a heads-up first?"

Adam finally glanced around the office and then met his gaze. "Personally, I think she might be on the up and up, but there's some that think she's in this neck deep."

"She?" The caffeine had yet to kick in or his brain hadn't woken up yet. Either way, nothing about this was making any sense.

"Your little psychic friend."

His stomach soured. "Sam? What does she have to do with this?" Brandt checked his watch. She should be out front waiting for him by now. "Has she arrived already?"

Adam looked at him, puzzled. "She just left."

"Left?" Brandt searched the large open room, hoping to catch a sign of her. "Why? I asked her to come in at eleven. I wanted her to meet with the sketch artist."

Adam lowered his voice and leaned closer. "She arrived hours ago. They just let her go."

Black, blinding anger coiled deep inside, stirring in anticipation of freedom. "They?" Brandt's voice was cold and thick. Who the hell had gone after Sam without talking to him first? Who the hell dared? Because that asshole had a surprise coming. Sam was *his* source and no one else's.

Adam ducked and peered from side to side, checking to see if anyone was watching them. The two of them always talked. They were on the same team for Christ's sake. Brandt leaned closer. "Talk to me," he ordered the younger man. "I want it all, and I want it all now."

Adam flushed even redder. "I don't know the details. Ask Kevin."

Kevin. Brandt thought about it for half a heartbeat. Yeah that made sense. Kevin's black-and-white view of the world matched his black attitude. Kevin didn't appear to trust anyone. Damn it. It was time to have a talk with Kevin. Brandt hated feeling like he'd been targeted.

Just then, Dillon joined them. Both men half-turned away from Dillon who belonged to one of the other teams. He wasn't privy to their work.

"What secrets are we discussing now?"

Both men gave him a baleful look. Adam walked away without saying a word.

Brandt studied him. Why would he even begin to step in where he wasn't wanted? Brandt had little to do with him, thankfully. He'd always appeared a little too slick. That had nothing to do with his fancy suits. Today, he wore another pinstripe suit and what appeared to be a damask shirt. This kid was looking the part. Brandt just didn't know what that part was.

"No secrets here." Every department had a misfit or two. This station was no different. The captain here was quite tolerant – as long as everyone did their job.

Brandt didn't know Captain Johansen well. Big, beefy, and built, his physique gave rise to the nickname of B-cubed. He kept a military-style haircut that showed more white than gray and had a huge squared off jaw. Buzz Lightyear anyone? Yet, he had a reputation of being a straight shooter with his men, and fair on most issues. But on the question of psychics, well Brandt had no idea where he stood.

It was hard being an outsider. He was here to do a job, allowed to join the team in order to complete a job, yet not quite a member of the team. Obviously some of them thought differently about him. But going behind Brandt's back was never acceptable.

Dillon half-laughed and shifted his position, his hands sliding into his pants pockets. "Are you sure? It sounded juicy when I went to walk past. Couldn't help but stop and ask."

He grinned in a way that pissed Brandt off. He needed to talk with the captain now. He needed to find out what the hell was going on. Brandt spun on his heels, slopping coffee on the floor and headed for the captain's office.

11:00 am

THE DOOR TO the captain's office was closed when he arrived. He knocked hard.

"Come in."

Brandt strode in and stopped short. Kevin was seated on the left. The captain sat behind his huge mahogany desk. There was a sense of expectation. They'd been waiting for him.

His defenses went up.

"Come in, Brandt. Take a seat."

"I'd rather stand." He struggled with it, but his voice actually sounded normal. Tight but calm.

"Fine. Whatever you're comfortable with. But you also need to be comfortable with the fact that Kevin is entitled to speak with any witnesses he sees fit. That includes this Samantha Blair." The captain's beetled brow met in the middle as he peered over his glasses at Brandt. "That is why you're here. Isn't it?"

Brandt choked back the words clogging his throat. He had to remember he was a guest here. "Correct. And it's possible that detectives at this station work differently than they would in most other stations – but that would surprise me."

Normally detectives built a rapport with their witnesses. They might ask another detective to go and talk to someone, to see what shook loose. Most detectives, as a basic courtesy, would mention to the other detective that they needed to talk to one of his connections before they interviewed someone involved in his case.

Captain Johansen cleared his throat. "Yes, we do things a little differently here."

Brandt's gaze cut to the captain. "That different?"

Once again, Captain Johansen exchanged glances with Kevin.

"We deal in good old-fashioned police work here. Not black magic." Kevin couldn't stay quiet any longer.

"That's what this is all about? Because she's a psychic?" At Kevin's nod, Brandt snorted. "Then you could have had the decency to talk to me, couldn't you? I've worked with Stefan

Kronos for over a decade."

"I'm not sure that I believe his work either. However, many of my friends do, given his success record. This woman is a flake, pure and simple. I don't want her involved in my cases." Kevin's sarcasm underscored his point of view.

Interesting that Kevin had heard of Stefan. "You haven't given her a chance, have you?" Brandt turned to confront him. "I believe in her. She's given valuable information and I think she can help."

"I interviewed her. She doesn't have anything to offer." Kevin stood up. "I don't have time for this. As long as you have something reasonable to offer to my cases, feel free. But if you're going to bring in a psychic, use her for your cases, not mine. She can hang you, not us. You're only visiting here. And you won't destroy *our* reputation with your fucked up ideas."

Kevin strode out, leaving an uncomfortable silence behind.

Brandt looked back at Captain Johansen, who stared back. "Is that the official stand?"

He pursed his lips, thinking. "For the moment. I'm certainly not a fan of using psychics. But I do know Stefan's work. So I can't discount them either. Let me know if she comes up with anything we can use. Other than that, don't confuse the issue between hard work and easy answers."

11:20 am

KEVIN WALKED THROUGH the commons, staring straight ahead. Most of the office knew what had just happened. The interior walls were very thin.

He didn't give a shit. Let them talk. As long as they didn't bring it to him, he could care less. He had work to do, and gossip wasn't one of his job duties.

Neither was dealing with flakes. Even harmless ones. But he'd had to check it out further. Now he'd done so, and now he could wash his hands of her. Good riddance.

If only Brandt would see things his way. He'd expected more of this 'visiting detective.' Brandt seemed to be a straightforward kind of guy. He'd always dug in and helped where needed and he sure as hell knew how to get the job done. But this psychic stuff was just plain weird. That he'd trumped Brandt's witness, wasn't something he was prepared to get into. Not on a murder case.

Besides, like religion, there was just no telling where individual beliefs lay.

That was fine with Kevin. He didn't push his beliefs down anyone's throat and expected the same courtesy – especially at work. Kevin shook his head. Christ, a psychic!

Even his wife had laughed at him.

12:30 pm

BRANDT PULLED THE truck up to the cabin in a spew of dust and dirt. Moses stood on the porch barking at him. At least the dog showed some sign of guarding the place. He cut the engine and hopped out, slamming the door behind him.

"Hey Moses, how are you doing, big guy?" Brandt eyed him warily, certain that Moses posed no threat. Still, one never knew. He climbed the steps, hand outstretched toward him.

Moses walked a step closer. Just as Brandt was about to touch him, a deadly growl erupted from the far side of the porch before rising into a hideous howl. Moses backed up and took up his fierce barking again.

Brandt started. "Jesus. What the hell is that?" He could just make out the oversized cage further down the porch, half covered in old gray army blankets. He took a hesitant step closer, only to stop as the growl grew to crescendo.

"Easy, take it easy." He didn't know what Samantha had inside that damn cage, but if it were relative in size, it had to be huge.

He glanced at the closed front door, sure he was being watched. Samantha had to be hiding behind the curtains. Ignoring the cage for the moment, he rapped on the door. Samantha opened it promptly, confirming his suspicions.

"Hi."

The door shut in his face, leaving him staring at worn, peeling wood.

He closed his eyes and groaned. Shit. After what the team had put her through, he couldn't blame her. Then neither could he blame the team. He might have done the same thing under different circumstances.

"Samantha, I had nothing to do with this morning's appointment. The detectives called you in because they had questions. I'm sorry for the way it went down. Still, it's our job to ask."

Silence.

"Crap." It would take a bomb to get her out of there now.

"Would it help if I said I didn't know about this morning's meeting until after you'd left? I had nothing to do with it. Honest."

More silence.

"That was the rest of the team. They don't have much faith in psychics and wanted to check you out for themselves."

Dead silence.

Shit. He so didn't have time for this. He searched for ideas. Moses had slumped to his usual position of full-relaxed mode on the porch. The cage was quiet, but Brandt sensed the awareness emanating from the wire structure.

"Nice pet you've got there. Sounds dangerous. I may have to put him down as a danger to society."

The front door crashed open. "Don't you touch him," she snarled as she raced toward the cage.

He grinned. Like taking candy from a baby.

As she caught sight of his grin, she stopped her headlong rush and changed direction to charge him instead. He laughed even as he deflected her blows.

"You bastard. You did that on purpose." She took another swing at him, her knuckles grazing the top of his nose.

Still laughing, he snagged her wrists.

"You're right. That was low, but I had to get you out of the house."

He was loath to let go of her wrists. Not wanting to get clipped was only one reason. The ire in those velvet eyes spoke volumes about her temper. No, it had more to do with the shape and fit of her against him. He switched to holding both her wrists with one hand. The fingers of his other hand sank deep into the always-present sweater – this time a deep forest green one – before finding her warm flesh below. Her frame – surprisingly solid. The purple fire shooting from her eyes made him grin. Even as he watched, she ran her tongue over her lips.

His stomach clenched. He reached and tugged her long braid.

He stared at her hands gripped in his. Blue veins wound from her fingers up and under her sleeve. He frowned and loosened his hold.

"Sorry." He grimaced as pink rushed through to her pale fingertips. "I didn't mean to hurt you."

Samantha tugged her hands free and stepped away from him.

"I'm not hurt."

He glanced from her hands to her face, frowning. Somehow, he didn't think she'd tell him if she were. She wasn't going to change on his say so.

"May I come in?"

She shuffled her feet, but refused to look at him. More evasiveness. Not a surprise, coming from her. He waited for a moment before adding, "Please."

CHAPTER 8

1:15 pm

SAM DIDN'T WANT to let him into her space. She didn't know how her ire had died so suddenly. But she didn't want to let it go just yet.

"Are you okay?"

She twisted around, brushing her hair from her eyes. "What the hell do you care?" The words burst out with more punch than she intended. Better to appear calm and rational than let him know how hurt and betrayed she really felt.

"We need to talk." he responded.

"What could there possibly be left to talk about?" She turned and walked into the cabin.

Brandt came in behind her.

She strode to the fridge and pulled out a jug of cold water. "Why won't you leave me alone?" she asked, without turning around.

A large muscled arm reached into the glass cupboard above her head, pulling out two tall glasses. He set them down on the counter and tugged the jug free from her fingers.

He appeared so in control, she wanted to scream at him. Her life was in turmoil. She watched as he poured two glasses.

Pissed at her reaction, she snatched one up and walked outside. Her nerves were rubbed raw. She could only take so much.

"I can't."

His answer hurt. She escaped toward Soldier. Her stocking feet whispered along the porch. Soldier still heard her. She couldn't see him, but she sensed his attention. "It's okay, boy. It's just me." The sensation of wariness coming from the cage never relaxed. She couldn't blame him, hers hadn't disappeared either.

A low growl erupted in the far corner.

"What's in there?" Brandt asked from behind her.

Sharper, higher pitched growls had the two of them backing up a few paces.

"That's some huge cage," Brandt said, his voice carefully moderated.

"He's a good-sized dog. And he obviously likes his space."

Brandt snorted and walked to the stairs and sat down. "You think?" He took a big drink, still staring at the cage. "Is he dangerous?"

"No." She amended her answer after a quick thought. "At least, I don't believe so."

He arched his eyebrow. "You mean you don't know?"

"I just got him," she muttered. She didn't think Soldier would really hurt anyone – unless they got too close.

She could feel Brandt's gaze burning her face. A hot flush washed over her cheeks. "So why are you here?" she asked.

Silence. She heard his heavy sigh on the air. From the corner of her eye, she saw his head turn, his focus on the view before them.

"I came to explain. I went to meet you for our eleven o'clock appointment. That's when I heard they'd called you for a visit earlier."

"Visit." Disbelief made her shake. "Did you say visit?" Her voice rose alarmingly high. "How could anyone call that a visit? How about calling it a Gestapo session, or maybe an interrogation?" She glared at him. "But a *visit,* it was not."

With Moses at her side, she headed down to the end of the dock. The water glistened in the late sunlight. Her knee buckled sideways as Moses leaned against her, whining.

"It's okay, boy. I'm fine." She laid a gentle hand on his bushy fur, enjoying the comfort of his touch.

"Are you?" Brandt faced the lake. "That's actually why I came – to check up on you."

She stiffened.

He hesitated. "I'm sorry I wasn't there, I might have been able to ease it slightly. But don't get me wrong, they would have brought you in regardless. They needed to check you out after you reported the third victim."

Sorry? She threw him a stunned glance. He wished he could have been there? Well, so did she. Overwhelmed and unaccountably relieved, Sam dropped to sit down on the dock, her suddenly weak legs dangling over the edge. Somehow, the day didn't seem so bad after all. Moses slumped down to the ground at her feet.

Brandt stood beside her, looking as if he wanted to say something. Sam didn't care. She had enough to deal with keeping the bubbling lightness inside from making its way outward. The last thing she wanted was for him to see her relief.

The silence grew uncomfortable. "What?" She didn't like the indecision on his face.

He shrugged.

"Come on, fess up. What?"

He sat down a little apart from her. "Do you have other skills? You know like telekinesis or telepathy – anything?"

His tone came across light and amused, yet Sam sensed a serious thread through it all.

"You mean like mind reading? She sharpened her gaze, trying to figure out what he meant. No, he was too sensible for that. Wasn't he? Searching his face, she had to ask, "You don't really think I can read your mind – do you?"

He shifted his weight and stared out across the lake.

She grinned, her first real one in a long time. As the realization swept through her, a giggle escaped. She slapped her hand over her mouth, astonished at the sound. Moses raised his head and whined. She giggled again. Then she couldn't help it; she laughed aloud. When he cocked his head to one side and stared at her, she laughed harder, threw her arms around the dog, and hugged him close.

She watched Brandt shake his head, as if he only just realized he'd crouched down beside her, his puzzled look clearing.

"What's so funny?" he asked, aggrieved.

Another giggle escaped even as she fought to control herself.

She wiped her eyes. "Sorry. God that felt good. I haven't laughed that hard in years." It took another couple of minutes before finally, she heaved a big sigh and relaxed. Peace settled upon her, ill fitting at first, but she slowly grew more comfortable with it. Another sigh escaped, and she stretched out on the dock. The sun had lost most of its heat, leaving a slightly cooler air to wash over her heated skin.

"Well?"

"Well what?" Then she remembered – mind reading. Another giggle escaped. He shot her a dirty look, and she tried hard to stifle the rest. There was no way to stop the grin that split her face. "I'm not telepathic. I can't read minds. Okay?"

He peered at her intently. She stared back, still grinning, but serious.

He nodded once and lay down on the warm dock beside her.

Sam smiled, the wooden boards warm beneath her shoulders. It was a gorgeous day.

She was dimly aware of Brandt stretching out on the other side of Moses. She could feel his gaze. She smiled slightly and closed her eyes. Content.

Her thoughts free floated in the newly created space in her mind. Stress had fled in the face of her laughter, leaving room for peace and contentment.

Images, both colored and not, danced, enjoying the freedom to roam. Faces, images, names, and places. Nothing followed a pattern as free association flowed. In an uncharacteristic move, she let them. Amazed at the clarity, Sam could only watch in awe. Where did these come from? She recognized some of them – and some she didn't.

"What are you thinking?"

"Hmm?"

"I asked what you were thinking."

"Not thinking – seeing. Pictures, images, events." She smiled lazily, never opening her eyes.

"Anything on the murderer?"

She froze. It didn't help. The moving images sped up, tumbling over each other, impatient for their moment in the light. One face flashed, followed by another and then another. Without warning, the film stopped. A camera trained on one woman. But Sam was inside that woman staring at the camera lens. The faint reflection on the camera lens showed the vague outline of a beautiful laughing brunette. The woman smiled into the camera, amused at something the photographer said. She turned her head. Sam caught glimpses of a huge green park, flowers in brilliant vibrant beds. Several other people mingled. Someone called out a name. Her head twisted around. Her name. She was called Annalea. Sam recognized her basic essence. Sam had connected to this same soul the other day.

"Annalea."

"Who?"

She knew. "That's her name." Sam opened her eyes to a slowly darkening sky.

"The murderer?" he asked. His voice sounded stunned, his

tone disbelieving.

"No," she whispered, grief already clogging her heart, breaking up her voice. "He's stalking his next victim. Her name's Annalea."

2:10 pm

EVEN AN HOUR ago, Sam would have said what she was doing was impossible.

It defied logic. But there it was.

She stood on the steps of the police station, staring up at the imposing front. What was even worse, was that somehow…somehow she'd been convinced to do this willingly.

Un-freakin-believable.

"Problems?"

Sam started. Brandt stood several steps above her, staring down at her with a questioning look on his face. She rubbed her damp palms on her faded jeans, glancing at her scuffed runners showing too much wear, then up at him. She wrapped her arms beneath her breasts, not quite knowing what to say. Her thick sweater was long and didn't seem to make a bit of difference to the chill deep in her bones. She stared around at the busy street before turning her gaze on him again.

"Yeah, this isn't exactly my favorite place to 'visit.'"

He grinned at her. "It will be different this time."

Should she believe him?

"I promise."

Sam raised her face to the sun, took a deep breath, got a grip on her whacked-out emotions, and strode the remaining few stairs. Once inside, she kept her focus on Brandt and followed his lead. Within minutes, she was sitting at a large table in a spacious lived-in room. It was much more pleasant. This looked like a meeting or a conference room. The sideboard held papers and books. One of the tables held used coffee cups and even a dirty plate.

"Do you want a cup of coffee before we get started? I'm not sure we have any tea."

Feeling as if she'd been caught snooping, Sam quickly nodded. "Thanks, coffee is fine. Black, please."

Brandt flashed a quirky grin as he left.

On her own, Sam glanced around at those passing through. There were no windows in the room. She'd have felt better if she could have seen the world outside – to have less of a caged feeling. She did much better in open air. She tilted her head. Maybe she should look at going into horticulture. That was outside, away from people. Yeah, she'd do well with plants. Too bad they didn't do well with her.

"Here you go. Careful, it's hot."

A cup of steaming coffee was placed before her. The heat drew her like a magnet. She wrapped her hands around the mug, almost moaning with joy.

At that moment, she looked up to catch Brandt's quizzical gaze. She flushed.

"I'm a little cold, that's all."

He raised one eyebrow and refrained from commenting.

Sam returned her attention to her coffee, staring at it longingly. With the steam still rising, she tried a sip. She choked, hastily putting it down again. She coughed again, trying to clear her throat. Dear God, how could they call that coffee? She snuck a glance at Brandt. He hadn't noticed.

Sam didn't know what to say. Brandt sat down across from her, sipping his own coffee. God, he actually seemed to enjoy it. He flipped through a file on the table. Every once in a while, he stopped and wrote a few notes on a pad of paper.

"You'll get used to it."

Surprised, Sam asked, "Get used to what?"

"The coffee." He flashed a grin at her. The wicked glint in his eyes caught her sideways. Her heart stopped, before suddenly thundering on.

"Like hell," she said when she finally managed to speak.

"You're right. I lied. You never get used to it."

A sudden commotion at the door caught their attention. An older woman, hauling a large case bustled into the room. "Sorry I'm late, Brandt."

"No problem, Irena. Grab a seat."

Irena banged the case down and shrugged out of her coat. "The weather has gone to hell out there."

"Has it started raining?"

"Not yet, but the sky is ready to explode at any minute." Irena opened her case.

Sam gawked. Wow, what a kit. She watched as Irena pulled out an art pad and a small case of art pencils.

"Okay, so what are we doing today?"

Brandt quietly explained. Sam listened, watching Irena's face intently. Her expression wrinkled once before settling into the same old cynical look. Whatever.

Brandt stood up. "Sam, I'm going to leave you in Irena's hands." He smiled at the two women. "I'll return in an hour or so to see how the two of you are getting along."

Sam watched him walk out.

"So." Irena pulled a large sketchpad toward her and reached for a thick art pencil. "Let's get started."

An hour later, Sam was so engrossed that when a heavy hand landed on her shoulder, she shot out of her chair and spun around to face the danger. Brandt.

"Jesus," she snapped when she could, her hand still covering her pounding heart. "Don't do that."

"Sorry." He held his hands out in supplication, yet his twinkling eyes paid lie to that statement.

Sam glared at him before slowly retaking her place.

"If you two are finished, can we get at it?" Irena glared at them both. "We're just about done."

Brandt walked around to stand behind the artist. He gave a quiet but deadly whistle. "Wow."

2:34 pm

IRENA SHOT HIM a look. "I'm not done yet. Get lost."

Brandt glanced over at her. He reached for the picture beside her on the table. "Is this yours, too?"

Irena took a quick peek in between her strokes. "Yes. We started with that one."

Sam slid lower in her chair under Brandt's intense gaze. "Why?"

"I do that sometimes. I started with a strong visual to help her to focus on the details. Why?" Irena frowned at him.

Brandt didn't answer. He studied the diagram. Something twigged, but he couldn't place it. The detail depicted was incredibly scary. Christ, she was good. Inside, he turned cold. His team members were going to have a heyday with this. Anyone would point out the three possibilities – either she was an incredibly gifted psychic, had a deadly twisted imagination, or she'd been there. He knew which one Kevin would lobby for.

He studied Sam, slouched in the chair. She lay with her eyes closed; gray smudges underlined her eyes, accenting her translucent skin and the fatigue.

The picture disturbed him. Irena was good. In this piece of work, she'd been damn good. The eerie details made it come alive – or appear even deader. In fact, the picture was damned near perfect. Tossed bedclothes, half on and half off, portrayed the violence with uncanny accuracy. The pool of blood on the mattress and the overturned lamp on the night table added to the impression of a great wrong having been committed. She'd given a death scene a terrible sense of life.

Softy, he questioned her further. "Sam – this level of detail?" He paused shaking his head. "Did you tell Irena about the blood dripping down on the mattress or the lamp overturned?"

Stretching her arms over her head, Sam shook her head. "I knew the bedding had been tossed around and that there was massive blood loss. I thought the lamp had dumped because the light came from the floor region. The layout details are all from Irena."

"You realize this level of detail is what will bother the other detectives?"

Sam bolted upright to stare at him. "Bother them, how?"

Pulling a chair up beside her, Brandt laid the sketch down. "They're going to say this picture has been envisioned from someone in the room, not from someone in the body, because if you were to see from her eyes only, you wouldn't have these details in your viewing area."

Sam peeked at Irena, who was listening to the conversation. "I gave her some details, her years of experience in this job allowed her to fill in the rest. But make no mistake, that picture..." She stabbed the sheet once again in his hand. "Is from one of my visions." She ran her hand through her hair. "Sorry, maybe I'm just overreacting from this morning." She turned to Irena who'd kept working, her pencil swiftly forming and pulling visions off the page.

Silence ensued in the large room. Brandt knew they were the center of attention. He cleared his throat and cast a glance in Irena's direction. She was studiously working on her drawing, keeping her head down.

"I didn't mean to imply anything. But for anyone who doesn't really understand how your abilities work, this...stuff seems, well I guess it's a little freaky, and they're going to question it."

She nodded, refusing to face him.

"Brandt, Captain Johansen wants to see you."

Damn. He glanced around at Adam, who tilted his head in the captain's direction. Brandt shook his head and motioned toward Sam.

Adam grimaced. "That's why."

Great. Cops preferred to work with what they could see, hear, and touch. That's why he'd brought Sam in today. For these pictures. That, and to hopefully shake loose more details from Sam's psyche.

"Now. And you're to take the picture with you."

Brandt glanced around the room only to find everyone suddenly busy – heads down. He glanced at Sam's bent head. "Don't panic. I'll talk to him. Everything's going to be fine. I promise."

Her eyes said she didn't believe him.

Frustrated, picture in hand, he strode past the younger detective to Captain Johansen's office. It felt like walking a gauntlet as everyone openly watched. He rapped hard on the closed door.

"Come in."

Brandt pushed the door aside and entered the room. The shades were now open, showing the heavy storm clouds of Portland beyond. Tall office buildings mixed with high-rises in the skyline. A busy world operated out there and for once Brandt wished he could join it.

"Sit down."

"I'll stand, sir." He stared straight at the captain and handed over the picture.

"What do you think?"

Surprised, Brandt could only stare at him. The captain glared up at him. "I think the two of them did a hell of a job."

The two men exchanged hard glances.

"Did she add anything new?"

"Not to this one. They are working on the next picture right now."

He nodded. Taking his time, the captain examined the picture in detail. "Does the photo match the crime scene?"

"I haven't had a chance to compare it yet. Still it lines up with what I remember."

The captain nodded again. "Does Stefan Kronos know her?"

That threw Brandt off balance. "I haven't asked him."

A keen glance came his way. "Maybe you should. Kevin doesn't feel this woman is to be trusted. In fact he puts her at the top of the list of suspects."

"He would." Brandt couldn't hide his disgust. "Kevin has yet to listen to her seriously."

"What makes you think she knows anything?"

Brandt pointed toward the sketches. "That."

The captain stared at the black image again, his lips pursed. "The question is whether the picture is too exact?"

"I'd have to compare it to the crime scene photos."

The captain nodded once. "Then do that. While you're at it, get her fingerprints and if she's willing, her DNA. That will either clear her or implicate her. She's either who she says she is or she's a suspect." He handed the sketch back. "Make sure we know which."

Brandt couldn't believe what he'd heard. "You might want to remember she came in willingly. She doesn't have to be treated with suspicion."

"Then don't. Just ask her. If she's innocent she won't mind." The captain's lips twitched into a wolf smile that made the hairs stand up on Brandt's neck. He returned to the stack of papers on his desk, clearly dismissing Brandt. "Now get those fingerprints and DNA and get her out of my station before I have a mutiny on my hands."

Brandt pulled open the door and shut it quietly behind him. Fingerprints weren't out of line; the DNA was.

Somehow, he had to gain Sam's cooperation.

Thankfully, she was still focused on the pictures. He watched for her reaction as he asked, "Would you mind offering your fingerprints so we can convince the naysayers that you weren't involved?" He tapped the paper for emphasis. "Like I said, some will take this the wrong way," he added in a low voice.

Sam froze. Irena even stilled for a long moment before her pencil returned to scribbling furiously.

Once again, Sam straightened. Calmly, she studied him. Once again, Brandt felt like a lowlife. It didn't matter that this was needed to rule her out, and it was only commonsense. No. It was the right thing to do and would stop the many conjectures and innuendos that were going to fly. Still, he felt like he'd kicked a puppy. Or maybe a cornered barn cat. "It's common to take fingerprints to rule out people."

"Only when they've been at the crime scene." Her voice was

low and troubled.

Brandt tried again. "I know you're telling the truth. I've just finished telling the captain that exact same thing. That doesn't change the fact that some people here aren't going to believe anything you or I have to say."

That brought a sharp glance his way.

"If you do this, it quiets the talk and shuts up those that want to put you as the prime suspect."

"No, it won't," she scoffed. "It will rule out that my fingerprints match those you have on file, but anyone who wants to disbelieve is still going to say that I could have worn gloves."

Damn. He was hoping she wouldn't figure that out so quickly.

She hopped to her feet. "I have nothing to hide. I came here to help so take my damn prints." She walked over to stare out the window, her face lean and hard, hurting.

Brandt hated feeling like a heel. It would help if he could explain it further. This wasn't the time or the place.

"I'm sorry. This really is the best way."

"Whatever. Just take the prints and let me go home."

"Fine." Brandt knew his irritation was unreasonable. She had a right to be dismayed, upset even, but this tired out acceptance upset him. Now that she'd agreed, how could he approach the idea of DNA? He hesitated, wondering how to start.

She gave him a long flat stare. "What?"

He sighed and rubbed the top of his head. "The captain would also like your DNA while we're at it."

She closed her eyes and swayed unsteadily.

"Easy. Don't faint on me. This is just a Q-tip in the mouth kind of thing. It's not major." He studied her pale face. "Did you eat?"

Her eyes opened, showing black unreadable pools. "Not much."

"Let's get this over with so you can get some lunch."

Sam checked her watch. She was so tired. She'd probably need food before making the drive back to Parksville. Right now, though, all she wanted was to be home alone.

"Make it fast. I need to return to the clinic."

Where she felt loved and supported, he had no doubt. He understood how she felt. "By the way, have you called Stefan yet?"

"No. But it might be the first thing I do when I get home."

He nodded. "That's probably a very good idea."

CHAPTER 9

4:14 pm

FOR ABOUT THE hundredth time, Sam wiped first one hand and then the other on her jeans. Her fingers clenched on the steering wheel. Weariness still pulled on her, although much less so. Going to work for a couple of hours had helped some. Especially considering she'd managed to sneak in, take care of the animals, and sneak out without seeing anyone. The last thing she'd wanted was company.

Moses lay in his usual place, his tail wagging. There was no sign of Soldier. Sam parked and went inside.

She scrubbed her fingers, up one side and down the other, then she washed them all over again. Using a tea towel, she dried her hands and inspected them again. That there'd been no fingerprint ink to wash off, didn't change the fact she saw it every time she looked. She shivered and tugged her worn sweater around her tighter. Even though the sun shone high overhead, her bones were chilled. It had been a hell of a day.

Sam could only guess at what Brandt and the other detectives were learning about her now. She reached for the hot water and soap again.

4:25 pm

BRANDT REFUSED TO feel guilty. He'd done his job. That's all. That picture of hers changed everything – and had cemented the captain's opinion. At least he'd agreed to make good use of what she had to offer, with the caveat to keep him in the loop.

He pushed his chair away from his desk and reached behind his head, locking his fingers together. The captain was right.

Brandt needed to ask Stefan about Sam. He'd give Sam another day to contact Stefan on her own, then he'd bring the two of them together, regardless.

He'd worked successfully with Stefan for years. He knew good psychics could offer invaluable help unavailable through traditional police work. He also knew they were unusual people. They didn't see the world the same as the rest of the population. Senses overloaded easier and they retreated to spaces that soothed their raw souls.

Sam had her home at the lake for a physical retreat, did she have anything else? Stefan had a beautiful log house, yet his real solace was his art. His stunning, but tortured paintings were known the world over.

"Brandt."

Brandt frowned. Kevin. He sighed inwardly. "Kevin. What's up?" He eyed the other detective warily. They hadn't spoken since the meeting in Captain Johansen's office. Right now, Kevin sported a huge smirk on his face.

Kevin walked to the desk, holding out a sheaf of papers. "Just some research for you. Maybe this will convince you she's not quite what you want her to be."

He dropped the papers on Brandt's desk and walked out.

The top fax was a newspaper article. Brandt checked the date, March 10, 1998. The headline read *Young Psychic Leads Police on Merry Chase.*

Shit. Brandt sat down for some heavy reading.

4:45 pm

KEVIN COULDN'T HELP feeling satisfied. Damn that felt good. Vindication. Now maybe Brandt would get that witch off his mind and off this case. And the same went for himself. Since this morning's meeting, he'd had a hard time focusing.

Finally, he'd broken down and researched Ms. Blair's background.

He'd gotten lucky. After just an hour, he'd managed to get enough information to convince anyone – even Brandt. At least it should be enough. As a precaution, he'd copied them and given one set to the captain to read as well.

Handing the papers over to Brandt felt good. Damn good.

This woman was treacherous.

He didn't want her anywhere near his cases.

8:25 pm

WANING LIGHT FLASHED on the ripples in the lake. Sam swam effortlessly through the flickering rays. The evening was silent, except for the splashes as her arms cleaved through the water. The long shadows drooped after the heat of the afternoon, dipping deep into the lake for the refreshing coolness. Even the birds were silent.

Sam continued to swim for another twenty minutes. Tired and content, she dove under the surface before rolling over to float on her back. She closed her eyes and rested. The serenity of the evening slipped under her anger and pain, gently tugging them free to disperse amongst the ripples. Deprived of all else, but the sensation of water lapping on her heated skin, Sam lost herself in the moment. Her breathing slowed and she relaxed deeper. How healing. A heavy sigh, coming from nowhere, released into the air.

A short bark cut through the tranquility. Sam rolled over to see Moses at the end of the dock, waiting for her. He barked again and jumped around, wagging his tail. Sam laughed, slowly swimming toward the dock. "I'm fine Moses. Don't worry, I'm coming in."

Moses barked once more before lying down to watch her approach. She'd almost reached him when Moses sprang to his feet and turned to face the house. He barked once.

Hugging the dock, Sam peered through the shadows. A shadow slowly separated from the tree line. Soldier. Sam watched in wonder as the big dog limped toward them.

Tears of pride melded with droplets of the lake as Sam hopped out of the water. "Hey, Soldier. Good to see you on your feet, boy."

She stayed at the end of the dock, her feet dangling in the water and watched his progress anxiously. "You can do it, Soldier. Just a little more." He seemed so weak. Head down, his spine hunched in pain as each foot touched down. Still, he kept coming. He stopped at the end of the dock and lowered his haunches. He stared down at them and whined.

Moving slowly but confidently, Sam stood up and walked the few steps over to the dogs. Soldier curled his lip, although he didn't growl. Sam bent over and patted him gently on his shoulder. His fur was stiff with dirt. She glanced at the fresh water all around them. It would be a bad idea.

Soldier glared up at her, his lip curled higher.

"Yeah, I hear you. Not quite ready for a dip in the lake are you? Maybe in a couple of days, okay?"

She picked up her towel and dried off. Wrapping it around her, she slipped into her sandals and calling to the dogs, she walked up to the cabin. Single file, they trooped behind her. At the front door, she waited for Moses to come in. Surprised, she watched as Soldier ambled in behind Moses. She felt honored. He'd obviously decided this was home.

Sam smiled, whispered, "Good night guys," and headed to her bedroom and a good night's rest.

That night, her dreams were wild and even more colorful than usual. The scenes were brighter than normal. They screamed at her overloud and overbright – overwhelming her in their sensory onslaught. A sexual haze had her twisting and moaning as her body moved to an internal heat she'd never experienced. Large capable hands stroked upwards over her belly, caressing the smooth contours. Slowly the fingers slid higher and higher.

Sam caught her breath when the hands stilled, the tension coiling tighter inside. She wiggled closer, trying to move into his hands. Warm laughter tickled her ear. She groaned, not understanding the driving need that had overtaken her body. A part of Sam struggled to clear her mind. She didn't have a lover.

His hands moved again. She sighed with relief, her breath floating out into the blackness of the night. That small part of her rational mind questioned the unusual sexual overtones and the wild colors floating through her mind.

The rest of Sam's awareness centered on the tormenting fingers and sparks igniting along her nerve pathways. Sensations burned as fire seared over her skin. She churned with an inner heat, a heat that built to the point of pain. Finally, the hands reached the swell of her breasts – and stopped. Sam couldn't help herself, she tried to shift into those magic hands, but they gripped her ribs, stopping her. A groan escaped.

"Shhh," whispered the dark voice. "We have all night."

Sam shuddered at the promise. The promise and something else. Something wrong, something off. It bothered her, except she was too caught up in the sexual tension to want to figure it out. She arched high off the bed as he cupped her full breasts and squeezed gently. They coaxed then relaxed then returned to torment her again.

Sam cried out.

Dark laughter wafted through the room.

She shivered. There it was again. That nebulous feeling of something wrong. What was it?

The hands returned to torment her again. "Please..." She tried to reach for him, needing him closer.

And found she couldn't.

Just as the sensation of wrongness returned, Sam realized her arms were caught above her head. Caught and held by one of his hands. And the clouds in mind, blurring her clarity.

He laughed again. Dark laughter became black as his other hand, the one that had so gently cradled her breast, squeezed hard and then harder again.

Sam arched up, screaming in agony.

And woke up.

Still in shock, Sam curled into a tight ball and rocked back and forth under the comforter, her hands cradling her tender breasts. She bolted upright, peering into the dark corners of her bedroom. Relief washed over her. She was alone. "Dear Lord. Thank you." It had only been a dream.

A dream. Was it possible?

She stilled. A dream or a vision. She shuddered, the shakes wracking her body once again. Dear God, is this what that animal was doing? Seducing his victims with their own sexuality then turning on them? No. Sam examined the memories. Something had been very wrong, but she couldn't put her finger on it. Everything had a surreal look, an overly loud and overly colored appearance to it. A thought burst into her consciousness.

Drugs. The woman had been drugged.

Had the other victims? Sam realized her earlier visions had started too late to be able to identify something like that. She wouldn't have noticed a needle prick amongst the other pain. Panic for her life would have dispelled the rest of the drugged dullness away from her thoughts.

Sam started crying, quiet painful sobs of possibility. She didn't want to know any more. She couldn't deal with it. Not this. After tonight, she might never let another man touch her again – ever.

Touch.

She froze. The guy in her dreams hadn't worn gloves.

Had it been him? Another asshole? Or had it truly been just a nightmare? She shuddered. It had seemed so real. A wet dream gone bad in a big way. Sliding deeper into her bed, Sam pulled the covers to her chin. Only it wasn't enough. She hopped out of bed, snatched up an old nightshirt from the box on the floor, and pulled it over her head.

For the second time that day – she felt violated.

9:35 am, June 18th

BRANDT STRODE DOWN the hallway. One of his priorities this morning was to connect Sam with Stefan. He'd finally managed to reach him early this morning. Now all he had to do was to get Sam to agree to meet him. And he needed to talk to Sam about her past workings with the police.

The research Kevin had brought him had been less than flattering. Still, Brandt knew that Stefan had some less-than-stellar moments at the beginning of his career as well. The article hadn't given her age and was years ago. She'd have been young and green. Not to mention untrained, which she still was. Hence his push to connect her to Stefan as soon as possible.

Nothing he'd read had given him any reason to disbelieve her. He suspected Sam could be instrumental on his proposed task force. Not to mention many other ongoing cases. He hoped to cultivate her skills on a regular basis. Even if that meant returning to his old station. At least there, his old captain was amiable to psychics. Ideas percolated through his brain. He'd talk it over with some of his friends – and Stefan, of course.

Brandt never had liked authority. He still didn't, but with age came understanding that those above were just doing their job to make it better and safer for everyone. Or at least it was supposed to work that way. However, just as there were good and bad guys on the streets, the same could be said of the police department. One still had to believe that most of the bad guys were outside the force.

"Hey Brandt. Ran the fingerprints you asked for. She checks out."

Brandt lifted his head. The youngest of the three technicians walked into his office. His name eluded him – something European like Pieter. Brandt smiled and held out his hand for the papers being offered. "Anything interesting?"

"No rap sheet, if that's what you are asking." The tech pointed to the second page. "This might be of interest. Yeah, she was also a suspect in a missing child case in Spokane, Washington, years ago."

Brandt's gaze sharpened on the younger man's face. "What? A suspect?"

The tech shook his head. "Apparently she had information for the police, only they didn't believe her. The end result made her a suspect for a while, until the child was found safe and sound."

Brandt digested that as he scanned the paperwork. "Thanks, I'll take it from here." Now he understood Sam's odd reaction yesterday. She'd already been through this. Once again at his office, he pored over the report. So, eight years ago she'd tried to help and failed – been mocked even, based on Kevin's material. This file showed she'd tried again five years ago. The Spokane P.D. hadn't mocked her; they'd made her a suspect.

Brandt shuffled through the file. What was missing in the report was how the child had been found. Had Sam contributed to the little girl's safe return? He might need to call the detective listed on this particular case file. Grabbing a folder, he wrote Samantha's name on the tab and stacked the growing collection of material inside. Brandt leaned back in his chair, hands locked behind his head.

Her connection to this killer bothered him. It could be the same asshole that he'd been tracking. Both of them changed the method of death, but as far as he could tell, they both favored beautiful young women between eighteen and thirty-five – and all were middle-class, working females.

His mind flitted through the elements he knew. Sam's killer wore a ski mask, which didn't make sense. Usually the guys who planned on killing their victims didn't bother with masks. After all, there wasn't going to be anyone left behind to identify them.

He had no way of knowing if the other cases in his files were the same. The victims were all dead. There were never any witnesses, and little forensic evidence left behind. Then there was the ring. If Sam had anything concrete, the ring might just be it.

She was also connecting with a lot of victims. Most serial killers took time between kills. Sam's visions occurred with only days between them. Some killers went on a killing frenzy until whatever drove them, drained out of their system. Then they went quiet. Sometimes the quiet period lasted months to years. Brandt knew his best chance of catching this killer was before he went off the radar again. Who knew how long it would be before he resurfaced again.

9:50 am

DILLON WALKED INTO the conference room. Not only had he missed the meeting this morning, he'd also missed breakfast. He was hoping there'd be some scones or a Danish left over. Walking to the sideboard, he smiled. One huge blueberry muffin. Perfect.

He snatched up his prize and walked toward the double doors. Several papers lay discarded on several chairs. He turned the closest one over. It was a picture of a ring. Wasn't that the one Brandt was researching? He'd heard about it, but this was the first he'd seen it.

Walking to his desk, he muttered about the dinosaurs in the office. It was hard being a forward moving kind of guy in this place. The mantra around here was always about 'good old fashioned detective work.' Christ, who needed all that legwork? Technology was meant to be used. The same for the media. They were always helpful. At least Dillon had found them so. The Internet was, of course, the best. Why didn't the station have a website where pictures like this could be posted and give the public an opportunity to email or phone in with their information?

Of course, this was an old argument, and he'd gone several rounds with Captain Johansen over it – and lost every one. Dillon had wanted to host a regular five-minute slot on both the local television station and the radio stations. That had been shot down, too. Still, accessing the public was the cheapest and fastest way to gain information. The department's man-hours, logged trying to find and interview people, were incredibly expensive.

He took a large bite of his late breakfast muffin. He could understand Brandt not wanting to take that step. Like Dillon, Brandt was new here and didn't want to rock the boat. Dillon stopped chewing as an idea formed. If he arranged everything correctly, Brandt would get the information he needed, and Dillon could prove his theory. More ammunition to take to the captain. In a way, Dillon would be doing this to help Brandt. Who knew what new information could come to light.

He grinned. He'd have to think this through. Yet…it sounded like a hell of an idea.

10:15 am

BRANDT RUBBED THE back of his neck. The screen scrolled, searching for more cases linking to his killer. Just then, his phone rang, distracting him.

"Hello."

"Detective Sutherland. This is Nancy from Willow Health Clinic."

The manager from the long-term care home. He groaned silently and closed his eyes, his fingers pinching the bridge of his nose. "Hi, Nancy. How are you doing?"

"Umm, I guess I'm fine. The thing is I need your help with Maisy again."

His shoulders slumped. He knew it. His mother was up to no good again.

"What's the problem?" He winced and held his breath.

"Umm, well…" She stopped.

Brandt shook his head, he knew already. Checking his watch – did he have time to whip down there? "Is she causing trouble again?"

"It's not so much causing trouble…more like she's stirring up the other residents."

He shut down his laptop. "Would you like me to come by and talk with her again?"

"Yes, yes. That would be wonderful. She's such a fun lady to have around. I hate to even ask you. But the Board has already stretched the rules for her several times, and I'm not sure that she can skate by on this one."

Brandt ran fingers through his hair. "How bad is it this time?"

"She's setting up pools again."

Brandt grinned. "That doesn't sound so bad."

"No," the harried woman on the other end of the phone said. "It's the subject matter that's the problem. Would it be possible to have you stop in sometime today?"

"No problem," he said. "I'm heading in your direction soon, so I'll be there before lunch."

"Oh, thank you. I certainly don't want to upset her. She's interjected such life here," Nancy said warmly.

"No problem. I'll see you in about an hour." Brandt rang off. Standing, he grabbed his briefcase and coat then locked up his desk.

Dillon stuck his head around the door.

"Hey Dillon. What's up?" Brandt barely withheld his grin at Dillon's suit of the day. This was the classic pinstripe with a matching tie in reverse stripes. But it was in forest green, black, and white. Mafia anyone?

"I'm just checking that you still need information on this?" He held up the sketch of the ring. "I missed whatever you said at this morning's meeting." Dillon raised an eyebrow in question.

"I'm looking for the owner. If I can trace it to a store, sorority, or something like that, I might be able to figure out who bought it."

Dillon stared at the sheet, frowning. "It's a simple enough design. But I don't think I've seen one like it." He turned the page slightly. "Is one of the stones missing?"

"Yeah, the last time it was seen, one stone appeared to be missing. The others are clear – diamond or zirconium, maybe."

"Gold, white, brass – do we know?"

"No. Gold in color is all I have."

"Shouldn't be too hard to track down. Have you talked to the jewelry stores here?"

Brandt walked around his desk to stand at Dillon's side, giving the sketch another glance. "I talked to several so far, I've faxed it to several more. So far, the same thing. Not in stock anywhere and no one remembers one quite like this in the last decade or so." Brandt considered the pattern. "It could be a custom job. I'll have to contact the local designers and see."

Behind him, Dillon asked. "Have you checked online?"

"Yes and no. I have a couple of people working on it."

Dillon nodded. "Okay, I'll keep an ear out and let you know if I find anything." He turned and walked toward the doorway. He stopped and turned around. "Oh yeah, while I have the chance, I also wanted to ask if the rumors were true?"

"What rumors?"

The younger man grinned, a perfect toothy smile. Some serious money went into that look. "That you've brought in a psychic on this case."

Brandt refused to let irritation show. "Love rumors, don't you?"

Dillon smirked. "Yeah. The grapevine here is rampant."

Brandt frowned at him, hoping to quell his interest. "Well,

you can't believe everything you hear."

"True." Dillon turned, as if to finally leave again. "Let me know if you need any help with anything."

"I'll be fine, but thanks for the offer." He motioned Dillon to precede him out of the office. "Time to head out." Brandt checked his watch. He was running late.

CHAPTER 10

10:45 am

SAM FOUND IT hard not to worry while she worked with the animals. It's not as if she lacked for topics. After last night's vision, she was now worried about *not* telling the police. Her instinct reaction had been *no way*. Not after yesterday. Today in the light of day, she knew she needed to tell Brandt.

The worry about what information the police had dug up on her, nagged at her. What if Detective Sutherland contacted that deputy from Nikola County? There was a lot of ancient history there and none of it looked good for her. Chances of the detective believing her story over that rogue deputy's version were nonexistent. She already knew that law enforcement protected their own. What were the chances the deputy had forgotten her? Not great.

"Sam, can you give me a hand?" The voice called through the swinging double doors.

Sam quickly closed the door to the rabbit cage she'd been cleaning and headed for surgery room one.

She pushed open the door. "Jesus." She jumped forward to help. "You could have called me earlier." She reached out to support the large, sleeping Newfoundland dog that was in danger of sliding off the small table. "Time to get a larger table?"

The other two women laughed. "Careful with the front legs. He's got stitches across the ribs on that side." The three women carefully maneuvered the large animal onto a second table. Then waited to receive him and then move him into an even larger cage.

Once inside, the dog's wounds were checked, his tubes adjusted for the cage walls and the door closed. Sam stepped over to look at the injured animal. He had to be a hundred and fifty pounds. "What happened to him?"

Dr. Valerie Brown, the older of the two, smiled and said, "You don't need to whisper, he's not going to wake up."

Sam's lip twitched. "I know. He's beautiful."

The other woman, Dr. Brenda Torrance, stripped off her gloves. "Yup, he's gorgeous alright, only he needs to stop arguing with cars."

Sam sent a sharp question her way. "What, another car accident?" She glanced at the sleeping animal. "How horrible."

"We'll move him to the back room after he wakes up from his anaesthesia."

Sam narrowed her gaze. Funny lights played over the surface of the dog's thick fur coat. Weird. Shivers raised goose bumps on Sam's skin. A vision reached into her brain and took over her sight. The dog was hurt worse than the minor repair held together by the stitches. Images crowded her – the dog up in the air, tumbling before hitting his left hip on a fire hydrant.

"Did he get the cut from the car or from the landing?" She focused on the animal's body, searching for any clues as to what else could be wrong.

"The front grill of the truck ripped a strip of hide off him. Why?" Valerie asked.

Sam gazed at her vaguely. "What? Oh, his left hip doesn't look right. But I'm sure you took x-rays, so that hip must be just bruised and not broken."

Deliberately, Sam left, as if to return to the cages to finish her job. In the other room, she stopped outside the door and listened.

Behind her was a weighty silence.

"What was that all about?"

"Damned if I know. Were x-rays done?"

A rustle of papers. "No, the owners brought him in for stitches. They saw the accident. They didn't want to go through the expense of x-rays, if not required. A check-up was done before we came on for the day." More papers were shuffled. "What do you think, should we do x-rays?"

"I hate taking over cases already in progress. I was told this animal just needed stitches. Shit."

Silence except for a brush of clothing and soft muttering. Sam could only hope they were checking the dog's hip a little more closely. Nodding encouragement that they couldn't see, Sam followed their actions with one ear to the door.

"Damn. We need to x-ray his hips. Let's call the owners."

"She's right?"

"I don't know, but there's something wrong. Who did the intake on this animal?"

"I'll have to check the paperwork when we're done."

Sam grinned. She whispered to the empty room. "There you go boy. Now you'll be fine." She listened for another moment before heading to finish her work.

It wasn't until later that she realized this was her first vision around an animal. Sam had actually seen the energy over the injured part of the body. The goose bumps had been the first inkling of something wrong. Her heart positively lifted with joy. To be able to do something for animals would be wonderful. Now, if she could learn to control it so she could use it at will. More questions for Stefan.

"Sam, can you run and do a pickup for us?"

Sam spun around, her hand rushing to her chest.

"Sorry." Valerie reached out an apologetic hand. "I didn't mean to scare you."

Sam blew out a noisy breath, letting her hand drop down. "I must have been miles away."

"It's these shoes. They should be sleuth shoes." Valerie lifted her practical working shoes to peer at the soles.

Sam waited until she had Valerie's attention. "What do you need?"

"I need you to run over to where Lucy's daughter works and pick up an injured cat. If you don't mind. It's about fifteen minutes from here." Valerie checked her notes briefly. "You were right, by the way, the dog's hip was dislocated and the ligaments and muscles are badly torn."

"Oh, how sad. I'm glad you could fix him." How could she refuse to go get the cat? Her shift wasn't over for at least an hour. Besides, they were doing right by the dog.

"Of course, we'll pay for your time and your gas."

Sam brushed her hand in the air. "It's no problem. I'm almost done here. Give me directions. I'll just wash up and get ready."

"Great. I really appreciate it. We've been so busy that I haven't taken the time to say how much I appreciate your efforts here. Thanks." With a grateful smile, Valerie headed to the office.

Sam stared, bemused, at the flapping doors. It's a good thing she'd left. Sam didn't have any response to give. She couldn't remember the last time she'd received a compliment like that.

It was kind of nice.

11:00 am

IT HAD BEEN a busy morning already. And still Bill wasn't quite done. He shuffled the contents in the bed of his truck. He'd promised to bring the dogs over to the palliative care center. Those patients loved seeing the animals. It was the least he could do for those dying folks. It was either make their last days a little sweeter or knock 'em off early.

He grinned. It would be so easy. Only, it wouldn't mean the same thing for him. It wasn't just getting his rocks off – well that was a huge part of it – but he needed certain things in order to get there. It used to be easy. Now everything had to go exactly right or he couldn't enjoy himself.

Starting with the victim – just anyone wouldn't do. The right victim was everything to him. He was a selection specialist. And he'd made a mistake last time. Not on the girl, but on the method. He'd tested a new drug on her. Bad decision. She'd reacted terribly, slipping into unconsciousness before he could really enjoy her. He'd left – beyond pissed. Now, he'd need a fix again...and soon because of that.

He'd expected to hear about her on the news, but so far nothing. Stupid cops, they'd probably written her off as a suicide. He grinned. That worked for him. Fooling the cops kept things challenging. Over the years he'd even wondered what drove him, but had come to the conclusion that it didn't matter, as he was past the point of stopping. He refused to dwell on it.

He also didn't like the mask thing. The bloody wool itched. He preferred to stay anonymous. Not take any chances. When he'd first started, he hadn't taken the same care. During the first couple of rapes, he'd sweated with the droplets falling onto the women's skin. Early on, he'd tried using alcohol on one woman's skin to remove any sweat or saliva and had quickly discarded that. He'd ended up with a bloody mess. If being uncomfortable was the price then that was fine with him. The gloves also didn't thrill him because he wanted the skin-to-skin contact. Every once in a while, he still succumbed to the temptation, but was always careful to put them on immediately afterwards. Why the hell it mattered at that point, he didn't know, except he'd been doing it that way for so long logic couldn't even begin to win over superstition. What worked, worked and that was all there was to it.

A shrink would have a heyday with him. Yeah, he was paranoid. Still, he was in this for the long haul and didn't plan to screw up anytime soon.

11:10 am

BRANDT PULLED INTO the parking lot at the Willow Health Center. He parked at the front and walked inside. The offices were off to the right. He headed there first.

"Hi, Nancy."

The tiny older woman looked up in surprise. Then a big smile broke out. "Detective Sutherland. Thank you so much for coming."

He shook his head. "She's my problem, not yours."

Nancy grinned. "Except that while she's here, she's also our problem."

There was no arguing that logic. "I'll walk down and have a talk with her before she goes for lunch."

"Good. She might be in her room, or she could be over with the animals today. I'll be there in a couple of minutes."

"Oh, right. It's pet day, isn't it?" The center had a well-loved program where family members were allowed to bring pets in to see the various residents for an hour to two. Sometimes, special dogs and cats came in to keep the people company or put on small shows. The older people loved it. It was a highlight for them.

Brandt walked down to his mother's room.

"Mom?" He knocked gently.

"Come in."

Brandt pushed the door open to find several other people in there. A hushed silence descended when they recognized their visitor.

He heaved a sigh. "Yes, the cops have been called. Mom, what the hell are you up to now?"

Maisy ran over to him and gave him a big hug. "It's lovely to see you dear, however, there's no reason to use profanity."

What could he do? She was his mother. He rolled his eyes and wrapped his arms around her frail body in a gentle hug.

He grasped her shoulders gently and held her at arm's length. "Mom, we have to have a talk."

11:20 am

"HERE IT IS." Sam slowed, pulled into the long driveway, and parked. There was a familiar truck parked to the right. She frowned. There's no reason it should be Brandt's truck. There had to be hundreds of those here in town. Her pulse jumped, and she couldn't help searching the area for him. She didn't want to see him, not really, yet couldn't hold back the pulsing excitement at the thought of it. Traitorous hormones.

She walked inside. Large and open with multiple comfy couches, the lobby had a friendly atmosphere. Sam could see people feeling welcome here. Bright yellows and moderate oranges blended with the lush palms and overgrown dieffenbachia plants filling each corner.

The front counter stood empty. Sam pursed her lips. There didn't appear to be a bell to ring for service either. Sam frowned. She checked her watch. Surely, it was early for lunch? Not knowing how a place like this worked, Sam found herself choosing between two corridors and took the left one. Various doorways along the hallway were identified by numbers. They appeared to be apartments or self-contained suites of some kind. They didn't look like the hospital rooms she'd assumed they would be.

Having never known anyone living permanently or temporarily in a place like this, she found herself wondering at the circumstances that would leave them here. Did these people not have family, or were they alone like she was?

Were they happy here? Or did they pine away, always wishing for a better life? Living alone for so long, a place like this could seem like a prison. Surely, some of these people had families to live with?

Laughter drifted toward her. Curious, Sam followed the sound. Glancing back, she saw the reception desk remained empty.

The hallway opened up into another large sitting area with many tables surrounded by people. Some played cards, others were engrossed in chess, and still others were petting several dogs. Animals. Now that was a nice touch. Sam smiled at a particularly large feline that strolled regally between several legs, her leash getting caught up – to everyone's enjoyment.

Sam looked around for someone in charge. Everyone appeared to be in the same age category – old. There was one younger man with a basset hound on a leash. The dog appeared comfortable, sprawled in place and showing no interest in being dragged across the room. Sam smiled. The dog was gorgeous. Evidently, several of the residents thought so too. Several bent to pat the dog's long ears and rotund belly.

No one appeared bothered by Sam's presence. In fact, no one even seemed to notice her. She continued past the group and headed down a quieter corridor where there were several more doors.

One opened, and a small woman with a nametag on her shirt walked out. *Finally.* Sam stopped. "Excuse me. Do you know where I can find either Sarah or Nancy?" Belatedly, Sam read the nametag.

"I'm Nancy. Sarah has gone home for the day. How can I help you?"

"I'm here from the vet hospital in Parksville to pick up an injured cat."

"Oh my goodness. You've been walking around here looking for me, haven't you? I'm so sorry."

Sam smiled at her. "No problem. How is the…?" Her voice trickled to a stop as a large man stepped out of the room behind Nancy. "Brandt?" She blushed and quickly corrected herself. "Detective Sutherland, I mean. What are you doing here?"

Nancy jumped in. "Oh, do you two know each other? That's wonderful. Why don't you stay here for a moment while I try to locate the poor cat?" With a bright smile the cheerful woman hastened down the way Sam had come.

"No, I'll come…" But Nancy was already gone.

"Too late. Nancy can move very quickly when she wants to."

"Brandt, who are you talking to?" A spry lady with bottle-blue hair came to the door. "Oh." She smiled, a little too brightly. "How nice. Brandt, invite your friend inside." She turned to Sam. "Hi, I'm Maisy and Brandt is my son."

Sam smiled weakly. "Hi." Of course, this was Brandt's mother.

"Come in, child."

Sam found herself manoeuvred into the small suite where several curious seniors instantly surrounded her. Behind her, she could hear Maisy whispering loudly to Brandt.

"Now I know why the others wouldn't do. All you had to do was tell me about her. This is wonderful." Maisy beamed.

Sam closed her eyes. Uh, oh.

"Mom, don't start with me."

"Of course not. I'm too happy to argue with you." She bustled over to regard Sam like a unique species under a microscope. "Move everyone, give the child some space." She snagged Sam's arm and led her to the couch. "My goodness there's not much to you, is there?"

"There's enough. I'm actually quite healthy." Sam tried to defend herself while allowing Maisy to shove her gently onto a flowery couch that probably had many stories to tell. For all the gentleness behind this woman's gestures, Sam sensed a steel core. She might be Brandt's mother, but Sam doubted she had let him get away with much.

A warm cup of tea was placed in her hand, followed by a small plate heaped high with cookies.

"Oh, no. The tea is just fine, thank you."

"Nonsense. You need to eat more."

A polite way of saying she was too skinny.

Another silver-blue head popped around the corner. "So your son is here, is he? Now you're going to get it, Maisy."

"Nonsense. He can solve this." This came from one of the people that had been in the small room the whole time.

Brandt interrupted. "Let's return to why I'm here. Mom, what are you up to now?"

She rose with a gentle smile on her face. "Surely, they didn't call you over this little bit of fun we're having, did they?"

Multiple voices chimed in with their take on the situation.

"Mom, this is the third time this month. What's gotten into you?"

"Why nothing. Besides, this isn't my fault. This time it's your fault."

Brandt shook his head, clearly confused.

Sam couldn't believe it. She watched in bemusement, drinking her tea, as fifteen elderly people in the room crowded around Brandt, all of them talking at once.

"Okay, one at a time. Come on everyone, calm down. Jackson, you take it easy – I don't want you having a heart attack again. Colonel, good to see you. Do you know what Maisy is up to this time?"

The colonel laughed a deep Santa laugh that charmed Sam. "Of course. She's acting as a bookie again."

"Mom?" Brandt spun around to see his mother calmly counting a column of figures. "What are you doing?"

"Nothing much. Just taking bets on Joshua's love life." She snickered. "Or lack of it."

Several giggles and guffaws filled the room.

"Joshua?"

"Yeah, the sour puss that runs this place. He has a new girlfriend, so we're betting on how long before it all goes south. Personally, I don't see it making it to the end of the month."

More laughter as several other people boasted what time they'd bet on.

Brandt groaned. As always, his mother had fired up her social circle. Brandt just stood, his mouth working, only no words came out.

Sam giggled.

Everyone spun to stare at her. Maisy hopped to her feet and walked around her son. A delighted smile lit up her face. "Oh my, child, that sounded a little rusty."

Sam's eyes widened at that comment. She knew she didn't laugh often, but surely calling it rusty was a little extreme.

"Brandt, I like her. Except she's all skin and bones." She turned to Sam. "Surely, you're not one of those hung up on all those fad diets are you?" Disapproval swept the room.

"No, ma'am. I'm not dieting." Fat chance. Sam thought of the belt she'd had to notch tighter this morning. She was losing weight quicker than she could eat.

"You're all eyes too. Life has been hard on you, hasn't it?" Maisy didn't wait for an answer, which was a relief as Sam had no idea how to answer. Maisy grabbed her arm, tugging the sweater up her arm. "Dearie, you're positively skinny." The blue veins pulsed along the top of Sam's arm. Hurriedly, Sam pulled the oversized sweater down to cover the top of her hand.

Maisy patted her hand before releasing it. "It's okay child. We're not criticizing you. We're all friends here." She smiled up at her son. "Brandt, tell me about this beautiful waif in your life."

All eyes turned to Brandt. Sam's were wide with horror.

Brandt found his voice, just not the volume control. He bellowed, "Mom, stop."

Maisy stared at him, affronted. "Now you listen to me, young man, I haven't even begun."

Grimly, Brandt glared down at her. "You can stop right now. This is a semi-official call because once again you are creating a disturbance. Do you *want* to be evicted from this place? Go somewhere else where you won't have all your friends? This has to stop."

"Harumph."

"Don't give me that. I've told you before, no more betting. Taking a simple wager between two people is one thing, Mom. Setting up a betting book on something like the administrator's love life is going too far – again." Brandt was adamant.

Sam sat bemused as chaos erupted around her. It went on for at least ten minutes before Brandt managed to calm down the outrage.

Watching him, Sam realized that several of the elderly people were staring at her openly. She probably wasn't the norm for Brandt's women.

Her lips quirked in a tentative smile at several of them.

They all smiled big fat grins back at her.

"What's your name, dear?"

Turning to look at Maisy, Sam replied, "My name is Samantha."

"That's a beautiful name." Maisy beamed at her, apparently having no trouble ignoring her son glaring down at the two of them.

Sam wasn't having the same success. Her glance darted between Brandt and Maisy.

"Mom, are you going to behave? Or must I arrange for you to go back to your apartment?"

"Should I ask Samantha if you're behaving?" Maisy asked archly, to the amusement of the audience. She stared innocently up at her towering son. The twinkle in her eye couldn't be missed.

The colonel interrupted. "How about we change the subject? When are you guys going to catch that killer? I heard about them finding that poor woman the other day."

That started the seniors all over again. Brandt threw up one hand in a classic stop gesture. "Silence!"

As Sam watched, Brandt's gaze slid over the seniors, his mother, and finally rested on Sam. He frowned. The room quieted, except Sam didn't think he'd intimidated anyone but her. Maisy's cronies were obviously used to him. They treated him like one of their own. Maisy looked like hell on wheels, for stirring things up.

"I don't know what case you're talking about. We're after several killers. You know I can't talk about any specifics. But the police are following up several leads. We're doing everything we can. So if you know anything that can help us – great. Otherwise, let us do our job." He sent a cutting look to his oblivious mother. "And don't set up a pool on it."

"Well, if we do, we'll bet on you. See? We know you'll solve these cases." His mother beamed up at him.

Brandt shook his head. "Is it safe to leave, Mom? Do you think you can behave for a while?"

"Of course she can." Several of the seniors glared at him.

Brandt rolled his eyes. "Sam, let's go."

Sam hopped up, but had to tug her hand free from Maisy's clasp. "I have to find Nancy and the cat."

"We'll stop at her office on the way out."

Maisy rose and wedged herself between the pair. "Sam, please come for lunch next week. Brandt, when can you bring her?"

"Oh no, I couldn't do that." Sam shook her head.

"Why not?"

Sam didn't know how to answer. She slid a sideways glance at Brandt. Their eyes met. She shrugged, not knowing how to answer the question.

"Mom, Sam and I will discuss it, and I'll get back to you." He tugged Sam further away from his mother. "Now, we're leaving."

"Not without a kiss. Official visit or not, I'm still your mother."

Brandt obediently bent to give his mother a quick peck on the cheek before snagging Sam's arm and pulling her down the hallway.

Sam felt the dozens of eyes following their progress out the door.

"What was that?" Sam glanced behind, sure she was being watched.

A line of curious faces watched every step they took. Maisy stood in the doorway, a satisfied smile on her face.

"The other side of my life," he muttered.

Sam easily read the adoration for his mother in his eyes. Her heart warmed. A guy who loved his mom had a lot going for him. "Uh, oh. Has she got the wrong impression?" Sam shook her head. "I don't know what just happened. I came to pick up an injured cat."

"What happened? My mother happened," he said wryly. "She's a force to be reckoned with."

Sam motioned behind her with her hand. "Is she always like

that?"

"Yes. Unfortunately."

"She's lovely. You're very lucky." Sam couldn't help but wish she had someone so lively and bright in her world.

She felt, more than saw Brandt's eyes upon her. She refused to face him. Thankfully, they'd arrived at Nancy's office, so she didn't have to.

Just then, an overly large box appeared, hiding the skinny man carrying it.

"Thanks, Jeremy. Brandt, can you carry the cat out to the lady's car?"

"No problem. We're both leaving."

"Thank you, Nancy. The hospital will fix this guy right up."

Sam tried to peek under a corner flap of the box. An unholy howl erupted, warning against going any further. She grimaced. "I'll definitely be leaving him in the box." She smiled at the other woman. "Thanks again."

Sam held the door as Brandt carried the box outside. Sam rushed to unlock the passenger side of her truck.

Brandt gently laid the box inside on the seat. It was a tight fit, which would help stop it from sliding around.

"There you go." He straightened and studied her. "Sorry about my mother."

What could she say? "I thought she was sweet. Thank you for carrying the cat." She unlocked the driver's door and got in, anxious to avoid awkward good-byes. "See you around." She cranked the engine and backed out of her spot. After turning the vehicle around she was ready to head onto the highway but Sam was forced to hit the brakes.

Brandt stood in front of the truck, stopping her from going anywhere.

CHAPTER 11

11:50 am

PUZZLED, SHE LOWERED her window. "What's the matter?"

He grinned. "You ran away so fast that I didn't have chance to ask you about Stefan." He held out his hands, palms up. "If you have time, I thought we could go see him later today. What's your schedule like?"

Sam stared at him in shock, as excited jellybeans jumped in her stomach. "I can't right at the moment. I have to get the cat to the hospital for treatment."

"And I understand that. Stefan is only about fifteen minutes from here so we can go later. But if today doesn't work, we can plan it for another day."

"Really." This would be a godsend. She needed to talk to someone who would understand. "What about Stefan? Don't you need to check with him?"

"I spoke to him earlier. He suggested we come mid to late afternoon. I was going to call and ask you what would be convenient, then you showed up here."

She didn't want to lose this opportunity by putting it off. Who knew when this chance would arise again? "This afternoon would be great. Where do you want to meet? Here? Or at his house?"

"No, it would be easier if I come to Parksville. How about we meet around three at the vet's office, then we'll go in my truck."

"That would be great." Sam beamed. "I'll see you then."

"Bye."

Brandt waved as she drove past. Sam was grinning so hard, she almost didn't see it. She honked the horn once and drove off. The trip home went fast.

It was a good thing as her thoughts were in turmoil. She had a million questions to ask Stefan and didn't know where to start. Then there was the prospect of spending the afternoon in Brandt's company.

Thoughts and ideas popped and submerged, yet more mixed and brewed. She wasn't the same person she'd been a month ago or even a week ago. What had changed exactly, she couldn't say. Only that she didn't wear her skin the same. Looser, maybe – and not from losing weight. Maybe it was just a better cut, more suited for who she really was.

Strange ramblings from a troubled soul.

Sam sighed. Glimpses of who she was and what she was doing with her life flitted in and out like a hummingbird. Enough to see the color and glow. Not enough to grasp the meaning or details.

A black pickup pulled in behind her. Too close for comfort, but not quite tailgating.

Sam peered into her rear-view mirror, wondering if Brandt had followed her. The truck might be his. She couldn't quite see the driver's face through the tinted windshield. Did Brandt's truck have gradient tinting like that? She couldn't remember. Still, she'd have recognized him behind the wheel, and this wasn't him.

The truck moved closer.

Definitely, tailgating.

The big truck dwarfed her Nissan. She knew nothing about vehicles and this one gleamed in the late sunlight with enough chrome trim to blind anyone. The pair of ram horns on the front identified it as a Dodge. A wave of relief hit when she was able to identify that little bit.

Then the truck came so close she thought it would hit her. Sam's heart shot into her throat, and her stomach heaved. She tried to pull over and let him pass, but he slowed down behind her. When she was almost stopped, he drove forward and deliberately bumped her.

"Shit." Sam hit the gas hard, pulling onto the road. She searched her pocket for her cell phone. She punched in Bandt's number. Sam switched her gaze from the road to her rear-view mirror.

"Hello. What's up, Sam?"

"Some asshole is trying to run me off the road," she yelled as the truck zoomed closer. The driver grinned down at her. His features were little more than a white blur – vaguely familiar, only too far away to be placed.

"What? What are you talking about?"

"This truck pulled in behind me just after I left you. He started tailgating me so I slowed down to pull over, then he deliberately hit my truck. I couldn't help it. I panicked and hit the gas. Now he's on my ass and grinning like a madman."

"What kind of truck?"

"Like yours. Exactly like yours."

This time he was all business. "How far from Parksville are you?"

Sam searched for landmarks. "I think about 7 or 8 miles."

"Anyone else on the road?"

"There's been the odd vehicle. Right now the highway is deserted."

"I'm on my way. Keep driving. Don't pull over if you can avoid it. You don't know what this asshole wants."

Shivers worked down her spine. "Great. I feel so much better now."

"Hang in there."

"Then you'd better drive like hell because I'm doing thirty over the speed limit and this guy is still on my tail."

He snorted. "Don't you worry about that. I'm not that far behind you. You focus on staying alive. I'll be there in a couple of minutes."

Sam turned off the cell phone, keeping a wary eye on the truck staying on her tail.

The highway was flat and wide. It was also deserted. There'd be little danger of an accident if she did go off the road. Yet, the idea of having this guy stop while she was stranded out here alone, kept her foot on the gas. Her little truck rattled and shook at the high speed.

Alternately scanning the rear-view mirrors and staring out the windshield, Sam increased her speed again. A double lane opened up. She surged ahead into the slow lane hoping the truck would take off.

Nerves locked down as tight as her fingers on the steering wheel. As she watched the truck sped up. He pulled into the fast lane to drive neck in neck at her side. Sam felt the first stirring of anger. It helped to check the fear bubbling through her blood. The asshole was playing with her.

From her position, she could see the lower portion of the passenger side panel, and huge monster wheels flashing silver lights.

Anger fuelled her next move.

It might not have been the smartest. Still, a compulsion unlike any other took hold.

Sam hit the brakes hard. The black truck raced past her. Sam whipped her small truck in behind the black one. It had no license plate. Crap. Fear shot skyward. Everyone honest and open had license plates.

She let the distance between her and the truck widen. She watched anxiously to see if he would slow down to torment her more or if he'd had enough. She wasn't looking for a confrontation.

The truck pulled ahead, gaining speed before racing around a corner ahead of her. Thank God. Sam settled into her seat a little more comfortably. And breathed. It had probably been a punk kid playing power games. The band around her temple loosened.

She called Brandt. "He just took off." Sam could see flashing lights up ahead.

"Did you manage to see the license plate?"

"There wasn't one. Another reason for my panic."

"Did he go straight ahead?"

Sam checked all her mirrors even though she knew the black truck was nowhere to be found. "Yeah. He's long gone by now."

"And where are you now?"

"Almost at the first intersection in town. I'm just a couple of minutes from the vet hospital."

"Okay, I should be in the parking lot by the time you're done in there."

Sam shut down the phone and proceeded at a sedate pace. The poor cat. She glanced over at the box, but it hadn't moved. There hadn't been a sound out of it either. She made a face. It had damn well better be in there. She didn't want to have to go back.

Sam kept a wary eye on her surroundings, but never saw the truck again. Once in the parking lot, she struggled to free the large box from the seat. The cat howled.

Moving slowly, she carried the cat into the first examining room and on to one of the small patient rooms. Valerie joined her almost immediately.

"I really appreciate you stopping to pick this guy up for me."

She glanced at her in surprise. "It was no problem. I was glad to help."

"Good, good. Now let's see what we've got here." She smiled

at her. "Would you mind asking one of the girls to join me? I'm going to need another set of hands for this job.

Sam nodded. "Yes, you will. That cat is pissed."

The vet grinned at her. "And with good reason. Not to worry, we'll put him to rights, if we can."

Five minutes later, Sam stepped outside, not noticing the black truck until she was halfway across the lot. She stopped, her hand going to her throat.

"Sam?"

Oh thank God, it was Brandt. She blew out her pent up breath and walked toward him, relieved and comforted that he'd raced after her. "Hi."

"Hey. How are you now?"

Good question. Sam tried to take stock but found her mind shrinking away from what had almost happened. "I'm fine. Part of me thinks I might have overreacted. Yet, another part says I didn't react fast enough." She shrugged. "I don't know what that was all about."

"Could you see the driver?" Brandt stood, hands fisted on his hips, his gaze penetrating.

She frowned. "Not really, the truck was so much higher than mine. I only saw a vague blur." She hesitated, then figured what the hell. "I caught a glimpse of his face in his rear view mirror, and although I couldn't get a close enough look there was something…I don't know how to describe it. There was something familiar about him."

"Was he tall? Short? Could you see his shoulders above the dashboard? Was his head close to the top of the cab? Hair, bald?"

He fired the questions at her so fast, Sam stopped and blinked. "Tall, his shoulders were above the dash, and his head did come close to the top of the truck or it looked like that from where I was sitting. He had hair, some, I just don't know how much."

Brandt nodded. "Anything defining about the truck?"

"Yeah, no license plate." She bent down to check out the rusted back end and the bumper. "He hit me once and more than a little tap, but I don't see any paint."

Brant squatted down, inspecting the rear of the truck. "The height of the truck would determine where he hit you. His chrome bumper might show traces of paint from your truck, but not the reverse. The chrome won't leave any trace on yours. It might have left a dent – not that we'd be able to see it if it had."

Sam could see that for herself. Her truck body was a mess. There were dents and dings all over the place. Bits of colored paint plastered the truck in odd spots. Some paint showed through the truck's outer layer while some sat over top of it.

Brandt glanced sideways at her. "The techs might be able to lift something off it, but chances are good that the bump shook your paint loose, confusing the issue entirely."

"Great. So no proof again." Sam stood up. "That's the story of my life."

"It's tough. These assholes know that cops follow a set pattern of evidence and when that's not present…"

"Makes sense. I suppose that the killers of the world learn police techniques to stay one jump ahead. She pointed to the tailgate. This killer…not the asshole who bumped me, "but the *killer* – he's playing with you. He considers himself some kind of pro. A specialist that's evolved over time."

He stood up, his gaze sharpened to a laser point. "What makes you say that?"

Leaning against her truck, Sam crossed her arms over her chest and thought about what she'd said. That it felt right wasn't going to be good enough for him. Slowly, formulating her thoughts as she went, she said, "I think it's the impression I've received. I've connected to his energy once or twice when he's gotten excited."

"More killings."

"Maybe." Sam shifted, uncomfortably. She hadn't told him about last night's victim. "I don't know if it's the same or not. But I woke up inside a woman who was being seduced."

His eyebrows jumped straight up. "Is that normal – for you?"

She flushed, heat creeping up her neck. "No. I don't normally wake up in other people's sexual fantasies." She hesitated.

"What?"

"The thing is, this woman was drugged. Some kind of hallucinogenic. Everything looked bizarre and felt over the top."

"But it was consensual?"

Sam couldn't help the grimace. "That's the thing. I don't think it was. He hurt her. Oh not at the beginning. No, in the beginning he made her feel a lot, but there was some sort of resistance going on in her mind that was hard to sort out. I think it was the drugs. I don't think she'd invited him in. I still can't identify him because the drugs distorted her vision and therefore my senses and view." Sadness tinged her voice. "It's almost like he's trying out new things. Like a new drug."

"Then he might try this again?"

"No. Not the same anyway. He didn't like what it did to her. I couldn't stay until the end because she faded into some kind of drugged unconsciousness." Sam shifted uneasily at the reminder. "I don't quite know what happened. If she died at that point in time, she didn't know it. She just went comatose."

Brandt stiffened. "Can you describe her?"

Describe her. Hmmm. "Not really. Just as my vision saw really weird things, her thoughts were the same." A nagging memory touched her again. "There was something off about this. From her impression, I got the feeling she knew him."

"Which could help a lot – if we knew who *she* was?"

"I don't have many details. She could be considered a suicide. Or a drug overdose. It was just last night, so would she even have been found yet?"

Sam studied her memories. "It's possible she didn't die, but was taken to Emergency." She shifted slightly, dismay wrinkling her face. "Even worse, she could be slowly dying in her bedroom right now."

"Horrible thought. I'll follow up with the morgue and the hospitals." He eyed her carefully.

She frowned. "What?"

"I'm concerned about you." He shifted closer, peering into her face. "That was a traumatic drive home for you. I want to know that you're okay." He reached out to grasp her gently by the shoulders. "Are you sure?"

Sam gently rubbed her face, feeling the weight of the full day pull on her. "I'm fine. I still can't decide if I overreacted, or if he really was toying with me."

"It's a busy highway. To be empty for any length of time would have been abnormal. That meant the attack had been spur of the moment. Someone had taken advantage of the opportunity presented. But why?" Brandt studied her carefully. "Who would want you dead? Have you pissed anyone off recently? Not so recently? Or this could be just some crazy asshole and not a targeted hit, but on the off chance…"

Sam heard his words, but they stopped making any sense after his suggestion someone might be trying to kill her. She could feel the blood draining from her face. There was one person. Only one person who had reason to wish her dead. But why would he be after her now? She stared at Brandt, horror dawning. The police checked into her history. Could that have triggered this? What's the chance Brandt had spoken to him? Nightmarish possibilities swirled through her mind. Did she dare tell Brandt? Did she dare trust him?

Brandt frowned. "You need to tell me the truth here. We've already got a crazed killer running around. If there is a second asshole, then I need to know about him."

Sam sighed. "Do you have time? This could take awhile."

12:15 pm

"HEY MAISY, I hear your son came today on 'official' business." Bert, a retired plumber, yelled at her from the far side of the room. There might be something wrong with his hearing, but there was nothing wrong with his voice.

Raucous, good-hearted laughter broke throughout the large dining room. Maisy smiled at everyone. "He did indeed. And did you also hear – he brought his girlfriend?"

Ooohs and aaahs from the group of seniors filled the room.

"Maybe he'll finally settle down now, huh?"

Maisy made her way slowly over to her table and took her place. "I sure hope so. You should see her."

Rosie, a retired yoga instructor seated at the table behind her, asked, "Is she pretty?"

Maisy thought about that for a moment, then shook her head. "No, not in the sense that a little girl running through a bed of flowers is pretty. She's…" Lost for words, Maisy glanced over at the colonel for help.

He nodded. "She's unique."

"Aaaah," said the collective voice of everyone listening in.

Maisy nodded. "Fine boned, long hair past her waist and eyes that make you want to cry. She's got my boy tied up in knots. He wants to protect her and devour her at the same time."

Knowing grins broke out on the other faces.

"So, it's serious then?"

Maisy couldn't see who'd spoken. She thought it was Jim, a permanent resident. "You know, I think it might be."

Silence reigned as the first course of hot soup and fresh bread was eaten.

The colonel, with a twinkle in his eyes spoke up. "I can't believe I'm going to be the one to say this, but how come you haven't set up a betting pool for when he asks her to marry him?"

A gentle chuckle rose around the room.

Maisy, acting as if insulted, said, "Brandt was just here telling me I'm not allowed to do that anymore."

The chuckle grew louder.

"And since when do you listen to him?" The colonel beetled his heavy brow in a leer.

She grinned. "Never." She pulled her notebook from her pocket and opened it to a clean page. "Okay, who's placing the first bet?"

The room erupted with voices clamoring to get their dates of choice before they were taken by another person.

With a big grin, and a fat wink at the colonel, Maisy set up a pool on her son's love life.

CHAPTER 12

2:30 pm

SAM AND BRANDT left their trucks behind the vet's office and stopped at the crosswalk. There was a cafe across the street with an outside patio. Traffic zoomed past until the lights changed.

It had already been a hell of a day. So, it was no surprise that the thought of answering the upcoming questions made Sam nervous. Questions always made her nervous.

They grabbed a table slightly away from the others.

A waitress walked over with menus. Sam shook her head. "Just coffee for me, please."

Brandt snorted. "Like hell." He motioned to the waitress. "I'll have coffee as well. Bring two chicken Caesar salads, please. Just make mine bigger with a side of garlic bread."

Sam stared at him. "And what if I'm not hungry?"

"Too bad. You need to keep your energy up to make the most of our visit with Stefan."

She didn't have an argument for that.

The waitress returned with two mugs of steaming coffee. Sam murmured her thanks, wrapping both hands around the cup. She stared out at the traffic whizzing by.

"Hey, are you there?"

Sam glanced up to see Brandt staring at her. "Sorry, my mind is just wandering."

"You do seem distracted. So talk to me."

She sat back and toyed with the cutlery. "It's not that easy."

"I presume this is about the car incident today?"

"I don't know if it is, or not. I guess so." She sighed. "Can I ask you a question first?"

"What do you want to know?" He took a long drink of his coffee, his eyes on hers.

Her lip curled. "That's the thing. I'm not too sure that I do want to know."

The waitress returned with their order. Taking a bit of food, Sam noticed the other customers. The table across from them had a family of five sitting around enjoying a cool drink. Sam watched their normal activity with a hint of jealousy. She'd never been able to have that type of experience. And she never would unless she could put this behind her.

She pursed her lips before lifting her own cup for a sip. "How much of my history have you dug up?"

"I had a surface history on my desk the first day you walked into the station. After taking your fingerprints and DNA, I learned a bit more." He toyed with the sugar packets. "I know you were in a bad car accident several years ago. I know you spent time in a mental hospital."

She closed her eyes, letting her head drop.

"I know you've helped the police in the past and at times, your help appeared to be more of a hindrance." He reached across the table, his hand covering hers. "I know you went to college where your best friend was murdered. You went to the police to offer your help and together, you managed to catch the killer."

"Lucy," she whispered. Memories flooded her mind. Lucy smiling with her wild and crazy coffee cups. She'd haunted curio shops for her next best mug. She'd been so open, so caring, and now she was so dead, just like the other victims. "You have it wrong. I went to the police to see if I could help. I thought I was getting somewhere and then Lucy was murdered. You see, she was murdered because of me. The killer, after finding out I was helping the police, came after me. He got her instead." Guilt tore at her. Her head bowed even more under the weight of the memories. She sniffled. "I couldn't save her. I couldn't save any of them."

"So you ran away. From your education, from your friends, and all of society."

The accusation stabbed into her. "That's not fair," she whispered. "I tried so hard to help those women. It broke my heart when I couldn't."

Brandt squeezed her hand gently, his thumb stroking the soft skin of her palm. Sam watched the slow movement, mesmerized by his gentleness. "Do you realize that's what I do, day in and day out? There are so many people I haven't been able to help. And some that I have. I can't quit just because I don't always succeed. It's important we just keep trying to save the ones we can."

She glanced up, caught by the strength of his gaze. "I didn't totally quit. I tried again, when several children went missing. I found I couldn't ignore the pleas for help. Not when I thought I could do something."

"Did you help?"

She beamed, a lightness inside, bursting forth. "Yes, I found a little girl that was missing. We saved her in time."

He grinned. "It feels great doesn't it?"

The light inside grew stronger. "Yes." Her smile dimmed and fell away. "Then, when the next child showed up dead, the suspicion fell on me again. It got pretty ugly."

Brandt nodded. He could just imagine. When a ship started to sink, all the rats either bailed or turned on each other.

She grimaced. "There was one cop, in particular. He disliked psychics. I think they all did to some degree or another, but he...he hated me." Picking up her cup of coffee, Sam bathed her face in the warmth drifting upward.

"Is that what you were afraid I'd find out about?"

The corner of her mouth tilted. "Yeah, sort of. If you'd talked to this guy, he'd have told you a whole lot of nothing good."

"To tell you the truth, I think I did talk to him."

Sam's stomach curdled, tossing the salad around inside. "Oh." She ran her fingers through the loose curls at her temple, the weight of her braid hot and heavy in the sun.

"Is that a problem?" He leaned forward watching her.

She grimaced. "If I show up dead, look to him first."

Brandt stopped and stared at her – his cup stalled mid-air. "Seriously?"

It was all she could do to meet his eyes. Eventually, taking a deep breath, she said, "We had a difficult last meeting." She ran her fingers across her neck. "As much as he hated me, he believed in my skills. It's just he wanted them solely for his use. I ended up taking off. Yes, running away and hiding from everyone. It was better than letting this asshole control my life. He threatened to kill me if I ever told anyone."

"But he was a cop."

"Deputy, actually. And a drug dealer on the side."

He glanced over the cup at her. "Are you sure?"

She nodded.

"Are you saying he could have been behind the wheel of the

truck that tried to run you off the road?"

Her shoulders slumped. "I don't know," she half-wailed. "He hated my guts and…" She stopped talking, unable to tell him the whole story. Tears clogged her eyes, emotion clogged her throat. She couldn't believe that after all this time this deputy still had the power to destroy her. Surely, she'd moved past that. "I disappeared and hoped he'd forget about me."

"But once I called him, then he knew where to find you?"

She nodded again as she finished off the last bite and moved her plate on top of his empty one.

His gaze was intent on her face. Sam felt heat rise that had nothing to do with the sun.

He stirred his cup until Sam reached across and stilled his hand. "Go and get a second cup so you have something to stir." Even as she picked up her own cup, relief slowly spread through her limbs. Relief to have someone to share this burden with. Relief that she was no longer alone.

A smile twitched at the corner of his mouth. "Do you want another?"

"No, not if we're heading to Stefan's house soon."

"If you're done eating…" Brandt glanced at his watch. "Let's head out then. We'll talk on the way."

"Great," she muttered.

"You'll be fine. We'll figure this out."

They crossed the street to his truck. He walked to her door and unlocked it before walking around to the driver's side. The small concession to old-fashioned courtesy made her feel good.

Getting into the truck was a different story. Her truck was lower to the ground. His had huge tires and no running boards. Fine for a six-foot male, but she barely crested five-foot-four and struggled to get up to the seats. Flustered, Sam finally managed to shut the door and get settled. A sidelong glance at Brandt's face didn't help. He was trying to hold back a grin.

Sam harrumphed and refused to look at him again.

As they passed the town's welcome sign, she ventured to break the silence. "How long have you known Stefan?"

Brandt glanced at her quickly. "Close to ten years now."

Sam raised her eyebrows at that. "That's quite awhile. Is he your age?"

That question brought a frown to his face. "I don't know how old he is. I'd say he's mid thirties. Then again, he doesn't look a day older now than when I met him."

Older would be better than younger, in this case. Sam could only hope he had decades of experience handling what the psychic life dished out. She needed to talk to someone who'd already figured this stuff out.

Brandt took a left turn off the highway and drove further into the country. Peace surrounded the area. Heavily treed on the left and rolling hills on the right. Stunningly beautiful and something she hadn't expected to see.

"He lives just a couple of miles further."

She nodded. "And he prefers to live away from people, just like I do."

"Yeah." Brandt snorted. "Stefan is different. There's really no other way to describe him."

Pursing her lips, she thought about that. In a way, the same description applied to her too. Better to wait and see just what that meant to Brandt. Maybe it would give her an idea of how he saw her.

3:00 pm

BRANDT NAVIGATED THE last turn onto Stefan's twisting driveway. The man had chosen a hell of a spot for a hideaway. Now that Brandt lived closer, he had a chance to visit and not just talk on the phone. Stefan didn't like phones. Then he bordered on antisocial at times.

Brandt regarded Sam's profile. Something was bugging her. In typical Sam style, she sat worrying on something instead of outright asking him.

The house winked at them from between the trees. Brandt drove around to the far side and parked. One side was glass that twinkled like diamond facets in the light. The rest was built of logs – huge logs. Evergreens surrounded the house on three sides. Stunning in colors, the air almost vibrated with an otherworldly appeal. Birds approved as they flitted and dipped between the foliage, chirping happily.

Sam appeared awestruck. Remembering how he'd felt the first time he'd arrived, with the sun bouncing off all the glass, he could fully understand her reaction.

"Ready?" He couldn't wait. Putting these two together in the same room should be interesting. Stefan wasn't the friendliest of males. But all women reacted to Stefan – one way or another. Over time, Brandt had come to understand the type of woman each was, by her reaction.

For that reason alone, he'd wanted to be on hand when Sam met Stefan for the first time. He needed to see Sam's reaction and see into the depths of who she was.

3:18 pm

SAM SHUT THE truck door gently. Turning, she tried to take the scene in. She couldn't imagine being the man lucky enough to own such a place.

Brandt, several steps ahead, turned to her, one eyebrow raised. "Coming?

They walked toward the front door. "How long has he lived here?" Sam couldn't help it. Her head swiveled from side to side at the spectacular foliage, and unique wooden carvings peering out amongst the brighter-than-believable plants. The strong scents blended and fused into a fresh woodsy smell. "Everything appears like it's on drugs, for God's sake."

"Or you are." Brandt grinned at her. "He's got plants from all over the globe. Everything about Stefan is unique and indefinable."

"I'll say." Sam stopped at the front door. It was made from one solid block of wood with faces pushing out of the wood grain. Some laughing, some crying, yet all of them glowing with life. "Christ." She didn't know if she was praying or swearing, but there was no way not to react. Everything she'd seen so far came under the heading of stunning. Maybe not comfortable, yet undeniably thought provoking.

"Quite the place he's got, huh?"

"That's an understatement. I can't wait to meet our host."

Sam barely caught Brandt's sidelong glance. She wondered at it as he pounded on the door – stalling any chance of asking.

"Come in." The shout came from deep inside.

Brandt pushed open the door. "Hey Stefan. It's us."

"Yeah, I caught that. Let me just wash up. I'll be right there."

The voice came from the far left. Sam noted that in a distant part of her mind, as she stood in the front foyer, her mouth hanging open. The inside of the house shone with warm yellow sunlight bouncing off wood floors and ceilings. Streaming light struck and highlighted vivid paintings hung on every wall. The room had a surreal energy. The entire house was an artist's canvas.

"Hey Stefan. Good to see you." The two men slapped shoulders. Brandt's large shoulders blocked Sam's view.

Brandt stepped slightly to the side and motioned between the two people. His voice light and easy. "Stefan, meet Sam. Sam, Stefan."

Sam stared at Stefan. Her soul stirred. Overwhelming love and warmth flooded through her.

Stefan gazed into her eyes, his gentle lips curved into a welcoming smile. That same warm loving smile from her vision, that same man from Louise's car accident. Then he opened his arms. Without warning, she burst into tears and ran into them. They closed securely around her.

3:20 pm

BRANDT'S MOUTH FELL open. He didn't know what to think or even how to jumpstart his brain. He was on shocked standby.

He'd never seen a woman react like Sam had. Ever.

Without trying to be too obvious, he tried to assess the clinch they were in. It didn't look lover-like. Neither did they resemble two strangers. He didn't know what the hell was going on. He'd sure like to though.

Interrupting them was out of the question. Whatever was going on was intensely personal. Even standing in the same room was uncomfortable. He walked over to stare out the huge window. The acreage around the house was as wild and impressive as the rest of the property. He heard soft voices behind him. He turned around to see the two smiling in a strangely intimate way.

He took several steps in their direction. "I gather you two know each other?"

They both stared at him in surprise.

Sam's answer stunned him. "What? No, we've never met."

3:25 pm

BRANDT MOTIONED TOWARD Stefan and then at her. "Is that how

you greet all strangers?"

Feeling heat rise on her cheek, Sam glanced over at Stefan, who stared at Brandt, an odd twist to his features. Christ. Stefan was as gorgeous in person as he was in her vision. A charming smile graced the model face. She turned to Brandt. "Oh that."

Brandt made a choked sound. "Yeah that?" He stared between Sam and Stefan. "So an explanation, please."

Sam glanced at Stefan to find him watching her.

"Go ahead."

Sam glanced down at the floor, knowing she was rocking slightly in place. Making a decision, she looked up to find Brandt's suspicious gaze firmly planted – on her. "Remember the car accident that I told you about. Louise Enderby? What I didn't tell you was that I saw a man in that vision. Not the killer, but a man who…at the time…I thought might have been someone close to Louise that had already died. Like her husband, a long-time lover, at least someone like that. He was trying to help me…her…get out of the car and cross over."

She glanced over at Stefan who had a benevolent smile on his face. "The guy left a very strong impression *because* there was so much love in his face. It radiated throughout his energy. He glowed like an angel."

Stefan snorted.

Sam smiled and continued. "I had no way of knowing who he was. Still, it isn't uncommon for a loved one to show up at the time of death to welcome the dying person. Except this guy had an incredible impact on me because he had such loving energy – and it was directed my way."

She gazed into Stefan's eyes. "That man in my vision was Stefan."

Brandt reeled backwards as if from a blow. "What?" He stared at Stefan, searching for confirmation. "Is that possible?"

Sam shrugged. "I don't know how, but it happened."

Stefan stared at them both. "It's a first for me too. I've never come across another psychic in my visions."

Brandt focused on Sam. "You're saying that you recognized Stefan here from your vision. And the emotions from that vision were so strong that when you saw him, you burst into tears and walked into a stranger's arms?" Hands on hips, head titled sideways, he stared at her in disbelief.

Sam knew how important her answer was. It was also important to her that he believe her story. She hated to admit it, but she'd come to enjoy his acceptance and now wanted his respect. "It is hard to understand. You have to consider the circumstances.

"I was caught in a horrible vision inside a burning car and a dying woman. Stefan appeared – yes, I'll say it again – almost angelic in appearance, and he saved me. The emotion that existed at the time was overwhelming. This man cared about Louise. I don't understand that part."

She glanced sidelong at Stefan who was listening casually. "But for me, it was as if he loved me, cared about me, and was trying to save *me*." She implored Brandt to understand. "It was pure instinct to cry when I saw him again. I thought he didn't exist…that he wasn't real. Then suddenly he's here, in front of me." She shrugged. "I just reacted."

Brandt shook his head, his fingers running raggedly through his hair. "Wow."

"Precisely." Sam found little satisfaction in his comment. She hadn't had time to adjust to this scenario either. Questions crowded her mind. She didn't know where to start and her energy levels had dropped alarmingly. "Stefan, can I go and sit down?"

Brandt made a funny sound. She glanced over at him, but he'd already reached her. His arm wrapped around her shoulders. "You look like you're ready to pass out. Come sit down."

Stefan moved ahead of them both. "You two get comfortable, and I'll put on coffee. It looks like we have a lot to talk about."

CHAPTER 13

3:45 pm

STEFAN WALKED INTO his kitchen, happy to escape the emotional energy of the other two. Coffee made for a great excuse.

Sam was an interesting development. As was Brandt's reaction to their meeting. Stefan wouldn't have said she was Brandt's type, but then she didn't fit his own type either – and he found her fascinating. That she'd managed to see and communicate on the etheric field was impressive all over again.

He stayed in the kitchen until the coffee dripped to a full pot. Pouring three cups, he carried them out to the sitting area. "Anyone need cream or sugar?"

"No, black is fine. Thank you." Sam reached for her cup and huddled over it as if needing the warmth.

Stefan considered her for a moment before sitting on a chair between them. He understood power positions and being between these two wouldn't be his normal choice, yet they obviously had issues.

"Sam, are you always cold?"

Both Brandt and Sam turned to stare at him. He allowed a small smile. "Not a trick question, just a simple inquiry."

Sam nodded. "Yes, I am. And that's getting worse with every vision."

"Is there any particular time when you are colder than others?"

Her head cocked to one side and Stefan studied the fleeting expressions washing over her face as she considered his questions. She had no guile, this girl. She was a newborn babe in the world of ageless freaks. He sighed inwardly. She needed a lot from him. Her survival potential, without it, didn't look good.

She was powerful but open. Her energy shone and flashed

with no control. Worse, she didn't even seem to know there was such a thing. She bled energy like a hemophiliac bled blood.

She shook her head. "No, I don't think so. I'm cold all the time."

Settling deeper into his chair, Stefan ran a few basic tests. First, he checked her life force. Strong, this girl was a fighter. Next, he checked her aura. Right now, it spat in several directions while being conspicuously reticent about going in Brandt's direction. Interesting. She didn't want Brandt to see too much.

He smiled to himself. While everyone was busy not looking at each other, Stefan took advantage of the uneasy energy and opened his inner eye.

He turned to focus on Sam. And found Sam staring at him. He reared back in surprise. She frowned at him.

"What's the matter?"

Stefan quickly switched to his normal sight to find she still stared at him. Could it be? Could she flip between the two views or did she not know the difference? With a quick glance at Brandt, who hadn't appeared to notice anything, Stefan decided to ask.

"Do you recognize when you are using your inner eye?"

His question seemed to surprise her, only she answered readily enough. "Yes. I use both equally and switch between them easily."

That made sense, given what he'd just seen. It also elevated her skills another notch. This was a very interesting woman. Without any formal training, she'd found her own way. Without anyone to say right or wrong, she'd developed in ways that worked for her. Stefan could count on one hand the number of psychics the world over that could switch their inner vision as simply.

"Brandt has told me something about your visions." He stretched out his legs, crossing them, and with a quick glance at Brandt, he centered on Sam. "Maybe you could explain to me exactly what happens to you."

Sam winced. She stared at her coffee cup. It didn't take long to fill him in. Stefan didn't interrupt her. He waited until she ran down before asking questions.

"So you have no trigger that you know of? You have no awareness outside of the vision when you're in one, and you've been having these particular visions during the night?"

"Right. There have been a couple of other odd insights as well." Quickly, she filled him in on when she thought the killer had been hunting a new victim, and the car accident where she'd seen

Stefan.

Stefan considered what he'd heard. "What would you like from me?"

Sam's face became a mix of contradictions. She looked hopeful, confused, and even full of trepidation.

Stefan leaned forward. What did she want?

"I was wondering if you could help me."

Stefan shifted, surprised. That's not what he'd been expecting her to say. "Help? In what way?"

Sam glanced toward Brandt.

Was she gaining strength from his presence, or expecting criticism? Stefan filed her action away to contemplate later. "The visions are extremely violent. My recovery takes quite awhile. I'm wondering..."

"Yes," he encouraged.

"Well." She stopped again, as if gathering her thoughts. Then the words rushed out. "The visions are hard on my system. My blood loss is huge. I was skinny before, now the pounds are falling off. I can hardly sleep." Her stream of chatter slowed down. "I'm scared these visions will kill me," she admitted softly.

Stefan didn't know what to say. She was right to be concerned. "Normally, the psychics with physical manifested visions, don't show the blood loss to a dangerous level – at least not for long."

She didn't seem to hear the last part, for she leaned forward, her eyes intent on his face. "There are others like me?"

"Absolutely. Some people will wake up with blood on their hands and not always know why. In this case, they've had an empathetic episode." He rubbed the side of his temple. "Some people walk in the gray area between life and death and will become comatose depending on how long they stay there. There are some who have died because they couldn't return to their bodies in time."

With a quick glance at Brandt – who sat quietly listening – he refocused on Sam. "I've often discussed with Brandt the number of misdiagnosed patients in mental hospitals who have psychic talents they never knew they had."

Sam did a double take. "Are you serious?"

Brandt nodded. "Unfortunately."

"Control." Sam jumped on that term. "That's what I need to do. I need to learn how to control my talents and to disconnect from the visions. The last time, I managed to keep one foot in both realities, only for the briefest of moments, then I lost it."

"Right. There are several techniques. But it's not going to happen overnight. It will take practice. I can help, but it will take effort on your part."

Sam smiled. "That's fine. The more control, the more I can use my talents to benefit others."

Brandt interjected for the first time. "What do you want to do with them?"

A becoming pink blush that started at her neck, washed upward. Stefan watched Brandt's mesmerized gaze follow the color trail. No doubt about it, he had it bad.

Sam licked her lips and Stefan almost laughed aloud. Brandt looked like he was choking on something.

"I want to be able to help people. Or maybe animals." She told them about the incident with the dog at the hospital. "I don't know yet the best way to help. Partly because I don't know my own abilities and therefore don't know what is possible *to* do. I just know that I don't want to hide, and I don't want to be helpless."

Interesting. "First let's set up time to work on your control. We'll sort out what your talents are, which are strongest, and which need developing. You can go from there."

Both Brandt and Sam nodded.

"That makes good sense." Brandt glanced at his watch. "We're going to need to go soon."

Stefan took note of the color surrounding the two. Their energy danced around each other, close enough to blend, yet staying separate – at least for now.

Long fingers of sunshine touched and warmed the atmosphere. Stefan watched the sunlight dance with their energies.

Sam spoke again, interrupting his musings. "Stefan, can I ask you about the vision where I saw you – what were you doing there with Louise?"

Stefan smiled. "I knew her, years ago before she married. By the time I arrived, it was too late for her. All I could do to help was escort her to the other side."

"Escort?" Brandt's curiosity jumped out. "You mentioned this before."

Sam stared at him. "Crossing to the other side. Death."

Brandt shifted in his seat, one eyebrow raised, listening.

Sam turned back to Stefan. "Was this an unusual occurrence

for you?"

Stefan thought about it. "It doesn't happen weekly or even monthly, but if there is a connection on any level, then I usually know what's happening."

"Were you close?" Sam flushed. "I don't mean to be personal, but when I was inside Louise I felt…different."

Intriguing. "I loved her. But she couldn't handle my life."

Sam nodded as if understanding what he meant. Maybe she did.

"What was she thinking about?" He admitted to being curious. He'd never experienced a psychic vision like hers. He studied Sam's face, searching for the truth.

"It's hard to say. My visions are overwhelmed with the physical trauma, though a little of their thoughts mix with mine. I don't remember much of hers, though. We were both more concerned with the car that wouldn't respond, then the crash, the fire…you know." Sam held her hands out. "That's about it until I saw you. Then it was my thoughts. I wasn't sure whom you were talking to – Louise or me." She waited for his answer.

He frowned. "Louise mostly, trying to get her to leave her body. Until the end, when I was talking to you because at that point, you were holding her back."

Understanding dawned in Sam's eyes. "That makes sense now." She cocked her head sideways. "Do you know how she died?"

"She was in a car accident. Her vehicle drove off the highway at Emerson Point."

"You know that?" Brandt shook his head.

"Sure, I could see her memories. One of the last things to happen before death is a rewind of the movie of your life." He glanced at Sam. "Don't you see that part?

She shook her head. "No. Mine are always violent deaths, and they don't have much time." She sat up straight. "Could you see why her car went over the cliff?"

Stefan stared at Sam. She almost vibrated with energy. "No, I came in later. What about you?"

"Only that her brakes weren't working. She pumped them hard." She shrugged. "Then she went off the road."

"What connects you to your visions?"

Sam shifted uneasily. "Usually violence. Lately it's been murder."

Stefan studied her. "You think Louise was murdered?"

"I think so, yes."

He frowned. "Did you connect with the same killer, in her case?"

"I don't know. I think so. It's his energy on the car."

"At the time of her death?

"Just before." Sam rubbed her hands together to warm them up. "No. As we went over the cliff, I thought I saw his signature. Once we crashed and burned, I wasn't looking at anything, but the flames and then you."

"What does that mean to you?" Brandt interjected, sitting on the edge of his seat. "I don't understand this energy signature stuff."

Stefan explained. "When you touch something, it leaves a bit of energy behind."

"This energy can dissipate quickly or hang around, depending on the energy of the person touching it and depending on how long the contact lasted."

Brandt jerked his head, urging them to continue. "That still doesn't mean much to me. Are you saying this guy owned or drove the car? Or did he just work on it for a little bit?"

Both Sam and Stefan shook their heads.

Stefan said, "It's not that easy."

"No. I'm not sure I can say very much about his energy in this case. I only saw it long enough to recognize it. For me that means he's responsible for Louise's death." She wrinkled her nose at Brandt. "The how and whys, well, I thought that was your job."

"Except, there's nothing left to investigate. The car burned to a crisp."

4:45 pm

BRANDT AND SAM drove to Parksville in almost total silence. Brandt's mind crowded with all he had to mull over, and he could only imagine what Sam was thinking. She'd set up the first session with Stefan in four days time. In the meantime, she had homework to do.

He, on the other hand, had regular work to do. He turned into the parking lot and pulled up beside her truck. Checking out the report on Louise Enderby was another priority. Stefan couldn't confirm that her brake line had been cut, yet he agreed that it was likely she'd been murdered.

"Are you okay?"

She nodded. "Yes, I'm good. Better than I have been in a long time." She collected her purse. "In fact, I should go home and review everything I've learned." She shifted to leave. "Thanks for taking me."

She opened the door and hopped out. "I'll talk to you later. Thanks again."

He walked around the truck to stand beside her. "Are you hungry? Do you want to go someplace to eat?"

Sam stopped and considered his offer. "You know, I think tonight I'd just like to be alone. My mind's a little overfull and I'd like some time to digest everything."

Brandt nodded. "Maybe another time?"

"Thanks, I'd like that."

Brandt didn't know if he should try to pin her down or not. He could understand her wanting to be alone tonight. He was the one that didn't want to be alone. Still, she'd been through enough for one day. Yet he couldn't leave it like this, he needed more. "I could pick up something and come down to your place tomorrow. If that works for you?"

Sam glanced back at him, startled. "That would be nice. Thank you."

"Good. I'll call you with a time when I see how the day is going." He walked to his truck. "Remember…" he said frowning, "be smart and stay alert. The killer is still trawling for victims."

"How could I forget?" She frowned at him. "I'm the one with the insider knowledge, remember?"

"Speaking of which, let me know if anything new pops up. Okay?"

"Alright."

Sam reversed her truck and pulled out of the parking lot in the direction of her home.

Brandt watched for a few minutes then headed back home. He could retrieve his messages from there just as well as from the office.

The house sounded hollow as he shut the front door behind him. Today was perfect for a cold beer and a medium rare steak – too bad he didn't have either in the house. By the time he'd showered, the coffee had finished dripping and he'd decided on a hefty ham and cheese omelet with hash browns. Easy, doable, and fast.

With a plate of hot steaming food, Brandt clicked on the television. His stomach growled with hunger pangs. He dug in while listening to the local news.

"The police have issued a press release requesting the public's help in identifying the owner of this ring."

The television screen flashed to a sketch of a ring with a four-leaf-clover pattern and missing one stone. Brandt bolted to his feet. "What the hell?"

He circled around the coffee table to get a closer look. There was no doubt about it. It was his sketch. His stomach warred with his nerves. How had the media gotten this picture? The announcer had said something about the police asking for help. The picture must have come from his department. From his office. Only not from him.

Trying to be fair, Brandt ran through those who knew about the ring. Basically everyone. He'd brought it out at the meeting after explaining it could be connected to the killer he was hunting. He'd been trying to identify the owner for Christ's sake.

"God damn it." He paced around the living room, his mind working furiously.

He couldn't believe someone had jumped him on this. Surely, that could only have been the captain – or someone on his team. But why? This wasn't even an official case. Sam's information was a tip, yet that's all it was. The others didn't even believe her. Damn it. This could blow up in the department's face. And put him into hot water. There were few people willing to own up to having a psychic help out. If the information wasn't any good, many people would be up for crucifying the idiots who brought the psychic in. And the psychic.

Jesus, what about Samantha? His heart stopped beating. No. Sanity swept in. No there was no way she could be identified by this. Relief sent his heart racing again. There could be serious repercussions. If Sam were right, and the killer saw this newscast, he'd be seriously wondering how the police knew about it. The killer could just laugh it off, or it might drive him into a killing fury.

There was just no way to know.

8:05 pm

THE EVENING NEWS rippled outward to another man enjoying an evening alone in his apartment.

"Life is good." Bill walked to his refrigerator and pulled out a cold beer. Raising the bottle to the sky, he took a long swallow. The television was blaring from the other room. He heard something about the police asking for help and walked to where he could see the broadcast.

"What the hell..." The tall slight man leaned forward, slamming the bottle down on the hewn wooden table beside the World War II airport model he was building. He stared at the picture on the screen.

No way. No fucking way. How the hell did they know about his ring? He glared at the item still on his left hand. It had been his lucky ring for so long, he'd forgotten he was still wearing it. Pissed, he tore the offending thing off and threw it against the far wall.

Why would anyone be searching for his ring? He wiped his mouth with the back of his hand. What did they know? Could they have connected the ring to his women? No. He thought about it. There's no way anyone could connect the ring to his victims. The cops would be pounding on his door if they were that close. So who else? They couldn't have captured a picture from a camera as he always wore gloves.

Disturbed, he slouched into the couch. The newscaster's voice washed over him in a continuous drone. What had he missed? What could he possibly have forgotten?

God damn it. No, there's no way anyone could know. He didn't make mistakes.

In a dour mood, he drank his beer and went over every move he'd recently made. He shook his head, feeling better. He hadn't missed anything.

Unless the last woman had survived.

He shot to his feet, disturbed. Not possible. Surely not. She'd been cold when he'd left her. She had to be dead. Except her death hadn't been reported.

The problem was, anyone could have seen the ring. He'd worn it as long as he could remember. Someone was sure to have noticed it somewhere along the way. He pondered the implications. First, he needed to make sure that woman had indeed died, then he needed to find a similar ring and wear it to fool anyone who may have thought he'd had on the ring the police were asking about. That way when anyone doubled checked, it would seem like they'd made a mistake. And last – he needed to never, ever leave a victim until he was sure she was dead.

9:35am, June 19th

SAM FINALLY SLEPT through the night. No nightmares, no visions, just sleep. Stefan's homework had helped. Lying in bed, feeling rested for the first time in several days, she rolled over and curled deeper into her blankets. Relaxation rolled through her.

If it weren't for the animals waiting for her, she wouldn't bother getting out of bed. Then, room service was a little lacking when you lived alone.

Moving easily through her morning routine, Sam made it to the kitchen and fed her canine family before they had a chance to get upset at the wait. Soldier ate then stood at the front door. Sam opened it and stepped out on the deck. He moved stiffly under her watchful gaze as he managed the steps and the few feet to a clump of trees.

While she relaxed with her morning tea, the two dogs started a ruckus. Sam frowned. Soldier's bark was hoarse, almost a cross between a growl and a bark. Like one long unused.

She walked toward the door and heard the vehicle. Instantly, her nerves reacted. She rarely had visitors, but it was only recently that the sound of an approaching vehicle brought out a sense of dread. Her tension eased when she recognized Price Coulson's car.

The rent wasn't due for another couple of weeks and her landlord came about once a month to check up on her.

"Good morning. How are you today?" She opened the door wider to let him in. She did it every time he came and every time, he refused to step inside. A married man in a single woman's house wasn't proper according to his generational rules.

"The wife sent over a loaf of bread and some cookies for you." His face creased into well-worn wrinkles. "Also wanted to make sure you're doing okay."

"Of course, I'm fine." Sam leaned easily against the doorway. God, she was becoming a good liar. How sad was that?

The old man glanced at her, sharp intellect shining beneath the heavy folds of his eyelids. "It's very isolated here. Aren't you worried about intruders?"

Shaking her head, Sam hastened to reassure him. "No. I've always been comfortable living out in the country."

He shoved his gnarled fingers into his jean pockets. "Now that may be, only it's not the same world today as it was a few decades ago. There are some bad people out there."

"There always have been. The communication systems of today are better so we hear about more cases."

"Aye. True enough. Just last night the news said the police were searching for the owner of an odd-looking ring." He turned to look at the calm waters of the lake. "The wife, she said it looked like a devil's ring, what with the snake twisting through a garden."

"A ring?"

"Yeah. You don't have television down here so you wouldn't have heard about it."

Sam went cold inside. "They said the police wanted this guy?"

"Just that they were looking for the owner of the ring so they could talk to him."

Almost numb with the ice that had settled into her limbs, Sam shook her head. "Then it's probably nothing."

He pulled out one hand to run through the white fluff around his ears. "Aye. I told the wife that. But well, she worries."

That was the reason for his visit. The pair of them were concerned about her. Unaccustomed warmth melted through her. This was a new feeling. She savored the sensation. Someone actually cared enough to worry. And he didn't even know her.

She shook her head in bemusement. "Are you sure you won't come in for a cup of tea? You can tell me all about it inside."

Price shook his head. "No, no. I promised Mary that I wouldn't be longer than a few minutes." He twisted, pointing out Soldier. "I didn't know you had a guard dog. Mary will worry less knowing you have him down here."

Sam's lips twitched at the thought. "I don't know how much help he'll be. He's with me because he's recovering from surgery and needed a home to heal and be rehabilitated."

The old man's gaze sharpened. "Is he dangerous?" His wrinkles rearranged downward. "Don't really want something dangerous living here. He's too old to be rehabilitated." He stared at the dog. "A bullet might be kinder all around."

Sam refused to take offence, understanding his old-timer ways. After all, he hadn't said anything different than the vets themselves had expressed. "No, he was mistreated, and then hit by a car. Since he's been with me, he's spent his time healing. I don't think he's dangerous." She couldn't help crossing her fingers. "He'll be a great deterrent for anyone out to cause trouble. I think he's a trained watchdog. At least that's what one policeman told me."

The older man's shoulders relaxed slightly. "That's good then. If the police and vets are involved, then he's probably fine." He nodded as if satisfied. "Mary will be happy to hear this."

A little later, Sam, with cell phone in hand, watched his pickup head up the hill. Dear God. The ring had been on television. Surely, not the same ring? Why would Detective Sutherland do that? What else had the broadcast said? She didn't quite understand how she felt about this development.

"Hello."

"Hi Brandt. This is Sam. Did you release a picture of the ring to the media?"

A hefty pause stretched out over the line. "I didn't, no. One of the members of the department must have. The first I knew about it was when I saw it on television last night."

"The whole point of telling you about the ring was to help – I just hadn't expected to have it released to the media. I guess I'm more surprised than anything." She took a deep breath. "The thing is, I'd really like to keep my name out of this. I've taken care to build a new life here. I don't mind helping, but I'd just as soon do it privately"

"Understood. I'll make sure your name isn't connected. I don't know who contacted the media, but I will find out." His voice came across strong and determined, and that helped reassure her a little more.

Sam rang off and went to get ready for work. A quick brush of her hair and a check to make sure her face was clean, then Sam grabbed her keys and purse and headed for work.

She couldn't quite stop the flutter of nervousness inside. Why had it never crossed her mind that the police might go public with her information? Why had she never once considered the risk that her identity would be exposed?

And why had this realization come when it was too late to change her mind?

CHAPTER 14

10:10 am

BRANDT STOOD WITH his legs apart, shoulders straight and his hands locked behind his back. What the hell? He struggled to keep his mouth shut. He couldn't believe what he was hearing. Captain Johansen had called him into his office and Brandt was getting his ass kicked.

"Sir? If I could just interject for a moment." Brandt tried to interrupt the captain's rant, only the man was steaming. Brandt relaxed slightly, and stuffed his hands into his jean pockets. He eyed the chairs stacked high with papers. An empty chair sat off to the side – one Brandt hadn't been offered.

"Brandt? Brandt, are you listening to me?"

At the first call, Brandt studied the man opposite him. At the second call, he raised an eyebrow. "Are you ready to listen to me?"

"Damn it." Captain Johansen blew hard and rubbed his temple. Reaching for his coffee cup, he glared at Brandt. "Fine. Talk to me. What the hell were you thinking?" The captain's face flushed red as his voice started to rise again.

Brandt held out his hand to slow the man down. "I didn't do it." He enunciated slowly and clearly. "I did not give that picture to the media."

The captain stopped cold. He fixed his hard stare on Brandt. "What?" he growled. "If you didn't then who did?"

"I don't know," Brandt admitted. "I'd planned to ask you that question."

"Why?" demanded Captain Johansen. "I sure as hell don't know. Any ideas? And why wasn't it you?"

Brandt stared at his boss. "I'd prefer to have proof before I say anything."

"Not good enough." Johansen pounded a fist on his desk. "I

want to know what you know – and now!"

What could he say? Brandt shrugged his shoulders. "I don't *know* anything, sir. I showed the picture at the debriefing meeting yesterday, so anyone who'd been there knew. As would anyone they might have shown the picture to."

"And yet, a couple of names on the force came to your mind." The captain glared at him, waiting.

Brandt avoided answering. "It's the why that bothers me. If someone wanted to help, you'd think they would have included me in the plan. Which means someone may be out to discredit me instead."

The captain glanced at his desk, a frown furrowing his brows.

Brandt added one other point. "Or the department." He paused for a moment, considering his next words carefully. "I'll tell you this. Kevin doesn't appreciate me having Sam onboard, except he appears to hold the department in high regard. And Dillon barely speaks to me except yesterday he came to talk to me about the ring. If he did this, he may have thought he was doing me a favor." He shrugged again. "In both cases, it could mean nothing."

"Did you give Dillon the picture?"

"He walked into my office with a copy," Brandt clarified. "All I know is I didn't give it to the media."

"Therefore someone else did." Captain Johansen played with his pen, thinking hard. "And because so many people had access to the sketch, anyone could have leaked it."

"I did fax it to two jewelry stores yesterday asking if they recognized the pattern. It's possible the media may have found out from them." The more he thought about it, the more possible that sounded. "Except they said the police were asking for help."

The captain picked up the phone. "Dillon, come into my office please."

Brandt straightened up. "Sir, I'd like to be able to call these jewelry stores before we accuse anyone."

"And so you should, but I want to know what his take is on this mess."

"Then I'd like to leave so he doesn't suspect me of pointing a finger."

Brandt turned and walked to the door. "In fact, it might not be a bad idea to question everyone," he suggested thoughtfully.

"I know how to do my job, thank you."

A knock sounded on the open door.

Brandt turned to see Dillon standing there, waiting. He smiled. "Hey Dillon. Your turn." He nodded at Captain Johansen and walked out. "I'll get to work, if there's nothing else, sir?" Without waiting for a response, Brandt walked out. Feeling like he'd just barely escaped, he headed to his desk.

Once there, Brandt sorted through the sizeable stack of files on his desk and pulled out two. He tried to focus on them, only his thoughts refused to organize. They kept returning to the news broadcast and the person responsible. Who could have done that?

Still, of bigger concern was the case itself. Picking up the phone, he continued to work down his list of jewelry stores.

10:30 am

THAT WAS CLOSE. How the hell had his name come up – and so fast? Self-consciously, he glanced around to see who might be watching. No one appeared to notice as he poured a cup of coffee and walked to his desk. Captain Johansen hadn't known much so maybe he was doing a check on everyone. Dillon grinned. Good thing he had such an honest face.

Besides, what was the big deal? So what if anyone saw the stupid sketch. After all, the whole point was to learn more about the ring. Who cared if the media asked the public for information? It was more or less a problem regarding chain of command. The captain was pissed because he hadn't known about it. Dillon smirked. Damn well time someone shook his goat. The old man was a control freak.

What had the department come to? What a joke. A psychic for God's sake. She was a joke. A pair of anorexic eyeballs. Talk about someone who should have been shown the door the minute she walked in.

He had to admit, there was an opportunity to cement his reputation here. He didn't know what form it would manifest, but he wanted to make the most of it.

Then there was Brandt. As far as anyone knew, he was here only temporarily. Dillon didn't think so. Brandt had plans he was keeping close to his chest. Dillon could respect that. He did the same thing. Yet, he wondered what was brewing. Brandt had managed several private meetings with Captain Johansen.

Plans could involve the psychic. Whatever she had going for

her, Brandt seemed interested. And that was just as ludicrous. Unless mercy fucks were this month's good deed. Dillon chuckled. Yet, she had something to offer or Brandt wouldn't waste his time. Dillon quickly pulled a notebook from the left side drawer and wrote some notes on what he'd found out about her so far.

He didn't have much, just bits and pieces of gossip gleaned from hanging around Kevin's team. Adam was a great source, and of course the office grapevine. That had kicked in days ago. In a place like this, it could usually be counted on for accuracy. It was a start. He'd source out her history and all the rest soon. Very soon.

The bottom line? She needed watching.

10:35 am

BRANDT SPENT THE rest of his day following up leads. He'd put several phone calls out to hospitals and morgues, checking for anyone fitting the right age and sex of a victim that had been brought in with a drug overdose or as a suicide. He'd found one possible – in a coma at Portland General Hospital. Asking the doctors to let him know about any change on that woman at the hospital, he carried on with his phone calls.

The city morgue offered a second possible victim. This one had little to no paperwork at this point, as she'd just been brought in and would still need to be autopsied for cause of death. He asked to be notified as soon as they knew anything.

Brandt frowned. Thanks to Sam, he had a very good idea of a time frame. Sam. He had trouble explaining his interest. She pulled at his heart, his mind, his emotions. He felt a dull pain in areas he didn't know existed. She made him ache for better times, for happiness, for a life filled with joy.

Spending time with her was like a drug. He liked the effect while under, and hated the sensation when it wore off. After his head cleared, he wondered why the hell he kept going back. Except he knew. He'd been intrigued since the beginning. Sex had never been his goal. He'd long since outgrown his adolescent hormones. He certainly wasn't searching for a mate to have the little white house with a picket fence and the customary two-and-a-half kids like so many of his friends.

When attraction slapped him up the side of the head, normally he ran with it. This time, the way forward held a few roadblocks.

Still, he didn't think they'd stop him.

Sitting at his computer, Brandt checked his watch. He had a few minutes before his five o'clock appointment at the university.

5: 25 pm

THE SUN DIPPED behind the mountain, casting golden beams rippling across the lake. Sam tilted her head sideways, wincing as the pounding inside her head increased. The sun's rays twinkled and disappeared under the water. Mother Nature had outdone herself. Exhausted, she lay in numbed limbo. She was still dressed in jeans and t-shirt because she hadn't had enough energy to go for a swim this afternoon.

For someone who preferred her own company, she'd been overwhelmed by people, recently. She had to watch out and keep centered.

Animals offered a respite for her senses. They exuded calm, peaceful energy waves.

People, on the other hand, lived on emotion. They constantly projected erratic bursts of painful energy. The larger bursts from strong emotions hurt her the most. Happier, lighter emotions were easier to tolerate. But when people were angry or upset, overwhelmed in grief or even sometimes when they were ecstatic, they exploded with energy. For Sam, these waves became almost solid walls pounding against her.

Everything impacted much more when she was tired. At those times, on top of lowering her defenses, her own talents increased because her ability to keep them shut down was weaker. Her energy both bled outward and sponged inward.

Working at the vet hospital had allowed her to make gains on her protective shields – in part, due to the animals and their energy. Stefan had given her hints on how to release the energy afterward. She should be euphoric at what she'd accomplished, instead she was too exhausted to feel anything except the headache clawing the inside of her head.

Today had been a tough day. It had taken everything she had to feed her dogs once she arrived home. She'd grabbed a chunk of cheese and an apple and walked to the dock. She'd actually slept in the warm sun after consuming that little bit of food.

A vehicle growl filtered down the hill. Moses raised his head, not growling, yet not totally at ease.

Sam tensed.

In the same half-aware state, she watched as Brandt's truck drove into view. Her heart leaped. She'd forgotten. He was supposed to pick up something and bring it down for dinner.

Sam rolled over to lean on her elbow. Blood pounded in her temple making her grimace. She closed her eyes halfway against the pain. Headaches were the bane of her health problems though she'd never seen a doctor about them. Her lips twitched, imagining trying to explain her issue to a local MD. She'd be referred to a shrink immediately.

Groaning as she stood up, Sam had to stop and breathe deeply as the hammer in her head was put down and a sledgehammer took over. "Oh God," she whispered to the empty air. "I so don't need this right now."

Walking very slowly, Sam made her way up to the cabin.

"Good evening." Brandt walked toward her with a large brown bag.

Sam nodded and immediately wished she hadn't as pain stabbed her right temple. Chinese food? Her stomach gurgled. The apple and cheese hadn't gone far and the food smelled delicious. Now if only the pain would go away.

"Are you alright?"

A wan smile slipped out. "Just a headache. I'll be fine." She eyed the bag he carried. "Is that Chinese food I'm smelling?"

Brandt's eyes narrowed as he searched her face. "I found a new restaurant to try. Let's go inside where you can sit down. I'll find some plates and serve." As they walked into the house, he added, "I also have a few pictures to show you."

Interest flared briefly before being pounded down. Sam navigated the stairs and led the way inside. As much as she hated to, she took a painkiller for the headache before collapsing on the couch. She let Brandt deal with the food.

She closed her eyes. Paper rustled, china clanged, and the aroma made her stomach sing. She hoped he picked up her favorite dish – Chicken Chow Mein.

"Sam, sit up and eat. You'll feel better."

She opened her eyes to see Brandt holding out a plateful. She placed it on the table between the two couches. Brandt sat opposite her. He'd heaped her plate high with saucy noodles, chicken, and lovely crisp vegetables. She'd be lucky to eat half of it. The hot steam wafted toward her, both soothing and comforting. She took several bites and moaned with pleasure.

"I love Chinese food. Thank you for this."

He smiled and kept a steady eye on her. "You're welcome." After another quiet moment with only the sounds of food being enjoyed, he asked another question. "Are you sure you're okay? You look a little pale."

Sam nodded gently, her mouth too full to speak. "Yes, sometimes I get these bad headaches." He'd been right, she was feeling slightly better. The headache, although not gone, had receded slightly. To change the subject, she nodded to several pictures upside down on the table. "What are those?"

He flipped the pictures over and spread them out.

Four different pictures of snake and leaf designs lay in front of her. Interesting. She leaned forward to study them.

After a few minutes, Brandt shifted his position. "Well?"

"Hmmm."

"What does that mean?"

Sam looked up at him. "It means they're close, just not the same as the one I saw."

"How can you tell?" Brandt leaned forward pushing the papers closer. "They're all so similar."

She took another bite of noodles.

"Similar but not the same. In the left one, the snake wraps around the outside of a leaf, not a cloverleaf. In the right one, you can't tell if it's a snake or a rope or something similar."

Brandt, shaking his head, collected the pictures together.

At her nod, he stacked the pictures into a pile. "Have you had any more visions or seen anything else?"

"No, nothing yet."

They continued to eat in contemplative silence for a few more minutes. The corners of Sam's mouth slid downward and her eyes closed. God, she was tired. She put down her half-full plate.

"Are you sure you can't eat a little more?"

She shook her head without opening her eyes. "Sorry, it's my headache. Let me just close my eyes for a few minutes."

"No problem. Lie down and rest. I'll clean up."

Sam was past arguing. With a warm full tummy, fatigue drew her in, and she slept.

CHAPTER 15

10:05 pm

WITH THE DISHES washed, Brandt sat on the couch opposite Sam. Now what? Should he leave her alone to sleep? Odd to be so unsure. Staring at her, he had to admit, the idea of staying and watching over her was winning. He glanced at the pile of blankets on the floor. Picking one up, he opened it and covered Sam.

There was something wild about her. Not necessarily in a good way. Maybe untamed was a better description. She appeared awkward in crowds, uneasy in close confines, and hated confrontations – she wouldn't walk away from a fight if she thought it mattered. She could hold her own.

She was trying to improve her life now, but what had brought her so low? Had it been the last incident with the deputy? He frowned. Had that car accident long ago wiped out her savings or had she been unable to work afterwards because of her injuries? He surveyed the small room. He doubted she'd had insurance. There was no sign of money here. In fact, poverty had moved right in. She dressed in oversized thrift store clothes that would fit any large man.

She needed a keeper. Someone to make sure she ate and rested. If there was no one else, then maybe, just maybe the job fell to him. That he'd even had that thought showed how far he'd come. A few weeks ago, he'd have run at the thought of caring for someone like her. This was stupid. He needed a decent night's sleep himself. He should be home in his own bed, not here keeping an eye on her. Still, it was early yet, and she'd looked wiped when he'd arrived. Staying awhile wouldn't be a hardship.

Moses slept on the floor in front of Sam and Soldier sat on guard at the end of the other couch – watching him.

Brandt peered into the blackness outside the window. Moments later he closed his eyes, too tired himself to muddle through the confusing array of reasons for staying there.

An odd muffled noise woke him.

Brandt turned his head, groaning as pain exploded through his neck. "God, what did I do?" Rolling his head from side to side, he leaned forward, trying to remember where he was. A muffled cry from the couch had him bolting upright, now wide-awake.

Sam jerked her legs out straight and arched her back. Her mouth opened, the muscles on her face and neck clenched into long cords, straining with effort. She screamed – silently.

The hairs on Brandt's neck stood straight up.

Sam jerked, her back bowed even tighter.

Brandt reached out to wake her from the nightmare, then hesitated, his hands inches from her shoulder. How many times had Stefan told him not to touch someone in a trance? But how did he know whether she was in a trance or a nightmare?

Sam collapsed, her legs sprawling at awkward angles. Her breathing stabilized, returning to a more even pace, slowly picking up a normal rhythm again.

Just when he thought she was fine, Sam's face twisted, her eyes opened wide with an opaque glassy look. Brandt bent over and stared directly into her eyes.

"Sam," he whispered. "Sam, wake up."

Sam arched again, then jerked spasmodically as if struck by invisible blows.

Jesus. Brandt backed up a step and stared at her. Ice raced through his body. What the hell was going on? He searched her face, watching every nuance, every tiny expression – it was easy to see she wasn't really here. She was seeing something, experiencing something that Brandt couldn't. Brandt had never seen any nightmare like this one. He wasn't sure he'd ever want to, either.

He glanced at his watch. 2:30 am. He must have fallen asleep. He could have sworn he'd been out for only a couple of minutes.

Sam made a gurgling sound, arched once, then twice before collapsing into a shuddering tremble. Then she fell silent. Brandt stared in horror. Cuts appeared in the blanket. He reached out, the raspy wool scratched his fingers. When he'd covered her up, the blanket had been tatty but whole. He couldn't see it completely from the awkward way it lay over her, but he could see several slices in the thick fabric.

His jaw dropped. More cuts appeared even as he watched. He leaned forward, shock making his hands tremble. This could not be happening. This was not possible. His rational mind knew that, yet his eyes wouldn't stop receiving the images. There, another cut over her abdomen appeared. No way. He leaned closer and sat again as bile rose up into his throat.

Blood seeped slowly from the last cut. Impossible. Brandt sat in horror as blood slowly oozed from the dozen cuts, soaking the blanket covering Sam. Was she hurt? She couldn't be – the cuts had just appeared. Only there was nothing there that had caused the injuries.

Soldier arrived at the couch, a high whine sounding from deep inside him.

"Easy boy. I don't know what's going on either."

Brandt studied his hands, not surprised to see them shaking, shudders even now moving up his arms. Christ, no one would believe this. Hell, he could hardly believe it himself – and it was happening right before his eyes.

His gaze dropped to a second blanket on the floor. Reaching down, he shook the folds loose and went to fling it across her form, when Stefan's warning drilled through her. *Never touch a medium when they are in a trance.*

The blanket dropped to the floor. He didn't know if a blanket counted as a touch and decided he didn't dare take the chance. A sudden thought jolted him. No one would believe him, just like no one believed Sam. Oh God. His stomach knotted and bile seared his throat, threatening to make him sick. Is this how she felt?

He watched in fascination as the blood dripped and ran to pool on top of the blankets beside her. Her face paled to a milky white, making his nerves jump again. Shit. He wanted to call for an ambulance. But what could he tell them? He knew logically there was no rational explanation. And he could be killing her by leaving her alone to bleed. Shit. Doubt paralyzed him.

Soldier stuck his nose closer to Sam, sniffing the blood. He whimpered.

Brandt grabbed his cell phone. Stefan, Goddamn it, please be home.

"Hello?" A thick sleep-filled voice growled at him.

"Oh thank God. Stefan, this is Brandt."

"Brandt." A thick throat-clearing cough bounced through the phone. "What's the matter?"

"It's Sam."

"Sam? What's wrong?" His voice turned businesslike.

"I'm in trouble."

"What else is new?"

"No, I'm here with her now and she appears to be caught in a vision."

"And?"

"Stefan. I've seen a lot of things in my life, but I've never come across anything like this. It's happening right now." Brandt took a deep breath and willed some stability into his voice. "There are cuts appearing in the blanket that's covering her and there's blood. Oh my God, there's so much blood. It's dripping on the floor." Brandt drew a shaky breath. "There's no weapon, or anyone, just the slashes without reason."

"But she's still in the vision?"

"That's what I'm saying. It's like she's experiencing someone else's attack. As I'm watching, she arches and reacts as if being stabbed, then slashes appear in the blankets around her. Within seconds, blood appears and drips to the floor. Christ, Stefan." Brandt bent, dipping his fingers in a pool of blood. He rubbed his fingers together. "The blood is real. It smells real, and it feels real."

There was silence for a moment.

"How can she survive something like this?" Brandt needed Stefan's reassurance. That it wasn't forthcoming, made him more nervous.

"Is she breathing?"

Brandt, his heart racing at the thought, bent over Sam. "Christ, she'd better be." He checked her chest for the telltale rise and fall movement. There. Ever so faint. He placed his hand to hover above her mouth. Yes. A faint waft of air. "Yes, she's alive. But not by much."

"That's okay. The deeper her trance, the more her body vitals slow down."

Brandt checked her over again. The blood had settled in, staining the gray material to rust. The smell flared his nostrils – the same metallic odour he knew all too well.

"Can you see any damage to her body, or are we just talking blankets and blood showing?"

"Is it safe to touch her? Hell, Stefan, how many times have you pounded it into me not to touch you when you're in a trance?"

"Lift the blankets and don't touch her body."

"Why is it I can't touch her again?" Brandt stared at Sam, trying to figure out a safe corner of the blanket to lift without touching her body.

"You'll snap her connection to whatever energy she's attached to. She could stay over there, snap back here, or get caught somewhere in between."

Brandt winced. "Right." Working carefully, he shifted a corner of the blanket away from her shoulder to peer at her slight body below. A slice deep into her abdomen made his gut clench. He groaned softly, sadly. She was dying, and he'd done nothing to help her.

"Christ, her abdomen is split open."

Stefan's voice remained calm and patient. "That's fine. Is she still experiencing new injuries?"

"That's fine! What the hell, Stefan? She's dying."

"No, she's not. In about twenty minutes, she should be almost as good as new. Check again. Are new injuries still appearing?"

Brandt stared at Sam, trying to check all of her at once. After a moment, he answered, "I don't think so. I think that part is over."

"Good, the blood should stop seeping too."

"It will?" Brandt studied the welling blood. Relief washed over him. "Actually, it appears to be slowing."

"Good. She should wake up soon."

"Should? I need her to wake up now!"

"Don't touch her." Stefan's voice was sharp, leaving no room for arguing. "When she wakes, she could be groggy, disoriented, and possibly scared. Give her both time and space. Try not to startle her, just watch as she recovers."

"Right. I guess that makes sense." Brandt moved over and sat across from Sam. "I'll call you in the morning. Or in a few minutes if she doesn't wake up."

"She'll wake up. Trust a little more." Stefan hung up.

Brandt tucked away his cell phone, Stefan's final words ringing in his ears – time to recover and heal. The heal part blew him away. If she experienced the same physical damage as these woman, then no wonder she looked like she could use a good square meal. Her body had to burn calories at a horrific rate doing something like this.

Sam stirred. Brandt rushed over to her side. She rolled her head from one side to the next before coming to a stop. A deep heavy sigh worked its way up from her chest. She opened her eyes, ones that widened in shock when they landed on him.

"It's okay Sam. It's just me. Take it easy. Take your time."

Understanding seeped into those beautiful eyes before she closed them again, drifting off into a light resting state. She licked her lips and whispered in a voice so low he had to bend to her lips to hear it. "I'll be fine in a couple of minutes."

Soldier whined and flumped down at her feet protectively.

Brandt ran a hand through his hair, relieved to hear her talking, but having trouble with the concept that she'd could be okay that fast. Was that possible? He wouldn't be – how could she? He watched her carefully. Could she recover from something like this on her own – without a doctor? How? Did Stefan go through this as well?

In amazement, Brandt watched as the blood thinned and actually appeared to be less. He leaned forward. The droplets on the floor remained. The slices in the blankets remained. What about her? Getting up, he gently lifted the corner of the blanket and checked her abdomen. Even as he watched, the wound shrunk down. It was only a couple of inches long now. He shook his head. He'd never have believed it. And he was open-minded about this stuff. He couldn't imagine Kevin's reaction.

"Brandt?"

"I'm here, Sam. Take it easy."

"I'm almost there. Just another minute and I'll be good."

"Right. Like I'm going to believe that." He snorted and sat on the coffee table across from her, accidentally nudging Soldier who lay protectively in front of Sam.

Soldier lifted his head, his lip curling at Brandt.

Brandt glared down at him. Soldier glared back.

"No, I'm almost there. Wait, let me check." She lifted her head to look at him. And cried out in agony, her body curling into itself.

Instantly Brandt was at her side. "Jesus, Sam. What the hell?"

Sam gasped for breath her face slowly gaining color with the effort. "It's okay. Honest."

Frustrated, he fisted his hands on his hips. "How? How can this be okay?"

He crouched down beside her, reaching out a hesitant hand. He desperately wanted to give comfort, yet was scared of hurting her further.

She opened her eyes to stare at him again.

"Oh God, Sam." Brandt breathed her name almost in prayer. The depth of her suffering and pain hurt his soul. Her eyes had gone black from her agony.

Helpless, he could only watch. "I'm so sorry, honey. What can I do to help?"

A tiny smile peeped out. "Wait."

He didn't think he could do it. "Sweetheart, there is blood everywhere."

The smile disappeared as she shuddered once, then twice. "Always is."

Brandt sank into a crouch beside the couch. "God, how can you do this – day in and day out?"

Her answer, so succinct and so honest blew him away. "Easy. I have no choice."

3:48 am, June 20th

SAM FOUND THE shift through transition harder this time. Having someone watch while she healed and returned to normal reality wasn't exactly fun. Self-conscious or not, she couldn't move before it was time. Shifting her glance to catch Brandt's expression, she winced and stared up at the ceiling. Barely concealed horror still rippled across his face.

She closed her eyes. She couldn't help him deal with this. It took everything she had to deal with it herself.

The research she'd done said that blood rarely manifested in visions. But in special cases, people woke up with their hands or bodies stained with the stuff. For her, the blood appeared wherever the injuries manifested, but less blood than if she'd truly been the one attacked. Apparently, the amount of physical manifestations should decrease as she learned to control her gifts. She could only hope.

Gently, Sam swung her legs over the side of her couch and sat up. Feeling dizzy, she took several shuddering breaths before fixing her gaze on Brandt.

Wild eyes stared back at her. She couldn't blame him. This stuff came straight out of a horror movie. She wanted to curl up and hide in shame. She'd hoped he'd never see her like this. Never see her so exposed, so…freakish. She could only imagine what he thought of her now.

A few last tremors worked up her spine. It was almost over. Her eyes still burned, swollen and dry. Even her bones ached.

She focused on Brandt instead of the pain. His rumpled hair looked adorable – at total odds to his eyes. She glanced at the clock, yawning at the same time. It was close to four in the morning. He must have stayed all night.

She slid her gaze over him again. He still appeared shell-shocked. It said much about his perception. He'd never be able to accept this part of her. The pain from her vision was nothing to the sudden pain in her heart.

Brandt sat down suddenly. She studied his features. In truth, it looked like his belief system, his very foundation of existence had been ripped out from under him.

Sam couldn't handle any more. Tears of shame burned. Freak.

"Christ." Brandt's whispered words were a soft prayer for understanding.

Sam knew how he felt. She also knew her prayers had never been answered. "What's the matter?"

He snorted, rose, and reached to poke a finger through one of the many slices in the blanket covering her. "This is what's the matter." He stuck his fingers through a bigger cut and waggled them.

Confused, Sam watched emotions whisper across his face.

He stared at her. "Does this mean…?"

Her bottom lip wobbled and she nodded. "It means another woman has been murdered."

Hearing her own words broke the dam holding back the anguish in Sam's soul. Brandt sat on the couch and tugged her into his arms. Sam went. Hurt, she curled into his chest and let her tears pour. Brandt rocked her gently, her broken sobs so soft they could hardly be heard. The pain behind them could hardly be ignored.

Brandt hugged her tight.

After the worst of the storm had passed, Sam thought she heard him speak.

She shifted slightly to peer up at him, wiping away the tears on her cheeks. "What?"

"I'm sorry to have to do this. I need to ask you some questions while this is all fresh." His gaze glanced off the blanket. He shook his head in a daze. "About the victim, not so much the process – which I admit to having some trouble with." As his hand continued to stroke her sore muscles, he became lost in thought. After a moment, he tugged her close for a quick hug before setting her back slightly.

Holding back a few stray sniffles, Sam shifted into a more comfortable position and let herself relax slightly.

"What happened was in real time." Tears welled again. Sam struggled for control, using her sleeve to wipe her eyes. "The slashes you saw appear on the blanket and on my body were the same injuries the victim received. The blood and cuts to the blankets correlate to the victim's injuries."

Brandt started.

"Are you saying that you are stabbed every time the victim is stabbed?"

The tears slid from the corners of her eyes. "Yes." Her voice was barely more than a whisper.

"No." Brandt shook his head. "No one could survive those injuries. They can't be happening to you, because..." Brandt shifted enough to remove the blanket. "Because you're fine. You'd be dead if that had happened to you. Like those women are dead."

Teary eyed, and tormented by the poor woman's fate, Sam nodded. "You still don't understand." She sniffled, rubbing her eyes with the sleeve of her sweater. Recovery might have taken a while longer tonight, it had also taken all of her energy. She was exhausted.

Sam locked her gaze onto his. "In a way, I am exactly like those other women." A quiver ran down her spine, shaking her entire body. Wrapping her arms around her chest, she took a deep breath.

"As each woman dies...so do I – I die every time."

10:10 am

"SO WHAT ARE you going to do about it?" The colonel shifted further out of the sun, the buckles on his ever-present suspenders glinting in the bright light. He hooked his cane onto the arm of the overstuffed easy chair as he sat down. He glanced over at Maisy again. "Well, you said it. Enough is enough." He grinned at her sour face. "So what are you prepared to do? The boy is full grown."

"Pshhh." Maisy snorted delicately. "Grown he might be, know his own mind, he doesn't."

The colonel grinned at her. "Oh, he knows his mind. It's just not the mind you want him to have. You don't like that he's choosing to live his life the way he wants to." He reached for his cup of tea. "Admit it. You want him to do it your way."

"Behave yourself, or you can go somewhere else for your tea." She harrumphed and busied herself straightening her sunflower yellow skirts.

The colonel chuckled and relaxed further into his chair.

"The boy should be married and have a family by now. That's all I'm saying." She tilted her face more into the sun. The heat from the sun's rays was wonderfully strong for this hour of the morning. It did her old bones good to soak up the healing rays. "Besides, I like this one."

"Which one?"

"You know perfectly well which one. The skinny one that's all eyes."

"I don't think they're really going out. That boy wouldn't recognize staying power even when it's there right under his nose. He's after other qualities." The colonel waggled his thick white eyebrows at her.

"He's a normal male." Maisy grinned at the colonel. "He probably doesn't even know what staying power is."

"Too bad. A girl like that – well she's a keeper."

"She looks like she's survived hell on earth."

The two sat in comfort, enjoying the simple things of life that had taken them decades to appreciate.

The colonel spoke up again. "Did you hear about that case the police are working on?"

Maisy glanced at him. "Which one?"

He waved his hand at the television. "The one they talked about last night. The police are trying to identify the owner of a ring with a four-leaf clover pattern and some sort of snake wrapped through the leaves. Apparently, one diamond is missing from the ring. They didn't specify why they were looking for the information, though."

Pursing her lips, Maisy thought about the many jewelry pieces she'd seen over the years. None had been in that pattern that she could remember. She loved jewelry, particularly unique pieces.

"Can't say that I've seen anything like that – at least not recently."

"When are they coming for lunch?"

Maisy recognized the sly twist to the colonel's face. "Meaning you don't give a damn about seeing him, you'd like to know more about the cases he's working on."

The colonel scrunched his shoulders like a young child who'd been caught with his hand in a cookie jar. "Call him. We need something new to talk about here." He stared at the blank television. "I'm pretty sure I saw that ring somewhere. I just can't remember where."

"Really? That's so exciting."

He harrumphed at her. "It's only exciting if I can remember where. My memory isn't that good."

Maisy smiled. "Isn't that the truth?" She surveyed the courtyard and the other seniors taking the time to enjoy the morning sun. Life was peaceful here – too peaceful. Stimulation was hard to come by and her son's career was the source of much of it. Still, it was a good excuse to get him over where she could work on him a little more. Besides, she shouldn't need an excuse. He was her son. She reached for the phone, ignoring the low chuckles from the colonel. "Brandt, good morning." She smiled at his sleepy voice. Poor guy, he didn't get enough sleep. "I wanted to catch you before you went to work this morning and got all caught up in your cases."

He mumbled something in response.

Maisy wasn't fazed. He was always like that. "The colonel and I have been talking. He saw that bit of news on the TV about a ring the other night. It triggered something for him."

"What does he remember?"

"That's the thing, he can't quite remember and he's getting really upset about it." She sniffled. Then she frowned. What was that?

Brandt cleared his throat. "We don't want him doing that. He'll remember better when he's calm anyway."

"Well, I know that. But try telling him that." Maisy caught a second sniffle halfway. She glared at the grinning colonel. "I'm really worried about him, Brandt."

"Tell him to relax about it, and if he remembers anything to give me a call. I won't be able to stop by today."

"I will." She hesitated. "Brandt, don't forget to bring Sam by for lunch one day soon."

"I know. It won't likely be this week though. Things are busy at work."

Voices sounded in the background. Maisy widened her eyes.

"Brandt, where are you?"

Silence.

"Why?" He cleared his throat.

Another voice came through the phone, faintly recognizable. Maisy strained her hearing. Something about tea. Brandt and tea? She gasped. "Brandt, you're with Sam!" She squealed in joy.

Brandt groaned, "Ouch, my ears. And it's not what you think, Mom."

Maisy bounced on her chair. "I'm sure it isn't, honey." She grinned at the colonel, her thumb in the air. "When are you bringing her for lunch?"

"Not today."

The colonel poked Maisy. "Tell him I want some advice."

She glanced over, frowning at him. But the colonel kept nodding his head. She shrugged. "Brandt, I don't know if this changes anything, the colonel says he wants your advice on something. You know how he is. He'll worry himself into another heart attack until he gets the information he needs."

The colonel blustered at her side. She grinned unrepentantly.

"Okay, I'll try to stop by later today – alone. If I can't, I'll give him a call tonight or tomorrow morning. I can't promise any more than that."

"Oh, that's wonderful dear. We both appreciate you making the effort."

"I said 'try.' I may not make it."

She smirked at the colonel, her cohort in fun. "No, no honey…we understand. Your job has to come first over things like this. That's fine. It would be nice if you brought Sam though."

After saying good-bye, Maisy hung up the phone and turned to grin at her companion. "He said he'll try to get here later this afternoon, or he'll call you later today." She leaned forward slightly as she squeezed the phone to her chest. "He spent the night with Sam."

The colonel nodded. "Good. We should have a few hours to ourselves too."

She plumped her blue white hair and smiled teasingly. "What did you have in mind?"

CHAPTER 16

8:25 am, June 21

BRANDT FOUND HIS mind wandering. After what he'd witnessed last night, it amazed him that he could function at all. Sam had been fully recovered this morning. He checked his email, hoping for leads of some kind. He needed progress. He already knew that the stone found in the bedroom of the one victim was a diamond. So, the news broadcaster had gotten it right. The police had nothing to go on – no semen or DNA was ever present. The cold cases he'd collected under his project were similar in that they also lacked forensic evidence. That alone made him wonder if Sam's killer could be the same man he was chasing.

It also reminded him that, according to Sam, another woman lay dead, waiting to be found. It could be days before this one was called in.

He tossed his pen on his desk and glared at the stack of papers waiting his attention. Maybe he should go and talk to the colonel instead. See if he could shake some details loose.

Shutting down the multiple open tabs on paranormal research on his desktop, he rubbed the bridge of his nose. He'd hardly slept. He'd stayed and tried to doze on Sam's couch until it was time to leave for the office. Now fatigue made it hard for him to focus.

His cell phone rang, pulling him out of his reverie.

"Hello." Brandt leaned forward, reaching for a notepad and the pen. At the familiar voice, he closed his eyes and sighed heavily. "Hey Stefan, glad to hear from you."

The thin voice on the other end sounded tired but well. "How is she?"

"She's fine. Better than I am." That was an understatement.

"Of course, she took a totally normal trip into the psychic world, and you've just blown your mind. Figures."

"I find I'm searching for an explanation today. What I saw last night, I'm doubting now in the morning."

"Also normal." Stefan sighed. "Your rational mind refuses to accept what your heart already knows."

"And what do I do about it?"

Stefan laughed. "You ignore it. You saw what you saw – now let it go." The irony in his voice was hard to miss. "If you stay with her, it won't be the last time you get to experience something on the wild side.

Brandt's mouth widened. "It's been a little nuts already, I have to admit."

"She's an interesting woman."

"Is that all you can say? Interesting?"

"Absolutely." A heavy, amused pause filled the air. "What would you call her?"

Brandt shifted uncomfortably on the computer chair. He didn't know what to call her at this point. Unfortunately, his friend had insider knowledge that gave him an advantage. Brandt winced, knowing what was coming.

Warm laughter filled the air. "You haven't figured it out, have you? Any woman that can twist you up like this, is...well, definitely interesting."

"Stefan," he started hesitantly. "I was way out of my element last night. She scared the hell out of me."

Stefan paused. "I have never met anyone with these abilities, so it's new for me, too. To have the cuts and the blood is an interesting twist."

Wrinkles appeared in Brandt's forehead with his confusion. "Why?"

"There is probably less than one person in ten million with her abilities. Maybe even one in a billion. Because of that, we don't know much about them. She has more than one gift, by the way. She's incredibly talented. As she learns control, these physical symptoms may change. Could disappear entirely."

Brandt shook his head. "Well, the whole thing left quite an impression."

"Does it change the way you view her?" Stefan's voice reeked with curiosity but not surprise.

Brandt shifted uncomfortably. "I'd like to say no, but I'm not sure that I can."

Heavy silence filled the phone line.

"Take some time and think about this. Particularly take some time to think about this from Sam's point of view."

"I know." Brandt rubbed a hand down his face. "God, her life must be hell."

"That's probably all she has known. Consider the amount of in-depth knowledge she's gleaned about the dark side of humanity. Take into account the amount of disbelief and mockery she's faced, and then consider how different she is from others. None of that is going to bring her hugs in this world. Kicks, however, are free."

Stefan was right. "She's spent some time in a psych ward. Just under four months."

Stefan's voice was tinged with weariness. "Haven't we all. It's society's answer for the unknown. If she is fully functioning at this stage of her life, she's learned to adapt, to cope, and to hide. All three are required to survive."

"And she's all alone."

"Easy to understand, isn't it? You're wondering why you haven't high-tailed it for the hills yourself."

Brandt couldn't argue that point. He didn't know what the hell he felt about Sam now. She required a little more acceptance and understanding than he had yet to be asked for in a relationship. He was sure he could give that – eventually, should he choose. That was the problem – he just hadn't worked it out in his head yet.

Stefan read his mind. "If you care at all, watch what you say and do right now. She's spent a lifetime under suspicion and receiving disapproval. If you want to be accepted by her, she needs to know that you can handle her gifts." Stefan coughed a couple of times. "If you decide that you can't handle them then don't let her know right away. The worst thing you can do today is to walk away. You'd be reinforcing what she's had a lifetime to learn – she's unacceptable in the eyes of the rest of the world."

"But that's not true," Brandt protested.

"Maybe not, but you'd have a hard time convincing her of that." Stefan tried again. "Look to her history. It's all there. Fear, distrust, hatred even. There's no acceptance handed out for people like her and me."

"You're different."

"No. No, I'm not. It took you time to trust me as it took me time to trust you. This is the same position you're in with Sam – learning to trust. Remember – it takes time."

Brandt was silent. "Can someone really live a life like hers?"

"She is." Bald and clear, there was no arguing with the logic.

"What if I can't?" There it was – the secret fear. The fear that had kept him awake all night as he lay on his couch as she lay opposite on hers. That sat stewing in his mind all morning, keeping him from focusing on his job. What if he couldn't accept Sam, couldn't accept the life she led?

Stefan's heavy sigh came through the phone. "If you can't, you can't. It would surprise me though. I've certainly pushed the envelope of your beliefs – so what's different this time?"

"This time I find I'm searching for an anchor, a point of reference. Something to help me place what I witnessed into my belief system, my reality."

"That is exactly how you felt the first time I spoke to you about a killer on one of your cases. I even told you something similar at the time."

Brandt vaguely remembered that time in his life. "Was I that bad?"

"Absolutely. You might also remember something you've said to me in the past. You told me that you'd never married because you couldn't see anyone accepting your life. Now you're thinking about rejecting her because you can't accept *her* life."

"I'm not rejecting her…" And he wasn't. He was rejecting her gift. God he was an ass. But Stefan continued to talk.

"Good. Think about this. See how you feel about it all tomorrow. Call me if you need to talk."

Stefan hung up after that, leaving Brandt alone with his thoughts. Brandt had seen a lot of things in his life. Police work often demanded finding a way through lies and deceit to arrive at the truth. In this case, the truth stared him in the face. He could no longer doubt what he'd seen. It had just taken some time to accept. That something impossible, something that broke all the laws of life as he knew them – had happened – whether he liked it or not.

11:45 am

NOT WORKING A normal nine to five, Monday to Friday job made for a great week, but damn it, she hated to work on weekends.

Peering into the mirror, Sam curled her lip. It's a good thing Brandt had left early this morning. She resembled the homeless woman everyone thought she was. Her hair hung lank around her shoulders. If there were any highlights then they were hidden in the shadows. Pulling a brush through hair she didn't have time to wash, she ran.

She was ten minutes late.

Two other staff members worked at opening the front office while Sam started feeding the animals. It must have been a busy day yesterday. There were several new animals and Sam's heart bled for each and every one. It took hours to make them comfortable. The hospital was short-handed. Twice, she was called away to help the front staff, once with an unruly canine, and the second time with a tomcat that wasn't interested in having his wayward ways changed.

Working with the animals out front, helped Sam to see other aspects of the business. Working with the injured animals in the cages gave her a lopsided view. She loved seeing them before they ended up in her care.

"Good morning, Sam."

Lost in thought, she spun around, almost falling to the floor from her crouching position. "Good morning, Dr. Wascott."

"How is Soldier doing?"

A big grin split her face. The vet stopped, a stunned expression emblazoned on his normally peaceful face.

"Soldier is doing wonderfully. He's walking around more and slowly gaining strength. He had his last medicine this morning, and he should be fine now."

The doctor moved his head from side to side. "Honestly, Sam, I don't think I've ever seen you this happy. I'm glad the dog is bringing some life into your world."

Heat bloomed on her cheeks as she realized she'd been babbling. "Sorry," she muttered.

The older man sported a boyish grin. "No problem. It's quite a nice change, actually."

Still, she couldn't help a sheepish grin, feeling a little more of her normal reserve drop off. She felt more comfortable with him than she ever had before.

"There's a phone call for you, Dr. Wascott." One of the vet assistants walked into the room, smiling. "Good morning, Samantha. How are you today?"

Feeling unnaturally peaceful, Sam nodded to the other woman. "I'm fine, thank you."

"Good. There's fresh bread, a new grainy recipe from the corner bakery, in the lunchroom. Lucy also brought in some fresh creamed honey. Make sure you have some before your shift is over."

The idea of fresh baked bread made her mouth water. "Thanks, I'd like to try it."

"You're done now. There's a fresh pot of tea in there, too. Go enjoy." Dr. Wascott nudged Sam's arm before walking out of the room.

The treat sounded too irresistible to ignore.

Sam slipped into the lunchroom, slightly disappointed to find it empty. With a frown, she considered that. How long had it been since she'd relished company?

The bread smelled luscious. A fresh yeasty aroma wafted free as Sam cut off a thick slice. An open canning jar full of creamy honey sat on the counter. In the light, the honey had a deep opaque milkiness to it. Opening the lid, Sam sniffed the contents. Using the tip of her knife, she tasted a small bit and rolled her eyes as the flavor exploded on her tongue. Oh my God, that was so good. Quickly, Sam slathered the top of her bread with a thick layer before sitting at the small table with her tea.

"It's good, isn't it?

Sam started in surprise, so lost in the snack she hadn't heard anyone enter. With her mouth full, she could only nod.

Lucy grinned, cutting herself a slice.

Afterwards, Sam headed to the library for more research books. From there, it was a quick hop over to the grocery store for a couple of items.

She stood in line, waiting to pay for her purchase. She should have come here earlier and avoided the rush. Crowds gave her a headache. She reached up to rub her temple when she felt it.

A long finger of evil reached out and brushed her soul.

The grocery store disappeared, the line of people morphed into a small tidy room. The smell of medicine and aftershave assailed her nose. A gruff cough poured from her chest. Sam bent to rub her sore leg, surprised to see a cane in her right hand and plaid slippers on her feet.

Her hand went to her chest as she shuffled over to an easy chair, stiff movements jarring her spine with each step. Evil surrounded her – *him*. Only she didn't think he knew about it.

"Hey, old man?"

The male body she inhabited jerked in surprise, turning somewhat awkwardly. The other man had a huge old lady's hat with flowers…and Christ, something that resembled a bird on top. A silk paisley scarf wrapped around the lower portion of his face, obscuring all, but his dark voracious eyes. Sam's stomach dropped. She knew that gaze. She wanted to close her eyes but they weren't her own. She wanted to jump free, but she was tied to this soul.

"Who are you and what are you doing in my room?"

"Just taking care of details. The mark of a professional is in giving every detail the same level of attention – no matter how small." The voice was muffled and rasping. Sam knew she wouldn't be able to identify it in real time.

"What do you want?" the old man asked querulously. "Get out of my room." Sam wanted to run from the room, to force the old man to move toward the door. She had no control over his limbs or tongue. She could only watch, paralyzed with horror, knowing what was to come. She tried to catalogue the details for later.

"Oh, I'm leaving, Colonel. But I'll be back – you on the other hand, won't be."

Pain exploded at the crown of Sam's head, colors danced, blinding her. She groaned. The carpet rushed up to meet her, as she collapsed to the floor.

Darkness swirled, coaxing her into the center of the morass before becoming an all-encompassing shroud then blinking out all together. Sam hung suspended between time and reality. Not moving one way or another. Caught. Lost.

At the last minute, Sam heard a faint voice weaving through the darkness, "Serves you right, you old bastard."

Then the darkness was complete.

"Excuse me." Sam was nudged gently and then again, not so gently. "Excuse me? Are you alright?"

Sam came to, woozy and still in a half-blind state. She could hardly focus. A woman's concerned face, blurry and of an odd size came into partial focus. "Yeess." Her tongue had a fuzzy, thick feeling and if that was her voice, something was wrong. Very wrong.

"You don't look it." The woman spoke bluntly, tugging Sam to a chair nearby. The grocery basket was removed from Sam's arms and she was gently pushed into the chair.

Sam's eyes went black with pain. This wasn't transition, it

wasn't reality either. It seemed a step in between – still painful with any movement, yet no bleeding, or other physical manifestations as far as she could tell. It would be a couple of moments before she'd be able to check.

"Are you a diabetic? An epileptic?"

Sam managed to shake her head slowly. "No," she whispered. "I'm fine."

The woman didn't appear convinced. "Do you want to just sit here for a few minutes?" She rose, taking several steps away. "I can return in a moment or two and see how you are doing?" She stopped her escape. "Or I could call for an ambulance?"

Sam eyed the woman again. Her eyes were huge with worry. Sam closed her own for a moment then reopened them again. The process worked much better this time. She gave her a tiny gentle smile. "Thank you," she murmured. "I'll just sit here until I feel better."

"Okay." Relief washed over the woman's face. "As long as you are feeling better, then I'll leave. I'll check on you in a little bit."

Sam said thanks and couldn't hold back a sigh of relief when the woman left. She really didn't feel well. Yet, neither could she say that she felt really bad.

She couldn't explain in a way anyone would understand. Whatever had just happened had drained her energy. She needed rest, and soon. First, she needed to get out of the public's eye.

Surveying the area around her, she couldn't find her basket of groceries anywhere. They could be sitting close, waiting for her, not that she had the energy to look or to care. She'd shop later. For now, she'd be happy with getting to her truck.

Staying upright was a challenge. Using the wall for stability, Sam slipped through the double doors to the parking lot. Her truck was somewhere in the middle. She closed her eyes and leaned against the outside wall. The fresh air helped. Several deep breaths later, her eyesight had returned to normal. If she waited just one more minute, she might be able to walk there like a normal person.

Once at her truck, she struggled inside, shutting the door with more force than necessary. She took another deep breath and evaluated her state of health. Most functions had returned to normal. She didn't know about her speech. But the pain was gone. Achiness remained, yet that was liveable. Her motor functions had returned to normal.

She pulled her cell phone out and dialed Brandt.

"Hello."

"Brandt." She winced. No, her voice wasn't quite normal.

"What's wrong?" His voice had no problem – it damn near split her eardrum.

She held the phone away from her ear, groaning as her head pounded. "Don't yell, please."

He modulated his tone. "Then tell me what's wrong. You sound terrible."

"I'm just coming out of a vision." Sam coughed gently. "This one was weird. This time some old man was hit over the head."

"What?"

Sam could almost see his brow furrowed with concentration.

"Did you see the attacker?

"He was disguised as an old woman. The old man knew him. I think I've been at this place before. Not the same room maybe, but something similar."

"Sam. I have another call coming in. I'll call you right back. Where are you?"

"I'm sitting in the shopping center across from work. While waiting in line at the grocery store, the vision damn near crippled me."

"But you're okay now?"

"Yes. Call me soon." Sam rang off. She rested her head against the side window and closed her eyes.

CHAPTER 17

1:20 pm

BRANDT ANSWERED THE second call impatiently. He needed to call Sam. Damn it all to hell. His fingers rubbed the ridge of his nose.

"Hello." He couldn't help the shortness in his voice.

He listened for a moment, and with the cries from the other end of the phone ringing in his ears, Brandt grabbed his keys and ran out the door.

It was a short trip, barely fifteen minutes before Brandt drove into the parking lot of the senior care home to be greeted by the all too common sight of an ambulance. He strode forward into the empty hallway. Arriving at his mother's suite, he was surprised to find that empty, too. But maybe he shouldn't be. She could always be found at the center of any gathering – and medical emergencies definitely qualified.

He raced to the colonel's quarters. Turning the corner, his steps slowed. A crowd had gathered at the doorway to the colonel's apartment.

Brandt pushed his way through, his heart dropping at the sight. The colonel was on the stretcher, strapped down. An oxygen mask covered most of his face.

Pulling his badge out, he addressed the paramedics. "What happened?" He leaned over the prone man. The colonel's wrinkled gray face resembled clay that had been baked in the sun too long. Unconsciousness hadn't smoothed the deep wrinkles splitting his face. No injuries were apparent.

One of the paramedics walked over. "He was found on the floor. His pulse is strong and he appears to be suffering from a head injury."

"Head injury?" Brandt bent for a closer look, but only the

corner of a blood-soaked bandage was visible.

"He might have fallen and hit his head," offered one of the many bystanders. "He wasn't as steady on his feet as he used to be."

Brandt nodded absentmindedly. The colonel used a walking stick most times. Sure enough, there it was leaning against the wall by his big recliner. The room was so full of people it was hard to move. He stepped out of the way of the stretcher as the two attending men pushed it out to the waiting ambulance. It was only as Brandt turned around to survey the rest of the room that he saw her.

His mom sat with her knees to her chin, her arms snugged tight around her legs like a young child. She swayed gently on the chair, tears in her eyes.

"Mom?" Brandt approached and sat close beside her. Wrapping one arm around her, he gently rubbed her arms. "Are you okay?"

She nodded. "I will be. Just a little upset."

"Were you with him when he collapsed?" Brandt hugged her gently, concerned at the frailty of this feisty valiant woman. She came across as such a powerhouse, then when knocked off balance, she folded.

Giving her time to collect herself, Brandt stared at the other curiosity seekers. Many had started to wander away in search of something more exciting. Still others were waiting, hoping to hear what Maisy would say. Brandt didn't intend to have anyone overhear them.

"Come on. Let's go to your place." He led her through the thinning crowd to her suite. Once inside, he set her in her favorite chair then closed the door on the concerned well-wishers mingling outside. "She'll be fine folks. She's just a little upset."

Turning back to his mother, he added, "I'll make some tea, and you can tell me all about it."

Without waiting for an answer, Brandt put on the teakettle and returned to her side. "Now I need you to tell me what happened. Why are you so upset?"

She lifted her head to peer at him. Torment and guilt gleamed through.

"Did you have something to do with his collapse?" asked Brandt, confused.

"I don't know." Maisy's eyes welled. "The dogs came today, so everyone was in the meeting rooms enjoying their visit. Everyone talked about everything, but the colonel was center stage because of the ring the police are trying to find and what the colonel was trying to remember."

Maisy chewed her bottom lip and didn't continue.

"Then…" prompted Brandt.

"We walked to his apartment where I left him while I went for lunch. After lunch, I came home to lie down."

She glanced up at her son, her bottom lip starting to curl downward. "When I woke up, I called him, except there was no answer. So, I knocked on his door." She shifted uneasily. "He didn't answer so I used my key and that…that's when I found him."

Brandt raised his brow at the mention of his mother having keys to the colonel's apartment – but that was the least of his worries now. "So you feel guilty for falling asleep and leaving him?" he deduced.

"If I'd stayed with him, he wouldn't have been left to lie there unconscious for so long."

Brandt frowned. "How long is so long?" He'd received the impression that the injury was recent.

"Probably half an hour."

"Half an hour is nothing to feel guilty about." Brandt reached over and brushed his fingers over her cheek. "He probably fell just before you arrived."

Her eyes begged him to be right. She suddenly blurted out, "The thing is, I locked the door when I left, and it wasn't locked when I returned."

Brandt shook his head. "Didn't you say you used your key to get in?"

"Yes I did, only I didn't need to because it wasn't locked."

"So why did you use your key?"

"I took it out, expecting to use it, only I didn't need to," she said, exasperation adding life to her eyes and fire to her voice. "Pay attention, dear."

Right. At least she was returning to normal. Speaking of not normal, he had to call Sam. Surreptitiously, he checked his watch. The call would have to wait.

Ignoring the key for the moment, he asked his mother, "Why are you concerned about whether the door was locked or not?"

"I don't think he fell."

Brandt sat up straighter. "What? What do you think happened?" He studied her face. She didn't appear to be in shock. "You think he was attacked?"

Maisy nodded.

"Why would anyone do that?"

"He said he'd remembered the significance of the ring and wanted to think on it a bit, try to figure the pieces out first. Then I fell asleep and now he's injured."

"Even if he did remember, it's unlikely someone would have attacked him over it."

Maisy leaned toward him. "They would if they were involved."

"True. I doubt anyone here is involved. They aren't strong enough for one thing," he said grinning.

She sniffed, such a haughty sound that Brandt had to laugh.

"Not everyone is ancient you know. We all have families that come to visit, and several members of the staff are certainly young enough to have committed murder."

Brandt had to concede her point. Still…it was unlikely. "But how would anyone know what the Colonel was trying to remember?"

Maisy's cheeks flushed pink then paled to pure white. She didn't say anything. Curious, Brandt pushed. "Mom, how would anyone know?"

She straightened her legs out in front and studied her bright red toenails. "I may have had something to do with that."

Brandt pinched the bridge of his nose with his fingers and closed his eyes. "You didn't set up a betting pool on it, did you?" He opened one eye to look at her carefully.

She reddened again. Guilt in pink. Damn.

"So in other words, everyone in the building knew and probably a dozen more besides. All because you wouldn't listen to me."

She opened her mouth as if to protest, then slowly closed it again. She nodded, her eyes full of remorse. "I didn't think it would be dangerous." She shrugged her shoulders in a dainty movement. "We just like to have fun here. You know that. So, we were all taking bets as to when the colonel would remember. There were some people who even bet that he'd never remember, given his age and all that." She sniffed in disgust at that suggestion. "He did remember though, and we were all cheering the winner of the pool. Then someone struck him down before he could tell us what he'd remembered. He said he was going to wait until he could talk to you first."

Brandt sat back. It was too stupid not to be true. Now he had to wait until the colonel awoke. Which, given his advanced years, could be the case *if* he woke up.

"Right." Brandt stood up. "Let's go to the hospital and see how he's doing."

It was a quiet trip with both of them deep in thought. Once there, Maisy insisted on waiting in a chair beside the colonel in the Emergency room. He'd been stabilized, but there was no prognosis yet. Two hours later, there was no change. Still the colonel hadn't woken.

A tall stooped man in green scrubs approached and offered his hand. "Detective Brandt."

"Hello, Doctor Sebastian. How are you?" Brandt watched the multiple frown lines smooth out into a real smile.

"I'm fine. Are you here officially?"

Brandt nodded toward his mother sitting, head bowed at the colonel's side. "We're here for a friend."

"Colonel Bates?"

"Yes, that's right. How is he?"

The doctor glanced at the apparently sleeping patient. "We're keeping him sedated at this time. He has a skull fracture. We'll keep a close watch on the bleeding and the swelling. If he makes it through the night, he should pull through. Given his age and health, well… It's hard to know how he's going to do. There's very little chance that he'll wake up before morning." The silent 'if at all' was very clear. The doctor nodded at him and left the room.

Brandt glanced over at Maisy who appeared to be lost in her own thoughts. "Did you hear that, Mom?"

She didn't answer.

Brandt walked over to crouch in front of her. "Mom, do you want to stay here for a while?

Maisy lifted her pain-filled gaze to stare directly at him. She couldn't speak.

Brandt's heart ached for her. "I'm sorry, Mom. But he's in good hands here. Why don't I leave you here for a bit and I'll come by in a couple of hours?"

She shifted her head in a minuscule imitation of a nod. "Find out who did this," she said, her voice thin and reedy.

Brandt frowned. She didn't sound very good. "Mom, I'll look into it, but that doesn't mean there is a 'who' to find."

Her gaze turned fierce. "This was no accident. Someone hit this dear old man over the head. Find him," she demanded. Then her shoulders sagged as she stared at her friend. "Find him, Brandt."

Brandt stilled. His thoughts turning to the phone call he'd cut short. Maisy's words a mirror of Sam's.

Maisy walked over to the colonel, taking hold of his hand. "Leave. I'll be fine."

Brandt couldn't help but feel dismissed.

2:15 pm

SAM OPENED HER eyes, surprised to find herself sitting inside her truck, still parked outside the grocery store. Almost an hour had passed. She felt better physically. Mentally, there was a sense of uneasiness that wouldn't listen to reason.

She wanted to be home where she felt safe. She started the truck, remembering that Brandt hadn't called her again. He'd probably been called out on yet another emergency.

Or she'd missed him? There were no messages on her phone. Disappointed, she sat for a few moments to get her bearings. Brandt had somehow taken up residence in her life, in her heart even. She shook her head, surprised as the speed her feelings had developed. Her hormones had gone into overdrive too. From dormant to wanting to jump his bones. She laughed lightly. As if. Just because she might be willing to go a little further didn't mean he was that interested.

She frowned. Odd to think that she could only know someone for such a short time and already be at this point. She didn't do one night stands. So what was different this time?

Trust.

As she mulled it over, she realized she trusted Brandt. Probably for the first time, she could honestly say she trusted a man. Love, now that was a different thing altogether. That she was interested was obvious. That she might go out of her comfort zone and have an affair – was also a possibility. But the permanent ever after thing, she didn't think would ever happen. It would take a very special man to accept her gifts… Then there was the teensy weensy problem of living with them.

Not every man would want to wake up to find her in the

middle of a vision.

A family walked beside her in the parking lot, laughing noisily, their laughter shaking her out of her reverie.

Time to go home. Not sure of her reaction time, she drove slowly and carefully down the highway. Her mind twirled around the various tidbits, trying to find a solution. Surely, the killer had better targets than an old man.

The traffic light turned yellow. She slowed before coming to a complete stop at the red light.

A black truck pulled up beside her.

Sam glanced at it, then away, before zipping back again. Her heart jumped. She glanced around at the truck. She couldn't see the driver as the truck was on the left of her and much higher up. Her gut clenched at the sight. It was identical to the truck from a couple of days ago…

The opposite traffic moved sluggishly through the intersection. Sam stole another glance up at the truck. A man stared at her.

"Shit." She glanced away and back again – just to make sure. And swore again. That face! Surely it couldn't be? Was it really *him*? That one person she'd hoped to never see again.

Her gut clenched. Her fingers flexed on the steering wheel. Trapped in traffic, panic clutched at her insides. Always, she felt so damned trapped. The cars ahead lurched forward. She punched the gas, made a quick right at the corner, whipping into a break in the traffic. She glanced in her rear-view mirror and couldn't see the truck. Oh God. Get a grip, Sam.

She checked to see if she were being followed. Theoretically, he shouldn't have been able to as the car behind her had moved up and taken her spot. Not wanting to take a chance, she turned several more corners and fed into the main road, where she could only hope she was miles behind the truck now.

Prying her right hand off the steering wheel, she wiped it on her jeans.

The trip couldn't end fast enough.

She hit a bad pothole, reminding her to pay attention. Still nervous, Sam found herself searching the surrounding countryside, afraid to find a boogeyman hiding in the trees. She still couldn't determine if it had been him. She'd thought so at the time, but now…?

Brandt hadn't called her back yet. She wanted to call again, yet hated to. He'd bolted so fast out of the house this morning, she wondered if he'd ever come back. It had been a lot for him to deal with last night.

But, she'd love the comfort of hearing his voice right now.

3:45 pm

DILLON STRAIGHTENED HIS charcoal tie to a perfect line. He liked to stay professional at all times, even mid-afternoon. One never knew when opportunity might knock.

He had plans, and he'd be damned if he'd let anyone get in the way. That included Brandt. Earlier, he'd seen Brandt bolt from the office. Very curious. Dillon wanted badly to know what was up, and whether it involved the little psychic chick.

After lunch, Dillon walked naturally into Brandt's office – Brandt's empty office. He grinned then wiped off the smile just in case anyone saw him and wondered. Better not to stir suspicions. Not that anyone would see him. Brandt's office was at the end of a long line of offices. Besides, the station was dead. Only a couple guys manned the phones and there would be the standard group hanging around the coffee machine, only Dillon wasn't planning on talking to them yet.

Even if someone saw him, he had a good excuse. He was looking for a specific file. It should be in Brandt's office. If he happened to find something at the same time, something that furthered Dillon's own career that would be good. If it helped him to put a finger on what made Brandt tick – even better. He didn't know if Brandt was going to be a problem or not, and he'd much rather be prepared just in case.

Quickly, he rounded the desk. The computer was still on. Perfect. He smirked and rubbed his hands in anticipation. Then he got to work.

4:15 pm

BRANDT LEFT MAISY visiting with the colonel. He quickly punched in Sam's number on his cell phone.

"Sam, let's go over that vision again."

It only took a couple of minutes, just enough for him to clear his head, connect the dots between the colonel's attack and Sam's vision. If he trusted Sam's abilities, then it followed that the colonel had been the old man she saw attacked. The only reasonable explanation for such an attack was if someone needed to silence the colonel – particularly when the attack was undertaken in complete daylight in a home full of people.

"Brandt?"

"Sorry honey, I'm here." Shaking his head, Brandt returned to the conversation and filled Sam in on why the room felt familiar. After giving her an update on the colonel's condition, Brandt headed to the station. Unfortunately, the incident was likely to be classed as an unfortunate accident until the colonel woke up. Without more information, Brandt had no reason to ask Kevin to open an investigation. A list of who had been at the center during that period was mandatory. Maisy was compiling hers and Nancy should have a partial list of visitors, repairmen, and staff.

Once back at the station, Brandt grabbed a mug, poured coffee and headed to the privacy of his office.

"Hey Brandt. Did you ever find out who gave that information to the station?" Adam called out from the common room.

Brandt didn't even turn around. "No, not yet."

He had one hand on his office doorknob before realizing it was already open. Frowning, he pushed the door open and stepped inside. The room looked the same. Brandt hated the suspicion coursing through him. He spun around to his desk. Where was his file on Samantha? It wasn't there. Right, he'd started locking it up in his desk. Pulling out his key ring, Brandt unlocked the drawer on the left.

There was the file as he'd left it. Opening it, he found the information on Sam lying on the top page and frowned. Had he left it there? Normally, he had those papers buried in the middle of the file. Uneasily, he replaced the material, taking care as to how he sequenced the information in the file.

Relocking the drawer, he searched around the office for anything out of place. It appeared to be the same. It didn't feel that way. His chair. He frowned. He'd rushed out of the office and couldn't remember how he'd left it. He didn't think he'd have pushed it in that far.

His monitor flashed for his login information. Brandt hesitated. His keyboard sat off center and further to the front than he normally had it. His hands didn't automatically rest on the keys properly.

Suspicion nudged the back of his mind. He had no way to know if someone had snooped through his office. His work wasn't exactly a secret. Logging on to his computer, Brandt quickly checked his files. Everything seemed normal. The knots in his spine eased, he rolled his shoulders, pushed his sleeves up, and started in on his emails. Communication was the mainstay of his network these days. However, he didn't share everything and made good use of security passwords to keep some information private.

He'd planned on putting in a couple of hours then heading to the hospital to pick up his mom. He opened a file where he typed in his notes from Samantha's call and the colonel incident. He saved the material with a different code. He admitted to a heightened sense of paranoia, but still…

CHAPTER 18

8:20 am, June 22nd

"HEY BRANDT, THERE'S someone here to see you." Adam stood at the open door of his office the next day.

Brandt raised one eyebrow. He wasn't expecting anyone. "Who is it?"

Adam shrugged. "Deputy Brooker for Nikola County."

"What the hell?" Brandt's stomach twisted. He lurched part-way out of his chair.

Adam grinned. "You don't look so happy."

"Very odd," he murmured to himself. "No, I'm happy," he corrected Adam. "I'd like to talk with the little piss ass."

"Oh, there's nothing little about this guy."

Brandt, in the process of clearing off the top of his desk and locking up sensitive files, scowled. "Big? How big?"

Adam snorted. "This guy makes me look like an infant."

"Scary."

Adam nodded. "If I had to describe him, I'd say he was one hell of an arrogant SOB, far too used to getting his own way."

Shit. So, Sam was probably right about him. Well then, time to go see why he'd come and what he knew about Sam.

"Thanks, Adam. Anyone in the conference room?"

"I don't think so. Is that where you want to talk to him?"

"Yeah. I'm not sure yet, but this guy quite possibly needs to be behind bars himself. Don't want to extend too much courtesy, just in case."

"Sounds good. I'm heading down there now. Why don't I deliver him to conference room one for you?"

"Good. That saves me a trip and gives me a little more distinction. I could use that in this case."

"What kind of trouble is he?" Adam walked out of the office

with Brandt.

"I think he's been a lot of trouble for a young girl."

"Then no special treatment for him. We don't need more of his kind."

"According to my information, he's also into corrupting law enforcement and running drugs."

He shared a look with Adam. They both knew other assholes just like this one.

"I need to make a quick call, then I'll be down."

Adam left and Brandt called his mom.

His call went to voicemail. Last night, Maisy had convinced the hospital staff to bring a cot into the colonel's room so she could stay with him. Brandt's protests had been shot down immediately. Chances were she was still there, but he'd feel better if he'd reached her. A second call to the hospital confirmed that his mom had spent the night and that the colonel hadn't woken up. As luck would have it, his mom was at the desk speaking with the nurse too. He spoke with her briefly, confirming that she'd gotten some sleep. She sounded more chipper this morning.

Brandt then headed to the conference room, quickly scratching down a few notes and questions he wanted to ask as he walked. Entering the room, he found a huge man with beefy shoulders – not a beer belly, rather a beer barrel that completely covered the belt holding up his pants. Dressed in uniform, the deputy's beady eyes held a voracious gleam that belied the smile on his face.

"Detective Sutherland?" At Brandt's nod, the older man stepped forward, his hand outstretched. "Thank you for taking the time to see me. I appreciate it."

Brandt shook the man's hand. Then motioned to a seat opposite his. He sat down, sliding his hand along his pants to wipe it clean before opening the conversation. "I'm surprised. Did you just happen to be in this region?"

"Nope. I came specific. This case, Samantha Blair, is way too important to leave to chance."

"Oh, you didn't mention that there was a case when we talked on the phone?"

Deputy Brooker shifted his bulk into the big boardroom chair. "I thought long and hard about it. But decided I needed to come and check this out. I'd just about given up finding her when I got your phone call."

"What do you want with her?"

"She caused me a bunch of trouble a few years ago. I believe she stole something from my family that I would really like returned."

Brandt frowned. Sam hadn't mentioned anything about that. "Stole something? Like what?"

"Files and folders. Our family history. We went to a spell of trouble to collect this material and we'd surely like it back."

The man was full of shit. Still, he was here. Therefore, whatever he wanted was important. Brandt didn't think any of it would be good for Sam.

"What was she like the last time you saw her?"

The beefy man hitched the front of his pants up over the lower portion of his belly. He shifted his weight; the chair creaked in protest. "She was a mouthy know-it-all. Just like she'd been every other time I'd seen her. The things that come out of that girl's mouth were something else. She's surely a liar, she is."

"A liar." Brandt barely restrained the desire to jump across the table and strangle the bloody fool. "A liar but not a fraud?"

"Nope, usually her visions were spot on. But that girl's a social misfit. She's not the same as you and me. She needed a keeper then and I'm sure things haven't changed."

"What is your intention when you meet her?"

"Just talk to her. See if she's had a change of heart in the meantime. Maybe she's ready to give the material back now. Or has she ditched it somewhere along the last few years?"

Brandt took a few notes, more to calm the fury inside than for later information. There was no way this asshole was getting close to Sam.

"She had a bad car accident after she was in your neck of the woods. Did you know that?"

"I'd heard. And in truth, I thought maybe she hadn't survived. I'd called the hospital a time or two, but word was she was in bad shape and not expected to live. That's when I put it all away in my head. Until your phone call, then I hopped into my truck and came here."

Shit. Brandt *was* responsible for this mess. Truck? As in black truck? "Long trip. When did you pull into town?"

"Oh, I arrived a couple of days ago. Didn't want to come knocking right away. Figured you'd be mighty busy."

Brandt sighed, keeping his head down. The asshole was lying through his teeth. So he had been around when Sam called him screaming on her phone about some guy trying to run her off the road. Through the DMV, he could find out what this guy drove – putting him on the highway at the same time as Sam was a different story. How to prove that? "Yes, we're swamped. Portland is a big city and it's not like there's ever a down season."

The deputy laughed. "Crime never takes a holiday."

"Isn't that the truth?"

As much as Brandt would like to cuff this guy with the information he had from Sam, he knew in good conscience that he'd need to hear what Sam had to say about the deputy's truths.

Then he'd have another talk with the deputy…on his terms.

10:48 am

IT HAD NOT been a good day. As a matter of fact, as days went, this one sucked. Bill had finally located the right hospital only to find out his drugged victim was still alive and in a coma. What the hell? If she died – great. If she stayed in a coma for the rest of her life – even better. He kind of liked that concept. But if she awoke, that was bad news. It couldn't be allowed to happen. He'd have to think this one over while monitoring the situation.

Then he'd gone on to the care center with his dogs. The dogs had been great, the staff had been great – the people however… What was with those old people? They all had a gambling problem for one thing. And for another, they were a bunch of busybodies. Like that one old geezer. Apparently, he knew something about the ring the media had flashed on the television. Those damn old folks were betting on when he was going to remember just what it was. Who could have predicted such a problem? Well, he'd had no choice, had he? The guy couldn't be allowed to remember anything about him – ever.

That little bit of violence had been just enough to whet his appetite, to rouse the beast inside, yet not enough to sate either. It had been too fast, not well planned…and that bothered him a bit. Yet, he'd had few options. Prudence said he should be home and out of sight right now. He'd actually been driving in that direction when he'd seen her.

She was perfect.

He pulled off the road to a small parking lot so he could watch her sashaying down the sidewalk.

The glare shining through the windshield irritated him. It limited his view. Rummaging in the glove box, he finally came up with a scratched pair of sunglasses. Better than nothing. Putting them on, he quickly searched the area in front of the drugstore that she'd walked into a few minutes earlier.

There. She was laughing at something someone had said, her head turned as she walked out the door. She strode with confidence in the sunshine. God, he loved that. Loved to see a woman sure of her sexuality, sure of who she was.

And she was so wrong.

That was the best part. Stripping away their innocence and teaching them about the real monsters of the world.

He leaned forward for a better view. She turned left and moved smoothly down the sidewalk. Look at her walk – liquid honey. He grinned.

Perfect.

He hopped out of the truck and followed behind at a steady pace. When she entered a small clothing boutique, he found a bench on the sidewalk and sat to enjoy the sunshine. He had nothing better to do, except follow her around. She loved her little boutiques and before the month was out, he'd know every one of them.

2:20 pm

THE AFTERNOON WAS gorgeous. Sam felt like shit.

Leaning against the front doorframe of her cabin, looking out to the rest of the world, Sam mentally ran through the various options. She still had a couple days before she started working with Stefan. In the meantime, she had some homework to do. If these visions would stop, she might actually have the energy to work on them.

Her phone rang. Butterflies took flight in delight at the number on her phone display. He'd slid into her consciousness like he'd always belonged there. When had he gone from a cop to a friend, and now to mean something so much more? "Hi Brandt. What's up?"

"I need to see you today. There's something I need to go over with you and it's better to do this in person. Are you going to be home this afternoon or evening?"

Sam's stomach dropped. In person would be great, except nothing about this sounded good. Now what? "I'm here all day and night. I'm going to work on Stefan's exercises this afternoon, then head to the lake for a swim." She hesitated for a moment. "What's this about?"

"Deputy Brooker came into the office today. His story is a little different than yours."

She snorted. "What? He's in town?" Sam gripped the cell phone in her hand, her knuckles turning white. "When did he get here and what is he driving? I think I saw that same black truck yesterday."

"What? Why didn't you say something?"

"I didn't know if it was the same vehicle or not. I was still in town, so took off around the corner. I never saw him again."

"He is driving a black Dodge truck, but that doesn't mean it was him. We're running a check on him now. You stay there and just be careful. If anyone shows up, but me, hide unless you know them. I'll get there in a couple of hours – earlier if I can."

She shook her head. Not good enough. Not even close, only what were her options at this point? None. "Then you damn well better show up soon, or I'll be coming in after you."

The phone closed with a snap. Sam let out a shaky breath. Okay. Another problem. She was good at those. She snorted. Like hell. In the past, she'd run. So what did she do now?

Stick around and fight.

CHAPTER 19

5:45 pm

THE LATE AFTERNOON sun danced on top of the glassy lake. Sam studied the inviting landscape. Yeah. That's exactly what she needed.

"Hello, Soldier." She smiled at the dog lying so peacefully in the sun. Healthier now, his coat was thick and although still grimy, it was no longer covered in blood. Most of it had dried and fallen off. She'd love to get him into the lake, except he still had stitches. The last thing she wanted was to have to manhandle the dog into the truck and back to the vet's office. Soldier accepted her presence as a necessity, but only as long as his independence and freedom never came into question.

Soldier surged to his feet and started growling.

Sam frowned. "Soldier?"

The dog turned to face the wooded area behind the house and growled again.

Sam peered into the trees, but couldn't see what bothered the dog. He growled again at the bushes behind her. The woods appeared calm, and should have been teeming with life. None of it showed.

The energy had a peacefulness to it. Then maybe it was the energy she was projecting. Stefan's exercises had a phenomenal effect. It was what she imagined meditation could do for a person. A sense of ease, comfort, had slipped under her guard. It's not that she felt she could do anything, because she knew she couldn't, however she did have a better understanding of just what she was capable of doing. The exercises were basic. She had to start at the beginning, according to Stefan. Working on seeing energy, understanding the colors around people, animals, even plants. Then to understand what the markings and colors meant.

Sure she was tired, but a good tired. Her energy muscles, something she never knew existed, had been well and truly flexed.

It felt great.

So many things in her life felt great – especially Brandt. She had no idea where the relationship was going, or when. All she could think about was where it would end up – in bed. At least she hoped she was reading the signals right.

Delight wiggled in her belly. She hoped he felt the same way.

With Soldier on guard in the late afternoon sun, Sam headed for a swim. It was the perfect temperature for a cool, relaxing dip. Feeling physically stronger than she had in years, Sam stretched her abilities to the limit, swimming strong for thirty minutes before rolling over onto her back and floating. Calm and filled with peace, she waited for her breathing to return to a calm gentle rhythm. It took longer than she expected.

With a groan, she realized she may have overdone it.

In the aftermath of exertion, her body chilled quickly. Turning over, she fluttered her hands enough to propel herself gently in the right direction.

The silkiness of the water slipped over her skin, making her sensitized skin come alive. The chill quickly morphed into heat as she moved through the water under the setting sun. Now, if only Brandt were here with her. His hands sliding across her skin instead of the gentle waves. She stretched, reveling in the freedom of the night.

"Sam. Goddamn it, what the hell are you doing?" The yell stormed across the water.

What was that? She raised her head.

"Get over here."

Well, that was hard to miss. She rolled over in the water and searched around the house and the dock. Brandt strode toward the water. Even from that distance, she could see his grim face. Her pulse sped up at the sight of him. Even if he was mad at her.

"Sam, you're too far out."

Too far. Sam twisted around her and realized she'd unintentionally floated out even further. Still, she wasn't in trouble. At least, not yet.

Striking out strong, Sam headed in. Her energy petered out before she managed a dozen strokes. She shifted to breaststroke and continued shoreward. When she made it to roughly fifteen feet from the dock, Sam slowed and treaded water.

She watched Brandt's loose-limbed stride carry him to the end of the dock, heard him yell, "God damn it, woman. Get your sorry ass in here."

Tall and lean, he looked incredibly good with a gentle wind ruffling his hair. Moses whined beside him. Now, if only she hadn't spent the last hour imagining him in the water with her.

"Sorry buddy. It's not you I'm mad at – it's her."

Moses sat down.

Sourly, Sam watched their interplay. Moses may not have anything to worry about. Obviously Sam couldn't say the same thing. She felt like hissing. Damn it. She was swimming in the nude.

6:55 pm

BRANDT COULDN'T BELIEVE it. The last time he'd seen her, she'd been caught in a heavy vision and experiencing huge blood loss. Now she was out there swimming in the middle of the damn lake. She'd have been better off relaxing and regaining her strength. He watched as she struggled the last few yards. She was worn out, but if he jumped in to help her, she'd be royally pissed. Go figure.

He scowled at the dog at his feet. Even Moses knew better than to swim right now.

Jesus. She needed a babysitter. She was as bad as his mother.

Watching Sam swim closer, he realized he'd probably overreacted here. Swimming would help rebuild Sam's strength and endurance. Exercise had many benefits and as long as she didn't overdo it, then swimming was a good way to go.

Somehow, that logic didn't matter because he was still pissed. Scary. He stopped suddenly, hands fisted on his hips. And all because he was worried – about her. He blew his breath out in a gust. Oh, God, this was getting bad.

The balmy evening breeze wrinkled the water before smoothing it flat again.

He frowned. The cabin was a long way from everything. Not only that, if she were to run into trouble, no one would know for days. Not until she didn't show at work. Damn it. His frown deepened.

The bushes rustled behind him. Instinctively, he dropped and spun around.

Deep yellow eyes glowed in the darkness.

That damn watchdog.

"Hello there, Soldier. How are you feeling? I see you're moving better." Keeping his voice even and calm, he kept a wary eye on the dog's reactions. He wasn't exactly growling. On the other hand, neither was he wagging his tail with joy.

The two males glowered at each other. Both silent and watchful. Both waiting for the other to move. Brandt knew better than to break his gaze first. The alpha male was the one who held the gaze the longest. If he were ever going to get close to Sam, then the watchdog had to accept his presence.

Splashes alerted him to Sam's approach. Keeping his eyes trained on the dog, he called out, "Are you okay, Sam?

She coughed gently, then again a bit stronger. "I'm fine." Her voice was reedy and thin. "I'm just getting out now."

Brandt stared at the dog, relieved. "You sound exhausted. You should never have gone for a swim. Or at least not for so long," he admonished.

"Like I'm going to listen to you," she scoffed. "You're arguing with a dog."

Brandt started. Indignantly, he said, "I am not."

Sam brushed past him, a towel wrapped around her body, droplets of water flying off with every step. She deliberately walked between the two males. Both sets of eyes immediately switched to the distraction.

Brandt swallowed. Her towel snuggled around her curves, shifting to accommodate the gentle movements as she walked. Water had soaked into the thin material, making it almost transparent. Brandt's imagination fired up. The towel hung loosely down the center of her spine. There were no straps on her shoulders.

He swallowed.

The towel cuddled her bottom, just barely covering the gentle curves. He couldn't see any sign of a bathing suit. The tantalizing thought both enraged and delighted him. Didn't she realize that anyone could have come down here?

This lady was just asking for trouble.

Yet, the thought of all that female flesh floating sensuously free in the cool water was a huge turn on. And gave him an intimate insight into her true character. Watching her walk ahead of him and not knowing whether or not she was nude, was an even bigger aphrodisiac.

The bushes rattled again. Soldier, now in front of Sam, turned. His lip curled, his spine humped up and the hair on the back of his neck stood straight up.

Samantha stopped.

Brandt instinctively freed his gun, staying close to her as he peered into the woods. "What is it?" he whispered.

Sam shrugged, her eyes searching the woods. "I can't tell." Her voice was low, balanced. "Soldier doesn't like it ...and neither do I. Something doesn't feel...right."

Brandt scanned the area for anything abnormal. He didn't know what she meant, but he couldn't help agreeing that all wasn't as it should be.

Sam hurried to the cabin, running up the porch steps. Brandt followed at a slower pace, a wary eye searching around him. Soldier growled and lunged into the woods.

"Soldier, no!" Sam watched and listened as the noises trailed off to the left. She turned to Brandt. "I'm going to get dressed then go after him."

Brandt couldn't stop his eyes from following that perfectly formed backside, highlighted by damp circles in the towel as she climbed the stairs.

With a shaky breath, he turned to search the twilight. The evening sun was setting, throwing long shadows across the yard. There was no sign of Soldier. Moses sat on the top stair staring off in the same direction. He wasn't growling, but his tail wasn't wagging either.

Sam came running down the stairs still tucking her shirt inside the waistband of her old blue jeans. Over her arm was the inevitable oversized sweater. Her skin sported a blue tinge. She held a leash in her hand.

"Damn it, you're cold. Stay inside and get warm. I'll go after him."

Sam shook her head. "I'm going. He doesn't know you, and he won't come if you call." Turning around, she spied Moses at the edge of the bushes. "Moses, come here." Moses trotted forward obediently. Sam snapped the lead on. "Only one dog missing at a time, please. Let's go find Soldier."

Brandt scoffed. "Moses won't find him, and Soldier won't come if you call either."

She shot him a dirty look before walking past him into early the night.

"Soldier," Sam called from the doorway, looking around. But the wooded darkness had swallowed him completely. They left the porch and headed across the lawn.

Howls and screams split the air, followed by a couple of quiet spits. Sam ran forward and stopped. A heavy crashing through the woods could be heard for a moment before dying off in the distance.

"Jesus," she whispered, her hand at her throat. Her heart smashed in her chest. "Brandt, were those human screams and gunshots?"

"Maybe. You stay here with Moses. I'm going to check it out." Brandt pulled out his gun and raced into the woods. The trees stood thick together. He headed in the direction of the shots. The silence blanketed everything, except his own passage. Leaves and twigs crushed beneath his feet. The wind started. Branches swished sending whispers through the night. Brandt moved quickly through the area. Nothing. He circled around to Sam.

"Any sign?" she called out to him.

"No. Whoever or whatever it was is gone." A few feet from the porch stairs, Brandt stopped and looked around again.

Ignoring Brandt's protests, Sam took a couple of steps into the darkness. "Soldier?"

Brandt came to stand beside her. "Can you see him?"

"No, but he has to be here?" She spun to the left. "Wait, what was that?"

A small whine sounded several hundred feet away.

"Soldier? Soldier! Come here, boy."

Twigs broke and the brush rustled with movement. Darkness had descended quickly. Sam backed up a couple of steps. "Soldier, come here, boy."

Peering through the darkness, she thought she saw something move. "Soldier," she whispered, "Is that you."

Soldier limped toward her.

Sam ran and put her arms around him in a quick hug. She coaxed him forward. "Come on boy. Time to go home."

"Is he hurt?" Brandt surveyed the large animal. The damn thing had to weigh at least a-hundred-twenty pounds. Uninjured and cooperative, he might be able to move him…injured and cranky – no way.

"I don't know." Sam gently ran her hands over the dog's

limbs, ignoring the warning growls. "Come on Soldier, let's get you inside."

Once on the porch, they could see fresh blood on his side.

"Damn it, Soldier." Sam checked his wound, accidentally touching a sore spot. Soldier spun around, his lip curled, an ungodly howl erupting from his throat.

Brandt trained his gun on the injured animal. "Sam, get back." The evening stilled. "Don't touch him. He's dangerous like this."

Soldier turned slowly toward Brandt, then his spine arched, and the howl turned menacing.

Sam shuffled behind Brandt. Soldier had eyes only for Brandt.

She said in a quiet calm voice, "Brandt, I think it's the gun – put it away."

"Are you nuts? He could attack."

"It's the gun that's upsetting him. It's easy to check my theory. Just put the gun away."

Brandt snorted. "I've seen too many aggressive animals to do that." He kept his eyes on the dog, sparing a quick glance at Sam.

"Let's just try it – please."

He stared at the dog for a long moment, then slowly lowered the firearm and slipped it behind. Out of sight but not away.

The dog watched every movement. The growling lessened ever so slightly.

"I wonder." A sudden impulse rolled around inside. Using hand signals, he ordered the dog to sit. Soldier howled.

Brandt repeated the command.

Soldier howled louder.

Brandt made the command sharper, harder.

Silence.

Then in a shuffling movement, Soldier slowly lowered his haunches.

Brandt shook his head then gave the command to heel. Wanting the dog to walk at his side was safer than having Sam try to coax him up to the house.

This time, Soldier obeyed on the first go around, the movement slow and awkward, but he did it.

"Brandt?"

"He's been well-trained. I don't know to what extent though. There are some commands I can try. From the look of him, I'm almost ready to suggest he's been a police dog in his past."

"Really?" Sam stared from one to the other. "Do you really think so?"

"I think he's a trained guard dog and chances are good his training was more formal. It's possible he didn't work out and never finished the training."

Once at the cabin, the slow moving party made it inside. Brandt ordered the dog to lie down. Soldier, small growls from deep in his throat, grudgingly obeyed.

Sam quickly checked out Soldier's wounds again. Brandt and Soldier glared at each other.

"It's not too bad. Looks like he ripped a stitch or two and he's limping. That could just be his old injuries with the unexpected chase in the woods." Sam gave the dog a quick hug. "Poor boy."

Brandt snorted. "Why's that?"

"The vet thought he'd been abused. As far as Soldier's concerned, it's people who aren't to be trusted." Sam paused for a moment, sniffed the air, bent closer to Soldier's back then raised her head. "Did someone just shoot my dog?"

7:18 pm

BRANDT SAT ON the porch steps, speaking with his mother.

Sam studied him for a long moment, waiting for his call to end, before walking out to join him. "I just poured you a cup of tea." Sam handed the cup to Brandt. "How are the colonel and your mother?"

He glanced at her in surprise. "No change."

"So can we talk then?" At his confused look, she added, "Deputy Brooker. Remember?"

"What? Oh, right. He's here. As I told you earlier, your Deputy Brooker came to see me today."

"Oh, God." Sam sat down – hard. She didn't need to look in a mirror to know that all the color had leached from her face.

"He's been in town for a couple of days already." Brandt sat opposite her. "I know it's easy to jump to conclusions, but we don't know any more than that yet."

It was too much. Sam had hoped to hide her history, hoped that past events wouldn't have to be dragged into her future. "Damn it."

"Keep in mind, he doesn't know where you live."

Hope unfurled deep inside then she remembered what had just happened. She searched his face. "You're dreaming," she scoffed. "He was probably the one doing the shooting out there tonight." She added, "I have no illusions. He'd kill me any time he had a chance."

Brandt studied her face.

She stared calmly back. If there was one thing he needed to believe, it was that Brooker was slime, dangerous slime.

"Alright, I can see you believe that. He said you stole something from his family. Information of some kind? Any idea what that's all about?" Brandt's supportive gaze gave her strength.

She laughed, a broken sound that made him wince. "I didn't steal anything. Don't you see? The information he thinks I have is what I picked up from him. My psychic abilities told me a lot. That's what he's afraid of. That I know too much." Pain knotted at the base of her spine, shooting up through her temple. She shivered. "And he's right. I do."

Brandt mulled this over.

She stared blindly out the dark window. "Remember my car accident?"

"The one where you were injured or the one where you saw Louise Enderby die?"

"No, the first one – where I almost died. That was him. He caused my accident – he tried to kill me."

CHAPTER 20

8 pm

SAM BENT HER head.

Brandt stared at the delicate tendrils of hair curled around her neck. The rest hung in long locks down to her waist. Really? He mentally drew up the deputy's countenance and conceded that, yeah, just maybe it was possible. That guy had an agenda. One that had nothing to do with his supposed visit to Brandt's station.

Staring at her bent head, he needed to ask, at least once. "Are you sure?"

Lifting her head, Sam stared straight at him. Her eyes shone with tears. "I don't have any proof if that's what you mean. But I saw him."

"You saw him?" Brandt leaned forward, to search her face. "Are you sure?"

Sam got up and walked to where she could stare out the window, her hair dangling down her back. "After the crash, I couldn't move. The flames had just started to reach the windshield. The seatbelt buckle had locked, my leg was broken, and my collarbone had been dislocated."

She closed her eyes and leaned her head against the cool glass. Tremors started at the base of her spine and moved up. "He walked up while I was wrestling with the straps." She paused, her breath coming out in shaky gusts. "I pounded on the window and screamed for help. He laughed at me." Sam swallowed. "There I was in total panic, thinking that help had arrived and he…" she turned to face Brandt, "And he pulled out his gun and pointed it at me through the window.

Brandt swore. Then swore again. "Bastard."

"That he is." She stared at him, a tiny smile on her face.

"Thanks for believing me. That helps a lot."

He snorted. "So what happened? Did he actually shoot you?"

Sam shook her head. "No, or I wouldn't be here. He just walked away. As he drove off, another man – a retired firefighter – arrived. He shattered the glass on the driver's door, unlocked it, cut my seatbelt strap, and dragged me free." She walked over to Brandt and sat down again. "So yeah, to answer your question – I am sure."

He watched her shorts ride higher on her thighs, wishing she'd sit closer. His senses were awash in 'what ifs.' With a shudder, he stared off in the distance. Clearing his throat, he asked, "Did you tell anyone?"

"No." She snorted. "Who would I tell? He *was* the police."

Right. Brandt groaned and leaned back. "God. What a mess." He ran his fingers through his hair. "The bottom line is that this asshole is here now, and he's searching for you."

"Right. Hence my question – did bullets score Soldier's shoulder?"

"Christ." He stared at her, seeing past the old fears and tough memories. She was a fighter, but against a stacked deck, she'd run – until now. There'd be no running now. She wasn't alone any more.

"Let me make some phone calls, see if we've got anything on him yet. One of my team is running his background."

Sam frowned.

"That means we can track him down and have another talk with him. Adam did confirm that Brooker drives a 2004 Dodge truck – a black one."

She shuddered. "So it could have been him on the highway." After a moment of contemplation, she shrugged. "Not that it matters, he's not going to admit to anything. Why would he? You'd need proof, like bullets or casing from tonight to match to his gun."

"True, but if you recognized his black truck…" he said, waiting and watching for her comprehension to kick in. Her eyes opened wide as understanding filtered in.

She frowned. "Yes, only how would he know what vehicle I'm driving?"

"The same way we can find out about his truck, run your name through DMV to find out what vehicle is registered under your name." He glanced at her truck outside the window. That thing should have been deep-sixed a long time ago. Surely, it wouldn't pass a safety inspection?

"But he couldn't have known that it was me on the road until he came right up to me."

Brandt considered that. "It's not out of the realm of possibility, that's exactly what did happen. And then he took advantage of an unexpected opportunity."

Sam wrinkled her face. "That's horrible." She grimaced. "At least, he doesn't know where I live." She chewed on her lower lip, her arms wrapped tightly around her chest. "Then again, it wouldn't be that hard with his connections, would it?"

Brandt tried not to watch as her breast plumped out against her skin. "As much as I hate to even suggest it, it's possible that he could have followed you, or even me."

Sam's eyes opened wide. "That's a horrible thought." She tilted her head, carefully considering him. "He couldn't have followed me, I haven't been anywhere today."

"No. Are you sure you lost the black truck yesterday?"

Her eyes widened in horror. "Oh, God."

He leaned forward gently patting her on the knee. "Don't panic. We're working on it. As soon as we have more information, I'll bring him in for a second and more informative talk." Excusing himself, Brandt headed outside to make the phone calls that would put things in motion. This needed to be dealt with now. As did something else. Just as he was about to walk out onto the porch, he called out, "Oh, yeah. I'll also be sleeping here tonight."

8:22 pm

"YOU WANT WHAT?" God, the last thing Sam wanted to remember were other victims. She shook her head, hair flying widely about. No. No way.

"Please. It might help."

She stared at him. He didn't know what he asked. He couldn't. He'd gone outside to make his phone calls after dropping his first bomb. Then he'd come inside and had dropped a second one. The last remnants of her control fractured, splintering apart. He'd asked for details on other visions. She shook her head. This isn't how she'd imagined the evening.

"I suppose this could be difficult for you."

She half laughed, half cried. "You think?" she said, her voice rising. "You have no idea!" She spun away from him, her whole body shaking.

Brandt winced. "I'm sorry. If it's that hard then we won't discuss this. I didn't mean to upset you." He walked over, one arm outstretched to touch her gently, hesitantly before dropping it down to his side. "I thought it might help to give the victims a voice." This time, he placed an arm around her shoulders.

She stiffened, but didn't move away. In truth, she wanted to snuggle in deeper, only couldn't trust her emotions. "All victims or just those from this same killer?" She reached up gently to massage the nape of her neck. She hated her immediate defensiveness. There was no reason not to. After all, she'd wanted to be able to make a difference. Although, it might be a lot easier if she had a chance to talk to Stefan first. Maybe he knew how to help her through the process without the damage she knew would happen. She needed to ask him at the first opportunity.

Surprise lit up his voice. "I didn't know you could choose." He mulled over the concept. "If given a choice, and if there is the possibility of this killer having other victims, then that's where I'd like to start." He paused for a moment. "Although, if you have information on other cases, that would be a help too. We have an incredible load of unsolved cases."

"I don't know. I suppose I can try," she said. Her voice so soft and so sad, he thought his heart would break. "It might be easier on me if we do this after I work with Stefan a few times. Maybe he'll have a few techniques so I can protect myself." Sam watched the puzzlement wash over his face.

"Protect yourself? I don't understand."

He wasn't going to like her answer. "During recall, a lot of the same energy returns. I tend to slip between the visions and this reality."

"Whoa! Come again?"

A wry smile played around her lips. "Sometimes, the same method the person died from will manifest again – although to a much lesser degree," She rushed to add this last bit because she saw the horror starting to overtake his face.

"So you're liable to start bleeding again?" He shook his head. "Uh, uh. No way are we going there."

Sam couldn't help it. She laughed aloud. "The bleeding can be the easy symptoms."

He glanced at her in disbelief.

"Don't forget, one woman burned alive in a car accident."

"But we don't know that it wasn't an accident."

"No, you don't know. I do. Not only that, I know it was the same killer. I don't understand how or why, just that there was some connection."

Brandt shook his head as he pulled a small notebook out. "You're certain that these are all victims of the same killer?"

"Sure enough that you should do a search and link everyone they knew and every activity they participated in. The killer is there somewhere in the mess. Personally, I'd add Louise Enderby in there. She's the exception that could show you the rule."

Sam wondered as Brandt spent the next five minutes writing down something in a notebook. Then she realized she had something that might help, while not hurting her. "I'll be right back." She strode into her bedroom. They were here somewhere in one of the boxes. She rummaged through the first, and then the second stacked box before finding what she was searching for at the bottom. Sorting the books out, she grabbed up the one she wanted.

Brandt was on his cell phone when she returned. Not wanting to bother him, she refilled their cups with hot tea then sat down to wait.

"Right. Graph it out. I know it's far-fetched, but we haven't got anything else to go on so let's give this a try." He glanced over at her and smiled. "Let's pull all the data and cross reference with these other cases. If the information isn't there then let's get it." Brandt jotted down several notes in his notepad. "No. I'll come in early tomorrow. We can map out what we have then."

The conversation carried on a little longer and Sam blanked out. She flicked through the book in her hand, wincing at the notes. Very graphic and way too painful to read again, she wondered at her compulsion to write all this in the first place.

"What have you got there?"

Surprised, Sam looked up. "What?"

He put away the phone. "So what's that you've got?"

"Here." She took a deep breath. Then as if making a decision, she handed the cheap, worn book over to him.

Brandt accepted it, glancing from her to the book and back again. "What is it?"

"My journal. It will have some dates and some details."

Brandt flicked through the lined pages, daunted by the sheer outpouring of her soul. "Is this about your visions?" He stopped, read a note, then turned the page. "How far back does this go?"

"It's close to being the first half of this year."

"This year?" Shock threaded through his voice.

"I have one I'm currently working on." She shrugged, unable to stop the self-conscious feeling. "I feel compelled to write down every detail I can remember after a vision. It's my way of letting the victims speak." She crossed her arms across her chest. "The thing is, I've never told anyone about these journals."

"Ever?

"No."

He bent forward, placing one hand on her knee. "Thank you."

A shaky sigh escaped. She nodded, a tiny smile on her lips. "You're welcome."

Brandt squeezed her knee gently, then sat up again. "So this is everything written here?" He slapped the book on this thigh, studying her face.

Soberly, Sam nodded. "Of those visions. I have more upstairs – at least twenty more."

9:05 pm

BRANDT COULD FEEL the blood leach from his face. One of them? She had twenty more journals? Holy Shit. What kind of life had she had?

"A terrible one."

Brandt's head shot up in shock. His mind spun out of control. Did she just do that? Please, no.

"No I can't read minds. Your face on the other hand…" She grinned at his sour grimace.

He stared at the gold mine in his hand. He couldn't figure out what to focus on. She'd just handed him an incredible gift. Sure, he'd have to find proof, depending on her information, but she could give him a direction to start digging. Some of these cases might not even be in the files. Some could have been ruled accidental. Some could have been solved by now. Some killers could literally have gotten away with murder.

Sam's hesitant voice broke through his heavy thoughts. "I might be able to help in other ways."

He glanced at her in surprise. "You already have," he said lifting up the journal. "Can I take this?"

She cringed. "I don't really want the information shared with the rest of your team. Maybe read it over and see if there is anything useful. Take notes or photocopy the pages. I would like the original back."

"Absolutely. Photocopying is a good idea. And don't worry, I won't let Kevin or anyone else get their hands on this." Brandt knew the value of what he held. He wasn't planning on letting anyone else in on it until he could find the proof to match with the information. He flicked through the journal, stopping to read a page, wincing at the pain and the horror that dripped from the pages. Sam had come up behind to read over his shoulder, her long blond hair falling over his shoulder.

His nostrils flared as her fresh womanly scent sank in. He glanced up, still caught by her feelings so transparent, her torment so real, before just focusing on her now. How quickly she'd slipped under his guard. This gentle woman had experienced so much pain already. He wanted to make her feel better, to make the pain go away. Setting the book aside, he stood up and stepped up next to her.

She stilled, her eyes wide like a deer caught in headlights.

Brandt grinned and dropped a kiss on the tip of her nose. Sliding his arms around her, Brandt tugged her into a gentle hug. When she relaxed against him, he rested his cheek on the top of her head and smiled.

He hesitated. Should he even broach the subject? Still, if this wasn't a good time, when would there ever be a better one? "You know you're never far from my mind, don't you?"

Sam tried to pull back slightly, when he wouldn't release her she contented herself with tilting her head up instead.

"Really?" Her voice came out as a gentle whisper, full of wonder and enchantment. Brandt immediately fell under her spell.

"Really." He stared down at her porcelain skin, the huge eyes that said so much, yet nothing at all, and those lips. He hadn't noticed them the first couple of times he'd seen her, now they were all he could think about – so red and full, so very inviting, so very ready to be loved.

He couldn't help himself. He bent and claimed them for his own.

9:15 pm

OVERWHELMED BY HIS words, Sam was blindsided by the touch of his lips. They coaxed, yet entranced. She'd never been kissed in such a way before. She wondered if she'd ever truly been kissed. She craved his touch. She wanted so much more. That there couldn't be a forever, didn't matter. She needed this, right now, right here…with him.

Letting herself slide under the spell he wove so magically, her hands slid up to either side of his face, and she kissed him back.

Her lips twitched at his startled pause. Excitement surged through her as he turned the tables on her and deepened the kiss.

A moan escaped. Oh, Lord. Her legs had turned to jelly – she'd never felt so weak. He tightened his arms, supporting her against him. He lifted his head.

"Sam?"

She opened her eyes. God, he was beautiful. Inside and out. She wanted what he offered. She wanted not to be alone – at least for one night. "Yes."

"Yes? Are you sure?"

Her smile turned to a full-blown laugh. "Yes, I'm sure."

Her answer darkened his eyes to an almost jet black. She smiled, reaching a hand to stroke the side of his face. "Yes, yes, and yes." She snagged his ear and tugged him toward her. "So what are you waiting for?"

"For you. For a very long time."

Sam's heart swelled. She knew exactly what he meant. She felt the same. She'd waited so long, she'd become so accustomed to the sensation, she'd forgotten what it actually meant. Now, she knew. She'd been waiting – for him. For this.

Still, she couldn't promise much. She frowned, not knowing how to let him know. He placed a finger against her lips.

"Don't. Don't think about tomorrow. Don't think about any of the many 'what ifs,' just think about us – tonight."

She closed her eyes, the tension draining from her shoulders, and relaxed against him. "You're right."

"I know. That wasn't so hard, was it?" He grinned at her even as he scooped her up in his arms and carried her to the bedroom.

"Always got to be right, don't you?" She couldn't resist teasing him. He set her on the bed, only she bounced to her knees and started opening the buttons on his shirt.

"Nope. Like right now. I think you're right." His grin blew

her away. She couldn't help but respond to the lightness of his tone. She never knew lovemaking could be so much fun. She quickened her pace, pulling his shirttail out of his jeans and down his arms.

"Whoa, take it easy. We've got all night." He shrugged out of his shirt, dropping it to the floor.

Sam snorted. "Like hell." She reached for his belt buckle, when the tantalizing bulge just below sidetracked her. Her fingers wandered, caressing with exploratory strokes before finally wrapping around and gently squeezing.

"Jesus Christ," he yelped, trying to put some distance between them. "This will be over before we ever get started if you don't stop that."

Sam grinned, feeling a lightness to her soul she'd never experienced before. "I don't care."

"What?" he responded, outraged. "Oh you don't, huh? Well, two can play that game." In a smooth move she hadn't even seen coming, her sweater and t-shirt were pulled over her head and wrapped around her arms, holding them above her head. He applied gentle pressure and Sam found herself lying on her back. Using only one hand, Brandt easily held her there while undoing her jeans and tugging them down her hips, to send them flying across the bed.

He grinned, his smile sensuous and teasing. "Now, it's my turn."

Sam's eyes widened. Expecting to be ravished, his slow sensual assault slid under her defenses.

Ever so gently, his tongue stroked around her nipple. First on one breast, then the other. Tiny nibbles followed the moist path, close, but not quite touching her nipples. She sighed and moaned, twisting closer, then moving sensuously away.

When he did finally take her nipple into his mouth, she arched her back. "Oh God," she whispered almost in prayer.

"You don't need his help tonight. This is nothing you can't handle."

She groaned as he teased the other breast, his lips nibbling and nudging, but never quite taking. She struggled to free her arms, but he'd have none of it.

"Please, I want to touch you. I need to touch…you."

Her arms – instantly set free – wrapped around him, pulling him down on top of her. He groaned as his bare chest slid across her heated skin. Sam slid her hands down to his belt, only to find it and the jeans they'd held up were missing. Her hand stalled, then slid down to the smooth, muscled buttocks. His skin was so soft. She couldn't get enough of the silky expanse.

He willingly offered her every part of himself for her pleasure. Sam took full advantage. Pushing up on his shoulders, he rolled over onto his back, swinging her on top of him. Sam laughed joyously and accepted the invitation. Using her fingers, her lips, and her tongue, she traced, teased, and tormented Brandt until he could stand it no more.

Without warning, Sam found herself flipped over, tucked under him, her legs hooked over his hips. Brandt waited until Sam gazed into his eyes. Then dropping his forehead to hers, he plunged deep.

Sam cried out. Her back arched, sending him deeper. The sensations roiled through her. Her head dropped to the side, her eyes drooped slightly…she was overwhelmed by sensation.

Brandt moved once slowly, then a second time. Need twisted through her, sending her higher and higher. Fragile and yet edged in steel, Sam twisted against the tension whipping through her.

"Brandt," she cried out, almost afraid.

"I'm here sweetheart. Let's go together." He hooked her leg higher and seated himself at her very center.

Sam's senses exploded.

Dimly in the background, she heard Brandt cry out as he found his own release. A long moment later, he collapsed on top of her, rolled to one side, and tucked her firmly up against him.

Well-being and satisfaction permeated the air. Sam curled against him and closed her eyes.

2:10 am, June 23rd

THE PHONE RANG.

Brandt opened his eyes, struggling to orient himself to the unfamiliar lack of space. He raised his head to find Sam splayed out, fast asleep on his chest. Her bed wasn't intended for someone his size.

The phone rang again.

"Shit." Carefully, he extricated himself from her arms, reaching for his discarded pants and the cell phone in the pocket.

"Hello." Brandt's heart dropped at the voice on the other end. "Right, I'm about a half-hour out."

Standing up, he put the phone away and searched for his briefs. He didn't want to wake her. Neither did he want her to wake up alone. Putting on the briefs, he grabbed his jeans next. While closing the buckle, he glanced over at Sam. She stared at him.

He immediately went to her. "I'm sorry sweetheart." He bent down and kissed her. "I have to go. We have a new victim."

CHAPTER 21

2:15 am

ICE SLIPPED OVER Sam's soul at his words. At least they'd found her. She'd been waiting for someone to call this last victim in. She wrapped the blankets tighter around her. The cabin temperature had dropped with the news. Blue crept through her fingers, and her legs had already turned numb. She tucked her legs under and reached for yet another of the cheap blankets stacked on the floor beside her.

"It's her. The one we've been waiting for. The brunette. Her name..." Sam's voice caught in the back of her throat. "Her name is...was Caroline."

A shadow crossed Brandt's face. He nodded to her as he walked out.

"Brandt?" Sam raced to the front door.

Brandt turned to gaze at her, one eyebrow raised. "What?"

"Be careful."

He acknowledged her comment with a nod then he strode over to her, gave her a seriously dangerous kiss, and walked out into the night.

2:55 am

ON ANY OTHER day, Brandt would have made record time. But it was just after three on a Sunday morning, and the Saturday night partiers had the city in full swing. Getting to the city was no problem. Navigating to the crime scene was.

"Jesus, Brandt, you must have had a hot date tonight. You aren't usually this late showing up." The forensic team had already arrived. Brandt took their ribbing in good humor, without offering any clue to his whereabouts.

Walking into the suburban brick house, the sense of normalcy struck him. How often did a family-oriented neighborhood hide a heinous crime? Regular two-story homes on city-planned lots surrounded him. Somewhere close would be the elementary school with a high school a little further away, and within walking distance would be the standard corner store.

Bad things did happen to good people. Grimly, he walked into hell.

The odor hit him first – the flies second.

The crime scene had to be several days old. A body in the heat of summer decomposed quickly.

Photographers worked at detailing every little thing. One of the CSI crew stood over the victim, the flashes from his camera creating an irregular staccato pattern. A victim with brunette hair. Brandt stopped in his stride. Amongst the dried blood and body fluids, the pasty white skin shone with an eerie light. Brandt struggled for objectivity. He walked through slowly and calmly, giving each area close scrutiny. Not knowing what to search for, yet he knew he'd recognize it when he saw it.

At the victim's bedside, all attempts at a cool demeanor vanished. The scene was incredibly familiar. Too familiar. Not the hair, not the features…but the injuries. God, the injuries were all too familiar.

Her boyfriend had been out of town. Caroline was supposed to have picked him up at the airport. When she hadn't, he'd come looking for her.

"Hey Brandt. The killer took a trophy this time."

With a sinking feeling, Brandt turned to face Kevin and Adam. Kevin couldn't wait. "He cut off her ear."

Christ.

Brandt paused for a moment to honor the dead woman. Now, more determined than ever to catch this killer, he got down to work.

9:10 am

SAM CHECKED THE roster. There were two new surgical cases to deal with. One still under anesthesia, while the other was awake and definitely pissed. She couldn't blame the poor thing.

He was a lop-eared rabbit who'd lost part of an ear to a dog. A large bandage covered the right side of his head. Sam quickly cleaned his cage and moved on.

With the basics taken care of, Sam headed to the lunchroom to find a cup of tea. She'd held her thoughts locked up until she saw the lunchroom was empty. With a sigh of relief, she collapsed at the table and dropped her head to her arms. Her heart and mind were a mess. She couldn't help being worried about the colonel's fate. Maisy was such a warm loving character, Sam hated her to be suffering the pain of waiting and not knowing.

Brandt had been on her mind all morning, then that was to be expected after last night. Her heart smiled as memories flooded her. Only to be shut down as Deputy Brooker slammed into her thoughts. She looked around nervously. Could he have tracked her to her place of work?

The door opened, startling her.

"Good morning, Sam." A chorus of greetings startled her. She smiled at the group of noisy women collecting around her. Somehow, she'd managed to create friends, without even trying. She didn't know how or why, but found gratitude welling up inside. It helped not to be so alone.

Their chatter swelled and receded and swelled again. Sam rode the waves of utterly bewildering topics from the latest color trend in shoes to the murder victim reported on the morning news. She stayed quiet, not wanting to listen and found it hard not to. The last thing she wanted to do was relive the experience. The thoughts turmoiled around, keeping her off balance and struggling to focus. She worked on keeping her emotions under control. The very name of the victim hurt her deeply. That poor woman.

Eventually, the coffee break ended, sending everyone to their jobs.

The friendly atmosphere followed Sam as she returned to the animals. She realized this was close to the normal life of other people. Instead of an inherent wariness with a guard always in place, other people laughed and joked, at ease with each other. Sam was suddenly hungry for more.

Dr. Wascott came to check on the dog coming out of his drugged state. Sam waited a few minutes, watching the dedicated caring so evident in his actions.

When he was done, she brought up the one subject she'd been waiting to discuss. "Sir," she said diffidently, "Soldier has re-injured himself."

The vet frowned. "How bad? What did he do?"

When she described the wound, the vet nodded. He went over to one of the many floor-to-ceiling cabinets and took out a small tube.

"Here is an antibiotic cream. Use this on the open wound for a few days. If it doesn't get better then you'll have to bring him in."

"I don't think he'll like that."

The vet grimaced. "Truthfully, neither will I. Only we can't have him getting an infection from his ripped stitches."

"Okay, I'll see how he responds to this."

Her day almost done, Sam quickly finished up, grabbed the new cream, and headed out. Once free of work, her thoughts automatically returned to the one subject she'd refused to focus on. Caroline.

She grimaced. Caroline had become the ultimate victim and Sam had been acting like one all along as well. She'd let this asshole control her every waking moment and many of her sleeping ones too. In order to regain control, she had to stop being afraid. In order to control the fear she had to be progressive. And just how the hell was she supposed to make that happen? The fear wouldn't stop overnight. She'd possibly have it forever.

Running a hand over her tired face, Sam vowed to stop letting fear control her. It was going to take constant vigilance to stay on top of this. She'd been afraid most of her life and this wasn't going to stop simply because she'd decided differently this moment. Still, power welled deep within her. She couldn't just sit here any longer and wait for him to pull her strings like a puppeteer.

It was time she pulled a few of her own.

9:24 am

"FINALLY." HE PUNCHED his heavy fist in the air. Jesus H. Christ, he could die himself before the fucking police actually got their heads on straight. He bet this was all over the Internet.

Bill rubbed his thick fingers over the top of his almost bald head. He'd need to shave again soon. But now he could relax. His victim had been found. Finally. He was tired but happy. There was no joy when his prize was decomposing without someone to watch and fuss over her. He grinned – that lopsided endearing movement as women described it. Before they got to know who and what he really was.

How long before the police actually received his surprise. He felt a moment of misgiving at his spontaneous action, then tossed it off. They'd never figure it out. He rubbed his thick hands together and gloated.

The gift should be nice and ripe by then.

10:03 am

BRANDT YAWNED, FEELING his face crack and splinter. God he was tired. He shouldn't have come in to work without catching a few hours of sleep, only he'd felt driven by the need to do something constructive. Besides, he might never sleep again. Not after that crime scene. That poor woman had been sliced and diced and Brandt could only feel grateful the killer hadn't been into cooking and eating too.

The forensic evidence wasn't in yet. The autopsy would be soon. All Brandt could do was wait.

He laid his head down on his crossed arms on the desk. He'd just rest his eyes for a minute. That's all he needed.

His phone rang a little later. Bleary-eyed he stared, uncomprehending at the noisy black machine. Sam? Rubbing his hand over his face, he reached for the receiver.

"Hello," he mumbled in a grainy voice. Reaching for his coffee cup, he took a drink to ease his throat. He choked and spluttered on the clammy cold drink, grimaced, and drank another sip. Caffeine was caffeine.

"Brandt, are you okay?"

Not Sam.

His mother. Damn, he'd forgotten. "Mom, I'm fine. How's the colonel?"

"He's still unconscious, but he does appear a little more peaceful now."

"But he hasn't woken up?" Brandt tried to smother a yawn and failed. He needed to talk to the colonel, if and when that was possible. He wanted to call Sam too, just to hear her voice. A warm light wrapped around his heart.

"No. Not yet."

Maisy sounded as tired as he felt. He hurt for her. It was hard to sit and wait when someone you cared about was hurting.

"Brandt, are you there?"

Brandt shook himself. "Yeah, Mom, I'm here." He checked at his watch. "Are you still at the hospital?"

"I'm here again now. I went home, had a shower, and came back in. I don't want him to wake up alone."

"It's almost lunchtime. Why don't I come by and pick you up? We'll go out for a bite to eat together." He could still check in with Sam, take his mom out for lunch and be back in time to tackle his heaped desk.

Maisy hesitated.

"Mom, come on. It would be good for both of us."

She capitulated. "Alright. But just for a bite."

Brandt checked his watch. "Good. I'll finish up here in another hour or so. Then I'll come by and pick you up."

Brandt rang off and stretched. He needed to check his emails and talk to his boss. Neither should take too long.

Bringing up his email, Brandt checked the couple of dozen messages waiting for him. One of them was from the librarian he'd met a couple of days ago. The librarian confirmed various ring patterns used over the decades for class rings and the similarity of the sketch to one used by a specific fraternity.

Brandt couldn't believe it. Finally, a breakthrough. His euphoria died as he read on. The ring design was in use for close to a decade with variations by year. Except it had been out of circulation for two decades. Over five hundred of them could have been purchased. The professor who'd informed the librarian, didn't have any figures or names available as the system hadn't been computerized back then. He did offer a few names of other people who might be able to help.

Brandt weeded through his messages, taking care of priorities. Before leaving for lunch, he walked over to the largest of the file cabinets and carefully hid, then locked Sam's journal inside. That would do for the moment.

"Hey, Brandt."

Brandt turned to find Kevin at the door. "Hey what's up?"

Kevin grinned. "The captain wants to see you. And for a change, I had nothing to do with this one. The grapevine apparently told him about Sam's vision and the latest murder."

"How the hell did the grapevine, or you, even find out?"

Kevin shrugged. "I don't know where I heard about it first,

but it's true, isn't it?"

"Is what true?"

"She saw this victim as she died, didn't she?"

Brandt groaned and closed his eyes. "Shit, did I slip up and say something to Adam? God I must have been really tired to have done that."

Kevin snapped his fingers, almost laughing out loud. "Yeah, that might have been who told me."

Captain Johansen's door was ajar when Brandt arrived. He knocked and pushed it open.

"Come in, Brandt. Take a seat." The captain gestured toward the single chair not piled high with file folders.

Closing the door behind him, Brandt made his way to the lone chair and sat.

The captain glanced at him. "Brandt. What's this about your psychic and another murder?"

Brandt said, "It's true. Sorry, I haven't had a chance to catch you up on the latest since coming in from the crime scene."

"You know what will happen if this gets out?" Captain Johansen always had the department's image on his mind. "How close was she?"

"Spot on."

"Damn."

Brandt understood how he felt. "It's not as if we're the first department to have used psychics." Brandt swept his arm toward the wide expanse of glass. "Besides, this is department stuff and the media shouldn't ever know – unless someone tells them."

Captain Johansen glared. "What about her? How are you going to stop her from stepping into the limelight? She could make a huge promo out of this case."

"Sam's not the type."

Brandt watched in fascination as Captain Johansen's beetle brows crinkled, almost meeting in the center of his forehead.

"Everyone is the type. You just have to have the right circumstances to bring it out."

Brandt stared out the window, refusing to be drawn. Captain Johansen was a hard-ass who'd apparently run the department fairly for many decades. His beliefs were little enough to put up with.

"Well, I'm saying that Sam isn't like that – but believe what you want."

The captain shuffled the papers on his desk. "So what did she see and what did she miss?"

It took a few minutes to give him the rundown. He finished with the one thing Sam hadn't seen. "She didn't mention the trophy. And we don't know why her ear was cut off or where it is."

"That's how it works with psychics. They get some of the information right and they get a lot wrong." Captain Johansen doodled on a notepad in front of him, obviously deep in thought.

"True enough." Brandt leaned forward. "This isn't for discussion with anyone else, but I actually saw her go through a vision." He gave a brief version of what he'd seen at Sam's cabin that night. The memories of the cuts appearing on Sam's fragile body haunted him.

"You saw these cuts appear and disappear – and you weren't drunk?"

Brandt stared into Captain Johansen's eyes. "God's truth. I swear I watched the cuts appear and then disappear. There was blood everywhere. Jesus, I panicked."

"Why didn't you call 911?"

Brandt's lips twisted. "I almost did. I managed to get through to Stefan first."

The captain squinted up him. "That would have helped. Did Stefan have answers?"

Brandt nodded. "And thank God he did. I would have caused more damage if I'd touched her. Maybe permanently."

"I don't know what to think about this stuff, however, I know several good cops that swear by Stefan."

"Sam isn't as strong or as secure in her abilities as Stefan. The good news is he's going to help train her. Sam's fragile. She needs to learn to protect herself." Brandt geared for the blow. "And that includes being protected from this department."

The captain leaned forward, glaring at Brandt. "What does that mean?" Larger than life, the captain never backed down from a fight. He had no trouble calling a spade a spade, and he always stood by his men. At six-foot-six, he was built like the football player he used to be.

Brandt glared back. "I can't forget about the ring diagram incident. Someone could also take it into his head to release personal information about Sam." He paused.

"But why?" The captain pounded his fist. "It wouldn't be someone from here. They'd know the damage something like that could cause the department."

"More likely to discredit me."

He waited a beat. "There's another possible complication."

The captain leaned forward. "Let's hear it."

Brandt quickly related what he knew about Deputy Brooker and what had been done to Sam, years ago. And the couple of incidents in the last few days.

The captain very clearly, very succinctly, said one word, "Shit." He shifted his great bulk deeper into his chair. It took another few minutes before Captain Johansen spoke again. "Bring her in. I think it is time I met this person."

"And how am I going to do that?"

"I don't know. That's for you to figure out. Just do it."

Ten minutes later, Brandt reached Sam by phone. "When?" Her tone somehow managed to convey weary acceptance. Damn she sounded tired.

"Today. Now would be good." Now that she'd agreed, he didn't really care, just the faster the better.

"I'm at work. I have roughly another hour-and-a-half before I'm done. Say about 1:30 pm. Does that work for you?"

"That would be great."

He hung up the phone and then remembered. Crap. His mother. He glanced at his watch. He was going to be late. Ah hell. Grabbing his keys, he locked his office and ran.

CHAPTER 22

1:07 pm

SAM SAT STIFFLY in her chair in Brandt's office. As soon as she'd arrived, Brandt had excused himself. What the hell was up with that? He'd mentioned something about the captain wanting to speak with her.

Hearing a noise, she turned to watch as one of the clerks walked in, smiled, and dropped a stack of mail onto Brandt's desk. Of course, there was no Brandt.

Just when she'd determined to go searching for him, Brandt walked in, followed by a huge man who dominated the small office.

Sam shifted to the side, slightly intimidated at the outright bulk of the two males. She tucked her fingers under her thighs, hoping to still the nervous rapping on the chair.

"Sam, this is my boss, Captain Johansen."

Surprised, Sam could only smile and nod. She shifted to the one side of her chair again.

The captain gave her a gentle smile that was at odds with his size. "It's nice to meet you, miss." He sat down on the chair beside her.

Sam could feel her eyes grow wider. She struggled against the nervousness threatening to overwhelm her. The captain smiled again. It didn't make her feel any better.

"What can I do for you, Captain?"

"I've spoken to Detective Sutherland here." Captain Johansen glanced at Brandt. "And he's told me a lot about you."

Sam whipped around to stare at Brandt. "Did he now?" Her eyes bored a question into the hapless target. When he nodded slowly, she slumped into her chair and closed her eyes, just barely holding back a groan. "Great," she whispered barely above an audible tone.

"Now I'm not saying that I agree with all this stuff, but I'm willing to trust Brandt. He says you have some impressive data. The problem is, I don't really want the public to know that you've been helping us."

That made sense, sort of. "Good. Neither do I."

He pursed his lips, gave a decisive nod, and continued. "Then we agree on that." The captain fell silent, Brandt stayed quiet, and Sam didn't know what to say.

"Why are you're telling me this?" She felt suspiciously under attack again.

The captain gazed at Brandt, one eyebrow raised.

"Stop it. No silent conversations between you two. Talk to me," she snapped. She glared at the two men.

Brandt hid his smile.

Captain Johansen opened the discussion. "We'd like to be able to use any information that you have for us. Like the ring. You know about the ring sketch on the news, right?" At her nod, he continued, "That wasn't supposed to happen. Still, it is bringing in tips on our hotline. There is a slight possibility that other information was accessed at the same time, but only a very slim chance."

She didn't know what to say. "Am I in danger?"

Again, the two men exchanged glances.

"I don't think so. Your address is a PO box and not a house address, so that would slow down anyone searching for you," said the captain. He took one of her hands in his. "I just need you to be careful until we get to the bottom of this."

"That's a little hard when you don't know what the threat is or where it's coming from."

Captain Johansen spoke up. "The killer doesn't know about you – does he?"

That was a horrible thought. "No I don't think so. Unless someone told him, or he's psychic, too. The chances of that aren't great."

He nodded. "Right. So just be careful."

Paper rustled as Brandt casually sorted the stack of mail on his desk. There was a small padded envelope in the stack. Grabbing scissors, he cut the tape.

Sam watched him. "An early Christmas present?"

Brandt snorted. "Not likely. The paper came off and the top of the box followed.

"Ohh, God. What is that?" Sam cried out as a nasty odor permeated the room.

The captain dropped her hand and damn near pounced on the parcel. Bits of paper went flying. The lid was slapped down and both men donned gloves from a box sitting on the filing cabinet. As Brandt reached for the box again, the captain held his arm and nodded in Sam's direction.

Brandt, realization coming into his face, nodded and walked around the side of his desk. He put an arm around Sam's shoulders and urged her out the door. "Sam, come sit out in the hallway. I'll get you a coffee. There might even be a fresh pot, if you're lucky."

Before she had time to register the offer, she'd been seated outside, and he'd already returned with a hot cup of coffee and a stack of magazines. "I'll be right back. Sit tight."

Sam, her hands burning with the heat of the Styrofoam cup, sat in numb silence. For all their efforts, there was no way to hide the smell or the fast glimpse she'd seen. She couldn't be sure, but she thought the box contained an ear: a bloody ear, still wearing an earring.

Several men came in and out. She watched, blind to most of it. The office swelled with people. Someone dropped a stack of paper on the chair beside her, someone else came and picked it up. Sam saw a small piece of paper on the floor. Not bigger than a half inch and was mustard colored like the package. Surely, it was important, too. She couldn't let the idea go as people walked over it and beside it – yet always missed it. Taking advantage of a lull, Sam snatched up the tiny piece, before plunking down on her chair again.

Instantly, the station disappeared as an unexpected door opened. She couldn't think. She couldn't focus. She couldn't see. She was lost in a black haze. Her hand holding the hot coffee ceased to hurt. Her surroundings ceased to exist. She walked in a gray fog, pulled down a path she'd never walked before.

Evil called to her, laughed at her, and even caressed her arms as she travelled. She knew there was something she had to do. Some reason for being here. But what? She didn't want to be here. It was dark, scary, and so very cold. The smell, God, the smell resembled a garden planted full of decomposing bodies. She felt compelled to walk forward. The fear and uncertainty diminished. The need increased. By now, the blackness soothed even as it hypnotized. She walked forward, uncaring where she went.

Then she heard it.

Mocking laughter filled the air, her ears, and even her soul.

Sam screamed.

1:30 pm

JESUS. SAM.

Brandt bolted in her direction and still came in behind the group filling the hallway. Where was she? Her high-pitched scream shut off abruptly. Brandt wrestled through the crowd to her side.

The captain was already yelling at everyone. "Give her room. Come on everyone, move back."

The crowd grumbled, giving way under his orders – slightly. Brandt spun around and glared at them. "Come on. Give her some air for Christ's sake. Sam? Sam, are you alright?"

This time several of the spectators broke away and headed back to their own duties. Only a few of the braver souls remained.

One of them asked, "Do you want us to call for an ambulance?"

Brandt checked Sam over. Pallid whiteness defined her face. Blue veins pulsed steadily down the gentle line of her throat. She was breathing slowly, evenly. She was either right out from a vision, or she was comatose from an injury. As she hadn't been on her own long enough and there were no visible signs of injury, he presumed she was reacting on a psychic level. Her hands gripped a piece of brownish-gold paper clenched in one hand.

Not sure if he should be touching her at all, Brandt plucked the offending piece out of her hand and took a closer look. It appeared to be a piece from that grisly package. If so, it could explain her fugue now. Turning around, he found only the captain and Kevin remained.

"Is she okay?" Kevin stood to one side, doubt and confusion in his eyes.

"What's the matter with her?" whispered the captain, crouching down beside him.

Brandt opened his hand to show him the paper. "I think she touched this, unwittingly, and it's sent her in a psychic state."

"What does that mean?" The captain studied her. "She's awfully pale. Is she okay?"

"I think so. I don't really know."

Her position looked so uncomfortable. Her body slouched sideways. She'd fall any minute. His office wouldn't offer anything more comfortable. The captain was obviously thinking along the same lines.

"Can we get her into my office? We can lay her on the couch there."

"Only we're not supposed to touch her."

"But we can't leave her here. She's going to hit the ground in a minute."

Decision made, Brandt slipped his arms under her legs and back and carried her to the captain's office. Once there, he gently laid her down, her head on a pillow. She moaned with the jostling movements.

"Sam. It's okay. Take it easy."

Her eyes flickered. Brandt eased back in relief. She was waking up. He didn't know what had happened, though he could make an educated guess. She really had no control. When visions took her over, it was as if she stepped out. He couldn't protect her – not from her own abilities. Not an easy thing to admit. He admired her guts. But he was damn sure he could *not* live her life.

Sam's eyes had a glazed look as awareness slowly returned. She glanced around the room, a frown wrinkling her face. "Where am I?"

"This is the captain's office. We moved you in here so you could lie down. How are you feeling?"

"Huh? Did I have another vision?" Her frown turned pensive as she thought deeply. "There was such blackness. The world smelled dead." She turned to him, a wave of sadness making her eyes huge wells of pain. "It was her ear, wasn't it?"

At the reminder, Brandt winced. "I'd hoped you hadn't seen that."

"Just a glimpse." She rolled her head against the couch. "That was enough."

"I'm sorry. You should never have been exposed to that."

She grimaced. "Really, what do you think my nightmares are like?" Bitterness tinged her voice, melding with the sadness. Brandt managed not to wince again but just barely.

Staring around the room, he found the captain sitting at his desk, listening in. Kevin stood beside him, watching, a deep frown of concentration across his forehead.

"Did you…" Brandt hesitated, "Did you learn anything useful

while you were in this place? Wherever it was." He studied her reaction.

"I don't know where I was either. I think..." she hesitated.

"Go ahead."

"I think I connected with the killer this time. But I can't be sure." She looked at each man, one at a time. "I think I was inside his mind. A black pit of darkness that lost its way a long time ago. He thinks you're all useless idiots and that you'll never catch him."

Kevin butted in. "That covers every criminal out there."

Brandt nodded, but kept watching Sam. "Anything else?

"He's old energy. He's been doing this for decades. He won't ever quit. You'll have to kill him."

"My pleasure." And Brandt meant it. He'd bring him to justice if he could. However if not, well sometimes that was the best way all around. "Do you know anything about what he's planning next? Where he is? What he's doing?"

Sam's eyelids drooped and a faraway look came over her pale features. "He's waiting. He's rubbing his hands gleefully and imagining your face, your reaction when you open the gift."

"Why? That *gift* doesn't make any sense. We already have his victim. The ear makes no difference." The captain spoke up for the first time.

A large tear welled up in the corner of Sam's eye. Brandt reached over and gently wiped it away.

"It's not her earring. It's her ear, yet another woman's earring."

"Another woman?" Captain Johansen surged to his feet. "What, there's another victim?"

"He thinks you won't figure it out. It's an older victim. His trophy from the drugged one. He doesn't want to keep it. She's not a memory he wants to honor. She was a failure for him."

"Sam." Brandt gently tapped the side of her head. "Sam, wake up."

"Is she aware of what she's saying?" Captain Johansen came around his desk to bend over and see for himself.

Kevin jumped in. "Do you think she was telling the truth?"

"The truth as she knows it. Yes." Brandt stroked her cheek gently, willing her to come to awareness. It took another moment before she opened her eyes again.

"Please quit doing that, will you? It scares the hell out me." He was rewarded with a half-smile. "Are you back now?"

It was weak but it was a nod.

"Then sit up," he said and half tugged her upright to lean against the overstuffed couch cushions. "Maybe now you won't go under again."

Sam curled into a small ball, huddling with her knees to her chin. A blue color highlighted her cheekbones.

"Jesus, you're freezing." Brandt searched the room for something to cover her. Captain Johansen walked over to a coat stand in the corner and pulled down a large wool overcoat. Sam gratefully snuggled under the warm material.

Captain Johansen asked in a diffident voice, "I know you're not exactly recovered but…do you have any other information that would help us?"

Brandt jumped in. "If you connected to the killer, does he have his next victim picked out?"

Her answer came out on such a soft breath the three men bent to hear her.

"Yes."

Kevin looked to Brandt, shrugged sheepishly, then returned his gaze to Sam. "Can you give us any details? Anything helpful that might help us to find her?"

Sam shook her head slightly. "Only that she's close to him geographically. He watches her, follows her everywhere. His hunger is building. He's enjoying this stage. Soon though, he'll have to appease his appetite. Not yet. He has time to play."

Brandt wondered. "Do you get a sense that he works or has a career? Does money ever enter his mind?"

Captain Johansen added, "What about his location? Can you see any landmarks? Anything that tells you where she might be?"

"Only stores, a drugstore, a coffee shop, sidewalks. I saw only some of the scenes from his mind." Sam rested for a moment. "She's Caucasian."

All three men stared at her, startled. "You can see her?"

"Only bits and pieces." Keeping her eyes closed, Sam, in a monotone voice, said, "She's tall. He's taller. She's young, mid-twenties with long brunette hair." She fell silent again.

The men exchanged glances, everyone anxious for the one or two details that could make the difference between finding her, or not.

Not wanting to disturb her if she were getting more information, only he didn't want her zoning out again either, Brandt murmured, "Sam, you there?"

She opened her eyes slowly, as if they were weighted down. "She has a vehicle."

Kevin snapped forward. "Can you see a license plate? Make? Model? Color? Sam – anything?"

Brandt shot him an approving nod. At least Kevin appeared to be taking a solid step toward accepting Sam's abilities.

"Red, small, two door. Can't see a license plate. He's watching her get in the car."

Brandt, on a sudden thought, asked, "Sam, is he sitting inside his car?"

After a long moment, Sam nodded. "I can't see much. The windshield is tinted blue green. The seats are dark green."

"Bench seats or individual?"

"Bench."

"Old or new?"

"Can't tell."

After that the questions came hard and fast from all sides. Some she answered and more she couldn't. After fifteen minutes, all three of them had run out. Brandt couldn't believe it. He was exhausted, so he could only imagine how Sam felt. In fact, he leaned over to find she'd fallen asleep. He reached to tug the coat higher up her shoulders.

Nodding to the others, Brandt followed the men outside and closed the door behind them. Once in the hallway, Brandt leaned against the closed door and looked at the other two. "So, what do you make of it?"

Captain Johansen grimaced. "I have no idea. I sure as hell hope she's giving us viable information. But we don't have much else to go on. Period."

Kevin spoke up. "We might find a different DNA on the earring versus DNA of the ear. That will give us some idea."

"That will help. Sam had mentioned this victim before. I came up with two possible women. One is in the morgue and one is in a coma at Portland General. We can check to see if one of the women was wearing the matching earring. If the victim is dead, then we're too late to help her. We'll need to check her for forensic information, but other than that, we should be trying to find his next victim."

Pursing his lips, Captain Johansen agreed. "I'll go to the lab now and talk to them. What do we do about her?"

"She needs to sleep this off. Her energy level drops quickly with these visions." That was a given. "I don't want to leave her for too long. She shouldn't wake up alone."

Kevin nodded. "Stay with her and I'll start with phone calls and running car data. I may just owe her an apology." Leaving, Brandt staring after him open-mouthed. He smiled and walked to his office. Brandt raised an eyebrow at Captain Johansen who shrugged. "Don't know, but I'm heading to the lab to make sure they don't screw this up."

Ten minutes later, after making a few phone calls of his own, Brandt opened the captain's office door to check on Sam. He must have woken her for she sat up, startled and nervous.

"Shh, Sam. It's okay. I'm sorry. I didn't mean to wake you." He walked in and sat at the edge of the couch beside her, close, without touching. She peered at him, still groggy.

"Wow. I guess I fell asleep?"

He smiled. "That you did. Not for long though, maybe fifteen or twenty minutes."

She stood up uncertainly. "What time is it? Can I leave now?" She searched around anxiously. "Where's my purse?"

"Take it easy. First, it's not that late. You've been here for just over an hour. Your purse is in my office, and yes, you can leave." He opened his arms, closing them around her as she walked into his embrace. "There, that wasn't so hard was it?"

She stared at him, fatigue pulling at her features.

Brandt hurt for her. She had to be exhausted. "I want you to stay and rest for a bit."

"I'm fine." She visibly straightened and produced a stronger smile. Brandt wasn't fooled in the least.

"Have you eaten?"

Confusion clouded her face. "I think so."

He nodded. "I may have found the drugged woman. She came in during the right time period – and with one earring missing. Her name is Annalea Watson. I'm on my way over to check it against the one that just arrived. The lab has taken swabs of it to match DNA, if need be. The woman is alive, but she's in a coma."

Sam's eyes widened. "But that's wonderful."

"So far so good. Come on, let's find your purse and get you some food."

1:50 pm

KEVIN HURRIED TO his desk. He couldn't believe what he'd seen. Or heard. His mind had been blown, and it still had a frazzled edge to it.

If he hadn't been there and seen it for himself... Well, he couldn't even go there yet. All his life, he'd thought he understood the ways of the world. He just didn't know anymore.

He did know one thing – she couldn't have been making this up. He'd watched her very carefully. Her eyes had been blind, the pupils dilated and unfocused. She'd been almost comatose at one point, then completely awake at another.

Her face had gone dead white, then flushed cherry red on her return. Her skin, God, her skin had been so thin and so blue. He shook his head.

No one could have faked that.

2:15 pm

NOW WASN'T THAT interesting? Dillon kept his face impassive as he watched the chaos going on around him. He'd been on the phone when the woman had screamed. Detective Sutherland had a hell of a reputation with the ladies – but not this kind.

Thinking she must be an informant of one kind or another, Dillon had initially ignored her. Until she'd screamed. Still he'd thought, hearing about the gruesome delivery, that it had to have been her reaction to the gift. But not after the preferential treatment she received in the captain's office. When that was followed by an intense session later, Dillon's interest was truly piqued.

So this was the psychic Brandt was working with. Unbelievable. He laughed.

By the time she walked out of the office, he had to admit, she did appear as if she'd been pushed through an old wringer washing machine. Brandt's careful handling confirmed one thing. Brandt must be sleeping with the weirdo witch. Brave man. And smart too. That was the best way to control a woman.

And while Brandt stayed focused on her, it gave Dillon a chance to move in and on up.

CHAPTER 23

7:48 pm

THE SUN HAD lost its heat by the time Sam managed to get home. Seemed Moses couldn't contain his joy. She knew he hated it when she came in late. Soldier wagged his tail, his only concession to her arrival. It was a step in the right direction.

She should have gone home after the vision, except working around the animals helped recharge her psychic batteries faster than anything else. Though working didn't help her physical energy levels, they would recharge faster once her psychic energy levels were high again.

Sam survived by shoving everything to the back of her mind and staying on task. Only once, had she fallen off balance – when she'd noticed the blue dangly earrings in Lucy's ears. It had been all she could to hold back the memories…and the tears. After that, Sam had stayed away from the others.

Only when she tried to make it up her porch stairs and inside the cabin did Sam realize the hamburger Brandt had bought for her had been a long time ago.

The kitchen seemed empty and cold. Leftover dishes in the sink, and an almost empty fridge added to the forlorn atmosphere. It took a moment of rooting through the cupboards before she found a can of soup and half-a-package of crackers.

"Yeah, food." She turned on a burner and slowly warmed up the soup, munching on the crackers while waiting for the rest of the meal to catch up. Just before the soup had heated enough to eat, Sam fed her animals. Then it was her turn.

She turned off the kitchen light and sat in the fading sun's rays. At some point in the last few days, the atmosphere inside the cabin had changed. The normal sense of security had disappeared. The darkness, instead of giving her peace, threw long scary shadows. It didn't feel right anymore. The loss of its solace devastated her.

Feeling chilled, she cupped the cooling soup bowl, needing what warmth remained. She drank down the last of the broth then headed outside.

With Moses at her heels, she walked to the dock. Hearing something behind her, Sam spun around, surprised to see Soldier hobbling after her. Happy with his progress, she ran toward him only to stop at his warning growl.

"Damn it, Soldier. What do I have to do to gain some acceptance here?"

His growl deepened.

Crouched down close to him, Sam didn't know whether to continue outside or head in. The sound of an approaching vehicle decided it for her. She stepped further into the shadows, glad she'd left the house in darkness. She knew the sound of Brandt's truck by now only it appeared identical to the asshole's truck who tried to run her off the road. She wasn't taking any chances.

Silently, the dogs at her side, Sam kept to the darkness of the trees and watched as a vehicle approached. Powerful lights lit the way.

At the house, the vehicle parked and a man got out. Sam squinted through the darkness. He looked like Brandt, yet she couldn't be sure. She refused to be the first to make a sound.

The man approached the dark house warily.

Sam watched just as cautiously.

The man jumped up the stairs and knocked on the front door.

He knocked again. He pivoted, searching the encroaching darkness. There was no way anyone could miss her truck parked out front. "Sam, are you in there?"

It was Brandt. Joy lit the dark areas in her heart and filled them with a sense of security. Misplaced feelings or not, she was glad to see him.

"I'm over here."

Brandt turned in her direction. "Where?"

"Down toward the dock." Still, she didn't move, waiting instead for him to approach her.

"Why the hell are you wandering around outside in the dark?" He stormed in her direction. "And why the *hell* didn't you answer the phone?" As he approached, his face switched from worry, to exasperation, and finally to a building anger. "Do you know how many times I tried to call? Did you ever consider that someone might be worried about you – especially after the day you had?"

Sam stepped forward so he could see her. "Hi." She pulled her phone out of her pocket, saying, "It's a beautiful night. Why shouldn't I be out?" Flipping her phone open, she groaned. "Shit. My battery is dead. I'm sorry, I never even checked."

He shook his head. "Right. Of course, it is. There's no reason to be extra careful or accessible, huh?"

Sam defended her actions. "I said I'm sorry. Besides, I have the dogs with me."

"Not a lot of good they are going to be against a bullet or two, are they? Remember the last time?"

She didn't need this. "So did you have an official reason for this visit or did you just come to yell at me?"

"Sorry." He smiled slightly, reached out and snagged her into his arms where she cuddled right in. "I am sorry, but you scared the hell out of me when I couldn't reach you by phone. I've been trying for hours."

Leading the way, Sam walked to the cabin. "As you can see, I'm fine." She didn't wait to see if he caught up with her. As she passed his truck, he stopped and opened the passenger door. Curious, she turned in time to see him pull an overnight bag out before locking up the vehicle.

Sam glanced sidelong at the bag, but reality didn't hit until she'd opened the door. Excitement unfurled deep in her tummy. Her breath hitched even as a kernel of outrage sparked at his audacity. She didn't know how to react. How to feel. Excited and comforted, all mixed up with relief. She needed to know for sure. She turned around. "What's the bag for?"

"If you won't look after yourself, then someone has to do it for you." Brandt walked around her and stepped inside. "Therefore, you have a houseguest." He walked over to the worn out couch and dropped his bag with a heavy thunk. "Besides, I have a couple of questions I need answered."

Sam didn't want to give in so easily. He had a lot of nerve making this decision without her. And yet, she couldn't be happier. "Did you ever consider asking me?"

"Asking – oh yeah, that's one of the questions I'd planned on putting to you earlier. But… Oh right, you wouldn't pick up the phone. So now I don't need to ask, do I?" He kicked back on the couch, his arms behind his head. His grin split his face in two.

"Whatever." Sam pushed the door shut with a little more force than she'd planned. She reached for her answer to all life's ailments – tea.

"So why didn't you know about the souvenir?"

Sam stilled. Turning away from him, she pulled out two cups from the cupboard.

"I won't go away."

Sam sighed, poured two cupfuls before walking over to sit down opposite Brandt. "Are you sure?"

He grinned. "Positive."

Sam sat in silence, then sipped her tea, staring quietly at the irritating and highly amused man in front of her.

"Get it through your head. I'm here for the long haul."

Sam tilted her head to stare at him in confusion. Quickly, she glanced down again. Surely, he hadn't meant that, had he? But God, she hoped he had. She didn't know much about long hauling, but she'd like to.

He sat up and leaned toward her. "So tell me why."

She tried to focus on the conversation. As much as she didn't want to revisit the case, she knew he wouldn't lay off. "I didn't know because it was sliced off after the woman died. After I disconnected."

Brandt's face was a study of emotions as he considered her words. "Then I guess it's a blessing that you didn't know."

With a frown, Sam sat back. "I'm not always so lucky." Sam stopped, as emotion rose dangerously high. She swallowed heavily. "Once the victims die, I have a couple of minutes of adjustment. How they die and how long it takes them to disconnect, determines how long I am caught in limbo. Sometimes, I'm aware of what happens to their bodies after death if I'm still stuck there."

Staring down at the table, her fingers traced the old pattern showing through the melamine top. "And sometimes," she said, raising her gaze slowly. "And sometimes, people think the victims are dead, but…" Tears clogged her voice. "But they aren't a hundred percent gone yet." Sam wiped her eyes with the back of her sweater sleeve. "They, and I, can feel every little thing then."

Her vision blurred with tears and through it all she tried to see if Brandt understood. The look on his face broke her heart.

"I'm sorry. I shouldn't have told you."

"No. No. Don't feel that way." He reached across the table, his hand a protective cover over hers. He squeezed her hand. "It's just disturbing that you have to go through this all the time." His thumb stroked across the soft skin beside her thumb.

"Working in law enforcement, I'm exposed to every horrific human experience. I should be used to it… It still catches me sometimes."

Sam gently caught up his fingers in hers. "I know. It's the same for me. People can be vicious to each other."

His lips twisted in a wry grin. "That's often why relationships don't work for law enforcement officers. If we marry someone *not* in the same field, then the partner doesn't have the understanding of what we go through every day. And if we marry another officer, then there is no leaving the work behind. Living with this level of violence every day, slowly wears down the relationship until nothing can hold it together."

"How horrible."

Moses barked, startling her. An odd sound rustled outside the cabin. Frowning, she went to the front door and stared out the window to the one side. The blackness showed nothing untoward. She opened the door to let both dogs outside then followed them. Brandt was suddenly at her side.

"What did you hear?"

"I'm not sure. Something was moving out here."

"Wildlife?"

She shook her head. "No. The dogs wouldn't react like that."

In the distance, a faint rumbling sound could be heard. A vehicle.

"Can you hear the highway from here?"

"Occasionally. It depends on the weather." As her voice died away so too did the engine sound.

"It has to be on the highway."

"Unless someone drove part way and then walked the rest."

The two stared at each other, uneasiness hanging heavy on the evening air.

Sam stepped closer, linking her arm with his. "I forgot to say thank you for coming. I really don't want to be alone tonight."

Survival had meant being alone before. She didn't know what to do with Brandt. Having sex once was one thing – didn't other people easily toss sex off as a momentary passionate lapse? Twice well, didn't that constitute a relationship? She didn't do those. Or she hadn't done in a long time. And she was pretty sure, he didn't do them either. Better to clear the air and tell him, no matter how uncomfortable.

"I need to tell you that I don't do relationships." Oh wasn't that smooth, Sam. Good job, Sam? How to advertise your inexperience and total lack of social skills.

Brandt slowly turned around to stare at her. "Why not?"

Heat pooled in her tummy at the sensuous vibes emanating from him. Her cheeks warmed, but she stood her ground. "I'm no good at them," she said baldly.

"How would you know if you don't do them?" he asked in a reasonable tone of voice.

Sam stared at him, unsure of how to go on. "I tried."

"So that's it. You tried and failed so you're doomed to a life alone? Haven't we been around this block once before?"

"Yes. No. I don't know. Maybe." Sam shut up, too flustered to answer clearly.

"You don't know because you're too afraid to go on."

"So?" she challenged him.

"So live a little. Don't spend your life so afraid of trying and failing that you live alone. Take a chance and let someone in your world." He reached out and cupped her chin, raising her face to meet his gaze. "I want to be a part of your world. I thought I'd proved that already."

He was saying the words she'd yearned to hear all her life. Moisture collected at the corner of her eyes. It's all she could to not start bawling. In spite of herself, her bottom lip trembled.

His thumb smoothed even as it rubbed her lower lip, gently teasing it to a smile. Sam couldn't resist. She kissed his thumb as it made its next pass.

He stopped. "Dangerous."

Sam's lips twitched. His thumb moved again, this time much slower, more seductive in its sensual mission. The tantalizing movement slowed when it reached the middle swell, where it sat heavy and waiting. Sam raised her eyes to his.

His asked a question.

Sam hesitated. Did twice mean a commitment. Or given her lack of social skills and inexperience did twice mean still dating? Could she really walk away? Did she even want to? No. If at the end she was devastated, then so be it. At least she'd have enjoyed life…and him for a little while.

Closing her eyes, she let her body answer for her. Her lips parted slightly. Her tongue slipped out to caress his thumb. Sliding first to one side then to the other.

Brandt bent his head, his eyes absorbed with her every tiny movement.

From under half-closed lids, Sam watched his eyes deepen, darken. Sliding her tongue out further, she slowly curled it around the top of his thumb. Instinctively, she'd invited him inside. He didn't resist. His thumb gently caressed the inside of her lips. Sam closed her teeth on his skin, tugging his thumb ever so gently inside. She sucked it lightly, her eyes wide, watching him watch her.

His eyes became heavy-lidded, his breathing harsh and rasping. Sam half smiled. She sucked harder.

His mouth opened, his tongue gently licking across his own lips. His nostrils flared.

The wait became unbearable. Sam closed her eyes to enjoy the simple sense of arousal. Nerve endings she'd tamped down surged to life, making her body tingle in places she didn't even know could respond.

Then he pulled his thumb away.

Her eyes snapped open. Blinded by sensation, her whole being focused on his mouth as he lowered his head and replaced his thumb with his lips. Stunning, hot liquid engulfed her as Brandt kissed her slowly, leisurely, and very, very competently.

When he lifted his head long minutes later, Sam sagged against him.

Holding her close, his lips against her ears, he whispered, "Too much?"

She shook her head, and whispered, "Not enough."

He needed no encouragement: bending and lifting her in his arms, easily carrying her up the stairs to the single room upstairs. He lowered her feet to the floor. Lowering his head, he gave her a long, slow kiss. When he broke it off, she stretched on tiptoes to recapture his lips.

"Sam, I need to know – are you sure? I don't want just a moment. I want to see where this goes. To give it a try. To give us a try."

Sam didn't want to talk, but Brandt reached up to hold her face in his warm hands as he dropped soothing kisses on her forehead, her cheeks, her closed eyelids, and even the corners of her mouth – but never on her lips. "Are you sure?" he murmured insistently.

Sam moaned as his teasing lips moved to her ear and down the smooth line of her neck. Shivers ran down her spine. She melted deeper against him.

"Sam."

She smiled. Her tongue slid against his lips, darting inside to stroke his tongue. Brandt took her mouth in a deep drugging kiss. He finally broke off the kiss, breathing in deep sharp rasps. "Sam, answer me," he ordered.

Sam forced her heavy eyelids open to stare at him in confusion.

"Say yes."

With her gaze fixed on his, she whispered the promise they both needed to hear. "Yes."

11:00 pm

BRANDT STUDIED HIS surroundings. The bare bedroom fascinated him. What an insight into her personal life. All walls and the painted ceiling were bare, not even a poster to break up the bleakness. There were no dressers, closets, or storage of any kind. He could only imagine how her life had been up until now.

Her bed held cheap army surplus blankets with even more stacked on the floor. He glanced at the odd stack of blankets. His face grew grim as understanding crashed in on him. They were spares in case what happened to the one on the couch, happened again.

His cell phone rang. His heart sank. Gently, disengaging himself from Sam's arms, he hurried to find the phone before she woke up.

"Hello." His cell phone showed it was just past eleven. Moonlight cast a pale shadow on the bedroom floor.

"Brandt. We've got trouble."

Brandt listened, glaring into the night. "What the hell? Not again. Who. Did. This?"

"I don't know. I have called the station, but no one is talking. If it takes a court order, I will find out. The ring incident was minor compared to this. You need to warn Samantha."

"Oh I will. Don't worry about that. I get first dibs on the asshole that did this."

"Don't go jumping to conclusions," warned the captain.

"I'm not. Go ahead. Get all the proof you need – then he's mine." Brandt's mind fired on all cylinders. "They actually gave her name? How irresponsible is that?"

"They say it never occurred to them that she might be in danger. Many psychics need publicity to stay in business. I don't think they understand what they've done. But don't worry. You look after Sam, and I'll sort this out."

His voice brooked no argument.

"Fine. You get the first shot. Sort it out…or I will." Brandt hung up.

11:05 pm

"OH SHIT!"

Dillon leaned forward to stare at the television newscaster, his handful of chips frozen in midair. Sam's face filled the screen. Dillon's chest constricted. He hadn't done this. He hadn't given the media a picture of her. Oh, crap. He dumped the chips into the bowl and rubbed his hands through his hair. It wouldn't matter if he'd done this or not. If anyone found out what he had done, he'd be blamed regardless. He was so fired.

He'd talked to the reporter, but had only mentioned a psychic being part of the investigation. How could they have put the rest together? He hadn't given them any details. He sure as hell wouldn't have given them her name.

They had to have a name to get a picture. Or the reverse. That's it! Someone could have seen and recognized her at the station. Then it would have been easy to have followed up on her.

Not that it mattered. Once the others knew he'd talked to the media a little bit, no one would believe he hadn't given them everything. Everyone would assume the worst. Given his behavior to date, he couldn't blame them.

The woman's face stayed on the screen so long Dillon wanted to throw something.

What was he going to do?

There was no doubt about one thing. If Brandt and Sam were right about a killer taking out women in the area, there was no doubt which woman would be his next victim.

He needed to save his neck. Shit. There was only one way.

He reached for the phone.

11:06 pm

"WHAT THE HELL!" Beer spewed out of Bill's mouth. He leaned forward to hear the newscaster's voice clearer. "A fucking psychic."

The small apartment closed in on him for a long moment. The picture on the screen wavered before focusing in tightly again. Whoever she was, she looked like hell. The picture was grainy and old, the woman hardly identifiable.

He leaned back, unsure what to think. After a minute, he started to laugh. A slow rolling-barrel laugh pealed across the small room. "Oh God, that is too funny. Fucking incompetent cops. They can't solve anything. Their heads are stuck so far up their asses they had to bring in a goddamned psychic."

With his beer safely down on the long pine coffee table, he laughed and laughed. This was so perfect.

Abruptly the laughter died in his throat. He glared at the picture still on the screen, committing her features to memory.

She'd better not sense him. He'd fucking kill her.

CHAPTER 24

11:15 pm

BRANDT GAZED DOWN at the sleeping angel beside him. God, help him, he was just as much to blame for this mess. There were so many things he could have done. He could have talked to the station himself about who supplied the picture of the ring. He could have put the fear of God into Dillon and Kevin – let them know he was suspicious of them. Most of all, he should have beat the shit out of that asshole deputy from her past. He closed his eyes and groaned. Guilt squeezed his heart. Stupid.

He'd never knowingly do anything to hurt her. Ever. But just as bad…he'd promised to keep her involvement private and he'd failed.

His arm tightened around the tiny woman that had broken into the locked places in his heart. Lowering his head, he dropped tiny caresses to the side of her face tucked into his shoulder. Unbelievable. He cared so much and just the thought of anything happening to her made his arms squeeze tightly.

With a muffled protest, Sam, still asleep, shifted slightly out of his grasp. "Sorry, sweetheart." Brandt shifted to give her more space.

His phone rang again. Casting a worried look at Sam, Brandt slid upward to sit against the wall, cell phone in hand.

"Hello."

Captain Johansen's next words had Brandt hopping out of bed to the far side of the room. He stopped in front of the window. "What?" he hissed.

Brandt shook his head at the next piece of information. "He what? What the hell was he thinking? Yet, he says he *didn't* give them her picture and name?" Brandt, remembering Sam was still asleep, took several deep breaths. "Do you believe him?"

Brandt, tucking the phone against his shoulder, quickly pulled on his briefs and pants. Trying not to wake Sam, he walked downstairs and into the kitchen.

The captain's heavy sigh was unmistakable. "Yes. I do. He's an idiot, mostly a harmless one. Do you have a picture of her in the file?"

"No, I don't."

"Right, and he wouldn't have gone to the trouble of digging one out. He's too damn lazy for that. Chances are someone else did it. I just don't know who yet. The station did admit this information came from a different source than the one who provided the ring – which confirms Dillon's story."

"Christ, what a mess." Knowing the captain agreed didn't help any.

"Brandt – you know what has to happen. I'll deal with Dillon. You have to get her to a safe house."

Brandt laughed a short angry bark. "That's not as easy as it sounds. She's not going to be happy."

"To hell with keeping her happy. At this point, I'm only concerned with keeping her alive. If she won't come willingly, you know what to do."

The captain rang off, leaving Brandt glaring at the phone in his hand.

Someone had deliberately put Samantha in danger. Whoever had done this might as well have pointed a gun at her head and pulled the trigger himself.

What if that was exactly what this asshole intended? Deputy Brooker came to mind. The more he thought on it, the more his suspicions grew. It shouldn't be too hard to pick him up. Adam had been working on tracking where he was staying earlier today. Brandt quickly made a couple of phone calls. Within minutes, an APB was put out on the vehicle, and Adam was heading into the office to pull a photo off the database to circulate as well. Then he'd be taking the photo to the newsroom to confirm Brandt's suspicions.

Could anyone else have done this? Sam said only a few people knew about her skills. After today's mess at work, that select few had grown considerably. Several of those might have wondered about her skills before – not after today. God damn it. He highly doubted Kevin would have done something like this, particularly after seeing Sam in action today. Besides, he'd have never put the department at risk.

"What won't make me happy?"

Startled, Brandt turned around to find Sam, with a blanket wrapped around her shoulders, leaning against the doorway. Tousled and tiny, she appeared so lost Brandt couldn't help himself. He walked over, tugging her into his arms.

He didn't want to tell her. Brandt grimaced. There was no way around it. She had to know.

"That was the captain. One of our detectives has fessed up to telling the media that you were helping the police with this case. He swears that's all he said. But on the news tonight there was a little more to it than that."

"Exactly how much more was there?" Her voice was quiet, too quiet. So were her eyes.

His heart sank. She already knew.

"Your name and picture."

She froze. Brandt rubbed her back soothingly. "It's okay. I won't let anything happen to you."

Stiff and unyielding, Sam didn't answer. After a few moments, Brandt tilted her chin so he could gaze into her eyes. Searching deep, he tried to find out what she was thinking.

Her eyes were frozen blanks.

"Oh, God, Sam. I am so sorry." Brandt tugged her closer, rocking her gently in his arms. "Captain Johansen wants you to go to a safe house where we can keep an eye on you."

Sam shook her head vehemently. "I'm not going."

Brandt winced. "I'm afraid it's not a choice."

Sam reared up, glaring at him. Brandt, damn his hormones couldn't resist noticing the gentle sway of her breasts. Now that he knew what those God-awful sweaters covered up, he wholeheartedly approved of them. He didn't want every other male getting an eyeful. Christ, she was gorgeous when she was mad. Peach flushed her normally pale skin, giving her a lively bloom that was so often missing from her skin.

"Like hell. You can't force me," she declared defiantly.

He sighed and tried to tug her down against him, only she was having nothing to do with it.

"Actually, I can, but I don't want to have to." He shifted slightly, realizing his body's interest in her nude state wouldn't be received well at the moment, but knowing there was damn little he could do about it. "Sam, try to be reasonable. The killer now knows who you are and it won't take him long to find where you live."

"Do you realize what you've done? It's not just the killer. It's my job and my friends." Sam stopped, a stunned look on her face. She snorted. "Okay, so they may not be friends in the 'forever' sense, but they were friendly to me. Why is it, I'm only just understanding what that means, now that I'm about to lose them?"

"Not everyone will see the news."

Sam snorted. "This is a small town. Whoever doesn't see the news will be told by 9 am tomorrow."

She was probably right. "That doesn't mean they will treat you any differently." Besides, he couldn't let anything else matter. She had to stay safe. Nothing else was acceptable.

Fine tremors ran through her. "I don't think I can I live here if I'm an outcast again."

Brandt ran his fingers through his hair. He couldn't imagine what her life had been like up to now. She'd built herself a life here. He didn't want her to lose that.

"I can understand how you feel."

An angry laugh escaped. "Can you?"

Brandt could feel the slow burn he'd stomped on earlier, start to flare up. Her anger was nothing in comparison. He couldn't let it be. This was beyond serious. She had to leave and now. Staring out into the black of night, he realized they didn't have much time. The killer could already have found her location and be on his way. He voiced his thoughts. "You have to consider that he could be on his way right now."

Sam aged before him. His heart went out to her.

"I'm sorry, Sam. But this is the way it has to be."

Sam blurted out, "The animals. I can't take them to a safe house. Soldier needs this place as much as I do. To take him anywhere else will slow his rehabilitation, magnify his trust issues if you take him away from his new home."

She had a point – just a small one. He was concerned about her though, not the dog.

"Staying here is out of the question."

"Why?" she interrupted.

"There's too much cover for a predator. It would be hard to defend."

"Not true," she answered shaking her head. "Someone could stay in the house with me."

"We don't want to use you for bait. He's going to come looking for you and you know that. If we take you to a safe house, he won't be able to find you."

"Really? You mean until another detective leaks that information too. Thanks but no thanks. I didn't trust the police before, and the behavior out of your office hasn't changed my opinion one bit." Sam walked over to curl up on the couch with the blanket wrapped around her body.

Sadly, he watched as those beautiful curves disappeared from view.

"Besides, if he can't find me, he'll just kill other women. You..." her voice choked, "or someone else has already set me up as bait. So you might as well make good use of the opportunity." Bitterness edged her voice.

Shit. Brandt sat down beside her. "Sam, I'm wondering if this isn't part of Deputy Brooker's machinations. If the killer found you, it would be an easy solution to his problem."

Sam shot him a considering look. A sweater lying over the couch caught her eye. Dropping the blanket to her waist, she pulled the sweater over her head, tugging it down under the blanket. Oddly enough, it was that action that made him suddenly very nervous.

"God damn it Sam. *I* didn't set you up. You know what a media frenzy is like. Once they sniff out a story like this, there is no letting go."

"Thanks, but I don't need the reminder." Sam curled into a tiny ball and stared out into the night.

3:15 am

NOW FULLY DRESSED, Sam curled up in a small ball in the corner of the couch where she could look out. Darkness still blanketed the valley, giving it an eerie glow. She wasn't going to leave her home. The police had created this situation, so they could damn well fix it. She wasn't being stubborn; she was being sensible. They wanted to protect her, fine. They could do it here.

Moses pushed his cold, wet nose against her arm. "Hey boy. That's right, isn't it? We couldn't possibly move you and Soldier. He's just starting to adapt to this place as it is."

She peered around at the simple room. This was her home and

she wasn't leaving. She knew better than most what this killer was capable of doing.

Brandt walked down the stairs. Her heart twanged. She didn't want to see him. She didn't like this sense of betrayal. If Brooker had done this, then it wasn't Brandt's fault. Except he'd promised to keep her name out of this. Unfair or not, there it was.

She geared up for the fight to come. Still, the feelings of resentment were hard to maintain as he walked toward her. Her nostrils flared. Her heart and mind flooded with images of last night. It couldn't be. She refused to be swayed by sweet memories. Damn it.

Ruthlessly, she forced down tears.

Brandt gingerly stepped over the sprawled dog to sit on the couch with her.

"You may not be feeling very generous toward me at the moment, however, I need you to understand and believe in one thing – I didn't set you up. I wouldn't – couldn't – do that to you. And I will do everything in my power to keep you safe."

When she stared at him, but stayed quiet, his shoulders sagged.

"Please," he whispered, "Just believe in me, in us, that much. We'll work out everything else. I promise."

This time, she couldn't hold back the tears. They pooled at the corner of her eyes before slowly running down her cheeks. Burying her face in her arms, she tried hard to stifle the sniffles. When his arms wrapped around her, lifting her to his lap, the dam broke.

Brandt held her tight, murmuring nonsensical things in her hair.

Finally, her sobs ran down until she rested quietly in his arms. Where did she go from here? How to go on? She'd lived so isolated for so long, she didn't think she could handle being pointed and laughed at again. She shook her head slightly. Tough as that might be, losing Brandt would be the worst. For the first time, she was experiencing this connection, this sense of belonging with another person. He fit like her other half, making her whole.

"Honestly, I don't think many people will recognize you. Apparently, it's an old picture."

Sam stilled then tilted her head. "Did you read my mind?"

He smiled and dropped a tender kiss on her nose. "No. I figure that's your department."

She leaned against him, not sure how she felt anymore. She hadn't really thought he was to blame. That responsibility belonged with the asshole who'd released the information. Still, how much did she really know of Brandt? Sure, her mind mocked. You only know him well enough to have wild, uninhibited sex with him. Sam winced at the reminder.

"What's the matter now?"

Deciding to be honest, she answered, "I'm realizing that I've only known you for a few days."

His arms tightened. "You know all that matters."

She wondered about that.

6:10 am

SEVERAL SLEEPLESS HOURS later, Brandt walked into the kitchen expecting, even spoiling, for a fight. "I hope you've reconsidered."

She pulled the bread out of the toaster and buttered the two pieces and didn't answer.

"I hope you're prepared to be reasonable." Brandt knew he should shut up, yet found himself aggressively defensive. He needed her to understand, to care about staying safe.

She shot him a look. "Reasonable? Take another look at what has happened to my life, then tell me that."

"Damn it, I have. I wouldn't have wished this on you for anything. But it doesn't change the facts. You have to be protected, and we have to catch this asshole. This could be the same guy I'm hunting, or it may be an entirely different asshole. I don't care – we have to get him off the street. You have to stay safe." His voice rose at the end of his sentence. He visibly struggled to regain control, but it was tough. She was fighting him over something that was inarguable.

She finished buttering the toast on the plate and carried it over to the table. "I don't have a death wish, but I do want this to be over. I can't live in a cell, and I have to have some space for my..." Out of words, Sam wafted her hand in the air. "For my abilities or whatever you want to call them. I can't live the same as everyone else. Don't you understand? These things happen and I don't know when they will. I have to feel safe in my world." Glancing around at the cabin, she added, "It's not much, but it is home. I feel good here, rested. Being in the real world all the time hurts me." She paused briefly. “I don’t want to leave this place.”

Brandt leaned against the table, trying to give her a chance to express her needs. He didn’t think she’d had much time or opportunity to have anyone care about what mattered to her.

She turned to face him, her hand out in a beseeching way that wrenched his heart.

Her voice continued the tug. “I trust you to keep me safe, regardless of the problems with your department. But if I go to a safe house, I won’t have an easy time of it.” Sam reached out, covering his hand with her own. “Brandt I just want this over. I don’t want anyone else to get hurt – including me.” At the furious look on his face, she backed off slightly. “I think you should use me as bait. Go ahead and involve Stefan. He has a great inner warning system, so use it.”

Seeing his mouth open to protest, she held up her hand to forestall him. “But I will leave that up to you.”

Brandt placed his hand flat on the table and slowly sat down, deep in thought. She had a valid argument in terms of her abilities. She wasn’t the same as everyone else. Was it unreasonable to force her to go to a safe house? No. However, it would be intolerable for her. He had his orders, still… He straightened up and looked around the cabin, considering location and the problems of guarding her here. Using her as bait was out of the question. A policewoman now…that was possible. Stefan was also a hell of a good idea. He narrowed his eyes, considering her earnest face.

He knew what he had to do. Right or wrong.

“Alright. I’ll talk to the captain. Maybe we can find another way.”

She turned to look at him in surprise. “Really?”

At his nod, her smile burst free, warming and calming the fear inside him.

“Thank you.”

He smiled grimly at her. “Don’t thank me yet. The captain isn’t going to be happy and may order you to be picked up regardless. Even if that means bringing you in for questioning where we can hold you for forty-eight hours.”

She swallowed hard. “I understand and thank you… Thank you for considering my needs.” She shrugged. “Maybe, he’ll understand.”

Brandt didn’t think so, but he’d made his decision and he’d stand by it.

But he wasn't looking forward to telling the captain.

10:15 am

SAM KEPT TO the rear of the vet clinic as much as possible. It helped that business was brisk and there were plenty of animals needing her attention.

It also helped her ignore the six-foot-four security guard that stood just inside the door watching her every move. He'd arrived at her house just before seven this morning. Open-mouthed, she hadn't had time to protest. As this guy had walked in, Brandt walked out. Not a good way to start the day.

She tried to stay focused and give the animals a little extra of her time. These poor things needed a warm, caring voice and a shot of love. She needed to stay away from the chaos in her mind. Somehow, she'd thought Brandt would be the one to stay by her side.

She stole a glance at the tall, silent ghost beside her. He'd introduced himself, shown her his ID and had stayed quiet ever since. Watchful, ever present, quiet – Sam, so used to silence, found his unnerving.

Lucy pushed open the door and walked toward Sam. She cast a nervous glance at the man standing silently to the side. "Sam, can you give us a hand? We need another person for a moment."

Sam nodded and followed her into the surgical ward. There was no animal on the table. She turned around in confusion. "What do you need help with?"

Three women converged on her.

"Sam, are you okay?"

"Why do you have a bodyguard?"

"Was that you they were talking about on the news last night?"

Their questions came hard and furious. She stared from one to the other, more than a little overwhelmed. It didn't take long to realize their questions came from a place of caring.

Dr. Wascott walked in. He headed straight for Sam, where he gave her a quick hug. "I can't stay and talk. But you take care of yourself. That psycho could be after you."

A wry smile lit Sam's face. "That's why the bodyguard."

"OMG!"

The girls' excitement and fear melded and blended until sentiments were impossible to tell apart. It took several minutes of explanations before they finally ran down. They gave her a big hug each and ran back to their duties. Sam stood there bemused, a warm glow inside and out.

So that's what having friends felt like. She could get used to this.

11:35am

PLANS, PLANS, AND more plans. He'd done what research he could. There was little enough to find. Bill hoped she was enjoying her celebratory status. Because soon he'd make her famous. He could see the headlines now: Psychic Who Couldn't See What Was Coming.

Serve her right. He preferred to study his victims, to learn everything he could about them. That was the best part. He loved finding out where the women worked, who their friends were, and especially about the lovers they slept with. Every tidbit helped him to know them just a little bit better. Once he'd collected all the little details then he could choose the perfect time and method for her death.

There was not time for all this now. He couldn't take the chance.

She also didn't fall into the same category as the other women. They were chosen. She was just an irritation to be taken care of.

He smiled. Cutting her brake line would be too easy. He already knew that she owned an old Nissan truck. He'd found that out within minutes of hearing her name. He used that method sometimes, just not with the chosen ones. Besides he couldn't guarantee the success like he needed to.

Many people deserved death. Not every one of them deserved his personal attention. Sometimes, men needed killing too. His old boss was one of them. The asshole had the audacity to fire him. Bill hadn't liked the damn job anyway. He frowned. That reminded him. That asshole had escaped. His damn girlfriend had borrowed his Mercedes, dying in his place. His stomach soured. Now, he'd be sure to take care of that bastard personally. But there were more pressing issues to take care of first.

Parksville was only a few miles away. The psychic wouldn't

know what hit her.

The cops were particularly stupid. She'd be placed under police protection and the cops would be waiting for him. Bill was too smart for that. His mind spinning with ideas, he couldn't help but appreciate the extra challenge. It definitely added a little spice to brighten up his day.

CHAPTER 25

5 pm, June 24th

SAM SLOWLY FOUND a level of comfort with having a constant companion. Her daytime watchdog changed shifts regularly, and Brandt stayed for the nights. There'd been a suggestion of a policewoman moving into the house in Sam's place. She'd nixed that. What if the poor woman was killed? Sam didn't want that on her conscience.

Sam still looked over her shoulder at odd times. At unexpected moments, she felt eyes on her. No matter how fast she spun around, she could never find her stalker.

Still, as time passed, she adjusted.

The detectives were busy doing their thing. They'd found out where Brooker was staying. He'd denied anything to do with the media, and hadn't planned for Sam to identify that the picture shown on television had been taken during her time in Nikola County. He'd blustered for hours, but Captain Johansen, paired with Brandt and Sam's evidence, convinced the overweight bully into giving them a cowering confession. Kevin wanted him to confess for trying to run her off the road, but Brooker wasn't going for it – yet. A crew had gone to her cabin searching the area for evidence where Soldier had been shot, in an effort to pin that on him, too.

Sam didn't ask for the details. That asshole was a minor blip in her life now.

Brandt's mother was having an easier time of it, too, now that the colonel had woken up. He couldn't remember what happened, which wasn't unreasonable considering his injury and age, but he knew her. She'd stayed at his side these last few days, only leaving for showers and changing of clothes. Brandt would be heading over tomorrow to take both back to the care center.

As for Sam, she was surrounded by friends and her bodyguards were reserved, yet friendly. That suited her. Best of all, Brandt came home every night and slept on the couch he'd moved into her room.

She hadn't invited him into her bed again and he'd never mentioned it either. The unspoken word 'later' hung in the air. There would be time down the road to talk and sort through their convoluted relationship. Not that she didn't wake up in the night and reach for him, because she did, then hugged her pillows close when she found herself alone. The temptation to go to him often overwhelmed her. It was the knowledge that her advances wouldn't be welcomed that stopped her. He considered himself to be on duty.

She planned to present him with a ready dinner tonight. Return some normalcy into their lives. Not that they'd had a chance to experience such a commonplace thing yet. That was for other people, other relationships…

By the time she'd made pork chops with a creamy mustard sauce and stuffed tortellini on the side, with slices of cucumber and tomato in apple cider vinegar, she was feeling quite proud of herself.

Brandt arrived just in time, only stopping outside to speak with the guard briefly. Sam's heart lifted at the sight of him. Sam walked to the front door. "Hi, how are you doing?" There, that was just the right note, casual and friendly. She waved good-bye as the guard hopped into his car and drove off.

Brandt walked in, sniffing the air. "Whatever it is, it smells wonderful." He dropped his coat and laptop bag on the end of the couch and walked over to sweep her into his arms, where he twirled her around so he could check out the pots bubbling on the stove.

Laughing, she squeezed him before stepping back. "It's ready. Wash up."

"How was your day?" he asked, walking over to the kitchen sink.

Sam started serving the plates. "The same as usual. Yours?"

"Same old. How's Soldier?"

"Not impressed." Soldier had objected strenuously to the added male presences. One of the guards had made the mistake of walking too close. Soldier had barely missed snapping his hand off. Sam had been horrified, apologizing profusely and had gone to calm the dog down. The guard had been wary ever since and had passed the word on.

Soldier spent his days in peace and quiet, his mornings and nights on full alert. She appreciated the fact that he never ventured far away from her. The two of them had an unspoken truce. She helped him to heal and regain his strength while he kept her company and worked to keep her safe. That it kept the men away from her and him was a benefit to both of them.

By the time bedtime rolled around, Brandt and Sam had spent several comfortable hours talking. They discussed everything from global warming to hybrid cars and even favorite recipes. By bedtime, Sam had a warm glow of friendship around her. She'd really enjoyed tonight. Still smiling, she fell asleep immediately.

Sometime in the wee hours of the morning, Sam surfaced from her dreams to hear the unfamiliar sounds of voices in her living room. Listening from under her covers, she heard Brandt move around.

Something was wrong.

Concerned, Sam hopped out of bed, grabbed up her old terry cloth robe and slipped downstairs. Brandt stood at the bottom of the stairs, fully dressed.

"What's the matter?" she asked, frowning.

"The hospital' raised the alarm. Your suicide victim has been attacked."

Sam wrapped her arms around her chest. "Oh no," she whispered. "Is she okay?"

He shook his head. "I don't know the details. We put a guard on her too, once we matched the earring to her."

"You did?" Sam felt warmed at his concern for the unknown woman. He was a good man. "Why didn't you tell me?"

"Because you would just worry even more." He reached into his pocket and pulled out his keys. "The guard has been injured, as have two nurses."

"Oh, God." This asshole was a sick bastard. "What makes you think he's not on his way here?"

"The hospital security chased him outside and saw him take off in his car. The police have picked up his trail, heading north to Washington. He's probably planning to run across the border." He kissed her on the cheek. "Just in case, there's another cop on his way here. I'll wait until he shows up and then head out."

Sam wrapped her robe tighter around her. "I can't believe how many people he's hurting."

"He's a serial killer, and the noose is tightening. He's going to do everything he can to survive."

Lights shone through the trees into the living room.

"Here he is. I'll see you in a couple of hours." He walked to the door and opened it. "Get some sleep. Remember, the cops are on his ass and should have him in handcuffs within hours."

Sam frowned. "He's pretty smart for that."

"Not this time."

David, an older man, walked in, smiling at her. "Good news, huh?"

"Yeah. But I'll feel better when he's behind bars." With one last glance at Sam, he said, "I won't be long, but it's important to get to the hospital as soon as possible. We need every bit of evidence we can to nail this bastard. I shouldn't be more than a couple of hours."

Sam nodded, giving him the reassurance he needed to leave. She couldn't quite believe that this was almost over. This worry had been with her for so long. It didn't seem possible that the end was near.

She smiled at David. "Thanks for coming. I'm heading to bed. Maybe I'll be able to sleep for the first time in weeks."

David tipped his cap. "Go rest easy. We'll get this guy."

Sam nodded, as expected, and walked to her room. She didn't have the same level of confidence. She knew this asshole had evaded cops for decades. A car chase was small change for him. He'd taken out a guard and injured two nurses tonight alone.

Who knew what other damage he could inflict this night?

2 am

BRANDT DROVE FAST, carefully. The long, twisting dirt road didn't offer much opportunity for speeding. He hated to leave Sam. Reaching for his cell phone, he called Captain Johansen for the latest.

"I don't have an update. I'll get one and call you back. Where are you?"

"Almost twenty minutes out from the hospital." Brandt hung up, turned on his sirens, and slammed his foot down on the pedal. His stomach churned with nerves. Leaving Sam was the last thing he wanted to do. They'd better have this bastard locked up by the time this night was over.

His cell phone rang.

"Hello." Brandt glanced in his rear view mirror. Other than a semi that he'd passed a few miles ago, the highway was deserted.

"Brandt, turn around," yelled the captain. "The cops pulled the car over. A stupid assed kid had been paid a hundred bucks to drive the car north as far and as fast as he could. The cops tracked the car. It was stolen yesterday."

"Shit!" Brandt hit the brakes. His tires squealed loudly as the vehicle spun sideways before coming to a violent, rocking stop across the highway. He turned the wheel and hit the gas. "Call David and warn him. I'm on my way."

If Brandt thought he drove fast on the way into town, he burned rubber heading to Sam.

A diversion. A fucking diversion to leave Sam open – and defenseless.

Christ.

He tried calling Sam's cell phone. No answer. Shit! She hadn't turned the damn thing on. He called David. No answer.

Oh, God, please let him be in time.

2:24 am

SAM CURLED UP in bed. She couldn't help feeling terrible about the guard and nurses. She didn't even know how the victim had fared in that confrontation. Hopefully, everyone would survive. Sam really wanted a happy ending to all of this. With the blankets pulled up to her chin, she found herself listening for the phone downstairs announcing the good news. Uneasy, without explanation, Sam found herself giving extra thanks for her bodyguard downstairs. Brandt…well, he'd be home whenever he was done.

Home. That had such a nice cozy ring to it. Maybe when this mess was over… After twenty minutes of not being able to stop her mind from circling uselessly, she compromised and took a, herbal sleep aid. It wouldn't knock her out the same as a sleeping pill.

Brandt. A warm contentedness filled her mind. An irritating pinch on her arm made her frown, but then his hands slid over the smooth surface of her hips. Mmmm. Heat flushed through her veins, awaking nerve endings she'd forcibly capped for the last few days.

Moving sensuously under his soothing caresses, Sam moaned in joy. She reached for him, but let him turn her hands aside as his caresses explored the soft valley of her abdomen. He was purely delicious. He was also too good at what he did. Lost in the sensations of building lust and the unique experience of enjoying her lover's attention, Sam slid deeper under his spell. Placing her hand over his, sliding her fingers gently through and over his, Sam explored his strong muscled hands before sliding slowly up his wrists. They felt different.

He still had clothes on.

With a slight moue, she tugged at the sleeve that interfered with her exploration. Gently, he grabbed her hands and raised them over her head, holding her in place. She murmured in delight and tried to tug. It didn't work.

He bent his head and nuzzled the plump side of her breast through her pajama top.

Sam moaned and twisted under him. Her stomach roiled, at odds with the rest of the sensations happily flickering though her body. She frowned in confusion.

His mouth fondled the pouting nipple under the cotton material.

"Please," she pleaded.

Silence.

A tiny bit of doubt crept under Sam's guard. It seemed so real. But so were her visions. A weird fog rolled through her mind. Shit. Realization was slow to come. Brandt was gone. This was another vision. No. Surely not. Sleepiness mixed with the images overlapping in her mind – all in bright Technicolor.

Heat flashed over her skin at the memories of her previous lovemaking with Brandt. Overlapping were sensations on her skin even now. Hands moved to cup her breasts and squeeze gently. She sighed. But her mind wouldn't relax. Caught in limbo between worlds, she struggled to stay real in another woman's dream. Wanting it to be Brandt, yet knowing the killer had taken another victim.

His mouth tugged and teased, tantalizing her nipple, bringing her back to a sensual high, all the while her mind operating in the background, struggling to remember Stefan's lessons.

Teeth clamped lightly on the end of the sensitive nipple.

Then bit down hard.

The woman screamed. Sam screamed.

Her spine arched and she tried to curve away from the pain. Her hands were held above her head, keeping her captive. Her eyes opened. Then closed again in despair.

Oh God. It *was* him. She was caught in another vision.

Sam struggled to separate the vision from the reality.

Oh, God. Oh, God. The poor woman. Sam knew she could do nothing, but endure. Locked inside her mental labyrinth, Sam felt the victim's pain and horror, as she finally understood.

She twisted and struggled, hearing the words. "Please don't hurt me." Were they from the victim or her? Sam didn't know. It didn't matter. Both of them wanted this to be over. They wanted to be saved. And they both knew it wasn't going to happen.

Low masculine laughter filled the room.

"Please," pleaded the same voice. "Let me go."

Her arms were wrenched above her head and held in a punishing grip. The attacker pressed down hard on the wrist bones. Pain squeezed through injured nerve endings, ripping scorch lines throughout her body.

Sam, desperate to separate herself from the woman's pain, tried to seek the blackness of the etheric world. This torture was just beginning. Sam didn't want to be here and most definitely not this early on. She normally came in at the end, those precious few minutes to help the victims cross the line to death.

She was part of this experience to help the victims and if she could, to help the police find justice for the victims. She wasn't here to suffer. Her mind waffled then raced in different directions from what had to be drugs, sliding insidiously through the victim's veins. She wanted out. Stefan had given her some tips to try, what were they? Right. Grounding herself by following the line of her skeleton down to her feet and imagining them coming from the center of the earth. Except, she hadn't expected to do this under these circumstances. Concentrating was almost impossible. The woman's terror, her pain dominated. Sam struggled to free herself of the dark sucking energy.

"Samantha."

Sam's mind froze. Then her heart slammed into her chest.

Who called her?

Her eyelids flickered and she was suddenly more afraid than she'd ever been in her life. Never had a vision called her name. She wrinkled her nose. A fetid odor filled her head. Something awful wafted through the air. A metallic bloody smell. God, she didn't want to open her eyes and see what she knew would be there.

"Look at me, Samantha."

She forced her eyes wide.

And found herself in her own bedroom, staring up at the same whitewashed ceiling. She was home. Oh God. She was not alone.

This time, she was the victim.

2:29 am

STEFAN SLAMMED INTO awareness. Shoving his bedding back, he came to a standing position before he'd even realized what had happened. He couldn't see where he was, his bedroom was seeped in darkness. His curtains were open – still no light shone in.

Looking around, his hand went to his throat. Jesus. Sam. She was in danger. He reached for his phone. No answer. Shit. He called Brandt. It was busy. Fuck.

Pushing into a sitting position, he crossed his legs and sent himself deep into a trance. He had to find Sam. Soon. She needed help. Evil was wrapping her up in the dangerous torrent. He had to make her aware…and fast.

He tried to block out the unwanted thought, then realized it was stopping his gifts. Better to acknowledge the possibility so he wouldn't be crippled by the fear. He knew that before this night was over she'd be fighting for her life.

Or…even worse, he'd be helping her cross over to the other side – to her death.

2:39 am

NO!

She tried to struggle. Panic dimmed her sight as she realized there'd be no waking up this time. There'd be no last minute rescue for her. It was her turn to die.

It wasn't supposed to happen this way. Where the hell was Brandt? Even as she panicked, vestiges of old resentment rose to the surface. Why was there no one there to rescue her? Wait. David. Her security guard. Oh no, the poor man.

I'm here.

Stefan.

Call Brandt!

He knows. He's on his way. Keep fighting.

I'm trying.

Fight harder.

Stefan's voice started to fade. *No. Wait. Remember your lessons. Disconnect.*

Her mind cried out for him. There was no answer.

She glared at the asshole that had hurt so many people. She'd never even seen him before. This time he had no mask. Why? As she tried to focus in on the details of his face, his features zoomed out, leaving her with a faint impression of dark wide-set eyes with heavy brows and thick cheekbones and prominent nose – his eyes black empty holes. His face look oddly colored, out of proportion.

Drugs. Of course, he'd given her drugs. Different ones this time. Her mind tried to puzzle through the convoluted maze of thoughts, then quickly frazzled out. It didn't matter anymore.

"What kind of useless psychic are you? You couldn't even see this coming." His mouth twisted into a malevolent mockery of a smile.

"What did you do to my bodyguard?" She spat the words at him. She twisted in vain.

He reared backwards. "Must have been a cop. Just as useless as the rest of them." He shifted slightly for a better look at her face. With a big smirk, he added, "You were supposed to be a bigger challenge, being a psychic and all." Coarse laughter filled the room, grating on her ears and sending terror running through her soul. "I was looking forward to this." He stared around in disgust. "Nothing to it. Or you. God, what a loser. Look at this place. It's a dump."

Evil glistened from his eyes, sourced deep in his soul. It would be a bad day for those who'd crossed him. Like her.

She, remembering Stefan's lessons, searched for lightness inside her center of being. His blackness was overwhelming. The light sustained her. If she let the blackness gain control, it would be over. If it were her time to die like all the others, then she'd rather go kicking and screaming – and taking a piece of him with her.

She reached out in her mind's eye. She could barely sense the bodyguard. He was still alive. The dogs' energy was outside her bedroom door. She could almost hear them whining. The bastard had shut it, locking them out. No sign of Brandt or Stefan.

"Damn you to hell." She glared at him, furious at herself, and the situation.

He laughed. "Not like you planned, huh?"

She twisted her head to check the window. It was wide open.

If she screamed, the dogs still would not be able to get through the door. There was no lock, still she had yet to teach any animal to open the door latch. Soldier was an incredibly determined animal. He was strong enough to break the door down if he wanted to. Or if he were mad enough. If she could find the right trigger. What had she called him in the vet's office so long ago?

At the top of her lungs, she screamed, "Major, git!"

"Whoever you're calling – let him come. I'll kill him too."

His knife slid upward without warning, cutting her throat under her chin.

Sam screamed. The drugs gave him enormous size. Nothing was needed to emphasize his natural cruelty. He was too big for her to move. Furious and in pain, she struggled for freedom. He laughed again, placing a knee on her chest. In a startling motion, he stabbed the knife into the mattress beside her ear, cutting locks of hair and grasping her throat in both hands.

"I want to squeeze the life from your body myself, you stupid bitch."

Black dots appeared before her eyes. Static filled her ears. She automatically grabbed his hands, trying to free her throat from his grasp. She gurgled for air, bucking to get rid of him. To no avail. With her strength gone and almost no air, she collapsed back down. This was the end then.

Her mind went cloudy. The killer's face blurred. The rage and joy in eyes blended into something pure evil. Her arms fell to her sides.

The last of her air bubbled from her lungs. Suddenly, the weight was lifted off – she was free. Sam gasped frantically for air, her hands circling her own throat, protectively. She rolled over into a tightly curled up ball, coughing as she gulped for air. "Oh, God," she whispered, her voice barely recognizable.

Noises penetrated the fog in her mind. Growling, and yelling, thuds and blows surrounded her. She shuffled on the bed to huddle at the headboard, trying to avoid bodies that crashed down beside her. Teeth bared, fur flying, Soldier had locked onto the killer's shoulder. Moses had locked on the man's leg. The killer grunted and punched, kicking any area he could as the three rolled in mortal combat.

The bedroom door swung in the cold night air.

Sam winced at the heavy thud of boot on bone. Soldier howled.

God, Soldier was already injured. She had to help him. Her body refused to respond to her orders. The shine of the blade, still embedded in the mattress, caught her eye. She focused on the shine.

Her hand grabbed the hilt just as the killer grabbed her arm pulling her back. Sam punched with her free hand and tried to kick. There was too much dog in the way and too many drugs in her system. She stumbled.

Finding an opportunity, she collected the last of her cohesive energy and lunged, digging her right hand, fingers stiff like claws, into the soft spots of his throat. Her left hand stabbed upward with the knife. He raised his arm defensively. The blade caught his arm and sliced upward, deflecting off bone. He screamed. "Bitch."

His much longer reach latched around her throat. Sam screamed at Soldier again, "Major. Kill."

From the corner of her eye, she hardly recognized the dog. His fangs dripped saliva and blood, and the howl coming from the back of his throat was…otherworldly.

Soldier was on a mission, and she was in the way.

His lip curled, his shoulders hunched up. Sam pushed herself away in a clumsy movement that tumbled her backwards onto the mattress. She needn't have worried. Soldier's jaw replaced her hands, ripping into her attacker's shoulder. The knife was jerked out of her hand.

Soldier's howls, dragged from deep down and forced through his clenched jaw, scared her shitless.

She turned slightly. The killer had the knife raised to bring down on Soldier's spine. "No!" She grabbed his knife arm with both hands and tried to stop him. "You bastard, leave him alone." Her arms trembled. Still, she fought. He grinned at her. She couldn't beat him. He was too strong, and knew it. Soldier continued to howl, splitting the air with his tone. The noise drove through her brain. She groaned, her knees collapsing under her weakening body.

"God, Brandt, where are you?" She needed him. She screamed silently into the dark of night. *Now.*

2:44 am

"JESUS." BRANDT SWORE he could hear Sam yelling in his head. It was bad enough hearing Stefan screaming though the phone at him a few minutes ago and knowing no one else could get to her before him.

The sounds coming from inside the house sent terror stabbing through his heart. "Hang on Sam! I'm coming," he yelled. Brandt raced through the living room, barely noticing the body collapsed in a pool of blood on the porch. The screams and howls from upstairs pierced the night. He took the stairs two at a time. The scene that greeted him made his stomach churn.

Blood splattered everywhere. Soldier and Sam were locked in a death fight with a large male, Moses reduced to a crumpled heap of fur on the floor.

Brandt jumped into the fray, knocking the knife from the killer's hand and pulling Sam loose. She stumbled a few feet then collapsed to the floor. The killer ignored him. Bent on destroying the fury chomping through his shoulder, he immediately locked his hands around Soldier's throat, squeezing tight.

Bloody bubbles foamed out of Soldier's mouth. Blood coated his fur. The sound coming out from his mouth, an unholy alliance with hell.

His gun trained on the two still caught in a life and death grip. "Sam, talk to me. Are you okay?"

"Yes," she mumbled, managing a small nod to reinforce her statement. "I think so." She reached up to her throat, barely able to touch the raw skin. "Save Soldier."

He spared her a quick glance, slightly reassured that Sam had crawled to Moses and was talking – not very coherently, still she could communicate. "Stay back. I have to get Soldier off first. I don't want to have to shoot him."

Brandt turned his attention to the still-howling dog locked on to the killer's shoulder. "Let the dog go. I'll get him off you."

"Like hell.," the killer gasped. "This asshole should have died a long time ago. Worthless piece of shit."

Brandt didn't know what he was talking about, and it didn't matter right now. Somehow he had to save the dog. For Sam's sake. The killer be damned. "Let go of the dog, or I'll shoot."

"Fuck you." The killer grinned at him through bared teeth as he removed one hand from Soldier's throat and with a quick twist of his wrist slid a dagger free from his belt and threw it.

"Brandt!"

The dagger stabbed into the wall behind Brandt, missing him completely. Brandt didn't miss the killer. The bullet hit him low in the left shoulder. The grin fell off his face as he stumbled to the floor.

Soldier, now with the upper hand and caught in a blood lust of his own, lunged again. He reclamped his jaws into a tighter grip.

"Soldier!" Brandt ordered. "Soldier! Stand down." He repeated it twice before the dog stopped trembling and unlocked his jaw. Brandt stepped closer, the gun trained on the killer.

Soldier curled his lip at him.

"It's okay, boy. You've done good. Move, Soldier."

The dog dripped blood from open tissue shining wetly in the dark.

"Soldier. Down."

In the distance, the sound of sirens grew stronger.

Brandt didn't think the dog was going to listen. Finally in a crippled shuffling movement, the dog slid to the floor. He was hurt, and badly. Brandt kicked the knife away. The killer glared at him, blood pouring from both shoulders.

Sirens filled the air, colored flashing lights filled the room.

"It's okay Sam. The ambulance and police are here."

"Sam?"

Silence filled the room.

Brandt spun around to look, his gun still trained on the killer. "Sam?" Fear spiked his voice to a scream. Crumpled in a bloody pile on the floor, Sam lay between the two dogs. All three looked dead.

CHAPTER 26

SAM WALKED SLOWLY down to the dock, Brandt at her side. Soldier hobbled behind them. Moses, moving much slower, brought up the rear. Sam wouldn't want it any other way.

She tried not to dwell on the events of that night. She didn't remember much and that's the way she wanted to keep it. She'd been rushed to the hospital where the doctors had frantically tried to stop the spread of the poison from the cocktail of drugs guaranteed to kill her. If it hadn't been for Brandt she would have died. Chills ran down her spine at the reminder.

It had been late the next day before she'd surfaced – screaming. Brandt had been at her side, a place he'd stayed during the first week of her recovery. Once out of hospital, they'd enjoyed the time alone at the lake. A healing time. But then he'd had to go back to work.

Sam had returned to the clinic soon after.

At the clinic, she'd refused to talk about the events, hoping the chatter would die down and with time – it had. Still, David, a good family man and an off-duty cop pulling extra time, lost his life when he'd stepped outside for a cigarette. He'd wandered out to the deck and never had a chance to draw his first smoke-filled breath.

The dogs had been rushed to the clinic where they'd both undergone surgery. Thank God, the vets had done it for free. Sam didn't have that kind of money, and although Brandt had joked that his department should pay the dogs' medical costs, she hadn't wanted to ask for it.

She didn't know what the future held, although more people than she'd ever thought possible stopped her on the street to ask what she saw in their futures. Her fame as a psychic had spread after the details of the attack had leaked to the press.

Speaking of leaks, Dillon had been reprimanded and transferred to another station.

As for Deputy Brooker, Brandt had matched shells picked up from the woods around her place to his gun, finally. He'd followed Brandt to her place when Soldier had caught his scent in the woods. His truck was the same as the one who'd tried to run her off the road. He wasn't admitting anything more at this point. She didn't know what he was going to be charged with at the end of the ongoing investigation, yet she could count on Brandt to make sure he'd be out of commission for a long time. Sam had agreed to testify and help their case in any way. She wasn't looking forward to seeing Brooker face to face, only knew she could do it and survive. She was stronger now – in many ways.

Captain Johansen had apologized profusely. Every time he saw her, in fact. He'd even thanked her. Who knew how long William Durant would have continued killing women if not for her visions. She could grin at the captain now. It had taken awhile, but she was slowly getting used to being around people.

Brandt had helped with that. So, too had Maisy, Brandt's mother. The colonel had recovered. He'd recognized the ring as being on the hand of the dog handler that brought the animals in to visit the patients at the center. A very subdued Maisy confessed that the dog handler had been there when she'd established the pool on when the colonel would remember what he'd forgotten about the ring. She'd actually asked him if he wanted in on the bets. That had sealed the colonel's fate…or nearly.

Even Soldier's story might have been connected. Although, chances are they'd never know for sure. The dog had certainly known what to do when the time had come. William Durant hadn't survived surgery. Sam found it hard to care. The world was better off without him and this way she didn't have to go through two trials.

Brandt was backtracking the guy's life, searching for links to other murders in his files. He was hoping for evidence to close dozens of cases – not to mention bring closure to dozens of families.

It would take some time. As a dog trainer, Bill had exposure to people, care homes, and even the hospital where he took animals in to visit with the patients. This allowed him to travel to various locations without raising suspicion. Teaching obedience training gave him access to hundreds of women. An opportunity he'd taken full advantage of.

Louise Enderby's long-time partner had come forward after

seeing the news. He'd been on the board for the city's animal shelters – he'd fired William from a part time job at the pound where he was to rehabilitate last-ditch cases. He'd been caught abusing the animals instead. An organization that relied heavily on donations, the pound hadn't wanted any negative publicity and agreed not to press charges if Bill disappeared – for good.

They could only speculate, yet it appeared that Louise had become an innocent victim of a war she hadn't even known about.

The best that Sam could understand, Bill picked his victims out of numerous loving couples where the man had been supposedly considered to be 'the best' man – theoretically underlining that, Bill himself, wasn't good enough.

Sam didn't understand the psychology of it all. Who could understand a twisted mind like his? Who would want to?

Stefan had even shown up at her cabin during the first week of convalescence, threatening to do her serious harm if she ever got herself into that situation again. Said it had cost him ten years off his life. He'd also pulled her training forward to avoid a repeat of this mess.

Sam smiled. Stefan was a special man and she loved knowing he was in her life. They had a closeness that she had never known was possible. She could only imagine it was similar to the relationship between twins.

As for her and Brandt, well they were slowly adjusting to life as a couple. They both had things to learn and Sam wasn't sure she was ready to live together, although the topic was under discussion. At the same time, she didn't sleep nearly as well alone. Not that she had the chance to.

It was Brandt who refused to sleep alone. According to him, he was planning on always waking up with her beside him. She hoped he meant it. She wanted to believe in a 'happily ever after.'

Her visions weren't ever going to stop, but she'd become accustomed to them. It wasn't about accepting them any longer, it was about understanding and utilizing them. Progress.

Her visions didn't make her an easy partner, then Brandt's job wouldn't be easy on her. They'd work it out. For the first time ever, she could see a future. It was bright and rosy. She'd like to have had a vision that told her Brandt was her future and she'd be spending the next forty years happily at his side, but as she'd found out, visions didn't work that way.

BRANDT GLANCED AT Sam, standing at his side, staring out over the water. He couldn't help but feel protective of this woman, so slight, so strong, and so damaged. She'd been a tormented soul who walked with one foot on the dark side of the universe. Now there was a lightness to her.

She was everything to him. He stepped closer, wrapping his arms protectively around her shoulders. He'd do anything to keep her safe. In this world and the next. They were a matched set. Their future wouldn't be the standard two-storey house and white picket fence life. No. But it would have its own rewards.

And he was going to make sure they received each and every one of them.

HIDE'N GO SEEK

Book #2 of Psychic Visions

Dale Mayer

Dedication

This book is dedicated to my four children who always believed in me and my storytelling abilities.

Thanks to you all.

Acknowledgments

Hide'n Go Seek wouldn't have been possible without the support of my friends and family. Many hands helped with proofreading, editing, and beta reading to make this book come together. Special thanks to Amy Atwell and my editor, Pat Thomas. I had a vision, but it took many people to make that vision real.

I thank you all.

CHAPTER 1

DEATH SHOULDN'T BE so greedy. Everyone came to him eventually.

Kali Jordan surveyed the wet gray rubble, her heart aching with sorrow. Three days ago this giant pile of debris had been a small but thriving Mexican town. Today it was a deathtrap.

Thunder rumbled across the mountain. She squinted at the black clouds gathering on the horizon. Already the weather and location had hampered rescue efforts with fog preventing the helicopters from landing.

The disaster site had been treacherous before the earthquake, yet if the approaching storm deluged the area as predicted, search and rescue conditions would deteriorate even more.

Rubbing her throbbing temple, she dropped her gaze to the crumpled mass of concrete and glass ahead of her. So many people missing and, as always, so little time to help them. Shiloh, her long-haired Labrador Retriever, had worked this same quadrant all morning with the concentration and focus typical of her breed. This afternoon, however, her tail drooped. Kali could relate.

Strong muscles bunched as Shiloh jumped up to another boulder. Her bright orange K-9 SAR vest stood out against the dusty gray backdrop. Even dirty, the vest was striking enough to be visible. Although Shiloh's fur was an unusual fox red, the grime had an equalizing effect, coating everyone and everything with a uniform layer of dust.

An aftershock rattled the ground, shifting the pile under the dog's sturdy feet. Shiloh scrabbled to stay upright.

Kali's heart stopped for a second, her breath catching in her throat. The earth stilled. Shiloh caught her balance and kept going. Kali waited an extra moment before exhaling. She didn't want to be here.

Many disaster sites had huge influxes of help from the global community. Many sites had organization, management of some sort, experienced people to move resources and offer assistance to the survivors. Many sites – but not this one.

Kali and Brad, along with Jarl and Jordan, another set of old hands in this game, were one of the few groups on the spot. The roads had washed out after their arrival, hampering the army's efforts.

Right now everyone else was working on a different quadrant. Her intuition – her grandma called it the Sight – had insisted she search here. She'd learned a long time ago to listen. But that didn't mean she liked where it sent her.

Shiloh barked.

Ignoring her headache, Kali hopped over the mess of ripped supports and roofing. Shiloh barked again, then sat on her haunches, head high. She wagged her tail, sweeping away the dirt around her.

She'd found a survivor.

Excitement bloomed. Unbelievable warmth surrounded Kali's heart. A miracle, after three days in this heat, and one sorely needed to boost the exhausted search and rescue volunteers' flagging optimism. A rush of adrenaline sent her surging up the next pile of rubble.

A large block shifted, tossing Kali sideways. She scrambled to recover her footing. Shiloh yipped, her version of 'are you okay?' Kali grinned at her when she'd righted herself.

"I'm fine, girl. Not to worry."

Jumping onto a different cement slab, Kali climbed ever higher, to where Shiloh waited.

"Hey, Kali, what have you got?"

Turning, Kali spotted her best friend and fellow SAR member Brad, with his German Shepherd, Sergeant.

"Shiloh's found a survivor here." Kali reached for the next handhold.

"Really? Hang on. I'm on my way." With his long strides, Brad covered the height differences in the piles within seconds. Sergeant passed them both as he jumped up to join Shiloh. He barked and sat on his haunches.

"Good Lord, this is great to see." Brad's voice brimmed with energized exhilaration. Holding out a hand, he helped Kali up and over a broken wall. "We passed that all important forty-eight-hour window this morning. I hate this stage of the search."

"Especially here." From her high position, Kali stared at the surrounding chaos while she caught her breath.

Both dogs whined.

Groaning, she started climbing again. Her muscles ached with tension. The rubble shifted again. "Shit," she whispered. "It's touch and go."

"I know. Slow and steady. Let's assess whether we can do this on our own or if we need to bring a crew over."

Not that there were many crews to call.

Disorganization ruled here. Survivors scrambled in desperation to find their lost family members, along with the few volunteers who had made the trek to help. Volunteers were invaluable on disaster sites. Silent unsung heroes as they often made their own arrangements and covered their own costs in a bid to help out.

The army would probably arrive in time to organize recovery operations. Meanwhile, everyone was doing what they could at a location where just being on site was a huge risk. The ground trembled with aftershocks several times a day, shifting the wobbly debris under their feet.

Kali finally reached Shiloh. Digging into her fanny pack, she removed Shiloh's reward, her black-and-white, well-chewed teddy bear. Shiloh gently grasped her cuddly toy before bounding to ground level where she lay down to rest, her bear tucked under her chin. Brad sent Sergeant to join her.

Peering through the helter-skelter heap of broken flooring and walls, Kali heard a faint voice. She studied the small pocket of darkness off to the left. "Hello? Is anyone there? Can you hear me?"

The tiny feminine echo bounced upwards. "*Si.*"

Kali let out a whoop. "It's a child. Brad, call for help."

Brad searched the surrounding area to see if anyone was within shouting distance. Several people scrambled toward them. He signaled for assistance then turned back to her. "A team is on the way. Does she speak English?"

She shrugged. Peering into the dark opening, Kali squinted at what appeared to be a young girl in the murky shadows. Slowly, a small face came into focus. A small hand waved up at her. "She's pointing at her leg. Ah. I see it now. Her leg is broken just below the knee." Kali called to the girl, "What's your name?"

The weak high voice trembled in a new spat of Spanish.

From Kali's poor Spanish, she thought the child said her name was Inez. She could only hope Inez was old enough to understand what had happened and not panic. Although if Kali were the one stuck in that hole, she'd be panicking plenty.

The girl stared up, fear and hope warring on her face. Kali's heart ached. She looked so tiny. So alone. She had to be terrified. Hell, Kali was terrified.

Needing to help in some way, Kali tried to reassure the child by speaking in a calm steady voice. "Take it easy, Inez. Help is here. Don't try to move." The little one might not understand the words, yet the smile and easy voice would help her to relax.

A noisy hub of activity heralded the arrival of several other workers. Lilting voices flowed as singsong conversation bubbled between the suddenly animated girl and the crew. A hubbub of activity commenced. Brad grabbed Kali's arm, pulling her out of the way.

She frowned, but let herself be moved. She didn't want to leave Inez alone. She was too big to squeeze through the opening to the frightened child.

On a separate slab twenty feet back, Brad and Kali watched as the crew went to work. The crowd on the ground swelled as news of a survivor spread. Spanish and English mixed into a confusing yet understandable wash of conversation. Kali tuned out most of it, staying focused on the yawning pit that held the promise of life…and the threat of death.

A buzz of excitement rose as one of the smallest rescue team members descended on ropes. The opening was ringed with hardhats as everyone leaned over to watch. Kali shivered. Instinctively, she backed up several more steps, shifting to a different piece of cement. Brad followed.

"What's the matter?" he whispered against her ear.

"There're too many of them, too much weight. This could cave at any moment."

Brad frowned as he surveyed the straining men muttering into the cavern. "There haven't been any major tremors for hours now. Maybe it's all over."

Kali snorted, her eyes never leaving the action before them. "Right. And this could be a warm up for an even bigger one." Telling herself everything would be fine didn't help much either. Her instincts said otherwise. Holding her breath, she waited for someone to surface. It seemed to take hours. Kali knew the broken leg would need to be splinted. She knew the child would need to be secured into a harness. Fear knotted her gut. She knew all that. It didn't matter. A chill clutched her heart. She wanted to yell for the workers to hurry.

The earth grumbled again, a deadly reminder of the risk they all took.

The band of workers stood, heaving on ropes. Slow painful inches at a time, the crew struggled to raise their load. The top of a head popped into view, followed by a very dirty, tired face with a pained smile shining through the grimy tear tracks. Cheers erupted from the crowd. The girl waved as the rescue team worked to bring her up the last few feet. Finally, her splinted leg rose into view.

Kali gasped, her breath catching in her throat, her hands clenching and unclenching as fear dug its own claws into her more strongly. The child was almost there. Almost safe.

A hard tremor rippled through the region.

"Oh, God, no," she whispered. "Please, not."

The crowd cried out. Their yells morphed into screams of horror.

Grating sounds mingled with shouts and screams, followed by heavy grinding as rocks slid against each other, building to that one final destructive crash.

Kali screamed, falling to one side as tons of shifting material sent her tumbling. Debris rained on top of her. Curled into a ball, she held both arms protectively over her head, crying out as a small block smacked her left arm. She thought she heard a cracking sound, but she was too busy scrambling toward Brad, who'd been tossed several feet below.

"Brad. Brad! Are you okay?" Holding her injured arm against her chest, she leaned over him. Her heart stalled, then raced with relief when he swore and opened his eyes.

He struggled to sit up, shaking off the stones and dirt covering him. "I'm fine." He took several deep breaths before struggling to his feet. "Your arm, is it bad?"

She dismissed it with a wave of the hand on her uninjured arm. "It'll be fine."

Shiloh barked.

Tears of relief filled Kali's eyes. She searched the area and spotted her several yards away, Sergeant at her side. Thank God, they were fine.

Brad helped Kali to stand. She winced. "Better your arm than your head. Come on. Let's get away from this hell hole."

Kali realized suddenly that they'd ended up close to ground level. A horrible silence had fallen.

Of one mind, they pivoted to see how the rescuers had fared.

A horrible sense of knowing clutched Kali. She yelled, lunging forward only to be caught and held tight in Brad's arms.

"No, Kali. You can't go there. It's not over." His arms tightened as she struggled against the truth.

The heap surrounding the black pit that had held the little girl was gone. Dust floated several feet into the air, blurring their view. The walls of the pit had imploded then heaped with more concrete and twisted steel, burying the area under tons of new debris.

As the dust cleared, there was nothing to see.

No equipment.

No rescuers.

No little girl in a rope harness.

They were all gone.

CHAPTER 2

KALI CLOSED HER eyes in a useless effort to ignore her surroundings. She hated hospitals, drugs, even doctors. Her parents had died after a car accident killed her father outright and left her mother barely hanging on to life for a few days before she succumbed to her injuries. Kali hadn't been in a hospital since.

Today she'd had little choice.

After the disastrous loss of the rescue workers and that poor little girl in Mexico, Brad had taken control. He'd determined her arm was badly sprained, shipping her home with Shiloh crated and at her side. He'd stayed behind to continue the rescue efforts. Numb with shock, Kali remembered little of the trip home. Dan, her boss and mentor, had been waiting for her at the airport, his sparse gray hair sticking straight out in all directions as usual. He'd driven her directly to the hospital. Kali had been beyond arguing. Good thing, too, her left forearm was cracked, just below the elbow.

The painkillers Brad had stuffed down her throat prior to loading her on the plane accounted, in part, for her silence since landing. The loss of the little girl, Inez, hurt her beyond words. The loss of the rescuers was another painful reminder of the dangers inherent in her profession. Those poor families.

Kali had seen more death than eighty percent of the people in the world. She hadn't had much experience with the process, just the aftermath. A hot tear leaked from the corner of her eye. That poor child. In her mind, Kali could clearly see the grimy smile and the excited wave as Inez surfaced.

So much loss. The tears dripped faster. Kali hated breaking down. The litany of reasons she worked disasters repeated like an old broken record. *To save the people I can, bring closure to the families, and stand for the victim.*

"There, there, dearie. Are you in pain? The doctor's going to be here soon. We'll get that arm casted in a couple of minutes. Then you can go home and rest."

All nurses should resemble grandmothers. This one oozed comfortable reassurance that gave Kali the impression everything would be all right. That was the problem with impressions. They lied.

She wasn't sure anything would ever be okay again. Despite the many disasters she had experienced, the many rescues she'd participated in, she'd never been faced with a survivor dying the way this child had. And had never been this badly affected. Naïve? Maybe. Those who survived were always rushed away to a hospital. Sometimes they succumbed to their injuries, but they did so where Kali wasn't watching. Of course those deaths had hurt. But they hadn't been as up close and personal as seeing this child vanish before her eyes.

During the plane ride home, she hadn't managed to quell the disquieting sense that maybe she should have stayed and searched through those cement slabs herself. Maybe the other rescuers had missed an opening, a crevasse somewhere. Maybe Sergeant had made a mistake. Maybe life had survived in that heap of unforgiving rock and concrete.

But life wasn't fair. When Brad had called Dan to pick her up at the airport, he'd filled him in on the details. Details that hadn't included a happy ending.

Kali wiped her eyes with her good arm, staring despondently at the wet streak across her sleeve. She had to stop thinking about it.

The middle-aged doctor strolled in. "Kali, the x-rays look good. You just need a cast to immobilize it and time to heal." The doctor's smile was both gentle and understanding.

The nurse beamed as if she'd created this happy outcome by herself. Kali stared at them both, dazed. So what if her arm was a simple break? It was still broken. She still wouldn't be able to return to Mexico or help Inez.

The nurse escorted Kali to the treatment room. Twenty minutes later her left arm sported a deep-purple cast. Dan hovered, asking questions and pestering Kali to stay awake. He snatched up the prescription when the doctor handed it over and said he'd get it filled at the hospital pharmacy.

Kali wanted to get home and be alone with Shiloh, who currently waited in the truck. Dan returned within minutes a small white package sticking out of his pocket. "Let's go, kiddo."

Conversations flowed around her, bits and pieces floating through her awareness. Something about shock, see her doctor and rest. Kali rose and followed Dan blindly. Shiloh barked as they approached, her tail wagging hard.

"Sorry for the long wait, sweetheart." Kali hugged her tight, giving her a good scratch on her ruff. "We're going home."

Home meant a fifteen-minute drive south of Portland's center to her house on the coast. When they arrived, it was all Kali could do to make it up the front stairs.

Dan put her pain meds on the table, then hauled in her gear. Shiloh bounded inside, barking once.

Kali stood at the bottom of the stairs, weaving on her feet. Pain, drugs and exhaustion blended toward an inevitable collapse.

"Kali, can you manage a shower or do you want to wait until later?"

They both looked at the purple fiberglass cast on the one arm – with the clean white fingers poking through – and then at the other not quite so clean arm.

"Sleep first, then a soak in the bath," she whispered.

"Let's get you upstairs."

Like a mother hen, Dan laid down a blanket to protect her sheets from the grime coating her hair and skin. Turning back to Kali he helped her remove her boots.

"I'll grab you a glass of water, while you get undressed." Dan walked into the bathroom while she struggled to shimmy out of her soiled jeans and t-shirt before crawling under her duvet. She pulled the covers up to her chin.

A moment later, Dan returned to place a glass of water and her pills on her night table. "Get some rest now. I'm going to the center for a few hours. I'll check on you later."

Shiloh, ever the opportunist, jumped up beside Kali and curled up into a ball. Kali rolled over to elevate her injured arm on the dog's shoulder and closed her eyes.

Dan turned off the lights. Before leaving the room, he added, "Look after yourself, Kali. Everyone has to deal with death and disaster in their own way. Go easy on yourself. You did your best. That's all anyone can ask of you."

With that he walked away, his footsteps fading away in the distance.

All anyone could ask of her? What about what she asked of

herself?

TODAY SUCKED. ONE more day in a long series of the same. Clouds gathered overhead. They suited his mood.

"Hey, Texan. I wanted to thank you for your involvement here." Adam spoke around the cigar butt in his mouth.

Texan? He'd worked hard to minimize that drawl. Still, if that's what this guy saw, it was hardly an insult. He could tolerate it, identify with it even. He sat on one of the many large rocks that dotted the unforgiving terrain. Brown dusty bushes similar to the sage brush found across Texas dotted the Mexican hillside.

The rescue teams had taken a severe hit with that last quake. Seven rescue workers and the little survivor from the original quake, dead. Kali Jordan injured and shipped home. Her departure had hit them all hard. Especially him. Even though she'd laugh if she knew.

Chaos had ensued in the short term, depression, and lethargy in the aftermath. Things had yet to be reorganized. No one cared anymore, apathetically accepting what life dished out. It was as if the simple beliefs from the locals had come true. He cast his thoughts to the old woman he'd found on the first day. She'd clutched his hand, speaking in broken English as she died. What was it she'd said? Something about it being God's will? The earthquakes, their punishment for a lifetime of sins?

Now, hours later, shadows blanketed the area. People littered the ground. Not moving, not talking, just staring into the emptiness of their lives. He looked over at Adam squatting under low hanging branches, smoking. Blue white fog winding upward through the leaves.

What an idiot. Adam was one of the lucky ones, pulled free early on. He should have been dead, and could have been maimed for life. Instead, that caring old woman had died and Adam had survived with only a cracked wrist. A break that still allowed him to move the cigarette to and from his mouth. Disgusting. Adam made him feel old today.

God, he hurt. He'd worked the south quadrant of the main center. Mostly houses. Mostly dead inhabitants. Shifting on the rock, he tried to ignore the other man. Fatigue had taken over as despair settled on his soul. He closed his eyes, grateful for the last few moments of daylight.

Adam wouldn't leave him in peace.

"That's a good thing you did here, helping everyone out like that. Good job." Adam spoke around the butt in his mouth.

Another stream of smoke drifted his way. What a filthy habit. Nodding in response to Adam, he narrowed his eyes and waved off the smoke. Adam's skin was scored with wrinkles and his bloodshot eyes would have fit a man who'd spent decades searching for the bottom of a bottle – not a man in his mid-twenties. "Did you ever consider giving up smoking? You got a second chance today. Don't you want to make the most of it?"

"I'm going to. Tonight I'm going to find me a hot woman, and I'm going to fuck her until *she's* almost dead." Adam howled, his open mouth showing yellowed and missing teeth. Evidence of heavy tobacco and probable drug use. The drug of choice here was marijuana, wasn't it? Or maybe it was cocaine? Not that it mattered, Adam hadn't taken care of himself before the disaster and had no intention of doing anything about it now.

What a waste.

"Remember the rescue angel, you know, one of them SAR people like you? Now I wish I could ride her tonight. Those long legs, wowzers. That walk of hers should be illegal. Definitely put a spell on my poor pecker." Adam frowned at the lack of response. "You should know the pair. The furry bitch is Shiloh. Don't know what the two-legged bitch is called. She must be from one of them foreign Nordic countries."

Staring off into the darkening sky helped tone down the rage in his belly. His fists clenched. How dare this asshole talk about Kali Jordan like that? Of course he knew her. Not as well as he'd like to. He'd worked on many sites with her. Besides, with so many rescue totals to her credit, it was hard not to know of her. She was famous. She was special. His grip on his temper slid. His stomach knotted, barely containing the bubbling acid in his gut. The bastard had no right to even speak of her.

"Hmmm mmm. Adam took another long drag of the cigarette barely clinging to his lips. He cackled then coughed, loud wheezing rasps driving up from his belly. His red-rimmed eyes lit with unholy amusement. "A couple of centuries ago, she'd have been burned at the stake for that walk of hers. I'm gonna catch me some shut-eye and dream of a witch." With a carefree wave, Adam flicked the still burning cigarette to the dirt before returning to his shadowy hollow. Within minutes, guttural snores wafted out from the burrow. The dust settled on top of him, even as the light evening shadows crept over him as he slept.

A witch? Watching Adam sleep, he tasted the word, rolling it around in his mouth. Hardly. Kali's skills were hard to explain, harder to understand, even for those who did the same work. Her record unbeaten. How many jobs had he done? How many times had he wondered why Kali was always so blessed in finding people when he was the one who prayed? He was the one who honored Him. He'd tried to emulate her, hoping for similar success – without much luck. Now another reason surfaced. One he hadn't considered.

Did she have unworldly skills? Nah, surely not. She epitomized everything good in a person. Could it be that she was too good? Maybe Adam's interpretation was right on the mark.

It would explain why she had such phenomenal success.

Troubled, he realized the more he tried, the less anything changed. He worked hard. He went to church. He believed in the good of all people. So why, with all the effort he put into his work, did it never make a difference? It needed to make a difference. *He* needed it to make a difference. Otherwise, why was he here? Why was anyone here?

Studying the ground, his gaze narrowed in thought. That old woman from his first day was never far from his mind. She'd been so peaceful with her death. It was her time, she'd said then. He'd thought it unfair. What if he had it wrong? What if he had it backwards?

What if this act of nature, this earthquake, was really an act of God? What if God created these *natura*l disasters to call home the people He needed, when He needed them? What if they weren't the horrible accidents everyone said they were?

Once he latched on to that train of thought, he couldn't let it go.

God had created this planet and put Mother Earth in charge. She carried out his orders. Therefore, it followed that if she'd created this earthquake, it had been with God's consent. If that were what God wanted, saving these people buried by rubble was going *against* His wishes.

He sat back stunned. He looked around to see if the sky had turned purple or the trees had suddenly grown upside down. After all, his whole belief system had just flipped.

Glancing over at Adam's burrow, he could see a bare foot

sticking out from the overhang. Adam was the type of person he'd been rescuing these last few days. Sure, there had been a couple of children included in the group, yet several had been single, asshole males like this one.

"Why? Why bother?" He looked up to the sky for answers. "What do you want me to do, Lord?"

All these years he'd been told that God was the creator of all. He believed it...knew deep inside it was true. His faith had been the mainstay of his world. So, then God had to be the creator of this earthquake. How simple. Why had he never made that connection before? If God had made this earthquake happen, it was because He wanted these results. He wanted these people to die. And if He wanted it, He had to have a good reason. It was not Man's job to wonder or to question why.

God had called these people home.

Just as the old woman had said; it was God's will.

He straightened, his face brightening with enlightenment. By SAR's intervention, these people hadn't followed God's orders. He suddenly understood. These people needed to go home. Search and rescue work was going against His will. The best of them, being the worst of them all – Kali.

This new understanding reenergized him. That's why nothing he'd ever done had made a difference – he'd been doing the wrong type of work. He hadn't understood.

He walked over to where Adam slept. So stupid, so careless of the life he'd been graced with. No appreciation.

"Hey, Adam, wake up!" The Texan nudged Adam with his foot. Adam moaned and rolled over; his snoring continued, unabated. He kicked harder.

Adam opened a bleary eye. "Huh?" At that moment he sneezed. A thick black wad of tobacco-reeking snot splattered the Texan's work boots.

Staring at Adam, the Texan scrunched up his face in loathing. "That's disgusting." His leg lashed out, the tip of his steel-toed boot connecting with Adam's chin. Adam's head snapped back. He groaned once, then fell silent.

Kneeling, he studied Adam for a long moment. This was almost too easy. Shoving the brush to the side, he slid both arms under Adam and rolled him over and then over again. It took several more rolls before Adam's unconscious body settled at the bottom of a shallow ditch at the edge of a small hillock. Using his hands, he cascaded dirt and rock on top of the prone man.

Adam moaned as small rocks bounced off his cheekbones and forehead. His eyes opened, then slammed closed as dirt rained on top of him. He flipped his head to the side, sending dirt flying. He rolled over. Using his elbows as levers, he tried to push upward. He was kicked back down, landing on his belly. Bigger rocks pounded his back. He lurched lower under the blows. "Wha…t?" A small boulder crunched hard on his shoulder, sending him flat to the ground. Adam shook his head as if to clear it. He turned to stare, pain and confusion evident in his gaze. "Why…why are you doing this?" Blood trickled from his temple and scratches razed his neck.

"You weren't meant to survive. You were meant to go home."

Another large rock hit Adam's skull, dropping him in place. The dirt piled higher. Adam could still draw a breath, but blood bubbled from the corner of his mouth.

The dirt pile, now with a large hollow gouged out of one side, collapsed, sending yards of dirt tumbling onto the still form below. Not satisfied yet, Texan kicked, shoved and scooped the balance of the small mound until it reformed above Adam.

His chest heaved when he finally stopped. Sweat rolled off his face and soaked his back. The summer heat sweltered, thickening the air, making it hard to breathe. Dust filled his nostrils and eyes. He bent over to regain his breath. After a couple of minutes, he turned to search the area. It was deserted.

Of course, it was.

God was on his side.

What was that old saying, ashes to ashes, dust to dust? He'd sent Adam home – where he belonged. Underground.

He smiled, a beatific reflection of the new glow surrounding his soul.

He'd passed his initiation. Now his vocation could begin. Satisfaction permeated his being. He'd found his calling.

Simple, reasonable, perfect.

CHAPTER 3

Six months later

KALI CAME TO a sudden stop, staring at the deserted landscape. Dust whirled around her on scorching dry wind, adding yet another layer of filth to her face and clothing. Lord, it was hot. She lifted her hard hat to wipe the ever-present sweat from her forehead. Her nostrils flared at the smell of decomposition and despair. Moving carefully, she stepped over a broken plastic doll, its head crushed by rocks. A table leg jutted from under a cracked window half covered in construction paper depicting a hand-drawn map.

This pile of rubble had once been a small school. Now death surrounded her. A week ago, school children had laughed and played here, smiling their joy to the world. Bodies of twenty-two children had been recovered since.

Her lower lip trembled. She gripped Shiloh's harness even tighter. Children's deaths were the hardest. Especially after Mexico. Before that disaster she had been able to keep death at a distance. She might as well have been wrapped with cotton batting, protecting her, giving her space to function in the face of so much pain. Now the images of her past pulled at her, keeping her awake at night. The cotton no longer insulated or distanced her.

Everything was worse after Mexico.

Especially the Sight. Stronger, clearer, more insistent.

The instinctive pull had morphed into a knowing she couldn't ignore. It demanded her attention. Sometimes she saw dark-colored ribbons. Other days she saw shadows. There appeared to be little in the way of consistency. The only definite here was that it was changing. And whatever was happening was getting stronger.

Kali pulled her drenched t-shirt away from her breasts as sweat continued to trickle. Grabbing her water bottle, she took a healthy swig. The place had a desolate appearance with gray dust coating everything and everyone. A landslide in the Madison River Canyon had taken out part of the town center of the small community of Bralorne, Montana.

Most volunteers worked on the other side of the hastily established rescue center that served as a command post. It also served as refreshment area and medical center. She chose to search in this direction. The Sight hadn't given her an option.

Whup whup whup. The sound reached its crescendo as a helicopter crested the treetops and approached her. Drawn upward by the propeller, dirt was swept into a swirling storm that engulfed her.

"Shit." Kali dropped to a crouch, wrapping her arms around Shiloh, tucking both their heads low as the chopper passed. The dust settled slowly; still Kali stayed hunched over. Their eyes would suffer the most from the filthy air. Normally, the helicopters didn't come in so close. Her safety vest should have alerted the pilot.

Straightening, Kali reached for her water bottle again, this time pouring some into Shiloh's mouth. Carrying a recessive gene, Shiloh was an odd, long-haired crossbred in a world of short-haired Labradors. Another reason the two had bonded instantly. Both were oddities in their respective worlds.

Taking a firm hold on her frayed emotions, she tuned in to the weird energy calling her. She'd given up calling 'it' intuition. It had become so much more. Right now, the ribbons were twisting.

Dark tendrils beckoned her. She caught her breath. The murderous threads, black and violent, rustled in the space between life and death. More north. Taking several large steps forward, Kali stopped again to listen to the whispers.

Stop.

Kali bowed her head.

Facing her, lay something she found all too familiar – with a twist. A twist she'd only started to better understand since Mexico. Mexico and little Inez had provided a defining moment in her life.

The whispers spoke again – called to her. Insisted she follow them. It was rare for the Sight to be this strong, this insistent. She shifted her feet, easing the ache from standing too long. At least her heavy, steel-toed work boots grabbed the uneven ground with the solid grip of experience.

She looked around, then filled her mouth with water, to rinse away the grittiness.

Shiloh whimpered at her side. Death depressed her friend. Kali frowned, rubbing the back of her hand across her forehead. Didn't it depress everyone? Kali stroked the top of Shiloh's silky head.

"It's okay, sweetheart. We can't help him anymore, but we *can* bring him home to his family."

Him? Kali tilted her head in consideration. Yes, the victim was male. That knowledge sat confidently inside her soul. Another fact. Her intuitive hunches had become something she could count on as fact.

She didn't understand how her skills worked or why. Kali also didn't know the best way to use them or how to shut them off. She could only accept that they were there, refusing to be ignored.

Kali had morphed into a divining rod for violence – man-made violence. She had no trouble finding this victim.

And this poor man had been murdered.

GRANT SUMMERS LEANED back against his high-backed office chair and rubbed his temple. Working for the FBI always meant tons of paperwork. On days it went smoothly, he could burrow in and dig himself out. Then there were days like today. Delay after delay. He'd yet to get anything off his desk. Instead, dozens more red-flagged problems had joined the pile. He'd be lucky to clear it before the weekend.

His stacked inbox caught his eye: Big, brown manila envelopes, too many to count; white business envelopes, too many to care; and a magazine. Now *that* he could handle. Grabbing it out of the stack, he grabbed five minutes for something unrelated to his cases.

It was the latest edition of *Technical Rescue*, compliments of his brother in Maine. Rob wanted Grant to return home and resume the type of work they'd both done once, long ago. Grant chose to stay up-to-date on the industry and the idea percolated in the back of his mind that maybe one day…

Turning to the Table of Contents, he scanned the listed articles. He paused. His breath caught and held as his fingers raced through the pages to the name that had caught his eye. To a picture in the center of the page.

Kali Jordan.

The same damned baseball that had hit him seven years ago

socked him in the gut again. Time hadn't diminished her impact. His breath whooshed out on a long sigh as he feasted on the picture. Fatigue dripped from her features, dust coated her from her work boots to her hair drawn back in a no-nonsense ponytail. Obviously photographed on a disaster site, her dirty rescue vest dominated the picture. Tired, proud, Kali stood strong on a boulder, her dog at her side. A sunset colored the background.

Damn she looked good. Older, sure, but then so did he. Was her hair darker? He remembered a sun-kissed gold layer over deep rich brunette locks. And long. God, he loved long hair.

She wore a pained I'm-doing-this-for-the-cause smile. She had heart, that girl. And as he recalled, she was no media hound. He'd first met her years ago at a conference where she'd been a guest lecturer.

He'd been fascinated. The stomach punch at the first sight of her had been illuminating. He'd been new to auras and chakras and had never understood the various terms for the different psychic abilities back then, but even he hadn't missed the emerging sensation of rightness between them.

But *she* had.

It had been hard. In his head, the rightness of it was natural, automatic. She'd been *the* one. The perfect match. The synergistic yin to his yang.

Except – she hadn't been free.

That realization had stunned him. How could anything so perfect not work out?

He shook his head at the painful memories.

For seven years he'd had that gut feeling that it wasn't over. It couldn't be over. It might not have been the right time back then, but there would come a time when it would be right. Yet what if he were wrong? Had he let life pass him by while he waited – for something that might never come?

He stared at the picture and wondered. Would that time *ever* come? He'd avoided committed relationships, always wondering…always waiting.

His cell phone rang, yanking him out of his reverie. He reached into his pocket and checked the number. Stefan. Of course. Stefan slept when he wished, painted when he wished and channeled incredibly strong psychic abilities the rest of the time.

Grant leaned back in his chair and lifted his feet to rest on top of his desk. What did his wily friend have to say today? "Hey,

Stefan."

"You're wondering right now if you're going to see her."

Grant slammed his feet down on the floor as he leaned forward. "Shit. What?" He closed his eyes in frustration. His free hand pinched the bridge of his nose. Being friends with Stefan meant his mind was his friend's to read. Sometimes that became very irritating.

"But not today?" Stefan snickered.

"Oh, shut up."

"The answer is 'yes, you will. And soon.'"

Grant loosened his tie, swallowing heavily. His mind spun at the endless questions forming.

"She has the Sight but has no idea how strong she is. Ask to see her paintings."

With that cryptic statement, Stefan rang off. Grant frowned. Damn. Stefan was right ninety-nine percent of the time. What's the chance that this one time – the one time he was desperate to have Stefan be right – he was wrong?

KALI SWALLOWED, HER throat rasping like aged sandpaper on stone as she avoided looking at the mounds of rocks and crushed buildings around her. She was stuck in Bralorne. Hours filled with organized chaos had slipped away since she'd located the buried victim. Kali had continued to search for survivors, always keeping an eye on the crew and gathering throng. Now she'd finally allowed herself to be drawn to the drama like the rest of the crowd.

Shiloh whined. Kali tore her gaze from the heavy equipment sitting beside the open pit. The smell of death was hard to get used to – even for a dog. Knowing what it was didn't help. In fact, it almost made it worse. Still when it was your life's work, what choice did you have?

Except to wear a mask and breathe through your mouth.

Tugging once on Shiloh's bright orange lead, Kali took several steps back. The crime scene people needed more space. At least that's what she thought they were. Their white coveralls carried no labels, but proclaimed them 'official'. She was grateful they'd arrived to take over.

The crowd immediately swarmed forward to fill the gap she'd left.

"When did this crowd arrive?"

Kali twisted to face Brad. "Just after you left." She offered him a tired smile and wiped the dust from her eyes. "What took so long?"

Brad held out a tall takeout cup. "I was waiting for Jarl to show. I don't know where he took off to. That guy's a bloody ghost when he wants to be. Besides I brought this back for you. Forgive me?" He wafted the full cup under her nose. "Tall, dark and black?" The warm cup passed to her hands.

Kali moaned in delight. "Coffee. Oh, thank God. I'm so cold."

"It has to be ninety-two degrees. How can you be cold?"

With her fingers hugging the coffee, Kali blew at the steam coming through the small opening. "I'm exhausted," she admitted. "I don't seem to have much energy these days." She shot him a worried glance. "Jarl's gone missing? Again? What's with him? He's been acting different lately."

Several men jostled her, almost spilling her coffee as they made their way past.

Brad patted her shoulder and pointed to a spot away from the action. Shiloh who walked in front of them dropped and sprawled in a small patch of shade. A huge boulder provided a place to sit and enjoy their drink in relative peace. Kali sat with her legs crossed, while Brad stretched out his six-foot length. Covered in dust and both in jeans and black t-shirts – except for their bright fluorescent vests – they could have been any two tired people.

"Jarl could be struggling today. This gets to you after a while. We have to remember tomorrow is a new day."

Kali exhaled noisily, staring at the heat waves rising around them. "I don't know. We work so hard to free these poor survivors, then to have this happen?" She eased her sore body into a more comfortable position. "I don't understand how someone could do this. It's senseless."

Brad frowned. "Like what? Who? What did I miss?"

Kali motioned toward the commotion in front of them. "I don't know exactly what happened here, but remember the guy we found several days ago? Stephen? The one with the broken left arm that had been pinned between the two cement slabs?"

Brad narrowed his gaze as he considered her description. "Yeah, I remember. Construction worker or something similar. What about him, outside of the fact he's damn lucky to be alive?"

With a tight smile on her face, she said, "That's the problem.

Someone decided he shouldn't be. Alive, that is."

Brad shot her a startled look. "What?"

Kali swirled her cup, watching the black brew slosh around. Brad deserved the full explanation. He'd been in on the poor guy's original rescue. "Shiloh signaled when we were walking through here a couple of hours ago."

She glanced over at him. "Heaped on one side appeared to be freshly turned dirt. I requested a crew to check it over. When we found the clothing we went into recovery mode, thinking this was a slide victim. It didn't take long to realize we were wrong."

"Wrong?" Brad frowned, a crease forming on his forehead. "What could be wrong with finding another victim?"

Kali stared up at him, the ghosts from too many disasters, accidents and deaths swirling through her mind. "This one was murdered."

HOW WAS THE 'best of the best' now? Standing quietly, the Texan watched as Kali wandered along the temporary road, Shiloh ever at her side. His position was perfect. Close enough to keep abreast of the running conversations but far enough away to mask his interest in what was going on.

He'd orchestrated this lovely little mess, so why shouldn't he enjoy the results? After all, this was his debut. Well, his *public* debut.

People surged forward when the recovery team brought out the victim. The crowd's gasps and cries were his well-earned accolades.

Shifting his weight, he slid his hands into his dusty jeans pocket.

He hadn't realized how much he would enjoy hearing and seeing their reactions. How much he would enjoy being the only one who truly understood. How much he would enjoy being God's inside man. His stomach had roiled initially at the hands-on work, but he'd never been the squeamish type and he'd gotten over it quickly. Besides, practice had improved his technique. Less messy.

He straightened, rolling his shoulders as a sense of freedom washed over him. A heartfelt sigh gusted free. Such a difference this had made in his world. A small smile played at the corner of his lips. Life was good.

Kicking the loose dirt at his feet, he considered returning to the temporary command center, except that could mean missing something good here.

He watched Kali and Shiloh again. She'd almost reached the center. Several people stopped to talk to her as she walked. Everyone loved her. A little girl offered Kali a flower and a hug for Shiloh. He frowned with disgust. She'd been blessed with a model's body, a dancer's grace and a queen's regal air. Only he knew her now. It had taken him a bit, but he'd finally seen the light. She had no soul. How dare she defy God's plan? Shooting a dirty look in her direction, he refocused on the scene going on around him, determined to enjoy the fruits of his labor. He could bide his time. There was a natural order to everything.

Her turn would come…and soon.

CHAPTER 4

Four days later

KALI AWOKE EARLY. She ached deep inside. A weariness, a heaviness weighed on her as she lay in bed. Now if only she could go back to sleep.

There was such joy in saving a life. She could only liken the experience to what a doctor must experience in an Emergency. When one case offers little hope – yet a miracle happens, and the patient survives. Heart-wrenching, painful, satisfying.

It was easy to understand why Brad went on a bender after some of the bad rescues. Still, it was hard enough on his wife with him racing off to disasters around the world, without adding days of wallowing in it, as well. Several others, like Jarl, used God to help them get through the pain. Other rescuers depended on the people in their closest relationships to help them heal.

Rolling over, she dropped a hand over the side of her bed, reaching until a cold nose nudged her palm. Grateful for Shiloh's presence, she stroked the dog's furry head – the two of them inseparable as always.

"Let's go for our run, Shiloh, before it gets too hot."

Shiloh's ears perked up, her head cocked to one side. She barked once.

It took a couple of minutes to change into a black tank top and matching shorts and to pull her hair into a ponytail. Running on the beach was unlike any other type of jogging. It was much harder. The first couple of times she'd thought the run would kill her. Time and practice had improved her speed and technique. Now she loved it. She'd lived in Oregon all her life – on the coast for the last year. Now she couldn't imagine living anywhere else.

Kali and Shiloh navigated the fifty-odd steps down the cliff to the rocks and sand. Large boulders and crashing waves dominated this part of the coast. The sound of the ocean was always noisy and boisterous, adding extra energy to anyone lucky enough to be near it. Another reason for running here. No matter how little she might want to run beforehand, as soon as her feet hit the cold, moist sand they gained a will all their own to send her speeding along the waterline. Today was no different.

Shiloh barked and danced in circles, and Kali laughed. The miles churned under their feet as she dodged the tidal pools. They ran daily, when their schedule allowed. Staying fit was mandatory for rescue work. Besides, she loved the way running made her feel.

Thoughts tumbled around in her head as she looped back over several miles of beach. It was a good thing the tide was out, or she wouldn't have been able to go as far. The beach narrowed to a strip winding between the rushing water and majestic cliff face. The slope was unstable there. Made so by tumbling rocks and sand.

By the time they'd returned to the cascade of rocks below her stairs, Kali was covered in sweat. Life thrummed through her veins. She gasped for breath as she slowed to a walk and stretched her upper body.

The sun slipped behind the clouds. It gave her a brief respite from the sun and helped her cool down faster. She walked up the stairs and across the long wilderness stretch to her yard.

A small white envelope sat on her back doorstep.

She searched to see if the person who'd delivered it was still around. There was no sign of anyone. It hadn't been there when she'd left. At least she didn't think so. Wiping her sweaty hands on her shorts, she picked it up and flipped it over and back again. No return address and only her first name printed in ink on the front. Written in all capitals, it appeared more businesslike than personal.

Weird.

After unlocking the kitchen door, Kali stepped into the kitchen before ripping the envelope open. A small folded sheet of paper fell into her hand. She flicked the paper open and read aloud.

Game on

Start of round one

I hide and you seek, see

– it's simple

If you don't find them in time

– they die

So use those unholy skills
– and see
Are you really so much better
– than He?
Get ready, because it's
– Game on!

Kali dropped the letter on the table and backed away, almost stepping on Shiloh. What the hell was that? Her heart raced and it was all she could do to stay calm. She wiped her sweaty palms on her t-shirt. She studied the letter from a distance, searching for some clue to identify the sender. No signature, no letterhead, no watermark. Nothing. Reaching for the envelope again, she searched for clues she might have missed. Nothing. The note was printed in the same style as her name on the envelope, blocky hand-printed letters, only *not* all capitals this time.

Shit.

She took several deep breaths as confusion and disbelief argued with fear. Common sense righted itself. This couldn't be real. It had to be a sick joke. Giving herself another moment to calm down, Kali reread it, this time slowly, trying to analyze the words – and the meaning behind them.

What *game?* Who was going to do the hiding and what was being hidden? It sounded like a child's game. As part of her SAR work, she found people all the time. Did this person know her personally? Know of her? Know her enough to understand the type of work she did? Was the person a psycho or a sicko? Hard to tell. Best-case scenario, this was a stupid prank. Worst-case scenario…well she didn't want to go there.

That question about whether she was better than *He* made her stomach drop. They couldn't know. She closed her eyes. *Don't panic. Don't panic.*

Added to that line was the fact that the letter had been delivered to her kitchen door. Talk about scaring the crap out of her. The letter writer knew her – in ways she didn't dare contemplate. It might have been a coincidence that she hadn't been here at the time of the delivery, except she couldn't stop wondering if she'd been watched and the letter delivered after she'd left. The fine hairs on her arm stood straight. Unable to stop herself, Kali relocked the back door then ran to make sure the front door was locked too.

What the hell should she do now?

She had to inform someone. She'd never sleep again if something bad came of this and she hadn't spoken up. That it could be nothing more than a bad joke, didn't matter. Ignoring the letter and the envelope, she put on a small pot of coffee, then headed to the shower. She did some of her best thinking under hot water.

Twenty minutes later, her hair still wrapped in a towel, she walked out onto her deck and took a bracing gulp of her freshly poured java.

Kali stared blindly out at the garden, considering her options. The simplest answer was to call the police. They might come and inspect the note, take her statement and possibly make a couple of inquiries. Still, they weren't likely to do more until something else developed.

All she really had was a piece of ugly fan mail.

Great.

Or she could call Dan. In the twenty-something years since starting the Second Chance SAR Center, he'd received several threatening letters. Dan *was* the center. He was as well-known as Kali, maybe more so. Had he received a similar letter? She reached for the phone.

An hour later the sound of crunching gravel drew her to the front porch. Beside her, Shiloh stood alert, barking madly at the unfamiliar large black truck. Kali narrowed her gaze as it parked beside her Jeep. As she watched, Dan stepped down from the passenger side, waving at her. She relaxed against the doorframe.

"Hi, Kali." Dan's smile reassured her further. She waved back before turning her attention to the driver. Tall and slim, dressed in jeans and a black stretch Henley, he looked big, dangerous and vaguely familiar. Her stomach twisted. Energy stirred inside. A faint zap crackled between them. She puzzled on it as he fell into step behind Dan. The two appeared opposites. Dan had wizened into a small gnome of a man, while the larger man resonated health and purpose.

Dan gave her a quick hug. "I called an old friend for help. This is Grant Summers."

Kali welcomed them both inside. She'd known Dan a long time and couldn't remember hearing the other man's name before. Nudging the door shut, she led the way through to the deck. "Can I get anyone coffee? It's fresh."

"Always, thanks." Dan beamed.

Grant shook his head. As she walked into the kitchen to find another mug, she glanced back. Grant watched her, an odd look on his face. Kali flushed. She'd seen him before, yet more than that, her energy knew him. Did he sense it too? From where? When? Her stomach pulsed. Which was crazy – she didn't know him, yet she *knew* him.

The two men had taken seats at the outside table. "Here you go." Kali placed the mug in Dan's waiting hand. "Careful, it's hot."

"Thanks, Kali."

"No problem. I was ready for another cup myself." She motioned to the letter on the table at Dan's side. She'd placed it there earlier. "There it is."

Dan reached for it, when Grant interrupted, "Read without touching it – just in case."

Glancing over at Kali apologetically, Dan read the letter aloud.

When he stopped, Kali spoke, her tone wry. "It's covered in my fingerprints. Honestly, I never considered that issue."

Grant moved over to study the envelope beside the letter. "Is this the envelope it came in?"

"Yes. It has no markings either, other than my name."

He gave a short nod. A muscle in his jaw clenched and unclenched like he had a twitch.

Under lowered lashes, she studied his lean face and narrowed gaze. Jet black hair matched by imposing brows and squared high cheek bones led to a chin that said capable and strong-minded. This was not someone to cross. So still, so stern, she couldn't read him. And if she'd seen him before, surely she'd have remembered that air about him.

Yet his energy synced with hers. She didn't really know what that meant. Her energy and Dan's were comfy together. She'd always figured it was because he'd treated her as the daughter he'd never had, giving her the opening to treat him as the father she'd lost.

Grant's energy was different. Warmer. Hot. Sexual? Maybe. Except it was more than that – she recognized an instinctive surety…a knowing. She couldn't really explain of what or how. She'd never experienced this with anyone else.

He glanced up and his deep brown eyes locked onto hers. Time stopped. Energy leapt, pulsed between them. She forgot to breathe.

"Is there something wrong?"

She blinked. Heat washed over her neck and face. "Oh no, sorry. I didn't mean to stare. I thought I recognized you from somewhere." Dan looked over at her, curiously. Kali averted her face and moved to the red cedar railing where she took several bracing gulps of air. She was an idiot.

The men's conversation droned on in the background, helping her refocus on the more important issue – the letter.

Still, why had Dan brought Grant here? She spun around to study the two men. Her narrowed gaze logged the inner strength and confident air of the bigger man, then she remembered his comments on fingerprints.

"You're a Fed."

Grant and Dan both stared at her.

"What makes you think I'm FBI?" Grant asked, studying her face.

She snorted but managed to meet his gaze calmly. "Everything. It's written all over you."

Dan jumped in. "You're right. He is. After we spoke, I called him to get his take on this. We rarely get a chance to visit, so I suggested he come with me to see the letter. He's not here in any official capacity."

Pursing her lips, she leaned against the railing, her gaze traveling between the two of them. "So, what do you think?"

Glancing from the letter to her, he gave a small shrug. "Definitely personal. This could be serious – or it could be a prank."

Kali widened her gaze. "I'd figured *that* out on my own. What else can you add?"

His narrow gaze studied her. "You think this is for real?"

"I'm concerned that it *might* be," she stressed. "What if it is?"

"Then we'll deal with it. In the meantime, there's no way to be certain. I'll take the note and have it checked for fingerprints. Chances are it's clean." He motioned to the envelope. "Same for that." Glancing up, he added, "Show me where you found the letter."

Kali walked ahead of the men and through the kitchen to her back doorstep. "It was there. Resting flat on the top step."

Grant stepped over the spot and took stock of the area. "Gravel all around the house. No footprints. Cement steps, but the delivery person didn't have to step on them to drop the letter. If you didn't see the person who delivered it, and there's no other evidence where the envelope was found, then there's little we can do at this point. I can search the files for similar cases. Other than that, it's a waiting game."

Kali crossed through the kitchen to the deck, where she slumped back into her seat, baffled. "You mean there's nothing I can do?"

"I have to admit, this letter is a bit unnerving." Grant's gaze narrowed in consideration. "I'm leaning toward it being a real threat."

She choked. "That's not the answer I was hoping for."

"On the off chance that this isn't a joke gone wrong, I need to ask a few questions. If you don't mind?" Grant tilted his head, his dark compelling eyes studying her.

There it was again. That same ping of recognition. Why? Keeping her voice calm, casual, she answered, "Of course not."

"Does this letter mean anything to you? It talks about this being a game. Do you know of, or have any idea where that game idea is coming from?" At the violent shake of her head, he continued. "Rounds. Any games that have rounds? Competitions with rounds?"

Surprised, Kali glanced down at the letter. "No. I don't. Nothing about finding people is fun or playful. Most of the time the experience is horrible, depressing and full of disappointment."

"Don't think of it that way. Think of it more competitively. Back to the wording here. It says I hide and you seek. I'm presuming that is your search and rescue skills being called into play."

She shrugged. "I don't know. Probably."

"It's simple." Grant continued to read.

"The hell it is." Kali didn't see anything simple about it.

"And if you don't find them in time, they die. Not good. Who or what are *them*? And how could we find out?" He pursed his lips, studied the letter, her face, then the letter again. "Definitely a competition. Do you know anyone who is jealous of your reputation?"

"My what?" Startled, Kali glanced at Dan for help. "What reputation? And why would that matter?"

Grant explained. "I understand from Dan that you and Shiloh are considered one of the best teams in the Search and rescue field." He glanced at Dan. "That you recently received several awards and a rather large monetary gift."

She shook her head slowly. This wasn't real. It couldn't be.

"I'm good, yes. So are hundreds of other teams. As far as I know, I don't have a *reputation*." Kali blinked several times, trying to clear the fog his question had created. "That money went to the center to help offset the costs from all the emergency trips. We have to pay for flights and supplies ourselves more often than not."

"You were written up in several magazine articles."

Puzzled, she glanced at Dan. "I was?"

Dan answered, "A couple of times. Once as part of the team and you've been mentioned several times in write-ups on the rescue work we do."

"Sure, but so was everyone else."

Dan shrugged, adding, "Shiloh won that contest. You were interviewed over that."

"But," she protested. "That was last year."

He wrinkled his face. "Still counts."

"I need a list and preferably a copy of articles where you or the center have been featured. We don't know what might be important here. It seems obvious that this person is jealous or thinks you undeserving of your reputation. It's almost a challenge of some sort. Prove that you are as good as everyone says you are." Grant looked up at her.

"Challenge? Prove myself? That sounds so wrong." The whole concept sounded wrong. "I'm not the one saying I'm good. That's what other people say. More to boost morale than anything. The media plays up the successes at disaster sites. There's so much pain and suffering, no one wants to focus on the many losses." She hunched her shoulders, hating the influx of memories.

"I don't think it matters who said what. What matters is that this person believes what's been said. Supposedly, people are going to die if you don't participate. It sounds very personal to me."

Kali massaged the building tension at the base of her neck. This was unbelievable. "So, because he wants to make this a game, I have to play, too?" Running her fingers through her hair, she added with a touch of humor, "At least we know he's male."

Dan tilted his head, a puzzled frown between his brows. "How can you be so sure?"

Kali snorted. "This is classic male 'my penis is bigger than your penis' – the old I'm-better-than-you-are kind of male competitive behavior. The mano a mano style of competition. A shrink would get that immediately."

Grant appeared interested in his notebook again, a muscle

twitching at the corner of his mouth. "I imagine one would," he admitted dryly.

With a smirk, Kali leaned back, feeling marginally more in control.

"Now according to the letter, he said you're to use your mad skills. Even more troubling is that your skills appear to be competing against God. He – written with a capitalized H – is likely to mean God and brings the possibility of a religious fanaticism in play here."

"As if he's seeing himself as God?" Dan asked, shock and disbelief in his voice. He sat there with his hand to his throat, his face pale and aged. "That doesn't sound good."

Grant nodded. "Definitely a possibility. Although he might also see himself as a messenger, a servant of God. Back to the mad skills part, does that mean anything to you, Kali?"

She swallowed hard. "I'd have to guess my search and rescue skills."

Her face froze in place. Her breath caught in her chest. This letter writer couldn't know about the Sight. No one knew. Hell, *she* didn't know much about the visions. Her stomach knotted and the band around her temple tightened with each question. Somewhere along the line it all became too much and Kali dropped into silence.

"And the worst line of all is the last one. Game on." Grant stared off in the distance. "I'd interpret that to mean whatever this is, it's *about* to start."

Dan added, "Or it has already done so and we just don't know it yet."

Kali shuddered. Shivers wracked her spine and a horrible feeling of impending doom filled her heart, boding no good for whatever was coming.

The men left soon after, taking the evidence with them.

Kali closed her eyes in relief as they walked out.

Mad skills. Surely, that was conjecture.

It had to be. Nothing else was possible.

AS HE WALKED to his car, Grant forced himself not to look behind him. The energy tug telling him to return to her, was hard enough to deal with. His heart made a small jump for joy.

Kali Jordan.

She'd changed. Not surprising. Life hadn't been easy on her. Maybe it was due to the circumstances or what life had dished over time – now she appeared distant. To him she looked every bit as stunning as the first time he'd seen her. She'd been addressing a large group of government employees during a training seminar. A refined beauty with a ready smile, she'd been energized about her topic, her face animated with excitement, her hands waving wildly to make her point. Passionate.

She still was, only more restrained.

Stefan had been right. Again.

She was an incredibly strong psychic but quite undeveloped. Dan hadn't mentioned *that* fact. But then, he might not know. He wasn't the most intuitive type around. Grant wasn't either. If it hadn't been for Stefan, Grant might have missed the signs telling him to look deeper.

Only Stefan *had* told him. And with that tidbit, he'd taken a deeper look using the techniques Stefan had taught him. He'd seen something that made him and his almost nonexistent skills pause. He could see her energy. Lavender and teal color waves flowed around her like a breeze. So unusual a color and so rare for him to see the energy at all, he couldn't help but enjoy the vision.

Grant started his truck then waited until Dan finished buckling his seatbelt.

"So what did you think?" Dan asked.

"I'm not sure. It *feels* ugly."

"Horrible letter."

"Does she not have a partner?" Grant glanced curiously over at Dan, who grimaced. He didn't want to let on just how badly he needed to hear this answer.

"She's a loner most of the time now. Her last long term relationship was years ago. The guy turned out to be a greedy son of a bitch. She dated for a while but nothing serious. Then something went wrong on a site in Mexico. She's been locked emotionally ever since. She won't date or socialize. Hell, she won't even have coffee with the regulars at the center anymore. Just hides away in the offices."

Grant shot a quick glance Dan's way. "Hmmm."

"Oh no. Don't think she's involved in this nasty letter business. There's no way." Dan stuck his chin out. "I'd stake my life on that. Kali lives to serve."

Grant pulled the vehicle onto the main road. "I didn't say she was. However, someone wants her to play the game – willing or not."

"We don't know that yet. I'm hoping this is a hoax."

"Time will tell."

From the corner of his eye, he could see Dan settle deeper into his seat with a heavy sigh. Grant frowned. How old was Dan now? Grant tried to remember what he knew of his father's old friend. He had to be mid-sixties at least. Could even be a decade older.

It had been a while since they'd spoken. What a way to reconnect. Kali Jordan.

He grinned. She had reacted to him… *Dare* he hope she'd remembered him? Dare he hope she'd felt the same tug he had? Dare he hope it was the right time – finally?

CHAPTER 5

SLEEP WOULDN'T COME. She'd gotten up once already to double-check the locks on every window and door in the house. Shiloh whined softly. Kali stroked the dog's head, helping them both to relax. Glancing at the clock, she wondered if it was too late to call Brad. Her best friend had been in and out of the town on various jobs these last few days. She didn't want to burden him with this nightmare, but she really needed to talk to him. Giving in to impulse, she dialed his number.

"Hello." The cool voice of Brad's wife always made Kali wince. Susan was iced wine, Kali was beer. Susan was a first class traveler in life, and Kali could always be found in the back with the dogs. Susan was grace, poise and perfectly turned out. Kali was jeans, t-shirts and hair pulled back with hair scrunchie to stop it from bugging her. Sure, Kali cleaned up nice for special occasions, but she didn't start each and every day as if cameras would be following her. The two women were as different as caviar and hot dogs.

"Susan, it's Kali. Is Brad there? I need to speak with him."

There it was. That awkward drawn-out silence whenever she called lately. Kali tried to shake off the icy disdain directed her way but damn it was getting old. The two women used to be friends. Somewhere, somehow this last year that had all changed. Whether it was from Brad's extended drinking binges, Susan's wish for him to leave the industry or something else, Kali didn't know. At one time she'd tried to find out. The icy wall had been in place ever since.

At the continued silence, Kali double-checked the clock. Ten at night wasn't late, was it? "Susan?"

"He's not here, sorry."

Click.

What the hell?

Kali stared at the phone. Now she really wouldn't be able to sleep. What a bitch. She allowed herself a moment to mentally vent, then pushed Susan firmly from her mind, focusing instead on Dan's visit and his FBI buddy. Could anyone just pick up the phone and call the FBI? And she couldn't even begin to sort through the weird sense of connectedness she felt with him. Her mind tripped over the questions about the letter writer, all without answers. Time passed while she just lay there, covers up to her chest and a cup of chamomile tea sitting forgotten on the night table beside her.

A stranger could know *of* her. She wasn't proud or boastful, but she knew her name had been bandied about by those in the industry. A private person in many ways, she still attended conferences, spoke at charity events and had written various reports submitted to SAR organizations all over the world. The trust fund set up after her parents' deaths, while not huge, provided sufficiently for her modest lifestyle and allowed the money from her appearances to go to Second Chance. She worked as hard as anyone to keep the center running.

Though she wasn't famous, she was known. She sighed. Her headache slowly returned. Grant could be right. This was personal.

Her gut quivering, Kali threw off her covers, turned on a lamp and retrieved a notebook and pen from her dresser. Scrambling back under her duvet, she turned to a clean page and titled it 'Competitors.' Enemy was too strong a word.

Throwing her mind back ten years, she skipped from disaster to disaster to the odd conference, and training sessions. She wrote a list of every person who'd been mean, cutting or jealous of her. Those who had been openly antagonistic received an asterisk beside their names.

Then on a clean page she repeated the process, this time listing every person she thought was incompetent or dangerous on the scene and those she'd been forced to file complaints against.

Both lists ended up surprisingly short. She frowned and highlighted the couple of names that might be worth checking further. Several hadn't been around in years, and still others had left the industry.

Completing that task was like pulling a plug in her mind. She yawned then her eyes finally drifted closed as sleep overtook her.

Caught in a dream state, Kali walked across the remains of a cement city where buildings lay crumpled like tissue. Steel and glass littered the surface where agonized screams for help came from people buried alive, waiting for rescuers who would never come. Their screams echoed in her head. With her arms wrapped tightly around her chest, she scanned the devastation. It was too much. She couldn't help them all. Even as she stood there, the earth grumbled, sending her into an abyss opening beneath her feet. Twisted metal caught on her legs; stones tumbled on her head. She panicked as she tried to get free of the collapsing rubble. Something clamped her heart and squeezed. She flailed her arms and struggled harder. She cried out her terror.

And woke up.

Kali jerked upright, fighting against the endless darkness. Her blankets lay on the floor and the sheets tangled tightly around her legs. Her heart slammed against her ribs. A light film of sweat coated her skin. She shuddered. Her chest rose and fell as her breath gasped out into the empty room. The cool night air wafted over her already clammy skin, raising goose bumps.

"Oh, God."

Shiloh's warm furry head brushed her arm, a wet nose nudging her shoulder.

"Hello, sweetheart." Kali kicked the sheets to the bottom of the bed and swung her legs over the edge of her bed. She needed a drink of water. Sleeping pills were not an option. She hated – *hated* – drugs of any kind.

The warmth slowly filtered back into her body as she paced her room, trying to slow her racing pulse and catch her breath. Sleep was done for the night. It was three a.m. But it was morning somewhere in the world. She needed to take her mind off this mess. She needed her paints. She walked through to the second bedroom-turned-studio. A blank canvas awaited her on the easel.

She donned her favorite smock over her pajamas and grabbed her mixing board. Shiloh took up her usual position at the doorway – beyond spatter range. Kali couldn't help reaching for black and dark purple. With the brush in hand, she felt her emotions gather strength, reaching for release.

Kali drowned in the maelstrom. At her easel she experienced no hesitation, no decisions of what to create or how. Her brush moved in smooth, sure strokes. A little more here, a dab over there – her brush quickly filled in details. Somewhere along the line, she got lost in the image swirling in her brain.

Then she stopped.

Her hand hovered in mid-air, the brush ready for yet another stroke. She sagged, barely managing to stop herself from falling to the floor. She dropped her materials on the table. Without gazing at the picture, she wiped her hands on a nearby rag, removed her smock and headed back to her bedroom. Her mind felt like a bucket with a large hole in it, completely drained. The steps to her bed took forever.

Shiloh plodded slowly beside her. That was the last thing she remembered before collapsing on her bed already asleep.

THE CHIME OF her phone penetrated the fog inside Kali's mind. Stirring, every muscle heavy and sore, she reached for the handset.

"Kali? Are you there?" Dan's thin reedy voice gave her the shivers.

"Yes. I'm here." Her voice came out scratchy, as if rusty and unused.

"There's another letter. It was on the doorstep of the center this morning. It has to be the same guy." Excitement rolled through the phone line, disturbing Kali's senses. Clearly, this drama excited Dan. He sounded almost *pleased.*

Kali frowned in dismay. "Another one? At the center? Huh?" She cleared her throat, hoping it would clear her mind. "What does it say?"

"It's simple. The first part is just two words – Game on."

Game on. Dread gripped her throat. That could only mean the game, whatever it was, had started. She'd been included, whether she liked it or not.

Something twigged. "What do you mean – the first part?"

"Yeah. The rest of it…and I sure hope you understand this…says, 'Kali's the pro. She'll know what to do.'"

"But I don't," she wailed. "Dan, I don't know what to do!"

"Well, he seems to think you do."

"Well, he's wrong," she snapped, throwing back the covers to jump out of bed. "As far as I know, he's just another of the many loose screws wandering planet Earth. Have you told Grant?"

"Yes, he's on his way in."

She strode to the bathroom, shuddering at her image in the mirror. Purple bags. "Look, I'm just out of bed. Call me if Grant has anything to add to this. I need a shower – not to mention a chance to think."

"Good idea. I'll talk to you in a bit."

What a mess. Again, she had to consider that someone had been watching her house. Why else would this guy take the second letter to Dan's center if he hadn't watched Dan and a stranger arrive here…and leave with the first one? Unless he wanted the center involved in his game? And Dan?

Twenty minutes later, dressed and depressed, Kali made her way to the kitchen. She fed Shiloh on the deck in the morning sunlight. Running her fingers through her shoulder-length hair, she remembered last night's painting. She headed to her studio to take a look. She'd almost reached it when apprehension washed over her.

The door was closed.

She never closed the door after painting. It wasn't good for the wet canvases. Besides, the room only had a small window, so the paint fumes built up fast. A frown wrinkled her forehead. Had she simply forgotten? She had been deadly tired last night.

Bolstering her courage, she pushed the door wide and flinched as the fumes rushed out, stinging her nostrils. "Oh gross."

Holding her breath, Kali crossed to the window, shoving it as far open as it would go. Fresh air surged into the small space. She'd love a huge studio, except painting wasn't exactly a full time career for her – no matter how much she'd like it to be. It was a release she relied on when depression and madness overcame her soul. Maybe later, when she no longer did rescue work, she could indulge her art as a creative hobby instead of as an outlet for pain and turmoil.

Walking around the easel, Kali stopped mid-stride.

The painting stood where she'd left it. With surreal and strangely enticing clarity, blacks and purples and browns popped off the canvas. Heavy paint splotched at places, then thinned and stretched across the top.

She stepped back and frowned. Up close, the heavy amount of paint applied to the canvas resembled a distorted nightmare. Not surprising. Still, she caught a glimmer of an intentional design. She tilted her head and looked at it from a different angle. Nothing changed.

Sniffing the air, Shiloh ambled into the doorway.

Kali smiled down at the dog. "Not very sweet smelling, is it?"

She glanced back at the jumble of colors and stilled. There. She studied the abstract mess, letting the colors move and form to reveal the image hidden within.

Shivers slid over her spine.

Oh my God.

No way.

Kali blinked. It was.

There was no mistaking the image of a person buried under small bushes. Civilization of some kind crouched on the horizon, with a series of rough rock formations soaring behind the bushes.

"What the hell?" she whispered.

Kali was not a great artist, by any means. Blind escapism kept bringing her back to the process because it worked. She painted with wild abandon. The paint, slapped on canvas with no thought, discharged her emotions. For some reason it always worked.

And it always looked like shit.

This, on the other hand, was ingenious. Sure the subject matter was gruesome; however, given her volunteer work, it was not unexpected. Especially after she had found the letter.

The artistic abandon was still there. The paint was so thick in spots the picture was almost three-dimensional. The terrain had depth and movement. The light was dark and terse, yet still shone with gruesome clarity – and this was way beyond her artistic abilities.

"It's fucking brilliant."

It was also scary as hell.

IT HAD STARTED. Finally. He couldn't stop beaming. And he'd learned to be a master of keeping his feelings to himself. Six months. For six months he'd been moving forward, taking tentative steps to clarify his path, bringing events into alignment and planning. Always planning. Finally, he'd reached the stage where he would deal with the abomination called Kali. She couldn't be allowed to continue with her Godless ways.

Hunkering lower into his makeshift bower on her neighbor's beachside gate entrance, he used his high-powered binoculars to keep an eye on Kali's cedar house. He had a perfect view of both the back entrance and a large chunk of the sundeck. She'd been storming in and out of the house all morning. Something was up.

He smirked. He was up.

With a quick tug, he delved in his backpack for his water bottle and the granola bars he always kept handy. He should have brought popcorn for the show.

Pushing an evergreen branch aside, he studied the road to Kali's house. She'd chosen the property for the privacy and beach access. Even better, the corner of both properties led to a pathway along the edge of the cliff. He'd have to examine those possibilities later.

The heavily wooded properties, while designed for maximum privacy, afforded him a secure blind. And one far enough away from Shiloh's incredible nose. Settling into a more comfortable position, he relaxed, prepared to wait and watch. He had time. He wanted to make sure he got this right. She was a jumping-off point – the supreme test, so to speak. If he rose to the challenge here, then he knew he could handle all of God's work – whatever that might be.

CHAPTER 6

THE SMALL PLANE bucked in the heavy winds.

Kali stared out the window, happy her stomach had learned to adjust to turbulence years ago. Dark gray clouds glared back. She hated flying through storms. The lightning hadn't started…yet. Not her idea of fun.

But necessary today. An apartment building had collapsed on the outskirts of Sacramento, California. Sixty apartments lay in rubble. With the collapse occurring during the small hours of the morning meant the building had been occupied.

The only good thing about it was it took her away from the letter mess. She'd dumped it in Grant's and Dan's capable hands. Part of her felt guilty. A bigger part cried with relief that she had a viable excuse to leave.

She couldn't do anything about the game, regardless of what the author of the letter thought, but she *could* help these people in Sacramento. Her choice had been easy.

Thankfully, Grant and Dan had agreed.

Search and rescue teams were en route. Kali yawned. The call had come pre-dawn. As always, her bag and Shiloh's traveling kit both lived in the front closet, ready to go. Two and a half hours later they'd been airborne.

Several others had made the same flight, with Lauren, Brad and Todd in the back with the dogs while Jarl and Serena were up front getting briefed. The quiet in the plane was thick. They all knew what was coming. No matter how much preparation time was available, no one was ever ready.

Once they arrived on site, the first nine hours passed in a blur until she reached the end of her endurance. She was tired and dirty, dispirited. Shiloh didn't look much better. The Labrador Retriever's beautiful coat was gray with dust, her eyes sad but valiant.

"Come on girl, one more corner, then we'll take a break."

That was a unique aspect of these special dogs. They were always willing to go on, always willing to give a little more. Shiloh wagged her tail and headed forward. Kali followed. They were working the far left quadrant. She'd been given the map coordinates, but her brain was too tired to remember the numbers. What she'd really love was a full bottle of water. Dust clogging her nose and throat made her eyes run.

Picking her way carefully through the debris, Kali walked on ground level. Shiloh climbed up to walk atop the closest cement block. She sniffed around the exposed area before climbing higher.

"Kali?"

The voice was faint yet insistent. Kali pivoted to find Brad calling – Lauren at his side.

"The first teams are returning. Come and get something to eat and drink."

Kali waved acknowledgement. "Shiloh, come on, girl. Break time." How many times had she said that to this brave dog over the years? Breaks didn't always happen. During huge disasters like earthquakes the rescuers slept when they could, ate when food was available and kept bottled water on hand at all times. Time was always against them.

Kali and Shiloh strolled along the cleared path to the safety zone where sheets of canvas had been set up as tents for a makeshift command center. It offered some small comfort from the hot sun and provided a steady source of water and medical aid.

Kali gave Shiloh her much deserved meal and water in the shade beside Lauren, who'd already found a spot out of the way. Picking up muffins and coffee for herself, Kali collapsed on the ground between them. Kali studied her friend.

Lauren had aged. Weariness pulled at her dust-streaked face.

"How are you doing?" Lauren asked. Her German Shepherd, Halo, lay quietly beside her. She reached over to scratch his ruff.

"I'm okay. Just tired." Kali shifted to get more comfortable. "Shiloh's holding up well."

"At least we made it on site fast this time."

Kali studied what was left of the original structure.

This building that collapsed should have been condemned for shoddy construction. Everyone was trying to make a buck and no one wanted to put out the money to get the job done right. With the tough economic times, families were screaming to get in, glad to have shelter of any kind. Babies and children, parents and grandparents, all piled in together to save money.

Now glass shards twinkled in the sunlight, an added danger for the rescuers. Huge tents had been set up to shield the dead until they could be tagged and removed.

For Kali, one of the most difficult elements was the noise. Steel groaned under the weight of moving heavy concrete next to the workers screaming instructions. Loud wailing could be heard at the tents. A sudden crash sounded. Kali jumped to her feet, spinning around. As she watched, a loader lost a chunk of cement, adding a second crash to her frayed nerves. Rubbing her hand over the back of her neck, she shuddered and slowly resumed her place beside Lauren. Loud noises always made her jump at a disaster site, since they often meant more death and destruction.

"I'm getting too old for this shit," murmured Lauren, her eyes closed.

Kali smiled gently. In her late forties, Lauren was married with four boys – all gone from the nest. She was as sturdy and as dependable as anyone Kali had ever met. Every crisis they'd worked though, Lauren always said the same thing.

"I mean it this time." She laughed lightly and kept her eyes closed.

"Then quit. If your heart isn't here, maybe you need to be doing something else."

"Oh, my heart's here. That's not the problem." Looking older than she ever had before, Lauren lifted her water bottle for a long drink.

Kali glanced at her in concern. "Sore and tired?"

"No, I could handle that. At least I always have." Lauren shifted to a sitting position. "Not sure what it is. It's almost as if my soul says *enough*."

Kali's lips twitched. "Interesting way to put it."

"I know. I'm searching for an alternative description because it sounds nebulous, but that one feels right." Lauren sent her a sidelong glance. "How are you doing these days?"

The letter business flashed into her mind. Immediately, Kali squashed that thought. Lauren couldn't possibly know anything about it. She was asking about Kali's recovery from Mexico.

"Better. It's taking time. However, I am getting there." And she realized with surprise that today those words rang true. They weren't just a pat answer to stop others from asking personal questions. She really was on the road to recovery. She shifted back, relaxing yet a little more. Progress.

"Great." Lauren reached over and patted her knee. "You're a good person, Kali. Don't ever forget that."

A shout of excitement from the site disrupted the quiet lull. The noise was unmistakable. Rescuers had found something. Kali's energy surged and it was all she could do to stay put, not wanting to add one more person to clog up the area. Lack of coordination on these incidents was a nightmare – as were the onlookers. Desperate family members crowded for that first glimpse, and gruesome curiosity drew others close enough to see the dead. Finding survivors was a victory for all of them.

The noise continued to build into cheers and clapping.

Lauren stood, hope breaking through the fatigue on her face. "They must have found someone."

"That would be excellent. I'm tempted to go and see, but there's such a crowd now."

"Look, there is Brad and Todd."

Todd loped toward them, a huge grin on his face. His near seven-foot frame gave him a distinct advantage over the crowd. Almost a foot shorter, Brad powered along beside him. Vibrant energy beamed off them both.

"Hey, they found four people. All from the same family. Two kids, a baby and mom."

"Wow, that's fantastic." Kali hopped to her feet, giving them both a big hug. "How are they physically?"

"Cuts, bruises and possibly a broken bone or two." Brad watched the crew bringing the last of the children out. "They nearly didn't make it. Someone upstairs had to have been looking out for them." His smile dimmed.

Kali caught his change in expression and understood. Rescue missions were difficult for everyone.

"Even better," Todd said, "the kids said they heard people next door, too. So they're going to try and open up that pocket next."

Brad interjected, "That part of the building slid sideways, missing the weight of the rest collapsing on top of it. There's real hope of more survivors."

The volunteers returned to work with renewed enthusiasm. They worked long past the fall of darkness and even further – past point of exhaustion. They slept in relays. Industrial spotlights flung their weird yellow glow, magnifying shadows around every corner.

By dawn, exhausted determination ruled as they forced one foot in front of the other.

Soon rescue would turn to recovery.

The building had sprawled and shifted like a sliding deck of cards, with the center of the building taking the worst damage. The rescuers were focusing on the outer areas, where the odds of finding survivors were the greatest.

With no new survivors found since the two neighbors next to the family of four, most of the teams knew in their hearts that they were in recovery stage. Though there was always hope, there was talk of some of the teams heading home soon. After first aid checks, several of the survivors had slept out here with the rescuers, waiting, hoping that family members and friends would be found. Many were silent, frozen in place with shock and despair as the workers toiled on.

Kali tried to give them hope. She'd seen miracles happen. She never let herself forget that.

She returned to the rescue center. The local coffee shop had delivered huge urns of coffee and someone had dropped off cases of donuts, muffins and cookies. A sugar rush to boost the caffeine. Great. She had moved beyond tired and was happy to have sustenance. She'd gone from adrenaline junkie to numb endurance.

Just like Shiloh and everyone else here.

Standing beside Todd, Brad held a hot cup of coffee toward her.

Accepting it, she studied his weary face. Brad rarely missed helping out when he could. He always seemed to be one step ahead of her, anticipating her needs, her wants. She loved that about him. That he was a compassionate, sexy male with an endearing crooked grin didn't hurt either. She was just damn glad attraction hadn't gummed up their relationship. They were good friends. Best friends.

He needed to take a break. The stress and exhaustion had to be getting to him. She frowned, knowing he'd race for the closest bottle of booze when this was over.

Brad poured himself a cup of coffee before choosing a blueberry muffin. "They haven't gone into recovery mode, but it probably won't be long."

Todd stared across the huge area of destruction. "There's talk of some of us heading home soon. More equipment is coming to move the rubble. Should be here within the next hour or so."

Brad grimaced. Professional crews could handle much of the clean up along with local search and rescue crews. Almost thirty-five bodies had been recovered. Kali had no idea how many survivors were still buried. Due to the circumstances, they might never know. The building would have to be bulldozed and moved off while the authorities did their best to determine the lists of those that had and hadn't survived.

As she stood quietly enjoying her coffee, a twinge of energy bounced up her spine and latched onto the base of her brain.

Where it tugged – hard.

Kali casually looked around. Lauren spoke quietly with Brad. Todd had moved to the first aid area and appeared to be in a heavy discussion with the medics. She glanced in the other direction. The streets were full of crews and equipment, the noise deafening. Shiloh was in her crate in a tent behind Kali, sleeping. She'd worked hard these last days. Kali didn't want to disturb her unnecessarily.

Excusing herself, Kali walked away from the disaster site. The apartment had been the last building on the block. A large wooded area lay behind and to the left. A thick wall of trees started fifteen feet from the pavement, making it hard to see any deeper.

The tug happened again.

She frowned.

The tug turned to a yank.

Kali strode forward. Dark waves rolled off in the distance. Waves most other people had no idea existed.

She passed a couple standing wrapped in each other's arms. She walked by unnoticed. At the green edge, she stopped for a moment, checked her direction and walked forward a few more steps. The waves had slimmed, twisting and curling in anger, the remnants of a violent act left behind. She frowned. Hands on her hips, she pivoted in a slow circle, an ear cocked for the whispers. Ah. There.

She walked to the right about twenty feet and stopped again, searching for a physical sign, something to point to other people.

A small ravine, taken over by trees and brush, dropped in front of her. She surveyed it first, then discovering where the ground had recently been disturbed, she walked closer.

And froze. The waves of energy became more defined, separating into wide, twisting black ribbons. All centering from one spot.

Shit.

Another one.

CHAPTER 7

KALI CLOSED HER eyes as different visions poured through her mind, mixing, churning into a bizarre picture of someone's life. Someone laughed, a grim smile, then the image flashed to someone else crying with pain. Bizarre colors swept through her mind. She struggled to orient herself. Sacramento. Apartment collapse. Murder.

Her nostrils flared, already smelling what Mother Nature hid. Decomposition. It took minutes of focused deep breathing before her senses returned to normal.

She wandered toward the center, her thoughts consumed with the next problem...disclosing it without anyone knowing about her talents or putting herself forward as a suspect. This required Shiloh. And maybe a witness or two.

The coffee station had emptied of people. Kali poured herself another cup of java, even though her caffeine intake had her floating already. Then she went to check on Shiloh.

As she came into view, the dog whined, her paw lifting to the wire front gate, her chocolate eyes beseeching. Perfect, Shiloh needed a walk. Time to find a witness. Kali's gaze darted in one direction then the next. Time was of the essence. There. The two women enjoying donuts at the edge of the center had stopped to talk to Shiloh this morning. Now if they cooperated, she could get this thing done.

Unlocking the cage, she hugged Shiloh, laughing as he gave her face a wash. "Let's go girl. Walk time."

Shiloh woofed and danced at her side, wagging her long plume of a tail. Kali snapped on her lead. Shiloh sobered. "Yeah, you know already don't you, sweetheart?" The two headed over where the ladies were talking quietly. The older lady, dressed all in denim, went to pet Shiloh, then stopped and looked up at Kali for permission.

"Sure, you can pet her. She's not on the job now."

"She's beautiful."

Shiloh wagged her tail, her nose in the air, head tilted to one side. A perfect lady accepting her accolades.

The other woman, sporting long pigtail braids, asked, "How old is she?"

"She's seven." Kali gave the two women a friendly response. "Do you two live close by?"

They both nodded. The older lady answered. "We live a couple of blocks over. We wanted to help in some way."

Kali understood. "I'm sure everyone appreciates what you're doing."

The younger woman smiled warmly. "I'm Doris, by the way. It's been good to be able to do something. This is so horrible for the families."

"Do you want to stroll over this way a little so Shiloh can relieve herself?" Kali walked a couple of steps, still speaking with them. "In cases like this, it's the survivors I feel bad for."

The two ladies fell into step beside her, tired but happy to carry on the conversation.

"Those poor people." The older woman spoke angrily. "The apartment was supposed to be torn down in the spring, only the landlord managed to keep the matter tied up in the courts."

"The guy's just plain mean," said Doris. "We all knew people had moved into the building, but since most had lost their homes and jobs, we didn't want to make an issue of it. I'm one of the lucky ones. My husband is a policeman, so he's employed, but we have so many friends in trouble. Marian here..." She patted her friend on the shoulder. "Her husband was laid off at the beginning of this recession. He found a new job about a month ago, right?"

Marian glanced over at her friend, her face grim as she nodded once.

The conversation kept the two women busy and walking in the direction Kali needed to go. So far so good.

As they moved closer, Shiloh's ears perked up. They were at the green edge now, not far from the ravine and its grisly prize. Bending, she released Shiloh's lead and checked her working harness over again, tightening the buckle. Shiloh understood. Using hand signals she commanded Shiloh to go search.

The dog bounded into the brush. She jumped onto a fallen log before disappearing into the underbrush on the other side. Dew drops fell, splattering widely from the disruption. Birds scattered. A cacophony of beating feathers and bird cries rose to the treetops.

As the other two women continued to talk, Kali kept an ear tuned to the conversation and both eyes on the dog. Shiloh lifted her nose and went into action. It didn't take her a minute before she stopped at the exact spot in the ravine and barked several times. Then she lay down, her nose buried beneath her paws.

Both women stopped, twisting to stare into the woods.

Leaving the women, Kali hurried toward to Shiloh, stepping carefully over the underbrush and fallen wood. "I'm coming Shiloh. Hang on."

Patting the dog on the back, she whispered, "Good girl, Shiloh." Taking a treat from the pouch at her waist, she held it out. Shiloh whined, bolted the food down, then replaced her paws over her nose. She whined again. Kali kicked herself for forgetting Shiloh's teddy bear. Shiloh liked her teddy bear anytime. She *needed* it after finding cadavers.

Kali studied the area. Whoever had done this had taken advantage of the natural decline to the ravine and heavy brush, basically tumbling the bank over the body. It was a lot of dirt – many hundreds of pounds. If that person had been alive initially, they wouldn't have been for long.

"What's wrong?" Doris called. The women were curious, yet unconcerned, not understanding a working dog's signals. Not that other rescue workers would, either. Due to her special skills, Kali had been forced to create unique signals for Shiloh that could adjust to the different situations.

She glanced over at the women. "Shiloh says she's found something."

"Oh." They both ran closer.

Kali yelled, "No." She held her hands up. "Stop. Don't come any closer. We need to call the police. Do either of you have a cell phone?"

Both women immediately held up phones, shock on their faces. One phoned the rescue center and the other phoned her husband – the policeman.

ANOTHER SUCCESSFUL MISSION and another successful experiment. Kali had failed beautifully.

Now Texan – and damn, he liked that moniker – had proof

she was using unnatural skills. She had to have been to find the body this far away from the site. That had been his mistake with the Bralorne victim – he'd buried him on site where her finding the victim could have been accidental. And he couldn't have that. He'd needed a definitive answer. Now he had one. There could be no mistake here. Satisfaction permeated his soul. He'd caught her…and now she would pay.

Pleasure rippled through him. Safely tucked in the middle of the crowd, he watched as Kali sat and waited, unable to leave. The crime scene surged with waves of people. He carefully hid his smirk. Once again, she didn't appreciate the effort he'd put out for her. That was okay; this time she wasn't meant to. She would though. Eventually. They had time. It wasn't like he was going anywhere.

He studied Kali's face. Fatigue had aged her. Covered in dust, she sat hunched over, weary patience holding her upright. No longer a perfect princess.

Her night wasn't over yet either. The police were still going to want to talk to her. Again and again and again. He chortled.

Damn, he liked pissing her life down the drain.

KALI WONDERED HOW much longer. With the police short-staffed due to the apartment crisis, it seemed like she'd been waiting forever.

She knew the victim had been murdered. She even thought she knew how. She didn't know why or by whom. And that's where the problem stood. She'd considered volunteering more information to the police; only they were quite capable of finding out the cause of death on their own and would do it regardless of what she had to say.

She didn't understand much about these psychic tugs, except that they refused to be ignored. It wasn't as though psychic abilities came with an instruction manual.

She'd blundered along in the beginning. Visions had begun to slip into her head, sometimes of the victim's life or their death, usually vague and always as confusing as hell. Even when she wasn't on a disaster site, but sitting and watching television, the newscaster would mention a murder and Kali would receive a quick flash, a picture of the dead person. Even worse than knowing all that, was not being able to discuss it with anyone.

Her last freaky painting was a puzzle, too. So was this letter business. With any luck, Grant would solve the problem while she was away. She'd wanted to mention it to Brad but couldn't find the right moment. There'd been no time and too many ears to hear what she needed privacy to say.

Her butt had gone numb from sitting for so long. Kali sighed and shifted again. Most of the other teams had flown home. She thought she'd seen Lauren and Todd still working, but had no idea where Brad and Jarl had gotten to.

Powerful lights turned on suddenly, brightening the atmosphere. Another police cruiser arrived. Kali watched, hoping this would end her wait. An older, grizzled officer walked toward her.

"Hi, are you Kali Jordan?"

Kali straightened in relief.

"Sorry, you had to wait so long. Let me take your statement and you can go home."

The process was over in a few minutes.

"Kali! Jesus, there you are."

Kali spun to find Todd running toward her, a ragged look to him. She could relate. "Hey. Am I glad to see you. I was afraid everyone had left already."

"I saw you talking with the police, what the hell happened?" he asked, concern shifting away the fatigue in his face.

Kali winced. "Just the norm. Shiloh found another body."

Todd frowned, staring in the direction of the collapsed apartment building.

"No, not here." She pointed toward the direction she'd walked away from. "Over there. I walked Shiloh over to the woods to relieve herself."

Todd shook his head. "She shouldn't have been working there."

"Nope, she shouldn't have. You know yourself that it's hard for the dogs to separate from the intensity of a disaster site and the surrounding areas. Besides, what's the chance of another body that far from the site?" She linked her arm with his. "I'm glad you're still here."

"Lauren has left and I'll be leaving soon. A couple are staying behind." He searched her face. "Can you leave now? There's another flight in…" He glanced at his watch. "In an hour and a half."

Kali groaned. "I so want to be on it." She bent down and

scratched Shiloh behind the ear. "Yeah, you're ready to head home, too, aren't you girl?" Shiloh wagged her tail and licked her hand. "Come on then. Let's pack up and get the hell home."

Straightening, she realized the night had gone quiet. If she hadn't been staring blindly in the direction she might have missed it. Murmurs wafted through the crowd, growing in volume as one of the crime scene officers carried out something large and awkward. As he placed it in the back of the van, she caught a better glimpse. Her blood ran cold.

Tucked in a clear bag, tagged as evidence, was a large metal tank of some kind – shaped almost like an oxygen tank.

CHAPTER 8

KALI PULLED THE Jeep onto her gravel driveway, parking at the front of her house. She frowned when she noticed the dark truck parked to one side.

Grant. And a stranger.

This she didn't need. The door opened and Grant stepped out. Shiloh barked. Kali murmured to her, "I know. Bad timing, huh?"

Still, Kali had a hard time dragging her gaze away from the tight faded jeans that accentuated his muscled thighs. And the cream golf shirt stretching across his chest didn't help either. She swallowed. She might not want him here, but he was definitely eye candy.

The twinkling front bay windows of her house caught her attention. The rest of the world danced with the dawn of a new day, whereas she…she felt like shit. And probably looked it, too. She'd been gone for days and had spent the last twenty-four hours in the same dirty clothes, with her hair covered in dust and her skin gritty as sandpaper. Lovely.

The flight home from California had been postponed by a good six hours. She thought it was Friday. Her inner clock was beyond screwed. Thank God Dan had been waiting to pick her up when she'd finally made it in. She could have begged off the next step, too, except she'd been doing this for far too long to shy off work when everyone else was exhausted. Together, they'd transported gear and animals to the center for unloading in the large garage. Later, equipment would be washed and sorted…checked to see if it was safe to reuse, and kits restocked.

First, the team needed rest. Janet, a long-time volunteer and dog trainer, had sent Kali home. Her good humor had been a balm to Kali's stressed nerves.

Right now, all she wanted was sleep.

Grant strolled over as Kali let Shiloh out of the Jeep, then headed to the back for her gear.

"Good morning."

Shooting him a quick glance, she reached for her grubby travel bag. "Well, it's morning. I don't know about the good part. It's a little early for a visit, isn't it?"

He reached inside the cargo area and lifted her bags in a smooth easy motion before she had a chance to argue. She turned to face the second man and her brain stalled. Christ he was gorgeous, cool and classy, with Adonis type features. He wore black jeans and a silver knit shirt tight enough to show the rippling muscles with every movement, but not so tight as to label him a player. He nodded his head in her direction, a small smile playing on the corner of his mouth. "Good morning."

Holy shit. The warm chocolate voice rolled through her ears and down to her tummy. She couldn't pull her fascinated gaze away. She must look like an idiot.

She didn't need this. She needed rest. No matter how many male models Grant put in her path today, nothing was going to stop her from heading to her bed – alone!

Grant passed her on the way to the front door, his spine stiff, his movements clipped, bags carried easily in his hands. Sure, he hadn't been up for the most of night, she thought, disgruntled. Slamming the Jeep door shut, she made her way to her front door. If Grant wanted to ask questions, he was going to have to let her shower and eat first. Hell, no. Better to give him what he needed then collapse. Besides, what she really wanted was another look at her painting.

"Just put the gear by the back door, please. I'll clean it up later." She tossed her keys on the counter and faced him and the hunk who had walked in behind him. "I have to feed Shiloh. You have about five minutes after that before I collapse." She turned her attention to rummaging up a meal for the dog. With Shiloh happily wolfing her food down, she faced the men. "What's so important that you had to come this early? And who's your friend?"

Grant crossed his arms and leaned against the counter. "Stefan is a consultant for law enforcement. He knows about the letters. I thought he should be here to hear today's discussion first hand." He cast a glance at Stefan, then turned his gaze back to Kali. "You were part of an investigation down in California yesterday, I understand." He regarded her intently. "At the apartment collapse.

Apparently you found a body."

Shit. How had he known? And so fast? Was there anything the FBI didn't know?

She turned to face him, widening her gaze in what appeared, she hoped, to be casual interest. She kept her gaze on him, refusing to be sidetracked by the mind-blowing Stefan. This time there was no mistaking Grant's assessing look. Brushing her hair back off the side of her head, Kali realized just how weary she'd become. Grant and then bed.

Her eyes widened. No, not together. She blinked as her hormones stood up and shook free of months – hell, years – of dormancy. No way. They had a hell of a nerve rearing their heads right now.

Slamming a lid on her unruly libido, she met his gaze calmly. "We found several victims. I presume you're talking about the last one that Shiloh found separate from the disaster site."

He raised one eyebrow. "Can you tell me about that, please?"

Dan had probably told him. Then again, bad news always traveled fast, and anything linked to her name probably had been flagged. It took a few moments to explain. When she fell silent, he studied her for several long seconds. Kali stared back, refusing to let this man unnerve her. Still, he was an imposing figure, causing her belly to quiver uncertainly.

"They've identified him."

"Oh, good." Exasperation crept into her voice. "Does that mean I can go to bed now?"

"He was one of the survivors from the apartment complex. And he'd been buried alive."

"Oh no!" Kali's stomach heaved and she closed her eyes briefly. "That tank. Christ. I saw a tank tagged as evidence when they loaded it into the van I didn't understand the implication." Kali's shoulders sagged, defeated by such a horror. "Why? Why would somebody do that?"

"I don't know. That's what I'm trying to find out."

"You?" She frowned. "Why you?"

"Because I wanted in on this one." He shifted casually.

"You work in California?" Kali was really confused now. Why would the FBI in Oregon be concerned about a local murder from California? "I don't understand."

Leaning forward, he pinned her with a gimlet eye. "Can't you see a potential connection between the letters and this murder?"

Kali grabbed the closest chair, sitting before she collapsed. As the realization set in, she slumped lower. Thoughts frantically rushed through her mind, only to circle around in endless loops of confusion. The letters… "No," she whispered. "I mean it's hard *not* to think of them. Still, I didn't make the connection – it's a different state."

"Understandable." He pulled out a small notebook and sat down opposite her. "So now…let's focus."

For the next half hour, Grant *questioned* her. Kali felt more like she was being interrogated. By the time he was done, she felt like a wet dishcloth hung out to dry.

Stefan never said a word. Quiet he might be – stoic he wasn't. His gaze locked onto her with unnerving intensity. She struggled to ignore him.

"Good. I think that's it. Except I need a list from you of every person you recognized in Sacramento. Dan has given me a list of everyone who went from the center."

Kali struggled as the world she thought she knew shifted again. "You think it's one of us? A rescuer?" Defeat tinged her voice.

"I think it bears reviewing. The person has to be in the know somehow. I'm going to be at the center for a week or so, posing as a visiting SAR member from Maine." He stood up and stretched.

The golf shirt pulled across his massive chest, showing every muscle. Then there were the tight-ass pants. Why was it Grant made her throat constrict and the nerves in her stomach dance? The consultant, Stefan, was better looking, with some indefinable charisma she'd never seen before.

But it was Grant that interested her.

It was Grant's energy that surged toward her whenever they were close together.

It was Grant's energy that made hers brighten.

Forcing her gaze back up to his face, she swallowed a couple of times before trusting her voice. "Are you experienced enough in this field to answer the type of questions that come up?"

Grant dropped his arms to his side. "I volunteered with my brother for years. He works out of a center in Maine. Both training and rescue work."

"Then maybe we could use you regardless of the real reason. We're always short staffed."

"Good to know. I'll be around, if you get called out again, let me know where you're going to be." Pulling a card from his wallet, he dropped it on the table beside her.

Kali's face froze. Was that the same as *don't leave town?* "I can do that," she whispered.

Something in her face caught his attention.

"Tough couple of days, huh?"

"Yeah, just a bit." Intense weariness made it hard to get up.

Stefan spoke, smooth velvet that momentarily hid the punch of his question. "How's the painting?"

She froze for the second time. "How do you know I paint?" she murmured, her heartbeat knocking so loudly against her rib bones, she was sure the men could hear.

"You just confirmed it." His gaze locked onto hers. So intense she couldn't break away. It was as if he were trying to see inside her mind. She blinked…and he broke the connection. She'd been released only because he let her go. She exhaled slowly, a fine tremor wracking her spine. It should have scared her. He should have terrified her. Instead, she understood. She didn't know if she'd passed or failed whatever test he'd administered, but she knew he'd been assessing her.

Beyond strange.

She gathered her strength and stood, stumbled slightly, catching herself on the side of the table.

Grant reached out to steady her.

Energy zinged her.

She jerked back reflexively. He frowned. She bit her bottom lip.

His hand stayed in the air before dropping to his side. He studied her quietly.

Heat flamed her cheeks. Bravely she met his gaze. "Sorry, I didn't mean that the way it looked; you startled me."

With a curt nod, he accepted her excuse and turned to walk away, a slight clip to his step.

Stefan stayed behind. She glanced at him, expecting anything but what she saw – compassion. He reached into his back pocket and pulled out his wallet. He handed her a business card. "Here's my card. You're going to want to call me."

Kali watched the two men drive away. She'd handled that badly. She hadn't been able to stop herself bolting from Grant's touch and the freakin' scary need to touch him. She couldn't explain it anymore than she could explain the need to feast her eyes on him. Attraction was one thing. This was something else yet again. She didn't want to care about anyone. Not anymore. It hurt. And she'd had enough hurt lately.

The trouble was her hormones weren't listening.

She glanced down at the card in her hand. Stefan Kronos. Consultant. Psychic Investigator.

What the hell?

GRANT PULLED ONTO the highway heading back into Portland. Kali lived in Sorenson, a hiccup of a town nestled between Salem and Portland. By rights it should lose its town status as it had been all but eaten up by Portland's growth. He drove seamlessly in and out of traffic, his mind caught on Kali's last comment. And her reaction to his touch. Now that had hurt. He'd only been trying to save her from a fall.

He'd felt the zing. Reveled in the energy. She'd bolted from it.

And not in a nice way. How could something that powerful *not* be right?

Damn. His hormones went into overdrive every time he thought of her. Yet when he was *with* her, he went into professional mode. Calm, quiet and dependable. Not exactly every woman's dream.

He needed her to feel the same way he did.

"She does." Stefan spoke for the first time.

Grant snorted, easing the car into the other lane. "Really? How come she couldn't take her eyes off you, then?"

"Only at first meet. She got over me pretty quickly."

The smile in Stefan's voice had Grant studying his friend's profile. Grant wanted to believe him.

"And you need to."

Staring back at the highway, Grant realized he needed lots of things, but Kali in the middle of this case wasn't one of them. Kali in his arms, Kali in his bed, or how about Kali in his life? As if.

His logical mind struggled with the whole logistics of the Sacramento murder. It would be physically challenging to pull off alone. Moving bodies required a physical strength and a level of fitness few people had. The oxygen tank added to the weirdness factor. Although Kali was in great shape, she couldn't have lifted a man the size of the Sacramento victim. If she had a partner – maybe. A partner would open the suspect pool to include almost anyone. Something else to talk to the profilers about.

Working with Kali on this case would be like diving into a game of 'hide and go seek' with the devil. Finding buried victims was going to be a challenge. She needed to stay strong. If the press found out about this…not fun. And with her undeveloped psychic power… He knew all too well what happened to people who couldn't control that. Most of them ended up in mental institutions or committing suicide.

Stefan could help her.

"I left her my card. She needs a bit of time."

He would have to watch how she handled this mess.

"You're in trouble here. With her."

"How bad?" Grant couldn't *not* ask.

"Bad." Stefan leaned his head back against the headrest and closed his eyes. "She's very powerful. Untrained, not in control and her system surges with physic awareness."

"That's not necessarily bad, though, is it?" he asked cautiously.

As if almost asleep, Stefan murmured, "No, not bad. Except she's keeping secrets."

ONCE AWAKE, KALI lay still for a long time. The last few days had finally caught up with her. Shiloh snuffled and rolled over beside her. "Hey girl. You're as whupped as I am, huh."

Maybe it was time to quit. What had Lauren said? 'It's almost as if my soul says enough.' Kali had to admit a part of her felt the same way. She hadn't handled this last mission very well and finding a murder victim definitely added a nasty ending.

She rolled over and checked her clock. Noon. Kali yawned and stretched. Shiloh stretched her paws across the pillows, burying her nose against the blanket. A lady in all ways. Kali laughed. Not.

She hopped out of the bed, opened the glass doors for Shiloh in case she needed to go out. Having an upper deck with direct access to the backyard was a nice feature to the house. So was having a doggy door in the laundry room. Shiloh could take care of her own needs while Kali slept. Enjoying the clear blue sky for a brief moment, Kali walked inside to shower. By the time she finished getting dressed in cotton capris and camisole shirt, Shiloh had joined her. The two trooped into the kitchen, feeling rested and more ready to take on the day. Hopefully without the letter writer's interference. She didn't dare call him a stalker – even in her mind. That sounded more ominous than she could deal with.

Kali stopped. Energy pulsed from outside her kitchen. Someone sat on her deck, someone in a black suit. Grant. Again.

Shit. Her stomach jumped, her aura pulsed in welcome. *What the hell?* She so didn't need this. Or want this.

And if she kept repeating that, she might actually believe it.

What could he possibly need now? She opened the French doors and stepped into the afternoon sun.

He immediately stood and faced her. Grim lines etched his face.

Her stomach sank.

"Hello. Sorry if I kept you waiting. I gather you forgot to ask me something this morning?" She yawned as the fresh air caught her. "You could have just called, you know." She stretched. "I feel so much better. It's amazing what a little sleep can do."

A quizzical look came over his face. "So you should." He studied her expression. "I didn't come this morning, I was here yesterday. It's Saturday."

Kali stared at him in shock. "No way. I only slept for a couple of hours, at most."

"No, you slept all day and all night. I was here yesterday," he said firmly.

Her stomach growled. Maybe she *had* missed three meals. She spun on her heels and turned on her laptop. She put on a pot of coffee while the machine booted up. When done, she checked the date. Damn. No wonder she felt good.

Grant stood in the open door. "Do you believe me now?"

"I guess I needed more rest than I thought." She shrugged dismissively, brushing past him to cross the deck. "I can't say I'm surprised. These last few days were pretty hellish." Kali walked over to the railing to stare out at her half-wild yard – so different from the dust and grayness of the Sacramento site. She took a deep breath, loving the musky scent of the evergreens, warm and heavy from the hot sun. It was good to be home.

She turned to him. "Will you have coffee? It should be ready soon."

"Sure. Thanks."

Returning with two cups, she held his out. "I seem to be doing this a lot. So, tell me, now that we have the social niceties out of the way, why are you here this time?"

"Dan received another letter."

Kali's stomach clenched. Suddenly she didn't feel quite so well. Carefully placing her mug on the table, she returned to the railing, trying to find balance in the craziness. Turning to face him, she leaned back against the wood and narrowed her gaze at him. "Why Dan again, I wonder?" She winced. "Not that I want the letters here. Believe me, I'm happy to put some distance between them and me."

He glanced at his mug and back up at her. "That's not going to happen. And the most likely reason for delivering the letter to Dan is that the writer knew either you wouldn't be here to receive it or that you wouldn't be awake in time to find it." He took a sip of coffee. "Or maybe he's trying to discredit the center. Or directing the suspicion toward it and away from something else? We don't *know* anything at this point."

Kali rubbed her temple. God, what a horrible thought. "So many people would have known I was out of town. Also, anyone could have watched the house and seen me come home and collapse. And that's just creepy." Shivers rippled over her spine. That had 'stalker' written all over it. She tried to refocus. "Putting that aside for the moment, what did this message say?"

"It said, 'First round to me. Round two begins soon.'"

Kali's knees buckled. Grant hastened over to steady her, his arm curving around her back. "Easy, Kali. Take it easy."

She leaned into him, welcoming something solid to grab onto in a world that had suddenly shifted. Flashes of color flared, sparked between them. She blinked. Embarrassed and more than a little stunned, she pulled away and retreated to the closest chair.

Yesterday she'd pulled away. Today she'd leaned in, then pulled away. She was an idiot. Talk about sending mixed signals. Grant was still speaking.

"I'm sorry. There was no easy way to tell you." He studied her face intently.

She shook her head, a broken laugh escaping. "It doesn't matter. I would feel this way regardless."

"Maybe."

She considered his strong face. She'd thought he had brown eyes. Right now, they looked as black as the dead of night. She swallowed and leaned back. Grant straightened. He walked away for a moment, then came back.

"Have a drink of coffee. It will make you feel better."

She stared blankly at him. "Coffee?"

He held out her cup. "Here, drink. Do you have any brandy?"

"Brandy? Uh no, I don't think so." Kali accepted the cup, then closed her eyes briefly and took a deep breath. She needed to get a grip. "I'll be fine. I just need a minute."

Grant took a seat beside her, his cup of coffee in hand.

It took a few minutes before she trusted herself to speak again. "One more time, what did the letter say?"

Slowly, Grant enunciated, "First round to me. Round two begins soon."

She shuddered.

"Do you think the victim in Sacramento was his first?"

He studied her face. "I don't know. The timing, situation, people involved could all work. However, it's too early to be sure." Turning to look up at the bright sky, he added, "It's also possible there's a different victim. One we haven't found yet."

Another victim? Christ, weren't there enough already? "I can't even begin to contemplate that scenario." She struggled to reason through the message. She'd been so happy to put this from her mind. No longer. "So, if – and it's a big if – this first victim were the Sacramento victim, it would mean the killer was there when I was there – or close by."

"And possibly for the same reason you were – only he had a hidden agenda. So the question remaining now is who was there with you? Any chance you wrote that list of everyone you recognized there, did you?"

"No, I went to bed right away." She sighed. "You said Dan wrote you a list of the workers who went from our center. Besides, those people, there were teams from other regions. And the many volunteers who weren't SARs." She took a sip of hot coffee, hoping it would warm the block of ice forming in the pit of her stomach. "Overall, there would have been more than a hundred people involved. Tracking them would be next to impossible. Besides, anyone could have flown there and done this. We weren't all that far away from home. Honestly, someone could have driven there and back in the time I was stuck there."

Heavy silence settled between them. Kali couldn't even begin to understand the mindset of someone who could do something like that. Why? She certainly had trouble with the center being targeted, but that someone had involved her in this nastiness…well it didn't make sense.

"Think carefully. Do you know anyone who could do this?"

A strangled laugh escaped. "What a horrible thought." She stared up at the sky. "I started *a* list after I gave you the first letter. I have to tell you, everyone on it is ridiculously normal."

Grant stared at her soberly for a long moment. "So were the worst killers in history."

Frustration boiled deep inside. It festered, turning her stomach sour. "Why is he doing this?" she whispered. "What does he want?"

Grant laid a soothing hand on hers, squeezing gently. Sparks flashed. Amazed, she watched them spark and then become absorbed into both their auras. Why? She couldn't begin to understand the timing for this new awareness. So much in her life was screwed up – and all at the same time – making everything hard to sort through...and even harder to understand. Acceptance was a long way off.

She released her death grip on the armrest, her knuckles pasty white already. She sighed, relaxing her shoulders. Her stomach burned with remnants of the revulsion slivering through her.

"What matters is that you realize and accept that this is happening. And..." he paused mid-thought, stretching out his long legs. "He knows you very well, which means you know him, too."

That scared the crap out of her. She liked normal. She liked predictable. She liked routine.

She sure as hell didn't like killers who issued challenges. She hopped to her feet.

"I'll be right back." She strode to her bedroom to retrieve her notebook. As she returned, she handed it to him.

"What's this?"

She picked up her cup and walked back into the kitchen, continuing to talk. He followed. "My lists. I tried to think of any known associates that might have a problem with me." She hitched a shoulder. "I don't know how well I did."

He flipped through the pages. "This gives us a place to start. If you think of anything else, call me."

"I will. Is there...anything else I can do?"

"Possibly. We're forming a small task force that will coordinate with several different local law enforcement agencies. The FBI is working with the Sacramento Police to process the evidence from this latest murder. Time is in short supply. We need to know everything we can before he strikes again. Therefore, we need to know what you know."

"Except, I don't know anything." Kali closed her eyes briefly. "I wish there was a way to predict his next victim…and why he would choose a particular person."

Grant loosened his tie. "There isn't yet. We'll know more once we plow through the material we've collected. Then we'll have to wait. For forensic information. For autopsy results. For the handwriting analysis. For a profile." He stood. "If I need anything else, I'll give you a call. Do I need to remind you to lock your doors, watch out for strange cars and keep your cell phone handy?"

She winced. "I will. Thanks."

The house felt empty after he left. Empty. Cold. A chill had settled into her soul. Her stomach growled, again. Kali opened the fridge and rummaged for anything that hadn't spoiled. Something wrinkled and brown sagged in one corner and something blue in the other. Lovely. Shiloh barked once.

"You're hungry too, aren't you girl. We both lost a few meals." Kali opened cupboard doors. "Yours is easy enough." She would prefer to feed Shiloh a raw food diet, but the constant traveling and rough conditions made that impossible. Kali opened a can of food and portioned out crunchies to go with it. Putting them together, she gave the mix a good stir before offering it to Shiloh. "There you go, sweetheart. I added a little extra to help with those sore muscles."

Rummaging for ingredients, she rustled up a quick cheese omelet and toast. She'd have to go shopping before she could eat again. Taking her plate outside, Kali sat in the sun and slowly ate her first real meal in days.

Knowing the letter writer might be watching her even now, she tossed her hair back, and took another bite. She refused to let the thought of him drive her away from the simple joy of being home and sitting on her deck. That didn't make her stupid. Her cell phone sat beside her coffee cup.

She sighed and leaned back, grateful to be home.

People were funny. She'd seen what people called 'home' all over the world. Some were gorgeous million-dollar houses on the ocean with private waterfalls and their own airstrips. Most often the homes were commonplace – four walls and a roof with a middle class family trying to make a living and enjoy life while they were doing it. Then there were the rest. The smile slid from her face. She'd seen cardboard boxes sheltering complete families. She'd seen platforms with big leaves for walls and she'd seen dugouts into the sides of hills that held multiple families. In every case, the shelter meant just as much to those people as the million-dollar homes did to their owners. Usually more.

A shelter represented home, security and a place to call their own.

When Mother Nature destroyed homes, she didn't discriminate. They all fell to her will.

Disturbed by the sad memories, Kali took her empty dishes to the sink. In a few quick seconds, she had the kitchen clean. Drying the last dish, she paused.

The painting.

She'd forgotten about it.

Finishing up quickly, she walked down the hallway. The door was closed again. She couldn't remember if she'd left it that way or not. Damn she hated the shakiness that slithered through her.

Stupid. She pushed it open and strode in.

Christ.

Power streamed toward her, waves pouring off the canvas. The force of it stopped her in her tracks. Determined, she stepped forward a couple of steps. She frowned. No way. She leaned closer. She studied the detail, the accuracy, the emotion. The life. She shook her head. No. It wasn't possible. Digging into her memory, she compared those images with the painting. She blinked several times. There could be no doubt. Grim foreboding slipped down her spine.

The picture took on a new ugliness.

The panicked finger marks scraped into the dirt wall, as if the victim had tried to dig his way out, hadn't looked odd before. She'd seen this countless times. It was a natural reaction for anyone buried in rubble.

No, it was the tiny cylinder tucked into the image that made her blood run cold. As did the faint tube running to the victim's nose.

There could be no doubt.

The person in the painting had been buried alive – intentionally.

Kali knew there were too many similarities to discount, regardless of how ludicrous. The painting, the scene with a dead body and the oxygen tank, depicted the murder victim she'd just found in California. Not a similar scene but that same one.

Kali lifted a hand to her aching temples. That meant she'd

painted this before the murder had happened. Wait. She thought about that for a moment. Was that right? Did she know when that poor man had been buried? No. Grant hadn't offered a time of death or a time line of any kind.

One thing she did know was that this painting would be hard to explain, particularly if anyone knew when she'd created it. On impulse, she bent forward to check something else. No, there was her signature.

So, she'd actually created this. Now if only she knew how? And what should she do about it?

CHAPTER 9

KALI AVOIDED THE center on Saturdays, if she could. Today, Dan had called asking if she could come in to help with the accounts. He'd been snowed under since Sacramento and as usual, his bookkeeping had gotten out of hand. The parking lot was half-full when she arrived. With mixed emotions, she parked at the front by the stairs. Chaos reigned outside the building, making her tired and energized at the same time. Dogs could be seen and heard everywhere. And that was comforting. Normal.

In a way, this really was home.

Shiloh barked and bounced from side to side in the back. Kali opened the door of her Jeep. Gathering the leash and her purse, she walked toward the front door.

"Hi, Kali."

Elizabeth, a regular visitor at the center, stood at the top of the stairs with a tongue-lolling Newfoundland pup slouching against her leg.

"Hi, Elizabeth. This place is chaos today."

Elizabeth laughed. "That's Dan's doing. He organized weekend training classes for those of us that work. I signed up Jefferson." Elizabeth motioned to the dog at her side.

"Hey, Jefferson, when are you going to grow into those feet?" Kali grinned, then couldn't resist bending down and hugging the beautiful teddy bear. Jefferson took immediate advantage, swiping her face with his huge tongue. Kali laughed and used her sleeve to dry her face. "How did he do?"

Elizabeth winced. "He's the biggest suck of the class. Does anything for a cuddle and remembers none of the lesson five minutes later."

Kali grinned. She could just imagine. "Have you seen Dan?" she asked, her hand scrubbing Jefferson's thick black ruff.

"Nope. I think he's hiding. Starting these extra classes has ruined his peace and quiet." Elizabeth tugged on the dog's collar. "Let's go home. It's good to see you, Kali. Take care."

"You, too." Kali watched Elizabeth coax the Newfoundland toward her van, before she turned and walked into the center. She greeted several other people on her way. Dan would be in his office. She knew he preferred the old days when the center was more about rescues and less about dogs. He often forgot that he hadn't built a business, he'd built a community. People came to socialize – themselves and their dogs.

She appreciated his call today. Helping out should keep her mind off the damn letter writer. A win-win situation.

At the open doorway to Dan's office, she watched him stare at reams of paper in his hands. Wrinkles creased his brow; a brown color tinged his jowls. He looked unhealthy. Her heart lurched. She wasn't ready to lose him. He'd been a mainstay of her life for years now. She couldn't image life without him.

"Hey, Dan. Nice trick if you can manage it."

Her absent-minded friend lifted his head, confusion clouding his face. It cleared almost instantly. "Oh, hi, Kali. Thanks for coming. What was that about a trick?" He ran his fingers through his hair, making it stick out at odd angles.

Kali sat on the spare chair, Shiloh at her feet. "Hiding in your office. What's the matter? The center too full for you right now?"

His sheepish grin slid free, brightening her spirits. "You could say that. It's crazy out there. We've got obedience classes going on right now. I used to enjoy Saturdays. I enjoyed the center more when it was smaller, too." He dropped his pencil and leaned back. "You had a rough go this time, I hear. And made the headlines again with the Sacramento disaster." At her grimace, he added, "But then, what else is new, right?"

Dan fixed his gaze on her as if wanting to say something else. His eyes were piercing, yet sad. The salt and pepper hair that she remembered had turned to snow white. The wrinkles of his face sagged, reminding her of a topographical map. Every job he'd worked had contributed to those heavy lines. This man had heart. He'd spent a fortune of his own money helping others and keeping the center going. Mostly, the center survived on government grants, contracts, training classes and private donations.

Instinct prodded her to look closer. Something deeper was going on. She waited for him to continue.

"You know, I've seen some nasty sites in my time. I've also

learned more than I'd like about what one person can do to another. This letter business..."

Kali winced. She so didn't want to go there if she could help it. "That mess is bad news; I know." She hesitated. "Is something else bothering you?"

Dan wrinkled his forehead, a heavy sigh escaping. "It's probably nothing. Not like he hasn't done it before. Brad still hasn't reported in from Sacramento. He shipped Sergeant home that last night, isn't answering his phone and he hasn't been seen since. Susan's called several times already today."

"Oh no. Not again." Kali didn't know what to think. Brad often disappeared for a day or two, particularly after a bad disaster; still it was rare for him to let Sergeant travel alone. "If he's gone on a bender, he wouldn't normally check in for several days."

Brad's drinking binges often lasted three to four days. His wife hated them and usually called his friends to see if he'd bunked on their couches. Susan hadn't called her yet. Apparently they weren't friends anymore. Truthfully, Kali couldn't remember if she'd checked her messages when she woke up. Grant's visit had thrown off her routine.

"I wouldn't worry yet." Kali injected hope into her voice.

"You're right. We'll give him a day or two to check in." Dan's face lightened, the wrinkles eased as a happier look appeared on his face.

"Let me know when he calls." Shiloh nudged her hand and Kali refocused for a moment on her furry friend. Shiloh always knew when she was upset. "I'll worry until I know he's okay."

"Me, too." Dan's fingers played restlessly with the stack of papers in his hand. When he looked up at her, the dread revealed in his eyes shook her. "I don't know, Kali. I'm not sure what's going on, but I've got a bad feeling about this."

So had she. That didn't change anything.

THE KITCHEN DOOR lock snicked open. Kali had been gone for hours. She'd probably gone to the center again. He knew he could be cutting it close, but he'd wanted to deliver his gift in person.

Careful, he placed the plate on the table and tucked the note half inside the wrapping. His gift stood out like a centerpiece. She couldn't miss it.

Perfect.

Backtracking to the door, he stopped. Her car lights would be visible well before reaching the house. He'd have lots of time to get away. What could it hurt to look around?

Decision made, he headed straight upstairs to her bedroom. He opened her dresser drawers, neat stacks of cotton underwear lay inside, his black gloves a strong contrast to the pristine whiteness. The need to touch the smooth cotton was a temptation he couldn't afford. Slamming the drawer shut, he opened the next and the next. He moved toward the large closet, examining clothes and shoes layered inside. Only then did he allow himself to focus on her bed.

He sighed. A cream duvet covered the chocolate sheets, with one corner turned back as if in invitation. As if. He forced himself back, angry as lust twisted against his purpose. She was the devil's tool, and the sooner he proved it to the world, the better they'd all be.

He walked downstairs, determined to erase the intimate picture of her bedroom from his mind. He cast a quick glance at the plain but comfortable living room with several arm chairs and couches arranged around the well-used fireplace before heading down the hall. He passed the laundry room and main bathroom. The next door was closed. Curious, he pushed it open.

A studio? She painted?

Her easel stood in the middle of the room, a sheet tossed over the top. Unable to resist, he walked over and lifted the sheet.

And jumped back.

He hissed his fury. Witch. Evil spawn.

Control, cold and clinical, returned his focus. He had to study her work – to know his enemy.

And that knowledge sealed her fate.

KALI ENJOYED BOOKKEEPING. Seeing the overall picture of the financial state of the center, stable and growing, gave her such a great feeling. She was part of something good, worthwhile. And she needed the distraction now. She couldn't get Brad out of her mind. She'd tried to call Susan several times, only she wasn't picking up. Kali had left messages. Susan hadn't returned her calls.

She thought about the teams she'd met in Sacramento. Her industry was relatively small and the dogs and handlers, well known. Who could have stayed behind and worked with Brad? It took her a few moments, then it hit her. Jarl.

Pulling out her cell phone, she dialed his number. No answer. She left a message. She hoped he'd call her back. Their ten-year friendship had hit the rocks late last year when she realized he'd been pilfering little things from the center. He'd stopped after she'd confronted him about it. Their friendship had taken a hit for a while. Still, things were cordial now.

Kali picked up a receipt, read it and placed it down on a pile. She snatched it up again, reread it and placed it on a different pile. She needed to get a grip or she'd really make a worse mess of the accounting than Dan.

Her mind refused to let go. Someone was killing people. Could Brad have somehow run afoul of this killer? She closed her eyes. Please don't let him have been a victim of this killer. She didn't even want to think about Jarl in the same light. That he hadn't returned her calls yet, surely didn't mean he'd been kidnapped, too. This nightmare was making her crazy.

No. Brad had to be drowning his sorrows. Like the last time and the time before. He'd check in soon.

Determined to complete the job, she reached for another handful of paper. This load had phone bills mixed in with several crumpled restaurant receipts. One for take-out Chinese food. Burger King. Stamps and envelopes. Kali groaned. Damn, Dan had entered the last batch of figures. That usually meant she had to review all his postings. Another hour of trying to read his writing. Honestly, he shouldn't be allowed close to the bookkeeping.

"Kali, good to see you." Janet stood at the doorway a big cheery grin on her face.

"Janet." Kali threw her pencil down on the desk in relief. Any interruption was welcome at this point. "Hey, thanks for finishing the cleanup from the last trip. I appreciate it."

"No problem. You were exhausted and I was glad to help," Janet said, leaning her tall willowy frame against the wall. "Besides, Brenda was hanging around, so I put her to work, too."

Kali rolled her eyes at the thought of her cute bouncy friend being put to work by Janet. Brenda loved to help out – for a little while. She wasn't great on sticking around. Janet, on the other hand, was one of those rare individuals who could see what needed to be done and then do it.

Janet's happiness seemed so genuine. If only Kali knew her secret. Janet was like a breath of fresh air and her light-hearted laughter was just what Kali needed right now. "Still smiling I see."

"Of course. Life is too short for anything else."

Kali avoided that topic. It was easier to present a front of peaceful contentment than to open up about the unsettled emotions chewing up her insides. Life was too short. And she had too much death in hers, as it was.

"What are you doing today?"

"The new guy is helping me this afternoon. He worked at the Maine center years ago. He does have a magical touch with the dogs. If he works out and stays around, we should consider hiring him as an instructor."

Kali blinked. New instructor? Maine? Jesus, Janet was talking about Grant.

Janet glanced behind her to see if anyone was close enough to hear, before she stepped further into the office. "Did you see him? Oh, my God." Her eyes gleamed with humor, her voice a conspiratorial whisper. "He's stunning. That tall-dark-and-take-charge look always does it for me." The tall redhead fanned herself and rolled her eyes, a huge grin on her face.

Kali sat back and watched her as-good-as-married friend rhapsodize over Grant. Kali didn't dare voice her opinion. She'd give herself away, for sure. Besides, she didn't need to say anything. Janet was right. Grant was stunning. And a little unnerving. "That good, huh?"

"Oh yeah, that good." Janet looked furtively behind her again. "Not only that, he's going to be here full-time." Her face split in huge smirk. "I'm about to volunteer every day."

"So much for Dennis." Dennis was Janet's police officer boyfriend. They were perfect together. Both would do anything for a person in need.

"Maybe not. Dennis wouldn't mind if I played a little." Mischief lit up her deep brown eyes. "I won't ask him about it, though. I'll just go ahead and snag this guy. Maybe, we'll have a threesome."

There was no help for it. Kali laughed. The thought of Dennis letting anyone close to Janet was comical. He was loving, possessive and never let her out of his sight when he was off duty. Even on duty, he called her several times a day. "I can't imagine Dennis with another guy."

"Well, I'd be in the middle of course. So technically, it wouldn't be Dennis with another guy." She jutted out one hip in an exaggerated imitation of deep thinking. "This has possibilities. Hmmm."

"Jeez, woman. How am I going to get any work done with you putting those damn images in my mind?"

"You need to laugh more often. You're serious these days. As if the weight of the world is on your shoulders. You need some fun in your life." She grinned. "Jesus, I bet you haven't been laid in months."

Like she needed thoughts of Grant rolling around in bed mixed up with her bookkeeping. Kali narrowed her gaze. "Like I'd tell you. You'd just post it on the bulletin board."

"How about I post a job ad for someone to apply for the position?" Janet wiggled her eyebrows rapidly, sending Kali into fits of laughter.

"What ad are you looking to post, Janet?" Dan had arrived, unnoticed, behind her and stood in the doorway.

Janet half choked. "Nothing, Dan. I'm just hassling Kali."

"That you are," declared Kali. Energy hummed into the room. Grant. She didn't need to see him to know Grant stood behind Dan. A lightness she was starting to recognize and respond to filled her.

"I brought someone for Kali to meet." Dan looked expectantly at Janet.

Janet took the hint gracefully. "I'm heading out. I'll talk to you later, Kali." Smiling coyly at Grant, she sidled past the two men and left.

Dan moved inside the office, whispering, "I wanted you to know Grant's going to be—" He looked behind him and dropped his voice further. "You know…around."

Kali barely withheld her smile. If it weren't for the deep worry lines on Dan's face, she'd almost think he was enjoying the cloak and dagger event. As much as she hated the reason for it, it was good to see the normally frail man energized by something.

Studying Grant's casual jeans and a white Henley, she could see he'd fit in perfectly as their new instructor. He didn't need power suits like he'd had on this morning – power radiated off him. His persona came across as large and in charge. Comforting. And attractive.

Power had a seductiveness few women could ignore. "Hi, Grant. Welcome."

He studied her face intently before nodding as if satisfied at something. "Thanks. By the way do you help out with the classes?"

Kali looked over at Dan. "Sometimes. If I'm needed. It's not what I've been doing lately, but I've taught in the past. Why?"

"Just wondered how many people know you well and how many might know of you?"

She groaned. "You're after another list of names, aren't you?"

He tilted his head in acknowledgement.

Kali reached for her bag and the list she'd started. "This list is those people I could remember seeing in Sacramento, I put an asterisk beside those that that aren't fans of mine and vice versa."

"Everyone loves you." Dan was nothing if not loyal.

A half laugh escaped. Kali shook her head. "If only that were true. You know perfectly well that some people resent me."

"They just don't understand."

It was Kali's turn to nod.

"Don't understand what?"

Both Dan and Kali looked at Grant, surprised at his question. Dan looked over at Kali. "Does he know?"

She wrinkled her nose at him. "I'd have thought so at this point."

Dan turned to face Grant. "Kali is financially independent. Some small minds would like to blame her success on her wealth. You know, she can afford better equipment, do more advanced training. Things like that." He straightened his back. "I, for one, would be lost without her help."

Grant studied her for a long moment.

Kali flushed and stared at the stacks of papers piled high in front of her.

"Has anyone ever said anything about it to you?"

Startled, Kali looked up at him. "Pardon?"

Pulling out his notebook, Grant asked, "Has there been anything more than usual grumbling. Like arguments? Threats?"

Kali and Dan exchanged looks. "No. At least none I know about." She looked over at Dan. "Have there?"

He shook his head vigorously, sending tuffs of hair flying in all directions. "No, I don't think so."

"Okay, but if you do remember anything let me know."

"Will do." She waved toward the stacks of paper on the desk. "Dan, this is the biggest mess yet."

"I'm sorry. I tried to stay on top of it, but…it ran away from me."

"Yeah." Kali groaned. "It always does. Take off, you two. I've got work to do."

The men left.

The soft hum of warm energy hung in the air. Reminding her. Teasing her.

Did she really want to open her heart again?

And was it already too late?

CHAPTER 10

KALI WORKED ON the accounts late into the evening with Shiloh sprawled at her feet. Dan had tried to send her home at one point. She told him she'd rather finish than come back tomorrow.

When she finally locked up, the sun had set and the intense summer heat had dissipated slightly – a welcome relief from the stuffiness of the office. Shiloh perked up in the fresh air. She explored the brush and pranced through the cool grass.

"It's past time to go home, isn't it?"

Kali yawned as she unlocked her Jeep, holding the door open for Shiloh to jump into the back seat. As she threw her purse to the passenger side, a rustling noise sounded by the trees to the left of the front stairs. She spun around. Jesus. Her heart pounded as she searched the deepening shadows. "Hello?"

The outside light from the center cast a yellow glow that barely reached the edge of the parking lot. A half whine, half growl slid from Shiloh's throat. With a last nervous glance, Kali scrambled into the front seat. "Let's go home, Shiloh."

Cranking the engine, Kali locked the doors and peered through the tinted window. Nothing. The eerie sensation of being watched would not dissipate. Kali left the parking lot and drove toward home. She kept one eye trained on the rearview mirror. She didn't think she was being followed...yet couldn't shake the sensation she was.

Uneasy enough to not want to go to an empty house, she drove instead to a late-night coffee shop at the mall and parked close to the patio seating. Kali clipped Shiloh's leash on and walked to the takeout window before choosing a seat close to her vehicle. Hating that she'd let a simple noise unnerve so badly, Kali hugged her latte and tried to unwind. Several tables were full. A couple of teenagers sat off to one side, heaps of whipping cream topping their concoctions. A man sat at another table with an open laptop, working diligently on something.

"Kali?" someone called, startling her. "Wow, I haven't seen you in a long time."

Squinting into the gloom beyond the cafe lights, she finally recognized the speaker. "Jim. How are you?" Kali was happy to see anyone she knew right now, even a stocky, fun-loving, very ex-boyfriend. She thought he'd gone north to work on the oil rigs. "I haven't seen you for a couple of years. How are you?" She motioned to the empty seat. "Join me."

"I've only been back in town a couple of months." He grinned down at her, spinning a chair around backwards and straddling it. Dressed in jeans and a lightweight plaid shirt, he looked like he had filled out some since she'd seen him last.

"That's great. I'm sure your mom is delighted to have you home." She watched as Shiloh greeted Jim like the old friend he was, before sprawling at her feet again. Kali relaxed some herself. Jim was safe. He could never be the letter writer.

As soon as the thought crossed her mind, she questioned it. Did she know that for sure? How? Jim could have changed. For that matter, how well had she known him to begin with? They'd had a hell of a fight before they split. A fight that hadn't been easy to resolve. Kali had bolted from the fight, from the relationship, from him. Then again, that had been years ago. And their relationship hadn't been serious back then. They'd both known it. The breakup hadn't hurt either of them. They'd seen each other enough since then to know they'd both moved on to new relationships. It was actually nice to consider that they could visit on a friendly basis now without all that 'relationship' stuff to interfere.

Shiloh grunted and stretched on the cement, reminding Kali that if anything was wrong with the company, Shiloh wouldn't be so relaxed.

They spent a pleasant hour catching up on their years apart. Then the conversation lulled.

Slowly that same sense of unease returned. She sat nursing her empty coffee cup, stalling. She wanted to see Jim drive away before she headed home. Stupid, she knew, but that didn't change how she felt. Her cell phone rang. She frowned. Who'd be calling at this hour? Pulling it out of her pocket, she didn't recognize the number. "Hello."

"Kali. Are you all right?" Grant asked.

"Ahh, yeah," she said, hating the instant relief washing over her at the sound of his voice. Her world righted itself. The sense of unease slipped away. "Why?"

"Because you look like you're trying to get rid of the guy at your table." His voice deepened, sending delicious shivers along her back.

"Where are you?" Kali smiled apologetically at Jim, and continued to search the area around her.

"Close. I'll walk your way in a couple of minutes. Feel free to act like I'm an old friend," he said and hung up.

She stared at the phone in her hand. For the number of times she'd seen him lately, he almost was an old friend. And how had he known where she was?

As she glanced at Jim, smiling reassuringly at him, another thought occurred. If Grant was that close, maybe he'd been the one following her? No, that didn't make sense. He had no reason to.

She searched the parking lot and patio again. Grant should have shown up by now.

Jim stood. "Home time. You take care of yourself, you hear?"

Kali waved good-bye and watched Jim walk away – unsettled again. His exit seemed abrupt, making her once again suspicious of him, though moments ago she'd been wishing he would leave. God, it was horrible thinking like this about people she'd known for years.

There'd never been an energetic connection between any of her past friends and lovers like she had with Grant. There'd never been this sizzle. That reaction was for Grant alone.

She watched as other people came and left.

Grant didn't show.

Sitting long past the time manners would dictate, she finally had enough. She considered phoning him and decided against it. As she walked to the Jeep, her phone rang again.

She checked the caller ID. She didn't recognize the number. She ignored it, not wanting to be sold any more free trips to Costa Rica. It rang again as she unlocked the Jeep. Same number. She ignored it again. Then she reconsidered, chewing on her bottom lip. It could be something important. Calls at this hour were often emergencies.

As she reached to answer, it stopped. Figures.

Kali put her key in the ignition. It rang again – from the same number. "Damn it."

Shiloh whined.

"Sorry, Shiloh. I'll answer it this time, okay?" She hit the talk button. "Hello?" No answer. "Hello?"

Still no sound. Then a faint coughing chuckle sounded in her ear.

"What the hell?" Kali stared at her phone then held it to her ear again. "Who is this? What do you want?"

The same chuckle sounded again, followed by a distinct click. They'd hung up. Kali searched the darkness as she turned the key to start the engine. Placing her phone in the holder, she hit the automatic power lock on the door. She knew locking her doors would not stop her creepy phone calls – however locking them did make her feel marginally better.

Where the hell was Grant, anyway?

Someone pounded on her driver door window. Kali shrieked. Shiloh barked. Her heart banged against her chest as she peered into the night – and saw the swirls of energy.

Grant.

She closed her eyes as relief and anger rolled through her. "Where the hell have you been?"

Grant motioned for her to roll the window.

Relieved, and now mildly pissed, she lowered the glass.

"Take it easy."

"Take it easy!" she snapped. "I'm getting freaky prank phone calls and—" She unlocked her door and pushed it open, forcing Grant to move back. "You were supposed to be here close to an hour ago."

Stepping out of the car, she stormed away a few feet to stand staring at the stars, hands on her hips. Damn it.

"From the beginning, please. What's made you so jumpy?" he asked, concern warming his voice.

Just hearing that caring helped. Kali closed her eyes and focused on Grant's energy. She drew in two cleansing breaths as she regained control. The last thing she wanted was for him to think she was so easily rattled. In truth, tonight she had been. She wasn't proud of that fact. Until this letter writer mess was over, she didn't think there was much she could do about it.

The next deep breath and the knot of tension in her spine loosened. She turned to face him. "Several things," she said. "It started when I left the center. A noise in the bushes rattled me,

Shiloh didn't like it much either. Then I thought I was being watched as I left."

Grant's eyes narrowed and he frowned at her but didn't interrupt.

She continued, "Not wanting to go home to an empty house, I came here, where I met Jim. That worked for a while. Then the visit got weird. You called, he raced off, and I sat here waiting for you." She glared at him. "Only you never showed up." She took another deep breath. "When I finally decided you weren't coming, I headed here to my Jeep when three phone calls came in, one after the other. I didn't know the number and chose not to answer the first two calls." She rifled her fingers through her hair before meeting his eyes. "I answered the third call." She caught his frown. "There was no answer at first, then some weird laughter before the asshole hung up."

Grant held out his hand.

Kali frowned. "What?"

"Let me see your phone, please."

Blasting him a fulminating look, she walked to the Jeep and pulled the phone from its holder. Handing it over, she added, "Then you scared me half to death."

Grant wrote down the number of her mystery caller. "No, I didn't. You'd already scared yourself half to death before I ever got here. I only knocked on your window." He passed her the phone. "I'll have this number checked."

"The laughter sounded weird, almost mechanical."

Shiloh, still in the Jeep, barked. Kali opened the driver's door and sat half-in and half-out in a way that allowed her to put a calming hand on Shiloh's neck. "It's okay, girl. It's just a crazy night." She turned so she was sitting properly in the driver's seat and reached to pull her door closed. "What happened to you anyway? Why didn't you show?"

Grant moved and closed it for her. "I followed your friend."

"Jim? Why?"

"I saw him leave and thought his timing a little suspicious. So, I followed him to a bus stop and waited until he got on a bus to downtown Portland." He shrugged. "Then I came here to find you freaking out."

"Okay, I resent that." She hadn't been that bad, had she?

"Almost freaking out, then," he amended with a small grin.

Damn that smile. It did make her feel better, though. The

heavy surge of emotions had taken its toll on her energy levels. Kali looked at the shadows surrounding them and shivered. The warm energy wafted between them. It wasn't enough to dispense the darkness. "I'm going home. I've had quite enough of this for tonight, thank you."

"I'll follow you home."

"Why?"

"So that you know no one else is."

"Oh." That made sense and made her feel stupid at the same time. "Okay, thanks." She turned the key in the ignition.

"Just a moment." He pulled out another business card. "Keep this in the Jeep. And call me the next time you think you're being followed."

Kali tossed the card in the coin holder on the dash. "I hope I won't need it. I never thought to call you tonight. What if I'd been imagining things?"

He snorted. "Better to call and be embarrassed over nothing than not to call and get into trouble."

She sighed. She knew that. "Except, it's not me he's after."

He bent down and looked her in the eye. "What makes you say that?"

"He's taking victims to challenge me. If I'm dead, there's no fun in it for him." She allowed herself a moment of relief. She was right. She could feel it. This asshole didn't want her – at least not yet.

"That may be – only this guy's not rational. You can't attribute normal reasoning or behavior to him. He could switch in a heartbeat and decide that it's more fun to hold you captive for a month or two."

A month or two. She gulped. That was *not* something she wanted to consider.

Grant continued, "And what about when he decides the game is over? I'm sure he has final plans for you, too."

Oh, God. That didn't bear thinking about. Kali avoided answering by shifting into reverse. True to his promise, Grant stayed behind her the whole way home. As she neared the house, she couldn't decide if she should invite him inside.

Still undecided, she watched to see if he'd park or, now that she was home safe, leave again. Locking the vehicle, she headed to her front door, not wanting to appear obvious.

Shiloh sniffed the long pampas grass by the front steps, enjoying the fresh air. Behind her, she heard Grant's door slam and the crunch of gravel as he followed her. She unlocked the front door, pushing it open for Shiloh, who wiggled in ahead of her.

Shiloh howled and raced down the hall.

Kali stepped inside. Shiloh stopped at the entrance to the kitchen and started barking madly. Kali halted, fear demolishing what little calm she'd regained earlier.

Grant raced forward. He grabbed her arm and tugged her onto the front porch behind him. "I'll go and check. Stay here until I tell you it's safe."

Kali's eyes widened. Good. She wasn't a hero.

"Call Shiloh back."

Kali called Shiloh to her and snagged her collar. Both retreated to the front porch. Together they watched as Grant, gun out and ready, took several deliberate steps into the hallway, assessing the scene. He reminded her of herself on a SAR mission. Survey, assess, identify, catalogue the elements that need to be dealt with before moving forward. At the kitchen, he stopped.

Exactly where Shiloh had stopped.

He glanced at her, still huddled under the outside light, before he entered the kitchen.

She waited. And waited. Finally, she couldn't stand it anymore and called out, "Grant. What is it?"

He reappeared, talking on his cell phone – as usual. Completing his call, he closed his cell phone. "I've called in a team."

Kali swallowed hard. "What's wrong? What did you find?"

"A package with a note from our letter writer."

Her stomach clenched. Nausea stirred in her stomach. The killer had been inside her house. She'd left it locked up. Shit. She forced herself to ask, fearing the answer, "What's in the package? And what does the note say?"

Grant sighed. "Kali…"

She held up her hand. "Don't. Don't try to protect me from this. It's way too late for that. To stay sane, I have to know what I'm dealing with." She closed her eyes for a moment. Opening them, she said, "Now, what did you find?"

"A bloody gold and emerald earring."

Kali swallowed hard as relief rushed through her. "I don't know what I'd imagined it could be, but I hadn't expected something as benign as an earring. That's good, right? This poor woman could be still alive. Right?" Kali felt a little better at his nod. "And the note?"

"I only read the part that showed – without touching it. It said something about, Round Two to me. Someone close is gone forever. Now it's on to Round Three."

CHAPTER 11

"ROUND THREE?" KALI squeaked. Shock reverberated inside. Not possible. How could they have missed round two? "Are you serious?"

"That's what it says. I haven't moved it yet. There could be more to the message."

"What happened to the second round?" Kali closed her eyes, pain washing through her. She leaned against the wall, grateful for something stable. If only she had something to grab onto emotionally. "He's already kidnapped, buried and killed someone, and we didn't even know about it? Didn't even know this person was missing? How is that possible?"

Grant slid his hand through his hair, exhaustion and frustration in his voice. "Unfortunately, it's all too easy to do." Hands resting on his hips, Grant stared, grim-faced, into the vast blackness beyond the yard. "Kali, I need you to look at the earring. You might recognize it."

She stared at him wordlessly. Through her own shock and disbelief she could see years of experience in scenarios like this one etched in his face. His job had to be harsh to live with. The things he'd seen. The things he surely wished he'd never seen.

She took a deep breath. "Show it to me."

Pushing the door open wider, he led the way. "I don't want you to disturb anything. I'll take you to the entrance first." He led the way down the hallway, pulling on thin latex gloves from his pocket as he went.

His broad frame blocked her from entering. "First, take a good look at the kitchen. Can you tell if anything has been disturbed?"

Kali perused the room. Nothing popped out at her. Except for the item on the table. She took her time, then finally said, "I can't see anything odd from here." At his nod, she drew a deep breath, then walked to the table.

The earring lay on a paper plate. No napkin, no wrapping, just a mistletoe pattern marred by the contents. Through the flecks of dried blood shone a stunning starburst earring with a half dozen emeralds. From its position, she couldn't tell the type of closure. It appeared to be a post style. The deep yellow color of the metal made her think it was real gold set with real stones. She didn't know for sure.

Bile rose in her throat. Kali swallowed hard. Her eyes flew to the note tucked slightly under the plate.

The sheet of standard printer paper had been cut in half; the message printed again in block letters, but this time in black ink. She couldn't see anything to indicate the location, identification or where to start looking for the owner of the earring. Neither was there anything to denote the identity of the letter writer.

Unless something else were written on the note. Her hand at the ready, she glanced over at Grant. He stopped her and used gloved fingers to pull the note free.

"Round two to me –
Did you even see that someone is missing?
She's a beaut and she's a charm,
Love her, leave her and no one to release her.
Back where she belongs – free
Even better, she's where she should be
Now, it's on to round three."

"Oh God," she whispered.

"Does that mean anything to you?"

Kali shook her head, incapable of speaking for a long moment. Finally, she cleared her throat. "The 'no one to release her' part, I'm presuming means she's contained in some way. As I search for buried victims, I can only assume she's also been buried. And, yes," she added bitterly, "I know we can't assume anything with this psycho. Back where she belongs? That could mean all kinds of things – and none of them nice. But free? Since when is death, death through being buried alive as the other victims were, an avenue to freedom? And what does it mean that she's where she should be? She should be buried? Dead? She should be dead?" She stared wordlessly at Grant. "Chances are good that no one *will* find her because I don't even know where to begin looking for her – so she will be dead."

"Do you recognize the earring?"

Kali shook her head, studying the emerald design. "I don't remember it." She shifted her position, trying to see from a different angle. *Have I?* When was the last time she'd even noticed other women's clothing? "Sorry. I'm not really one that notices that type of thing."

He nodded. "Understood. What about the note? The killer must think that means something to you."

"Sure. It means this asshole has taken some poor woman and I'm supposed to help her. But I *can't*. I don't know how," she cried out. She gave her cheeks a quick scrub. "Sorry. I didn't mean to lose it."

"Shh. It's understandable. Stop kicking yourself for it. Let's focus on what's here. See if we can find anything useful. The earring has older styling, like something worn by a mature woman. The jewels, if real, are expensive. Someone had money."

"Or had a *friend* who could afford it. Not to mention it could have been a family heirloom handed down."

"True."

Kali stared at the plate with morbid fascination. As much as she wanted to turn away, she couldn't. The cheerful seasonal print contrasted so sharply to its contents. "Does the plate have any significance?"

He shrugged. "Possibly. It may have been a convenient way to deliver the item, or it could signify something much darker, uglier. Does anything here give you an idea of where you'd go to look for a person?"

Kali glanced at the plate, then away again as her stomach roiled. "No," she whispered in despair. "Nothing."

Grant gave her a brief hug. Energy warmed and sparkled between them, not energizing but soothing. For a moment, the chaos faded. Safety surrounded her. Then he dropped his arms as if realizing what he'd just done. "Let's change tracks. Who has keys to your home?"

She barely tracked the conversation. Bereft of his heat, so brief and so tantalizing, Kali couldn't help but wonder if he felt anything of the energy that hummed between them. How could he when he'd stepped back so casually. Did he hug all the women?

"Kali?"

Blinking, Kali focused on his face, grateful for the momentary shift back to reality. "What?"

"Who has a key to your house? Who would know you weren't home tonight? Who knows the layout of this house?"

Kali's mind raced to grasp something concrete. "Many people have been in here over the years but I haven't given out spare keys to friends and lovers, if that's what you're asking. I don't do that. I'm gone constantly and Shiloh always goes with me. I don't have plants that need to be watered or other animals to be taken care of, so I don't need anyone to check on the place when I'm not here."

"What about Dan? Does he have keys?"

Kali frowned. "Sure, he did. I'll have to ask him if he still has one. I stored a bunch of stuff for him while the center was undergoing renovations. Most of the boxes were kept in the garage. The financials were stored in the spare room."

"I'll check with him. That thread leads us back to the center again." He paused. "Do you think this," he pointed to the earring, "could have been worn by someone from the center?"

Her gaze followed his movement, nonplussed. The question had to be asked. She understood that. Really, she did, but to contemplate who might have worn the earring meant acknowledging that someone she knew could be the victim…waiting in eternal darkness for rescue.

That the murderer was likely to be another person she knew was beyond thinking about. Too much had happened recently. Kali couldn't wrap her mind around it. She didn't want to. She wanted it all to go away.

Not that it was going to.

"Of course she could be from the center. If you're asking in a roundabout way if I know who the wearer was – the answer is no."

"What about anyone else from the center? Julie? Brad? Jarl? Do any of them have keys?"

She reared back. "No. I don't think so." Bringing up Brad's name just brought up the fear. She took a deep breath and asked, "I can't help but wonder if Brad could be the missing victim. He was working the Sacramento disaster with me, but has been missing ever since."

Grant opened his mouth to respond, but it was his beetled brows that had her rushing in to say, "I know he goes on benders after a rescue. So I know it's probably nothing, but…"

Grant reached out and squeezed her shoulder. "Take it easy. We don't know what – if anything – has happened to Brad. Dan told me and I alerted the local authorities in Sacramento. If he's there, we'll find him."

A nerve twitched in her cheek as she struggled to hold back the sudden tears. "I didn't even know that he was missing until today. I would have found out yesterday, if I hadn't slept the day away."

He nudged her toward the double glass doors and outside. "Let's go sit on the deck until the team comes."

Kali let him lead her onto the deck and her favorite chaise where reality hit her all at once. "Oh God. The bastard probably taunted them. Saying I'd be looking for them. They'd have been waiting for me. Hoping I'd come to save them. And I never even knew they were missing." Tremors washed over her. Grief brought tears to her eyes. "Now there could be another one."

Grant swooped down and grabbed her by the shoulders, giving her a light shake. Energy flipped off them at his movements. Yet he didn't appear to notice. "Take it easy, Kali. You can't blame yourself. You didn't know."

"But maybe I should have." Bitterness colored her voice. "You already said that the Sacramento victim was likely to have been his first." Haunted, she stared into the night, as if the surrounding darkness would offer up the answers she needed. "Do you think the earring is from the round two victim or from the round three victim?"

"Stop. It's. Not. Your. Fault. Got that?"

With effort she tried to listen to him. Not just listen, but hear his words. Rationally, she knew it wasn't her fault. And that didn't matter one bit. She bowed her head, rested it against his chest, letting his confidence and calm seep into her soul.

And with it came anger. A deep down pissed off fire that ripped through her – burning, cleansing, firing up her soul. She lifted her head. "You're right. He's responsible. He's been playing on the fact that I consider the center as much mine as Dan does. I'm not there out front like he is, but it's my life's work. Any failure at the center or any loss of life feels personal. Like I should have done something to stop it."

"But you couldn't."

"Exactly."

After a moment she glanced toward the kitchen, then she said, "It would help if we had a time line. Like when the victim went missing. To narrow down which SARs workers were where, although I can't imagine any of them being involved. I slept for a day and a half to recover. There's no way another of the rescuers could have kidnapped and murdered someone in the same time."

"Unfortunately, a couple of hours would have been long enough." Grant checked the time on his cell phone.

She dropped back into her deck chair, her emotions churning inside. She needed her sketch book or, at least a piece of paper. Something to dump the tension winding up inside. "Would you get my sketchbook bag? It's hanging in the hall closet." As Grant walked back inside, Kali let her body relax slightly; there was no relaxing her mind.

Shiloh nudged her hand, a soft whine escaping. "Hey, girl. I know, someone was in there who didn't belong. Not nice, huh?" She gently scratched the dog's head. "If only you could talk. I wonder what you could add to this."

Her blue cloth bag landed in her lap. She dug through it, withdrawing the sketchbook immediately.

Grant eyed her curiously. "What are you going to do?"

Her art was deeply personal and not something she cared to share. Need clawed at her. The need to dump the images in her mind. The need to find a peaceful center again in the midst of the chaos. "Doodle. It helps me to calm down when I'm feeling overwhelmed." She shrugged dismissively, hoping he'd take the hint and leave her alone. "No big deal."

Choosing a pencil, she opened the book to the first page. She loved a new sketchbook with its pristine blank pages waiting for her creativity. Within moments Grant ceased to exist. She let her fingers flow and move, transforming the page to a jumble of emotions. She knew the result would be garbage. That wasn't the point. She needed to pull the plug and let her mind drain.

Once she paused, arrested by sounds in her house. Twisting, she could see Grant in conversation with several men. The team had arrived. Fear, pain spiked again. Kali picked up her pencil, her hand moving at a furious pace.

"Kali?"

She stopped and tried to refocus on the face in front of her. "Grant. Are they done?"

"Not yet. A team is searching the property, but we need you to do a walk-through to make sure nothing else was disturbed. Are you up to it?" He held out a hand. "We'll also need your fingerprints to rule them out from the ones collected tonight."

With Grant's help she stood, her stiff muscles a sure sign she'd been in one place for too long.

Kali stretched, closed her sketchbook and dropped it on the table. She followed Grant into the house. Putting on gloves, she went systematically through each room, standing first at the doorway, then walking in and checking drawers and cupboards. Everything appeared normal and undisturbed. At her bedroom, she opened dresser drawers, night tables, even her cedar chest at the foot of her bed.

Her walk-in closet appeared normal, disorderly and disorganized…but normal. "I don't think anything has been disturbed," she said. "Everything looks untouched."

"Okay, that's good. Let's check the rest."

They moved downstairs to her studio. Shit. She hadn't considered they might need her to go in there. The door was also closed. Again. "Lately I've been forgetting to leave this door open." The possibility that the killer had been inside and closed the door on her made her skin crawl. She shoved that thought away.

Uneasy, though she didn't know why, she opened the door and stood still, her gaze sweeping her small studio. Her painting stood on the easel, a drop sheet draped over the top. She tilted her head. Had she done that? She might have. The rest of the room appeared undisturbed. The paints sat where she'd placed them. The spills and smears had been there before. She really needed to clean up in here. Checking the door, she found her paint smock hanging on a hook where she'd left it.

Kali pivoted to return to the kitchen, hoping to avoid her easel.

"Don't you want to check that the painting is untouched?"

Double shit. No, she really didn't. Kali glanced at it, then at Grant. "No. I don't really care if the intruder touched the painting, and if he didn't, then nothing has changed."

"Please. We need to know where he's been and what he might have done."

Kali bowed her head briefly, then sighed. He was right. She walked to the easel and lifted the cover. She flinched. It was the same as before. She dropped the sheet and walked out. "He didn't touch it."

Grant didn't say anything. "Can I see?"

She froze. "Why?"

"Your reaction as much as anything. I want to know what

caused that pained expression." Not necessarily true.

"Maybe I'm just a bad artist." She tried to quell her nervousness. When that didn't work, she nibbled on her lower lip. Would he understand the significance? Or would it throw suspicion on her?

"Please."

Kali knew she could refuse. The painting certainly didn't come under his jurisdiction – at least she didn't think it did. A refusal *would* arouse suspicion. She didn't want that. Neither did she want to explain the picture. She couldn't. Finally, she walked over and flipped the drop cloth over the top, turning so she could see his instinctive reaction.

Confusion. Intensity. Then comprehension.

He stepped closer. "Bloody brilliant, yet bloody horrible at the same time."

"Now you have the explanation for the look on my face," she said lightly, reaching for the drop sheet.

His hand stalled her movement, his gaze never leaving the painting.

"You must have awful nightmares." He retreated a step.

"You have no idea." She stared at the victim in the painting, knowing a second person could be in the same situation even now. Bile crept up her throat.

She could sense him studying her and the painting, shifting back and forth. Yet he didn't ask. It surprised her, but she was grateful. It was a temporary reprieve. He wouldn't be able to leave it alone. Not forever.

At least he didn't know she'd painted this *before* her Sacramento trip.

CHAPTER 12

AN HOUR LATER Kali sat on the porch and hugged a cup of fresh coffee while Grant's team worked over her house. She'd lost track of time. Surely bedtime had come and gone hours ago. She wrinkled her nose at Grant and yawned. His energy clung close to his body. He was tired, too. "What? Sorry, I was miles away."

"I asked if I could look at your sketchbook," he asked gently, sitting beside her. "That painting you did was damn powerful. I don't think I've ever seen anything like it. Remember Stefan Kronos, the consultant that came with me a couple of days ago? He also uses art to purge his demons."

She paused, uncertain where this conversation was going. "I imagine many people do," she said cautiously.

"Of course he's different in another way, too. He's a psychic. He often paints his visions. It helps him set the details."

Her breath caught and held. "He left me his card. Something about him being a psychic consultant?"

Grant nodded. "And famous. His success rate is phenomenal. He works with law enforcement all over the world." He shifted casually in his seat. "Of course, that work is often the source of his demons."

She considered the point. "The disasters are the reason I paint. Occasionally I paint for pleasure, but it's more an outlet for my pain, instead. If I draw something, it's concrete and clear and real. Once it's on canvas, it's out of my mind. If I leave the stuff in my head, it rolls around in an endless rewind."

"Sounds like the system works." He reached for the sketchbook, paused and looked at her.

She nodded, returning to blowing gently on the hot brew in her hand.

He flipped back the cover to the first page and stopped.

"Kali?"

"Huh," she looked over at him.

"Is this the picture you worked on today?"

"As it is the only picture in there, yes, I'd say so. Why?"

Grant quickly leafed through the rest of the pages before returning to the front of the book.

"Do you remember what you drew?" His curiosity was palpable enough to make her uneasy.

"I didn't draw anything. It's just doodles. An outpouring of pent-up images and emotions."

"Where do these images come from?" His voice held an odd tone.

She looked over at him. "Like I said, my SAR work supplies a never-ending film of horror stills. Why?"

He stared at her intently, ignoring her question. "Do other people know about your art?"

She leaned her head back and closed her eyes. Surely there was something more productive for him to do. "Probably. It's no big deal. Artists are everywhere."

"Kali?"

She opened her eyes to find him holding the sketchbook in front of her. At first glance in the poor light, she couldn't make anything out. "I can't see in this light."

"Sit up. Look." Urgency threaded through his voice. He changed the angle of the sketchbook.

Shifting forward, she took another look.

And froze.

"Oh my God," she whispered.

In stark black and white, dominant strokes depicted a woman in a fetal position, jammed inside a box of some sort, and buried under the ground. A pipe extended upward to the surface to let in fresh air. Blood dripped from a head injury. The woman appeared to be unconscious or…dead.

Kali shook her head. "I didn't draw that."

"Didn't you?" he asked, leaning closer to study her face. "It's the only picture in the book."

She glowered at it. "I suppose I *must* have – but I didn't realize what I was drawing at the time. Not sure I believe it now, either," she muttered. Her pencil *had* moved at a furious pace. She'd let everything pour, not caring if it made sense or not. Like her painting sessions, she'd hoped to lose herself in another world when her physical one had became too much.

And just like the painting sessions, something very unexpected had popped out. Reaching for the drawing, she studied the details intently. She bolted upright.

"Oh no." Her shocked voice faded to silence. Her fingers clenched around the pages.

"What?"

"I know this woman." She tapped the picture with her finger, unable to tear her eyes from the sketch. Then she stopped and frowned. "I *think* I know who it is?"

"You do? Who is she?" Grant leaned forward and peered closer to the sketch. "How can you identify her from that little bit?"

"Her name is Julie." Kali choked back the emotion threatening to overtake her. "I'm not sure, though. Her hair looks like Julie's, the line of her nose, the body shape." She studied the sparse details. Doubt crept in. "It's hard to see when she's bundled up like that. It could be her." Tears sprang to her eyes. She swiped them away. "Julie comes to the center a lot. She likes to help out because she's a survivor herself. She was in Thailand when the tsunami hit in 2004." Kali looked over at Grant. "She's a very sweet lady. About 35 and single – at least I think she is."

"Do you know where she lives?"

"Close to the center. That's all I know. Dan will have her contact info."

Grant pulled out his cell phone. Kali reached across to grab his arm. "What are you doing?"

"Going to call Dan and ask."

Her fingers clenched on his forearm. "Because of this?" She lifted the book. Her painting prodded at her memory too. She'd never drawn or painted anything like these two images before. She wasn't about to count on them being right, though. Far from it. And there was no way she'd have bet this picture depicted Julie. It could represent any small-framed woman or teen.

He paused, his gaze going from the book to her. He shrugged. "Yeah."

Shit. "Uh. This is just a sketch. Something I drew while I was upset." She shook her head. "It's not a photograph. It's just a combination of random drawings. It probably means *nothing*."

Closing his phone, he took a deep breath and faced her. "Where did that image come from, Kali?"

She stroked a finger along the edge of the book. Her gaze locked on the image rendered with horrible clarity. "My mind?"

"Kali, is there is something you want to tell me? You know you can, right? I'm not going to judge you."

Uh-oh. Here it comes. She shifted uncomfortably. He could say what he wanted, but that didn't mean she believed him.

"I've worked with Stefan a long time."

She wrinkled her nose. Stefan the psychic. Maybe Grant would comprehend. Still…

"Kali, surely you recognize what's going on?"

She swallowed hard. She didn't know how it had happened, but for the first time she had to talk about something she'd kept hidden from everyone. He stared at her so patiently, his gaze seemed so understanding.

Did she dare?

How could she not? "I've never spoken of this to anyone."

He reached for her hand, cradling it in his large capable ones. His thumb stroked the side of her fingers gently.

"You're psychic?"

There. He'd asked her a direct question. She sighed heavily. "Honestly? I don't know what I am. My grandmother called it the Sight. She had it, too. I see things. Know things."

"Paint things?"

She half-laughed. "Apparently. And sketch them, too."

"Can you explain what happens to you? How you perceive the information?"

She shrugged. "Not really. It's been changing so much I don't have a handle on it. When I think I understand how it works…it changes. Sometimes, I just know things. Sometimes, I see ribbons of energy that point me one way." She frowned. "That painting in my studio is a first. I woke up in the morning with paint on my hands and a faint memory of my actions." She stared into his deep eyes, more than a little unnerved by what had happened. "I went into my studio and there it was."

His eyes widened. "Wow."

She gave him a lopsided grin. "Yeah."

"Is it the same way with your sketches? You just close your eyes and draw?"

"I don't know. Now that you mention it, that does seem to be my process. I close my eyes, as if I'm asleep." She thought about it. "All I can say is this is all new to me. Six months ago, I was working a different disaster. We lost a lot of people, including a little girl that Shiloh and I found. The loss really affected me. After that, all this stuff," she tugged one hand free to wave at the sketchbook, "went wild. Before then I had some inkling of where to search for victims on a site, just an instinct that told me where to go. I could find my friends' lost jewelry, keys, pets when I was growing up. It was always minor stuff. Now..." She shook her head, unable to finish the thought.

Silence hung between them.

"Then maybe we should give it free rein and see what comes." He straightened, still holding her right hand. Waves of energy slid off him and toward her.

"Huh?" she eyed him and the energy curiously. The more time they spent together, the easier their energy blended, almost joining into a single color. Odd. Comforting. Intriguing.

But he'd gone from being a friend to being an agent in that nanosecond it had taken her to understand. And that switch – no matter how intriguing their energy match – was disconcerting. Now he was making calls...again. He dropped her hand and stood up while he talked on his phone. Then he strode inside to his team.

Kali stared at the sketch. Just when she'd figured he'd forgotten about her and the stupid picture, he returned, all business again.

"Kali, Dan's headed to the center to find Julie's contact information. Apparently she moved recently. We're going to meet him there."

Kali jumped to her feet. It didn't matter that it was past one o'clock in the morning. Shiloh watched her, waiting for the signal to say she'd be coming along. She'd be needed if Kali had to search, but that would mean figuring out where to start looking. It would, however, be nice to have her with them. She packed up the sketchbook and pencil to bring along, just in case.

"It's not likely to be Julie, you know." She muttered glancing sideways at him. "Just saying."

"Maybe it isn't. Let's find her and we'll know."

"The doodle might mean *nothing*," she told him. "I'm not Stefan. I don't do this stuff."

"And it might mean everything." Grant's lips curved in a grim smile. "I'm willing to take a chance. We'll take my car."

KALI FOLLOWED GRANT, letting Shiloh into the back seat. Moonlight danced between the clouds. A chill had settled in. They pulled into the center a few minutes later. Dan's car was already there. Kali pulled out her keys and opened the front door. "Dan?"

"I'm in my office," he called back.

Shiloh raced toward him.

They walked in to find him frantically searching through drawers and stacks of papers; his sparse hair sticking out at all angles as usual. "I can't find it, Kali."

"Find what?"

Dan lifted another stack of papers before dropping them again. Frustration marred his face. He tugged at his shirt collar.

Was he still wearing pajamas?

"The volunteer list. The one with all the names and contact information on it."

Kali frowned. "The last time I saw it, you were carrying it and updating the information as you saw people. That was before Sacramento."

"Right. Several people had moved recently, Julie being one of them. Damn. Where did I put it?"

Kali stared at him, a growing pit of darkness in her gut. The list was important, and she had a good idea why it was missing. Then a new idea struck her. Horrible, but a possible explanation as to why Julie might have been targeted. "Dan, are there just names and phone numbers on the list? Or does it have more personal information?

He looked up at her, puzzled. The usually vague expression sharpened. "It has names and contact information. So addresses, phone numbers, emails and some information concerning their volunteer status and what areas they worked in. Also information on their readiness to leave at a moment's notice. So if they had kids, did they have a caregiver lined up? Or did they live alone; did they work for a living; were they retired and could they come to help out at odd hours? You know we come in and out of here all the time. Some people are good with that. Others only want to help out on weekends." He shrugged. "We need more volunteers. We've had major changes here, so I was trying to see who was available to do what and when. Like always."

Oh God, if the killer had somehow gotten that list, he'd have information on Julie that he might not have gotten anywhere else. "Did Julie ever talk about her time in Thailand?"

"Often. You know it helps victims to share their experiences. Even though it's been years for her, it still helps to have someone listening, who understands."

Kali scrunched up her face and glanced over at Grant. "There wouldn't have been anything on that list to indicate she'd been a survivor from another disaster – would there?"

Grant went still. Kali kept her gaze casual but firmly locked on Dan.

With one hand running through his hair, sending the spiky mess into a new formation, he said slowly, as if thinking it through. "I don't think so…it said that she lived alone, worked at the bank, her hours, work number." He paused, an odd light coming into his eyes, before adding, "And that she would prefer to not be called on Thursday, as she meets with her online support group that night."

Online support group night? Kali shot Grant a quick look, to find him staring at Dan, a hard look in his eyes. She could just imagine how he'd feel about that level of information missing on so many people. "That's fine," she said to Dan, watching as his shoulders sagged slightly, relief washing the dread out of his eyes.

She didn't want to discuss this here. "Wait." Dan came to a stop, his eyes widening as if his brain and thoughts just clicked. "You're thinking the list has something to do with the letter writer?"

"I'm *afraid* it might. It's just one of many possibilities."

Dan nodded. "Then we better find it." He walked to the filing cabinet by the door. He *was* wearing pajamas and shoes.

Kali lowered her voice as she spoke to Grant. "Julie was a survivor from a disaster. So was the last victim in Sacramento. He'd survived the apartment collapse. Could that be a link? That letter said something about *even better, she's back where she's meant to be* or something."

"So since they survived a disaster they should be returned to the state where they were found?" Doubt colored his voice. "Both being survivors of a disaster is a link. Whether it's pertinent in this case, I don't know." Frustration glinted from his eyes.

"I don't know that they'd have to be returned to how they were found, but consider that the Sacramento victim was buried under the rubble of the apartment collapse. He was found buried close to the same location. Hell, the oxygen tank could even represent air pockets from the building that collapsed." She frowned. Damn it. They didn't have enough information. They needed more on the second victim. Whoever that was.

"It's also likely to be sheer coincidence that Julie and the first victim are both survivors. The first could just have been a victim of circumstance. In the wrong place, at the wrong time. We know nothing about Julie at this point."

Damn him and his logic. Kali's mind tumbled over the possibilities. Then she noticed how silent the room had become.

Dan stood stock-still, eyes wide, jaw slack as he stared at them. "Oh, God. You think she's been snatched. Where's that list? Damn it to hell. I figured you needed to talk to her. That she knew something, someone...damn me for being an old idiot. Shit." He frantically pulled out files, looking for the right one.

"Don't you have her number in another place? On your cell phone, in the bills, somewhere?" Grant's hands fisted on his hips.

"Dan, you have a master list on the computer, don't you?" Kali strode over to the desk and pushed the power button. It would take a minute or two to load.

He shook his head. "That's the old one. That's what I was trying to update the other day."

Typical Dan. Still, she could understand. Sometimes she had trouble with priorities, too. Any other time the contact list wouldn't have been critical. The log-in screen came up.

"Dan, come log in. This is your computer, not mine."

"What? Oh, yeah." Dan stepped up to the keyboard and pounded out a series of numbers and letters.

Kali waited impatiently as the computer finished booting. Then she navigated to the main directory.

"Here it is." She double-clicked on the document, her fingertips pounding out a rhythm on the desktop as it opened. There. "Okay. What's Julie's last name, do you know?"

Dan leaned over her shoulder. "Taylor. There. Wait, you just passed it. Go back."

"Okay. Here she is. We have her old address, old phone number of..." She rattled off the number to Grant, who wrote it down. Kali quickly rattled off the cell number, too. Both men snatched up phones and started dialing.

"No answer." Dan said. Grant was talking to someone. They both waited until he was done. "Grant?"

"I have her new phone number and address." Even as he spoke, he was re-dialing. Everyone waited to see if Julie would pick up.

Kali absentmindedly stroked the top of Shiloh's head. She watched Grant's face as he left a message on her answering machine.

"Let's go," she said. Grant headed to the door.

Dan looked at her, confusion wrinkling his face. "Go where?"

"To her home."

"Did she have a vehicle?" Grant asked abruptly.

Kali shrugged. She had no idea.

"Yes, she *does*." Dan stressed. "But I don't remember what."

"We'll find it. Let's go."

Kali was already through the door and heading back to Grant's car. "Dan, I'll call you if we learn something." She snapped her fingers. Shiloh came running.

Dan trailed behind them. "Is there anything I can do to help?"

Kali started to shake her head, then stopped and considered. "Pray?"

Dan shuddered. "Call me when you find her," he cried as they drove away.

THEY ARRIVED AT Julie's townhouse within minutes. Kali jumped from the car before Grant had the engine off. Racing to the front door, she pounced on the doorbell. Then rang it again. The brick townhouse remained dark and silent. Where had Grant gone? She searched the surrounding area, spying him walking through the parking lot to stand behind a small red car.

"Is it hers?" she asked.

"I'm having the plates run now."

She watched as he checked the parking space number. It matched the townhouse number. They both walked around the car, as if it would give up the answers they sought. Grant's cell phone rang.

"Right. Okay. Yeah, I'm going in. No. Yes. Fine."

Grant put away his phone and approached Julie's front door where he knocked first. Then again. Then he called out, "Julie? This is the FBI. Answer the door, please."

Silence. He pulled out a small tool and had the door open within seconds.

Kali watched, astonished. "Isn't that illegal?"

"Not if we have just cause. The car is hers." He pushed open the door and stepped inside.

"Julie," Kali called out behind him. "Julie, are you home? This is Kali."

"Julie?" Grant ran up the stairs two at time. Caught up in his energy, Kali raced after him.

There was no sign of Julie.

But she'd been there. The bedclothes lay crumpled, half on and half off the bed. Several days' worth of clothing decorated a rattan swivel chair. Untidy but normal-looking.

Grant strode over to the night table and turned on the lamp. A halo of light filled the room. Grim lines wrinkled his forehead as he assessed something on the floor.

"What is it?" Kali whispered.

"Blood."

His words punched her in the gut. "Oh no." Her imagination took flight. Now all she could think about was that Julie was missing and possibly injured, and Kali was trying to find her, with no idea where to look. Shit.

Panic set in. Julie didn't deserve this. Kali had known her for years, yet she didn't really *know* her. She was a great woman who'd already survived so much. Kali wished she'd taken more time to visit with her. After Mexico, Kali had ignored the people around her, the changes going on in the world and especially at the center.

She stood in the middle of Julie's bedroom and held her throbbing temple. "Think, damn it. Think," she whispered. Where could Julie be? What was the chance she'd be doing something ordinary like visiting friends or staying over with a boyfriend? Just because she wasn't home didn't mean she should hit the panic button. And yet...Kali's nerves refused to be calmed. She spun around looking for a jewelry box. "What's the chance the matching earring is here?"

Grant frowned but checked the dresser and night table. A small one sat open in the top drawer. Kali walked over to see. No missing earring.

"It makes sense that the earring wouldn't be here. If he has her, she's likely to have started out wearing both."

If she'd been taken, she couldn't be far. There'd been no time. Or had there? When had the earring been delivered? She'd been at the center for hours, followed by at least two hours at the coffee shop. So where could he have taken her within...say an hour's drive? Although, even that was an arbitrary time frame.

"What are you thinking?" Grant asked, the phone open in his hand.

"I'm sorting through possibilities." Kali motioned out the

window. "If the letter writer has her, this isn't exactly the easiest place to kidnap or bury her. Presuming he buried her. There are always people around – someone should have seen him. She's small, but surely he's still going to be noticed carrying a body, isn't he? She might not have been in the box until she was buried."

"If she didn't walk out on her own. We'll have to get a team out to canvas the neighborhood in the morning. It's in the middle of the night, but if we're lucky, someone saw something."

"But chances are we won't find them in time to save her." Kali couldn't keep the bitterness out of her voice.

"This is not your fault," he reminded her firmly, a gentleness in his eyes.

Kali wanted to believe him. Shaking her head, she struggled to concentrate. "My brain understands, my heart, however…"

"I know."

His voice soothed her tattered nerves. She welcomed the comfort, but the deepening connection between them confused her more. So much for locking people out. Grant had wormed his way inside.

"Let's stay focused," Grant said. "*If* she's been taken, and, yes, we're jumping to a conclusion here, where could he have taken her?"

"Anywhere. Everywhere. Within an hour's drive, there are millions of places to bury someone so they'd never be found." Places flashed through her mind, ditches, fields, gardens, empty lots. The opportunities were endless.

"You found the last victim."

"Sure. But I was already on the scene with a SAR dog in hand." She threw her hands up in frustration. "That was the right location with the right tools. Yes, I have Shiloh with me now, only she won't be able to help unless we can narrow the location."

"Okay, now think. He knows you and how you work, so he must be expecting you to do something. There has to be a clue somewhere."

"Yeah, somewhere." Tears of frustration turned her voice into a croak. Damn it.

"What about your sketch? Can you identify a location from your picture?"

"Maybe," she said, relieved to have something constructive to think about. "I can take another look." Grant retrieved the sketchbook from the car while she waited at the front door. Using the bright kitchen light, they studied the details.

"No mountains or major identifiers." Grant bent over the map. "It's hard to pick out anything."

"I know," Kali whispered. "Yet…"

"What?" Grant straightened, his sharp gaze zeroed in on her face. "What do you see?"

"It feels familiar." Kali reached out and motioned toward the slope and ground cover surrounding it. She chewed on her bottom lip. "But I can't be sure."

"What about it looks right?"

"It's hard to explain. That single line captures Julie's profile." She pointed it out. "This line here captures a hill on one of the training areas we use for cadaver training."

"You have a special training area for that?"

Kali shook her head. "It's not full of dead bodies or anything. It's where we run training exercises for the dogs, especially young ones."

"Would you have trouble finding Julie there?"

She understood what he meant. "No, Shiloh can separate live from dead and, although it may take her awhile, she will eventually find everything buried, dead or alive." She pressed her lips together, thinking. "It would be a good hiding spot, because the ground is easy to dig." Kali dismissed her words with a head shake. "Then again, it's an area that Shiloh knows well so, this wouldn't be much of a challenge."

"Maybe the challenge is to find the location, knowing you'd have no problem finding the body."

Kali recoiled. "What time is it?"

"Just after two in the morning."

"Sunday morning. Already."

He put his hands on either side of her face. "Focus for a moment. Is there anything else in the picture that calls to you? Anything recognizable?"

Kali closed her eyes against the tumultuous thoughts crowding her head. Opening them, she stared at the picture one more time. Instead of seeing something new, the picture cemented the location in her mind.

"She's there." Kali knew it in her heart. Julie was buried somewhere in their training ground. "I need to go home and get my gear."

Grant held the front door open. "I'll pull a team together. And

I'll get a uniform over here to wait in case she comes home. Just in case this is a wild-goose chase." He headed for the car, already talking on the phone while Kali waited impatiently. Before opening the door, he asked, "Directions?"

Quickly relaying them, Kali hopped into the car, wishing he'd hurry up. Her heart pounded and her palms started to sweat. Julie was dying. Kali knew it, even though she couldn't prove it. Urgency morphed into panic – they weren't going to be in time.

Tears blinded her.

Grant drove back to her house. He glanced at her several times, and Kali appreciated his concern…and his silence. She needed time to collect herself.

Back at her house, lights blazed because Grant's people had never left. Kali shook her head at how far her life had slid out of control. Shiloh barked. Kali bent and hugged her tight.

"Okay girl. Let's go to work." Kali quickly gathered up a vest, Shiloh's lead and some dog treats. As an afterthought, Kali filled a couple of water bottles and stuffed several granola bars in her pockets. It took a moment longer to find Shiloh's teddy bear. She tucked it inside her jacket.

A fine-edged focus calmed her by the time she'd finished. *Time to go to work.*

"Ready?" she asked Grant on her way to her Jeep.

"We're right behind you."

Kali held the door open as Shiloh jumped into the back. Kali slammed the door, hopped into the driver's side and took off, spitting gravel in her wake. The training ground was a good twenty minutes out of town. Wooded areas and meadows dotted the hilly terrain there. Shiloh's playground.

As she drove, she had to wonder who knew the industry and the center well enough to know their training ground's schedule, setting their plans in motion when they wouldn't be disturbed accidentally. Detailed records were always kept of who had been where, and used what for each training session. Who knew enough to access the schedule?

Kali's cell phone rang as she pulled onto the highway. Shiloh whined, an odd note in her tone.

She pushed the button, leaving the phone in the holder on her dash. "Hello."

Eerie laughter filled her Jeep.

"Hello? Who is this?" Kali snapped.

"You're too late." The strangled whisper ended with a click as the line went dead.

Kali's heart stalled. "Oh, God. Shiloh, please tell me that doesn't mean what I'm afraid it means." Her hands started shaking. Shiloh whined and nudged her nose against Kali's neck.

Leaning forward, Kali rummaged through the front cubby-holes for Grant's card. Damn it. Where was it?

There.

Keeping one eye on the empty highway, she punched in his number. Grant," she said, "the killer just called me." She quickly relayed the conversation. "It had that same mechanical sound as the voice from the other night."

"Chances are he's disguising it. It's easy to do with today's technology. My team will have traced it. I'm betting it's a dead end again."

Tears collected in the corner of her eyes. "Shit." She pounded the steering wheel. Frustration and anger warred with grief and sorrow, all of them threatening to collapse her very foundation.

"Keep steady, Kali." Grant's voice sharpened. "Let's stay focused. There's always hope."

"But what if I'm wrong and she's not even here?"

"Then we're wrong and we have to accept that. None of it means you're to blame."

Kali sniffled. She checked her rear-view mirror, noted the steady headlights of the FBI following her and changed lanes. "The turn-off is ahead."

"We're right behind. Let's see this through to the end."

Kali hung up and made the turn. "Right. To the end then." Shiloh woofed behind her.

She parked beside the small shack that served as a basic shelter against the elements, and hopped out. Shiloh scrambled behind her. Kali snapped Shiloh's working leash on, then turned to the huge area ahead of her.

The other vehicles pulled in beside them in a flurry of dust. Kali ignored them, grabbed her flashlight and stepped out. Shiloh urged her left. Kali had considered snatching up a piece of Julie's clothing, but that wasn't Shiloh's forte, and if the victim wasn't Julie, Shiloh's focus would stay on that scent, potentially missing a different victim.

Shiloh barked once, lowered her head and got to work. The flashlight was dim and the heavy cloud cover made the terrain treacherous. She hadn't taken the time to put on her work boots and her runners slipped on the leaves littering the ground. Kali scrambled up the short incline, her hands digging in the thick natural loam. Behind her, the sounds of the team trying to follow chased her. Shiloh tugged hard on her leash. She wanted to go. Kali didn't dare let her run free. She'd never be able to track the dog in this dense blackness. Instead, she picked up the pace giving Shiloh more lead.

Left, then a little more to the right, around the trees and into a clearing on the right. An eerie glow shone. Kali blinked. The light was gone. She blinked again, opening her psychic senses. There it was. She turned toward a soft tumbled hill. Kali unsnapped Shiloh's lead. She bolted forward. Circled the hill once, twice and whined.

"What is it girl?" Kali reached the hillock and didn't need her flashlight to see the dark purple glow. "This is it, isn't it?"

Shiloh barked once, then lay down, her head on top of her paws. Kali jogged the last bit toward her. She could hear the sounds of the men catching up behind her. She ignored them, trying to understand Shiloh's reaction. It was unusual. And it gave her hope.

Kali shifted her vision, allowing the psychic threads to light up further. In the darkness, they held an unmistakable luminescence. Only they were dark, deep colors in snaky thin threads, acting unlike anything she'd seen before. They snuggled low to the ground, weak and reedy instead of reaching upward. She frowned, trying to understand. Noises rustled ten feet in front of her and off to the left. Kali sucked in her breath. What was that?

"Grant?" she yelled into the blackness. An odd sound burst through the brush in front of her. Kali spun around. "Grant, are you there?"

Heavier thuds clumped into the eerie darkness before fading away. Kali's heart thudded in panic. Oh, God. She hadn't been alone. Kali snapped off her light and hunkered down in the darkness, motionless beside Shiloh.

"Kali!" Shouts sounded behind her.

"Here!"

The men's high-beam flashlights broke through the blackness, picking up Shiloh and her. Kali stood up, pointing in the direction of the receding footsteps. "Grant, someone was here. He took off that way."

Men scattered.

Grant grabbed Kali's arm as she moved. "The men will look. Now," Grant took a deep breath. "What did you and Shiloh find?"

"Shiloh," Kali stressed, "stopped here."

Grant used his flashlight to survey the ground. "It's been disturbed recently." He shifted position, scooping the dirt away with his hands.

Kali joined him. "It looks different from my sketch."

He glanced over at her. "Does it?"

"There's no air pipe."

Grant stopped for a moment, then shone his flashlight over the area in a quick perusal as Kali continued to dig frantically at the end where she knew the head would be. "No, there isn't." He resumed working beside her. Two other men with shovels joined them. Grant pulled Kali back. Exercising caution, the men went to work. There was no time for proper procedures. Julie's life hung in the balance.

"Look," Kali cried out.

Flashlights beamed in her direction and locked onto where she pointed. A piece of plaid fabric shone in the light. A shirt. Shovels were tossed aside as careful hands scooped and lifted, clearing the dirt from around the head area. Grant followed the shirt to the body underneath, sliding his hands underneath. He tugged a body upward. With effort, he pulled it free. First a pinkish arm flopped out and then another as the dirt grudgingly slid to the side, unwilling to give up its secret.

Kali stood fixated on the chaos, Shiloh cuddled up at her side. The lights created weird shadows in the sky as men went to work on the victim. An oxygen tank landed off to one side.

Kali's heart stopped. She closed her eyes briefly. "Is it Julie? Is she still alive?"

Just then, the sea of men parted.

"Grant?"

Grant stepped back a pace as the light flashed on the victim's face. Kali stared. It wasn't Julie.

It was a man.

THAT HAD BEEN too close. Hidden in a hollow less than two miles away from the craziness, Texan struggled to control his breathing. Crap, he shouldn't be this winded already. He went for much longer on disaster sites. He hadn't expected panic to steal his strength. Groaning, he rolled over and flopped on his back. Dampness soaked into his shirt, cooling the raging sweat he'd worked up. Kali's black magic was strong. Scary strong. If he hadn't seen her painting, he'd never have believed how strong.

His heart had pounded so badly when he'd heard Shiloh coming up behind him he'd been afraid of having a heart attack. When Shiloh worked, nothing threw her off. He'd bolted, as far and as fast as possible.

No easy feat in the dark.

Tugging his jacket loosely over his chest, he coughed once, then twice. He'd take just a minute more. His car was quite a distance away yet. The last thing he needed was to run into a roadblock. The dark would hide him for hours until the searchers brought in high-powered lights and really got to work. He had to be long gone by then.

He'd survived this far by being careful and faithful to God's plan. He wasn't about to screw up now.

Damn Kali, anyway. She'd gotten lucky this time. He'd underestimated the strength of her evil. Forewarned was forearmed. Next time, he'd plan better and make damn sure she came out the loser.

CHAPTER 13

KALI STOOD, A silent island amid the sea of men surging in the eerie moonlight. Where was Julie? And who was this poor man?

Someone bumped her, jarring her to awareness. She looked around. Grant's men blended with paramedics, at least she thought that's who they were. Having led the way the whole time, she'd had no idea how many people Grant had called in, until she was drowned in the sea of people. High-powered lights had been set up, throwing weird shadows across the area as men moved about their tasks. Energy wafted high in the night sky. Colors flung and retracted with the movements of the men. So many men, so much energy. She blinked several times and tried to shift her awareness away from her own personal borealis. Nudging the agent closest to her, she asked, "Is he alive?"

Looking up at the sky beginning to lighten ever so slightly, he gave a small shake of his head. "No." His voice dropped to a low whisper. "But he's still warm."

"Oh God," she whispered, pulling her light jacket tighter. That explained the low to the ground and barely black visible threads amongst the brighter waves. It also explained Shiloh's reaction. Crouching down, she hugged Shiloh, who lay with her teddy bear under her chin. Shiloh understood. Kali buried her head in the thick pelt as hot tears pooled. They ran and mingled as sorrow overwhelmed her. They'd been so close, so fast. Had almost saved him…almost.

Where could Julie be? And if Kali had gotten this wrong – was Julie even missing? Some psychic she was. Kali sniffled softly as she stared out in the night.

The picture clicked into her mind, drawing her attention back to the missing air pipe from the victim to the surface of the ground. She'd been so sure the picture had depicted this location, yet she'd found someone else. God. Another victim.

She reached for her phone. Damn, she'd left it in its holder in her Jeep. Stupid.

Grant came up behind her. "Not exactly the end we'd hoped for."

She flushed at the reminder and stood swaying in place, so tired and confused that nothing made sense. A firm hand grabbed her and tugged her forward. Before she realized it, she was tucked close to Grant's chest. She accepted the gesture as tears threatened to fall. Not Julie. A stranger. Some poor soul buried out here all alone. Her lip trembled then firmed. "No," she whispered. "Not exactly."

"Kali, you're beyond exhausted." Giving her shoulders a gentle squeeze, he added in a voice that made her want to weep with its tenderness, "It's over. Let's get you home."

It would never be over. "It's not over. Julie is still missing." Kali opened her eyes and stared at him. "Who is he?" she asked, grief warring with the pain in her voice.

"We don't know yet." Turning her slightly, he pulled up her vest zipper before stepping back, putting a slight distance between them.

"I'd hoped—" She swallowed, her throat dry and rough. "I really hoped to find someone alive."

"We all did." Nudging her gently in the right direction, he led her forward. "Let's get you home and into bed."

Kali didn't fight him. "I doubt I'll be able to sleep." A choked laugh escaped. "We can't forget about Julie. We have to find her."

"And we will. I'll have a team continue to track her down. Don't worry about it now. We'll handle it. You need rest."

She did need sleep. Having burned through the adrenaline rush, she had nothing left. Maybe come morning everything would make sense. "The caller was right." The words blurted out on their own. The emotion threatened to overwhelm her. She stumbled, righted herself and then stumbled again, her feet like ungainly blocks of wood. "We were too late."

"I know. Take it easy. We're almost there." Grant's voice echoed from the shadows.

Kali kept moving forward. Her eyes focused on the shifting beam of light as it moved over the uneven ground. They passed several team members carrying gear one way or another. Grant spoke to them. Kali kept moving forward. She wanted to go home.

After another ten minutes Kali recognized the small shack and the outline of her Jeep.

Thank God.

Shiloh, quiet for the whole trip, barked once as they approached the parking lot. "Yes, Shiloh. Time to go home." Kali opened the back door of the Jeep for Shiloh before collapsing into the driver's seat. She leaned her head on the perforated steering wheel cover. And caught sight of her phone.

She checked for messages.

Julie's voice, faint and reedy sounding, came out clear. "Kali, what's going on? Call me back."

Relief overwhelmed her. "Kali." Dan's voice signaled the next message. "Kali, I found Julie. She's fine. She went to the hospital last night for a bad nosebleed. She's home now. I hope you get this." The next message was an exact repeat.

Grant crouched and leaned in on her driver's door. "So now we have the answer to the Julie mystery. And yes, we'll have someone go talk to her. Warn her, just in case... Okay?" At her tired smile, he added, "Kali, let me get someone to drive you home."

"I'm fine, just tired." She shook her head. "And I'd rather be alone right now."

Grant stood, understanding evident in his expression. "Call me when you get home." He started to turn away but stopped. "Remember, I set up surveillance on your house, so don't worry and sleep well."

Kali lifted an eyebrow. How easily she gave up her prized privacy. Her mind was numb, on overdrive, and yet nothing fit together in there. Too exhausted to sort this out, she stopped trying.

All she could focus on was that it wasn't Julie. Julie wasn't in danger. She'd never been in danger. Or was she? What about her painting? She'd painted that before they'd found the victim in Sacramento – if it even depicted that victim. She was good at what she did, finding people. As a psychic, she sucked. Big time. Her earlier sketch and even her painting were nothing but twisted meanderings of an exhausted mind.

Confusion, fatigue and she'd admit a little shock linked and twisted everything together. She needed rest. Then she'd sort this out after a few hours.

Putting the Jeep into reverse, she backed out of her parking spot, stopping when Grant walked toward her again.

"You two did really well tonight. Don't forget that."

She whispered to the dark empty interior, "So why do I feel like such a failure?"

"DAMN IT." AS soon as Kali turned onto the highway, Grant regretted not driving her home. She might want to be alone, but she probably shouldn't be. He was needed here. Yet he couldn't shake the bad feeling in his gut. He wasn't really psychic, with effort he could see some energy, like Kali's, but he'd learned to trust his intuition. He called to one of the junior team members returning with equipment.

"Grab a car and see that Kali gets to her house safe and sound." He pointed to the taillights disappearing down the road. Grant watched the second car peel out after her. With a marginally better frame of mind, he returned to the crime scene. Clouds whispered across the moon, giving the night a surreal look.

That went along with the surreal events of the night.

Thomas approached. "I don't know, Grant. You sure collect weird friends."

Grant laughed, a sound at odds with the scene open around them. Still, he appreciated the easing of the macabre tension. "That I do. Have you ever seen anything like this?"

Thomas, his demeanor grimmer than usual, said, "Never. To imagine one person carrying this guy all this way is pretty unbelievable. He is small and wiry, but still…unless he was forced to walk in at gunpoint."

"I mentioned that to Kali. She said the training is not only extensive, but also intensive, with some people becoming fanatical about their fitness levels. She said this level of fitness wasn't out of line with some of the stronger people."

"Then those are the ones we should be focusing on." Thomas glanced over at him. "Did she really draw a picture of this scene?" He waved his arm to the controlled chaos going on around them. "Cause that's beyond bizarre."

"I know. I need her to connect with Stefan. He could help her a lot."

"I have to ask." Thomas hesitated. "I know you don't believe it, and that people are working in the background to verify it, but are you absolutely sure she isn't involved? It wouldn't take much for an artist to draw this image if she'd participated in the events."

Grant knew Thomas well. They'd worked together for over a decade and often spent time off, together. He'd been Thomas's best man three years ago. In fact, Thomas had attended the same seminar where Grant had first laid eyes on Kali. They'd spoken about it several times.

"I'm asking you, both as a friend and as an FBI agent, do you believe Kali is innocent of any wrongdoing here?"

"Yes." Simple, clear and the truth. "She had nothing to do with this. In fact, I'd wager my career on it."

"You realize that's exactly what you're doing?"

Grant stared calmly back at his friend. "I am and that's fine. She didn't do this. I know it, and the truth will prove it."

Some of the rigidity slipped off Thomas's shoulders. He slapped Grant on the shoulder. "Good enough. So who the hell did?"

KALI WISHED SHE could have slept longer. Sandpaper hid under her eyelids, and her muscles ached after her midnight run. Shiloh joined her, limping, her joints moving stiffly as she walked into the kitchen. Last night had been hard on both of them. They needed a week of physical and mental healing time.

In the kitchen she turned on her computer and checked her answering machine as she waited. Pressing the play button, she listened to the messages. One from Dan, updating her on Brad's disappearance – no word on his whereabouts. The next was from Brenda, who wanted to do lunch now that Kali was back from Sacramento. The last two were business calls.

Kali wasn't up to returning any of them. She forced herself to the beach for a short run to loosen up her legs. She couldn't shake her awareness of the security Grant had provided for her protection. Just to make sure, she checked that her cell phone was tucked in her pocket.

She'd just made it back to the bottom of the steps when the phone rang.

"Kali, it's Jarl. You called yesterday?"

His thick European accent came through loud and clear. Still gasping for breath, it took a moment before she could speak normally. She started to walk in a circle to cool down. "Hi, Jarl. Glad to hear you're home safe and sound."

It took her a moment to remember why she'd called him. All thoughts of Brad had been forced from her mind after the crazy midnight hunt.

"Except I'm not home yet. Should be there tomorrow. God looks after those that do his work."

Kali frowned. Though she didn't share his beliefs, she was happy to leave him to them. "Did you see Brad over in Sacramento this last week?"

"Sure I did," he said comfortably. "Why? What's the problem?"

"He's gone AWOL again. I was hoping you might have seen him after I left."

"That I did. Saw him a couple of times, in fact. That Sergeant of his is hell on wheels with cadavers, isn't he?"

"Isn't that the truth?" Shiloh was better at finding live victims, Sergeant had made a name for himself in recovery operations locating the dead.

"Time is still messed up for me. All this traveling and weird hours. If you're wondering when I last saw him, it was right after you went home. I passed him outside drinking with some of the locals." Jarl's disapproval laced his tone.

"He does struggle with his demons. It's the work we do."

"Aye, a man's got to do what he's got to do."

"Okay, well, I thought I'd check." Kali had hoped for better news.

"Let me know if I can help you with anything else."

Jarl rang off, and Kali climbed the steep set of stairs cut into the cliff.

Showered and refreshed half an hour later, she poured a glass of orange juice, then sat down at her computer to check her emails. Forty-two. Several were spam telling her how to enlarge her penis. She snorted. As if. Even with her email filters, she received several a day. There were a couple of work-related emails, one from The Picasso Gallery owner who carried a few of her prettier paintings. Good news. They'd sold the last painting and wondered if she'd be interested in placing more with them. A good idea, if and when life returned to normal and she could actually think in terms of *pretty* again.

She clicked on the last email. No sender listed. She frowned. "The game is up. If you don't tell, I will."

Kali could feel the tension build inside of her. "What the

hell?" she whispered. As she scrolled down, her shoulders slumped and tears came to her eyes when the picture came into view.

The picture showed a dead or dying man, an oxygen mask on his face.

It looked like the man they'd found last night.

Kali reached for her cell phone and called Grant.

"Finally woke up, did you?"

"I have an email from the killer."

Grant's voice snapped to business mode. "I'm on my way."

Kali signed off and returned to the kitchen. She put on coffee and turned her attention to food. Anything to stay busy and keep her mind off that email. Besides, Shiloh had missed enough meals. Searching the fridge, she realized it had to be a skinny omelet and toast again for her.

Shiloh dug into her breakfast with gusto. Kali ate hers more slowly, her mind now locked onto her weird sketches.

If they'd come at any other time, she'd have assumed they were an outpouring of ugly memories. Yet they'd proven vital in sending her, for all the wrong reasons, straight to the wrong victim – but a victim nonetheless.

Kali stared at the Julie sketch, as she'd come to think of it, even though it had led to a man and not Julie. It looked the same as it had five minutes ago – if anything, a bit freakier. She'd used it as a map straight to a dead body last night. That would freak anyone out.

She needed to take another look at her painting.

Kali opened the door to her studio, grimacing at the mess. Tubes and brushes were now sitting amongst her paints, fingerprint dust covered most surfaces and her stack of canvases had fallen askew.

Snatching up a cloth from a cupboard under the counters, she quickly put things back to rights. While she worked she puzzled over the time frame. It really bothered her.

Turning her attention to the canvas, she flipped back the cover, struck anew by the power streaming off the painting.

Then it hit her.

She'd done this painting *before* she'd traveled to the apartment disaster in Sacramento. If, and it was a big if, she'd done the same thing again, it meant that her doodle of Julie, should have happened *before* Julie was snatched. Then, theoretically, Julie should not have been kidnapped...yet.

Which meant she was in danger even now. Thank God, Grant had left someone at her house last night.

And she needed to talk to him.

But it was a hell of an assumption to think this sketch had anything to do with her oil painting. Or that either picture depicted real-life murders, which brought her full circle to one indisputable fact. The last sketch *had* led them to a victim.

Hearing the crunch of tires, she raced to the front door. Grant walked toward her as a second vehicle pulled in behind him.

She sighed. How was it that he could appear handsome despite his exhaustion? She sighed. "You don't look like you got much rest."

"Thanks for reminding me. Where's the coffee?"

"In the kitchen," she answered tartly. "Go get a cup."

Leaving Grant to direct his men as needed, Kali walked straight out to the porch with her cup, biting her lips to keep from blurting out her fear about Julie. She'd give him some time before she dumped that on his shoulders. "The email is up." From the porch, she heard another vehicle arriving. More of his team, she supposed.

Turning, she found Grant standing in the doorway. "Did you get the name or email of the sender?"

Grant shook his head. "I can't, our specialist…" He nodded toward to the man she could barely see behind him. "Should be able to."

"Does he have to take it away? I need my laptop."

It was Grant's turn to shrug. "Probably." Frustration colored his voice.

"Did you learn anything about last night's victim?" She hadn't wanted to think about him, and therefore hadn't been able to put him out of her mind.

"Yes and no. His ID said David Stewart. A fifty-year-old trucker. We're waiting on confirmation but there's no reason to doubt that's his name at this point."

Kali stared at him. "A trucker. How did this guy get to him?"

Grant looked up into the sky and then dropped his gaze to her. "We don't know. Or what the connection is to the killer or to the other victims.

Bitterness rose up. "We don't know very much at all, do we?"

"Without you, he could have been left there for a long time." Grant reached out and squeezed her shoulder gently, before dropping his arm. "You brought him home. For that, we are all grateful."

Tears rose, surprising her. How could such a simple touch comfort her? Disturbed, she blinked the tears away, rubbing the back of her neck, feeling a stiffness she hadn't noticed earlier. "He'd have been found soon anyway, since we do regular training there."

"The killer probably counted on that."

"Only it happened sooner, rather than later through dumb luck." Kali looked over at him. "We focused on that stupid picture."

"Regardless, we did hit the right destination."

"But not in time." The bitterness returned.

"Chances are David wouldn't have survived anyway."

Kali stared at him in shock. "What? I thought we'd just missed saving his life."

"That's what we all thought. His head injury was severe and the oxygen mask hadn't sealed around his face. The coroner should be…" Grant looked at his watch and finished, saying, "Doing the autopsy right now."

Kali's cell phone rang. Turning away slightly, she clicked it open. "Hello."

"Hi, Kali. Did you get my message?"

"I did, Dan," she answered. "Sorry for not getting back to you sooner."

She could hear the happiness in his voice. "No problem. I'm calling about Julie. We upset her last night. Can we give her a better explanation now?"

"Ask Grant. Here."

Grant raised an eyebrow and accepted the phone. "Hi, Dan."

Kali shut off the rest of the conversation and headed to the far end of the deck where she could catch a glimpse of the ocean through the treetops.

Grant joined her a few minutes later. "We're done here. The email was sent through a special server and that account has been closed already. I doubt we'll get anything from it." His voice shifted, becoming brisk. "I need you to take another look at your sketch to see if you notice anything else we can use."

"Damn it, Grant, I've stared at it for hours already. I thought it was Julie. Honestly, I'm still afraid it is – or will be – Julie."

Silence.

"You think she's the *next* victim?"

Kali turned, propped one hip against the railing and closed her eyes, her head bowed in thought. "I don't know what to think." That was the truth. At least as far as it went. She'd refrained from telling him one tiny little detail. He'd freak.

"Yet something is bugging you."

She gave him a sideways look. "I think it's fair to say that a lot is bugging me."

He narrowed his gaze. "You know what I mean."

Wrinkling up her nose, she admitted, "I might not have told you everything."

That same eyebrow shot up. His cheeks hollowed as his chin firmed. When she didn't speak, a glint came into his eye. "Speak."

Kali didn't know how to begin.

"Kali? Please."

She nodded. Reaching up, she ran her fingers through the strands, collecting her thoughts. "It's about my painting."

He glanced in the direction of the studio. "That painting?"

"Yes."

She hesitated, then the words erupted from her mouth. "I painted it before I went to Sacramento."

He blinked. Then he got it. "Precognitive painting?"

Kali stared at him. "Is there such a thing?"

With a half laugh, he asked, "You tell me?"

"It was only when I got home from that trip and took a closer look that I understood."

"Except we don't know when that victim was kidnapped. Does the rest of the painting fairly represent the scene you found down there?"

Mute, she considered the question. "Yes, it does. So now I have to wonder if this Julie sketch is something similar. I'm just too new to this psychic stuff to know."

"Has this happened to you before?"

"Drawings like this? No. Never!" *Or had it?* She frowned pensively. Would she have recognized other paintings for what they were? Not likely. "At least I don't think so? I've drawn for years, like I told you. I've never mentally connected the image to a specific event before. Especially not something like this."

"Could *they* have been precognitive in nature?"

"I don't know."

"Maybe you should check?" He studied her features curiously.

Kali spun around and headed to the small studio, Grant at her heels. Opening the door, she walked in. "Uhmm, there should be some around here somewhere." As she talked, Kali opened cupboards and drawers. The big storage closet held her overload of art supplies and it was full, very full.

"Wow. Maybe check your artwork from the last couple of years. Your precognitive skills could have been developing for a long time."

The smaller closet contained an organized stack of her sketchbooks. "Maybe when this mess is over and I get a minute." She turned to face him. "Still *if* I'm right, Julie could be the *next* victim."

Grant's eyes narrowed, his focus shifting inward. She could almost see him tick off each point in his head. "We'll talk with her."

Kali closed her eyes briefly. "Thank you. I should have considered it earlier, but, honestly, it only crossed my mind just before you arrived."

He snorted. "And when were you supposed to think of it? You drew the picture last night. We found the trucker within hours and you've caught a few hours of rest. There hasn't been any extra time. Stop with the guilt trip. We'll speak with her."

He strode to the front door. "I'm going back into town. I'll call you later."

Kali felt torn as she watched him leave. She connected to the nasty turn her life had taken, yet he was comforting to have around. He'd become a rock in her world of quicksand.

She hadn't thought she'd be willing to lean on anyone else again after so many years alone. True, it was a rare disaster where she didn't break down at least once. Death and hopelessness did that to a person when blended with exhaustion. Dan had lent his shoulder a time or two, as had Brad. Her heart swelled. God, she missed him. Though she wasn't as tough as everyone assumed, she always pulled up her socks and carried on. She was no quitter.

So what now? Grant had set up security, surveillance but she hadn't asked him about new locks. That she could do. The last thing she wanted was another visit from this asshole. She should have done it earlier. Kali picked up her phone and by promising to pay extra, she secured the locksmith's promise to come out within the next hour. That done, Kali noted down things she had to do.

Talk with Julie.

Catch killer.

Figure out what she wanted from Grant.

But no pressure, Kali!

JULIE WANDERED THROUGH her town home, hating the sense of vulnerability. It was hard to believe the night could have gone so wrong. Her nosebleed last night had been so bad she'd gone to the hospital. She hated hospitals. She hadn't even been able to drive herself there.

And to come home to have an officer waiting for her…

She sighed. Surely she had a forgotten bottle of wine stashed somewhere. It didn't matter what time of day it was. Finding out everyone thought she'd gone missing was bizarre, and Dan's explanation had been over the top.

Kidnapped, for heaven's sake. They'd really lost it with that assumption. And what about coming in and searching her place? In a small way she felt violated. Better make that in a big way. It no longer held the same comfortable hominess. Her house was full of energy – their energy. She'd need her feng shui specialist to clean it out properly.

Dan had been so apologetic that he'd made her laugh. He reminded her of her father, his actions coming from the right place, even if Dan appeared to have lost his head. He was the epitome of the forgetful professor. Harmless.

Kali was downright scary. How could she do the type of work she did with such eerie calm? Julie shook her head as she opened her fridge.

Wine. That would take the edge off. She popped the cork, breaking off a little into the bottle in the process, and poured herself a hefty glass. Carrying it out to the porch, she chose a seat in the shade.

A sparrow hopped through the garden, pecking away at the ground. Julie smiled at its antics. She'd like to be so carefree. According to her shrink that wouldn't happen until she 'made peace' with herself. Julie snorted before taking another hefty swig of her drink. The place was a connection to what she'd experienced. The SAR center an irresistible lure, a chance to connect to people who understood. Most people couldn't understand; the people at Second Chance did.

As far as she was concerned, she didn't need a shrink; she

needed a new life. And she'd been hoping that was in progress.

Until this.

Julie shuddered.

Men in her house. Going through her drawers, her bedroom, her papers and her life. Yuck. She knew they believed they had just cause. It was supposedly for her benefit, still… Her personal space was everything to her.

Checking her watch, she realized it was time to get dressed. Her new man should be here soon. They were going out for lunch and to the conservatory. She hadn't yet decided if this would be the night. She'd held him off so far, wanting him to work for it a little. In her opinion, women gave in too easy these days. Then the guys became spoiled and expected the same treatment all the time. Julie loved a good romp, but not because it was expected of her. Besides, the guy was married. It's not like he wasn't getting it on a regular basis.

Julie preferred her men married. Short term and private, with no complications. Her phone rang. Checking the caller ID, she smiled. "Hi," she sang into the phone. "Are we still on for lunch?"

CHAPTER 14

DAMN DRAWINGS. SINCE when had her barely existent extrasensory skills extended to paranormal artwork? Was there even such a label? Or did she have the dubious distinction of being the only weirdo who created 'kidnap art'?

Kali reached for the cold iced tea sitting beside her on her patio table. Grant had been gone an hour, and her thoughts had already dropped into chaos.

Her phone rang. Grant.

"Last night's victim died of a heart attack," he said brusquely. "He'd most likely been comatose for hours."

"What? What about the head trauma? Being buried? Lack of oxygen from the dislodged mask?" Kali had a hard time taking it all in.

"All of that would have sped up the process, but what I'm saying is you couldn't have saved him. He was a dead man anyway."

Relief and pain washed over her. Poor guy. At least he wouldn't have known what was happening. Shit. "So, if he hadn't had that heart attack, he'd have been there waiting for us?" Relief vanished. Shakes wracked her spine. God, if he hadn't died, he could be still lying there, waiting in agony and terror, wondering if his life were over. Understanding hit. "We weren't meant to find him that fast."

A heavy sigh slid through the phone lines. "I'm thinking the same thing. That's why the killer felt safe being there. We were supposed to look for the owner of the earring."

"How does he think I'm going to find these people?"

"What's the chance he knows about your paranormal skills?"

"Not likely. I don't talk about it. At all."

"Feel free to contact Stefan if you want to talk."

Right, the psychic who worked with the police. Grimacing,

she asked, "Do you think he'd mind?"

"No, he won't. Have you got a pen?" He rattled off the number as Kali jotted it down on her notepad. She had Stefan's card somewhere. This was easier.

"Have you spoken with Julie?"

"Not yet."

Kali stared around at the old fir trees on her property. "I'll call her again in a few minutes. I was hoping you had contacted her."

"We're working on it. She was told to check in this morning and hasn't yet. We don't know if she forgot, didn't feel like it or..."

His businesslike tone of voice told her nothing. Did they have any idea where Julie was? What were they doing to try and find her? So many questions. Yet she didn't feel she could ask any of them. He was doing what he could. That things weren't moving fast enough for her didn't mean Grant was sitting on his ass doing nothing.

"Right. I don't imagine she was pleased about last night." Kali massaged her forehead. "She's probably fine. We don't even know if he's after her." And they didn't. She'd latched onto the idea based on her pictures. Stupid. "I can't get rid of the idea that he's targeting disaster survivors. However, that only works if David were a survivor himself."

"We haven't found anything like that in his history so far."

Then why him? She couldn't begin to understand the methodology, the craziness of a killer's mind. Especially a killer like this. "He has to be picking his victims somehow."

"Is there a registry or something for survivors?" The sound of a pencil scratched as he took notes.

"I don't think so. There are support groups where people go to deal with the guilt of being the person who survived." She thought about it. "Both online and in person."

"So he'd have had no problem finding out who belongs to these groups?"

"Maybe initially, but once he tapped it, there'd be a huge supply of victims."

"We can ask Julie about new members to her online group. She's been told to stay in touch, so she's not likely to be too far away. If you reach her, let me know immediately," Grant said, his voice brisk and focused. "Meanwhile, we'll work on finding the connection between these victims."

Grant rang off, leaving Kali to stare at the dead phone. She dialed Julie again.

Julie didn't answer. Again dread rolled through Kali. She'd been out of communication for too long. Even for someone who valued her privacy. She dialed Dan next.

"I can't reach Julie. Do you know if she belongs to groups or associations involving other survivors?"

"She did therapy afterward, and still belongs to at least one online group. I don't know which one." The fatigue in Dan's voice worried her. Dan's health had been slipping *before* this mess. Now…

"Right," Kali said. "Grant wants to talk to her. This killer has to have a way of selecting his victims, a pool to choose from. It could be a support group."

"Oh, God."

She hung up.

Tension ran through her and into everything she did. Like fine wire tightened too far. She knew that anything more and she might snap. She straightened magazine stacks and reorganized her almost empty bedding closet to keep busy.

When the phone rang, she dropped everything. Maybe Dan had good news for a change. Unknown caller. She frowned.

"Hello."

Laughter answered her. The same voice punched her in the gut. Shit. Anger burned away the shock. "Stop it. Quit calling me and quit killing people, you asshole."

Kali slammed the receiver down. Grant's men should have picked that up, too. There. It rang again. She thought it could be the same monster but she hadn't written down the number of the last call. She did this time and refused to answer. Then doubts crept into her mind. "Shit."

She snatched up the phone and answered it.

The same laughter answered her.

"What do you want?" she screamed into the receiver.

"You missed one."

"What?"

But Kali was talking to a dead phone.

"Shit."

Fingers trembling, she had to dial twice before she punched in the right numbers. Grant answered on the first ring. "He just called. We missed one." She started crying. "He said we mis–"

"What?" Sharp tension shot through the phone. "Kali, calm down. Take a deep breath."

Choking back a sob, Kali released a shuddering breath. She wiped her eyes.

"Sorry," she whispered. "Just a second." She wiped her eyes on her sleeve and sniffled back the tears.

"Better? Now again, slowly, please."

After a slow deep breath, Kali repeated what he'd said. "I've been trying to reach Julie; I'm only getting voicemail." Kali glanced over at the clock, frowning, her stomach knotting. "It's early. I want to believe her cell phone battery is dead, but…"

"Now you're afraid she won't be coming home." His grim voice added to her queasiness. She could hear him talking to someone in the background, asking for a copy of the call. She vaguely remembered him saying he'd put a trace on the phone. Good, maybe they'd catch this asshole after all.

"I don't know what to believe," she whispered. The horror of the previous night rose to clog her throat with tears again. She walked outside into the early afternoon sun. Her slippers clicked on the cedar slats. Shiloh joined her, nudging her nose against Kali's bare legs. Bending down, Kali hugged her close, needing the comfort as much as giving it.

As she straightened she looked surreptitiously across the property. "You're sure there's surveillance on the house? I'd hate to have to stay inside, but it feels weird out on my deck."

"Go in and stay in when you're alone. We don't want to give him any opportunity." His voice sharpened. "And yes, there's a team watching. Twenty-four hours a day."

That helped. Rotating her shoulders, easing back the tension, she could look around without tearing up again. It truly was a beautiful day. Sun, blue sky and a warm breeze… She took a deep breath of the salty, tangy air. That helped, too. Now she'd follow orders and go inside. Refocusing, she asked, "I'm really hoping he's referring to the round two victim. I'd hate to think there's another one we don't know about."

His silence was agreement enough.

Soberly she asked, "What now?"

"We're working on it."

"Great. The waiting game." Kali couldn't stop the sarcasm from slipping into her voice. "Please call me if there's any development."

Kali hung up the phone. This asshole had to be stopped. A thought glimmered in the back of her mind. She didn't know if it would work or not, but she needed to try. Gathering her art stuff, she poured herself a cup of coffee. This might take a while.

What she really needed was Grant's friend. What was his name? Stefan? Yes, he could be a big help.

STEFAN LEANED AGAINST the front grill of his beamer and watched the seagulls floating on the wind. The sense of freedom from the physical plane, achieved through an out of body experience, was a sensation like no other. He'd come to crave it after all these years. Being a sensitive, a psychic, meant he was often buffeted by factors other people couldn't imagine.

For some, it was all hocus-pocus bullshit. For others, like him, it was a strange hidden world coexisting in the same time-space continuum as theirs. For him, the rest of the world appeared to be sleeping. They didn't see what he saw. They didn't hear what he heard. They definitely didn't know what he knew.

It was lonely in the ethers. Probably why he'd started to build a network of friends who were like him. With the world being as judgmental and disbelieving as it was, anyone struggling to understand his abilities had nowhere to go. No one to talk to.

He'd been there with hellish results.

Leaning back, he tilted his face to the sky, letting the sun beam on his skin. He hated traveling. Being in traffic with all those tempers and personalities put him in a maelstrom of other people's emotions.

They were like children. They let everything out, verbally, physically, and for him almost worse was the endless blasting they did mentally.

Keeping his shields in place was automatic, but in rush hour especially, he needed a suit of armor to repel the energies. He loved the water. It held a life force that drew him, calmed him.

Sitting there watching the waves, enjoying the respite, he heard his name whispered. Opening his eyes, he considered the speaker.

Kali.

And what did he want to do about it?

Checking his watch, he smiled slowly. "I know exactly what I'm going to do."

The real question was, should he tell Grant?

KALI OPENED UP her sketchbook, stared at the old picture for a few moments, then turned to a clean page toward the end of the book. The two previous pictures had come about as a result of exhaustion and mental overload.

"Neither of which applies here," she muttered to Shiloh.

Kali stared at the blank page, hoping for inspiration. None came. Frustrated, she realized she didn't know what to do. She knew the desired result but not the methodology.

Just when she was ready to throw her sketchbook down in disgust, the doorbell rang. Shiloh jumped to her feet, barking crazily.

She followed Shiloh to the front door where she stopped to look through the small peep hole.

"Holy shit," she whispered. It was Stefan, Grant's psychic friend. There was no forgetting that face. He was tall, and his golden hair had a hint of a curl, just as she remembered. He stared down at her, amusement glinting from liquid chocolate eyes.

Double shit. She looked behind her toward the kitchen where she'd been when she'd wished he could be here with her…and here he was. Coincidence? Surely he couldn't know she'd been thinking of him. Could he? She opened the door and her brain hitched. *Christ, he was beautiful.*

She stared as something else triggered. His energy was warm and soothing, captivating…yet contained. It didn't reach for her. It didn't tease her, attract her…it wasn't for her. And hers didn't respond to his either.

His lips curved. "Hello, Kali. Remember me?"

Stefan, Grant's friend.

Grant.

Her world righted itself.

She sighed happily. "The artist in me would love to paint your face. The woman in me is glad I have other interests."

He laughed with honest humor. "Thanks. I'm glad for Grant, too."

Heat washed her cheeks. She gave an embarrassed laugh. "Oh, that's great. You can read minds too."

"Only wide open ones."

"And mine is? Ouch." She didn't like the sound of that.

"It was when you opened the door." He said. "You've slammed it shut now."

"Yeah, duh. Do you always have that effect on women?" She opened the door wider for him to enter. With her own perspective back in balance, she took a closer look. He really was male model material. "It must be quite a burden for you."

He cocked a brow her way.

"I'm serious."

As if just realizing she was speaking to him, he nodded. "It can be. Few people look beneath the surface."

Not nice. She wouldn't appreciate that herself.

As she led the way to the kitchen, she tossed a curious look at him. "Did Grant suggest you come by?"

"No, I'm here because you were looking for my help. The question is for what?"

Amazed, she stopped in her tracks. "You're saying you're here because I was thinking I'd like to have your help with something?" She couldn't quite get her mind wrapped around it. "Surely you don't hear every time someone thinks of you or says your name? It would drive you crazy."

Some of the light in his face dimmed. His voice deepened; a weariness entered. "That's quite true. I have to keep guards in place for just that reason."

"Christ." She was almost bereft of words. "That is so not nice." Back in the kitchen, she motioned toward a seat beside her own. "Take a seat. Can I offer you a drink of some kind? Coffee?"

A boyish grin whispered across his face. "You do like your coffee, don't you?"

She couldn't help but laugh. "You don't have to be a mind reader to pick that up." She lifted her mega-sized cup from the table and took a sip.

"I'm fine for right now." He motioned to her sketchbook lying open on the table. "What type of help are you looking for? Artistic or psychic or both?"

She winced. "I'm sure Grant told you a little about me." She sent him a questioning look. At his nod, she quirked her lips. "The thing is, even though I'm doing this stuff, I don't know how to do it. If that makes any sense. My drawings always just happened – usually when I'm horribly exhausted."

"Meaning your abilities just happen when they will, without you having any control? As if you're along for the ride instead of being in the driver's seat?"

"Exactly! And now that I'm trying to consciously connect to these abilities, I can't."

"That's because your mind is getting in the way. When you're exhausted, your subconscious can shut your conscious mind down easier as it's too tired to fight back."

Her confusion had to have been evident, because his lips curved and he pulled the sketchbook closer and picked up her pencil. Looking sidelong at her, he raised an eyebrow in question.

"Go for it." Kali hitched her chair closer.

"When you draw, you look at your page, determine where you're going to start and then you start. When you draw psychically, you don't follow the mental process. You've shifted, for whatever reason, into another consciousness that controls how your drawing looks. It's not that you don't know how – it's that you're working with the wrong part of your brain. You need to let the subconscious have control."

She grappled with the concept. "So I need to draw with my subconscious to tap into the psychic side of things? How do I do that?"

"That's where practice comes in." He wrote a series of numbers down on her sketchbook. "I do have a few techniques for you to try. These aren't things you can go to school and learn. Practice is required. It's the only way to gain control."

"And presumably, I'm not going to get it right off the bat?"

"Most people require some time. It depends on the wrestling match between the two consciousnesses. Some people have no trouble switching from one to the other."

"Like you?"

Stefan glanced up, warm eyes twinkling. "Like me, yes. And you will get there."

He wrote quickly and, before she realized it, he had made a list. His hand moved smoothly across the page. She could see the artist in the simple movements. The sure confidence on the paper, the hand positioning. He was comfortable with who and what he was.

Finally, he tossed the pencil down and turned the page so she could read his notes.

1. *Start by turning off all distractions and find a place to be alone.*

2. *Next – go into a meditative state – by whatever means works for you – soft music, candlelight, yoga position.*
3. *Relax. It's only through relaxation, that we free the mind.*
4. *Pick up your pencil and sketchbook and wait in this same relaxed state.*
5. *An image will form, at least this is how it works for me. I draw what I see.*
6. *If you are distracted, feeling pressured, or try to force it, the image will disappear.*

"Disappear? Really?"

"Absolutely." He waited while she reread the instructions. "It's simple to understand, much harder to do…damn near impossible to do well."

"I have no doubts about that." As she glanced his way, she saw he'd risen. "You're leaving?"

"You need to draw. I can see the energy around you. And what's the first thing on that list? Be alone, if you can." Snatching the pencil up again, he quickly wrote his name and number below the instructions. "That's if you need to contact me." His mischievous smile flashed. "Now you have my number for the third time."

His fingers brushed hers as he handed the notebook back to her. His gaze met hers as he said, "You are not alone."

For the first time she understood some place deep inside her psyche. He was right. She wasn't the only one dealing with these abilities. He was, too. Her heart eased. He wasn't deserting her.

"And there are more of us. One lives not too far from here. She's unfortunate enough to connect with murder victims *as* they are being killed. A skill that damned near killed her as her body would manifest the same wounds as the victims during their attacks."

"Oh no. That's horrible." She couldn't imagine having to deal with more than one murdering bastard…and to physically be harmed in the process… That was just wrong.

He nodded. "It is indeed. But Sam is learning to control that ability and her many other gifts. The more you open yourself up to this…" He motioned toward her sketchbook. "The more your abilities will be enhanced. They can strengthen, and new ones can develop. We really don't know what the limit is."

"That's enough to make anyone think twice."

"Exactly. Like Sam, you will find a level of satisfaction and self confidence you can't imagine, as your abilities let you see and understand more about how the world you live in operates."

She couldn't help asking, "Sam… Is she okay?"

"She is now. She's found a partner, a cop in fact, who understands and accepts her for who she is. He helps her to stay grounded. I'll have to introduce the two of you. You have a lot in common."

Before she'd realized it, Stefan had reached the front door with her trailing behind. She hated for him to leave. "I'm glad for her."

"Be glad for yourself, too. That's one of those things you have in common." Without a backward glance, he walked out to his car, leaving her sputtering in his wake.

She couldn't even form the right question in her mind before he was gone.

Light shone and left. Like sunlight going behind a cloud, her world dimmed. Then she remembered his words…she was not alone.

He was something else. And what the hell did she have in common with Sam? Psychic abilities? Being at the learning stage…a cop who understood and accepted her? She couldn't go there right now. That he was comparing the cop in Sam's life to Grant seemed obvious on one level and ludicrous on another. She forced Grant from her mind.

One thought lingered as she wandered across the deck. Even with all the pain she was going through right now, she wouldn't want what Sam had gone through.

She returned to her kitchen chair, the sketchbook open in front of her. She didn't know if his instructions would work, but couldn't wait to try.

Her house was being watched. That gave her a vulnerable, almost invaded sensation.

Collecting her art materials, she moved into the living room. After lighting several cinnamon scented candles, she gave Shiloh a chew treat, then sat on the recliner. The candles weren't needed for light, but their warm glow added a comforting mellowness. Kali shuffled her chair closer. She reopened her sketchbook, ripped off the sheet with the instructions then turned to her old picture for a few moments. Shaking her head at the artistic skill, she picked a clean page in the middle of the book.

Letting herself relax, she freed her mind. Pictures flowed. She watched and observed but never engaged. After a few minutes she could feel the tension in her spine easing. It drained from her toes, leaving a limp weakness behind. Staring out the big bay window, she watched the clouds above swell in brilliance. The entire sky shone in rings of pearls above her. A stunning display. A deep sigh worked through her, shaking her to the core, and adding to the limp feeling.

Such an odd sensation. Kali stretched, her pencil coming off the paper as she relaxed after. What had Stefan said at the end? Relax and step outside your mind. Right. Easy for him to say.

Leaning back, Kali slipped into an altogether different state. Peaceful, floating, free of cares and worry. Happy. The last couple of days had been tough. She now realized how much stress that had been on her body. Aches and pains had shown up in places she barely recognized.

She shifted into a more comfortable position. A heavy sigh worked its way up and out.

A tiny picture formed in her mind. With her art pencil in hand, she drew what little she could see in her mind's eye. Within minutes, another tidbit showed up. She translated it to paper. By the time that had been completed, a little more appeared. Slowly, step by step, she pushed back the fog. Still unable to see the whole picture, she focused harder. The fog immediately moved in.

Kali stopped.

Aha. Forcing the picture wouldn't work; she had to relax to let the information flow.

Kali leaned back again and took several deep breaths.

And closed her eyes.

There. A tiny twig of the picture emerged again. Her pencil moved at a furious pace. Kali lost herself in the process.

The crazy pace continued for fifteen minutes. Then everything stopped. Kali's pencil stilled.

Drawing blind? Who'd have considered that as an artistic system? Not her.

She opened her eyes.

And couldn't see anything. The soft light sent a weird flickering glow over the black lines. She turned on a pole lamp beside her. Laying the sketchbook down, Kali sat back and studied the drawing.

It was a picture at least. Not a messed up series of scribbles on top of each other as she'd feared.

But what a picture. A tiny woman or child lay curled up in tight ball, surrounded by intense darkness and almost nothing else. A few sharp lines set the scene and a minute bit of shading finished the job.

Another victim.

Kali stood up to look at the picture from a different angle. Grim foreboding hit her in the gut. The picture had a very different look than last time. Was it the missing victim, a new victim or a figment of her imagination? *God damn it.* If her mind could produce the image then it could damn well produce some parameters.

So how?

Kali studied the picture and then backed off and closed her eyes. The information had to be there. She just had to access it somehow.

Closing her eyes, she relaxed into the picture. Out of the bubbling cauldron of emotions and self-doubt came a day. Friday.

Letting the information roll around inside, she sat quietly to see if anything new came to mind. Studying the picture, so dark and black, it was hard to imagine any hope existed for her. *Her?* Then like she had with her painting, she turned to study the room round her and then glanced back. Yes, it was definitely a woman. So dark and depressing. Almost as if devoid of life.

That was it. This victim was dead. She'd died several days ago. Alone and unknown.

Kali's heart broke.

She reached for the phone.

CHAPTER 15

THE DOORBELL RANG as the coffee finished dripping. Two hours. Not bad. Grant had made decent time, considering he'd had to conclude a meeting before he could leave. Kali rushed over to let him in.

"Hi. Thanks for coming so quickly." Behind him, a second car arrived. *Dan's.* She frowned. "I wonder what he wants?" Motioning in the direction of the kitchen, she said, "Please, go ahead. Dan has no idea about my pictures. I don't want him to see this one, either."

Grant headed obediently into the kitchen while Kali plastered a welcome on her face and waited for Dan to reach her. "Hi, Dan." At his worried expression, her heart sank. "Are you all right?"

"No. No, I'm not. I've been driving aimlessly, hoping to spot Julie. I don't know why, but it seemed like something I could do." He glanced up, an almost blank look in his eyes. "Somehow, I ended up here."

"I've called her several times, but got no answer. Grant's got people looking for her, too." She tried to keep her voice positive.

"I left her a message on both her cell phone and her home phone asking her to meet me at the center this afternoon. She never showed up."

"Maybe her phone isn't on. Or her battery could be dead. Not everyone remembers to keep phones charged. Hell, she might not want to talk to you or me, for that matter."

Dan stomped his feet on the outside mat and stuffed his hands in his pockets. "I'm worried, Kali."

"I was worried last night," she muttered. "Grant's here. Come in and we can ask him what he knows."

"Oh good. I hoped it was his car." Dan bolted for the kitchen. Kali followed at a slower pace. The late afternoon heat had dissipated and the early evening brought a chill as the sun descended behind the hills. Kali detoured to her bedroom and snagged a sweater. Pulling it over her head, she walked into the kitchen.

In the middle of the kitchen, Dan stood wringing his hands, his gaze switching between Kali and Grant. "Grant, I can't get rid of the feeling that, this time something bad has happened."

"I hate to be the voice of reason; however, we also need to consider other possibilities," Kali interjected.

Both men turned to face her.

Kali threw up her hands. "Sorry, I'm worried, too. I also remember searching in a mad panic for her last night, only to find she'd made a trip to the hospital."

"Would she get a nosebleed two nights in a row?" Dan pulled his cell phone out, checking for a message. He put it away again. "Surely, she'd check her messages."

Kali eyed Dan. Flushed and on the point of weeping, his frail build appeared even more fragile. Kali glanced over at Grant. "Have you heard anything?"

Grant sighed. "No, nothing. Dan, we're looking for her. There's nothing you can do but wait for us to call. We'll let you know as soon as we find her."

"Thank you." Dan's face crumpled, fatigue morphed into despondent acceptance. "I'm too old for this shit. I'm heading home. Call me if you find out anything. I won't rest until I know Julie's safe. First Brad, now Julie." Shaking his head, Dan walked out, his steps slow and shuffling. Poor Dan. His world was crumbling.

Kali's shoulders slumped. She knew how he felt. She walked over to Grant. Shiloh passed her, heading to a patch of sunlight on the deck. "Now that he's gone, did the team have anything new to add about Julie? And thanks for coming alone."

"No. They don't know anything yet. And you're welcome. I considered bringing Thomas along, as he's fairly open, but decided I'd hold off a little longer, for your sake." He watched her, his eyes level, his voice steady. "Why so tense about Dan?"

"I didn't want you to mention my sketches to him." Kali brushed past him as she led the way to the deck. "Dan is a staunch Catholic. I don't think he'd see them as a gift from God."

The sketchbook lay closed on the table where she'd left it.

Grant followed. As she reached for her sketchbook, he noticed the page with the instructions for relaxing. His gaze locked onto the name and phone number on the bottom. "Stefan was *here*?"

She paused. "Yes. And what a weird visit that was."

"You're lucky to have seen him at all. The man's a hermit." He hesitated. As if the question was dragged from him, he asked, "What did you think of him?"

Kali studied his face, sensing but not understanding the insecurity that colored his energy when he asked. "I think he knows his stuff. He arrived out of the blue. He said he 'heard' me call. I'd planned on phoning him when the door bell rang and there he was."

"He's very powerful."

"And gorgeous." She shook her head. "He should be a cover model."

"I believe he's been asked. He's a very private person. You should feel honoured that he came here."

That made her pause. She thought about Stefan's visit and the sense of urgency she felt to practice his instructions. "He could have called me. Or waited until I phoned him. He didn't. He came here to talk to me. To assess me, maybe?" She looked up at Grant. "It was a good – but really weird visit."

Grant's face turned grim. He didn't offer any comment on Stefan's behavior. "He obviously helped you, since you called and told me you'd drawn a new picture?"

"Right." Opening the sketchbook in her hands to the proper page, Kali studied her sketch. Next she flipped to the first picture she'd drawn. The one they'd followed to find David. Grant's curious gaze followed her every movement.

"I believe this first picture depicts Julie and that it's precognitive in nature. So it foretells the future."

Grant stepped closer and studied the picture with her. Kali flipped to the new one. "In this one, I think the event has passed and the victim is dead."

"Julie?" His voice was so neutral, she wanted to kick him. She wasn't sure what she'd expected. The drawing screamed at her. From his reaction, he could have been looking at a sunset scene.

"No, I don't think so." Neither the lines of the face nor the body fit.

"Why do you think this victim is dead?"

Again, the neutral tone. Did nothing get to him? Or had he so much experience with psychics drawing weirdo victim pictures that nothing fazed him?

"The blackness, the absence of light – of hope," Kali explained as she flipped to the first picture. "Here, for all the horribleness of this one, there exists a lightness or sense of life." As she flipped to the latest picture, she said "On this one, it's dead, buried, empty, the picture…lifeless. The woman depicted is dead." She took a deep breath. "I think it represents the other victim. The one we missed."

He raised his gaze to lock onto hers for a long moment. Had she said neutral? There was nothing neutral in his eyes. Determination, hope and fear burned deep in those gray eyes. She realized he feared she was right, yet hoped that she was onto something. She wanted to hug him, tell him that everything would be fine. Odd. They both knew it would never be okay for the missing victim.

His eyebrows came together at a fierce angle. "Why wouldn't you have done a precognitive of this woman instead of seeing the event afterwards?"

She laid the sketchbook on the table. "I thought about that. I think it's because I was in Sacramento or sleeping off the exhaustion from that trip at the time."

He considered her point. "No sketchbook, time or energy."

"More than the lack of time and energy, my focus was on helping those people right in front of me. I might have picked up on this victim if it hadn't been for that disaster but…"

Grant reached for the book, flipped between the two pictures. Finally, he said. "I can see what you're saying, based on the pictures."

"Obviously, it's all interpretation – guesswork, if you will."

"So yesterday was all about locating Julie, but instead, we found a different victim. And today is about finding the 'missed' victim who may or may not be Julie."

Kali blinked several times, processing his statement. "Sounds bizarre when you put it that way." Studying the new picture, she added, "The problem here is…nothing speaks to me. I have no idea where she's buried."

Reaching for the sketchbook, she returned to the old Julie picture. "I really thought we'd find Julie last night."

"At least we found David. Could the second picture represent David?"

Kali studied the sketch, slowly shaking her head. She dropped the book on the table. "No. This person is smaller yet again and slightly built. Female." Hands on hips, she turned to face him, her chin on an angle. "I'm beyond confused. Why so many victims in such a short time span? Has a time line been developed?"

"We're listing the Sacramento victim as the beginning of the time line. Unless you can offer a different one." He studied her. "With all the deaths you've seen, have any others been similar, connected even in the smallest way? Other murdered victims that have been buried?"

Bralorne. Kali stared at him in shock. How had she missed it? She blinked, sinking into her chair as she thought it over. Speaking slowly, trying to focus her thoughts, she said, "I don't know. Maybe. I hadn't considered it before. Everything surrounding the other victim was different. I didn't connect the dots."

Grant crouched in front of her. "What victim? Tell me."

Kali filled him in on the murder victim she'd discovered in Bralorne. "The man had been buried. There didn't appear to be any attempt to keep him alive. No oxygen tank." She swallowed hard, trying to remember details. Guilt plagued her. Why hadn't she made the connection? "This guy had survived the disaster with only a broken arm and bruises. He'd been one of the lucky ones."

"That connects." At her nod, he continued, "A very distinctive MO. Potentially, he's our first victim. Possibly the one that set this killer on his path. That's huge. Each victim gives us information about the killer. We need to run the lists of suspects. See who was at Bralorne and in Sacramento." He withdrew a notepad from the back pocket of his pants and jotted notes. "What else can you tell me about that event?"

Kali's cell phone rang. Shiloh whined. She got up and walked over to Kali, butting up against her leg. Kali frowned at her reaction, dropping one hand on the dog's head. Picking up the phone, she checked the number. She didn't recognize it and displayed the number for Grant. He wrote it down.

"Go ahead and answer it."

She put the phone close to both their heads. "Hello."

The same damn laughter.

"Still trying to figure it out, huh?" His voice had the same tinny sound as before. "You're not making this much of a challenge, are you?"

"Why the poor trucker? What did he do to you?" she said, her voice tight and controlled.

"David? Oh, David never did anything to me, except live. No, David was supposed to die years ago during the San Francisco quake."

"Wait, you mean you killed David because he had the gall to survive?"

Laughter floated through the line. God, she hated that sound. She held the phone a little away from her head so Grant could hear.

"An interesting way to put it. God called him home, David refused to answer. It's my job to make these people show up for their appointment, even if they're a little late."

"And Julie? What could she have done to you?"

A heavy silence took over the space between them. An ugly silence.

Tight anger threaded his voice. "That's good. That's very good. Julie's a survivor. I'm sure she'll survive for a while."

The killer laughed again, a more normal laugh than earlier. If anything, that terrified her more. Then he hung up.

Kali very slowly, very carefully closed her cell phone. Taking a deep breath, she said, "All our fears were correct. The asshole has Julie."

Grant, already punching in numbers on his cell phone, disappeared inside.

Kali dropped her head to her arms. Everything hurt. Her head ached, her heart wept, her soul cried for this to stop. God, she was so tired. Her adrenalin and excitement were long gone. Her eyes drifted closed. A minute or two of respite, that's all she needed. Just until Grant finished making the necessary calls.

And she fell asleep.

JULIE OPENED HER eyes; blinding pain stabbed the back of her eyeballs. A moan escaped – the sound barely audible. She shifted her head, confused. Scared, she tried to move, only couldn't. Where was she? What had happened? Darkness surrounded her. Blinking rapidly, she struggled to clear the black spots before her.

She couldn't see anything.

Her eyes drooped, her head sagging to one side. She tried to swallow. Sandpaper scraped the delicate tissues of her throat in a futile search for saliva. Cloth filled her mouth. Panicking, she struggled to push the material out of her mouth with her tongue. Managing to get it out far enough to breathe easier, she got her first swallow. Several attempts later, her throat eased. A shudder of relief worked up her spine and she sagged in place. Carpet scratched her cheeks. Where the hell was she? What the hell had happened?

Weird shapes formed in the darkness.

Squinting, she tried to focus. Nothing changed. Shifting her position, she gasped. Her shoulders hurt, her back ached. Her hands were constrained. Every movement brought her up against a wall.

A wall?

No. She blinked as reality seeped in. Consciously, she moved experimentally.

She'd been tied up.

As that understanding filtered in, the odd look of the area surrounding her made sense. She was in a small, enclosed space of some sort.

Kali had been right.

Someone had been after her. She'd been kidnapped.

Julie screamed.

HIDDEN IN HIS bower deep on the neighbor's property, Texan adjusted the binoculars so he could see the drama playing out in Kali's house. He could hardly contain his glee.

Plans, plans and more plans. He'd jumped into this scenario a bit recklessly and a little quicker than normal. Now adjustments had to be made. Anticipation rippled through him.

The phone calls…well, he really enjoyed them. Except this last one. The smile dropped from his face.

They knew about Julie. How?

Even though he knew about Kali's black magic, it had been a stunning blow to hear Kali mention Julie. Still, knowing he had Julie wouldn't help Kali find her. Not this time. He'd stashed her for the night and would move her tomorrow. He couldn't contain the ripple of excitement. Finally, Kali was in the game.

She probably thought she was safe, her evil strong enough to go against anything. So naive. A contented sigh washed over him. Evil aligned with evil, but good always won out. It had just taken him awhile to understand his true mission and how SAR rescues were negatively impacting the Lord's wishes.

And Kali was the queen of the infidels. She had to be stopped. First, though, she had to learn the error of her ways. He owed her that. They'd been friends once. She'd be given a chance to turn the devil aside…to fess up to her black magic before he returned her to her Maker.

Slipping from the bower, he wandered to the edge of the woods and a favorite tree stump. The leaves crackled, dry and crisp under his feet. The summer heat had baked the earth. Surprising for this time of year. The undergrowth usually kept the ground dank, if not actually moist.

Tilting his head back, he beamed a smile into the night, his eyes closed, almost in benediction. His soul walked lighter these days. He was grateful.

He hoped Kali slept well tonight.

She'd need it for the challenges that lay ahead.

She had to prove herself worthy of salvation.

CHAPTER 16

KALI'S HEAD SNAPPED up. *What the hell?* Dusk had started to settle, giving the sky an odd half light. She searched her surroundings, groggy and disoriented. Rubbing the sleep from her eyes, she frowned. Surely, she'd only closed her eyes a second ago.

"Hi. Feel better?"

Grant's face came into focus. "Hey." She cleared her throat and tried again. "How long did I sleep?"

"Ten to fifteen minutes."

Her mind struggled to put the foggy pieces of reality back together. She massaged her stiff neck. "Julie?"

"No news yet. We're waiting for update from our profiler. We tracked the phone number to a disposable cell phone."

He dropped a piece of paper on the table in front of her.

Kali yawned, her brain fuzzy. "What's this?"

"The short list of names."

Her brain clicked on, and she was suddenly wide awake. "Of potential suspects?"

She picked the sheet up and peered closer. And blinked. The first name listed caught in her throat before shocked surprise took over. "Brad? *Are you serious?*"

"Not really, but we have to consider it. He was at the site where the first victim was found."

"So were many other people. He's gone missing, remember?" She was outraged that her best friend was being considered.

"Kali, this isn't about personal feelings, it's about who had motive and opportunity. Please. Take a look at the names and cross off the ones you don't feel could have done it – just give me a reason." He held out a pencil.

She glared at him, snatched the pencil from his hand and with a thick bold stroke knocked Brad's name off the list. "If you put him on *this* list, you might as well add him to the list of potential victims."

Silence. "I did."

She winced and turned her attention to the other eleven names. She knew four from the center. Francoise, a Frenchman, was a good man and a close friend of Brad's. Briefly, she wondered if anyone had told him about Brad's disappearance. Then she remembered, no one was to know yet. "Francoise works with several centers, so I'm not sure where he is right now. You'll have to check on that. I haven't seen him in years."

She crossed the third name off the list. "Sam had a back injury two years ago on a site. He can't do any heavy lifting."

Grant raised an eyebrow and jotted the reason in his notebook. He'd probably double-check everything she said. Then again, he had to… Didn't he?

"Johnson was supposed to go to the Sacramento site but pulled out at the last minute when his wife went into early labor. His name would have been on the original manifest, which probably has yet to be updated." She put a line through his name.

"Good. Keep going."

Eight names left.

All male.

All white.

All young.

But not all single. That surprised her. "I can't see anyone who is happily married doing this." She glanced over at Grant, but his face was a blank slate. Did he suspect anyone here more than any others? She didn't want any of them to be the killer. She knew them all, friends, coworkers, people she depended on at disaster sites.

Kali swallowed hard and studied the other names. "I saw Zane and Ron from the San Francisco center at Sacramento, but didn't have much to do with them. I've worked with them on various sites. They're both good hard workers."

She put question marks beside two names. "Allen and Joe are both happily married, a half-dozen kids between them and are heavily involved in community affairs. I can't see them having the opportunity to kidnap and murder these people."

"Strike them off and I'll make a note of them here."

Six names remained.

"As much as I want to, I can't find a reason to cross these guys off."

Grant accepted the list. "We'll check them over."

"Ask Dan, too. He knows stuff about everyone – way more than I do."

"Okay. I'll turn this over to the team to start on."

Kali frowned. "So what's next? How else can I help?"

"Rest. Do laundry."

She glared at him. "Aren't you funny?"

Tapping his thigh with the rolled up list, he tilted his head and considered her. "Draw?" His face turned earnest. "We need any and all help possible. I know that's not FBI policy, but I know what Stefan can do. And Stefan hasn't connected to this guy. You have. Let's see what you can do."

Kali considered him. "We need tangible leads, not more conjecture. I may have been right once or twice, but I can't count on being right all the time."

"Leads are good; yes. But as we're lacking those, we have to consider everything. And we don't expect you to be right all the time – we won't know what you can do though, unless you try."

Giving him a disgusted look, she agreed.

"I have to go inside and make these calls, as much as this area is under surveillance and this deck isn't accessible from the ground, I don't want you out here alone..."

Kali blinked. Then shuddered. She'd never given it a thought. She followed him inside and locked the door behind her.

With the sketchbook open to a clean page, she sat under the golden halo of the light in the living room and pondered the strange turn of events in her life. How had her only constructive input become her psychic art, when she excelled at searching for victims, especially murdered victims?

She sat back, stunned.

Could she find the missing victim?

And if she could, then why was she sitting here?

If the victim was dead as depicted by her sketch, she could find her if she managed to get close enough. But what did 'close enough' mean? She had no idea. It was as if she'd accidentally fallen over the energy of the various victims before this. More or less. Pursing her lips, she considered the concept.

She went to locate Grant and test it out. She located him in the kitchen and she said, "I need to go out."

Grant frowned. "Where?"

Kali sighed and wouldn't meet his gaze. "I don't exactly

know."

Grant's gaze narrowed. "Explain."

This time Kali met his gaze, calmly. "I need to try something." She waved toward the sketchbook. "It occurred to me that my specialty, up until now, has been *finding* not *drawing* people." She came to a stop, not knowing how else to explain. With a defiant toss of her head, she added, "I want to give it a try."

"I'll go with you."

Kali stared at him, nonplussed. If nothing came of her attempt, she'd feel like an idiot. Who needed an audience to that? "You don't have to. I can go alone."

The niggling sense prodded her. *Go. Now.*

"No." Grant placed a hand on the small of her back, propelling her forward. "It's with me or not at all. There's a killer loose, remember?"

"Fine." Kali hurried to the front door. At the familiar sound, Shiloh bounded toward her, her tail wagging. Kali bent to cuddle her. "We're just going driving for a little while. We won't be long."

"You don't want to bring her?"

Kali paused, frowning. "What I'm trying to do tonight isn't something I've tried before. I don't want to be distracted or influenced by Shiloh and her energy. As we're only going to drive around for a bit, I think I'll leave her behind. She could do with a rest, too."

Opening the door, she stepped into the cool night to check the temperature. Turning back, she snagged a jacket from the hooks by the door. Glancing at her slip-on shoes, she opted to change into sturdy hiking boots…just in case.

Grant waited for her on the gravel path. Stern, patient, professional, he was never really approachable. No, that wasn't quite true. With a casual glance his way, Kali blurted, "You rarely smile. Why?"

He raised one eyebrow and frowned. "That's not true. I smile a lot."

She hid her smile and said lightly, "Really, have I seen you smile?"

Shooting her a look, he added, "Yes, you have. Besides, there isn't much to be happy about right now."

That was a great conversation killer.

Grant continued to his car, opening the door for her. "We'll take my car. You can tell me where to go."

"Love to." She smirked and slipped into the front seat. Grant started the car and pulled up to the edge of the road.

"Which way?"

Kali closed her eyes and let the sensation roll over her. When she followed one of her twinges, a fuzzy bristling would usually nudge the back of her neck, sending her in a specific direction. She felt no such sensation this time. Knowing that Grant watched her, she closed her mind and opened the door to her alternate senses and relaxed. Since he'd witnessed odd behavior from her before, surely this wouldn't throw him.

"Left," she whispered. Kali slid into a relaxed state and blocked out the world. She kept her eyes closed for a while as they drove onto the main road. Sitting blind gave her an eerie insight into the bizarre world of darkness and trust.

She trusted Grant to keep her safe.

Her mind hiccupped. Her eyes opened. What the hell did that mean? Safe in the car? With her life? With her body? Oh God. She couldn't do this right now. She couldn't do energy work with all the unanswered questions. She had to focus. Slamming her eyes shut, she forced herself to draw on Stefan's instructions. Calm down. Relax. She was so caught up following his instructions, that the twinge on the back of her neck came out of the blue, making her flinch.

"Whoa!"

Grant hit the brakes.

Kali opened her eyes as they passed a road sign. They were on the outskirts of the city. "Left again."

Grant glanced at her, but obliged.

The road curved through hillsides and wooded areas. She searched the region. Now where? She waited for a couple of minutes. Nothing. She settled into the seat and closed her eyes again. Bringing thoughts about the victim to the forefront, she imagined her lost and alone and needing to come home. Kali concentrated on the fear, pain and horror of her last days, then brought in conscious awareness, a willingness, a need to find her.

Nothing crystallized. Frustrated, she set up a map in her head, waiting for the next step to appear, only to find herself blocked. Of course. Like her drawing, she'd tried to force the information highway to give up its secrets.

Kali relaxed the building tension, releasing a heavy sigh, shutting down her mind.

"Problems?"

Kali shrugged. "I don't know where to go."

"You knew the last two turns. They came clearly, didn't they?"

"Yes."

"So, let's not doubt the process. We'll keep driving in this direction until you say otherwise."

"Fine. But that's an odd attitude for a black and white FBI agent." How disconcerting to have him so amiable. Contrarily, she wanted to prod him out of the reasonableness. "What if I'm wrong?" she muttered. "What then?"

"Then we drive home and...no harm done." He shot her a curious glance. "How did you get the idea that I am a black and white kind of guy? Haven't we spent most of the last few days living in a gray area?"

Kali addressed the first comment and chose to ignore the rest, stymied for an answer. "I was wrong last time."

"No. Don't say that. You might have been wrong regarding the identity of the victim, but you weren't wrong about there being a victim or where he was located."

"It might be different this time."

"Relax. The inklings won't come if you don't give them a chance.

"Maybe, but it's never worked like this before."

A pregnant pause.

"Before."

"That's something I haven't mentioned yet." Kali stared out at the window. Christ, she'd look like a certifiable nut case when this mess was finally over.

"Explain?"

"Shiloh makes a great rescue dog because she finds people that are alive. Finding dead people upsets her, but she can do it."

"Can she tell the difference?"

Kali glanced at him. "Definitely."

"And you're saying you can do the same thing?"

"No, not quite." Kali answered slowly, considering her words carefully. "Shiloh uses her nose and I...well, I use the Sight. With it I can find cadavers, but a certain type stand out for me. Shiloh can find them all."

"Cadavers come in types?"

"Yes." Kali took a deep breath, bracing herself. She'd never told this to anyone. "I see dark, seething energy in ribbons. They are always attached to people who have died violently, especially people who have been murdered."

GRANT CONTINUED TO drive, even though he had trouble processing her statement. He'd known about her psychic talents, but this? Could she mean it? Years ago he'd have run like hell to get away from such a concept. It had taken Stefan to open his mind.

Now this woman continually surprised him, too.

He gave her a sidelong glance. The information might not scare him; still he had to wonder how she could deal with it all.

With every new tidbit she revealed about herself, he became more fascinated and alternately, more disturbed. This was heavy stuff. She'd turned out to be a complex myriad of witch, siren and philanthropist. Impossible to ignore.

Grant snuck a glance her way again. Returning his gaze to the road, he shook his head. He had it bad.

His lips quirked. Here he was working through his feelings and she was staring at him, wondering at his lack of reaction. Her abilities disturbed her, while he found them fascinating. It was his concern for her ability to *handle* them that disturbed him. That didn't say much for his state of mind.

A sigh escaped. He was an idiot.

THE SILENCE IN the car grew to deafening proportions. Kali stared out the window, anywhere but at him. Had he taken the news with his usual stoic attitude or had he decided to drive her to a mental hospital?

"Hmmmm."

"That's it?" She glowered at him. The dark interior of the vehicle couldn't begin to hide his knowing look.

"Sure. There's not much I haven't heard after working with Stefan all these years, you know. And 'hmmm' means I'm thinking."

Kali couldn't believe it. "Good. Fine." She waited a beat. "You know, you may have *heard* a lot from Stefan, but I've never told anyone, ever."

"Right. A little too mild a reaction, huh?"

"Ya think?" Kali couldn't believe it. It would be the last time she shared a secret with him.

Grant glanced at her, a light shining in his eyes. "So tell me how you really feel."

"Ohh. Ohhh, you…you," Kali stuttered to a complete stop. Her fists clenched and unclenched. Closing her eyes, she focused on deep breathing. In the silence of the car, she heard a sound. One she'd never heard before. No way. She turned to look at Grant. He was sputtering. Sputtering for Christ sake. Unfreakin' believable.

He caught her staring at him. His lips quirked. His smirk widened to an outright smile. Before her astonished eyes, he broke into a guffaw, his laughter infectious.

Good Lord. She hadn't thought he had it in him. She laughed. "Wow."

Grant shook his head, a goofy grin decorating his face. "I'm not that bad. Surely?"

"Yeah, you are." Kali bolted upright to stare into darkness. "Where are we?

Grant pointed at a sign up ahead. "We're heading north to Portland. Remember?"

"We've been out for a while."

"A bit. Any more directions?"

Kali dropped her head against the headrest. "No. What a stupid waste of time."

"Not necessarily. Now you know I can laugh."

Smiling, she answered, "There is that. Maybe we should just turn back." Endless darkness surrounded them, with only the beams of the headlights to light their way. A prophetic sign maybe. Her eyes drifted closed under the hypnotic influence of the steady hum of the engine.

Her neck throbbed; she reached up to massage the muscles, but the pain worsened. Kali twisted her head to the right. Sharp, stabbing pain shot upward. She moaned softly.

"Are you okay?"

"Yes. My neck started hurting."

"Your neck or your intuition?"

Raising an eyebrow, she glanced over at him. "I don't know. Maybe?"

"Yes or no?" Grant raised an eyebrow, sending her a sideways glance.

"I usually get a funny prickling at the back of my neck, not sharp pains." And normally, she wasn't deluged in weird colors.

This time her normal mental state of lavender blended with a dark blue, becoming almost black in color. She sensed the anger building in the seething morass.

"Maybe we aren't supposed to go back yet. There's a turnoff ahead. Tell me if you get more twinges." Grant pulled the vehicle up to the corner, edging the vehicle slightly off the road.

The pain stabbed into the back of her brain. Her stomach heaved. "Ouch."

Grant stopped the car. He looked at her, then turned the steering wheel, directing the vehicle onto the side road.

Immediately the pain eased. "Ahh, much better. Not perfect, but not stabbing at me either." The dark energy also eased back to a dull purplish black.

They hadn't driven more than a few hundred yards when the pain and the angry colors bashed into her consciousness.

She gasped. Bile crawled up the back of her throat, bringing a sick taste to her mouth. She coughed slightly.

Grant hit the brakes, peering in her direction. "Well?"

The stabbing stopped. Kali sighed in relief. "It's gone."

They peered through the window into the gloomy surroundings. A dirt road loomed on Kali's right. Even in the dark of night she could see the ribbons twisting toward her. Her neck twitched. "Turn here. She's up here."

Kali no longer had any doubts. Images slammed into her. Children playing, a family gathering, laughter and arguing combined as faces and places flashed too quickly to catch as the impressions kept rolling on.

Grant shook his head as he drove the car onto the dirt road. "We are going to have a talk after this. I can't believe that even after seeing your sketches, you didn't tell me about this."

The visions receded, letting Kali catch her breath.

"Shiloh is my cover. To make it look like she's the one finding the bodies." Kali leaned forward, peering through the windshield. "The paintings and sketches are a new development. Not expecting them, I didn't have a cover story ready."

"Anything else you've hidden from me?"

Shearing pain stabbed through the back of her neck. The colors throbbed.

"Stop!"

Kali held her breath, waiting for the pain to ease as the vehicle rolled to a standstill. Kali pointed to his window in the direction where angry ribbons twisted in the night sky. "She's over on the crest."

"God."

Kali hopped out.

Grant exited the car, flashlight in hand and walked over to stand at her side. "There's nothing here."

"Yes, there is. I wish I'd brought Shiloh now. She'd have picked up the decomp." Closing her zipper against the chill of the night, she pointed at storm clouds off to the north. "We need to hurry to beat the storm."

Grant lifted his head to study the horizon. "Why didn't we bring Shiloh, again? If we find anything, I'll have to get a team here fast."

"We didn't bring Shiloh because she's tired, because I didn't expect to actually find anyone and besides…we don't need her," Kali said, her tone grim. "The victim is just a few yards up." Sand and loose gravel grated under their feet. The hoot of an owl sounded far off in the distance. With the stormy weather coming in, the air practically crackled with static.

"How'd the killer expect you to find her way the hell out here?"

"I have no idea. No one, and I mean no one, knows about my weird psychic skills." She thought about that for a moment and realized it was no longer true. "Except you and Stefan."

"The killer may have suspected it anyway. Even if only as an explanation for your successful record," Grant said.

She glanced at him, his face a pale circle in the dark. "Except these skills are relatively new. That reputation was established long before these weird twinges showed."

Grant frowned. "But this person wouldn't know that."

"Christ." The killer could be putting her years of success down to otherworldly reasons instead of experience. By being forced to play the killer's bizarre game, Kali could actually be proving the killer right about her 'mad skills.'

The clouds separated, releasing the moon from its shadowy hold to highlight the violent energy twisting and churning at one spot.

"Why don't we do this stuff in daylight?" Kali asked, knowing there was no answer, but wishing there was anyway.

Grant strode forward, passing her slightly. "You tell me. This is your show."

"No, this is the killer's show." Kali stumbled in the dark,

caught herself and carried on. The terrain leveled off. They angled around a crop of bushes and stopped. They were at the top of a knoll with the ground dropping off on the other side.

Kali stopped, hands on her hips, to catch her breath. "Right, she's here. At least I think she is. Normally, I have Shiloh to confirm something like this."

Grant walked closer. "The dirt is loose and the slope accessible on the downward side." As he shone the light over the surrounding area and the big evergreen in front of them, Kali saw some of the dirt had fallen away. Moonlight highlighted the skeleton roots, exposing huge hollows underneath. The dirt pile underneath suggested something was buried here.

She bent over, scraping up a handful of soil, before letting it slip through her fingers. "It's sandy. With the dry spring and summer we had, interspersed with heavy storms, this is a perfect burial place begging for a crazy killer."

"I need to call a team."

"And if she's not here?"

"Is she?" His gaze locked on hers.

"I think so. But are you willing to call out a team without confirming there's a crime scene?"

"How much information can you get about her? Can you show me a spot where there is less dirt that I might be able to brush away enough to confirm what we have? We have to make sure we disturb the area as little as possible though."

Grant rested the flashlight on a root where it cast a yellow light in the gloom. "And I'll try to grab a couple of pictures before we touch anything." He pulled a camera out of his pocket, surprising, and momentarily blinding Kali as several flashes went off.

When he was done, she suggested, "You're at her feet. It might be better to try for her face?"

"You can tell?" Poor light or not, she could see her statement had thrown him. He studied the ground.

Kali stepped forward. "Yes. She's in a relaxed fetal position with her head here." She pointed out the correct layout. "She's facing us." She placed her hand gently where the woman's head lay hidden. A large chunk of earth slid down. "Try there. The layer is thinner now."

Pulling thin gloves from his pocket, he bent to where she pointed and scooped one handful of dirt away. Sand slid into the newly created space. He worked gently for a few minutes. Kali was mesmerized by his gentleness as he brushed the dirt away from the pile. He treated the area with deference. Her heart warmed. He believed her. And he cared about the woman beneath the ground. An odd euphoria swept over her. Followed by doubts. What if she were wrong?

"There." Kali cried out. "Stop. I think I see something."

Leaning back on his haunches, Grant reached for the flashlight.

"I need more light." He flashed the light down on the spot – and reared back.

She crowded beside him. "What? What did you find?"

Eerie flickering light shone on the exposed surface. A small delicate nose blended into the grains of sand. A gold earring with an emerald starburst twinkled in the dirt. Kali sucked in her breath, tears gathered at the corners of her eyes. Although expected, nothing prepared her for the reality of what she faced.

And nothing could camouflage the eye that stared out – accusing them both.

Recognition slammed into her. Kali jumped back with a small cry.

Grant spun, reaching for her. "It's okay." He laid a gentle hand on hers. "We found her. That's why we're here. To bring her home." He tugged her trembling frame into his arms. "Take a minute. Breathe."

She shuddered. Closing her eyes briefly, she leaned into his comforting arms. Nothing could stop the image from burning into her memory, where she knew it would stay for the rest of her life. Sorrow washed over her. Pulling back slightly, she gazed up at him.

Pain speared her heart. "I know her. She's a regular at Second Chance. Her name is Melanie Rothschild."

CHAPTER 17

GRANT STOOD ON Kali's front doorstep. He should have let someone else make this call. Dan maybe. It would have been easier. But it wouldn't have been right.

The news would hurt her regardless of who delivered it. Maybe he could at least give her a few answers to go with it. Even worse, no one who knew about this was going to be able to talk about it. Not until the killer had been caught, just in case it *was* case related.

He rang the doorbell before stuffing his hands in his pants pockets. Inside the house, Shiloh barked. Kali's voice murmured softly. He loved the soft caring in her voice. Her voice took on an almost sing-song tone when she spoke to the dog.

He didn't want to break her heart today. But his news would. He glared at the low-lying clouds. Rain could break before he made it back to town. He didn't have this window of time but had made it happen anyway. He'd yet to make it to bed. Talk about a shitty night. He rubbed his whiskered chin, wishing he'd had time for a shower and shave first. Still, he was here. He could find an hour for her.

The door opened.

Kali's face lit up with surprise…and he hoped, with pleasure.

"Kali, may I come in?"

The surprise dropped away, a hint of dread slipped in to replace it. Wordless, she opened the door wide enough for him to enter. "I have fresh coffee. Would you like a cup?"

"Thanks."

She led the way to the kitchen. "I presume you have news about last night. I have to admit that I didn't sleep very well. Just the thought of—"

"I didn't come about last night." He hated to see her step falter, her back stiffen. Her shoulders hunched as if fearing a blow, but despite that, she slowly turned to face him.

"I'm sorry. I wish I had better news."

She swallowed. "Just tell me."

Shit. Still, straight out was best. "We found Brad."

"What?"

"He's dead."

Kali closed her eyes briefly and bowed her head. Her hand climbed to her neck as she sagged into the first chair. She tried to speak, but no words came out. Shiloh came to her side, whining deep in her throat. She laid her head on Kali's leg.

To give her a moment, Grant walked over to the coffee pot and poured her a cup. Returning, he placed it on the table beside her. He walked to the open porch doors and stared out at the sky that couldn't make up its mind.

"What happened?"

He walked back, pulled out a second chair and sat down in front of her. Reaching over he picked up one chilled hand and warmed it in his. "We don't have all the details at this point. His body was found a few hours ago. Apparently it had been there for a while."

"Where?" she whispered, her other hand buried in Shiloh's ruff.

"In Sacramento. He never left. The authorities are working on the theory that he stumbled into the cordoned-off area after a night of drinking. The area was unstable. Part of the building shifted, crushing him under a heavy load of concrete."

Kali placed her second hand over his and squeezed tight.

"Poor Susan." She stared at their clasped hands, but he doubt she saw them.

"Kali? Kali, I'm so sorry."

"When?" Clearing her throat, she asked in a hoarse voice. "When did he die?"

Grant stroked the side of her hand on his. "Don't know yet for sure. He was found in sector four at the site." His thumb moved gently back and forth. She watched the movement for a long moment, then lifted her head to face him. He didn't have much more information to give her. Except one thing. "He would have died instantly."

Her eyelids slammed shut. He could only imagine she knew exactly what condition Brad's body when it had been found. She had a wealth of images to draw on for that. Her bottom lip trembled as she struggled for control.

He admired her even more when her lips firmed, but his heart broke when she asked the next question.

"How do they know it was him? Could there be a mistake?"

Her shoulders hunched against his answer. There was no way to make it easier on her. He turned her hand protectively then squeezed her hand gently, bracing her. "I'm sorry. The victim's DNA is being tested to be sure, but there's little doubt. The victim had on a SAR vest and Brad's wallet was on the body. Everything else fits too."

Her shoulders slumped. "Oh." She produced a sad smile. "Being buried alive is every rescuer's worst nightmare, you know. It's something we see too often. Something that sits in the back of our psyche and festers." Kali closed her eyes, hot tears meandering downward at the corners. "It really hurts that he died alone."

"A couple of the locals said he'd stayed around for a while, drinking heavily."

Kali nodded. "He sent Sergeant home to Susan and stayed behind to drink away his demons alone." Tugging her hands free, she stood and walked to the railing. Shiloh followed to lean against her leg. Several sniffles sounded. He wanted to walk over and take her into his arms, but she'd walked away. A part of him understood. She needed to find her balance in a world that had suddenly shifted. As he watched, she wiped away her tears on her sleeve before turning her face to the breeze.

"Is there anything I can do?" she asked after a moment.

Grant joined her at the railing.

"I don't think so. Susan's mother is arriving tonight. Brad's body will be shipped home in the next few days. I'll keep you up to date on arrangements when they're made."

"Please do. How's Sergeant?"

"According to Susan, he's fine."

Kali cringed. "Sergeant will be lost. Brad raised, trained and worked him from a young pup."

Grant didn't have an answer for that.

"I wonder what she'll do with him."

"I doubt she knows at this point."

Kali sniffled, releasing a heavy sigh. "So much death."

"I told Dan. He said he'd be here soon." Grant checked his watch. "I can't stay. I'm meeting with the profiler, then I'll try to grab a few hours of sleep."

"Oh, I never thought. You've been out all night on the scene, haven't you?" She rubbed her eyes. "Any news on last night's victim? Do we know if it was Melanie, for sure?"

"Not yet. The coroner has her now."

She sighed. "I came home instead of hanging around, but I didn't sleep. It gets harder every night."

"It's difficult to rest knowing this killer is out there, isn't it."

She stopped. "Damn, this is hard. Could Brad have been a victim of the killer?"

Grant's heart ached. "No, Kali. All indications say it was an accident."

With a tremulous smile, she nodded. "Thanks. It does make it easier. I don't think I could have stood it otherwise."

"It's tough enough to deal with, as it is."

"Dan and I are both going to miss him." New tears formed at the corner of her eyes. She wiped them away. "I relied on Brad's laughter, his compassion and, most of all, his support. My world has become a darker place." She forced a tremulous smile through her tears.

He couldn't stand it. Stepping closer, he opened his arms.

And she drifted into them.

Enfolding her close, he held her while the tears poured. He'd be late. Too damn bad. Sometimes schedules had to adapt. He closed his eyes and rested his head against hers.

It surprised him how quickly the storm burned out. Finally she lay with her head resting against his chest, staring out toward the ocean. He just held her. When she made a move to retreat, he forced himself to drop his arms, allowing her to step back.

"Better?" He searched her eyes, beautiful deep blue, awash in tears. But, thankfully, not so lost as before.

"Thank you. It's going to take some time, but I will get there. Brad wouldn't have wanted me to wallow. He'd rather I open a bottle of champagne and celebrate his life. I'll talk to Dan, maybe plan something like that." She retreated another few steps.

He hated the widening distance, but the moment was over. "Hold off spreading the news. We've asked Susan and Dan to keep a lid on this for a few days. Try to avoid any interference in our investigation. Just for a day or two."

She attempted a smile. "Right. We still have a killer to catch. You need to go. I'm fine. Dan will be here soon and that will help. I want you to make your meeting with the profiler, then please get some rest. This madness needs to stop."

She hooked Grant's arm and ushered him back through the house to the front door. She opened it and damn near pushed him out.

"You're sure you're all right. I hate to leave you alone."

This time her smile had real humor. "I'm fine. Go. And…" she reached up and kissed his cheek. So gently, so tenderly, he almost snatched her back into his arms.

It was the first physical move she'd made toward him.

With that, he left. But in his car, driving down the highway, he couldn't stop grinning.

Progress.

KALI STOOD LOOKING out at the empty driveway long after Grant left.

She hated that sense of loss as the distance between them widened. Could he see the energy, the colors vibrating between them?

Even through her grief and tears, they'd been hard to miss. It gave her hope. Something she badly needed today.

Her eyes burned from the tears already shed, and she could only imagine how they'd be by the end of the day.

God. Brad, her staunchest defender and best friend since forever was never going to come home again. With this psychic murder stuff consuming her, she hadn't had time to really worry about him. She hadn't allowed herself to consider such an outcome. She'd been expecting him to show up out of the blue with that sheepish look of his. Instead he was already dead. And no one had known.

Picking up the phone, Kali dialed Susan's number. If Brad's death was painful for her, she could only imagine what Susan was going through right now. Her heart ached for the widow. Susan and Brad had been married for over ten years. Kali had lost a beautiful friend, but Susan had lost her partner.

"Hello?"

The ravaged voice made Kali's stomach clench in sympathy. "Susan, it's Kali. I just heard. I'm so sorry."

"Sorry?" Susan's voice had a dreamlike quality, as if she wasn't fully hearing Kali's words.

"Yes. I know how difficult Brad's death is for you. It's hard on all of us. These rescue missions can be dangerous, but we don't really expect anything bad to happen to those we love."

"Love?" Susan's voice sharpened. "What do you know about love? Brad was *my* husband. He was down there because of you. Because *you* needed him. This is your fault. Yours. He's dead because of you." Her voice cracked with tension; her blistering words singed Kali's heart. "Stay away from me. Don't call me again – ever. I hate you!"

Kali sat frozen. Logically, she could rationalize away everything Susan had said. Susan was upset, grieving and angry at the world. Kali knew that, but her heart didn't care.

It hurt.

Brad had been her friend. She'd loved him, too. And it hurt to know that to a certain extent, Susan had been right.

A couple of times, Brad had mentioned quitting, staying home with Susan because she wanted him to, instead of gallivanting off at a moment's notice. Kali knew Susan had made sacrifices. She'd endured missed birthdays, messed up plans, long absences. These had only gotten worse with Brad's increased drinking bouts.

Kali had always persuaded him to stay. Brad was good at what he did. Very good. The rescue world needed him.

But at what cost to Brad?

Guilt sat heavy on her heart.

Her world would never be the same again.

Sitting there, she heard the crunch of gravel as a vehicle drove in. Dan. At least she hoped it was; she didn't want to see anyone else.

Getting up, she walked to the front door and watched Dan park his car.

Her spirits lifted at the sight of him…until she saw his expression.

Grief had ravaged his face, wrinkles appearing where there hadn't been any. Skin folds deeper, but thinner, like all the substance had drained from him.

"Kali?"

She teared up. "Oh Dan."

They held each other for several minutes. Holding Dan's frail body, her grief receded as concern for him grew. Dan couldn't handle much more.

She pulled back slightly, gave him a sad smile and ushered him toward the kitchen. "God, I can't imagine not seeing Brad ever again."

"I know." Dan hesitated, as if wanting to ask a question but not daring.

Tiredly, she glanced his way as she automatically gravitated to the coffeepot. "What?"

With a heavy sigh, he asked softly, "I wondered if you had any news, preferably good news, about Julie?"

Kali blinked, her forehead creasing. What was he talking about? Good news. There wasn't any left in this world. "News? Julie? Oh, my God." She spun around. "That's right, you haven't heard."

"What? What did you find?"

"We found the other victim."

"What?" Dan grabbed her by the shoulders. "Where? Was it Julie? Please, tell me it wasn't." Kali, surprised by his outburst, didn't answer fast enough.

"Kali, please. Tell me." Agony threaded his voice.

She closed her eyes. She didn't want to tell him. They had too much pain now. Death surrounded them. "It wasn't Julie."

"Oh, thank God." Dan searched her face, but what he read made his shoulders slump. His arms dropped to his side, while dread hooded his eyes. "Who was it?"

Pain shattered Kali's calm once again. "The FBI people have to confirm it." She took a deep breath. "But I think it's Melanie."

This time tears washed Dan's rummy eyes. "Melanie? Little Melanie Rothschild? She's just a girl. A teenager."

"She celebrated her twentieth birthday a couple of months ago, I think." Kali's voice choked. "Not even twenty-one."

"Oh, my God! Why? What could she possibly have done to this guy?"

Kali had no answer.

Dan stepped through the glass doors into the sunlight shining on the deck, one hand over his face, his head bowed, his shoulders shaking. Kali gave him a few moments. She poured coffee and took her time carrying the cups outside. She sat down in her favorite chair and waited. The air was fresh and clean. There was no sign of the horror and pain going on in the world. There was no fear, or sense of threat out here. Maybe, because she knew about the surveillance team…that she wasn't alone. She didn't believe the killer was after her…yet. But neither did she want Dan to be a target.

Dan turned to face her, one last sniffle sounding. "I saw her at the center a couple of days ago." He screwed up his face. "Wednesday, maybe? I can't be sure until I check the schedule."

"Do you remember who else was there?"

Dan wiped his eyes with the back of his hand and frowned. "I remember a class had started, I'd escaped to my office and she stopped in to say 'hi.' Although, I admit my memory is a bit faulty lately."

A ghost of smile kissed Kali's lips. Dan's memory had long been an issue, but particularly this last year.

"Jesus, Kali. What kind of evil has found us? We have to close the center until this is over. He can't have any more of our people. Let's cut off his supply."

"I think it's way past that point. He already knows many of the people. We can ask Grant about closing the center." Kali dialed his number, hoping to catch him between his meeting with the profiler and his planned nap.

"Ask him about Melanie, too." Dan collapsed on the kitchen chair and rested his head on his hands. "Maybe it's a mistake."

As she waited for Grant to pick up, Kali turned to look at Dan. "What about Melanie's family, wouldn't they have missed her? Have they called her in as a missing person?"

"They've gone east for a couple of weeks. Melanie's in college part-time and didn't want to miss classes."

The mention of schooling twigged Kali's memory. "Right. She'd worked part-time in a vet clinic for years and wanted to become one herself."

"Yeah. I can't believe she's..."

"Let's find out for sure."

Grant's tired but welcoming voice filled her ears, easing some of the hard knots from today's series of shocks. "How are you?"

She understood what he was asking. "I'm okay. I'm adjusting. Slowly. Dan is with me."

"Good, I'm glad he made it. It's better if you're not alone right now. Probably better for him, too."

She glanced apologetically at Dan and moved her conversation into the kitchen. "Did you confirm ID of last night's victim? Was it Melanie?"

"It appears so, but we haven't located her next of kin. Also, I wondered if you knew if she'd been a survivor of some kind? If she had been that would help to cement the link with the others."

"Melanie lived at home, but her parents have gone back east

for a couple of weeks. Dan says she was a student here at Rosewood College. As to the other…I'm not sure. Hang on." Kali turned and asked Dan.

Dan's eyes clouded over and stared at her, thinking hard. Then he nodded. "Oh Shit. In New Zealand. Remember?"

Kali shook her head. "I don't think I ever heard about it. What happened? And how would the killer know?"

"She'd spoken of it several times. They were caught in a big rock slide. Her family survived, but a couple they were traveling with didn't."

She turned back to the phone. "Grant—"

"I heard. Let me talk to Dan for a moment."

"Yes, here." Kali handed the phone to Dan.

With raised eyebrows, he accepted the phone, clearing his throat before saying in an almost normal tone of voice, "Grant? What can I do for you?"

Kali slumped in her chair, letting the conversation drift around her. Too many shocks, too fast. Christ, she hated this. Her neck throbbed as she let her mind wander. She wanted to do something for Brad – and didn't know what. She'd wait until those at the center heard. Brad had been well-loved. Maybe shutting the center down until this craziness was over and the killer caught was the best idea. She couldn't bear it if anyone else was taken. Melanie and Julie were already too many.

Dan interrupted her musings. "Kali, they're putting cameras and some men in the center. They're operating on the assumption he's a regular and don't want to close the center in the event it might scare him off. It's been well over twenty-four hours. I know they have Julie listed as a missing person and there's an APB out there, but it doesn't feel like enough."

That made sense. She thought of something she'd meant to ask him before the bad news had chased everything else from her mind.

"Dan, do you know any religious-fanatic types at the center?"

His eyes narrowed in consideration. "No one comes to mind. Don't know about the groupies though." He shrugged.

Groupies formed and dissipated on a regular basis. Year in and year out there'd be a half dozen core members and a dozen that rotated between the various centers. For the most part, they were harmless, only wanting to belong, to be cool. To remember them all would take a miracle, as they came and went with regularity.

Kali eased deeper into her seat, slowly rubbing her thigh muscles. Everything ached today.

"What's on your mind?" Dan asked.

She gave him a dispirited smile. "The loss of innocence."

He stared. "Huh?"

"We've been naive. Cavalier with people entering and leaving the center at will. Our records are dismal, mostly covering payroll and expenses." She looked over at him. "We assumed nothing could go wrong. That because we worked to help people, we'd be protected. Instead, we've left ourselves wide open for this."

Dan hunched his shoulders. "Grant made a similar comment."

Kali shuddered. She could just imagine. "I don't understand. Why is this guy doing this? It's almost as if he sees himself as an angel of death, correcting the balance like in that movie, *Final Destination,* where Death comes after everyone who escaped him." Shivers rode her spine to her hipbones, making her consider the theory a little longer.

Dan's eyes widened. "These people are given a second chance by surviving a disaster. Their lives are changed forever. Many suffer the aftereffects every single day." His words burst out as if his frustration and emotion had finally boiled over.

"I know that, and you know that, but this guy isn't thinking with a full deck."

The conversation waned on that note.

Kali studied Dan's face, the fatigue, the dullness of his gaze. He'd been through a lot already. Did she dare ask him about something painful? Taking a deep breath, she plunged in. "Dan, I called Susan today to offer my condolences. I've actually phoned several times, but she wouldn't return my calls." Kali took a steadying breath. "I know she's hurting right now, but she sounded like she hated me. She blames me for Brad's death. I understand that. But something about the phone call, her words, her voice, made me think there was something else going on."

Dan shifted uncomfortably, his glance sliding away.

Uh-oh. Kali frowned. "Dan what aren't you telling me?"

His sorrowful gaze brushed her face briefly before flitting off again. "I don't want to spread rumours, Kali. Brad's dead. Leave the past where it belongs."

"But that's the problem; he's dead. I can't ask him. And I'd like to understand her behavior."

He ran a tired hand through his thinning hair. He stayed silent for a long moment, then his shoulders drooped. "Susan believed you and Brad were close, too close."

THE HACKSAW MOVED back and forth with swift sure strokes. Good thing he'd come prepared. The PVC pipe was just too long. But he would fix that. The cut piece fell to the ground as the blade sliced through the last edge. This time he'd planned ahead. Once again, things had fallen into place. The industrial cardboard box had been tossed in a dumpster close to the center. It was big enough for Julie and yet small enough to carry into the woods. It should be a breeze to bury. Good thing she was a little bit of a thing. She'd be fine for several days in here. And he really did want to visit with her for a while.

She'd made it easy for him. Almost too easy. No challenge. Of course she hadn't appreciated his efforts. No, she'd screamed at him something fierce. He grinned. The fighting spirit might keep her alive longer than his other victims. None of them had presented a challenge. Melanie had been docile and David, well, he'd gone out like a light after that blow to the head, never even whimpered. He frowned. Unexpected, that. Something must have been wrong with David in the first place. The guy had really let himself go.

At least it made it easy to send him home. If he'd been conscious and in a fighting mood, David had been wiry and strong enough to have caused him hell. Instead, he'd collapsed after one blow.

Not like Julie. She was a fighter.

He picked up the large PVC pipe sitting off to one side. At six feet long, the pipe would deliver air from the surface directly inside the box to Julie. The bottom of the pipe had been cut off at a long angle to let in lots of air at the bottom.

Turning his attention back to where Julie lay unconscious and trussed like a Thanksgiving turkey, he repositioned her head where she'd have instant access to the fresh air. Closing the heavy lid, he snapped the interlocking tabs in place then used the commercial staple gun to secure them closed. With the pipe positioned inside, he cut a hole on the top of the box. Perfect. He secured the pipe to the box with duct tape, letting it stand straight. Julie moaned from inside her makeshift coffin. He grinned. Her voice was barely audible now and with a hill of dirt on top she'd never be heard.

That ought to give them some time together. And give Kali a

chance to figure this one out. Not too long though. Maybe, a day or two? Julie would hold for that long. He could even 'up the ante.' Another phone call maybe? How about a letter? Or another gift? He doubted that she appreciated his last one.

With one last look around, he started shoveling dirt on top of the box. Julie moaned again. He smirked. A perfect time for her to wake up. She'd understand what was happening. On cue, the box shifted slightly as Julie struggled inside. A kick resounded at the bottom end then another. But with both hands and feet tied, her attempts weren't doing much. He laughed.

What was that old saying, 'do what you love and love what you are doing?' Yes. He'd finally found a service that he could enjoy.

Perfect.

With a light-hearted whistle, he lifted the next load of dirt.

CHAPTER 18

"TOO CLOSE? AS in more than friends close?" she asked cautiously, trying to wrap her thinking around Dan's words.

Dan's wrinkles scrunched before relaxing in defeat. "Yeah."

"But we weren't...we never...I mean...It wasn't like that between us." Outrage sparked. "Dan, we were friends and coworkers but nothing more."

He held up his hands. "Kali, I believe you. But I doubt you'll convince Susan."

"But why? We were never...never..." She leaned forward and emphasized the next word. "Lovers."

He squinted, considering her words. "Did you really *not* know how Brad felt?"

Memories crowded in on her. Brad finishing her sentences. Brad delivering coffee when she'd hit exhaustion. The caring hugs during emotional, overwrought times. The constant comforting presence at her side.

"I loved him," she whispered, hating the paradigm shift in her world. "Like a brother."

"And he loved you."

Dan said it simply, eloquently, and Kali accepted the truth. How could she not have known? How well had she known him, really, on the inside where it counted? Her chest hit lockdown. She couldn't breathe. Brad had cared; he'd wanted more from her and she hadn't noticed. She closed her eyes against the tears threatening to fall and slumped back. "I didn't know. Oh, God. I'm so sorry, Brad."

For several moments, Kali couldn't speak as regrets clogged her throat. Finally, Kali leveled her gaze at Dan. "How did Susan find out?"

"I think she probably suspected something for a while, but Brad asked for a divorce before leaving for Sacramento."

"He what?" Kali straightened in her seat. She needed the shocks to stop. "He never said a word to me. I knew they had some trouble but not divorce-sized trouble."

"He wanted to wait until everything had been finalized. Susan had said no, not wanting to change the status quo in her life."

"Status quo?" Kali blinked. What an odd thing to say. "Didn't she love him? Want her marriage to work?"

"Brad told me before he left that he needed time away and his wife needed time to think, to decide what to do. She'd asked him to stay home this trip and work things out. But he left – with you."

"Poor Susan. Oh, Dan. I never wanted to break up their marriage. I was happy for them. Proud to know someone in this day and age who could make marriage work."

"That's why you felt safe getting close to him."

Confused, Kali glanced at him. "What do you mean?"

"Kali, you haven't had a serious relationship in – what, five, six years – or dated for at least eight months. You've been emotionally locked down since Mexico," he said, talking right over her spluttering, "Brad shot to the top of your best friend list years ago because he was married and you thought he wanted nothing more from you. He was safe."

Kali winced. "Ouch."

"Brad understood, particularly how you'd changed these last six months. He felt that, once freed of Susan, he'd slide into a 'more than friend' relationship with you."

"Crap." Kali's mind bordered on overload. Safe and complacent, yup that was her motto. Except in Brad's case, she'd been blind and stupid.

"No wonder Susan won't talk to me." Kali struggled to compartmentalize the new onslaught of guilt. She'd failed everyone lately.

"Right."

Silence ensued. Hurting, Kali whispered. "I didn't know. Honest."

Dan placed a hand on her shoulder. "I believe you."

Kali offered him a wan smile, more exhausted than if she'd come from a three-day rescue with no rest. Done in. "Do I say something to her? Do I leave her alone? What?" And why was she asking him?

Because she no longer trusted her own judgment.

"Let her alone. Give her time to heal."

A common sense attitude, but one that offered no closure for Kali. She wasn't sure how to live with that.

"You might want to consider your relationship with Grant for the same reason."

"I'm not going to think about Grant." Not now. Maybe never – considering Dan's latest bombshell.

"Do you want a relationship?"

Kali quirked her lips and slunk lower. "I hadn't thought so. My life is chaotic enough."

Dan's steady gaze showed years of wise living. "And now?" He raised one eyebrow at her. "Grant is seriously interested. I've known him for years. I know how his job has changed him. But being around you takes years off his face."

"No." Dan was just being sweet. Then again, Grant's energy reinforced Dan's words. There'd be no blending of their energies if Grant wasn't interested, if being together wasn't right on some deep level. That didn't make this the right time or place. "He and I are all about the victims."

"No," he corrected. "That *is* your relationship. You see things the same way, think the same way and do the same work. With so much in common, you haven't realized you're working and growing together. *Growing together*. Did you hear it the second time or do I need to say it again?"

Kali hated the squirming child inside, as if she'd been caught in a lie. He was right. She knew it, but…she didn't know what she wanted to do about it. And what did Grant want with her?

"Right." Dan stood up. "I'm going to head to the center. I want to be on hand in case some of this news sneaks out so I can put a stop to the talk. I doubt they'll release Melanie's name yet. It's going to be hard to keep a lid on this for long. And you, well you need to think about what I said."

Kali gave Dan a good-bye hug at the front door. The phone rang. Hurrying into the kitchen, Kali answered it.

"Hello."

"Found another one, did you? Too late, again. Here, I'd hoped you'd be a decent challenge. Instead, you can't even get into the game."

Fury and pain exploded through her. "What have you done with Julie?"

An ugly silence filled the phone line.

"Julie is fine – for the moment. I've given her a fighting

chance as you appear to need the extra time." The voice cackled once before ringing off.

Fingers shaking, Kali struggled to dial Grant's number. Her words tripped over each other as she tried to explain. "He just called... He has Julie...something about a fighting chance... I don't know; he said something about I needed the help?"

Grant fired several questions at her. "Think. Did he say anything specific to help us find her? It's been recorded but give me what you remember right now."

Kali repeated the conversation the best she could.

"I hate to ask, but Julie's life is at stake. Will you please sit with your sketchpad and try to get another picture?"

"There's no guarantee," she warned.

"No. I know. But everything helps and at this moment, you're the best hope Julie has."

HA. STUMPED THEM this round. Damn straight.

A breeze slipped through the branches. He adjusted his stolen jacket, grateful for his foresight in lifting it off the neighbor's back deck. Anything to throw Shiloh off his scent.

Leaning forward, he adjusted the focus on his binoculars to peer through his heavily treed bower directly at Kali's deck. Kali leaned over the railing, her face, a picture of pain. Perfect. Let her stew.

The killer opened up his granola bar, ripped off a piece and popped it into his mouth. This was better than dinner and a show. He vaguely remembered evenings long past, spent in theatres. At a time when he believed in ever-lasting love. Right, those were his young and stupid years. His face puckered. He washed the granola bar down with lukewarm coffee from the thermos. Not a great meal. Still he wasn't ready to leave yet. The sun would be hot soon. Here in the trees, with a breeze blowing in off the ocean, the heat had yet to penetrate.

A great day, which promised an even better evening. He chortled. Later, once darkness fell, he'd go visit Julie.

She'd be waiting for him.

He didn't want to disappoint her.

KALI REACHED FOR the sketchbook and turned to the sketch that was supposedly of Julie. In the drawing, a pipe brought fresh air in for the victim, extending the person's chances of being found alive. Julie, therefore, had to be restrained in some way that prevented her from digging herself out. The fresh air supply meant the killer assumed she'd be buried for a while. If, and it was a big if, regardless of what had happened so far, the picture was viable, this could be the fighting chance the killer had talked about.

Or he wanted to lull her into thinking Julie was still alive.

"Who exists in Julie's world? Friends? Lovers? And who would know?" she muttered out loud. She laid the sketchbook on the table. "Brenda might." Brenda held a unique position at the center. Not a dog owner or a rescuer, she neither worked nor volunteered but she knew so many that did, she'd become a regular herself.

Picking up her cell, Kali called her. "Hey, it's Kali. Brenda, I have a weird question for you. Do you know if Julie has a current boyfriend?"

"Hi, Kali, how are you? Nice to hear from you. Aren't you wonderful about returning your calls. And why don't you ask Julie yourself."

Kali forced a snicker at her friend's sarcasm. "I would if I could, but she's not answering her phone. And maybe I'm arranging a party for the center and want to know if she has a 'partner' she might like to bring." Kali rolled her eyes at the lame excuse but it's all she could create on the spur of the moment.

"Oooohhh. Am I invited?"

Exasperated, Kali said, "Of course. I'm hardly going to call you about this and then not invite you, too."

"Oh, in that case. As far as I know, Julie does have a new man, but a married one. So I don't think they go out in public."

Not good. A married man meant a clandestine affair. No one would know the details. "That's too bad. I guess I'll have to wait until I get a chance to speak with her then."

And how else could she find out?

"So are you going to ask me?" Brenda's bubbly voice piped up.

Kali rolled her eyes. "So, Brenda, do you have a new man in your life?"

"I dated one guy off and on last month, but that fizzed out." Brenda giggled, obviously not terribly upset over that relationship. "Speaking of losers, I stopped in at the center early last week hoping to find you. Instead, I met a real weirdo. I never did get his name. He called me a couple of days later but I wasn't home. Thankfully."

The hair on Kali's neck quivered. Casually, she asked, "What made him weird?"

Brenda's voice dropped to an eerie whisper, "Fanatically religious."

Religious. Now the hairs on her neck bristled. Taking a deep breath, Kali tried to inject a casual tone to her voice. "How could you tell?"

Brenda's tone sharpened with disgust. "He kept arguing with himself, for God's sake, about how God meted out His own justice." She huffed. "You know me. Any talk of justice and I break out in hives."

Kali knew it well. Brenda avoided all conversations on morals and any mention of right and wrong. She'd enjoyed more than a few married men herself.

"He called and left a message on my machine, suggesting a date with a heavenly experience – a date with destiny." Brenda giggled. "Isn't that the corniest line ever?"

Kali's eyes widened. This guy had possibilities. "Did you erase his message?"

"Absolutely. Think I wanted to keep that?"

"How old is this guy?"

"Who knows – who cares?"

Kali understood. Brenda loved men. All ages, races, and normally, religions. "This guy must have spooked you?"

"It was weird. He called me at home even though I hadn't given him my number. Where'd he get it?" Brenda's voice dropped again. "He had a weird accent – like a bastardized French or Portuguese or something. Who can tell anymore?" A sigh worked through the phone. "The message kinda freaked me out."

"Would you recognize him again?"

"Absolutely."

"Brenda, I'm going to call you right back. Sit tight for five minutes."

"Wai—"

Kali didn't give her a chance to argue, shutting her off mid-sentence. She immediately called Grant. At this rate, the poor man wouldn't get any sleep.

"Grant," she said without preamble when he answered. "I just spoke with a friend of mine from Second Chance. She met an odd religious guy at the center who called her at her home when he shouldn't have had the number."

"Who?" His voice sharpened, cutting through the line like a knife.

"She doesn't know his name. We can ask Dan, but I don't know if he'll know him from her description either, Grant. I'm wondering about a police artist?"

"I'll call you back."

Kali clicked off the phone. Five minutes later, Grant called back.

"Can you two meet me at the office on Waterston Street?"

"Sure. When?"

"About half an hour. There's an excellent artist who works out of that office. Do you need the address?" Without waiting, he rattled it off. Kali grabbed for a pen, then stopped as she recognized the address. "I know where it is."

Kali hoped Brenda didn't have plans. A half hour didn't give either of them much preparation time. But Julie had no time. She dialed, relieved when her friend picked up on the first ring. "Brenda, I can't explain right now, but I need you to trust me on this. I need you to go with me to the police station and work with a police artist. I can come and pick you up and drive you home again afterwards."

Brenda's gasp came through loud and clear. "The police?"

"Yes, I need you to help me with this."

With a groan, Brenda said. "We've been friends for a long time, but this is just weird."

Kali chewed her bottom lip. "Please, trust me. I have a good reason."

"But why can't you tell me what's going on?" Worry fussed through Brenda's voice. "All right. I don't like it, but I'll do it."

Kali closed her eyes in relief. "Thank you."

CHAPTER 19

THE HEAT IN the small room at the police station made Kali melt. She sent Shiloh to a corner to lie down. After being away most of last night, she hadn't wanted to leave the poor dog alone today. Or maybe Kali didn't want to be without Shiloh. Today had already been hell. Thank God it had been a fast trip to the station. Brenda had peppered her with questions the whole way. Kali stalled her until she could confirm with Grant what she was allowed to say.

Kali removed her light sweater, draping it over one of the chairs before sitting down. "Hi, I'm Kali. This is Brenda. She's the one you'll be working with."

"Hi, I'm Nancy. Brenda, take a seat and let's get started."

Kali hid her grin at the trepidation on Brenda's face. Still, her friend willingly turned to Nancy's fancy computer program.

Once seated, Nancy got straight to work. "Brenda, start by closing your eyes and think back to when you saw this person. Block out all else and focus on his face. Do you see him in your mind's eye?"

"Yes."

"Good. With your eyes closed, give me your impression on the shape of his face? Don't focus on the details, let his face blur into giving you the shape. Round face? Squared off? Perhaps it's more triangular or maybe a heart shape?"

Kali watched as they worked through the various aspects of the face. The artist in her found it fascinating to watch. An irresistible process. A stack of paper sat to one side, with pencils sitting on top. At an opportune moment, Kali snitched one of each, a questioning look on her face as she caught Nancy's eye. Nancy nodded.

Listening to Brenda's answers, Kali sketched the oval face, the large oversized nose, followed with the deep-set eyes. She followed the conversation, understanding the insights as they surfaced.

Somewhere along the line, she slipped from awake and aware into something else.

Her hand moved at an incredible pace, filling in, shading, adding a detail here, thickening a line there.

As if a switch had been thrown, she came to an abrupt stop. She leaned back with a deep sigh and rotated her stiff neck. A deafening silence alerted her.

The other two women stared at her.

Kali frowned. "What?"

Brenda spoke first. "You're an artist?"

"It's a hobby of mine." Kali shrugged. "I paint more than I sketch but I'm comfortable with both."

"That's obvious." Nancy spoke up for the first time. Flipping her laptop around, she showed Kali the artistic rendering.

Kali couldn't help but stare. There was something about him she half-recognized. Like someone she should know. The picture, although clear, had a generic look to it. It needed something. But what?

"Now compare the screen to this." Nancy reached across the table for Kali's sketch. She held the sketch up beside the monitor so the other two could see the pictures side-by-side.

"Oh my God."

She'd drawn the same male face. Except her drawing was almost terrifying in detail. "I just followed along with your instructions and her answers."

Brenda peered closer. "How bloody freaky, Kali. You're my friend and I love you, but that drawing is plain scary."

Shooting Brenda a quick glance, Kali returned to analyze the sketch. Hot, fervent eyes stared out at her. A zealot peeped out. The large nose and thin lips represented a simple verbal description that translated into a hawkish nose and a cold angry mouth that promised retribution.

"Maybe my imagination just went wild." Kali avoided looking in their direction. These women had no idea of her weird talents. And Kali didn't want them asking for an explanation.

The door opened. Grant walked in. In the small room his energy surged her way. Tired and pale, it blended with hers – that very act strengthening his. Kali had never seen anything like it as she watched Grant throw off some of the fatigue that had been weighing him down. He even stood straighter.

Casting a surreptitious look at the other two women, she was relieved to see them focused on the drawings.

"Good; you're done?"

"Yep, we're done, but it turns out you didn't need me. Take a look at what Kali sketched while we worked on the digital version."

Kali watched Brenda's reaction to her first glimpse of Grant. Brenda was a notorious flirt. Nothing. Not even a smile for him.

Stepping closer, Grant peered at the paper and digital sketches. "Brenda, is the sketch a good likeness?"

"No, it's a freaking awesome one. Kali nailed him." She shuddered. "Christ, he gives me the chills."

Grant picked up the paper sketch. His eyes met Kali's and held.

Shivers slid down her spine. She understood what he was thinking. She couldn't help but wonder the same thing. Was this the killer?

Speaking slowly, she said, "I think I've seen him around. But this is like an exaggerated version of what I remember. I feel like I know him, but it's not quite right. Dan will know." She gave him an apologetic look. "I've spent too much time away, or hidden in my office at the center."

"Then let's go. We'll have him take a look before I circulate this as a 'person of interest.'"

Kali pulled out her cell phone and dialed Second Chance.

Reaching for her bag, Nancy asked, "We're done, aren't we? I'd like to head out."

Grant reached out to shake her hand. "Yes, thanks for helping. We appreciate it."

"You should convince her to go into the business." Nancy gestured at Kali.

"Nope." Kali shook her head. "Not for me."

Brenda snorted as she stood up. "Sure, you'd rather find dead bodies."

Ouch. Kali ducked the truth. "No, Brenda. I'd rather find live people."

"I say it like I see it." But she smiled at Kali, softening the words. "Can I leave too?"

Kali rose. "I'll take Brenda home, then meet you at the center afterwards, Grant."

"Good, and on the way maybe you can explain what the hell's going on?" Brenda stuck her chin out. "I've been patient Kali, but now it's time for answers."

Grant held the door open for them. "I'll need about ten minutes to finish up here."

Rain drizzled from the gray clouds overhead, forcing Brenda and Kali to make a dash for the vehicle. Shiloh beat them to the Jeep. Kali fired up the engine and drove in the direction of Brenda's home.

As soon as she pulled onto the main road, Brenda bubbled over like a water pipe that had popped a cap. "Now that we're alone, what's with you and Grant? He couldn't take his eyes off you. How come you didn't tell me you had a dish on the side?"

Kali shot her a disbelieving look and changed lanes.

"Typical. You didn't even notice," Brenda said wryly.

Really? Another quick look at her friend confirmed it. "Seriously?"

"Yeah, girlfriend."

"Oh." Warmth bloomed in her chest. Maybe there was something solid there. Good. She could work with that.

Brenda giggled.

She pulled up outside Brenda's house. "Home. Thanks for helping this afternoon."

Collecting her purse from the floor, Brenda commented, "You never did explain what's going on. I got that it's all hush-hush. Grant did give that whole thank you for coming…your cooperation is appreciated line. But still…a little more, please. You know my curiosity – it's going to kill me!"

"Several people have been kidnapped and two, possibly three have been murdered. This guy could be a suspect." Kali stared out the front windshield. "Don't go out with anyone you don't know really well."

"Good enough." Brenda shuddered as she opened the door. "The same warning applies to you. Thanks for a unique afternoon."

"Stay safe." The door slammed shut as Kali repeated the words to the empty interior as her friend disappeared into her house. Checking her mirrors, Kali reversed her car, and drove toward the center. She'd forgotten to call Dan. The traffic thickened but hadn't reached the critical point of no forward movement. The picture she'd drawn dominated her thoughts. She should know him. She did know him. She just didn't recognize him. How sad was that? She'd spent so much time hidden away from the public, she couldn't even place a new look on an old face.

Driving with deft skill, she maneuvered the Jeep forward, taking the next left and then the long stretch leading to the center. She hoped the news of Brad's demise hadn't made it here yet. It shouldn't have, but bad news always traveled. The more secretive the better. She didn't think she could deal with that kind of conversation right now. Tomorrow would be soon enough. Several vehicles pulled out as she pulled in. A class must be finishing.

Kali waited for a car to pull out before she took its spot close to the front. She checked out the lot but didn't spot Grant's car anywhere. She strode through the front doors, propped wide open as always.

Once again, the center was a mad selection of dogs and people. It seemed like Dan's plans to bring in more business were doing well. Laughter and conversation filled the air punctuated by barks and woofs from the many different dogs. Everything was so normal looking. How could the rest of the world carry on, oblivious to the danger that stalked them?

Needing a touch of normalcy herself, Shiloh enjoyed making the rounds, catching hugs and scratches from friends, old and new. Kali waved at a couple people she knew as she made her way to the coffee pot. Empty as usual. So what else was new? Dan could probably use a cup. She took a minute to make a fresh pot.

"You're gonna share, that aren't you?"

"Jarl." Kali gave him a big hug. Stepping away, she peered into his tired face. "Wow, where were you? You look like hell."

His weary face creased into a grin. "That feels about right. Been doing graveyard work. Hell's been a prime topic lately."

She laughed. "You realize the workers are supposed to do the digging."

Jarl tugged on his scraggly beard. "But I like playing in the dirt."

She shook her head at him. "What type of project this time?"

"Moving an old graveyard." His face scrunched at the memory. "When the land was resurveyed, the old one was outside the church's property lines."

He took a sip of hot coffee, watching as Kali filled two mugs.

Nodding toward the cups, he asked, "Thirsty?"

"One's for Dan."

"I didn't know he was here." Jarl checked the field outside the window where a class had started. "I searched earlier but didn't find him."

Kali smiled at the familiar line of dogs and owners. The owners tried to get the dogs to pay attention and the dogs tried to get the owners to let them do their own thing. "He's probably in his office. I'm trying to bribe my way in." Kali held up the two cups. She needed to make an announcement to let everyone know about Brad, but first she should see if Dan had mentioned it to anyone and what they needed to do for a memorial. Brad had been well-loved here. Everyone would want to say good-bye.

"There's a mess of things to catch you up on. First though, I have a few of the details to sort out with Dan."

"Perfect. I'll talk to you later." Jarl joined the long table of people on the veranda. A hue and cry rose at the sight of the fresh coffee and a stampede headed her way. Kali escaped.

Kali set the coffee cup on the large bookcase in the hallway beside Dan's door and knocked twice.

No answer. "Dan? It's me, Kali. Can I come in?"

Silence. Kali tried to the knob. The damn thing was locked. Shit. Kali pounded on the door. No answer. Something was definitely wrong. Checking her pockets, she realized she only had her car keys on her. She didn't carry the spares for Second Chance if she didn't need to.

Could he have gone home? Pulling out her cell phone, she speed-dialed Dan's number. His voice mail played immediately. Shit.

Kali jumped back when the strip of light showed under the door. Shiloh barked, sensing Kali's distress.

"Kali?" Grant walked toward her. "What's wrong?"

"Thank God, you're here." She motioned toward the door. "Dan's door is locked and he's not answering his cell phone. Something's wrong. I need to get in." She jiggled the doorknob again, despite her shaking fingers. The sense of urgency slammed through the roof.

"Step aside." Grant reached into his rear pants pocket, opened his wallet and slid out a thin metallic tool. Kali watched as he fiddled with the lock, then turned the knob. It opened under his hand. Kali pushed the door open and rushed inside.

The office light shone on the old scarred desk piled high with tumbling stacks of paperwork. There was no sign of Dan. Perplexed, Kali strode to the other side of the desk and gasped.

He lay in a crumpled heap on the floor.

"Oh no, Grant…he's hurt."

Kali fell beside the older man, but Grant beat her to him. "Thank God, he's alive." She reached for the phone and called 911. With so many SAR members at the center, she couldn't think if she'd seen anyone on her way through. They all had medical training of various levels, as she did. Some of her panic eased with Grant crouched at Dan's side. His movements were swift and sure. He opened Dan's shirt and ran his hands over the prone body, searching for injuries. When he withdrew his hand from beneath Dan's head, it was covered in blood.

"Oh, no!"

Grant gave her a sidelong glance but said nothing.

Dan's desk drawer sat open a couple of inches and his computer hummed. Odd, his monitor was off. She frowned. Using a pen, Kali clicked it on. The desktop appeared right away but showed no open documents.

Puzzled, she asked, "Grant, there are no open files on his computer, so why would the monitor be switched off if he was in here working?"

Pulling his attention away from Dan, he sent a fleeting glance toward the screen. "I don't know. Sometimes I shut off my monitor when I'm not using it. But don't touch anything, just in case."

"Do you...suppose someone attacked him?"

Grant countered. "Can you find anything he might have hit his head on?"

Kali walked around the office. The wall behind the office chair held a large map taped to its smooth surface. The corners of the desk showed no blood stains and the filing cabinets were on the other side of the room.

"Not that I can see."

"Thanks. Can you direct the paramedics here, please? Don't discuss details with anyone and no one leaves. My team's on the way. They'll want to question everyone."

Kali raced out.

JULIE PRESSED HER face against the rough edge of the pipe, sucking in the fresh air. Hot tears seeped down her cheeks. She didn't know where she was or what she was trapped in. It felt like paper under her fingertips but had to be something stronger. She'd tried kicking her way through, but the cord keeping her ankles together hadn't given her much freedom for kicking. Not only had she not made a dent in what trapped her, but with her knees snuggled up to her waist, she could hardly move.

Asshole.

Her mouth was so dry she had trouble swallowing. She wanted a drink of water badly. And a blanket.

The experts said time passed quickly when you floated in and out of consciousness. That a person wouldn't be aware of his surroundings. That he'd have no understanding of what was happening.

The experts were wrong.

Julie did drift in and out of conscious. She did float on a timeless vision of the reality she found herself in. But she fully understood what had happened. Somewhere in the mist, the fog wadded around her, holding the understanding close to her, just not sharp and in focus.

The pain did that.

Julie moaned again.

"Awake again? Lovely."

Julie opened her eyes, blinked against the falling dirt, before focusing on the small circle of light above her head. The pipe she'd found last time she'd awakened had become her symbol of hope. Anyone could find it anytime, accidentally or by design. Find it and her.

Julie struggled to remind herself that she'd survived once. She'd do it again. Then she'd show this asshole the reality of being buried alive. Julie closed her eyes, tears streaking her muddy cheeks. God, she wanted to go home. Home. Where Kali had searched for her, had arranged to have an officer waiting for her. And what had she done? Gotten mad. She'd worked herself into a full blown hissy fit and hadn't done what she'd been told to do. She'd been pissed at them all. What a hell of a time to come to her senses. When it was too fucking late.

Through dry lips, she whispered, "Bastard."

Laughter floated through the pipe.

A small surge of anger whipped through her. Where the fuck was Kali?

KALI BURST OUTSIDE through the front door; sirens were already audible approaching along the main road. People ran behind her.

"Kali, what's wrong?"

"Hey, what's going on?"

Kali shot them a frantic glance as the ambulance pulled into the lot. "Dan's collapsed."

"Oh, no!"

More people joined in the commotion. As soon as the EMTs emerged, Kali led the way to the office. There she blocked the stream of curious onlookers. The arrival of Grant's men shifted the crowd back.

Several moments later, Grant strode toward her. "They're stabilizing him now for the trip to the hospital. Do you want to drive or will I?"

She closed her eyes briefly. "You drive."

The paramedics were fast. Dan was wheeled out and loaded into the ambulance within minutes. Kali grabbed her keys and purse, locked up Dan's office and raced to the parking lot. Shiloh ran at her side.

Grant drove from the lot amid cries and good wishes to Dan. Kali waved to them through her tears. Dan was deservedly proud of what he'd built over the last decade. If anything happened to him, he'd be sorely missed. Kali immediately castigated herself for the negative thinking. Dan had hit his head, not collapsed due to a heart attack. His injury could be minor. It had to be.

It wasn't.

After almost an hour in the waiting room, Kali learned Dan suffered from a skull fracture complicated by intracranial bleeding. The doctors were monitoring his condition. Grant had explained the procedure the doctors planned to do if the bleeding and swelling didn't stop. Kali refused to contemplate anyone drilling a hole into Dan's skull. The idea of him with his lifeblood dripping away made her cringe.

Stay positive.

Kali rotated her neck to ease the ribbons of tension knotting her shoulders. She knew she should leave, but still hoped to see Dan – if only for a minute. Sitting there didn't help her mind-set. It gave her too much time to think. So much heartache. So many losses. David. Melanie. Brad. Julie. No, damn it, not Julie. Kali jutted out her chin. Enough was enough.

Her shoulders sagged. But what could she do? Grant and his team were questioning everyone at the center right now, according to what he'd said after she'd updated him on Dan's condition. The team had run the list of names she'd given them. The police report had arrived on the Bralorne murder. The profilers were expecting to have something soon. And then there was the sketch. According to Grant, the FBI was working on that.

Kali felt distanced from it all. For those minutes, her life had shifted, narrowing to a single focus – Dan. To lose him…well, she hadn't even dealt with the other recent losses. Emotion flooded her heart and salty tears welled. The losses had come so fast, there'd been no time to grieve. Time was a luxury she hadn't been afforded. When this hell finished, when there was time to honor her friends the way she should, then she'd say her good-byes.

If she were lucky, she'd have sorted through her bewilderment and a growing sense of betrayal, whether right or wrong, about Brad by then. How dare he have those feelings for her and not let her know? If he'd mentioned it, hinted at it just once, she'd have explained her position. Let him down gently. Hiccups happened in friendships. They'd loved each other – just differently. God, she missed him. Tears ran down her cheeks. Kali sniffled, wiping tears away with her sleeve.

As she sat there, her tears shifted to deeper frustration, then to anger. Something good needed to happen soon. She'd about had it with this bad news bullshit. Had the FBI found anything on Dan's computer? Or in his office? Attacking Dan didn't make sense. It was a dumb move, an obvious mistake, and she had no doubt that's what had happened. If the killer had been there, someone saw him. And if the killer had made one mistake, maybe he'd made another.

"Miss Jordan?"

Kali stood up at the arrival of the older man. He wore scrubs and just stood there, worry rising to the forefront. "Yes, I'm Kali Jordan." She wiped her eyes on her sleeve.

The man held out his hand. "I'm Dr. Poole. Dan is doing slightly better. The bleeding in his brain has slowed." The doctor offered her a gentle smile. "We're monitoring the swelling. If he continues to improve through the night, we'll be able to upgrade his condition by morning."

"Thank God for that." Kali beamed as the good news set in. "Is he awake?"

"No, and he won't be soon. We're keeping him in a drug-induced coma."

Kali's heart sank. She shoved her hands in her pockets, to stop from wringing them together. A coma didn't sound good. "Can I see him, please?"

He motioned down the hallway. "I'll let you in for just a moment. Come with me."

"Thank you." Kali grabbed her purse and coat then followed him. "I appreciate this."

"Hospital policy states only relatives are allowed in, but the FBI tells me that you occupy a similar position in this gentleman's life."

Sad but true. Kali knew of no relatives, close or otherwise, in Dan's life. His wife had died years ago.

The doctor led her into the intensive care room where Dan lay, covered in blankets, with tubes running in all directions.

"Oh, Dan," she whispered. The injury had aged him. His heavy wrinkles should be smooth in sleep. Instead, they looked thin and flat, as if piled up on top of each other.

"The swelling has distorted his facial features. But that's a temporary situation."

Seeing him lying like this, hurt Kali. He used to have so much vitality, so much to give. Lately he'd slowed down and his memory wasn't as good.

His skin was now the color of plaster; lifeless. "At least that's something." Kali walked over to Dan's bedside. She placed her hand over Dan's cool, still one. Beside him machines hummed with smooth efficiency.

"Yes, but head injuries are tricky." The doctor returned the clipboard to the bed. "He's not out of the woods yet." He met her gaze straight on, a small smile in place. "Not to worry. We're doing everything in our power to make sure he pulls through."

She hoped it would be enough. Dan looked so ill. "I know you are, but that won't stop me from worrying."

"Caring does that to a person. Everyone deserves to be loved."

True. Kali's heart ached. After she lost her dad, Dan had stepped in as a replacement. He'd become that father figure to talk to, to visit with and to offer well-meaning advice – regardless of how wrong it was.

"Can I sit here for a few moments? I promise I won't disturb anything."

"Just a couple of minutes. No longer."

"Thanks." She appreciated the bending of the rules. Dan deserved to know someone cared. Kali barely heard him. "You're going to be fine, Dan. It's okay. You're safe. Honest."

For five minutes, she whispered to him. It didn't matter if he heard her or not but she needed to talk to him. To reach him in some way and to hope that he heard her.

"Excuse me."

Kali turned to face the newcomer. A young nurse stood in the doorway, smiling apologetically at her. "I'm sorry, but it's time for you to leave."

Kali sighed. The nurse was right. It was time to go. On the way she smiled at the officer standing guard. Thank heavens for that. She had put aside her worries about Dan, in order to find Julie and catch a killer.

She'd almost reached the outside the front exit when her phone rang. "Hi, Grant. Any chance of a ride?"

"Good timing, I'm on my way. We have a face on the camera through the research center. Thomas is working on cleaning it up right now." His voice was sharp and businesslike. "I'm hoping you can identify him. I need you to come back to the station."

Walking out the front entrance, Kali tried to put a face to Thomas. She knew she'd seen him before through this case, and that Grant appeared to have a good rapport with him, but things being the way they were, she'd glossed over all those men. And that was wrong. They were working hard and she couldn't even put names to faces.

An oversight she'd have to fix.

Grant pulled up a few minutes later, Shiloh's head hanging out the window. She barked once at the sight of Kali, who laughed. Obviously Shiloh hadn't been upset by staying with Grant. She gave Shiloh an extra cuddle before getting in beside her. Minutes later they were on their way.

"You have a face from the center?"

"Yes, going into your office."

Kali frowned. "You realize it's not *my* office, right?"

The police station loomed ahead. She let Shiloh out after her, then waited for Grant to lock up the car before walking toward him, and the station. Shiloh danced around her. Kali called her over, bending slightly to put a calming hand on Shiloh's head.

Crack.

Pain burned in a fiery streak along Kali's shoulders and back.

"Ohhh." Kali's knees buckled. What happened? She glanced up, confused. Shiloh whined, her face nudging against Kali's cheeks. She tried to stand only to cry out before collapsing back into position.

"Stay down," Grant snapped, standing over her. She barely heard him for the agony burning her neck and head. Kali wrapped her arm around Shiloh's neck, huddling close. Her stomach really didn't feel well. Grant shifted, circling her, searching the surrounding area. Why wasn't he helping her? He should be, shouldn't he? What the hell had happened?

Unaccountably, tears collected in the corner of her eyes. Whatever the cause, he shouldn't have yelled at her.

She burrowed her face in Shiloh's side. Shiloh whined, nudging her cold nose against Kali's hand. Kali scrunched tighter. Somewhere in the background she heard Grant talking on the phone. What a time to socialize. Didn't he see she needed him? She heard him walking toward her.

"Kali, talk to me. Don't you faint on me? Buck up girl."

Lifting her head, she gasped with outrage. "I've never fainted in my life." She tried to shift onto her knees, only to fall forward. Her stomach knotted in a sudden fierce movement. "Ohhh, God, it hurts. Make it stop, please, Grant."

Grant bent, trying to lift her to her feet. "I will, honey. Let's get you inside. The attacker might still be here."

"Attacker?" Kali shifted upward into a half crouch before making it all the way to a standing position, with his help. "Someone attacked me?" Shiloh leaned against her.

Men poured from the building, spreading out to search the surrounding areas. Grant kept her snuggled tight against his chest while he yelled, "He bolted over there." Grant pointed toward the far back of the lot. Guns at the ready, officers fanned outward.

Kali tried to watch, but black spots kept getting in the way. She blinked, trying to see around them, but they moved with her.

"How bad is it?" One officer ran toward her. Kali turned her face into Grant's chest. Sweat dripped along her side. It tickled and bugged her at the same time. Irritated, she swiped at it. And cried out.

"Shhh. Take it easy, Kali. Don't try to move." Grant whispered against her ear, his arms loosely holding her in place. Through the haze of pain, she caught part of the conversation happening…caught the new arrival's last comment.

"I've called for an ambulance."

Kali lifted her head, pulling a frown at the men. "An ambulance?"

The two men glanced at each other, then at her.

In a soft gentle voice, Grant responded, "Kali, it's for you. You've been shot."

CHAPTER 20

S*HOT?*

Pain blasted through her system tenfold with his words. "You shouldn't have told me," she said peevishly. "Now it really hurts."

Grant hugged her close.

Bile floated up her throat at the movement. Kali closed her eyes and clenched her teeth. A moan escaped and she rested against his chest. A whine first, then the gentle paw on her thigh, caught her attention. Shiloh sat beside her, her huge chocolate eyes focused on Kali. Reaching down, Kali tried to reassure her…but damn, it hurt.

"It's okay, sweetheart." Grant's words were calming and he rested his chin on the top of her head. "You're going to be fine. Appears to be a flesh wound, maybe scraping through the layer of fat on your back."

"Ohhh." Kali reared back and slugged him. "How dare you?"

Grant stared at her in astonishment. "Whoa! What's wrong? What did I say?"

Kali snorted at the glint in his eyes. "I don't have *any*," she said, emphasizing the next word. "*Fat* on my back."

A telltale shaking rumble ran through his chest as he wrapped his big arms around her – her fists tucked up tightly against his chest. With a voice thick with mischief, he added, "If you say so."

"I do," she mumbled, burrowing deeper in his arms. Only the pain dug in deeper, grabbed on tighter. "I don't need an ambulance."

"No, maybe not," he whispered, his cheek resting against her hair. "But I might."

"What?" she gasped, pulling free to pat his chest and shoulders. "Where? Did you get shot too? Where does it hurt?" Damn the stupid male psyche, always having to play the big strong role.

With a tug, he pulled her back more securely against him, cuddling her closer. "I'm not hurt. You are."

"But..." Kali stopped fighting to free herself, trying to understand.

"But nothing. I want *you* in an ambulance."

"Why?" She slugged him once more for good measure then collapsed against his chest.

"Ow. What was *that* for?" Grant asked.

"For making me worry."

Grant shook his head at her. "You're making me crazy."

Sirens sounded in the distance.

Pulling free, Kali ran her fingers through her hair to smooth it down. A wave of intense pain bent her over double. She crumpled to her knees. Shiloh whimpered, nudging her nose against Kali's hands. Gasping for breath, she rocked in place.

"Stay with me Kali. Focus on your breathing."

Kali heard him, only that irritating trickle deluged into a stream of wetness. She slapped her hand over the spot. As she pulled her hand away, blood dripped freely off her fingers. *Christ.* Her stomach revolted; she wavered. Digging deep, Kali struggled to remain conscious. Lord, she hurt. Grant's face appeared in front of her. His forehead creased with worry.

Kali drew a deep breath. "I'm okay. It's just blood." Attempting to reassure him, she patted his hand while ice trickled along her spine. Pausing, her hand mid-air, Kali cast a puzzled gaze at Grant. "Something's wrong."

Ice pooled in her tummy. Kali gazed at her belly. The warmth drained from her face, converting her cheeks to frost. Grant's face blurred. Kali opened her mouth. The words froze inside.

She pitched head-first toward the pavement.

"KALI!" GRANT CAUGHT her before she hit the ground, immediately checking for a heartbeat. It pulsed slow and steady. Several other men joined him. Shiloh twisted between them, getting in the way. Her nose pushing against Kali whenever she could reach her.

"Where's the damn ambulance?" The sirens screamed louder.

"They're here, Grant. Take it easy."

The ambulance peeled into the parking lot. Two men hopped from the vehicle. One ran toward them, the second one opened the rear doors of the ambulance and withdrew a gurney.

"Move aside, please. Sir, please stand aside."

"Grant." Thomas placed a heavy hand on Grant's shoulder. "Move buddy. These guys need to do their job."

As if shaking free of a mental hold, Grant allowed his friend to pull him back. It was obvious Shiloh was anxious as the men worked on Kali so Grant stepped forward and tugged her toward him. "Come on, girl. Sit over here with us." He crouched, stroking her beautiful coat. Finally, the overwrought dog calmed enough to lie down. He straightened to speak to Thomas. "There was such an odd look on her face when she collapsed."

"Shock."

"Maybe." The two men watched the EMTs work on Kali. Grant puzzled over the shooting. "It doesn't make any sense. There's no reason to have targeted her."

"How close were you to her at the time? Any chance you were the target?"

Grant closed his eyes, picturing Kali walking toward him with Shiloh at her side. God, he hoped not. He didn't want to live with that for the rest of his life. As he thought on it, he realized the direction had been wrong. With a decisive shake of his head, he said, "No, she was the target."

Thomas shoved his hands in his pockets. "I wonder if the killer is changing the game. Or maybe he wants to end it?"

Grant shook his head. "Doesn't feel right."

"Then what the hell is going on here?"

The EMTs already had Kali on the gurney and were loading her into the ambulance. Grant moved forward. Thomas placed a restraining hand on his arm.

Frowning, Grant pointed to the ambulance. "I should go with her."

"No. Two men are going with her to stand guard. We'll check on her in a bit. Give the doctors time to do their thing. The best thing you can do is bring this to an end."

The ambulance peeled away, sirens blaring, leaving a parking lot of law enforcement officers staring after it.

Darkness settled on Grant's face. "Let's go. We've got an asshole to catch."

Grant strode toward the entrance, Shiloh at his side and the rest of the men scrambling behind him.

At the door, Grant turned back for one last glimpse of the pool of blood drying in the early morning sun. Fury spiked through him. "I want this asshole caught. Today."

"We'll get him. Don't doubt it."

With jaw clenched, Grant gave a clipped nod before heading inside.

KALI MOANED AS she tried to shift her position.

"Damn, we're almost done. Just need another moment."

Metal clattered, weird sucking sounds and soft squishy noises penetrated Kali's conscious. Sharp pins stabbed her repeatedly. Dimly, words registered. They didn't make sense. Nothing did. So much pain. What had happened to her? Her back burned with pain, making her twist away. "Hurts."

A hand soothed her shoulder. The movement blended into the confusion of sounds and sensations.

"Easy, sweetie. We're done. It's going to be okay."

Kali moved again, desperate to stop the deep aching pain. Her mind fogged. Why was she here? What were they doing to her?

"Try to stay still."

"Nooo," she moaned in protest as something jabbed her again.

"Let's go, people. We're not quite done. Put her under so we can finish this. We can't let her tear out the stitches before we get this closed."

Bright lights flashed in strobe symmetry as Kali blinked rapidly. Stitches. Injured? Hospital? Kali struggled to make sense of the distorted words and images interspersed with the pain. Then none of it mattered. Clouds and soft white cotton batting closed in.

Sighing with relief, she drifted under.

GRANT PARKED BESIDE several other vehicles at the front of Second Chance. A couple people wandered the large lazy veranda and there were less dogs than he'd become accustomed to seeing here. Shiloh woofed deep in her throat.

"That's right. This is a second home for you, isn't it, girl?"

"It's a busy place. So how do you want to play this?" Thomas studied the layout of the center and its adjoining fields.

Grant wanted to throw his cover and let everyone know he was FBI and meant business, damn it. And that could cost someone else their life if the wrong person figured out we're closing the net on him. "I'd love to go pound heads and get answers, but—"

"But we can't. No one here knows about your FBI connection, at this point, and we need to keep it that way. I wonder if anyone noticed the cameras."

Grant opened his door, "And I wonder who's in charge while Dan and Kali are out of commission." Not that anyone here should have heard the news about Kali yet. Dan yes. Hell, this place would erupt when the news of Melanie and Julie trickled through. Another day. That's all they needed.

The two men exited the car and walked toward the fields. Two classes were going on in the yard. Grant recognized Sam working the left side of the field with a group of owners, their dogs at their sides. Sam was putting Colossus, a brindle-colored Great Dane through the paces. Grant checked the opposite end of the field. There, Caroline, her diminutive stature almost obscured by the attendees, demonstrated obedience training with her Jack Russell terrier. His admiration went up a notch. Anyone who successfully commanded a Jack Russell had skill.

Returning to the white clapboard center, they walked into the general lobby. Shiloh raced over to Maureen. She bent and cuddled Shiloh. "Grant, any news on Dan? The place has been crawling with cops but no one's talking."

Good. Grant responded to the question voiced and not the palpable curiosity in her voice. "He's doing better."

Joseph spoke from behind the two men. "That's great. Fresh coffee is dripping if you're wanting a cup."

Turning to watch the younger man approach, Grant said, "Great. I could use one. The day's been a little rough." And that was the truth. He'd caught a power nap earlier, but sheer adrenaline was keeping him going at the moment. Later he'd crash and burn but only after he had answers and knew Kali was safe.

"Were you two here this morning during all the chaos?"

"No. We teach on afternoons, evenings and weekends and drop in the odd time during the week," Joseph answered. Grant glanced over at Maureen, who nodded her agreement.

Walking over to the still-dripping coffeepot, Grant thieved a cup for himself. "Thomas here," Grant motioned in Thomas's direction, "is trying to identify a couple of men. Maybe you two can help."

Thomas obligingly held up the first picture they'd recovered from the new cameras installed at Second Chance.

Joseph piped up. "Jarl. Jarl…Blackburn. He's worked here since forever. I heard he just returned yesterday or the day before."

"Any idea from where?" Thomas wrote Jarl's name on the back of the picture.

"Oregon, I think. I heard he moved part of a graveyard or some such thing – for a church."

Thomas paused, pen in mid-air, a blank look on his face. "Uh?"

Maureen grinned. "Bizarre, huh? The longer you hang here, the more normal the bizarre becomes. The story I heard was the church lost a parcel of land when the area was surveyed for a new development. The land held old graves. However, some of the markers were gone, so Jarl located the bodies for removal and reburial on the new graveyard."

Grant raised an eyebrow. "He can do that?"

"Jarl specializes in it."

How did that fit into his investigation? They'd have to confirm the dates, but it sounded like the timing, if what Maureen said were true, gave him an alibi for the early kidnappings and murders. So many of these people were experts at digging and burying bodies. Kinda creepy.

Thomas spoke up. "Do you know how we can reach him by any chance?"

Joseph stepped up to answer. "He'll be on the contact list in the office." He motioned toward the hallway heading to the offices. "If you can't find it, contact Kali. She'll know where it is."

Figures. Neither Dan nor Kali were in a position to help.

Holding up the second image, the sketch Kali had done at the police station, Thomas asked, "What about this guy?"

Maureen frowned. "I've seen him but don't know his name. I think he's one of Brad's friends."

Thomas adjusted the angle of the sketch so Joseph could get a better look. He studied it for a moment, then shrugged. "No. I'm not sure I've ever seen him."

"No problem. Thanks for helping us identify the first one."

"Anyone else here have access to the office?" Thomas studied the almost-empty center. "Someone who might be here now so we don't have to disturb Kali?"

The two instructors exchanged frowns. "I don't know. Those two run the place. A couple of us have keys but only to this common area and the bathrooms, not the offices."

Grant exchanged a glance with Thomas. "Okay, I'll ask Kali. Thanks for the help."

Thomas and Grant reached Kali's office a moment later. Reaching out, Grant tested the knob. Locked. Pulling out his pick from his wallet, Grant opened the door in seconds. Glancing at Thomas first, he stepped inside.

The room appeared normal, untouched.

Grant walked to the far side of her desk and booted up her computer. While they waited for it to load, both of them perused her desk, drawers and bookshelves. Unlike Dan, Kali's workspace was sparse and clean. Cold.

"Hardly looks lived in."

"Kali mentioned she didn't come in often, but when she did she mostly worked."

"Obviously." Thomas paced the small room, checking for anything of interest.

The computer requested a log-in and password. Grant frowned, sat down and entered several possible log-ins. None of them worked.

"No luck here."

"Head to the hospital and Kali?" Thomas asked.

Grant sighed and rubbed his eyes. His cell phone said four o'clock. Time to try the hospital again, for at least the fifth time that day.

This time, Grant reached the nurses' station and as luck would have it, the doctor. "Hi, Dr. Sanderson. Have you an update on Kali Jordan? The shooting victim from the police parking lot this morning?"

"Jordan? Oh, right. That's one lucky lady." The doctor coughed several times, clearing his throat.

Grant waited for him. "How's she doing?"

"I've put in close to thirty stitches. The bullet's path scored the trapezoid and triceps muscles. The skin will take the longest to heal, however everything's been repaired. Time will heal the rest."

"That's good news." He straightened as the load of worry slipped off his shoulders.

"Yes. If that bullet had gone in at a slightly different angle, she'd likely be dead."

"I understand." Grant didn't dare dwell on what-ifs. "Is she awake? Can I speak with her?"

"Maybe in an hour or so."

Grant finished the call to update Thomas. "She's still under. We won't be able to talk to her for a bit."

"Then let's try to identify this second man, then find Jarl."

CHAPTER 21

"HEY?"

Kali turned her head, rising up slightly onto her arms so she could see him. Lying on her stomach gave her a limited view. "Grant?"

His footsteps sounded first, then the sound of him moving a chair up to the front of the bed. He added a second one.

She twisted for another look, only the second person stood just out of view.

"Don't try to move, Kali. I brought Stefan."

"What?" Great, she couldn't even turn to sit properly. At least she wore a gown, though her back lay exposed, the blankets covering her lower half. She'd been so looking forward to seeing Stefan, again. She must look awful.

She swallowed hard before saying as nonchalantly as she could, "I'd say hello except it's a little hard to see you. Grant, can you give me a hand, please?"

Grant's strong arms grabbed her below the ribs and he lifted her free of both bed and bedding.

Kali shrieked as the world spun in a chaotic movement before righting itself. She snagged the blankets to cover herself as she settled down in a sitting position. "Unorthodox, but effective." She smiled up at him. "Thanks."

Arranging herself cross-legged on top of the bed, she looked up and lost her breath again. "Good Lord, I'd forgotten. You're too gorgeous to wander loose, Stefan," she exclaimed. Satan's angel stared at her, a barest smile casting a wicked glint to features already too stunning to assimilate.

His grin widened, his eyes flashing with appreciative humor. "And why would you say that?"

That made her sniff in disgust. "My mom didn't raise any idiots. And my dad would've bought a shotgun after meeting you."

Stefan laughed outright. "I'd have liked them both. My face was a gift from God. My heart and soul are my own. We're obligated to do all we can to be the best that we can be."

Grant stretched his long legs out in front of his chair, drawing attention to his presence. "How profound."

With a quick glance at Stefan, Kali turned her attention on Grant. "Must be tough to watch the women fall all over your friend, huh?"

His eyebrows beetled together as he studied her. "Sometimes. How are you doing, Kali?"

The subject change gave her pause. Maybe her words had struck home. Tucking the information away for later, she answered, "Fine. I'm learning a new appreciation for drugs." She couldn't resist asking, "Did you two come to bust me out? And how's Shiloh?"

"You'll leave when the doctor says so and not a moment earlier. And Shiloh is doing just fine. I'll bring her when I pick you up – later."

Her face fell. "Bully," she teased gently, remembering how concerned he'd been this morning. Realizing she was staring, she glanced over at Stefan to find he'd been watching their byplay. Heat washed over her cheeks. He already knew where her heart lay. Stefan's looks might blindside initially, but it was Grant who made her heart jump.

Grant's stoic voice interrupted her thoughts. "So, who's Jarl?"

She refocused on his question. "He's a big hearted goof who volunteers at the center when he's not out relocating grave sites."

"A big goof?"

"Yeah. In a good way."

"Dangerous?"

Kali frowned. Why was he asking that? What did he suspect? And was Jarl dangerous? She pondered what she knew of him. "Personally, I believe anyone is dangerous given the right circumstances. Jarl loves very strongly and I would imagine he hates just as strongly."

Stefan nodded, a curious approving light in his eyes. "As do many people."

This time Grant made no attempt to hide his exasperation. "We'd like to talk to him."

"Then do so," Kali responded lightly. "He lives a couple of blocks from the center."

"Where?" Grant pulled out his notebook, tugging a pen free from his shirt pocket.

"I've driven him home several times. Let me think." Kali mentally traced the trip. "Turn left as you leave the parking lot. Jarl's house is two blocks ahead. I don't remember the number. It's a two-story, cedar shingled bungalow hidden behind a six-foot plus high cedar hedge along the front."

"Any idea if he's struggling with any particular problems lately?"

"Not that he's shared. I know he's happily married with two full-grown sons."

"Money problems?"

"I don't know." Kali shrugged, then hissed in pain. "Stupid move." She gasped.

Grant leaned forward, concerned. "Do you need a nurse?"

"Hell, no." Kali breathed deep, then exhaled slowly.

With a frown, Grant sat back, sending a quick questioning glance at Stefan. "That sounded emphatic."

Stefan never moved, except for the knowing grin on his face. He appeared content to watch and listen.

Kali twisted her lips. "Nurses poke and prod and do nasty stuff. I'll skip it, thanks." Kali studied Stefan who studied Grant, a smirk on his face. Puzzled, Kali's gaze bounced between them.

Understanding struck. Grant was jealous! And Stefan knew it. Okay, she was dense. Had to be the damned drugs.

Her lips twitched at his male stupidity.

Grant kept the conversation on track. "Okay, so there's no financial or family problems that you know about? What about competitiveness? Does he like to be the top dog?"

It seemed impossible to imagine Jarl in that type of role. She shook her head. "I don't believe he does. I've never seen any sign of that. He teaches a lot and is well loved – has a great sense of humor, but...I'm not always sure what's going on inside. He's very private."

Grant scratched down notes while Kali watched curiously. "Why the interest? Surely you don't think he's a suspect?"

"The cameras shot him trying to access your office."

"So? That means nothing. It's *the* office, not my office. Dan could have asked him to go in and get something or do some work on that computer. Anything's possible."

"Only Dan lay unconscious in his office at the time we've

clocked Jarl's entrance attempt into your office."

"Maybe Dan asked him before he was injured? Jarl was at the center before we found Dan."

"What? He was?" Grant lifted his gaze to stare at her in surprise.

"Yes, I remember giving him a big hug. He'd been away for several days."

"I need to get into your computer."

"There's nothing worthwhile on my account but you're welcome to my login." Kali rattled it off.

"That's not very sophisticated." Grant glared at the number and letter combination on his notebook, his voice sharp. "You need a more complex password than that."

"Why?" she asked reasonably. "Apparently, even the difficult ones are hackable within hours anyway." What could Jarl want in her office? The shelves held a selection of books, and her desk held the financial files for the center. Then again…"

Straightening, she added abruptly. "My computer is the server."

Grant leaned forward. "What? Why your computer?"

"The budget didn't allow for a standalone server and Dan continually crashes his."

"So you use the server instead? That's not smart."

Kali grimaced, barely withholding a shrug. Since lying in the hospital bed, she'd realized how that one simple movement dominated her expressions. Maybe the injury had a benefit after all. She realized Grant was waiting for a response. "Dan's motto is 'do whatever works.' Speaking of Dan, how is he?"

"Still unconscious but stable. The bleeding has stopped altogether."

"And Julie," she whispered, petrified to hear the answer. "Any progress?"

"We're on it, Kali. The FBI does function even without you." Grant's voice was even…almost too even.

Kali shifted, her butt noticing the long stretch in that position. "Sorry, where's Shiloh?"

"I drove her and your Jeep home, then came here with Stefan. I'll head over there and feed her in a bit."

His words pinched. Shiloh was hers. She'd been the only one to feed her – ever. Stupid. She should be grateful that Grant was capable of caring for her.

"Grant." Kali stopped.

"What?"

"If you're going to my house anyway, would you mind bringing my art stuff?"

Stefan sat up. He and Grant exchanged glances. "Are you picking up on something?" Grant asked, hopefully.

Not wanting to get his hopes up, she compromised. "I'm not sure. My dreams…wow! But the drugs are problematic. Are they putting the pictures in or have they opened my mind up further?"

"It could be either or both," Stefan said, his liquid voice soothing her doubts. "We'll get you a sketchbook. You get the images down and then we can take a look. When your mind is overwhelmed with images it's hard to separate real from imaginary."

"Exactly." She stared at him in delight. He understood. Stefan smiled as they shared a conspiratorial look. Flashing Grant a look, Kali found his gaze narrowed on them both. She rolled her eyes.

"We'll head there now." Pushing his chair back, Grant stood, prepared to leave. At the end of the bed he stopped. "I have to ask, are these images related to Julie?"

Stefan had reached the door, but at the question he stopped to hear her answer.

"I can't be certain until I've drawn it," Kali said soberly. "Maybe."

"Back in forty minutes." He started for the door.

Stefan winked at her before walking out of the room.

"Grant."

Almost at the door, he pivoted and raised one eyebrow in question.

Crooking her finger, she motioned him closer. When he stood at her bedside, she reached up and tugged him to her level. Staring him in the eye, she said, "Your friend *is* gorgeous. That does not mean I'm nuts over him. Okay?"

A fine flush worked over his face, highlighting his strong features. "Ouch. I'm that obvious?"

"I understand, really I do. I'm sure women fall all over him. However, and get this straight, I am not other women."

His eyes warmed. Grant bent and dropped a kiss on her forehead. "I'll be back soon."

Kali listened as his footsteps faded away. Time for help. She reached for the call button.

A nurse arrived within minutes. "How's the pain, dearie?"

"Liveable. But I have to go to the bathroom."

"Good." With efficient practice, the nurse pulled the blanket back and tucked it over the bed. "Now, on your feet and let's see how steady you are."

A disappointing try, as Kali wasn't as steady as she'd hoped. Eventually, Kali wove her way back to her bed with the nurse's help. Then, bone-weary exhaustion invaded her limbs.

The bed loomed in front of them. Three full steps and a baby one. Climbing up onto the bed, she collapsed onto her belly, then buried her face in the pillow. Oh Christ, she hurt. Flames burned along her shoulders, tremors vibrated along her limbs. There'd be no more lifting her head. "Ohhh," she moaned against the crackling hospital pillow.

"Painkillers?"

Kali twisted her head sideways. "No, thanks. Do you know when I can leave?"

"Nope, but I can tell you going to the bathroom on your own is a definite requisite."

"Right. Failed that one." Kali closed her eyes and waited for her breathing to calm down.

She woke up an hour later and felt so much better; it was hard to understand how that was possible. Had she missed Grant? She frowned, searching her room. There was no sign of her sketchbook. A hospital tray waited for her with a large metal dome hiding its contents.

Kali pushed herself up and attempted to sit sideways on the bed. Awkward, ungainly and painful, but it worked. Kali sighed with relief as she settled into a more comfortable sitting position, her legs swinging over the bed. The blankets reached the floor when she tucked them around her lower body. The over-the-bed table was accessible too. Perfect.

The largest of the plastic domes held a bowl of tomato soup and a grilled cheese sandwich. Cold and greasy. Kali shuddered, dropping the lid. A small salad and a bowl of Jell-O or possibly plastic, wobbled in a small bowl at the back. Well, that wasn't happening.

Depressed and hungry, she was trying to shift back onto the bed when Grant walked in, sketchbook in hand.

"It's good to see you moving about."

Kali glowered. "You may enter if you brought real coffee; can't say a muffin or sandwich would go amiss either. It's supposed to be dinner time, but the meal here can't be classified as food. No Stefan?"

His lips quirked, his gaze switching from the tray to her. His eyes lit with amusement. "Stefan will stop by later, if he can. Here's your sketchbook and pencils, and I'll find you something to eat." He dumped his armload on the bed, dropped a quick kiss on her cheek and left.

Kali stared after him, shock rippling along her spine, her fingers pressed against the ghost of his kiss. He was getting very comfortable with those. She kinda liked it.

To take her mind off her hunger and Grant's behavior, Kali opened her sketchbook to a clean page. Julie had been missing for a full day now. Depending on her condition and the amount of oxygen available, her time was running out. Kali's thoughts turned dark and dreary. Depressed, she worried about how to end this mess. Her mind flipped from one possibility to another as she doodled. What if she went on TV and publicly admitted this killer had her beat hands down? It wasn't as if her ego cared. His ego needed the satisfaction. TV? Newspapers? Radio? Hmmm. She would mention it to Grant. Kali's hand moved aimlessly as her mind pondered the problems.

"That's a face to photograph and me without my camera."

Kali looked up as Grant entered the room carrying two take-out coffees and a paper bag.

"Oh yeah, food and coffee." Kali threw her sketchbook to one side and tossed her pencil on top. "The table is cleared and ready." She shifted, to sit over the edge again, taking her blanket with her. "What did you bring?"

Her mouth salivated at the rich aromas wafting from the bag. She opened it then pulled out two warm oversized muffins and below it, a small container of fruit salad followed by two large Kaiser bun sandwiches. "Perfect. Thank you." She broke off a piece of the muffin and popped it into her mouth. The banana nut flavor filled her mouth. She closed her eyes and moaned with pleasure. After several more bites and a long sip of her fresh coffee, Kali knew she'd survive. She turned her attention to Grant.

"Bring me up-to-date on the progress with the case. Did you talk to Jarl?" In-between mouthfuls, Kali listened, but her hope quickly sank to despair. For all the legwork, phone work and man-hours, they hadn't found much. No idea who'd shot her. No sign of Jarl. And no leads on locating Julie.

Not great dinner conversation. Pushing the table away, she leaned back and massaged her belly. "Okay. I'll survive a little longer. What about the police sketch, any luck identifying it?"

"Your sketch you mean?" Grant dropped his muffin wrapper to the table then reached for one of the two sandwiches he'd brought.

"Nope, the credit goes to the police artist. Her skill dragged the information out of Brenda. I translated the answers to paper."

"So did the police artist, but your picture hit the mark. We showed it to several people at the center and he's been tentatively ID'd as Christian LeFleure. No one seems to know much about him. The team is running a background check on him."

Kali tilted her head. "Christian. Hmmm. Sounds familiar but I can't place him. Dan will know him. We can ask him when he wakes up." A yawn worked up from deep inside. The warm food and drink, not to mention the drugs, were making her sleepy.

"Mind if I go through your sketchbook again?"

Kali glanced to the book at the end of the bed. "I did a bit of doodling while you were gone, but not much." Shifting slightly, she stretched out on her left side, tugging the blanket up to her shoulder. With the pillow crunching under her head, Kali felt lethargy take over. "I need to close my eyes for a just a moment," she murmured.

With eyes drooping closed, she watched as Grant picked up her sketchbook and started flicking through the pages. Snuggling deeper, she drifted off to sleep.

KALI'S 'DOODLE' SOCKED Grant in the gut. It also didn't make sense. He turned it sideways and still couldn't get the clarity he needed. "Kali? What's—" Catching sight of her, he smiled gently.

She slept, sprawled like a child, her breathing slow and regular. One blanket rested precariously on her shoulders with a second crumpled at her feet. Grant lay down the sketchbook, stepped over and pulled the second blanket over her prone body. Walking to the other side, he straightened the gown up to her shoulders. The gauze bandage gaped, showing the string of black stitches surrounded by red puffy tissue.

"Shit." Grant whispered softly, his heart aching at the damage. The good doctor had spoken true. She was damn lucky.

His gaze dropped to her sketch.

Kali had incredible talents, whether she believed it or not. Both as a psychic and an artist. Sitting again, he took his time to study the two sketches. The first one of Julie that had led them to David and he presumed the second was of her as well, but he didn't know that.

They needed something useful, landmarks, terrain – to lead them to her location.

Frustrated, he studied the sketch. The close-up showed only the underground hell with little to no above ground markings. He had the weird sense of missing something important. "Damn it. What's the missing link? Where the hell are you, Julie?"

"She's there."

Grant turned to face Kali. "Did I wake you? Sorry."

Kali's soft voice had an odd flatness to it. "Julie's so scared."

Grant studied her face. She appeared half asleep, half awake. Studying her face, he whispered, "Kali? Do you know the location in your sketch? It looks odd and I can't quite figure it out."

"What sketch?" she murmured, her eyes still closed.

"Kali, this is important. Open your eyes." Grant leaned closer, holding the sketchbook above her face.

She blinked several times, struggling to focus. With a big yawn, she shifted slightly and looked at the picture in front of her. "That's an underground stream."

"Underground stream? Huh?" Grant stared at the picture. With her explanation, he could identify the lines depicting water a distance beneath the body.

"Roystan Park. It's well known for the underground stream running through the length of it. Julie has to be at Roystan Park."

Grant wasn't familiar with the area, had never been to the park and knew nothing about underground streams. One thing he did understand, underground waterways like above-ground ones usually ran for miles. "That's a lot of territory to cover, Kali. Can you narrow it further?"

Kali didn't answer, her eyes drifted closed. She needed her rest, but he needed answers and Julie needed help.

He sharpened his voice. "Kali."

"What?" she answered, her voice groggy, her eyes flickering open briefly.

"Where on the underground stream is Julie?"

"Look at the tree from the first picture. There's a recently disturbed hill."

Snatching up the sketchbook, Grant flipped to the first Julie picture. The first picture showed a unique tree. Christ. "I need to borrow your sketch book, Kali. I need to copy these pictures."

Kali yawned, her eyes drooping closed. "Nurses' station."

"Back in a minute." Grant bent over, dropped a hard kiss on her forehead, only to hear her slow even breathing. She was asleep.

CHAPTER 22

KALI SHIFTED HER position gently, wincing at the tugs on her shoulders and spine. Hospital beds weren't comfy to begin with but for the injured, they really sucked. Opening her eyes, she watched the shadows stretch across the room. She yawned. The afternoon had long disappeared. With a sense of relaxation permeating her soul, Kali realized despite all the aches and soreness, she felt better. Less like she'd been hit by a bus.

The table and her sketchbook, slid into focus. Tidbits of conversation with Grant came back to her. Her curiosity spiked.

Shuffling upright, she stretched out a hand for the pad, flipping to the last picture she'd done. Bold, stark lines stared at her. What had she said? Roystan Park. Kali bolted upright, moaning from pain at the sudden movement. Damn it. Then she caught sight of her cell phone. Her pain forgotten, she reached for it. Yeah, connected again. She dialed Grant's number.

"Why aren't you asleep?" he growled.

"Hi, how are you doing? Nice of you to call," she said, her voice snapping in irritation. She threw back the blankets.

"Sorry, how nice of you to call. Niceties done, why the hell aren't you asleep?"

Kali slid off the side of the bed and walked over to the window. "Because I woke up. Cut the attitude and tell me what's going on. I remember something about Roystan Park."

"That's where we are right now."

"Good, what handlers have you called in?"

Silence filled the phone.

Kali's heart sank and she closed her eyes. "You didn't call any, did you?" Kali couldn't believe it. "Jesus, Grant. You need a canine team and preferably more than one. You'll never find her otherwise."

"I didn't know who to trust," he said, simply.

She paused and closed her eyes in acquiescence. What a nightmare.

"There are forty men here. I'll call you when we find her. Bye."

Frustrated, Kali stared at the dead phone in her hand. He was wrong to believe men, regardless of how many, made up for a canine unit. She lived that world. She understood just what these dogs could do. Yet, he was also right. Who could they trust? She doubted everyone, and no longer trusted those she knew.

Who could help?

Shiloh. And therefore Kali.

Grant would never let her…if he knew. But…was she capable of going out and searching? If she couldn't physically do the job, she'd slow them down – or worse, take valuable man-hours away from the search for Julie. Testing, she rolled her shoulders. A few tugs and a few pulls – and actually it wasn't that bad. Okay, she was lying. Still she felt so much better than she expected. Amazing what a paradigm shift could do.

Encouraged, Kali considered the situation. Julie needed her help. She was out of time. They had a potential location, and all the stops needed to be pulled to make the most of the next few hours.

Kali?

She stilled. Spun around. The room was empty.

Kali, it's Stefan.

"Stefan," she whispered. "Where are you?"

Warm laughter filled her mind. *At home.*

She smiled. *Damn. You're good.*

The same laughter wafted throughout the room. *So are you.*

He was speaking in her mind. And she was answering. A mess of questions rose to the surface, but even the concept of telepathic communication seemed too much right now. She shook her head. *Later. Right now. I have to help Julie. I need to search for her.*

Interesting. Why can't Grant's team handle it?

She needed him to understand. *He hasn't got a SAR dog! Shiloh and I easily replace forty men.*

A deep hum filled the air. Kali turned around slowly, finally laughing as she realized what it was. Stefan…thinking.

"I *have* to go." If heavy painkillers worked and allowed her to function at a safe level, she might pull this off. If she fell and ripped her stitches…well, better to not go there.

Definitely don't go there. I'll help. We will find her.

Kali walked experimentally around the room then attempted to twist and bend slightly one way and then another. Painful, but not agonizing – sore yet doable. She could do this. First, she needed to get the hell home, grab Shiloh and head to the park. Ticking off her mental to-do list, she didn't see any of it happening short of an hour. That meant starting her search and in the dusky light. Damn.

"What are you doing out of bed, Kali? I know you didn't want to stay overnight, but it is for your own good."

Kali smiled with relief. Her doctor had perfect timing. Quickly, she explained what she needed and gave a brief explanation why.

He frowned and shook his head.

She interjected before he could refuse her. "I know this isn't your recommendation. I understand this is a really bad idea. Except a woman is dying. I have to find her."

Thankfully, her doctor had dealt with survivors of several local disasters. His frown deepened and he pursed his lips. "Why can't someone else go?"

"Everyone who can – is. I understand the damage I could cause again, however, the bottom line is that even if I rip out the stitches, the damage won't kill me. If I stay here, Julie will die."

"Overdramatizing, aren't you?"

"No," Kali said softly, sadly. "Julie is out of time. We have to find her soon."

The doctor studied her face then made a decision. "Get dressed and come down to the nurses' station. I'll give you something for now. When you finish tonight, you're to return here. Not home, not the boyfriend's house, but here. Agreed?"

When she didn't answer immediately, he added, "That's the condition. Take it or leave it."

"I'll take it. I'll meet you at the station in five minutes." Kali turned away, opening up the locker at the far wall, searching for her clothes. The cargo pants, although blood stained, were serviceable. She pulled on what clothes she found, realizing belatedly she had no shirt and there was no sign of her sweater. Damn it. The doctor must have cut it off when she'd been brought in.

A nurse walked in. "I guess you don't need my help getting dressed. You've done just fine."

"I'm okay so far, but I can't find a shirt or my sweater. I'm presuming they were destroyed?"

The nurse walked over to look in the locker. "Possibly. But there's a pile of clothes in the Lost and Found. Give me a moment."

What a relief. Kali hadn't relished the idea of walking out topless. There was no way she was going to attempt to wear a bra. In the small bathroom, she washed up and ran her fingers through her hair. Dried blood clung to the ends. More blood dotted her arms and chest. Using the washcloth, she did a quick wipe, removing the worst of the mess. The pain made her shudder, yet it was the change in awareness that made it possible. Knowing Stefan was there, helping, made her stronger. She paused…or was he? She couldn't sense his presence any longer.

"Here. Try these on."

The same nurse held out a black tee shirt and a hoodie in royal blue. Perfect. The nurse dressed her as if Kali were a two-year-old with her arms in front sliding the tee shirt close to her chest before slipping it over her head. "Let's wait until the doctor gives you a shot, then put the hoodie on."

Then Kali tackled her shoes, a much harder proposition. Biting her tongue, she finally finished and stood up again. "Okay, let's go."

She walked out of her room.

And came face to face with a guard – one of Grant's men. Easily, six-foot-four, with steely eyes and linebacker build, he didn't look like compromise was in his dictionary. He raised one eyebrow and stared down at her.

"Oh shit."

The eyebrow went higher.

She sighed, and considered. "It would be so much easier if you overheard my conversation with my doctor." She waited a beat. "Did you?"

He nodded his head.

"Oh thank heavens. Sooo, I'm hoping, that like the good doctor, you'll understand? I have to do this? A woman's life is at stake?"

Again silence, then a clipped nod.

Were all Grant's men so taciturn? She brightened. "Then you'll let me go?"

"Yes. But I'm going with you."

She brightened. "Actually, I'd be pleased to have you. But…I can't have you telling Grant. He's not going to let me go or allow you to let me go."

The guard narrowed his gaze as he stared down at her and sifted through her words.

"I have to do this. Julie's dying. I might be able to save her."

One final clipped nod of that closely shaved head and relief flooded through her. "First stop is home to collect Shiloh, my SAR dog. Then to the site. We're out of time."

She raced to the nurses' station, where she signed papers and waited for the doctor. The guard, Scott – she'd managed to drag his name out of him – drove. She leaned forward but every bump in the road jostled her spine and threw her backwards. At her house, she headed inside where Shiloh waited, wiggling in excitement.

"Hello, sweetheart. Did you miss me? I'd love to cuddle, but we need to go to work." Kali walked into the kitchen and filled her pockets with granola bars and energy drinks. Water bottles had to be filled, dog bones collected and, what else? Another five minutes and Kali decided they were ready to go. Flashlights, rescue bag, snacks, drinks, warm vest and a blanket for Shiloh. At the last minute, Kali snatched up Shiloh's teddy bear. Shiloh understood and waited at the door.

You had to love a dog that gave her all, no matter where or when.

Stefan? No answer. *Stefan?*

Still no luck. Neither could she still feel his presence. As long as he showed up when she needed him…

Scott backed out of the driveway and headed in the direction of Roystan Park. Kali had to push her seat to the furthest setting and sit on the edge to avoid hitting her sore back with every bump. Chewing on her lip, she wondered how much ground Grant had covered. Then she snorted and laughed a little grimly. It didn't matter. She'd have to go over the same miles to confirm they hadn't missed Julie. Shiloh could pick up a human scent within a quarter of a mile and track it forward.

"Have you any idea where they are in the park, Scott?"

He shook his head. "Haven't had an update."

Kali called Grant. "So?" she asked. "Any news?"

"No, nothing yet. But it's early yet."

"How many miles do you think you have to cover?" Kali pointed and Scott turned the Jeep to the right. It should take her another five minutes to reach Roystan Park.

"About ten. The hydrogeologist gave us a map of the underground creek. It's on the west side of the park, running parallel to the back fence."

Her heart sank. Ten. That was likely more than she could do.

"What do I hear?"

Kali heard the frown in his voice and lied without a qualm. "The nurse's trolley is coming."

"Oh. You rest and heal. I promise I'll call if I hear anything."

"Okay. I'll talk to you later." Kali clicked off before he had time to ask questions.

Shiloh knew the park relatively well, as they'd spent many a happy day roaming the area, although, Kali didn't remember seeing a fence along the back. By the time they pulled into the parking lot, they'd already driven in several miles. The kidnapper could use the access roads to go wherever he wanted to, but she couldn't take the chance of missing Julie. She'd start this search in an orderly fashion. There were a couple of FBI vehicles in the parking lot; she could only presume the rest were using the service roads. There should be a dozen vehicles here.

"Scott, I'm going cross country." As she went to give him instructions, a group of FBI came out of the woods, powerful lights shining in eerie patterns in the sky. She needed to be gone before they saw her.

"Scott, grab the others and come behind me. You should be able to see my light easily to catch up. I'm going up this fence line." She pointed it out to him.

Unloading what she needed, Kali clipped Shiloh onto her lead and headed off, the adrenaline pumping, giving her a shot of energy. Feeling good and feeling strong, she let her body settle into a steady stride.

He'd said the underground creek surfaced south of here. The park was a huge rough rectangle but the entrance led to the parking lot in the center of the park. Left and right were the options. The left would offer an easier route with a slight downhill slope, but the creek traveled closer to the surface if she headed right.

Shiloh would decide.

"Shiloh. Go look. Let's find Julie."

Shiloh barked once, looked at Kali then took off left.

Of course. Right would have been the easy answer.

THE WIND HAD picked up, causing a brutal chill. The sun had long gone. It was the middle of summer and Grant couldn't believe he was zipping up a fleece vest and feeling cold.

Blame it on Roystan Park. Heavily wooded, neither sun nor heat reached deep or stayed for long.

He checked his section of the map again. The geologist had showed him which side of the park to search and the approximate width of the long strip that held the most potential. He'd broken the men into several teams and each had taken an area.

Kali had to be upset at missing this but she'd been through too much already. With any luck, they'd find Julie soon. If luck was on their side she'd be alive. What were the chances? Grimly, he returned his attention to the long red strip on the map in his hands. They'd be lucky to cover half this area tonight. Forty men weren't enough.

"Hey, Grant. Let's get these men moving."

Grant passed over the spare sheets in his hands. "Here are the maps. Let's go."

The hard work began.

THE COLD HAD settled deep under her skin. Julie hated the endless dark. Exhaustion had set in. Not enough, though. Her body still screamed with pain from the unnatural position every time she twitched.

How much longer? Surely, someone would notice the pipe in the ground soon. She wasn't done yet. That bastard could gloat all he wanted but she wouldn't give him the satisfaction of dying in this underground hell. She fanned the faint flames of anger. It kept her warm at night. Endurance had stepped in. Replaying memories of happy times kept her mind busy, which helped but reminded her of those people already gone from this world.

And that she might join them this night.

She was so cold. A part of her was ready to die.

Kali and Shiloh, Dan, all those SAR specialists probably didn't know she was even missing. How ironic. She'd been pissed at them for entering her home before and now she could only hope they were still concerned enough to check on her again.

Typical. You never knew the value of your friends until it was too late. Or the value of law enforcement; she hadn't even been nice to the guard waiting for her at home. She booted him out so fast.

She was a fool.

Closing her eyes, she twitched slightly. Nerve endings jumped to life like a thousand hot needles throughout her body. Julie spit the grime from her mouth but couldn't do anything about the hot tears streaming in rivers down her cheeks. Who'd have thought she'd end up like this – again?

She'd been saved once before. What were the odds of being saved a second time?

Kali, where are you?

CHAPTER 23

KALI THOUGHT SHE caught a faint voice on the wind. Not likely, but she picked up speed, giving Shiloh a long lead. She couldn't afford to slow the pace or allow Shiloh to take off. Whatever the doctor had given her allowed her to maintain a strong steady pace. Kali didn't want to sprint in her condition, if not required. Who knew when the shot would wear off?

Or when Stefan would show up?

She figured Scott would be behind her, possibly with one or more of the other men, but the pace had been brutal so far and the night was far from over. She couldn't waste time looking for him. He should be able to follow her light and catch up.

The twilight resembled a gray fog, blurring light and dark. Not a street lamp in sight. No, this wilderness park deserved its name. It housed many long-lived species of trees and plants. The tree canopy was full and heavily covered in green leaves, leaving the moonlight to illuminate pathways to the under layer. It was also cold.

Kali kept an ear tuned for Grant's group as she raced thirty feet along the fence. Gratefully, the stuff the doctor had given her hadn't smothered her other senses. The tingle at the back of her neck stirred, keeping her focused and moving forward.

Thank heavens for commercial flashlights. Hers scanned the woods in a continuous movement, adding a weird glow to the night. Nothing like adding gloomy and creepy to kidnapping and murder. Kali shook her head, throwing off the ugly vibes with determined effort. Julie. She needed to find Julie. Nothing else mattered.

As the miles churned under her feet, Kali searched for landmarks, anything that twigged. There were lots of flat heavily treed areas that wouldn't take kindly to digging. A sinking knot settled into her stomach. She faced a huge job, especially in the dark. Scott should be just behind her. This park was massive. People were known to get lost here for days. Tonight, Shiloh's skills came into play, with Kali's as the handler. As she moved through the bush, her mind locked on her weird skills. She'd yet to take the time to study them. She'd always assumed they happened naturally. Lately, though, natural had become wild and weird. It confused, terrified and if she were honest, delighted her on some level. Since she met Stefan she realized that she might learn to control her skills. Skills that had helped them find David and Melanie. Now if only she could find Julie…alive.

"Shiloh, how are you doing?" Kali found comfort to hear the sound of her voice. "Being alone out here is unusual, isn't it? Normally, we're surrounded by people." Although Scott should be here soon.

Shiloh ran toward Kali to say 'hi.' Her ear twitched as she accepted a caress then took she off again, her nose to the ground, her lead stretching a solid ten feet in front. Kali walked faster to narrow the distance between them, but then with the slack in the lead, Shiloh pulled forward.

"Take it easy, girl. We need to conserve energy."

Shiloh ignored her and ran ahead. Kali caught the same sense of urgency and quickly ran up to her, using the powerful light of the flashlight to shine their way. A wind picked up, filling the woods with a chill and odd sounds of dry leaves rustling. Kali pulled the zipper of her multi-pocketed vest up to her neck. The shiver that overcame her was a sign of her lowered health. The doctor's stuff wouldn't sustain her for long at this rate. Kali hunkered deeper in her vest.

The moon peeked out behind the clouds for a brief moment, illuminating the eerie darkness. Branches cast villains and bushes whispered dire warnings. Kali hurried to stay close behind Shiloh. Her watch illuminated the time. An hour had passed. One hour and she'd already reached the cold sweat stage.

Kali's cell phone rang. She jumped at the noise.

"Hello."

"Kali?"

"Hi, Grant." Kali closed her eyes, caught off guard. She struggled to regulate her heavy breathing. Shiloh tugged her forward, forcing Kali to quickly juggle flashlight, lead and cell phone. She shuffled the flashlight to her left hand and picked up her pace.

"Are you okay? Your voice is…shaking?"

"I'm fine, tired maybe." Just a little. "How's the search going?"

"It's in progress. It's weird though, one of the teams thought they saw someone else out here at the same time?"

Kali spun around, searching the woods, expecting someone to burst through the trees at any moment. Had she been spotted? An agent would have approached her, surely? Refusing to be deterred, she plowed forward.

"Kali, what do I hear?"

"What?" Kali glanced at her phone. "What do you hear?"

"You're at the hospital, aren't you?" he questioned, his voice rising. "Those noises make it sound like you're running? Puffing with exertion?" Kali couldn't stop the wince at the aggressive accusation in his voice. He didn't know the half of it.

"Uhmmm," she hedged.

"Kali, where the hell are you?" His voice rose in accusation.

The shit was about to hit the fan. She sighed heavily, and confessed. "I'm probably a couple of miles behind you."

"What?" His roar ripped through the night.

Shiloh whined. Kali slapped her thigh, calling Shiloh over. "It's okay, Shiloh. Everything's fine."

"Like hell it's fine." Grants voice roared his concern. "You're supposed to be in the hospital. God damn it, Kali."

This time, Shiloh barked at the voice thundering through her cell phone.

"Stop it. You're upsetting Shiloh."

Grant sputtered. "I'm upsetting the dog? What about me? What about how upset I am?"

"Get over it," she snapped. "I'm cold and tired and don't want to be out here." Kali shivered in the cool air. She wanted to be in her bed. Julie wanted the same thing and she deserved to have it. Kali wouldn't quit.

"Then don't try; turn around." The phone line crackled with bits of conversation trickling through from Grant's side. "Go home."

"I'd love to," she said, letting her irritation grow. It helped dispel the fatigue. "Except this isn't about you or me. This is about Julie. And I didn't come alone. I brought Scott, the guard from the hospital…except he was supposed to grab another group of men and catch up…only they haven't yet."

"Shit. There are forty good men here."

Kali shook her head, interrupting, "And not one dog team.

Shiloh's sense of smell beats your forty men in a heartbeat. And then there's me."

"Where are you?"

"I'm searching twenty feet off the west fence." Kali scanned the gloom to identify a landmark. "A hard walk for an hour plus, I'd guess we're about three miles in. Maybe only two and a half. Hard to say with the rough terrain." Kali tripped and caught herself as she spoke. "Shit."

"What happened?" Grant asked, concern overriding the anger in his voice.

She bit back the moan as the burning in her back heated up.

"Damn it, answer me."

"I'm here. Give me a second," she whispered. She took a deep breath, letting it out slowly. "I tripped on a root. I'm fine." And she would be. She had to be…for a while longer.

"Shit, Kali. I'll be there in a couple minutes. Don't move."

Like hell. "Grant, I haven't stopped moving." She searched the gloom for the halo of flashlights. Nothing yet. "Either walk toward me or wait and I'll get there in a bit."

"Jesus, you're stubborn."

Kali smirked. "I've heard that before."

Nearby, the brush rustled. Kali stopped, her hand to her throat. "What was that?"

"What did you hear?"

"Noises. In front of me." Shiloh growled deep in her throat, the sound raising the hairs on the back of Kali's neck. Kali's gaze followed Shiloh's stare. The shadows stilled, blending bushes to trees into a dark silhouette. Clicking off her flashlight, she hunkered close to the ground, one arm wrapped around Shiloh. "Grant. Did you say someone else is out here?"

"There are several teams out here. I have men everywhere, damn it. I don't have an update pinpointing everyone's location. Scott should have stayed with you. Where the hell is he?"

"I'm hoping that's him, but I don't want to call out…just in case." Memories of startling the killer at David's burial site filled her mind. Impatience gnawed at her. She hated the reminder that the killer could be here watching her. "I'd really like to know if friend or foe is in the area."

She did not want a repeat of the last incident where she'd come upon the killer in the dark.

"I can't get the information on the others because I'm talking to you. As I can see just enough to run, I should be within ear shot within five to ten minutes."

"Thank God," she whispered, wishing he'd already arrived. She could hear his uneven breathing on the phone as he covered the ground between them. Kali stayed quiet, hugging Shiloh. She knew Scott would have trouble finding her like this but she felt safer.

Poor Julie, she must be going through hell. Cold, tired, worn out with the effort of staying alive. Survival wasn't for the weak. Kali buried her face in Shiloh's warm fur and waited.

"Kali." *Who said that?*

Kali snapped upright, frowning. Had someone called her name? Grant? No, he'd call out several times. Not in a grated whisper. Her heart pounded. She wasn't alone.

Noises crashed through the underbrush up ahead. No attempt to be quiet. Kali slipped further into the shadows.

And was grabbed from behind.

Kali screamed and struggled to free herself. Shiloh barked and jumped at her attacker, dashing in for an attack before retreating, dancing out of reach of the kicks, then rushing in again.

"Shit." The man grunted, the muffled sound blasting in her ear.

A gloved hand slapped over her mouth. Kali fought, a scream gurgling past his leather-covered fingers. The strong arm pulled her backwards. Fire tore across her shoulder. She cried out with pain, tripping and falling to one side. Her movement broke her free of the one restraining arm. Pivoting, she kicked up at him, screaming at the top of her lungs for Grant.

"Kali?"

The distant shout sounded off to the left. *Grant.* Although she couldn't be sure because of Shiloh's constant yipping. At least Grant would hear her, too.

Her attacker dropped on top of her, trying to pin her arms down, his shoulder shoved against her mouth, pinning her head low. Pain stabbed at her constantly as her stitches argued with the hard ground.

Twisting and kicking with only limited success, Kali managed to slide one arm free. She immediately raked her nails across his face.

"Bitch!" But it was enough to loosen his grip on her mouth.

"Grant, help!" Pain enveloped her entire body. Fire licked

across her back and shoulders. Christ, she hurt. Kali ignored her injures as she strove for freedom and still the movements pulled at her stitches. Bile climbed the inside of her throat.

Shiloh added to the nightmare, barking and nipping at any body part she could reach.

Her attacker roared, his arms clamping on hers, pivoting her onto her belly, his knee slammed against her spine as his weight came down holding her there. "Fucking bitch."

Kali gasped for breath, but couldn't get any oxygen. Her spine felt seared and she couldn't imagine the damage to her back. "Shiloh," she whispered.

Shiloh charged. Her attacker screamed again. Suddenly, his weight lifted and Kali scrambled to her feet, bolting into the darkness in her panic.

"Shiloh. Here Shiloh." Kali raced ahead in the blackness of the night.

"Grant," she screamed. "Grant, help. I'm free."

"Kali."

Strong arms reached and grabbed her. She screamed and panicked.

"It's me." Grant pulled her tight into his embrace. "Stop, it's all right. Calm down. It's okay now. It's me."

His words finally penetrated the sound of blood pounding through her veins. "Grant." She burrowed against his chest, her body quivering in fear.

Grant held her gently, careful to keep his arm low and away from her injuries. "Easy. It's going to be okay. We'll get him. Calm down."

Kali twisted to peer into the darkness behind her. "In this light, he could hide out here all night. And there's nothing stopping him from going over the fence."

Grant considered her comment, pulled out his phone and within minutes, he had tapped another team of men.

"Wow," Kali said, pulling back to smile up at him through the tears that had arrived now that she was safe. "A man of action, I like that."

Grant snatched her close again, his chin dropping to rest on her head.

Several more men broke through the brush from the way Kali had come. Scott in the lead. He slowed down, shaking his head when he saw her. "Jesus, when you said catch up, Kali. I didn't figure you'd be sprinting for miles." The men with him dispersed, on the hunt for the killer.

Comforted, Kali closed her eyes and leaned in. Just as tension drained from her spine, Grant tilted her head back so she could see his face. "Why the hell aren't you safe in the hospital?" he demanded in angry frustration. "God damn it. Why the hell can't you stay in one place like you're told to? Do you know how much shit I'm going to give Scott for letting you out?"

"Don't. I begged him to. And it was the right decision. Besides, I'm not a damned dog," she fired back, glaring at him. "Nor am I ragdoll. Stop shaking me. You're ripping out my stitches." Cheap shot, yet effective.

Instantly, he stopped. "Shit. Did I hurt you?" His arms cradled her and rocked her back and forth. "I'm so sorry."

He shifted gears again, pushing her back again, his hands running over her. "Did he hurt you? One of my men will take you back to the hospital right now. Get those stitches checked."

"Stop." Kali placed her hands on his chest and pushed him backwards. "Of course I'm sore, but I'm going nowhere – not until I find Julie. Don't—" She held up a hand to forestall the words as he opened his mouth. "It's now or never for her."

Shrugging free of his grasp, Kali bent to pat Shiloh on her back. "I need a flashlight. I dropped mine when he attacked me. I should have hit him with the damn thing. At least then I'd still have it."

"Jesus." Grant splayed his flashlight across the area. Trampled grass, and broken branches were a testament to her panicked flight. His face grew grim.

Kali watched the hollows beneath his cheekbones deepen. "It's over and I'm fine. Let's get this job done." Before I collapse, she wanted to add but kept it in at the last moment. From the way she felt now, she could use some more of the doctor's miracle stuff – it had long since worn off.

"Take mine. I'm sticking close to you anyway." Grant handed his flashlight to Kali. "Now let's see if we can put an end to this madness."

Kali turned toward the fence line and stepped out. "Shiloh, back to work."

"What the hell, Kali?" Frustration oozed from Grant's voice but he fell into step at her side.

"We're close. I can feel it." It would explain the killer's presence and she had no doubt that's who'd attacked her.

Grant compromised. "One hour. If we don't find her in an hour, you're returning to the hospital and we continue without you."

"Like hell," she muttered under her breath. Hopefully, it would be resolved before that. Kali picked up the pace as Shiloh strained on her lead. She could feel the exhaustion and cold gnawing away at her. Even as she thought of her fatigue, energy surged through her, colors erupted in her mind, bathing her body in a warm lavender energy. Kali didn't dare stop. In fact, she suddenly felt like she could go all day. Then recognition hit her. She laughed inside.

Stefan?

A rumble of warm laughter wafted through her mind.

Thanks. I needed that boost.

You're welcome!

Can you connect to Julie? Tell her to hang on. We're coming.

That same weird humming filled her mind.

I'll try. Not getting much of a reading.

Shit what did that mean?

And he left, leaving a pulsing, throbbing surge of power in her legs and body. She didn't know how long it would last, but she was grateful to have it at all. She hadn't been sure she could go on much longer.

Kali raced now, focused and determined to finish this job before her body, or Grant finished it for her.

For fifteen minutes they raced forward in the darkness. Going left, then right, under trees and around brushes and hillocks as Shiloh tugged on the lead. Kali's determination waned as her energy declined. Her stomach growled. Grant pulled a granola bar from his pocket and handed it over. She snatched it with a grateful smile and devoured it in a few bites. Shiloh's focus had to be intense; she rarely missed a chance at a bite of Kali's bars.

Kali's tingle surged to the forefront, starting a musical beat on her spine. Excitement took over. This was it. She knew it. It had to be…she couldn't go much more.

Shiloh had caught the scent. She barked, tearing off in a flat out run. Kali was jerked forward, her flagging energy gathering for this final lunge. She raced behind Shiloh.

"Kali?" Grant caught up, running easily at her side. "What's going on?"

"We're close," Kali gasped.

Hearing footsteps, she checked behind her, to see a team of

men running at her heels. The eerie lights of multiple flashlights in motion, crisscrossing in all directions as the group moved across the rough terrain giving an otherwordly appearance to the landscape.

The knowledge that everyone believed in Shiloh, in her, warmed her heart. And scared the crap out of her. So much rode on this night.

Shiloh ran strong, making for an open area. There. Threads. Dark violent, angry reds and blacks twisting in the night, faint but visible to Kali. "She's here. I can see her."

"Are you sure?" Grant came to a stop beside Kali, walking the area searching for any sign of Julie's presence. "We searched this area already." Grant said. The team with them spread out to search.

Kali walked toward the ribbons, unsnapping Shiloh's lead. "You missed her. She's here."

Shiloh barked once, circling a ten foot radius, stopping at a heavy bush. She sat and barked again.

Excited, Kali ran to her side. "This is it. Shiloh says she's alive." Threads of energy wove through the brush. "Let's get some light over here, please." Men rushed over, flashlights blinding her. More men joined them.

One of the men spoke up. "We didn't spend much time here because the terrain's not right."

Kali circled the bush, making two laps before she spied it. A pipe rose from the ground up into the bush.

Clever.

"Here's the pipe."

The three men ran over to her. "Where?"

"How? It doesn't appear to be a burial site."

The bush had thrown them off. Willow bushes were notoriously hard to kill with their tenacious multiple roots. But had it actually grown here or been planted as a cover? Studying it, she realized none others grew close by. The ground consisted of fallen leaves and moss. Bending, Kali reached deep into the center of the bush, branches snagging on her hair, scratching her face. She grabbed on and pulled.

The bush lifted free easily, throwing her off balance. Strong arms took it from her, tossing it off to the side.

"See." Kali bent to the end of the pipe, shining her flashlight inside. She couldn't see anything. "Julie? Julie can you hear me?"

Silence.

Kali called a second time. "Julie. Julie, can you hear me. It's

Kali. We're here to help you."

There. She bent her head closer to listen. She waved the men to silence. "Shhhh."

Everyone stilled, holding their breath.

Kali bent her head and pressed her ear against the pipe. She strained to hear. There. She put up her hand. What was that noise? Kali closed her eyes and focused.

There again.

A slight moan.

"She's here."

A cheer went up.

HIDDEN HIGH ABOVE in the leafy bowers of an overgrown fir tree, the killer could see nothing below. But the conversations came through clearly.

"Son of a bitch," he whispered, spit rolling in his mouth. "They found her. That's impossible." How'd Kali pull that off? He'd had trouble finding Julie in the dark tonight and he'd visited the area many times.

His fury grew in tandem with the growing noises below. Were they cheering? How dare they? The assholes figured they'd won. He snorted. He wasn't stupid. Kali might have found Julie, but he doubted she'd survive the night.

He glared at the greenery hiding him from the men searching below. This was not supposed to happen. Not now and not tonight.

In his books, this round counted as a draw. He'd cut his losses and rethink his plan. He must have done something wrong. God had to be displeased with him. But he would sort it through. God knew he was loyal.

Then he could move on.

Kali would have no hope of beating him on the next one. Even with her black magic bullshit.

Good humor restored, he settled down to wait them out.

TRIUMPHANTLY, KALI TURNED to Grant. "Shovels, men and lights – lots of them."

Everyone moved back several feet looking for the best approach. Everyone but Kali. She sat protectively beside the pipe, not wanting to leave Julie alone, feeling the exhilaration morph into exhaustion. Still her pulse beat a nervous tempo as she watched the team organize Julie's release. Shiloh lay at her side, her chin resting on Kali's thigh. Nothing could dispel the sense of urgency. Julie hadn't made another sound. They had to get her to a hospital, and now.

The hill dropped to a hollow. The men started there. Other teams converged on their corner. A stretcher was carried in and medical equipment. Kali had lost her bearings. She didn't know if the men had found the road access or if they'd hauled this gear for miles. She hoped a vehicle was close by. Walking back wasn't an option.

Feeling moisture gathering on her cheeks, Kali reached up, not surprised to feel tears. She wiped her face on her sleeve. A sniffle escaped.

An odd tingle whispered through her mind.

Nice job.

Kali stiffened. *Stefan?*

Yes. You found her. Good for you.

Thanks to you. I was running low. Might not have made it without your help.

You would have. You tapped into the universal energy all on your own. I just helped to keep everything flowing properly.

Really?

A sensation similar to a warm hug, enveloped her.

Really.

The faint sensation slipped from her mind like it had never been there.

A warm hand squeezed her shoulder. "You did it, Kali. We've found her."

Kali lifted her head to see Grant at her side. She didn't want to mention Stefan's part in all of this – not with their audience. Standing up with his help, she smiled through her tears. "I know. I can't quite believe it." She glanced at the frantic activity. "I won't feel better until she's safe."

Julie had to be feeling the same. Kali leaned over the pipe, speaking down the tube. "It's okay, Julie," she said encouragingly. "We've got lots of men. You'll be out in a couple of minutes. Hang in there, Julie and you'll be fine."

"Kali?" A whisper so soft, Kali almost missed it.

"Julie, I'm here." Kali waved the others to silence.

The men stopped digging.

Her voice, tired and weak, traveled up the pipe. "Kali, be careful. He's here."

"He's here?"

"Yes…" A muffled cough sounded underground.

Kali exchanged looks with Grant. "Julie, who is he?" Several gasping coughs sounded. Kali repeated the question.

The coughing stopped. An eerie silence filled the night.

Grant raced to join the men, everyone galvanized into action. A palpable worry permeated the atmosphere. Kali's stomach knotted. She closed her eyes, repeating a litany of prayers. Shiloh nudged her hand and whimpered. Crouching, Kali hugged her tightly and buried her face in the warm fur. Kali's heart pulsed in tune to the fear throbbing through her veins.

A shout went up.

She surged to her feet. Hands reached out, pulling her back as the front of the hillside slid down, the pipe falling to one side. The corners of a large box slid into view. Men quickly brushed off the last of the rocks and dirt and pried against the crumpled corner. The medical team filled the area and Kali could see nothing but men bending over the opening.

"Is she alive?" Kali called out to Grant, who'd disappeared in the sea of men.

Tense silence worked through the crowd as they waited for news.

Grant stepped free of the crowd. "She's alive!"

The crowd roared.

Shiloh leaned against Kali. She didn't notice.

Kali stood in the cool night air and bawled.

CHAPTER 24

KALI DROOPED IN the hospital cubicle, her eyes closed and her body swaying from exhaustion in the overly bright space. As they said in the movies, she'd 'hit the wall.'

"Kali?"

"Mmmm?"

"Kali, wake up. The doctor's here."

Kali struggled to focus until her bleary gaze settled on a familiar face. She gave him a wan smile. "Great drugs, Doctor."

He grinned at her. "At least you put them to good use. I hear you found the missing woman. Good for you."

Kali straightened in her chair. "How is she? Do you have an update?" Memories flooded through her. The medic in the woods figured Julie had spent the bulk of the time sliding in and out of consciousness.

Probably a good thing.

"She's severely dehydrated, and suffering from a head injury. That's what I can tell you at this point. We're running tests now."

"But she's alive."

The doctor patted her shoulder, smiling. "She's alive – thanks to you. We'll do everything in our power to keep her that way."

Kali beamed through the dirt, and gave him a small decisive nod. "I know you will."

"Now young lady, let's see what kind of damage you did to yourself tonight." The checkup didn't take long. Kali was past the point of protesting. She slumped back down, lifting what he told her to lift and showing him what he wanted to see. She never protested at the poking or prodding. She endured in silence. Her eyes drifted closed.

"No new damage. A couple of stitches have torn loose. We can't restitch them. So your wounds will take longer to close. Nothing serious except you're worn out, which will slow your healing. Go home and rest for the next few days and that's an order."

"Hmmm. Sounds good."

"Nurse, bring in that bear of an FBI agent pacing in the hallway…before she falls asleep. Now."

"I'm okay." Kali worked to sit up, her leaden limbs refusing to cooperate. Grant must have been close by because suddenly his face was there, watching her with a grim smile.

"How is she?" he said.

"Exhausted. She needs to go home and rest." The doctor looked down his nose at Grant. "I expect you to see she does."

"Oh, I will. Don't worry." Grant's voice threatened retribution if she didn't do as she'd been ordered.

"*She'd* like to sleep now." Kali slid off the bed and would have fallen to the floor if Grant hadn't reached and caught her.

"Easy does it. Ten, fifteen minutes… Then you can sleep."

She snorted. "Five. You get five minutes and that's it."

Grant raised his eyebrows. "Right. Let's go then." With murmured thanks to the doctor, Kali let Grant help her to his car by the front entrance. Shiloh lay stretched out in the backseat. She gave a tired woof at the sight of Kali. The fresh night air filled her lungs, giving her a small boost of energy. Kali managed to slide into the front seat on her own.

"Home, James," she ordered.

Long minutes later, the house loomed before her. Every muscle ached as Kali made it from the car to the front door. At the bottom of the stairs, she wavered.

"Let's go. Upstairs."

Trembling with exhaustion, Kali grabbed the banister and made it up the bottom set before Grant picked her up and slung her over his shoulder, eating up the last flight in seconds. Shiloh raced to the top beside them.

Grant lowered her to her feet at the base of the bed. She stumbled forward, pulled back the covers and dropped. Shiloh jumped up beside her.

"Kali, wait. Let's get you out of those clothes."

"Too tired," she whispered. Grant didn't leave her alone though. He tugged her shoes and socks off, ignoring her grumbling.

"Typical male." She brushed his hands away as he pulled on the waistband of her pants and tugged her jeans halfway down her legs. "Cold," she murmured.

"I know honey. Come on. Sit up." Sliding an arm under her shoulders, he lifted her into a slumped sitting position. Sliding one hand along her waist, he grabbed the lower edge of her t-shirt easing it over her head. Kali flopped backwards and moaned as the gauze dressing over her stitches pulled on her tender skin. She immediately rolled into a tight ball.

"I'm sorry, sweetheart. You'll sleep better without the heavy clothing."

Kali wanted to comment, only her teeth chattered to the point she couldn't talk.

Grant pulled her duvet up to her chin and tucked it in along the length of her body. Then he left her alone.

Blessed quiet descended in the room.

She closed her eyes and sank deeper into the mattress. Grant returned in minutes.

"Just one more thing. Let's wash your face." Soothing warmth filled her as he wiped her face clean.

"Now you can sleep."

Kali sighed as a warm lassitude spread throughout her body. She fell asleep before he made it to the doorway.

SOMETIME IN THE night, Kali woke up aching…everywhere – tears drifting across her face. Grant's warm arms wrapped around her, tugging her into a comforting hug. The tears poured.

"Shh, it's all right, Kali. Take it easy."

Her shoulders shook as she burrowed deeper. The tears wouldn't stop. She cried in silence. Emotionally battered, her heart ached with the pain, the losses. Tension had knotted her muscles. The relief of finding Julie should have let it go. Instead, fear kept them tight and coiled…prepared.

What if they hadn't found Julie in time? What if there was someone else out there to rescue? Her heart ached too much for sounds to make their way past her throat.

"Shh. Stop crying, please, honey. You'll make yourself sick." Tender kisses landed on her forehead, the top of her head and her temple. His big hands massaged her lower spine, soothing away some of her aches and pains.

Kali's tears finally slowed. Easing her head back, she looked up at him, studying his beloved features. Heat spread throughout her lower body. She realized she wanted – no, needed – his touch. Energy warmed between them, making her realize that lying as they were, their auras had nestled together too.

With a last sniffle, she opened her mouth to speak only to find his finger up against her lips.

"Shhh."

A slumberous warmth slid through her.

Energy spiked, small flashes dancing between them.

What mattered was she wanted him. And had since she'd first seen him. With her eyes smiling into his, she licked the finger held against her lips, caressing the skin upward to the tip. His eyes darkened, deepened – then he shuddered. Kali loved it. Lifting her head, she slid his finger slowly inside her mouth and sucked gently.

"Jesus, Kali," he whispered. Or was that a prayer? "You're playing with danger."

"No, I'm encouraging it." A wicked grin flashed before she closed her eyes and sucked his finger rhythmically.

"Fuck," he whispered, closing his eyes briefly. Tenderly, he placed a hand on either side of her head and stared into her eyes, searching.

She reached up, whispering against his lips, "Yes, please."

Energy blossomed, heat whispering between them, through them.

His hands tightened, cupping her head and holding her fast as their mouths joined. The kiss started out light, tentative, an exploration…then ignited into something deep, intense. Kali felt the answering pulse deep in her belly. A moan slid free. She shifted her position, wincing as her back muscles tightened, pulling her stitches. Sliding her hands over his chest, Kali realized Grant was fully dressed. Searching out the top button of his shirt she moved with delicious pleasure and slid the button through the hole, one finger purposely sliding against the smooth skin of his chest. She reached for the next.

"Christ, Kali, you're driving me nuts." His lips slid across her neck to feast on the delicate shell of her ear. His hands touched her spine and froze. *Her stitches.* Kali sensed his withdrawal immediately, as he pulled back, a protest forming on his lips.

She beat him to it. "It's okay, Grant. We'll be careful."

"God, you're hurt. You need rest, time to heal."

This time her finger stopped his words. "And I will. I need to believe in life again, to believe in love again. I need this. You need this. I need you."

Grant closed his eyes and shuddered. "And I need you...have for a long time."

She smiled, and reached for his lips. "Good. Let's not waste anymore time."

When he took her mouth this time, there was nothing tentative about it. He devoured her, for the first time tasting her, enjoying her, knowing they had hours of pleasure ahead. Sitting up, Grant stripped off his shirt and went to work on his belt buckle next.

But her hands pushed his away and tugged the snap open. The zipper parted as her fingers delved inside.

"Christ." Grant sucked in his breath, backed away from her marauding fingers and stood up. Within seconds he'd stripped and stood nude before her.

Kali, kneeling on the bed, was struck by the male glory in front of her. She feasted on the sight of him, slowly studying his strong muscled body until she reached his hooded eyes. Their gazes locked. His breath caught.

"You're something, you know that?"

Shaking her head, she whispered, "No, you are."

Tearing his gaze away, he looked at the bed, then at her.

She narrowed her eyes, wondering what he'd suggest.

Walking to the far side, Grant stretched out fully. "I guess you'll have to have your way with me, after all."

Kali watched him in confusion.

He opened his arms. "Don't want to tear those stitches..."

Of course – her back. Kali grinned and went into his arms gladly; her kisses joyous and hot. A veritable buffet of manhood lay stretched out before her. She couldn't resist. Her hands stoked and caressed as she dropped greedy kisses down the heavily muscled chest. She explored everything in reach. Grant twisted beneath her, his hands caressing her curves.

He reached out to cup the weight of one breast. Kali shuddered and stopped so he could stroke her hardened nipple. But her need was too great – she couldn't wait. Straddling his body, she bent over and gave him a kiss that raised the temperature of the room. As his arms came up to hold her fast, she slid down his body. She dropped kisses over his heated flesh down to his navel and along the line of hair. Kali caressed him with her fingers and inched downward.

His erection cuddled between her breasts.

Grant's breath caught and held.

"Do I stop?" she whispered, her tongue teasing his belly button.

"Never," he answered in a whispered prayer.

She slid lower to place kisses along the long length of him.

"Shit."

Kali found herself dragged upward, her lips seared by his kiss. He maneuvered her back into straddling his body. His hands on her waist, he pushed her downward.

The head of his penis rested at the heart of her. Kali sat back. Her gaze locked on his face, she lowered herself ever so slightly and stopped. His eyes, darkened with need.

"Witch."

His fingers tightened on her hips, digging into the soft flesh. He tugged downward. "Please."

Kali gave him a smoky, languid look. "Is this what you want?" Inch by slow inch, she lowered her body, watching in joy as his eyes closed, his body twisted upward and his face flushed with pleasure.

"Yes. Christ. Yes."

Kali's heart swelled. To tease him and to prolong his pleasure, she paused her descent. Then slowly she slid upward.

"No," he moaned, his fingers digging into her hips. "No, don't leave."

"Look at me," she whispered.

Grant opened his eyes, searing her with his fiery gaze.

She watched him from under half-closed lids then lowered her hips again, taking all of him until he was seated deep inside. Grant pushed his hips firmly against her, sealing their flesh together. A long shudder rippled through them both. Placing her hands on his shoulders, she lifted and lowered, settling into a slow smooth ride.

His hands lifted to cup her breasts, his fingers teasing the hard nipples.

With her head tilted backwards, her hair flowing around her shoulders, Kali lost herself in her own pleasure as her blood heated and boiled. Her breath shortened; her movements becoming faster and faster.

Grant's hands clenched spasmodically on her hips as he tried to stop her from rising too high. He moaned, twisting beneath her.

Finally, his control broke.

Gripping her hips to hold her in place, he took control of the rhythm, driving his hips upwards, driving them both to the edge of the cliff. One. Two. Three hard thrusts and Kali flew, crying out as raw nerve endings exploded with pleasure, leaving her reeling in the intense aftermath.

Energy ballooned, then the boundaries broke, edges dissipated and their auras melted together.

With a long groan, Grant followed her.

Kali collapsed against his chest, her breathing coming in ragged gasps. But her heart and soul flew and soared. Still connected with his body, her breathing eased, became slow and even.

She dropped off to sleep, barely registering the beautiful deep purple aura surrounding the two of them.

Hours later, Kali surfaced to find she was lying on her side, wrapped in Grant's arms. Snuggling deeper into his embrace, she fell asleep again.

"CRAP." THE WHISPERED word barely made itself heard in his hidden perch. What a long night. His neck ached, his back had kinked and he didn't think his legs would extend fully again. Taking his time, he stretched one limb at a time, careful not to dislodge the branches. The assholes continued to work below, walking, talking. He could hardly leave, but damn he needed to take a piss. Damn his back hurt. Men weren't meant to sleep in trees.

Voices floated up to him. The murmurs rose and fell but remained indistinguishable. He still had trouble believing they'd found Julie. Just a little longer and she'd have been lost to them. Then again, he should have killed Kali last night too. She'd been in his grasp. His hands on her neck. And he'd lost her. That failed attempt didn't bear thinking about. And due to his failure – they found Julie.

He pondered on his system. He preferred that Julie had suffered longer. Maybe his design needed adjusting. The pipe provided a great communication link, her suffering a source of joy…maybe it was too big? Allowed in too much air? Then again he'd planned on her living longer.

Kali's success had caught him sideways. She'd been fast. Too fast. He wouldn't hand over a victory to her again. He had to stay on top. Prove to God that he was worthy.

Shifting again, he winced. His stomach growled, reminding him he hadn't planned for hours of hiding. At least not here. The hunting blind at Kali's place had been set up for the long term with snacks and water bottles along with a change of clothes. A couple of sandwiches were there as well. Plus he slept like a baby there.

Close to her.

The FBI were always around but they watched the road entrance whereas he always entered by the beach. With a fat grin, he contemplated the FBI sitting out all night every night – for naught. He hoped they were as uncomfortable as he. Thank heavens for this heavy jacket and work boots.

His jeans had stiffened overnight, but they would loosen as he walked – when he could walk. Hiding in the park overnight hadn't been in the plan.

Still, life was good. Stuck in a tree he might be, but he was also alive and not under arrest. He was free to plan his next step. And the cops had no idea who or when. That's the way he liked it.

Pursing his lips, he hunkered lower and considered his next move.

CHAPTER 25

KALI WOKE TO an empty bed.

Rolling onto her belly, she yawned and stretched, wincing at the pain in her back and shoulder. Memories flooded her mind. Julie. Grant. That couldn't help but produce a fat smile. They'd found Julie. Injured and unconscious – alive. Satisfaction wove through her heart. Monday had ended better than it started. Hopefully, Julie would come through this like a trooper. Obviously, she needed to heal, both mentally and physically. And she would, Julie was tough. It would take time but Julie would put this behind her and move on.

Grant was another matter. Kali had no intention of putting that behind her. She looked around her room. No sign of her clothes or his. Hmmm. A knock sounded on her open door. Shifting position, she watched as Grant entered, carrying a large mug. She smiled at the way his soft gentle energy brightened at the sight of her. Being this connected they'd never be able to hide from each other. Their energy would always show the truth of how each felt toward the other.

"Good morning. I just spoke with the hospital."

"How's Julie?" Kali shifted, tugging the duvet over her chest as she struggled into an upright sitting position. Grant passed her the mug.

Kali inhaled the rich coffee aroma, letting the steam float upward to bathe her face in its warmth. With her free hand, she tucked the duvet tighter. Even after a good night's sleep, her exhausted body felt chilled. "Thank you."

"You're welcome." Grant grinned at her as he took a seat toward the end of the bed. "Julie's in critical condition, and has yet to wake up. However the doctors are being cautiously optimistic she'll make a full recovery."

"That's wonderful news," Joy surged through her. "I've been

so worried. When the medics couldn't revive her, I was afraid we were too late to save her."

"She's got a long road to recovery." He shifted further back on the bed, crossing his legs at the ankle. "There's more good news. Dan is awake. We can go see him in an hour."

"Wow. So coffee, a shower, food and then the hospital. Sounds great."

"Good, but you'll have to speed it up. Breakfast is almost ready. Shiloh looks hungry but I figured you'd want to feed her."

"Thanks. I do prefer to feed her myself." She appreciated his consideration.

"Thought so." Grant stood and walked toward the door. "You've got fifteen minutes until breakfast. I have a confession to make and I need breakfast to fortify me beforehand. Okay?"

One eyebrow raised, Kali nodded. *Interesting.* "I'll make it quick."

Kali crawled out of bed and headed for the bathroom. Butterflies took flight in her belly. She didn't want anything to mar this morning. What did he want to tell her?

Outside of initial shyness, Kali couldn't help but be pleased at the naturalness of their relationship. It gave her hope for their future. That he wanted to unburden himself could be another positive – depending on what he had to say. Grant hadn't made mention of a future together, but she'd do her damnedest to see they gave it a chance.

Fifteen minutes later, she followed the appetizing aromas into the kitchen, where she found sausages, hash browns and eggs ready for the table.

With a look of disbelief at Grant, she said, "This looks great."

"I dug around in the freezer." Grant brought over two laden plates. "If you pour the orange juice, we can start eating."

Kali obliged, delivering two glasses to the table. "This smells wonderful. I didn't realize how hungry I was until I walked in here." Grant had heaped her plate. Picking up her fork, she took a bite and closed her eyes in bliss.

"Eat up. You're downright skinny as it is. The doctor ordered bed rest for the next couple of days."

She sniffed. "It's hard to keep the weight on when I'm working all the time. Rest will help me regain a pound or two."

"And that is what you'll be doing. One trip to the hospital and then straight back home again where you'll spend the next couple of days resting, eating and doing some serious sleeping."

Kali knew his vision was ludicrous. Not while a killer stalked her. Still, she'd let him play the caregiver role happily for an hour or so. She forked more food into her mouth, concentrating on the flavors. The man could cook. She polished off her plateful. Standing, she refilled their coffee cups and turned to face him. "So what do you need to tell me?"

GRANT REACHED FOR his mug of coffee, studying the pattern of steam as it rose from the hot brew. He grimaced, wishing he'd never initiated this conversation. "Six, closer to seven years ago, you gave a talk in Portland on SARs. I attended that talk."

Kali gave him a wry, lopsided smile. "How did I do?"

He studied the beauty of her face. "You made such an impression I haven't been able to get you out of my mind since."

Kali leaned forward to stare at him. "Really?"

"Yes, really." Should he show her? Why the hell not. Grant reached into his back pocket for his wallet. Flipping it open, he showed her his driver's license on one side and a picture of a woman on the other.

Kali studied the photo. "Is that me?"

Turning the wallet, Grant grinned. "Yeah. I cut it from one of the seminar brochures. How sad is that?"

Amazement lined Kali's face. "That's where I'd seen you before. You looked familiar but I couldn't place you."

"Not surprised. We spoke briefly. You gave your talk, answered questions then left." He didn't add that she'd left with a partner. A boyfriend.

"Seven years ago…" Deep sadness filtered into her eyes. "I lost my parents a few months after that talk. And I'd just realized my fiancé had more than a passing interest in my new-found wealth." With one long finger, she traced her features on the old photo. With the odd quirk to her lips, she handed it back. "How sweet."

"Sweet?" He put his wallet away. *Sweet? Was that good or bad?* He wasn't sure. It certainly wasn't what he'd expected to hear.

"I like the idea of leaving an impact profound enough that you thought about me over the years." Kali gazed into his eyes. "A couple of weeks ago, that might have sounded a little creepy because I didn't know you then. But now, well I think it's sweet."

The relief rushing through him made him sit back, his shoulders sagging as they dropped a heavy weight. But her next words made him stop in shock.

"It's a little unnerving though. What if you'd found me wanting after all these years? You didn't know me back then and after getting to know me, what if I hadn't lived up to your memory?" Kali paused. Grant searched her face. She was nervous, afraid even – that the real woman hadn't matched the one in his mind. She couldn't be more wrong.

Confident, caring, compassionate Kali, always concerned about others, lacked the assurance she needed from him. Gentleness whispered through his heart. He could take care of that right now. "You're right. Back then I did have an idealistic view of you. How could I not? I didn't know who you were as a person. When I saw you this time, you were quieter, more withdrawn than I remembered. As if life had dished out some hard years." He studied her face, noting the flash of pain. "Your parents, your fiancé and yes, Dan told me about little Inez, lost in Mexico." He reached across the table to gently cover her hand.

Her gaze dropped to the table, a sad twist playing at the corner of her mouth.

He squeezed her fingers tightly. "Listen carefully. I have never felt disappointed or short changed. You measure up in all ways." With his gaze locked on hers, he pulled her other hand free from its lock on the coffee mug and cradled both in his much bigger one.

"The truth is I didn't know what to expect. I didn't know who you really were, but I couldn't get rid of the feeling I needed to know you. That if I didn't have the opportunity, my life would miss a huge essential element and I'd feel bereft forever." His thumb stroked the soft skin of her palm. "Last night was special," he admitted with a slow smile. "Better than any fantasy I might have dreamed." He grinned. "But in the morning light, I can't be too sure. We'll have to repeat it and see. Often."

The sexiest look he could have imagined slid from her eyes and headed straight to his groin. He gulped.

"Glad to hear that," she whispered softly.

Staring back down at their entwined fingers, he added sheepishly, "My mom wanted me to call you years ago."

Kali blinked, shock on her face. "What? You told her?"

A laugh broke free. "Yes. And she's going to have a great time reminding me. She told me life was precious and if I was really interested, I should call you."

Apparently having trouble with the information, Kali sat back, shaking her head. "Did you tell her you were working with me these last couple of weeks?"

He snorted. "Are you kidding? It was bad enough that Stefan knew. My mom is quite capable of driving down here to meet you if she'd known."

Kali laughed. "A lady after my own heart. I will enjoy meeting her."

"When this mess ends," he promised. He glanced at his watch and raised an eyebrow. "However, if we want to go see Dan, we need to leave – now."

THEY WALKED THROUGH the front entrance of the hospital fifteen minutes later. Grant led her past a set of double doors and into a different hallway. Kali smiled at their clicking footsteps, amplified by the empty corridor. Visiting hours didn't start for another hour, giving the hospital the appearance of a rare serenity.

"I owe Stefan a big thanks for his help last night?" Kali murmured awed by the silence of the long hallway. At Grant's questioning look, she explained.

His eyebrows raised, Grant shook his head. "I had no idea he could do that."

Arriving at a large double door, Grant nodded to a guard standing on duty. Grant showed his ID to the officer who checked it before moving aside.

Kali whispered, "Did you set up security for Julie?"

"Yes, although I doubt the killer would go after her again."

"Maybe not, but she won't survive a second attempt."

"And she won't have to." Entering, Kali saw stark white walls, interrupted only by huge sunflowers standing in a vase beside the bed. Dan lay on his side facing the window, the blanket at his shoulders. Grant walked up beside her. The door snicked shut behind them. When Dan rolled over, Kali caught her breath.

"Oh, Dan." She threw her arms around him in a gentle hug.

"Hi, Kali." Dan patted her arm.

Pulling back, it was all Kali could do to stop the tears from spilling over.

His wrinkled face shifted and reformed into a parody of a smile. "Don't look so worried, Kali. I'm going to be fine."

Sunshine seeped into the room and fell on Dan's beloved face.

Kali sniffled. "Thank heavens for that. I can't take much more. Can you please tell us what the heck happened?"

"I'm not sure. I'd been working on the computer when I found something odd. I went to the files to check the information and the next thing I know…I'm here in the hospital."

Studying his face, Kali asked slowly. "Were you alone? Did you fall? Or could you have been hit?"

Grant stepped forward to rest a comforting hand on her shoulder. Kali leaned into him.

Dan noted the movement. A slight grin dimpled his cheeks. "Either case is possible. The office door was open so it's possible someone snuck up behind me." He shrugged. "I'm sorry. I don't know. I didn't see anyone. All I can say is there were lots of people around who had the opportunity."

It hurt Kali to look at him. His face, normally so full and healthy, looked thin and empty. The wrinkles, usually beaming with life, drooped in layers, lifeless. His changed countenance reflected more than a head injury; he looked seriously ill. Kali's stomach knotted at the thought.

"Listen I'm fine. I just need a couple of days to return to normal."

"You'd better." She sniffled and swiped her watery eyes.

Grant took several steps that brought him to the other side of Dan's bed. "You said you found something wrong on the computer and went to check the information. Do you remember what that was?"

Dan frowned, his forehead creasing into more wrinkles – if that were possible. "Not really."

Changing tracks, Grant reached into his pocket and removed a folded piece of paper. "Do you know this man?"

Dan, his shoulders shaking, struggled to sit. Kali reached out and helped him into an upright position. "Take it easy."

"I'm fine." He pulled the bedcovers higher. "Let's take a look."

Dan reached for the picture. Kali and Grant watched him for any signs of recognition. They weren't disappointed.

"Christian LeFleur." Dan took another glance at the picture, his face pinching tight before handing it back to Grant. "Christian pops in now and again. He volunteers for several organizations. He's training a young German Shepherd, with decent success I hear." He glanced up at Kali, his rheumy eyes revealing pain. "Brad and he were close. I imagine he's hurting right now."

Kali frowned. "I don't remember Brad mentioning him."

"He might not have. They were *buds*. You know, they talked about anything and everything, went and got drunk together – guy stuff. Brad mentioned a couple of times how he could be himself with Christian, unlike when he was with his wife. They shared similar backgrounds, interests, even looks. They also belonged to the same church."

Kali's frown deepened as she glanced at the picture.

Dan added. "They used to joke about being brothers. You had to see them together."

Interesting. It didn't help her place Christian in her mind. Nor could she see Brad's features in the sketch.

"Christian's an active SARs member, working disasters for over a decade but he's a loner – and a bit of a ladies' man, come to think of it. Has coffee when he's here, more often than not he takes off with Brad or works alone, if you know what I mean?"

Pondering the picture, Kali shook her head. "I can't really place him in my mind."

A half snort came from the bed. "Of course, you're one narrow-minded person when it involves men."

Grant stepped forward. "What do you mean, Dan?"

Dan cast a sideways glance at Kali. "Nothing bad. It's just she's blind to men. Many try to catch her eye, but she just doesn't see them. The more obvious they are, the more oblivious she is."

With an apologetic look her way, Dan added, "She only remembers men if she has meaningful interaction. Without that, they don't register on her radar. Brad worked for years to be allowed into her inner circle." He reached out to clasp her hand. "Kali doesn't mean anything by it. It's just *her*."

Kali hated the heat rising up her cheeks. "I'm not that bad."

"There's nothing *bad* about it. It's your protective mechanism. If you don't see the men and their advances, you don't have to deal with them."

She gasped in protest. "No one has ever made an advance at me."

Grant glanced between her and a ruefully smiling Dan who held his other hand up. "Like I said." To Kali he added, "And there have been many."

"No way." She shook her head, refusing to believe she'd been that blind. "Let's return to the subject at hand. Christian. What else do you know about him?"

"Not much. When he was with Brad, they loved to debate religious issues. You'd hear them arguing all the time. Both were strong believers but Christian was worse."

"Worse? How?"

"More voluble. The debate I remember was on who deserved to live and die. Restitution, right to life issues. At the time, I'd assumed they were discussing abortion or maybe assisted suicide. I left the room because…" Dan's gaze traveled between the two of them. "Well, I didn't want to know."

Kali understood. Dan hated discussion involving politics or religions as much as he detested girl talk. If any woman opened up on pregnancy, labor or marriage in his vicinity, he bolted. Divorce was the worst topic.

Tossing a glance at Grant, she watched in fascination as his eyes narrowed and he stared straight ahead, as if the room faded out of existence. Even his body stilled.

"Right to life issues fit." She mixed Dan's comments with what she knew regarding the kidnappings and murders. "The survivors cheated death. In his mind they have no right to life. He's helping God by making things right."

"Any apparent competitiveness or jealousy?" Grant continued. "Did he ever ask you about Kali or want to discuss her?"

Dan closed his eyes. Kali watched him in concern. They'd have to leave him to rest soon. His skin had taken on an even grayer tone.

Dan pursed his lips. "He wouldn't have to ask. Her record is well-known."

"Record?" Grant glanced over at Kali before refocusing his attention on Dan. "Is that like a recovery count? Do you people keep those kinds of records?"

"Not official records. Like any industry, some people do. Kali doesn't, but her success rate is often commented on because it's phenomenal. She can't work a disaster without her peers watching, taking note. Many journalists and politicians follow her progress."

Grant spun around to stare at Kali.

Embarrassed, Kali shrugged it off. "I do what I do."

"And she does it very well," Dan interjected. "The industry has noticed. Honestly, her work is a major reason why the center functions."

"You hire her services out?" Grant frowned, his brows forming a v-shape. He stood with his hands fisted on his hips.

Dan chuckled. "I do but she doesn't."

Grant shook his head. "What?"

Kali sighed. "It's not a secret. I mentioned it before briefly. I work pro bono and Dan uses the money to keep the center open and running. I don't need the money, however, the world needs the center. Dan does a lot of necessary work, and on a global level."

Heat rose on her face. She hated explaining herself. She was hardly a philanthropist, but she didn't need the money nor did she want to accept payment for helping people in need. That she gave money on a quarterly basis to the center as well wasn't something she wanted to discuss either.

"Do you get paid to help out when there's a disaster?"

"No. I don't." Clear cut and equivocal her voice left no room for doubt. "There are a couple of paid rescue workers here, for all others the center covers the costs but not wages. Mostly through donations, government subsidies and contract work similar to what Jarl did for that church."

Grant glanced over at Dan, who nodded. "She's right. To stay afloat, we run classes, take on contract jobs. That can be locating graves, missing dogs, people lost in the bush, etc. There's no compensation for helping out on disasters."

Kali jumped in. "It's the same for most centers. The bulk of rescue workers are volunteers."

"Before we leave you to rest, have there been any problems with Jarl at the center or on a disaster site?" Grant asked.

The question blindsided her. She chewed her lips and snuck a look at Dan. He stared back at her, then shrugged.

"What aren't you saying?" Grant's tone thickened with annoyance.

Reaching over, she patted Dan's hand. "I didn't consider it before but since you put it that way." Kali shifted back into her chair and pleated the folds in her shirt. "A while back, I thought Jarl might have been stealing from the center. I had no proof and honestly I could've been mistaken. I spoke to him about it, and he denied everything. He was quite upset about the whole thing. We had several uncomfortable months before our relationship regained a normal footing." Kali paused. "The thing is…after our talk the thefts stopped."

Dan spoke. "Until recently."

Kali started. "What?"

"I hadn't had a chance to tell you. Just recently I've noticed a few minor problems surfacing. Stuff disappearing, the petty cash empty when it shouldn't be. You know little stuff…nothing serious, more of an inconvenience."

Grant glared at the two of them. "And you're telling me about this now?"

They both shrugged. Kali said innocently, "Why would I have mentioned it earlier? It's not important."

"Christ." Grant threw his hands up in the air. "You do realize this might explain Jarl's presence in your office?"

Kali hated feeling guilty. She ran her hands through her hair. "I wasn't thinking of thefts – there were bigger issues like kidnappings and murders, remember."

"What's the chance he's moved from petty crime to stealing identities or banking information? Presuming, you keep information like that on your computer, Dan?"

"Aye, I do. And I suppose given the circumstances, it's possible."

Both Kali and Grant frowned in sync. "What circumstances?" she asked. As far as she knew, everything was fine in Jarl's life.

"Jarl's wife is seriously ill and their medical insurance won't cover her treatments. It's progressed to the point she can't work, so he's actively looking for ways to cover the bills."

"Shit." Pity hit her. Poor Jarl. She'd have helped him if she'd known. She brightened. Maybe she still could?

Grant, his cell phone already in his hand, headed for the door. "I'm stepping out to make some calls." He strode to the door. "Be back in a few minutes."

Kali waited until he'd left before moving to sit on Dan's bed. "You know we found Julie?"

His eyes lit up. He grasped her hand. "Yes, and thank God you did. The doc said she'll recover. I can't imagine what she went through."

"She's going to need time. Physically and mentally." Sadness pulled at her. No one should have to go through what she'd been through – and never twice.

"She's strong. She'll make it." Dan coughed, his voice hoarse and rasping.

Kali frowned down at him. "Do you need a nurse?"

Tremors wracked his thin frame. "No. They can't help. I'm feeling my age today."

"Is there something you're not telling me?"

A disturbing rattle worked its way up his throat until he coughed and coughed. Kali reached for a tissue and handed it to him. Dan sat, the coughs wracking his thin frame violently. After a few anxious moments, Kali watched his face turned beet red and witnessed sputum spewing. Finally, he could breathe easily.

Dan slumped onto the bed, taking several deep breaths. "That hurt."

Kali hesitated, unsure she should pry. "Have you asked the doctors to check you over?"

"No, they're doing it anyway." He closed his eyes briefly. "The results will take a few days."

The door opened as Grant entered, his face carved in stone.

Kali assessed his features. Time to go. Kali stood. "I'll stop by tomorrow." She dropped a kiss on Dan's forehead. "Rest and heal."

"You take care of yourself." He smiled grimly at the two of them. "Grant, get this guy before someone else is hurt."

"That's the plan," he answered. He opened the door, his hand on the small of Kali's back, nudging her forward. "We'll see you again, Dan. Take care."

Once outside, she asked, "Can we visit Julie?" The hand on her back eased off.

He shot her a quick sideways look. "No, I just checked. She's heavily sedated. And…she's not doing so well."

Kali stopped and stared at him. "Oh," she whispered.

Grant hooked an arm around her shoulders, tugging her into moving forward again. "Her body's gone through a horrible experience. She's injured. She's dehydrated and needs to heal. Her body has shut down to deal with the trauma. It happens and in this case, it might give her a fighting chance."

"I'd so hoped she would have recovered enough this morning for us to be able to talk to her."

They walked past the bustling nurses' station and out to his car. As they walked outside, Kali brought up the one question she'd forgotten to ask. "Why would the killer have been in the woods last night?"

Grant hesitated.

Kali waited until he unlocked the car. After buckling up the seatbelt, she asked, "He likes to watch them, imagine them dying, doesn't he?"

Grant looked at her and nodded before turning on the car and backing out of his parking spot. Once on the main road heading to her house, he spoke up. "Probably something like that. He could have religious reasons for his visits like enumerating their sins or gloating over what was happening. With a twisted mind, it's hard to tell."

"Was the pipe to give Julie fresh air or to talk to her, torment her?"

Surprise lit his face. "Possibly both."

Kali curled her lip. *Yuck.* Thankfully, they were almost home. They pulled into her driveway moments later. Kali hopped out. Grant stayed in the car. Kali bent to look at him through the window. "Are you coming in?"

He hesitated. "I need to go to the office. But I'll be back in an hour or an hour and a half at the most." Grant stared at her. "You be careful. Go in and lock the doors. This guy is a loose cannon. He could come after you next. Remember, the FBI has your house under surveillance but if you leave here you'll be unprotected. Stay smart and I'll be back as soon as I can."

She wanted to put on a pot of coffee, fill her travel mug and head to the beach with Shiloh. Kali switched her gaze from Grant to her house and back again. "I don't have anywhere to go."

"Good. I'll return as fast as I can. I'll bring an overnight bag with me this time." Grant reversed the car and headed down the road.

With a light heart, Kali ran to her front door. She'd have a house guest tonight. Kali laughed and ran the last steps.

Grant had no idea what he'd be letting himself in for.

CHAPTER 26

KALI HUMMED IN the kitchen as she waited for Grant's return. It had been ages since she'd spent time cooking. She loved to cook, only preparing a meal for one person wasn't the same as for company. She sliced onions and peppers, adding them to the cooking hamburger. Her spaghetti sauce recipe had been handed down from her great-grandma. She'd made several personal tweaks along the way, yet the essence remained the same. She couldn't help but wonder what her mom would have thought of Grant. She'd approve, Kali decided.

Shiloh lay in a sunbeam running across the kitchen floor. They both needed the downtime today. Rest and relaxation was good for the soul. Even with everything going on, Kali felt happy. They'd found Julie alive, Dan was improving and then there was her budding relationship with Grant. She had high hopes for tonight – if this asshole left them alone for that long.

Unfortunately, he was likely searching out his next victim right now. Kali turned and looked outside. The sun had slipped behind a dark cloud. She couldn't help think this was the classic calm before the storm.

Better to not go there now. What would happen, would happen. She'd deal with it somehow.

Kali returned to the kitchen and her sauce. Grant should be here soon. She moved through the mundane chores she'd missed out on recently – like laundry. Shiloh didn't appear to have the same sense of duty though as she lolled about around the house, watching as Kali worked.

Knowing the time was disappearing; Kali strode into her bedroom and quickly dealt with the clothes. As she started to leave, she turned to gaze thoughtfully to the bed. Checking her watch, she made a fast decision. Striding back over, she stripped the bedding off and made the bed up with fresh sheets. Better to be prepared and not have an opportunity than to have an opportunity and not be prepared.

Jamming the old sheets into the washing machine took another few minutes.

"Whew." Kali checked the laundry room over for dropped items. Then she headed back to the kitchen.

She walked around the corner when a hooded figure, dressed all in black, lunged for her.

Kali screamed. She spun and bolted back toward the laundry room. He grabbed for her arm, pulling her off balance. Pain streaked across her back. Kali stumbled, kicking wildly and heard him grunt. Freed unexpectedly, Kali screamed, "Shiloh, help!"

Shiloh barked and jumped. Kali didn't see anything else as she ran for the kitchen, bursting through the glass French doors, onto the deck, jumping the stairs two at a time.

"Shiloh," she screamed at the top of her voice. "Shiloh, come." The trees on the property weren't going to give her much coverage, only she'd take anything right now. She dared to look behind her. He wasn't following her. Shit. Kali stubbed her toe but didn't dare break stride. She could run ten miles without stopping, only right now, worry for Shiloh kept breaking her focus. She'd be running to catch up if she could. That she wasn't, couldn't be good.

She hid out in the woods and paused to catch her breath. Kali peered from behind a tree. Where was he? Kali closed her eyes and leaned into the tree. "Shit. Shit. Shit."

Her legs trembled in shock and she could hardly breathe. She took several deep shaky breaths. *Think. Think stupid. What are you supposed to do now?* Shit. Her cell phone. She slapped her hands over her pockets. There. Her fingers fumbled frantically. Finally, she managed to pull it free but struggled to punch in the numbers. She failed the first time and had to redial. She kept watching for any sign of him.

"Hello."

"Grant," she hissed softly.

"Kali. What's wrong? Where are you?" he yelled. Fear leapt through the phone and raised her own panic level. She peered nervously through the brush. Where were Grant's men?

"He's here at the house." She buried the phone in her shoulder at his yell. "I'm hiding out in the back yard at the bushes by the beach access. Grant, there's no sign of your men."

"Shit. I'm on my way. You stay put. Do you hear me?"

"Hurry." Kali couldn't stop the pleading tones. She didn't give a damn. She was scared and being alone was the last thing she wanted. "Something has happened to Shiloh. Either he has her or she's hurt."

"I'm in the car. I'll be there in less than ten minutes. There's two men on surveillance duty – have you seen any sign of them?"

No and damn it, she'd expected them to come to her rescue. Had counted on it.

Instead she was alone.

Cut off. With no sign of Shiloh.

And terrified.

Swallowing hard, she said, "No. Hurry, this is going to be the longest ten minutes of my life."

"Just make sure you're alive by the time I get there. If the bastard comes after you, run like hell."

"Don't worry I plan on it." She chewed on her lower lip, daring to peer around the tree. Her house sat silent and still. She searched the windows looking for any sign of movement...of life.

"Kali?"

"Shhh. I'm here." Kali pulled back behind the tree.

"Can you see him?"

"No." Her voice had dropped to a barely audible level. Kali scrunched up into a tight ball and sank further under the branches. "Hurry."

"Be there in a few minutes."

"Don't come alone." Kali's voice rose and suddenly remembering, she dropped it down to a hoarse whisper. "He's going to be waiting for you. I'm afraid he's hurt the surveillance team."

"I'm pulling into the driveway now. Stay where you are. Be there in minutes."

Kali's phone clicked off. She stared at it, then put it back into her pocket. The silence was eerie and unsettling. She couldn't stop peering behind her, afraid the asshole was going to pop up from nowhere.

It seemed like forever yet it was probably only three to four minutes before she heard the welcome sound of sirens in the distance. "Thank God. Please be okay, Shiloh. Please." Kali prayed for her best friend. Shiloh might be a dog to others, but she was family to her.

There. She peered around the tree, her head barely above ground. Someone was running toward her. Grant. She wanted to run to him but couldn't be sure of his identity. Her heart pounded. She peered out from her hiding place.

"Kali." Grant yelled, his hands cupping against his mouth. "Kali, where are you?"

A noise behind Kali had her spinning on the spot. Her throat constricted. The rustling sound moved in Grant's direction. *There.* A flash. Another movement. A heavy rustling.

Kali realized Grant, his gun at the ready, raced toward her right in front of the tree line. Exposed. An easy target. *Shit.*

And there was the killer…creeping up on Grant.

"No!" Kali bolted toward Grant. She hit him in a flying tackle but he twisted at the last minute – just as a funny spitting sound split the air.

Kali arched as her back hit the ground, tumbling into a mass of limbs. Men shouted and spread out into the wooded area.

Kali moaned and struggled to move.

"Kali? Are you all right?" Grant rolled over and regained his feet. He bent down to help her up.

"I'm fine. That was a rough landing." She smiled up at him. "He's a lousy shot. Go."

"Thank heaven for that. Still, he took out the two men watching the house. I have to find him." He cradled her gently, dropped a quick kiss on her forehead. "Are you sure you're okay?"

"Yes, yes. I'm fine. Go. I need to find Shiloh."

"Wait for me at the house. The rest of my team should be here soon."

Nodding, Kali took off at a run toward the house. Worry for Shiloh dominated – her own injury was forgotten. Maybe she was hurt, hiding somewhere. She burst into the house, calling out, "Shiloh?" Kali went from room to room, hating that she'd taken off without helping her friend. "Shiloh, where are you?"

Walking through the kitchen, she grabbed Shiloh's treat bag and walked into the bedroom, shaking it.

Kali stopped. She closed her eyes and reached out with the Sight. *Where are you, sweetheart? Shiloh?* Kali could feel her. She was alive, but hurting. Shit. Kali broke into a run and headed to the laundry room. The closet was open and on the floor back in the far back corner lay Shiloh, motionless. She didn't make a sound when Kali bent down beside her. Shiloh's fur was warm, except she didn't move when Kali touched her. Kali crawled into the closet and ran her hands over her friend. She stopped when she came to a sticky patch. She withdrew her hand to take a closer look. Blood.

"Oh God. Shiloh." Kali reached into the far back in the closet and slid her hand gently under Shiloh's chest and hips. Awkwardly, she backed out, shuffling on her knees, half-dragging and half-lifting Shiloh. The dog whimpered.

"Easy girl. You've been shot." Kali was already punching in the vet's number. "Oh God, please answer." It took just a minute to inform them that she was on her way.

Keys. Where were her keys? Kali panicked until she located them on the fridge with her purse. She made it through the front door and ran ahead to unlock the back door on her car. One agent saw her and ran to help. With his help, as gently as they could, they loaded Shiloh into the passenger seat. Kali raced around to the driver's side. She hit reverse and tore out of the yard, gravel spitting behind her tires. Grant would be pissed. Too bad. Grant had his responsibilities.

Kali had hers.

KALI DROVE RECKLESSLY. Shiloh was dying. Tears clouding her vision, hindered her driving.

"Hang in there, Shiloh. It's going to be all right girl, we're almost there." Kali ripped into the parking lot and drove up to the back door. She pulled the Jeep to a squealing stop and hopped out. There was a buzzer outside the back door. Pounding it several times, Kali raced to the passenger side. Shiloh hadn't moved.

Dr. Samson slammed the backdoor open and raced toward them.

"How is she?"

Kali stumbled in her reply. "I don't know. She's been shot but I have no idea how badly."

"Move over. Let me get her." Dr. Samson stood well over six-foot-four and was built like a linebacker. Kali didn't argue, was just grateful he was here at all. An animal gurney arrived at his side.

Shiloh was quickly transferred into the operating room and Kali was left standing alone. She didn't want to leave the surgical room, however the assistants ushered her to a waiting room and left her there. Paperwork had to be done, and her vehicle needed to be moved.

There was one more thing she could do. She leaned against a wall and sent loving healing energy toward Shiloh. She had no idea if it would help, but hoped it would. Could Stefan help? She didn't know how to contact him. Tears pooled in the corner of her eyes. It wasn't fair. Shiloh was family and Kali had lost too many people already.

I am helping her. Continue to send healing energy yourself.

Stefan.

Kali smiled through her tears, her heart full of hope. *Thank you!*

The wait was physically uncomfortable. Kali couldn't lean back and she couldn't sit still. Her phone rang on the fifth lap around the small waiting room.

"Where the hell are you?" Fear and anger sliced through the phone.

"At the vet's. The asshole shot Shiloh. I had to take care of her."

"And you couldn't fucking call me? You know this killer is hunting, right? What the hell do you think I thought when I couldn't find you?" His roar hurt her ears. "I told you to stay at the house."

Anger of her own spiked. "Well you haven't caught him and look at how many people have died. Don't tell me how to protect my family unless you think you can do a better job. And so far, you haven't."

Silence.

Kali cringed. She hadn't meant to be so harsh. "Look I'm sorry. Shiloh is in surgery and…I just didn't think." Kali stopped her pacing and brushed her hair back off her head. "She's been in there for over an hour. I don't even know if she's alive." Pain stabbed through her heart at the thought.

His voice turned soothing. "I know this has been tough on you."

"And, no, you don't understand," she cried out, her voice breaking. "This is your work. This is the stuff you deal with all the time. I don't. I don't want to either. I want this all to go away." Tears collected again in the corners of her eyes, and again Kali brushed them away. "He's hurt so many people. Destroyed so many families. When will this stop?" God. Her emotions were a mess. She sniffled quietly, but Grant still heard.

"I'm sorry, sweetheart. Stay close to Shiloh and I'll call you back in a little while."

Kali put her phone away. Every time she thought about him

and his work, she felt confused and upset. Talk about double standards. Her work had put off more than one prospective date. Yet, she was doing the same thing to him.

They weren't dating though. Yeah, right. So what did one call it?

"Kali."

She twisted to find Dr. Samson waiting to talk to her. Kali hastened over to him.

"How is she?"

"I think she's going to pull through. The bullet did some damage on its way through but missed the vital organs. We've patched her up. She'll need to stay here for a few days, under sedation, so we can keep an eye on her to make sure the bleeding has stopped."

Kali closed her eyes in relief. She swayed as every muscle in her body weakened.

"Here, sit down." Dr. Samson's concerned face stared down at her.

Kali smiled back at him. "I'm okay. Just relieved that she's going to make it."

"She's not out of the woods yet," he warned.

"She's a fighter and if she's given a fair chance, she'll do her part to pull through." Her heart suddenly felt lighter. Kali reached up and kissed the vet's cheek. "Thank you. Shiloh deserves to live. She's saved so many lives; I'm grateful you were here to save hers."

"We need Shiloh in this world. As long as she does her part and wants to live then I'll do my part and give her that chance."

The two friends shared an understanding look. "Can I see her?"

He shook his head. "You shouldn't. She's covered in blood with tubes coming and going in all directions. She wouldn't even know you."

It took some convincing but finally Kali headed back out to her car. Kali winced at the sun high and heat. She'd already been through so much today, surely it was bedtime. Before getting into the car, she called Grant. "I'm on my way home. Where are you?"

"Searching your yard. We've got a team sweeping the neighbourhood. I'll be at the house by the time you get back."

"Glad to hear it. See you soon."

Her shoulder had stiffened to the point where she could barely move it. Still Kali figured she could make the less-than-five-mile drive to where her bed waited. She drove slowly and carefully, not wanting anything else to go wrong today. She stopped at a red light.

Her phone rang. She snatched it from the holder. "Hello?"

The same horribly mechanical voice filled her ear. "You're too late…and now your lover is going to die." Laughter filled the Jeep's interior before being abruptly shut off.

Kali cried out in pain and horror.

The killer had Grant.

WALKING CASUALLY ALONG the tree line, visible enough to be seen, hidden enough to not be obvious, Grant closed the phone and tucked it away in his back pocket. He'd been glued to the damn thing all day. His mind raced over the information he'd just received. He was tempted to tell Kali but didn't dare until he'd had his suspicions confirmed. Besides she had enough to worry about.

But he might have just gotten a major piece of the puzzle handed to him. The DNA of the victim found in Sacramento was not Brad's.

"So you think you've figured it all out, do you?"

The cool confidant voice came from behind him. Grant gave a small hard smile. Then something small and hard dug into his back. Shit.

"Hold out the gun, real slow."

Grant's fingers flexed on the gun as he held his hands out. The gun was tugged free. Double shit.

"Now, turn around." Twigs rustled with the leaves as the gunman stepped back.

Tossing his options around in his head, Grant slowly turned to face a tall, muscular brown-haired male. Only by a stretch of a good imagination did it resemble the elusive Christian.

"Brad, I presume?" He narrowed his gaze at the smirk flashing across the other man's face, replaced only for a second by uncertainty and surprise. Brad might have been hiding out for days but he looked to be in peak physical condition. Except the eyes. The fervent glare shining his way looked anything but normal.

"Took you long enough, didn't it. Not so smart, are you? FBI trained and I still have the drop on you." He waved the FBI issue pistol in his hand, while he slipped Grant's gun into his pocket. "I'm going to have a decent collection of these by the end of the day."

Shit. That meant at least one of his team was down. There had to be a half dozen men out here. He cast a furtive glance around. Why had no one seen him?

"I've got a special hiding spot close by. A bird's-eye view of the place, so to speak." His lips might have twisted into a smile, but there was no reflection of it in his eyes. Grant could see the killer who lived inside instead. "It let me keep an eye on Kali. Pick my time to take you out. Or did you think I hadn't noticed how she looks at you, or you at her?"

Grant stared, his mind racing. He needed answers. He needed a way out. He needed to take this nutcase out before Kali got here. "I'm sorry. I don't know what you're talking about."

"Like hell, you don't. Do you know how long I've been trying to get her myself?" Brad snorted, pulling the gun to point at Grant's forehead. "God damn it. I let my marriage disintegrate for her. Did she care? No." Spittle formed at the corner of Brad's mouth as he worked himself into a more agitated state. He waved his gun around as he talked but was always careful to keep it pointed in Grant's direction.

"Stupid bitches. Her and that dog. Witches both of them. She had me cuckolded for years, caught up in her spell. Believing in her. I was an idiot. Not now. Not anymore. I've finally seen through her trickery."

Grant held back his retort, not wanting to slow the flow of words out of Brad's mouth. It might be the only chance he had of getting answers. His team should have them surrounded by now. It wasn't like Brad was making any attempt to be quiet or hidden.

Providing any of Grant's team were left alive to hear.

Brad's face turned mean. He motioned to Grant to turn down a well-travelled path through the trees. Obediently, with an eye to the surroundings and scanning for a way to escape, he wove through the trees.

Thankfully Brad kept up enough conversation for the two of them as they walked.

"I guess I'm not the brightest star around but I prayed to God for help. It seemed like nothing I did ever changed anything." Frustration bubbled through his voice gone hard and angry. "Not with Kali, not with the disasters. If anything, it seemed like the more people we rescued, the more people needed rescuing."

Grant started to turn around, but Brad nudged him hard with

the gun. "Keep moving. We're almost there."

They walked a little further. Kali's neighbour's house was off in the distance on the left – to the right, trees. They were descending slightly. Behind him Kali's house. In front…nothing but cliff and ocean.

Grant said, "Where are we going?"

Brad shoved him hard. Grant stumbled, and recovered. Three more steps and he could see the small clearing, barely big enough for the two of them at the cliff edge.

And a small hollowed out depression.

His stomach sank. Try to take Brad out now and risk a bullet and a fall off the cliff, or wait for the others.

Stall. "Why are you killing these poor people? I thought the purpose was to help all of them?

Snapping the words out, Brad said, "No. That's the problem. I didn't get it. Until Mexico." Brad snickered.

"I had a light-bulb moment. The reason things never changed is that I wasn't doing the right work. God created these disasters to call his people home. Natural disasters …are naturally occurring…as in they're manifestations of God's will. I wasn't supposed to rescue the buried victims. I was *supposed* to help God and finish the job on those people God missed because of interference."

He was crazy. That's the only explanation for the twisted excuse Brad was handing out. This was going to break Kali's heart.

"Then I made one last realization. I was supposed to enjoy my life. I hated to go home to my bitch of a wife, suffering in silence with unrequited love for the witch, and working my ass off to boot. That's no life for one of God's special workers. Not anymore. Life is fun now. This work is a joy." He laughed, pausing to wipe the sweat from his brow. "This is great. I'm dead to the world and you'll be…just dead."

Grant's mind raced. How to get out of this alive, before the madman with the gun started shooting? *Anytime, people.*

They are almost there. Keep holding him off.

Grant's knees almost buckled at Stefan's voice.

Thank God. Am I glad to hear you.

Kali is almost here. Hold on. Stefan's voice was sharp and urgent in Grant's head.

Grant straightened, spinning around. *No! Stop her. Brad will kill her.*

Too late. She's only minutes away.

"No!" Grant screamed, spinning around.

The blow came out of nowhere. It slammed into the side of his head, dropping him where he stood.

BRAD LAUGHED, WAVES of power flying through him. He could do this. He'd been off-stride all day. Driven by rage after last night's fiasco. But now things were pulling together… He thought he'd had the Julie stuff under control, but to learn that she'd lived through it had festered, eating away at him all morning.

Then he'd lost Kali in her own damn house. How stupid. By this time, he should have felled her several times over. Shooting Shiloh had hurt but when he recognized Shiloh also worked against God's will, firing had also given him an outlet for his rage.

And, he'd just redeemed himself. Still chuckling, he tossed the gun to the ground and bent over his latest victim.

What could Kali possibly see in this fool?

He dragged Grant the last few feet until he lay in the depression. Christ, this bastard was heavy. But the location was perfect. There was only room for him to stand. The cliff was so unstable here, no one would think about checking this outcrop. The eroded edge was ready to go as it were. Not that Grant would care. By the time the cliff crumbled, he'd be dead.

Brad stopped and took a deep breath; he mightn't have pulled this last one off if God hadn't been on his side.

He had to hurry. Kali could be here any minute.

He wanted to be ready for her.

CHAPTER 27

KALI GASPED, "GRANT. Oh, God, no. Please, no." She couldn't help the plea that floated around the interior of the car. She grabbed for her cell phone and dialed quickly. Cars honked. Kali hit the gas and sped toward home. She listened for his voice, but the ringing went on and on. Grant didn't answer.

Kali dug furiously through the front cubbyhole for Grant's card. She hit the brakes at the next stoplight. *Christ.* Where was it? Panic set in when she couldn't find it. There. Under several pens. She snatched it up. Good, there were the more formal channels on the card. Kali dialed the first number, wracking her brain for the name of the friend who worked with Grant.

Thomas, that was it. She asked the person on the other end to speak with him – explaining it was an emergency concerning one of their agents, Grant Summers. It took a moment but finally she had Thomas on the line.

Kali quickly filled him in.

Thomas wasted no time. "Where are you?"

"Almost home. I'm turning into my driveway now." She drove in and parked.

Grant's car was there. Along with two other FBI vehicles. Kali sighed with relief. She raced up to her front door and opened it. "Grant? Hello? Are you here?"

Silence. "Thomas, he's not answering and there's no sign of him. I think the killer has him."

"We're almost there. Don't go inside. Get back into your car and leave the property. Do you hear me?"

"Too late, I'm already here. Where's Grant's back-up team?"

She walked through the house checking for signs Grant had been here. There were none. She headed into the kitchen; the lingering aromas of her spaghetti sauce reminded her of their long forgotten plans. Kali walked onto the deck and searched the backyard. She returned to the kitchen. Surely, there should be other agents here? "The bastard must have circled and snuck up on Grant."

"There are several teams there now and I've got another one with me. They'll find this guy. Stay out of their way and let them do their jobs," said Thomas.

Kali surveyed the room. There were papers on the kitchen table. She walked over to check. On the top of the pile, a short ripped-off piece read: "Who's going to help you now, witch?"

"Shit! The bastard left a note on the kitchen table."

"God damn it, stop," roared Thomas. "We're almost there. Let us take care of this."

"As you've taken care of everything else?" Kali snorted. "I don't think so. I happen to care for Grant and I'm sure as hell not going to leave his fate up to you."

"Kali, don't do anything stupid. I know you want to help. So do we. We're only minutes away. Stay there until we arrive so we can at least assist you. This guy wants you to do something foolish. But unless he's huge, he's not going to move Grant too far."

"Not likely." Kali closed her eyes. Grim reality hit home. "That's why he shot Shiloh, so I wouldn't have her help to find the victims. Giving him yet another advantage. He's determined to have me show my true self."

Kali turned as she heard several vehicles roar into the yard. She raced to the front door and opened it. Thomas still had his cell phone and was talking to her. "True self? What do you mean? Don't you need Shiloh?"

"No."

He looked confused when Kali walked up to him. They exchanged grim smiles at each other as they put their cell phones away. The men collected in a group around them. Several stood listening to the conversation. She didn't think Grant would have told any of them about her abilities – except maybe Thomas.

She motioned for Thomas to walk a few steps away for a private chat.

"He thinks I'm using black magic," she said. "He called me a witch in his note."

"Why is that?" He frowned.

Kali was beyond caring about his opinion. Grant's life was at stake here. "Some of you saw Shiloh and me in action earlier. But it's not always Shiloh that does the finding. I do too."

Thomas stared at her.

"Shiloh isn't a rescue dog?"

"Yes, she is and a damn good one. But I often pick up on victims, too. She does well when Mother Nature causes chaos. My specialty is when men are responsible for the damage."

"Because you're psychic?" Doubt and skepticism were evident.

"I'm not really psychic. More a barometer for violence." Kali shrugged. "Shiloh and I work well together as a team. But I *have* worked and *will* work without her if I have to. Like now," she added grimly. "So if you don't mind, park your doubts and leave your questions for later. Let's find Grant before he's buried alive."

Thomas stood beside her, cell phone open, already texting his team. "Any idea where to start looking?"

Kali spun in a circle. She was Grant's only chance. If she could just find that faint trail of violent energy.

A faint sprinkle, like sunlight on dust – only much darker – floated to the right of the house. "Yeah, he's headed to the beach."

"Let's go then."

Kali summoned the Sight, easily picking up the scattered energy. She pointed the way and took off at a dead run. She could see the trail flattened through the woods in her mind's eye but hadn't caught sight of the actual trail in the woods yet. She didn't need to. A few hundred yards took her to the steep stairs. Energy fluttered at the top then continued along the top of the cliff. The stairs had been considered but had eventually been tossed. Opening her eyes she turned left. "This way. Hurry."

Kali crashed through the bush, knowing that sneaking was better than charging like an elephant, but she couldn't stop herself. Urgency rode her hard.

The men crashed noisily behind her.

She came to an abrupt stop. Clouds of energy billowed atop the bushes. She spun around and held up a hand to stop the charge behind her. Thomas walked quietly to her. "What's up?"

She leaned toward his ear, whispering, "He's just up past the bend. I recognize the place. The cliff is very unstable here. There's no space either. Enough for one man, maybe two – but that's all. You'll take the cliff down if anyone tries to rush him. You'll end up killing Grant anyway. And possibly other members of your team."

Thomas stared in the direction she mentioned. "So how do you know he's up there?"

Kali shot him a withering look. "I can see the energy."

He looked at her, a puzzled expression on his face. Then he said, "We'll fan out and come in from several directions."

"Quietly," she cautioned. Kali moved forward ten feet, twenty feet and then thirty. She heard a voice and came to a dead stop.

A pain worse than anything she'd ever experienced unfurled in her heart. Her soul was already splintering with the horror that came with the voice recognition. "It can't be. Please not." Pain and grief clogged her throat as Brad's voice roiled through her defenses.

Kali peered through the brush. She gazed on the face of the man she'd considered her best friend for the last decade. So changed by expression and his words, each one a fresh stab into her soul.

The crazed killer…the one who'd kidnapped and killed so many people, was her best friend…her dead best friend. Oh God, the same person who'd killed little Melanie and almost killed Julie, had been a friend to them all.

Brad.

Kali burrowed her head in her hands. Had Brad killed other people? People he was called to save…how many had he killed? Brad spoke again. Kali strained to hear the words.

"So you're coming around already, huh?"

Kali groaned softly. He had to be talking to Grant.

"Maybe that's good. Not that it will save you. That bitch needs to know my life, to live my old world. Feel that sense of failure. That knowing that nothing she does ever changes anything. Your death will teach her so much."

Kali's heart shattered. Brad's mind had broken. He'd morphed into this bizarre killer. She couldn't even begin to imagine who lay in the morgue wearing Brad's toe tag. His words reverberated in her soul. So much emptiness, so much pain, so much evil. A monster.

And *that* Brad had Grant.

Creeping closer, Kali wished for the first time in her life that she had a weapon of her own. She looked around for something that could do some damage. The sight of the men creeping toward the unstable area made her heart stop.

Rising up slightly, she tried to locate Grant but there was no sign of him. And Brad stood at the edge of the cliff. Shit.

Enough. She had to help Grant.

She stood up, calling out, "It's me you want. So why do you keep attacking everyone else? Brad, why are you hurting all these innocent people?"

All the while talking, she searched the area for any sign of Grant. Again nothing. Except she spotted a gun tossed off to one side. Her heart sank when she saw freshly turned dirt piled against the cliff rising behind the small jutting ledge. If Grant survived the burying, the cliff was poised to fall away at any moment, killing him anyway. Without air, he had only minutes. Who knew if Brad felt Grant rated an oxygen tank this time? Billowing clouds of gray energy engulfed the area. Signs of violence in progress. Kali could barely see through it.

Brad stepped back, his chest heaving, shock evident on his face. "No, you can't be here. Not yet."

Approaching slowly, Kali sought the right words. "Of course it's possible. I'm better than you."

She watched warily as his face turned purple and red, the veins on his temple bulging.

"No. I'm better. I've proved it."

"Proved what? That you're weak and useless and you like attacking innocent people?"

Anger speared his voice. "Innocent? They are not. You don't understand, but then how could you? You don't know I'm doing God's work. But you think these people deserve to be saved. They were supposed to die in the first place." His voice rose until he practically screamed the last words.

Kali stared at him. So that's what a broken mind looked like. Horrible.

"They deserved to die like this? Suffering for days? What disaster did Grant survive? You're only killing him because of me. How many other people have you killed?" She paused, then whispered softly, "You're crazy."

But not softly enough.

"I am not crazy," he screamed. "I'm sending these people home, my way. Sending them back. They were supposed to have died – like all the others. I don't know how many I helped God take home. I didn't kill them, God did. I'm just putting them back into the same situation they shouldn't have gotten out of. God's will must be done!" he yelled at her.

Then suddenly, he stopped talking.

He'd seen the men rise up behind her.

"You're too late. You'll always be too late."

Kali stiffened. "What have you done?" She ran at him, screaming in fury.

Before she could reach him, the pile of dirt shifted in waves and a hand reached out from the grave. And grabbed onto Brad's ankle.

Brad cried out and jumped back, breaking the hold on his leg. Just then a heavy rumble sounded. An odd look rippled across his face as the ground beneath him gave away.

Kali stopped in her tracks as a horrible scream filled the air. She stopped breathing but her heart pounded crazily as her mind filled with an instant replay of what had just happened. And froze on the glimpse she'd caught of Brad's face as he went over the cliff. The disbelief. The fear. The horror.

As if he saw, not God, but the devil.

Then he was gone but his shocked face remained in her mind for a long instant before fading away. Her breath whooshed out.

Brad was dead now. This time – for real.

But Grant… Relief filled her as he heaved up from the grave onto all fours… He was alive!

Later she'd deal with Brad's betrayal, but right now the only feeling rushing through her was pure happiness.

She raced to Grant as he struggled to his feet. His chest heaved as she threw herself into his arms.

"Christ, Kali," he said, choking on the words.

Kali didn't care about words right now. She squeezed him tight, relief bringing tears to her eyes.

It was over. Held tight in Grant's embrace, Kali's splintered world glued itself back into a cohesive whole. From the bits of conversation going on around her, she understood Brad was gone. The hillside had sent enough dirt and rock on top to require equipment and men to recover his body. Fitting in a way.

As she stood, her face buried against Grant's heaving chest, she came to a realization. The real Brad, her best friend Brad, had disappeared a long time ago. As she'd internalized her pain from the Mexico disaster, the Brad she'd known had fractured, becoming someone else.

She'd mourn the loss of her friend. She could only be grateful for the death of the madman he'd become. Maybe understanding in this way, would give her closure.

Her heart eased. She shuddered as the weight of so many lives slipped off her shoulders. Tilting her head back, she stared up in Grant's warm loving gaze. "I'm so glad it's all over."

"So am I." The glint in his eye was the only warning before he captured her lips in a devastating kiss.

The men surrounding them cheered.

By the time he lifted his head, Kali collapsed against his chest, exhausted, but smiling.

KALI GENTLY BENT over to scratch Shiloh's ears. She lay on the far side of the deck. She'd healed but hadn't fully recovered her strength yet. Kali didn't care; Shiloh had survived. That's what counted. Hopefully, they'd have many more years together.

"How's she doing, Kali?" Julie asked.

"She's doing fine. Although it will still be a few weeks before she's back to her normal bouncy self."

She straightened, twisting against the damn itchiness that was damn near killing her. "At least her stitches aren't bugging her as much as mine are. Damn." She tried to reach the one spot on her right shoulder and couldn't.

A large hand found and scratched the spot for her.

Kali moaned in relief, leaning her head against Grant's chest to give him better access. From the coziness of his arms around her, she surveyed the motley crew collected on Kali's deck. Grant had fully recovered. Julie had also pulled through. Her face could use some more color, yet she looked to be managing her recovery well. Dan on the other hand, looked to be managing his demise. He was dying.

Kali had shed many tears for him. Even now moisture collected in the corner of her eyes. As if sensing her distress, Grant whispered, "Are you okay?"

She tilted her head up and responded softly, "I'm just struggling with Dan's acceptance of his own death. Why refuse treatment. It could really make a difference."

His arms tightened around her. He dropped his chin onto the top of her head. "Because it would only give him a few months. He wants to go peacefully – the way God intended."

Kali flinched. "And that just reminds me of Brad. How could he kill Christian, his best friend, in order to gain a fresh start?"

A heavy sigh worked free of Grant's chest. "Brad brought a lot of pain and torment to many people."

Cringing slightly, she nodded. "True. I'd be happy to take Sergeant. He's a great dog."

"Give Susan a chance. If it doesn't work out then you can suggest it." His deep murmur sent shivers down her spine.

"And Jarl?" She tried to hold her bitterness back.

"You can't fix everything, honey. He shot you. He attacked Dan. I don't care how worried he was you'd finger him for the thefts, attempted murder is going to put him away for a long time."

"Well I hope he gets to stay with Penny until the end. She only has a few weeks left." It had to be hard on her to know what Jarl had done and the penalty he'd pay for trying to fix their situation. Not a nice end to her life.

"You're such a softy." He cuddled her closer.

Rational, sensible Grant. He'd been the stalwart one throughout all this. He'd calmed her when anger had overwhelmed her. He'd held her when despair had taken hold. He'd loved her when she hadn't loved herself.

He'd become everything to her.

Grant returned to gently scratching his hand along her slowly healing wounds. Kali moaned with pleasure.

"That feels so good."

"Didn't you say that very same thing last night?"

She flashed him an intimate glance. "Yeah, I think I did. Maybe it'll be your turn to moan tonight."

He winked. "I look forward to that."

"Hey you two, my old heart can't stand much more of this. Keep it clean." Dan's teasing voice brought them both back to their surroundings.

Stefan added his two bits. "Take pity on those of us unattached and unloved." He'd become a regular visitor as he was enlisted to help Kali develop her skills.

Grant snorted at his friend. "You're alone only when you choose to be."

And if Julie had her way, Stefan wouldn't be alone tonight or any other night. Kali surveyed her group with satisfaction, her gaze landing on Dan, his face alight with knowing laughter.

Grant reached out and captured her fingers in his. "So were you planning to do anything special in the next couple of months?"

She wrinkled her nose. "No, I don't think so. Other than enjoy life."

"Sounds good to me. How do you feel about having company?"

She glanced sideways at him. "I'd love to have some company.

Are we talking for a day or two? For a few weeks or a few years?"

Her fingers were squeezed in a death grip. "If we're talking that long, maybe I should ask how do you feel about a house guest?"

Wow. Kali raised an eyebrow. "I guess that depends on whether he's going to be a guest or if he's moving in." Kali gave him a saucy look.

Grant's steely gray eyes searched her face. Kali cast a warm glance from her partially closed eyes. His lips twitched. "Is moving in an option?"

"Hell, yeah. House guests are work. Partners share the load." Kali smirked.

"We do make a good team, don't we?"

"Damn right we do.

"Then partners it is."

Dan finally spoke up. "About damn time too."

They all laughed.

Grant squeezed Kali's hand. She smiled. Her future looked warm and bright for the first time in over a decade.

Personally, she couldn't wait.

MADDY'S FLOOR

Book #3 of Psychic Visions

Dale Mayer

Dedication

This book is dedicated to my four children who always believed in me and my storytelling abilities.

Thank you!

Acknowledgments

Maddy's Floor wouldn't have been possible without the support of my friends and family. Many hands helped with proofreading, editing, and beta reading to make this book come together. Special thanks to Amy Atwell and my editor Pat Thomas. I thank you all.

MONDAY

When you believed in the goodness of life, why did darkness always nudge up against you – test you – try to make you change your mind?

LATE AFTERNOON SUNSHINE poured through the window of The Haven casting warm rays across Madeleine Wagner's spacious office on the top floor of the long-term care facility. The early part of August had been hot and humid. Now, entering the last week, the dead heat had cooled to a comfortable temperature.

She stared at the paperwork stacked high on one side of her desk, then at a smaller mountain on the other. Groaning, she leaned back and rubbed her throbbing temple. *Why had she wanted to become a doctor anyway?* Although, today her career choice wasn't the problem; it was her other skills. The skills no one mentioned but everyone knew about. Dr. Madeline...was not only a brilliant doctor, but a medical intuitive.

And her unorthodox skills were the reason Dr. Johnson, from the second floor, had asked her to look at Eric Colgan. He wanted Maddy to try to find out why Eric's condition was deteriorating so rapidly – for no apparent reason – when all his tests were coming back negative.

She'd gotten her first inkling something wasn't right while Dr. Johnson had been explaining the case. Then he'd sent her an email with more details. As she read, a weird twinge settled at the base of her neck. A sensation something was wrong. That feeling had grown until just the sight of her colleague's email brought goose bumps on her arms.

She'd immediately printed the page off, dug out a new folder and buried it under a dozen others.

It made no difference.

It pulled at her. Sitting there.

Waiting.

She sat up straight and forced herself to continue through the large stack of paperwork, until the pull refused to be ignored.

Crap.

She pushed the open file off to the side and dragged the email out. Maybe she should take a quick peek. See if there was anything she could do, and if not, then she'd pass the case back – quickly. She wasn't able to help everyone.

She quickly accessed Eric's file on her computer. With his information displayed in front of her, she eased back from the heavy mahogany desk and mentally distanced herself from her emotions. She took several deep breaths to calm her energy. On the next breath, she opened her inner eye and focused on Eric's energy. Almost instantly, the outline of a young man's body formed; it stood upright in the center of the office, as clear as if he actually stood before her.

Sometimes the person appeared in street clothes, as if they'd just walked into her office, and she'd see the energy moving through them and over them. Other times she saw only a vague shape pulsing with colors. This time Maddy saw both the physical and the energetic forms of Eric.

Now the shell of Eric's body teemed with a swirling darkness as energy poured outward in hundreds of dark red and purple ribbons. Hugging the outside edge, his aura hung lanky and dark, missing the vitality of someone in good health and good spirits.

Colors swelled and receded in a grotesque dance. Stretching away from the body, they faded outward, filling the small office. Maddy rose and circled the desk to get a better view of this apparition. She reared back slightly and blinked several times. The energy still twisted and stretched in its macabre dance. She rocked slightly on the balls of her feet. She'd never seen anything like this.

Angry energy had one appearance. Hatred had another. But this…this defied description.

Maddy needed more information. Letting the vision dissolve, she walked back to her desk and laid one hand flat on top of the printed email.

Eric's energy reached out and grabbed her by the throat. She coughed and choked – tears filled her eyes. She snatched her hand back and bolted to the far end of the room.

Christ.

Maddy paced around the small office trying to calm herself.

Another 'first.' In the middle of the room she stopped, her hand on her chest. She took three deep breaths, and frowned. His energy was incredibly strong.

Maddy's mind stalled…reconsidered.

Was it *his* energy? She'd assumed it was his, but did she know that for sure? Not really.

Frustrated, she returned to her chair to flip through the online information. Changing tactics, and with her finely tuned control locked in place, she released a small amount of energy outward in Eric's direction.

It normally took a moment or two to see the pattern, feel the pain and locate the regions of distress in an unhealthy body. Not this time. This time, tidal waves of anger washed over her. Whatever had happened to this young man, she knew he hadn't come to terms with it.

That didn't surprise her. Few people came to terms with imminent death, whether it was their own or that of friends and family. Anger was an understandable reaction to learning you had less than three months to live. But what she'd experienced just now was so much more than anger.

Maddy hugged herself to ward off the unearthly cold now permeating the room. She tried to focus on Eric's physical condition, but emotional trauma blasted at her, disturbing her balance. This man was beyond angry. He'd moved into panic. Confusion and pain agitated his space. His outrage – palpable.

So was his terror.

Tapping into her inner eye, she brought up the same energy vision as before. The aura had thinned until it was snug against his body. Leaning forward, she studied the color patterns, searching for the origin. Energy swarmed throughout the different layers of the young man's body, refusing to stay contained. It was as if the shell were too small to hold it all. The colors darkened, the energy slowed – as if heavy – engorged.

Static energy filled the small room, strong enough to cause loose strands of her hair to quiver.

The image was painful to observe. It reminded her of the aftermath of a feeding frenzy. One energy feasted on the other. Then it hit her. Clearly.

There wasn't a single energy spinning endlessly inside this body – there were two.

Two separate and distinct energies fought a battle within his body as he stood before her.

Stunned, Maddy tried to locate and identify the two distinct energies. One energy, pale and indistinct, sat low and snuggled close to the center of the body. She frowned, recognizing the signs. This energy was weak, dying.

A wave of black swept down the front of the body so fast, Maddy barely saw the paler energy cringe beneath. The wave had depth, density almost. Instinctively, she stretched out her hand, tracing the slow pale ribbon closest to the middle of the image. Her hand went right through the strip.

She gasped as she understood this was in real time. Whatever battle was playing out in the young man's body, it was happening somewhere in The Haven…now. She moved back to the computer and checked the location of Eric's bed – number 242. He was almost directly below her.

As she watched, the energy waves to the right of his body zipped off somewhere out of her vision, speeding forward. The force was so extreme, it snagged the other ribbons, dragging them along in its wake.

A weird noise filled the room. *Laughter?* She spun around…searching. The room was empty.

Then a voice, so malevolent, so angry, that it was almost tangible, whispered through her mind's eye. *Just try to stop me.*

Was it possible?

Maddy jumped to her feet as the energy waves winked out of existence. Panic set in. The mocking laughter swelled to encompass her entire office. She raced out but still the faint laughter snaked through her psyche as she ran down the stairs to the second floor. Urgency fired her long legs as she tracked the faint thread of energy back to its source. She had to stop this – whatever *this* was.

She swerved to avoid a cluster of young people hugging in the hallway. Up ahead, a laundry cart rumbled down the main aisle, clogging it even further. She blasted through the crowd, heading for Eric's ward.

She had to be wrong – to be right would open up something unthinkable.

A horrible suspicion filled her mind, one too bizarre to believe – even for her. And suddenly she knew she was going to be too late.

Surely, no one was capable of doing this.

The laughter cut off as she came to a shuddering stop at the doorway to Eric's ward. The room was filled with frantic activity. A trauma team crowded around the first bed. A crash cart sat between two beds. The other patients in the ward watched on in fearful silence. Maddy stood at the open doorway, unable to see which patient the team worked on.

Confused, she tried to stay out of the way as the chaos heightened around her. Outside, people mingled in the halls. Nurses bustled in and left, and throughout it all, the team worked diligently.

Maddy opened her inner vision only to slam it closed again. Colors, images and sounds crashed into her mind from the chaotic emotions and the overwhelming number of energy systems of those around her. She doubled over with pain from the onslaught.

One nurse raced to her side to help, but Maddy waved her away before stepping back into the hallway to regain her sense of balance.

Several beds lined the hallway. An older woman, her bed in the middle of the others, slept through the commotion. A sheet barely hid her bony frame, decimated by disease. A grayish cast covered her thin, almost translucent skin. Maddy's heart ached for the poor woman. There were several beds with patients that looked in similar condition. A normal state for this half of The Haven that operated as a long-term care home.

Maddy heard Dr. Samuel finally call it, requesting a time of death. She stepped into the room in time to see him tug the sheet over the patient's face. A moment of respectful silence ensued. Maddy quickly sent out a prayer for the family of the unknown man. Death was an all-too-common event here at The Haven. This was the last placement for most patients.

The staff filed out, wheeling some of the equipment with them. The doctor closed the curtain around the bed, smiled at her quietly and left.

Taking advantage of the sudden calm in the room, Maddy walked into the room, nodded politely at the shocked patients whose eyes followed her every move. Then she checked the bed numbers. She stopped in front of the closed curtain and pulled it back slightly.

Bed 242. *Eric Colgan.*

Stunned, Maddy stumbled back to the hallway, taking a last, long look at the white-curtained area. Her heart raced and her brain stalled. Confusion and fear churned together.

What had just happened?

She stared aimlessly down the hallway, unsure how to process the event. Her glance fell on the same elderly woman in the bed in the hallway.

Maddy blinked. Surely, the old woman's gaunt frame hadn't thickened slightly? Her bony ribs seemed less pointed. That couldn't be right. Surely physical changes like that weren't possible? It had to be her imagination. Or possibly it was a different woman instead. There'd been several lined up in the hallway before.

Maddy peered down the corridor. One bed was being wheeled down toward the next ward, with another old woman propped up on the pillows. Maddy breathed a sigh of relief. That had to be the woman she'd seen before. Still, she couldn't resist a last glance at the first woman still positioned in front of her.

Damned if she didn't closely resemble the woman she'd seen earlier – when she'd first reached Eric's room.

Except…this woman's gray-tinged skin now sported a peaceful pink glow that made Maddy's stomach cramp and her heart seize. The old woman opened her eyes and stared at Maddy in surprise, a quick sly smile coming to her face.

Shocked, Maddy stared back as fine tremors of disbelief wracked her spine.

She had been too late.

But too late for what? What had just happened?

TUESDAY

THE SUN SHONE on the brick sidewalk leading to the front door of The Haven. It was late. Maddy's morning schedule was already off – on a day she could little afford it. Not with yesterday's bizarre happenings twisting in her mind. She'd had a horrible night. She'd worried well past midnight before managing to nab a few hours of sleep.

What she needed was a good dose of adrenaline to toss off her lethargy and kick-start her morning. The many floors of the building gave her a perfect opportunity. The meeting she had this morning was on the main floor beside the physio center and pharmacy. The first and second floors offered open wards and major storage; laundry and morgue were on sub levels. The small hospital serviced the community's needs as well as their own. Her special healing project occupied the top floor, known as Maddy's Floor. Her floor.

Walking to the tall narrow stairwell inside the massive stone building, she glanced around to see if anyone was close by. Nope. As usual, she was alone. Another good thing about the cage elevators – people loved them and that left the stairwell free for her to run. Slipping off her heels and flexing her bare feet on the rubber stair edge, she mentally counted to three then bolted upwards. She'd been running these stairs since she'd started at The Haven five years ago. Only twice had she met anyone in her mad dash.

She loved to run. The power she felt as her long legs took the stairs two at a time was addictive. She whipped around the first, then the second corner where the double doors to the next floor remained quiet and closed. Just the way she liked them.

Onward and upward, gaining speed, she felt laughter bubbling up. She had a reputation for being prim, proper and a bit staid. She hadn't cultivated that image, but it did give her a professional persona that made people listen, and in the medical world that counted. If only her coworkers could see her now.

The next landing flashed by. She laughed as she sped faster and faster. Most people tired out as they climbed. Not Maddy – the vertical climb energized her. The next landing went by in a blur. Maddy hardly noticed. Being so focused on the end goal, she pounded ever upward.

And ran into a wall.

"What the hell?"

Maddy stumbled, scrambling to stay upright even as hands reached out to steady her.

"Whoa, easy there."

Gasping for breath and waiting for her balance to reassert itself, Maddy struggled with the shock of hitting what appeared to be a linebacker in a charcoal suit. She stared, stunned at the oversized stranger before her. Then she frowned.

Maybe not a stranger – there was something familiar about him.

"Are you okay?" Concerned pools of blue steel stared down at her.

Part of her brain heard and understood his words. However, the rest of her understood something was seriously off-kilter. She recognized him, yet she was sure she'd never met him before. There's no way she'd have forgotten this man.

Maddy took a step back, blowing out a breath, and managed a light laugh. "Thanks. That was close."

"Do you always run like you're being chased?"

"I was laughing so it was pretty obvious I wasn't in trouble." She gave him a cheeky grin. "And yes, I do like to race up and down these stairs." His gaze dropped to the floor. Maddy glanced down and wiggled her toes self-consciously. Heat climbed her cheeks. Hurriedly she slipped her heels on again.

"Bare feet?"

"Bare feet or heels. I run in both." Maddy tossed her head, her jet-black, shoulder-length hair flipping around her face as she stared him in the eye.

The stranger's eyes widened. "Hardly the safest or healthiest way to start your day."

Her back stiffened. She hated criticism, especially from people who didn't know her enough to be an expert. "Better than a donut."

The stranger's hands fisted on his hips and his forehead creased as he scowled at her. "How'd you know I was a cop?"

Surprised, she arched a brow. "I didn't." She smirked, feeling on a more equal footing. "Maybe that's your guilty conscience talking, Officer."

"Detective."

Maddy acknowledged his title with a nod. "So why is a detective hiding out in the stairwell of The Haven?"

He snorted. "I'm hardly hiding, and I definitely was not expecting to be mowed down. I'm visiting my aunt and checking on my uncle's application to transfer in."

"Ahh, I can understand that. Good luck." She checked her watch. So much for making up lost time. "If you'll excuse me, I have to run." She grimaced at the automatic turn of phrase.

"Right. Back to full speed, I presume." He stepped aside.

Maddy walked up the last flight of stairs at a more sedate pace. She couldn't resist looking over the railing for one last glimpse of the stranger, disappearing below.

DREW CONTINUED DOWN the last few stairs, his mind consumed with his 'run-in' with the intriguing mystery woman. She'd worn no nametag, had on no jacket to identify her role in this mausoleum, but her height was a definite clue that would help him find out who she was. He should have come right out and asked her, except he'd been lust-struck by the sight of the six-foot Amazon running barefoot in such a wild fashion up the stairs. And that flash of red and black lace peeking through the buttoned-up blouse – yeah, mega sexy.

How odd. He was usually drawn to petite women. Then again, he also went for the helpless take-care-of-me-because-I-can't-do-it-myself type.

He snorted at his folly. Drew glanced up the stairwell. His mystery woman had vanished.

Though tempted to chase her down for her name and number, he held back. In an all-out race, she'd probably leave him eating her dust.

Still his fingers flexed as if remembering what had slipped through their grasp.

Drew walked down the remaining flights, his mind locked on her. Could she be the elusive Dr. Madeleine Wagner? He'd pictured her as a stiff professional with high-buttoned shirts and thick-rimmed glasses that hid a deep intelligence, not a barefoot, lingerie-loving wild woman flinging herself around the stairwell with complete abandon. How was he to reconcile the two halves to the whole?

If she were Dr. Maddy.

Aunt Doris had been here for close to a year. In that time, Drew had come to respect the staff and the facility. Uncle John, with his rapidly declining health, should be happy during his last few months here – if he could get in. Then again, his uncle was another wild card. He demanded and expected everyone else to hop to it – even though he'd retired a few years ago. Of course, he'd been forced to retire and that twisted his view of 'retirement.' John McNeil would still play the role of the 'chief of police' until the last breath left his body.

Uncle John had run roughshod over everyone all his life and he wasn't about to stop now. If the old guy could arrange life to suit him better, he'd do it.

Drew reached the busy parking lot. His uncle was a challenge, but he was family and that had to count for something.

MADDY REACHED HER office with barely enough time to clean up, calm down and grab her notes before her appointment. Today was important. The board meeting needed to go her way. Though she was progressive in her thinking, she was settled in many parts of her life…and change, for her, wasn't something that happened easily. Maddy wanted to stay exactly where she was – on the top floor – with her patient roster exactly as it was. She'd written the Board a nice letter explaining her reasons…that she understood their budget problems, but that if she had to take on more patients it would not be possible to maintain the quality of care each deserved.

Still, if it came down to the bottom line, she'd rather accept more patients than spend hours working on another floor. The latter would divide her energy and compromise the project – hence today's meeting. Tossing a grin as she passed Gerona, one of her senior nurses who marshaled the front nurses' station, Maddy strode to the elevators. Impatiently she pushed the down button – no stairs now. She'd already burned through the last of her time and energy, worrying.

The elevator descended, slow as a snake on a frosty day. She leaned against the back wall and tried to focus on anything other than the meeting ahead. Glancing down at her navy suit, she checked to make sure her outfit looked as appropriately somber as when she'd put it on this morning. Normally, she loved color. Today was all about conforming, at least on the surface. A grin slid out. A prize piece of her Victoria's Secret collection comprised the under layer. Maddy wiggled. No one knew. Except Visa!

Though Maddy was tall that didn't stop males from being interested in her, yet it did slim the numbers down some. Maddy considered that a blessing. If someone drop-dead gorgeous, with that extra something, walked across her path and thought she'd make a great playmate – well then, he'd be in for a happy surprise when he found out about her secret passion. Maddy loved to play – only she didn't do short-term.

It didn't bother her that she'd been alone for over a year now. Someone would show up eventually.

The elevator dinged.

Straightening, she brushed her jacket off and strode forward to face the lion's den, aka Gerard Lionel, The Haven's badass CEO.

GERARD STRETCHED, EASING his arms upward to erase the kink in his back. A bad night and a lousy morning gave his spine a feeling of being pounded to conform to other people's wishes. He was only thirty-nine, what was life going to be like by the time he hit fifty? He and the other five board members present were once again trying to cut the budget and keep The Haven viable and operational, an almost impossible feat in today's economic crisis.

"Have you considered trimming supplies? Surely, we can reduce this heavy laundry bill. Look at the expenditures on paper towel and tissues." Peggy Wilson, the most annoying, penny-pinching accountant Gerard had ever met, thumbed through the pages she held. "The budget cuts have to come from somewhere."

Gerard groaned silently. Not this again. This was a long-term care facility, for Christ's sake. "We trimmed that area of the budget a year ago. The staff is struggling to maintain this figure as it is. We can't cut things that could affect the spread of infection. You know that. By rights, we should be adding fifty thousand to this figure."

Peggy pouted, her stern countenance almost cracking with the movement. He knew she didn't like being thwarted.

"I do understand that. What is the answer then? We can hardly cut the wages of doctors or other staffers. As lucky as they are to have jobs, we're the ones lucky to have them here."

Gerard put down his pencil and sank back in his chair. "And I know that. We're going to have to raise the fees again and increase doctors' workloads instead of filling open job vacancies. There's really no other option at this point."

And there wasn't. Gerard knew that. He'd been to this point before, at other facilities as well as this one. The past year had been tough on all of them. Theirs wasn't a unique problem and neither was the solution. Yet telling Maddy she'd have to spend some hours each day working on the floor below was not something he was looking forward to. She might consider the alternative worse.

He knew he had to follow the dictates of the Board of Directors. He knew he was the boss below that. He knew she was bound by his decisions, and none of it mattered one bit. Dr. Maddy was...well...she was Dr. Maddy. Special and unique, with skills he'd never be able to replace. Without her, they'd lose a large percentage of their residents, and the huge donations for her project – something they could ill afford.

She'd worked on the top floor for close to five years, and had been running it for the last three. Sure, Dr. Cunningham ran it with her, but his presence fooled no one. Still, with over thirty years of impressive experience he'd lent his name and reputation to the project. But, it was called Maddy's Floor for a reason.

In addition to the special project she ran there, her light, her presence, just the person she was radiated something special. When she turned that light onto 'her' patients, they blossomed, improved, and in some cases, they even healed. Her personality or her 'skills' – whatever you called it – was a common thread of discussion in the lunchroom and meetings, but always behind her back. She had a gift that caused everyone to want to reach out and touch her – if just for a moment – to know that miracle healing was possible.

Gerard shook his head at the fanciful thought. These thoughts dominated every time he watched her work, and lately, every time he thought about her. Not good.

"What about extending the day clinic hours?" Peggy suggested. "Open up for more private consultations, have the doctors do an additional half-day a week...or something?"

"That's possible, but the best thing to do is involve the doctors in this issue. In its resolution too. They're all intelligent and aware of the problem. Ask them what they see as options," suggested Dr.

Jack Norton, seated beside Peggy. He rarely spoke and when he did, people listened. Jack knew his stuff.

Gerard considered the possibility. "We'd have to set up a meeting, which they won't like as they're strapped for time now. However, if we bring them in to discuss the problem, together we might brainstorm some solutions, or present a few options for them to consider."

"Don't give them too many options. That's asking for trouble." Peggy jotted notes down on her yellow legal pad. "One or two at the most and see what they think. There's a lot of brain power in that group and it's their future as well. It wouldn't hurt to give them a say."

A knock at the door interrupted the thread of conversation. Sandra Cafferty, Gerard's administrative assistant, opened the door and pushed in a coffee cart. "Coffee, everyone. Gerard, Dr. Maddy has arrived."

Gerard nodded and picked up his pencil again. Maddy's visit should be short, and probably not sweet. He needed her to accept the new patient and she wasn't going to like it – at all. Not that he could blame her, but The Haven needed to take in more patients as soon as possible to stay afloat. Even this patient.

"Good to see we can still afford a decent cup of java, hey Gerard?" Moneyman and Chief Financial Officer, Alex Cooper, stood and walked over to the trolley and doctored a cup for himself.

"Let's not joke about such a serious issue," Gerard replied. He'd cut what was necessary, but the team needed to focus on creating a bigger income stream, not just making temporary fixes to the expense drain. He rose and walked over to pour himself a coffee. Bringing it back to his place, he said, "If everyone's ready, let's bring Dr. Maddy in and deal with that issue so we can get back to the rest of the agenda. Sandra, please."

Sandra walked out, leaving the door open.

Maddy's presence filled the door seconds later. It was as if an air of lightness entered with her. "Good morning, everyone. So good to see you."

Even taciturn Jack had to smile at her. "Come on in, Maddy. Grab a coffee and take a seat. This shouldn't take long."

Maddy hurried over to the cart, quickly poured herself a coffee and glanced around the room. "Does everyone have coffee?"

Peggy lifted her gaze from her files, her brows beetled together. "Oh, I'd love a cup. Black. Thank you."

With a sunny smile, Maddy poured the second cup and placed it down in front of Peggy before taking a seat.

Gerard waited until he had her attention. "Now, the new wing, although it's not officially open yet, is causing a stir." Shuffling papers, Gerard, pulled out the one he required. "We have a long list of people waiting for beds."

Maddy remained quiet, her dark chocolate eyes watching his every move. That was a little unnerving, even after all these years. "As you know, there will be twelve extra beds on your floor. Theoretically, two or three of those could be filled now and the rest later."

He raised his gaze to Maddy.

Her eyes never wavered. "It won't be as quiet or as peaceful for them if the space isn't completely finished. There is still equipment to be installed and the finishing touches done to match the rest of the floor. You know the effect atmosphere has on healing."

En masse, the board members dropped their eyes to the various papers in front of them. Gerard studied the bent heads, knowing they were all thinking the same thing. This was a long-term care facility. People came here to die, not to heal. Unless you were on Dr. Maddy's floor. Then weird things happened. Good, but weird, and everyone who was sick wanted to be on Maddy's Floor. Hence, part of the current problem.

"Right. Unfortunately, that's not negotiable right now. The budget requires cash. Either we ask you to take over shifts on other floors, or we bring in the new patients early. Four residents means four more sets of fees, and we need that funding at the moment."

Maddy had tensed initially, yet now seemed to ease. He studied her face to see if she understood. So focused on patients and healing, many doctors didn't get the basics of dollars and cents.

She inclined her head. "That'll be fine. The patients will take several days to adjust anyway. The noise will be part of that."

Gerard let out a small sigh of relief then plunged onward.

"On the waiting list for your floor are, of course, many current residents, some you referred yourself." He looked up at her. "The waiting list for new patients is longer. We're in the screening process now and have two good possibilities." He frowned.

This floor stuff bothered him. A care facility should be open to all, and it was, except this issue of requests for Maddy's Floor had grown beyond him and beyond the facility. People offered an incredible sum to have a bed for their loved one on Maddy's Floor and sometimes refusing wasn't an option, particularly when the applicant fit the stringent requirements – like the one they were considering now. And Maddy wouldn't like this scenario one bit.

He forged on.

"Dr. Lenning has requested one of those beds."

Every person at the table stilled.

Dr. Lenning was not Maddy's favorite person. Not by a long shot. In fact, it was safe to assume she'd buck this choice any way she could. Gerard studied her calm face, wondering at the utter stillness of it.

Finally she spoke. "And why would Adam want to be a patient on my floor?" Her voice, so quiet, so calm, raised the bent heads. Everyone looked at each other before staring at Maddy.

Gerard cleared his throat. This is where it got tricky. "He says that he'd like to experience your healing magic firsthand."

One cool eyebrow rose, heat flaring briefly in her huge eyes. "Magic. Rubbish." Her gaze was clear and serene. "We all know these people are here to spend their last months as comfortably as possible. I repeat – why would he want anything to do with me now…at this critical stage of his illness? His feelings toward me are well-known. He tried to discredit me, to have my license revoked. So why my floor, now?"

"He may have had a change of heart, my dear. Dying men do, you know." Peggy offered an unusual insight. Gerard would have to remember to thank her later.

Maddy's gaze never wavered, a hint of suspicion remained. No one could tell what she was thinking. Finally, after a long pause, she said, "As I presume you've already made your decision, a discussion on this is moot."

Damn it. Gerard hated the burning frustration eating away at him. He dared her to pass up the size of the check he'd received to let their former doctor have one of the new beds. Morals and preferences aside, he had bills to pay, and Maddy needed to do her part.

"And the other patient?" she inquired gently.

"We're considering Dr. Robertson's request for Felicia McIntosh's transfer." Gerard had already approved transferring the seven-year-old from the local children's hospital as a boon to help Maddy deal with Lenning's impending arrival. Not to mention that any child would have outstanding results with Maddy's particular skills. For that reason alone, they tried to find a place for most children who applied. He watched the reactions flit across her fine-boned features. Instead of a beam of joy, her face softened, gentled and warmed. He actually felt like he'd received a pat of approval on his head.

"I'm sure she'll like that."

"As for the next bed to be ready, we're considering former police chief, John McNeal."

Maddy nodded, her features smooth and unworried. "I'm sure you'll make the right decision on that one." She drank the last of her coffee. "Was there anything else?"

"Not at the moment. Just know that we won't be hiring any additional staff. I'm afraid these extra beds will be added to the current workload without any budget additions. We'll still be within the state guidelines – barely."

Maddy stilled yet again – unnaturally so. Everyone watched without being overt.

When she inclined her head a second time, the occupants of the board room sighed with relief.

"That's fine. My team can manage – at least for a while. Thanks for letting me know."

In one smooth elegant arc, Maddy stood, replaced her cup on the trolley and strode from the room.

The board members once again looked at each other.

"That went well, don't you think?" Gerard relaxed his tight shoulders.

Peggy snickered. "Like hell."

Then Jack raised the real issue. "And why *would* Adam want to be under her care when he tried to have her license revoked? *Has* he had a change of heart?"

Ben, the marketing director, who had yet to speak, added, "Or is he going after her again?"

MADDY MADE IT back into the gilt cage elevator before her composure dissipated. Her stomach rolled in horrific waves of unease and yes, fear. Dr. Lenning. The world must really hate her right now to toss him her way.

Maddy worked to achieve her best all the time.

Sometimes she failed. Dr. Lenning was proof of that.

It wasn't that Maddy was a goody two-shoes, as some of the

other staff believed. She knew firsthand what difference her emotional balance made on the patients' energy around her. Anyone involved in energy work understood the impact negativity had on others.

Maddy leaned back against the wall, her hands against her belly. Two deep breaths later, she could almost straighten her spine. A third did the trick and with the fourth, some of the tension lifted off her shoulders.

So, Dr. Lenning wanted a bed on her floor and, of course, the Board buckled under his demands. He'd make their lives a living hell otherwise. He might also have tossed his checkbook around and bought his way in. The man wasn't as rich as King Midas, but close.

Maddy frowned. She had a hard time with the constant budget cuts. Money was often short and now it was critically so. It wasn't only in her sector. This lousy economy affected everyone.

The elevator slowed its upward climb before coming to a stop. The gated doors opened, letting her exit. Maddy strolled to her office, maintaining her calm as if her world hadn't just collapsed.

"Good morning, Dr. Maddy."

Maddy smiled at the nurse pushing a medicine cart down the hallway. In general, everyone on her floor was happy with their jobs and the people they worked with. Maddy strove to keep it that way. It took finesse and compromise. However, they'd pulled together and had created something special here. Everyone on her floor knew that a delicate balance was required to keep this floor functioning at a higher energy level than the others. Her staff fought any suggestion that they transfer out – as hard as the patients fought to get in. Maddy didn't take all the credit, yet she understood the synergy on her floor. It was important that new arrivals not disturb the delicate balance.

Dr. Lenning already had. It was about damage control until everything could truly be harmonious again.

Instead of disappearing into her office as she'd hoped, Maddy walked down to look at the area under construction. She'd prefer to wait until the workers had finished before moving new patients in, but that was out of her hands. Besides, the renovation was mostly complete. The inspector had been through and the fire marshal was due today. There were a few little finishing touches, and they waited for some medical equipment to arrive and be installed, but the rest was cosmetic. Everything that had been ordered for twelve new patients was coming in piecemeal. She hoped all this would be over before the first new patient arrived, but knowing Gerard, that wasn't likely to happen.

In truth, the renovations weren't the biggest problem. It was expanding the healing energy from the main area into the new area. With new people coming in over the next month, she didn't know how to make that happen without destroying the strong healing cocoon that the patients in the main part of the floor were enjoying.

Maddy considered the problem. Dr. Lenning would move in here – down at the far end. He couldn't complain about the location because he'd have a little more privacy there, plus a window overlooking the treed area behind the facility. The advantage of that location, from Maddy's point of view was his physical distance from the other patients who were actively working on their healing…and to be honest, the distance he'd be from her office was even better.

The more she considered the issue, the more she searched to distance herself from him and the problem of him. A light went on.

With a sharp nod, Maddy smiled. Dr. Paul Cunningham could take on Dr. Lenning. He'd agreed to take on a couple of the new beds so this would be perfect. He would do this just to help Maddy. He'd been a stalwart supporter of her and her project, and someone she'd come to depend on. He didn't put in as many hours on her floor as she did, but he spent many more over at the hospital side of The Haven where Maddy's presence was minimal. She preferred it this way but with extra patients coming in, she'd need him more than ever. They'd work that out.

On the plus side, Dr. Cunningham found it more difficult to deal with children. Maybe due to his grandfatherly age? Maddy, on the other hand, saw the potential of a young person's ability to heal, regardless of the disease wasting their body away. Felicia would be Maddy's patient and she was delighted to have her. *Perfect.* Everything would work out and calm would be restored.

Maddy strode back to the welcoming warmth of the main area. At her office, she emailed Dr. Cunningham on the upcoming changes and her suggestions for the first two patients. The other two patient would be determined at a later date.

With that email sent, she felt a sense of relief. Adam Lenning might be on her floor, only he wouldn't be under her care.

THE NURSE WALKED into the ward, a smile on her face. Sissy watched her approach.

"Good morning, Sissy, how are you feeling today?"

"I'm Occupant of Bed 232, not Sissy."

With an age of patience in her voice, the nurse asked, "Why do you insist on calling yourself something so impersonal?"

"It's what I am. How is that impersonal? Besides, the doctor says it has to do with my disassociation disorder or some such thing."

With a smile, the nurse left her alone with her thoughts, all of which centered on the knowledge that yesterday's session had relieved the soreness on her left hip, and what a difference. She shuffled slightly in her bed, pulling the thin sheets up to her chin. Thankfully, there should be no more tests for another couple of weeks. She hated being taken out of her room. Look what happened yesterday. She'd spent hours in the hallway, in an assembly line of the lost and forgotten, until someone had remembered why she was there.

It hurt to be treated as if she didn't count as much as that kid dying across the hallway. Of course, she counted. More than they could imagine. Now why hadn't they accepted her request to transfer upstairs? She wasn't unstable mentally, no matter what people whispered about her. She'd heard them talk. So what if she talked to herself? So what if she called herself Occupant of Bed 232? Everyone should be allowed to make fun of themselves. There was little enough joy in her life.

And so what if damn near everyone in The Haven had applied for a transfer to Maddy's Floor? Why didn't they just move the whole floor up there one at a time as beds became available? That was the fair thing to do. She snickered. Better yet, move Dr. Maddy down.

Besides, she'd been here for ages. She should get priority over the new arrivals. Let them put in their time like she had. She didn't want many more months like this – even with her private healing sessions.

Although, she did feel much better today.

CONFINED TO HIS bed at Summerset Home, dying from some stupid disease that none of the damn doctors could identify, former chief of police, John McNeil stretched out his full length. The foreign sounds of machinery droned endlessly at his side. They weren't attached to him, thank God, though his days were numbered. He knew that. The doctors and nurses could continue down their same bullshit-lined path, but he'd been a straight shooter all his life. He wasn't about to change now.

He did miss his work, though. The process of dying surprised him – it was plain boring. He needed stimulation. Watching bedpans being changed, tubes being adjusted and charts being marked didn't quite do it for him. Surely, dying hadn't made him useless.

The concept made him so mad, he wanted to growl. His body might be rotting before his very eyes, yet he'd be damned if he'd let his mind do the same. And it was almost dinnertime – good thing. Too bad the food sucked. At least he'd had his bath already. He shuddered. Who wanted to be treated like a goddamned baby at his age?

Thankfully, his nephew was on his way. There had to be some case he could offer advice.

DREW WAS PISSED. The meeting had run late again. "About damn time," he muttered, exiting the station and heading to his black Ford F250. Checking his watch, he realized he was already twenty minutes behind. His uncle had pre-chewed lectures ready to spit out at the least excuse, and by now he'd be spewing them at anyone who'd stop by long enough to listen. Particularly as it was after dinner, so he could lambaste them about the lousy food.

Unlocking his truck, Drew hopped in and started the engine then pulled out of the lot. At least he could update his uncle on his application to enter The Haven. Drew spoke with Gerard Lionel during this morning's visit. Good news. Now Drew would be able to visit both family members at the same time. There was still some uncertainty as to which floor Uncle John would be placed.

Drew knew John had his heart set on Maddy's Floor. There was no guarantee that he'd get that boon though. Twenty years of law enforcement didn't guarantee a spot in the 'angels' wing.' Drew snorted. Angels' wing. Who came up with this shit? On the other hand, he'd found there was more than a little to like about the head angel, having verified she was his running goddess.

The Haven had a reputation for caring for their patients. That's all. Nothing more.

Regardless of what rumors abounded, the only thing that happened at The Haven was that people eventually died.

Not him. No way. He'd rather get killed on the job than let one cancer cell into his body. Christ, all he'd done for the last decade was watch members of his family waste away to nothing. He'd eat a bullet first.

The access ramp to the highway loomed ahead. Threading the truck into the traffic, he checked his watch and groaned. At least the meeting that had kept him late had ended with good news. His transfer to the Cold Case Squad had been approved. Now maybe he could make a difference.

That was another move that would piss off his uncle – big time. Tough shit. Not everyone wanted to be the chief of police – especially him.

And following in his uncle's footsteps had never been in his plans. Regardless of what others thought.

THE VISITORS TO Maddy's Floor had gone. The lights had been lowered. The nurses were going through the special ritual to cleanse the day's energy from the floor to facilitate healing overnight. A routine Maddy had established right from the beginning. She had enough different energies to deal with without having to work around residual energy of grieving relatives.

Stiletto heels clicked on the bare marble floor, the echoes bouncing in the dimly lit hallway. Maddy strode from doorway to doorway, checking each sleeping occupant before moving on to the next.

This wasn't part of her job description. This was part of her self-assigned Maddy duties. Besides, it had been a tough day after a tough night, and she needed this. Her patients were family. She loved the journey called life and her beliefs allowed that death was not a crushing end.

The next room was Belle's. This eighty-nine-year-old wisecracker extolled the virtues of living life to the fullest. At every chance, she eschewed healthy eating and the rest of that 'mumbo jumbo,' as she loved to call it. Maddy leaned against the divider between the patients' open areas and chuckled at the shot glass, half full of golden whiskey. Belle's favorite replacement for sleeping pills went totally against regulations, making her doubly happy. Tonight, Belle slept deeply, her energy rippling along her prone body in soft soothing waves, revitalizing her body for tomorrow.

That's the way it should be.

Too bad most people didn't get to experience the same joy and level of balance. So many people took their stress and troubles to bed with them, manifesting their negativity into bad dreams as a result.

Maddy could see patients' energies easier when they slept – when they weren't trying to hide their secrets or control their futures. She'd learned that fear, pain and stress caused energy to drain from a person's body.

Maddy hesitated outside Belle's room. As a patient, Belle wasn't the easiest to deal with. Maddy knew Belle wanted to make peace with those she was leaving behind. She had more than a few relationship wounds to heal. As a healthy vibrant woman, she had been an unapologetic hell-raiser. Maddy had been trying to give her time to deal – but the end of the road was coming.

She entered Belle's room where it was very quiet. For all Belle's peaceful sleep, she was bleeding energy from her lower chakras like a hemophiliac bleeds blood.

Maddy continued her rounds, the soft staccato of her heels tapped out a comforting rhythm. On Maddy's Floor, the different patient areas offered privacy without the four walls and doors that one would expect. Several people on her floor had passed on over the years, although fewer every year and so few in the last several months that people had begun to notice.

Maddy didn't delude herself to think that she had unique, fantastic healing abilities that offered the fountain of youth. She chuckled softly. At least not yet. However, she knew that her patients tapped into warm loving energy to deal with their life issues and this often resulted in a prolonged life and healthier last years. In a couple of cases, the people had actually gone home with a new chance at life.

She ignored the whispers behind her back, the curious looks from nurses as they did their rounds, and the subtle criticisms from the rest of the medical team. If she let their doubts in, they'd affect the healing. All actions had an equal reaction – and negative action always caused a bigger reaction.

She hadn't gotten yesterday's weird two-energy incident and the death of a patient off her mind and then there was the board meeting and their bombshell about Dr. Lenning's placement on her floor. She shuddered. Those things alone were enough to rattle anyone's cage.

Consciously shoving away the memory, in favor of deliberate calm had worked throughout most of the day, only to bounce back to problems whenever her schedule eased and she had time to think. Really think.

Jansen Svaar's room came next. With the renovations, Jansen's bed had been shifted. He was not quite in the new area, but not as cozy as he'd been before.

Jansen hadn't minded. The big Swede had enjoyed every one of his seventy-eight years and wasn't ready to jump off yet. Big and robust in his prime, his physical body had withered to one battling diabetes that defied control, and cancer that defied remission. Yet, he was still here and looking so much better than when he arrived. Even his thick head of hair had returned with rich brown color. His last tests had come back with very positive indicators. So much so, Jansen wanted to stop his treatments. According to him, he was all better. If it were possible to heal by his word alone, then he'd see it done.

Maddy grinned as she recalled the many conversations they'd shared in the past.

At the entrance to his doorway, she stopped to survey his bed.

Something was wrong.

Purple energy hovered over Jansen; a thick blanket of colored haze covered his midsection. Frowning, Maddy studied the odd essence. Energy had a signature – like DNA, the energy was unique to each person. It just wasn't as easy to identify.

She'd worked with him long enough to know it wasn't his aura.

The smoky blanket moved.

Who or what did the energy represent? Her gaze swept the rest of the room before striding forward. The activity over Jansen did not shy away; it increased. She narrowed her gaze. The eerie silence of the room magnified the unearthly scene before her.

It wasn't what she'd experienced the night before, racing through the hallway into chaos. She expected noises of some kind. Not this hushed silence, as if sound would shatter the intensity of whatever was going on. She frowned. A struggle of some kind was going on.

She shook her head, panic stirring inside. Could energy fight with itself? With someone else's energy? Is that what happened to Eric? She studied the energy again. This time she saw it. The blanket of malevolence was moving over the bed and occupant, spreading and growing every minute.

Underneath, Jansen was suffocating.

His energy, tiny and thin, struggled to remain separate and distinct from the purple amoeba-like entity sucking the life force from him.

Fear shot through her. This couldn't happen again. Maddy raced to the bedside. "Stop," she cried out hoarsely, not wanting to disturb the other patients. "Leave him alone."

The purple energy quivered in place but did not dissipate.

Maddy wafted her hands over Jansen's body. Her fingers slipped into and through the mist, neither feeling it nor dispersing it. She fed her own energy into Jansen's heart chakra, giving him her strength and will to hold on. At the same time, she closed her eyes and surrounded herself and, by the extension of her hand on his, Jansen's body with white light. The old answer to keeping oneself safe and balanced.

The energy shifted, cooled.

She opened her eyes to find the energy still wiggling in place, the purple haze malicious in appearance. Then slowly, like fog blowing in the wind, the haze thinned before sending tendrils into the darkness.

Maddy reached out and checked Jansen's pulse. Her medical training took over on the physical level as her medical intuitive training took over on the energy field. She observed the thread-like cord of light stretching far out of Jansen's body, gently pulsating in a reassuring rhythm. Maddy coaxed his system to relax a little more, then to wake up gently.

"Dr. Maddy?" His paper-thin lids opened to reveal rheumy blue eyes blinking in surprise.

"Yes, it's me, Jansen." Maddy studied his face. "How do you feel?" He appeared fine, normal but surprised.

"Christ, I don't know. I had the most horrible dream." He coughed slightly and shifted position in the bed, tugging at his covers as if chilled.

"Oh?" Maddy kept her voice calm and soothing. "What was it about?"

"Like someone was pulling my soul from my body, one inch at a time." Fear filled the old man's eyes. His thin hands grasped hers nervously. "I don't know what the hell it was, but I felt on a precipice between life and death. It was like meeting Peter at the pearly gates himself, and him not being too happy to see me."

"Shhh." Maddy stroked his hands, noting with clinical detachment that his liver spots had begun to fade. "It was just a dream. Not to worry. It's over. I'm here, and you're safe. Go back to sleep."

Relief washed over his face. "Thanks, Doc. Don't know what I'd do without you."

Shifting sideways, Jansen closed his eyes and fell back to sleep.

Maddy walked to the doorway, turned around and glanced back.

No sign of the purple grim reaper. Jansen was safe.

For now.

WEDNESDAY

THE HAVEN BUZZED with activity. They had several hundred residents and more than that amount of staff. Without Gerard, the place would have imploded years ago. Maddy massaged her temples in an effort to draw out the tension.

She wondered if she'd missed a growing thread of discontent. One that had started or fed the horrible negativity – or, dare she say it, evil – that she'd observed over Jansen last night. She couldn't even begin to understand the source of the hellish energy that contributed to Eric's death, either.

After going home last night, she'd tried to contact several of the other medical intuitives she'd met over the years. She only managed to touch base with two. Neither had seen or heard of anything like that deep purple-black blanket of energy. A crime may have been committed in Eric's case, although what it was or how it was perpetrated was beyond her. Too bad she couldn't go to the police.

That handsome detective she'd barreled into on the stairway bloomed in her mind, making her pulse quicken. Damn if that man hadn't made her hormones sit up and sing. She'd obviously been single too long. Maddy didn't do one-nighters, but right now her body was pushing her to reconsider the concept. That the detective wasn't impervious to her, helped keep his smile alive in her mind and the 'what ifs' dancing through her body. The warm light of approval she'd seen in his eyes had been hard to ignore. She should have asked his name. Hell, she should have asked for his phone number. She could only hope his uncle would make it onto her floor so he'd become a regular visitor.

She walked out to collect the stack of papers waiting in her intray.

"Dr. Maddy. The ambulance has arrived with Dr. Lenning."

Silence descended on the nurses' station. All movement

stopped. Furtive glances came her way. Everyone knew about their new patient, and the impact it could have on Maddy.

Maddy nodded as if she'd been expecting the news. Gerard was nothing if not fast.

"Right. Let Dr. Cunningham know, will you Nancy? Dr. Lenning is his patient. Dr. Lenning's to be put into the new area, in bed 349. I'm presuming the bed is in place. If not, we'll need to get one brought up immediately."

"It arrived an hour ago. Except, uhm, Dr. Cunningham isn't in yet."

"Isn't he?" Already on her way to her office, Maddy spun around to stare at Nancy, her head nurse and confidante – not to mention best friend – who had been there almost as long as Maddy. A frown creased her brow. "Where is he?"

"He phoned in to say he'd been called to surgery unexpectedly." The two women looked at the clock.

"Ten o'clock." Maddy tapped her toes, thinking rapidly. She'd do a lot to avoid meeting Dr. Lenning, but she wouldn't be able to avoid that forever.

Shrugging as if it didn't matter, Maddy said, "You know what to do. Get our new patient comfortable and check his vitals. His information should have come with him. If it's there, bring it down to me and I'll see what we're looking at. If it's online, send me the link. I'll speak with Dr. Cunningham when he gets in."

After scooping up the stack of paperwork from her box, Maddy headed to her office for a little down time before facing the one man who'd managed to teach her quite a lot about fear. She walked the short hallway, feeling the eyes focused on her back, the whispers in her wake. Let them talk. Maddy only hoped they wouldn't indulge in a gossip fest. Gossiping destroyed a peaceful balance faster than anything.

Knowing this didn't stop it, however. People were human and reacting was instinctive. It's when the gossip didn't stop that it became a problem.

She dropped the paperwork on the corner of her desk and walked to her window to stare out at the courtyard. Having to deal with Dr. Lenning was not going to ruin her day. She wouldn't let it. Gerard knew what he was doing, and if he said this was a necessary step, even given her history with the good doctor, then she'd accept that and try to make it work. She was a professional.

One difficult patient, a dying one at that, wasn't worth making a major life-altering change. Not now. She'd put so much time and effort into this floor, and she could hardly abandon it. To do that would tear her soul apart.

Grimly, she reached for the paperwork on her desk. She had work to do. Making the new patient comfortable required at least an hour, possibly two. With any luck, Dr. Cunningham would show up by then.

DYING WAS A bitch and Dr. Lenning had sworn off bitches years ago. Until now. The trouble with dying was it gave him too much time to think. He'd been more than satisfied with his life until he found out he was losing it. He'd lost the best thing in his life when he'd lost the love of his life, Mark, five years ago. Even now, his heart ached at the memories. He'd loved and been well loved in return.

Four years ago, he'd lived a normal life – at least for him.

Then he'd seen Maddy and he'd lost the one sure thing he knew about himself – his sexuality. She had changed that. Her slim, lithe, vibrant femaleness had challenged his beliefs. She'd made him doubt himself and the choices he'd made. Made him wonder if he'd been fooling himself all these years. He'd hated feeling like he was betraying Mark. He tossed his head back and forth. He wouldn't be disloyal to Mark or his memory. He couldn't. But these feelings…

He detested the emotions Maddy had stirred up, the glow he felt when he was around her. He wanted Maddy and he *hated* her for that. He'd wanted her removed from The Haven. He had even gone so far as submitting a fifty-page document to the medical board hoping to kill her medical career. Only she'd had some powerful people on her side. So he'd spent the last four years alternating between a need so crippling he shook with it, and a hatred so violent he vibrated because of it.

Maddy's never-ending legs rose in his mind. Christ, he couldn't get her out of his thoughts. Knowing that made him angrier. He closed his eyes and shuddered. These feelings were worse than he'd experienced during puberty. He'd never had a woman and now, bedridden and dying, the chances were good he never would. That left him in endless torment. Teenage fantasies tortured him with excruciating 'what ifs.'

Why now, when he had no time to explore that side of life?

Why her? And why had he demanded to be on her floor where this exquisite torment would be that much worse?

Even as he asked the questions, he knew the answers. He was desperate, that's why. Not that he understood her New Age bullshit, but dying made him more open, more willing to look at other options. He hoped she did have some magical skill that would save him. He wanted to believe.

His education and experience said there were no second chances for anyone.

Plus, he couldn't resist an opportunity to get close to her.

"Stupid bastard. Why didn't you do something about this before? Why didn't you grab some pills and finish this once and forever?" But he hadn't. As long as there was one more day to live, one more chance of a life, one more hope of seeing Maddy again, he'd take it.

He grimaced. God, he was weak. The woman wouldn't give him the time of day. Not now. Not after he'd tried his damnedest to get her out of his life, his profession, his space – to where he'd never have to see her again. Then cancer had ground his life to a halt. Now he needed the special healing powers she was rumored to have. The same ones he'd used to try to run her out of the medical association.

She hated him.

He couldn't blame her.

He hated himself.

A HEAVY KNOCK on her door interrupted Maddy from her drug interaction research. "Come in," she called out.

The door opened tentatively. Gerard poked his head around the corner. "Maddy? Sorry to bother you. I just checked to see how Dr. Lenning was faring. He's not in a great mood."

Maddy raised a brow in surprise. Things couldn't be that bad. No one had come to tell her about any problems. With a discreet check on her watch, she realized only an hour had gone by. The patient would barely be in bed and checked over. Stifling a sigh, she leaned back to give Gerard her full attention.

"Not surprising. He's dying and any attempt to make him more comfortable requires more drugs, which leaves him moving up and down on the moody scale." She sighed and added gently. "It is normal and expected – regardless of whether we like it or not."

Gerard grabbed the spare chair, swiveled it around and sat on it backwards to face her. Slightly older than her, Gerard had garnered a lot of respect in the years he'd been here. "He says he hasn't seen you yet."

Maddy willed her patience to suck it up. "No, he hasn't." She glanced at the time on her computer. "It's early yet. I doubt the floor nurse has even completed her assessment. Dr. Lenning knows the length of time it takes to complete admission. There are deadlines to meet and we will meet them."

She held up her hand to forestall Gerard's next words. "Yes, I will go and welcome him to The Haven if Dr. Cunningham doesn't arrive in the next hour. I do want to see his paperwork first, however."

"Fair enough. I'll stop by before I go downstairs and let him know you'll be along in a little bit." He stood, flipped the chair back around the right way, and stepped to the door. "I want to tell you that I appreciate your cooperation on this. We all know that he isn't the ideal patient for this floor, but his money is good and our need is great."

Maddy smiled at Gerard who was doing his usual, putting money first. He exemplified tunnel vision. "I don't have a problem with either point. However, his presence on my floor is definitely not required. The rest of The Haven is just as great a facility. The staff is equally qualified." She stretched her arms forward, clasping her hands together and rested them on her desk as she had in grade school. "To have insisted on my floor doesn't mean he gets *me*."

"No, it certainly doesn't. You're carrying a large caseload as it is. However, this morning, if you would step in for Dr. Cunningham, we'd appreciate it."

"Absolutely." She firmed her jaw. "But should he cause any unrest or deliberately attempt to sabotage my floor, my people or my project, I will ship him downstairs. And I don't care about how much money he spent to get here. Do *you* understand?"

Maddy watched as surprise lit Gerard's eyes, followed by a tinge of anger and then finally his tensed shoulders relaxed and he nodded. "I suppose that's no different than for any other patient we take in."

His cell phone rang. Sliding it from his pocket, he looked at the number and grimaced. "I need to take this call." With a quick salute to her, he left.

He hadn't been gone ten minutes when Nancy arrived, rolling her eyes. "The new patient is settled in and complaining loudly." She held out a fat binder to Maddy. "This is his. He might squawk loudly, but I doubt he's going to die tonight or tomorrow. When you're done going over it, we'll enter his information online."

The binder sat on her desk. Maddy gazed at it as if it were a viper ready to strike. The Haven was more advanced technologically than many other facilities. She'd forgotten how much easier it was to have everything online.

How much longer until Dr. Cunningham arrived? She reached for her cell phone. He answered almost immediately. "Hi Maddy, the roof must have fallen in for you to need me."

"Maybe it has." She leaned back in her chair, relieved to have reached him. "Dr. Lenning transferred in this morning."

He chuckled. "So the pain in the ass is there, is he? I have to admit, I hoped he'd change his mind at the last minute." Paul coughed and cleared his throat.

Maddy waited until he was quiet. "No, he's here and would like to see his doctor."

"Par for the course. Well, buck up. This is one we have to have whether we like it or not."

She knew and understood that. But she still wanted him in to deal with the new patient. "That's why I'm calling you. When are you coming in?"

"I'm still going to be another hour here, so do me a favor. Give him the welcome speech, or the warning speech in his case, and tell him I'll be there soon to go over his medical information and current treatment. You have to face him sometime and this way he can't fault you for your lack of professionalism. I promise I'll be over soon."

And that was as good as it was going to get.

Maddy closed the binder on her desk, and stood. She'd grab a coffee, put on her most professional smile and be civil. She could do this. She had to. Maintaining the healing balance on her floor depended on it.

JOHN SHIFTED POSITIONS, hating the throb that raced down the outside of his right leg. Damn useless body. Piling the sheet at his waist, he shifted his cell phone so he'd hear better.

"Gerard, I want to confirm that my transfer's gone through."

John strained to listen to the voice on the other end of the phone. "Wanted to say thanks. I've been waiting to get onto Maddy's Floor for a while now, but it's not like beds open up there. Good thing that new wing was being developed. And that I donated to it, huh?" He laughed until a cough caught him out. "Damn chest. Can't stand all this coughing."

He reached for his glasses atop the small bedside table. "Speak up, boy. I know you're busy, however I want to know when the transfer will happen. I've waited all morning for news, and nary a peep out of your people. Haven't got all year, you know." He chuckled at his own joke as he pulled his day planner to his side.

"I gather Drew spoke with you."

"Yup, he did. Now I've got my calendar out. So when can we make this happen? I have lab tests this morning...the dietician's coming midafternoon – I'm happy to miss her. Lord, if I have any more fiber in my cereal I'm going to start to moo with the damn cows. I know there are a couple of other appointments here somewhere. Give me a minute..." He studied the handwritten notes that kept his daily activities organized. What a pitiful way to live. He knew the ward clerk kept it all straight, but he needed to keep track of it himself. A matter of pride. He wasn't that decrepit.

"What's that?" He'd missed Gerard's last comment. Damn the man, why wouldn't he speak up? Christ, the guy was big yet had the voice of a woman. He was probably a damn fairy; wouldn't surprise him, knowing his mother and the antics she'd been up to way back when. In his day, that wasn't talked about, but now, Christ, these men wore pink shirts to advertise the fact. What the hell was happening to the world?

"The logistics of the move aren't your concern. We have people who will take care of that. But I don't have the room assignments sorted out yet."

"Yeah, whatever. I don't really care about that. It'd be nice to look out over the back woods, though. I'd like a spot of nature to remind me of better days. Didn't I hear something about balconies in some of those rooms?" He rubbed his grizzled chin. "That'd be mighty fine."

Gerard sighed. A deep, long-suffering sigh that made John roll his eyes. "I know. However, the balconies are designed to be for everyone, as are the sitting rooms. There aren't closed bedrooms John. There's privacy, only not the same as four walls and a door would provide." He hastily backed up. "That's *if* you're getting onto Maddy's Floor."

"What?" John roared. "Of course I am. You said so yourself. What are you trying to pull here?"

"John, I said your transfer to The Haven had been approved. I didn't say you were guaranteed a spot on Maddy's Floor."

Panicked, John's face burned, his heart slammed inside his chest and it was all he could do to catch the next breath – the fear was so bad. He had to get onto that floor. It was his only chance. "Don't play games with me, Gerard. Maddy's Floor *is* The Haven and that's the only place I want to be."

"I can't just give one to you without going over all applications and making an unbiased decision, John. The beds are at a premium. More than that, there are strict requirements to gain entrance to the third floor. Requirements you don't necessarily fit. We have a stringent interview and selection process, for that reason."

Unbridled anger rose in John's chest at Gerard's words. His left hand pressed against the sudden constriction as he tried to breathe. The bloody bastard. "Why you little prick! This has nothing to do with the entrance requirements – this is all about money, isn't it? You want more to place me on Maddy's Floor. Haven't I paid enough? Or maybe it's you who hasn't paid enough. I thought we'd put the past behind us, but if you don't get me onto Maddy's Floor, the past is going to rear its ugly head and bite you in the ass."

Silence.

In an odd voice, Gerard asked, "Are you blackmailing me?"

"Hell, no. Nor am I threatening you. This is a goddamn promise." This couldn't happen, not now. He had so little time left. With so much panic surging through him, he almost dropped the cell phone. His breath came out in anguished gasps. "Don't you understand? I *have* to be on Maddy's Floor," he cried. "What makes someone else more important?"

"Well, for one, they've been waiting much longer than you. Some of the other patients have been waiting for over a year now. From their perspective, you should be on a lower floor and they should move up one at a time. You have to understand, John. I don't have a few applications, I have several hundred. Not everyone will qualify, but we have to consider them."

John sank back down into his wrinkled bed, tears welling up at the corner of his eyes. Not fair. So close and yet so far. He pulled up the corner of his sheet and wiped his eyes. Giving himself a hard mental shake, he tried to see the situation clearly. He understood that requirements had to be met, a set of criteria had to be established and followed. He knew that for these twelve beds to be filled, hundreds had to be rejected. He was a lawman. He understood justice. He'd played fair and square all his life ...and he'd bent the rules just once.

Now he needed the beneficiary of that one slip to bend the rules for him.

Gerard's voice turned brusque. "Listen, John, I know we go way back. I'll take another look and see what I can do."

John didn't dare speak. Sixty-six-year-old men didn't cry. Shit, real men didn't cry. He was being a wuss. He could blackmail the bastard into getting what he wanted. However, he also had money. Maybe he should sweeten the pot. Sniffling hard and coughing as if to clear his throat, John said, "Let me know if there is any equipment you're short of down there. I might be able to help."

There was silence for a moment before Gerard answered. "Will do. Give me a day or two to check some figures. Then I'll get back to you."

"A day or two is fine. Don't wait too long."

The meaning was clear. John meant to get what he wanted. And he'd pay his way if he must, but get it he would. One way or another.

GERARD STARED ACROSS his large executive office. His gaze landed on the huge oil painting on the far wall. He didn't bother to bring it into focus. What was he going to do now?

He didn't have much choice with the bed assignment issues. And in this case, he was good with that. Still, wouldn't it be nice if people took to their beds and were happy? But no, just like little children with desk assignments in school, everyone thought having a bed somewhere else – in some cases, anywhere else – would be better.

The hospital policy stated they were not to cater to the petty demands of patients and doctors. Fat chance of following that policy to the letter. Still, if making minor changes appeased the parties involved, then The Haven tried to accommodate all reasonable requests.

Then there was the problem of John's thinly veiled blackmail threat. He shuddered. However, if John were willing to pay a little more, then he'd pass his application through the Board no problem. With the budget shortfall they were currently experiencing, anyone who could pay would pay, whether the Board liked the system or not. This wasn't the time to raise the moral issues of better care for the wealthy. The doctors on the other floors were extremely capable. The Haven was known for the quality of care for all patients, not just those on Maddy's Floor.

Damn that man anyway. The same persistence that had made him a hell of a cop made him a hell of a lousy patient. Choices were limited. Bills had to be paid and patients needed care. Yada, yada, yada. That Maddy wouldn't be happy over this decision was a given. What choice did he have? He hoped John's life expectancy was incorrect, because that would be a sticking point. But if he did get John there without her knowing about it, then she'd find a way to make it work, she always did. Manipulative? Yes.

Desperate? Oh yes.

Well, there was no point in waiting. Grabbing up the correct application file from the top of his overflowing in basket, he picked up the desk phone. "John, I have good news for you."

JOHN ENDED HIS call and immediately placed a second one. His emotions were still on a roller coaster. "Drew, I got onto Maddy's Floor. It took a bit of finagling, but I did it."

"Wow," Drew's tired voice perked up.

That damn kid worked too hard. He'd have made a hell of a police chief.

"That's great news. Did he give you a date yet?"

"Nope. They have to finish the rest of the wing. I told him I'd move in with exposed lumber as long I made it out of here, but he just laughed and said it wasn't that bad. Apparently they've moved one new patient in already, however, the rest of the medical equipment and supplies will take a day or two."

Drew said, "Please tell me you didn't offer to pay for equipment…"

John's smile beamed across the room at the three other patients shamelessly listening in on his call. "What's the point of having money if it doesn't help you?"

Drew was silent for a moment. "I think that's called bribery."

"Bribery, smibery. Who cares what it's called as long as it

works? Gerard needs donations and I need a bed. That's called a *trade*." He wanted to get up and dance around the room. This was going to work. He just knew the famous Dr. Maddy would fix him.

"Hmmm. At least I'll be able to see both you and Aunt Doris at the same time."

John coughed. "That's the best part. I'm getting on Dr. Maddy's floor, but I doubt she is. She's going to be pissed."

"You have the money, *trade* her way up there, too."

What? Like hell. John couldn't help the harrumph that slid out. "She can pay her own damn way. Christ, the sibling bond doesn't stretch that far. Especially a step-sibling. She's a pain in the ass with all her ordering about. Do you think I want to listen to that to the end of my days? Like hell." He shifted in his bed, pulling the blankets up higher on his shoulders. This damn place was either cold or hot. There never seemed to be a happy medium. Cheap buggers, all of them. All they ever wanted was money.

Well, he'd spend his the way he wanted to. And he'd leave it to whomever he wanted and that person sure as hell wasn't his stepsister. He winced as his guilty conscience poked him. "Besides, look at her mental deterioration. It's not like she'd appreciate the difference in the floors. Why waste the money?"

Drew's long-suffering sigh, the one John had heard a million times before, sounded through the phone. "Whatever makes you happy. You do know you can't take it with you?"

"Hell, I know that. Otherwise I'd have kicked off and taken it with me years ago, before this old body decided to break down. Now I'll spend it when I want to and how I want to. Have to go. The dinner cart is coming."

John hung up on his nephew. Damn do-gooder. How the hell had Drew gotten so strong on family? Besides Doris wasn't really family. And she'd spent all her money on her loose lifestyle. Why should he pay for her care now? Drew was the only one worth helping, but if Drew kept bugging John to be nice to Doris, Drew wasn't going to get anything.

Just like Doris.

DREW PUT AWAY his cell. Why the hell couldn't those two get along? Didn't he have enough trouble on his hands without running interference between his aunt and his uncle? Jesus. For two bedridden people they caused a pack of trouble. Like he needed that, today of all days – his first day on his new job.

He stood in the doorway and surveyed his new space as part of the Cold Case Squad office space. He'd visited before, but now this was *his* office. The large open room featured windows down one long wall that opened out to the back parking lot. Bulletin and white boards filled the other walls. Some were filled with notes and pictures and others remained empty, waiting for cases. *Stacks* of boxes, file numbers written on one end, filled the back wall. In the middle of the room were several large empty tables and two desks sat toward the back of the room. Open and friendly looking. He liked it already.

"Drew, welcome. Glad to have you here, finally."

Wilson Carter walked toward him, arm outstretched. They'd worked together for years, then apart for the last two when Wilson had transferred to this unit. He'd worked on Drew, slowly, inevitably persuading him to join the Cold Case department. Drew hoped to find that sense of job satisfaction here that eluded him in his former position.

Solving old cases with forgotten victims and helping out the families that had been waiting for closure since forever, should give that to him.

He shook Wilson's hand and listened as his old friend gave him an overview of the work area and the cases in progress. "Wow, it seems like we have some work to do."

"Ya think?"

Drew grinned, feeling a weight slide off his shoulders. "And I'm damn glad to be here." He glanced at the one wall beside the doorway that held several kids' pictures. "Where do we start?"

"We have several cases that have been reopened. It's going to take you some time to get up to speed on everything so I suggest you start with one. Go over it so you can become familiar with it, and then go on to the next. However…" He walked over to study the board in question. "This isn't really one of them. Although, when we have a lull or spare time, feel free to look deeper. But unless you come up with some concrete lead – well, it's not in the budget. We have to use the limited man hours where we can make a difference."

Drew stepped closer to the old photos on the wall. Six of them, boys and girls, one black and one of mixed race, Mexican maybe. The others were Caucasians. The fresh happy faces tore at his heart. If they were on the wall, they were victims. Victims he'd come here to help. He read the brief notes interspersing the old photos.

Glancing over at Wilson, he said, "I'll find time to go over this case though, even if it's in my spare time. I remember my uncle telling me about this one. Fascinating stuff."

Wilson nodded. "And very odd."

DORIS GLARED AT the small black cell phone. Her hand trembled so hard, she could barely hold the receiver to her ear. Her perfect asshole of a brother was gloating. Again. *Jerk.* In truth, he wasn't really her brother. Her mother had married his father when they were young enough to share their parents and old enough to hate having to do so. A difference she'd come to appreciate over the years. She tugged ruthlessly at the blankets, pulling them higher on her chest.

"You got a bed on Maddy's Floor? I don't believe you." And she didn't. Her application had been in for months – if not years. Who could remember? The days rolled into one hellish moment after another. "How did you get accepted before I did?"

"Money. Something I have a lot of and you don't."

John's joy made her sick. How dare he bribe his way in? And gloat about it. No siree, she wasn't letting this slide. The Haven would pay for this insult.

With the new wing opening, she'd hoped her application would finally be accepted. So far, only a couple of new patients had heard about their transfer requests. If she trusted the gossip, there were another ten beds or so still to fill. Patients had been in a frenzy trying to get transfer requests in as fast as possible, only they needed their doctor's approval too. Surely, one of those beds had her name on it?

She closed her phone while her brother was mid-sentence. There was only so much gloating she could handle. Besides, the second floor of The Haven was chaos. Doris watched the organized mess continue, as it did at this time of day every day. There was no weekend off from being poked, prodded and asked silly questions, with answers noted on the clipboard for all to see. Who in the world cared if she'd had her fiber and whether it was working or not? Peace was a prized commodity. Still it was better than the being in the morgue. Doris shook her head, her busy fingers pleating the sheets on her chest.

She studied the others in her ward. She'd had the same three neighbors for the last six months or so. No one left here except in a coffin. They should paint the walls black to prepare everyone for that certainty. Instead, someone had painted a happy yellow color on the walls. Yuck.

Still she'd been here close to a year. If John would give his head a shake, he'd understand that she was the one who deserved to be on Dr. Maddy's floor – not him. She didn't mind if he joined later – after he'd done his time on the other floors.

The higher the floor here, the closer to God. At least that was the rumor. She could believe it. The few times, she'd been privileged to see Dr. Maddy, she'd given off such a peaceful serenity it made Doris want to reach out and touch her. So young and so beautiful… Doris just knew she'd been graced by God.

That her stepbrother should get to Maddy's Floor before her was intolerable. Settling back into bed, Doris pondered her next move.

Something had to be done.

MADDY, CARRYING HER big ceramic mug, clipped down the open hallway at an astonishing speed. She wanted this over as quickly as possible. She had to curb the negativity and the fastest way to deal with that was to face the issue. Smiling at the patients as she walked past, her steps slowed as she reached the new wing.

"Dr. Lenning." She turned her groomed smile on her new arrival. Only by drawing on her years of experience did she keep her shock at his appearance from showing. The tall arrogant doctor who had made her life hell had turned into a shrunken and obviously very ill man – a shell of his former self.

"Welcome to The Haven."

His response?

A glare.

She raised an eyebrow and waited him out. Everyone knew the only way to beat an aggressive dog was to make sure he knew who was boss. Maddy had no intention of backing down to anyone on her floor – especially him.

Keeping her professionalism firmly in place, she let him see the amusement in her gaze. If he wanted to pout, let him. She'd dealt effectively with similar patients before. To that end, she walked forward and straightened his sheet, tucking it up to his shoulders, shifting his little table closer so he'd be able to reach his water. Lifting his glass, she asked, "Would you like a drink? I'm sure your mouth must be dry from the air in here."

His glare deepened.

She smiled as if he were an obstinate child. "No? Okay, maybe you'll feel like it later." She replaced the glass and stepped back. As if by rote, she rambled off the traditional greeting. "Welcome to The Haven. Here your comfort, your health and your state of mind are important to us. Our guarantee, our promise to you, is to make your visit as happy as can be. We'll give you the best medical care we can and hope you enjoy the rest of your stay here with us."

As she finished, she grinned down at him. "That's the professional version. Now for my version. I'm not sure what brought you to my floor or why; however I take my responsibilities and my residents' care seriously. I will do everything I can to maintain a loving and peaceful state among the residents and staff. As harmony is a prime goal, those that find 'being nice' on a regular basis too challenging will be moved to a different floor immediately. This floor is for those who are interested in improving their quality of life for however long they have one to enjoy."

His glare, had it been lasered, would have left her in tiny pieces strewn across the floor. Maddy didn't care. For the first time, the reality sank in. So what if the high and mighty Dr. Lenning had made her life hell before? This man was dying. He was incapable of getting up off that bed and attacking her again. His words would never have the same impact they'd had before, and knowing this was his last stop before death's door put the control firmly in her hands.

She relaxed. She didn't need to fear him. She could sympathize with his situation.

It was a long way from compassion and love but it was equally far from fear and hate.

For her, life was all about balance.

She smiled at the silent patient and continued. "Your doctor, Dr. Paul Cunningham, will be here this afternoon. You know the drill. He'll review your information then make his way here to go over your treatment options with you."

Shock lit his eyes. "What?"

"Oh, didn't you know? My caseload is full. Dr. Cunningham, however, who has been reducing his load for the last year, has agreed to take on your case. So you are in good hands."

She stepped back, her heels clicking on the hardwood. "Now if you'll excuse me, I have other patients I must see." With a final nod in his direction, she repeated her greeting, this time with real feeling. "Welcome to The Haven."

THURSDAY

HALFWAY TO WORK the next morning, a light misting rain started, soaking Maddy. Typical coastal weather – although technically Portland wasn't on the coast. What a day to decide she needed fresh air. Just as she resigned herself to getting drenched, a car honked and pulled up beside her. Maddy turned and recognized Gerard driving his charcoal beamer. She smiled with relief.

As she slid into the front seat, her suit jacket started to steam and her hair started to curl. She clipped in her seatbelt. "What a mess."

He pulled back into traffic, his movements sure and confident like the CEO he was. "You will walk."

"I know," she said ruefully. "Most of the time, it's fine. Then there're days like today."

He shot her an admiring glance. "Even soaking wet and imitating a duck, you're damned gorgeous."

Maddy laughed. Gerard had been making backhanded compliments to her for years. She refused to take them seriously. It went against her personal policy. Dating coworkers was bad business. Messy. She didn't do messy. "Thanks, I think."

"I'll be sorting applications today to fill that bed as soon as possible."

She frowned, a knot forming inside. She had no empty beds "What bed?"

He frowned at her. "Didn't Dr. Cunningham call you?"

Alarm triggered her nervous stomach, making it want to empty on the spot. "No. What did I miss?" Maddy pulled out her cell phone. She checked but there were no messages and no missed calls.

She frowned. Dr. Cunningham was usually good at staying in touch as a professional courtesy. If something had happened to one of her patients, he'd have called her.

"Jansen Svaar passed away last night."

Maddy stared at him, uncomprehendingly. That wasn't possible. "What?"

Gerard kept an eye on the traffic before darting a quick glance at her. "Apparently he died in his sleep. He was found by the nurse around three this morning."

That didn't feel right. In fact, it felt incredibly wrong. She chewed on the inside of her lip as she turned the information over in her head. Jansen had not been on death's door. She knew that. She'd have known if anything were going on. In fact, she'd scanned his system two days ago, after that weird visitation that had scared her so badly. Everything had been fine. Strong and healthy.

She didn't have all the answers to life and death. In fact, the more she learned, it seemed the less she knew. Particularly with energy work. And people died all the time – except, the last death on her floor had been eight months ago. Eight months was a long time for terminally ill patients. And she wouldn't have taken Jansen Svaar for the next candidate; far from it.

Jansen shouldn't have died.

And Dr. Cunningham should have informed her.

Gerard pulled the car into the underground parking lot. Disturbed, Maddy strode with him to the elevators.

"I'll speak with Dr. Miko. See what she has to say about his death." The in-house pathologist hated mysteries and could usually be counted on to come up with the answers Maddy wanted.

He nodded. "Remember Maddy, people die. Especially here."

Maddy tilted her lips slightly. She knew Jansen's bed would be filled within hours.

She understood, although she didn't particularly like it.

An hour later she closed the door to her office, relieved. She needed a few moments of peace…to adjust. A few minutes to mourn the loss of someone who'd been a joy to have on her floor. She couldn't believe how personally devastating she found Jansen's death. He'd been doing so well.

A knock sounded on her door.

"Come in," she called out, trying to compartmentalize her feelings and lock them down until she had space and time to sort through them.

A tall imposing man stood in her doorway. "I'm looking for Dr. Madeleine Wagner."

Maddy's gaze widened at the dignified stranger in her doorway. "Yes, that's me. What can I do for you?"

He smiled, walked forward, held out his hand. "Nice to finally meet you. I'm Dr. Chandler of Madison House. I'd like to speak with you, if you have a couple minutes to spare."

She stood up, smiling at one of the most respected surgeons and researchers on this side of the country. "It's a pleasure to meet you, Dr. Chandler. Please, have a seat." She motioned toward the seating arrangement out on the covered deck. The earlier rain had stopped, letting the sun peek out. "May I offer you some coffee?"

At his surprised nod, she fussed at her machine for a few minutes, then picked up the two cups and joined him outside.

She sat across from him. "Now, what can I do for you, Dr. Chandler?"

SEVERAL FILES SAT open on Gerard's desk, applications under consideration. Another bed had just opened up on Maddy's Floor. Perfect. Who had money and who would be willing to pay handsomely for a chance to move up in life?

His office phone rang. Damn, now what?

"Hello. Oh, hi, John." Gerard rolled his eyes and sank deeper into his high-backed wing chair. "How are you doing?"

"Getting impatient. When is my transfer going through?"

"Soon. I haven't gotten the forms from your doctor yet. Being in a different facility means there's a mess of paperwork to complete."

"If that's the only thing holding you up, I'll take care of it." John's tone made it clear there'd be hell to pay if his doctor didn't move on the issue – and fast.

Gerard smirked. Better to have John target someone else for a change. "Go easy on him. He's probably swamped with work. And it's likely to be his nurse taking care of the paperwork. You may want to check before you snap at him."

John's snort blasted through the phone. "Like hell. It'll get done today."

Gerard pinched the bridge of his nose and did something he rarely did – he excused himself. "John, I'm rushing to a meeting. I'm sorry but I have to run."

"Right. No problem. I have someone else to chase now. Have a good one."

Gerard stared at the phone as he replaced it. Given a new target, John sounded positively perky. That man must have made his department hell for any lollygaggers. Still, he was off Gerard's tail for a bit. Thank God.

Sandra walked into Gerard's office, a large stack of opened letters in her arms. "How bad is it today?" he asked.

"It's an interesting mix. The bulk of them are applications, requests for applications and questions about The Haven, all of which are good things." She dropped the stack in front of him. "And they give me confidence that I'll still have a job at the end of the year."

"Yeah," he growled, "but you may have to take a pay cut."

"Not going to happen, so don't go there." She turned to leave. Before she reached the door she turned back as if she'd forgotten something. "Although, speaking of pay cuts and the employment issues in today's world, I thought I saw Dr. Chandler walking the halls this morning, heading upstairs."

Gerard glanced up at her, his mind already immersed in the morning's mail. "Who?"

"Dr. Chandler. You know the physician with that leading-edge-technology-stuff from Madison House."

Gerard's eyes widened. "What?"

She looked over her glasses at him and frowned. "Is that a big deal?" The glint in her eyes said she knew it was.

He pushed his chair back and stood. "Do you know why he was here or where he was going?"

"Nope. Haven't a clue." She pushed her glasses up the bridge of her nose and walked toward the door again.

Jesus, Sandra had been here since forever. Nothing much happened here she didn't know. Damn it. He sat back down and tried to refocus on the morning mail. He didn't see the words on the page. What the hell would the head of the most expensive, most prestigious hospital want with anyone upstairs?

Upstairs? His head snapped up.

Maddy.

Oh, Christ.

DREW PULLED HIS scratchpad closer. He had several pages full of notes so far, but he was a long way from done. He hadn't been able to resist a closer look at the kids' cases – on his own time. Wilson had explained that wall was a reminder page, a memorial so to speak, rather than a current case.

He remembered more the deeper he delved into the case. His uncle had spoken about the raging argument among the members of his department as to whether it was a criminal case – or a case at all. He couldn't resist trying to find out. The mystery behind it was addictive. He'd stayed late last night to catch up on the details.

In all six cases, the cause of death had been listed as inconclusive. No evidence left behind and no links between the children – none that anyone had found, at least. He picked up the folder and flicked through old detectives' notes, results and timelines. The first victim, Sissy Colburn, had been sitting at her kitchen table doing homework when she'd fallen to the floor dead. The last victim, Stephen Hansen, was found in the backyard of his home, fully dressed, backpack hanging off one shoulder and a half a chocolate bar in his hand. Dead. As if his last breath had just left his body and he'd collapsed on the spot.

Odd. For some unknown reason, all six healthy kids had just dropped dead, under what seemed ordinary circumstances.

Even odder was the tiny bruise on the base of the spine on all six kids. The doctors had no explanation, the autopsy hadn't shown a cause for them, and none of the parents knew anything that would indicate how each bruise had occurred.

The intriguing thing was that each victim had the same bruise. Six victims within a four-month span of time. No similar cases could be found before or after, according to Wilson's research.

He studied the old photos. The bruises looked insignificant, like an everyday small bruise.

The hairs on the back of his head rose. Spooky stuff.

Could he contribute anything to the case? Was there anything, any evidence that could be processed again with today's technology?

He set the boxes, four of them, off to one side and sorted through the swabs and clothing samples. It took the rest of the afternoon to determine that the detectives on the case had been thorough. Their notes spoke of their frustration with the lack of evidence.

Many cops expressed their doubts that a crime had even occurred, suggesting these were medical deaths – sad, but not their problem.

Then there was the evidence box full of diaries. Small, feminine diaries chronicled the years prior and the twenty years after the death of Darcy Durnham, the second victim of the six. According to Wilson, the father, Scott Durnham, had started dropping the diaries off a good ten years ago after the writer, Darcy's mother, passed away, in the hopes the police could find something helpful in them. Wilson had put them in order to find that there was no diary for the period covering Darcy's death. He'd expressed doubts that it had existed, but Drew figured it probably just hadn't shown up yet. Compulsive writing like Darcy's mother had demonstrated with her diaries rarely stopped one day to the next…and started again just as abruptly.

Scott showed up once in a while through the years when he found another one in the house. As always, it was logged in and added to the pile. So far, Wilson hadn't found anything of value in them.

Now it was Drew's turn.

Not an easy job.

BED 232 SMILED. No, not bed 232, she'd be Sissy today. She did feel so much better. She shifted slightly in bed. Mornings were always better. 'Good drugs,' the docs would say.

The long-term care aide stepped up to her bedside. "How are you feeling, my dear?" Bending over, she searched Sissy's gaze for a long moment as if trying to see who she really was. Satisfied, she pulled back with a decisive nod. "My goodness, Sissy, your color is so much better today. You're positively blushing. Is this a special day for you?"

Sissy eyed her slyly. "Maybe. One never can tell. I'd like to have breakfast out of bed this morning."

"Well, you certainly do look nice today. That's great that you are feeling well enough to get dressed. Shall we choose something special to wear? And how about your makeup, would you like some lipstick on today?" The aide bounced around the room, chattering happily and pulling out various pieces of clothing. "Let's try the pink sweater, and if you're feeling up to it, how about slacks?"

Sissy gave a graceful nod in thanks. "Pants and a sweater sound lovely, and maybe the Summer Blush lipstick to match."

Collecting the clothing, the aide walked over and laid everything on the bed. "Here we go."

With a fat smile, Sissy said, "Thanks." It had been awhile since she'd been in such good spirits. There was nothing like getting out of bed first thing in the morning to make life brighter and the day more positive. She could get used to this.

Of course, the buzz of excitement helped.

A new bed on Dr. Maddy's floor had opened. A flurry of excitement drifted through Sissy's ward. She sniffed. Like any of the old biddies in her ward had a chance at that rare lottery. She watched and listened as they all dreamed about moving up to that floor. As if that would change their lives. They weren't doing anything to help themselves. Hadn't they understood this whole concept? A bed had opened up because someone had died. *Died.* As in people died upstairs just as easily as downstairs. Stupid twits. Didn't they think at all?

A transfer upstairs for them would be a waste.

They weren't like her. She needed to do some serious thinking about the next step in her healing process. Sometimes, the days went by so fast, she had trouble keeping up. Probably her medication. Her old doctor had kept her so drugged out, no wonder she'd had trouble adjusting to the world around her.

It was his fault, not hers.

But he'd paid for that one.

ADAM LENNING LAY still, frozen in his bed as the first morning light warmed his corner of the world. The nurses hadn't noticed anything out of the ordinary. He'd closed his eyes to appear asleep. It had fooled them but there was no fooling himself.

He had seen something…wrong. Horribly wrong.

Yet, he couldn't say exactly what he'd seen.

The patient in the next bed had died last night. Adam knew the exact time. He'd been woken in the night by the cold. After growing up in Alaska, he understood cold. This part of Oregon did get chilly, except it was late summer, not the dead of winter. Last night, well, he'd have sworn the temperature on the floor was below freezing. Surely the furnace had quit unexpectedly? Although, given the time of year, there shouldn't have been the need for it in the first place. This eluded logic.

He'd tried to snag the blanket at the foot of his bed to spread it over himself, only the shivers that wracked his frame had made that virtually impossible. It's when he'd been lying there, shivering, that he'd noticed the shadows through the curtains surrounding Jansen's bed at the end of the open area.

Unlike the rest of The Haven, where you could barely walk for the people, Maddy's Floor wasn't crowded. This floor didn't have private rooms, but each person had privacy through partial walls and curtains, making the areas individual, homey, yet accessible in an emergency.

He liked it. The place offered companionship and medical care without cloistering each person in their own room for hours on end. There was room to walk and be social and yet, there was privacy.

Footsteps approached, the sound mingling with the gentle whisper of a small cart rolling forward. A cheerful voice called out, "How are you doing, Dr. Lenning?"

"Cold," he muttered, his teeth chattering uncontrollably. "So cold."

The nurse frowned and immediately pulled out a thermometer from the medicine cart. She checked his temperature, before returning to a small computer on the cart to make a notation on the file. "I'll be right back."

She took her cart back down the hallway. It seemed to take forever before she returned, but then she wrapped his shaking body in heated blankets. She put a second one over his shoulder and neck.

"Ohhh," he moaned, sinking into the welcomed heat. He turned his face into the blanket, feeling the warmth on his cheeks and against his eyes.

"It's okay. Let's give your body a chance to warm up. I'll come back in a couple of minutes."

The nurse disappeared again.

He didn't care. For the first time in hours, heat was seeping into his old bones.

Warm and feeling safe, he succumbed to fatigue and his eyes drooped closed. His sense of balance reasserted itself. He almost believed he'd imagined the whole thing.

Almost.

MADDY MOVED THROUGH the morning, trying to ignore the sense of foreboding hanging over her head. Not an easy thing. Something had warped through her world, leaving a trail of unease and confusion in its wake and she didn't know what it was or where it had come from. What she did know is that she couldn't let fear or unrest take over her thoughts.

Moving through the floor, she checked on each of her patients.

At Beth's bedside, she spent a few minutes with the sixty-four-year-old woman. The patient had a zest for life that Maddy admired. Today, that spirit had disappeared. Beth lay curled up in a ball, the covers pulled to her neck. Tiny already, she looked like a child now.

"Bad night, Beth?"

Beth shuddered, her pink scalp showing through her sparse white hair. "Horrible. I had nightmares about death and dying. Nasty stuff." She lifted her liver-spotted hand and reached out for Maddy. Though she tried to smile her lips had a tired droop.

Maddy sat on the side of her bed. She noted the pallor of the woman's skin and the tremors shaking her hand.

It was obvious, Beth, along with every other one of her patients, had been disturbed last night.

"Well, it's a new day, Beth, and that terrible night is over, sent into the annals of history with every other bad day in your life."

Beth attempted a bigger smile. It failed. "I don't know, Dr. Maddy. It scared me pretty good."

Maddy studied the position of Beth's bed. Looked around, wondered. Was it possible? Jansen's bed was at the far end of the floor. Beth shouldn't have seen anything, yet she'd obviously felt it. No surprise there.

"Beth, what was the dream about? Maybe if you tell me about it, you'll be able to let it go."

The old woman's trembling increased. "I don't think so. It seemed like death was sitting on my bed, watching me, waiting for me. There was no lightness or angels. Only darkness and ice." She gasped for breath, a thin film of sweat breaking on her forehead. "I can't think about it! I know my time is coming and soon. I'm petrified that death will be like my dream." Her eyes filled with tears. "Dr. Maddy, I'm scared."

Not good. Beth's attitude toward her own health and death management had been spot on since Maddy had first met her. This dream had really sent her for a spin. Maddy pulled out a small bottle of Rescue Remedy, a homeopathic tincture, and gave the old woman several drops under her tongue. The natural remedy was used by many paramedics for shock and trauma of all kinds. Maddy had found it worked well for frights too. And being all-natural, it didn't mess with patients' energy or medications.

Satisfied, once Beth rested comfortably, Maddy stepped over to her next patient. And found a repeat of the same story. Frowning, Maddy made her way through the floor, finding variations of the same theme. The negative energy ripple had a bigger effect than she'd thought possible.

As Maddy approached the new wing, Dr. Lenning called her over.

She frowned as she saw him bundled up, his head swathed in warm blankets. "Bad night?"

"Terrible, just terrible," he whispered. "Thank heavens this place is equipped with blanket warmers. So, what happened, Dr. Maddy? Did the furnace quit overnight?"

That surprised her. None of the other patients had complained of a debilitating coldness. Chills, yes, but not to this level. Although his reaction reminded her how she'd felt when she'd first seen Eric's energy. "No. There were no reported problems or dips in the temperatures. Apparently, several people did have a weird night, though."

"Honestly, it feels like I've had less than an hour's sleep."

Maddy frowned. "Any change in your medications?" She stepped closer, pulling up his file on her tablet. He wasn't taking anything unusual.

"Oh, it isn't my drugs. No, I woke up and thought I saw something going on over at that bed." He pulled a frail hand far enough free of the blanket to point at Jansen's old bed.

Maddy spun around, realizing that from this position, Adam would have had a good view of Jansen's area. Staring down at him, she also understood that Dr. Lenning really was a helpless old man now. Why had she given him so much power over her emotional well-being? Shaking free of the thought, she sat at the edge of the bed. "What did you think you saw?"

"When I watched the curtain, it appeared as though someone attached a rope to Jansen's body and was pulling him up toward the ceiling. He didn't lift clear off the bed, his back arched up and down several times. Then it was like someone cut him free and he collapsed back down again. It was almost like someone was trying to pull his shadow from his body." His hands folded the corner of his sheet over and over in precise uniformly sized folds, but his eyes darted up to see her reaction.

Maddy's spine locked in place at his first words. Oh no. She needed to call Stefan, her friend, mentor and fellow energy worker – and fast. Though worried, she did her best to placate Adam.

"I'm not sure what to say. I can't imagine Jansen being able to do that on his own and there's certainly no evidence to suggest anyone else was here with that physical strength. Jansen, like everyone else here, came to enjoy the last days he had. It was just his time to go." She gave a casual shrug, patting his hand. "Take it easy and rest." With a gentle smile, she turned and walked back toward the nurses' station.

"DR. MADDY, WAS there a full moon last night? I swear everyone is acting weird today," Amelia asked. Several of the other nurses gathered alongside the long-time nurse to hear Maddy's answer.

Maddy shook her head. "I have no idea." She reached for the schedule. "Who was on last night?"

Amelia handed over the staff roster. "Amber. So far today, I've heard that last night was the result of everything from a bad planetary alignment to the new government's spending."

The nurses chuckled. Over the years, these nurses had heard it all. And sometimes even they were surprised by the comments and actions of patients and their visitors.

"Susan mentioned patient concerns in the meeting this morning. I wrote it down." Nancy held up her notepad.

Maddy stepped over to read the note over Nancy's shoulder. "The thermostat registered normal temperatures; however, all patients were hollering about feeling cold. She says staff were kept running with requests for sleeping aids, water and hot blankets. *Hmmm.*"

"I know that hmmm. What are you thinking?" Nancy twisted to look at Maddy. Her gaze narrowed on Maddy's face. "Is this all related to Jansen's death."

"Maybe."

Nancy frowned, leaning in closer so as not to be overheard. "How?"

Maddy glanced around as the nurses resumed their other duties, then lowered her voice. "It's hard to say. However, energy is energy and whether it is used to heal or to kill, everyone will feel it or experience it in a different way."

"We've had deaths here before without everyone freaking

out."

"I know. This does concern me. I can only assume at the moment that as the healing energy here increases, everyone becomes more sensitive to changes in that energy."

Nancy walked to the coffee maker. "So this may not be a bad thing?"

"Let's say I'm not panicking over it yet. If it happens again, we'll have to look at minimizing the impact on those left behind."

"Can we do that?" Nancy was wise. Her years of working with Maddy had made her intuition more open and she was more receptive to new concepts. That they were best friends and confidants didn't hurt, either.

Maddy smiled. "To some extent." Something else occurred to her. "I wonder if patients on the other floors were affected."

"We can ask."

With a gentle squeeze on Nancy's shoulder, Maddy said, "Ask one or two of the nurses on the other floors, will you please? Find out if anyone there had similar reactions. Or was it localized to our floor?"

DR. ROBERTA MIKO sat at her overflowing desk, dwarfed by the stacks of papers and files circling her. The rest of the office looked the same. Tuning it out, she debated the issue for hours in her head. There'd been no reason to believe Jansen Svaar's death was suspicious, not with his history of Stage II mesothelioma and diabetes. He had been exposed to asbestos during his decades-long work in the shipyards. Chemotherapy and radiation had slowed the progression of the lung tumors for just about a year. Then the cancer had advanced. When he had moved into The Haven, his prognosis had been for less than seven months. He couldn't care for himself and had slid to skin and bone. That had been close to ten months ago.

She frowned. So, what had happened in the meantime? She walked over to the cooler and pulled out the drawer where the body was stored. Lifting the sheet, she gave the body a slow perusal. This man showed a healthy weight with good skin tone and elasticity. At first glance, he appeared to have been doing fine. These signs of health meant nothing except that they were in direct opposition to the condition he'd been in when he'd arrived at The Haven.

Something at The Haven had worked for him. Maddy again. Roberta hadn't been sent many of Dr. Maddy's patients down here, a fact she'd pondered more and more as time went by. When Maddy's patients arrived at The Haven, they were no healthier than the rest. Roberta cocked her head to one side, and considered possibilities. She didn't know how bed assignments were arranged here. Maybe those on Maddy's Floor had to fulfill requirements different from those of other patients. Something she'd look into.

She'd heard the rumors. She didn't have a basis to believe or disbelieve them. *Except…* She stared down at the interesting case before her. *What a perfect opportunity to learn more.*

FRIDAY

MADDY CLOSED THE door after the last of the nurses left and allowed her shoulders to slump. The daily meeting had cleared the air on several issues. Dr. Cunningham had shown up late as usual.

Her stomach grumbled. She'd missed lunch again. The small fridge contained the usual stash of yogurt and veggies, only she needed more today. Her eyes studied the stack of files on her desk. As much as she'd love an hour away, her workload also beckoned.

Her cell phone rang.

Maddy recognized the number and picked up. "Dr. Miko, hi."

The pathologist spared no greeting. "Look, I don't know what to tell you. Jansen Svaar's cancer was in remission. So whatever magic you were doing up there was working. There were several tumors of varying sizes in his lungs. However, there was no evidence they were growing or contributed to his death. I'm waiting on the tox screen so I have nothing specific at the moment. The only thing I can tell you is that I can't give you a direct cause of death at this point. And I have to tell you that I don't like that much, either. In fact, this one is liable to bug the hell out of me." By the end of her tirade, Roberta's voice was almost snapping with annoyance.

Maddy didn't like the information, either, but it wasn't as if it were the first time or indeed, unexpected. She said gently, "And sometimes, people just die. Jansen was seventy-eight. He'd lived a good life and he died a good death." At least she hoped he had.

Maddy had seen plenty of deaths that science didn't explain. Still, with any death, she always saw a blockage or a major energy system gone awry, or the energy cords thin and worn out. The body ready to go. Very rarely, did a person go to bed and disconnect their one link to their body – their own energy cord.

And when death did happen in this way, instead of being a

horribly sad event, it was usually a peaceful passing.

But Jansen's death didn't feel the same. Her misgivings stemmed from her sense of guilt over that purple-black energy she'd seen hovering over him – that same energy she had yet to identify. In hindsight, she realized she shouldn't have left him alone. Yet it was impossible for her to be everywhere all the time.

"Maddy, are you still there? What's wrong?"

Staring down at the phone in her hand, Maddy shook her head – hard. Lord, Dr. Miko was going to think she'd lost it.

"I'm here. Sorry. Lost in thought." She coughed several times, clearing her throat. "Roberta, were there any bruises to indicate perhaps he'd fallen or other signs of trauma that we may not have noticed? Anything out of the ordinary?"

"No. Except for…" A slight silence filled the line. "A small bruise at the base of his spine. But there was no puncture or damage to the spinal column or even the muscle tissues. It appears to be a superficial mark."

Maddy snatched up a notepad and jotted down the coroner's words. "Could you send me a copy of the autopsy report, please? Oh, by the way, that bruise, what size is it?"

"About that of a quarter, maybe slightly larger. As there was little else to put into the report, I have measured it out and documented it along with a photo should anything arise later."

"Right. Let's hope the mystery can be solved one day."

"So many never are."

"Isn't that the truth?" Maddy sighed. "Thanks for the call."

After she signed off, Maddy stared out the window. A bruise might mean anything, except in that location, it made her uneasy. Settled in behind the base of the spine in a spot most people referred to as the root chakra, or root energy center, lay the Kundalini energy. This powerful energy lay dormant at the base of the spine in everyone. It was less developed in children, but still an incredible energy source. *If* someone outside that body could access it… And that was a big *if*.

It also related to the crown chakra, another powerful energy center, at the top of the skull.

She'd forgotten to ask Dr. Miko if she'd checked Jansen's head. Should she call her back? Or let it go as a slim-to-none chance that Jansen had a matching one at the top of his skull?

Shit. She had to know. Maddy quickly dialed.

"Roberta, sorry. Did you happen to notice a matching bruise

on Jansen's head?"

"Hmmm. Checking the report now. At the base or the crown?"

"Crown. It would probably be around the same size as the other one." Maddy couldn't help chewing her bottom lip nervously as she waited.

"I don't have anything written down. Let me go check."

Maddy listened as Roberta placed the phone on the desk with a clunk, followed by soft-soled steps and a heavy metal slide. Her impatience grew, the longer she waited. What could be taking so long? Surely it was a simple matter to check? Then she remembered Jansen's hair. That man had a full head of stiff, wiry stuff. He'd always liked it long. In fact, he'd been quite particular about keeping it just right.

"Maddy?" Roberta's voice sounded odd, confused even. "I'm not sure. You might be right. I'm going to take a closer look and call you back."

Maddy's heart sank.

She'd hoped she'd been wrong.

DORIS HELD HER notepad firmly in one shaking hand and tried to finish the letter to the Board. No way was she was going to lie down here while her brother used underhanded tricks to get his way. That man thought way too much of himself. That he'd been able to buy the spot she'd been waiting for on the famed third floor was intolerable.

She cast a furtive glance at Sissy in the bed beside her. She hadn't been able to stop studying her all morning. How odd. She looked better every day. How did that happen? As Doris had steadily declined, that woman appeared to have steadily improved. In the last few months, the improvement had been noticeable.

Sissy wasn't friendly. She had that better-than-everyone attitude, so it wasn't as if Doris could up and ask her what she'd been doing. As it was, the two rarely spoke.

Who called their daughter 'Sissy' anyway? Doris had met one other person with that name, a child she'd taught piano lessons to way back when. The poor girl had died a mysterious death, as Doris recalled.

Doris kept her head down, tugging her focus back to the half-written letter in front of her. Surely, Sissy shouldn't be here on this floor anymore, at least not much longer. She didn't know what drugs she'd been getting, but Doris wanted some of the same for herself.

She'd have to ask her doctor. Maybe he'd prescribe the same thing. She stole a second look. Damn, that woman looked good. She offered Sissy a tentative smile and received a lukewarm response.

Doris returned to draft her letter, happier. Maybe they could be friends. Most of her other ones had died.

TIME TO MEET her new patient.

Maddy barely kept her bouncing step in control as she walked down the hallway to meet her newest arrival. She smirked at Nancy's eye roll. "What? I'm happy. We get so few children in here. Felicia's arrival is a huge deal." Hospice care differed from location to location across the country. Yet Maddy knew from experience that children responded better to her energy work than any of her other patients. Children didn't come here normally – it was considered an adult care facility. But the hospital was open to everyone and sometimes, on rare occasions, a child moved into The Haven. Often their family fought to have them here. They always came to Maddy's Floor.

Maddy came upon Belle, as she visited with her latest great grandson. Contentment whispered through her aging energy. Belle had come a long way these last few weeks. It was good to see her adjusting.

"Except the arrival of this child means she's deathly ill and there's not much great about that," Nancy reminded her.

"And that's why she needs to be here. Maybe we can turn things around." Maddy refused to let her joy dim with negative thinking. She wished she could work only with children. Her healing skills could do so much more with them. Unfortunately, the medical establishment was a long way from acceptance on that issue.

They passed the nurses' center, where two of her staff worked tirelessly, their energy calm and relaxed. That was so important here. People liked to believe they were independent of each other, but everything they felt and thought affected those around them. Children were particularly susceptible. The good news was the children also had the ability to heal – almost overnight.

The last two children had been released in steadily improving health. Paul Dermont had cancer that refused to respond to treatment. After his transfer to this floor, his cancer had gone into spontaneous remission within months of his arrival. Sending Paul home had been a highlight of Maddy's year.

Nancy smiled, her features softening. "Let's hope so. Felicia could use it. It's a good thing Dr. Robertson is on your side."

They shifted to walking single file, as two orderlies moved carts down the hallway. Maddy smiled at Horace, who'd been working here for decades. He was a favorite among the patients – always had a smile for each one.

Momentarily distracted, Maddy tried to pull the threads of their conversation together. Where were they? Right, Dr. Robertson. "How true. Unfortunately, it took him a lot of years to get there."

Convincing doctors at the beginning had been tough. Many misunderstood and viewed her work with dismay or distrust. They wanted proof. Something she could only provide after working with a patient – and she couldn't do that if they didn't invite her in on a case. Now, after seven years, she worked with two specialists and several doctors at the local children's hospital.

Felicia's medical history would be an interesting read. Maddy knew a bit about her condition, but not her full history. She'd have a conference with Dr. Robertson to discuss treatment options and to set up a pain management program.

Maybe Felicia would be lucky and experience something magical here, too.

Felecia was moving into Jansen's spot, a circumstance that had given Maddy pause, until she realized that had also been Paul's bed and he'd gone home to continue his recovery. Jansen's death was an anomaly. It had to be. Nothing else made sense. Maddy insisted Jansen's bed be moved back to its original position, tucked securely inside the protective energy. That didn't guarantee the child's safety, but it would help – and it made Maddy feel better.

The increased noise level said they'd almost reached the right bed. Gerona was there, paperwork in hand, to sign off on Felicia's arrival.

"Dr. Maddy, it's good to see you again." A tall, silver-haired man in a white lab coat hovered protectively beside Felicia's bed, holding out his hand to two interns. Dr. Robertson shook the two men's hands and thanked them for taking good care of Felicia.

One man grinned and waved at Felicia while the other chucked her under the chin before leaving. "You be good. This is the luckiest move of your life. Let's hope the next one will take you home… So behave yourself."

Maddy shook Dr. Robertson's hand. "Why am I not surprised to see you here with her? Did you follow the ambulance in?" she ribbed him gently. Felicia had been Dr. Robertson's patient since her birth. She was also his most heartbreaking case. Terminally ill children were hard on everyone – especially the children.

The sheet-covered body moved, a sock-covered foot slid out, then the toes wiggled. Maddy grinned. God, she loved children. As she reached to snag a toe or two, the sheet slid down and Felicia's head popped up. Shaved and bruised looking, yet the little girl wore a gamin smile that melted all who saw her.

"Hi, Dr. Maddy," she piped in the optimistic singsong voice of a child. And that was one of the reasons Maddy wanted her here. Her life force was strong, regardless of the brainstem glioma threatening to kill her and the unsuccessful radiation and chemotherapy that had made her life hell. Her spirit shone bright and free. That gave her a fighting chance.

"Hey, pumpkin. How are you doing?"

Doernbecher Children's Hospital had given her great care. However, it was Dr. Robertson's push that brought Felicia to Maddy. Paul, the patient who went home, was also his patient. There was nothing like success with one case to bring hope to another.

Maddy studied Felicia's energy field. Low, thin and pale, yet still strong. The core pulsed with possibilities. Maddy had watched her from the sidelines this last year and as each treatment failed, Dr. Robertson and the parents had become a little more desperate. She'd undergone surgery once, only the growth had returned. At that point, Dr. Robertson had thrown his hands up and asked for her help.

Medical practice required permission. Maddy had it now. Felicia was hers. Hopefully, it wasn't too late. Maddy immediately reached for a brighter thought to overcome the negative one. Lord, she'd been doing that a lot lately.

"I'm good. The ambulance ride was fun. Do you have television here?" Felicia twisted her head from side to side, checking out her new home.

Maddy threw her head back and laughed. "Of course, do you

think all these patients would stay if we didn't?"

Felicia giggled. "Maybe if you served chocolate ice cream."

Dr. Robertson reached out and lightly tapped her bald head. "Not everyone is as addicted to chocolate ice cream as you are, young lady."

"Then they don't have taste buds." Her eyes opened wide at several posters on the walls that depicted animals and kids playing sports. That would be Nancy's doing most likely. They'd be able to decorate the area more fully now that Felicia was here. There was rarely time before patients arrived.

Opposite was a large window that allowed the midmorning sun to sneak in. A super-sized balcony sat outside huge double doors halfway to the next bed, sectioned off by partial walls and curtains.

Maddy smiled at her patient's curiosity. A good sign. Activity bustled around them as nurses stepped up to complete the transfer of paperwork and equipment, and warm blankets arrived to take off the chill that had been induced by the move and any uncertainty the girl felt over the changes in her life.

"Mom said she'd be here." Felicia glanced around for her mother – the first glimmer of nervousness showed in her eyes.

"If she said she'd be here, then she'll be here. This place is huge. She's probably lost like we would have been if not for your terrific ambulance guys," Dr. Robertson said with a smile.

With a nod and a wink at the tiny addition to her floor, Maddy led the way to her office. Once inside, she offered Dr. Robertson a coffee from her espresso machine.

"Only you'd have a coffee station in your office." He shook his head, accepted the cup of Italian coffee from her and sat down in the leather seat opposite her desk. "I may have to reconsider my career options. Look at this place. High class indeed."

"The Board indulges me." Maddy shrugged. She'd also taken over from Dr. Newell, who'd been fastidious about his office furniture. She actually preferred light-colored wood furnishings like cedar or oak, but asking for a complete furniture switch had been prohibitive and unnecessary. She'd rather have the funds go to patient care.

"So what are we doing for Felicia now?" That turned the discussion back to business and they sat down to discuss the next step in Felicia's medical journey, hopefully one that would lead to an improved outcome.

DREW RELAXED AT his desk, enjoying the new office. So few people. So much space. So little noise. He finally felt like he was adjusting to his new caseload as well as his space. They had a lot of freedom to work here, but it was hard to re-evaluate old cases to find a new angle, find a way forward with the old evidence. He had to wrap his mind around a lot of information. Technology had changed this field tremendously, allowing them to retest old samples, provided they hadn't deteriorated. DNA samples were a huge boon.

The dead kids though, with their faces staring down at him from the wall, had affected him. Their unexplained deaths were a puzzle with no way forward. That hadn't stopped him from trying. He'd left a message with a contact in the FBI Behavioral Unit this morning, hoping to run some info through the MO databank. There'd been no return call at this point. Chances are there wouldn't be one.

Portland didn't have a similar database and he'd already run the bruise pattern through the Oregon State Police Law Enforcement Data Computer or LEDS system, with its limited MO files. No luck yet. Next were InfoNet and its system that allowed him to email anyone on the LEDS system. Maybe he'd get lucky and find someone who had seen this particular bruise pattern.

Then there were the journals. Sigh. He'd flicked through a couple, only he hadn't been able to find anything except the painful ramblings of an older woman. He'd put them in chronological order, yet hadn't devoted much time to them. He figured he might get through a diary a day. That would still take him a month or two, but at least he'd know that he'd done what he could in that regard.

He was about to reach for his coffee cup when the phone rang. Dr. Miko, the pathologist at The Haven. Interesting.

MADDY COLLECTED THE flowers delivered for Felicia and carried them down the hall. Painted bright and cheery with lavenders and turquoises, her area looked like any normal child's bedroom, complete with a bookshelf and a toy bin.

Felicia was awake and appeared to be playing with her Nintendo video game. Her hands and fingers were painfully thin as she manipulated the small buttons. Handheld computer toys were a great way to pass the time. As her condition was terminal and she was debilitated to the point she couldn't live a 'normal' life, Felicia had teachers visit for various lessons and she attended school online with her laptop. Her mother visited her each day to help with the homework.

"Hi, Dr. Maddy. Are those for me?" Her young face brightened at the gorgeous sunflowers in Maddy's arms. "Wow, those are beautiful. Who are they from?"

Maddy grinned as she placed the bouquet on the bookshelf. Pulling out the card, she handed it to Felicia. While the girl exclaimed about the flowers, Maddy opened her tablet to Felicia's file. Hmmm, Felicia's appetite was down. Not unusual given the transfer, but that couldn't be allowed to continue. Felicia needed her strength. Healing would only happen if the body had energy to spare.

She studied the drugs listed. The cocktail was daunting, particularly considering that nothing was working. Her radiation treatments had been discontinued and the traditional way forward appeared to be the only option – help her make peace with the future.

After her rounds this morning, Maddy planned to go into her office and do a full energy scan on her youngest patient – something Maddy needed peace and quiet to do. She'd like to do one here at Felicia's bedside while she slept. However, until the place returned to normal from the repairs and new arrivals, she'd do her scans remotely. Switching her vision, she checked Felicia's energy. It pulsed slowly and was snug against the tiny body. White with soft lavender ripples, but the pulses had a tenacity to them that gave Maddy hope. Still, the energy was low and fainter than Maddy would like.

There was no time to lose.

"Felicia, I have to go and run a bunch of tests. When I'm done, we'll talk again." With a bright smile, and a brief touch of her hand to Felicia's cheek, Maddy left and strode down to her office. At the nurses' station she stopped for her messages and told the staff she'd be working and not to disturb her.

They understood, at least to some degree.

Few understood the world of a medical intuitive. For Maddy, her special awareness was a natural complement to her medicine and as instinctive as breathing.

She closed her office door, drew the heavy curtains together and turned off her phones. She walked over to the wall beside her door, pushed the visitor's chair back and away and cleared a space where she could sit on the floor. She could do this standing or sitting; however, as yoga was her preferred method to unwind, she usually chose to relax into one of the many poses her body loved so well.

After unbuttoning her jacket and kicking off her heels, Maddy gracefully sank to the floor to sit cross-legged. She sighed deeply, rotating her neck and releasing the tension in her system. Tension was resistance. She knew that, and slowly eased her body into a state of relaxation and self-awareness.

Feeling a familiar calming detachment, Maddy went to work.

Using a technique called remote viewing, Maddy focused on Felicia until her awareness was right at her bedside where she 'saw' Felicia's body. It was almost as good as being there in person. She shifted her focus to Felicia's energy systems. Every physical body had a road map of energy like highways rippling across it, servicing all the main body systems. Maddy saw the energy flows and drains, as they moved to address worry, stress, past events or even joy.

Most people in The Haven had little energy dedicated to the good things in life. If they had, they wouldn't be as sick. The human body created and tapped into so much more energy than people understood. Instead of reaching for the energy so readily available, people 'used up' their stock of this resource with the little irritating things in life, leaving their systems short for healing. They could get more anytime, but rarely did. Most people, if asked, would say they didn't know where or how to get more energy.

Maddy had perfected another technique for use on her terminal patients. She moved from one end of the body to the other, seeing thin slices of the body similar to a CT scan, which allowed Maddy to flick through one area to another.

Starting at the toes, Maddy studied Felicia, making note of any issues on the way through the layers of the child's body. Energy buzzed or slugged its way through Felicia's circulatory system, shining with light, and in some areas, with a dark, purplish slow energy.

Working steadily, she familiarized herself with the ebb and flow of Felicia's life force, her health, her condition and her illness. The back of the child's neck and the lower portion of her head had a dead black pulsating look to it. This was the problem. She'd known that much already though. The question was, what fed this tumor's insatiable growth? Usually a growth of this type came when blockages prevented the normal spread of energy, causing new pathways to form around it.

Distancing herself slightly, Maddy studied the meridian lines tracing movement of energy the length of the child's body. Several blockages existed: one below her right knee, one on the left side of her chest. Slicing the layers lengthwise, Maddy scanned the holograph, studying the images from top to bottom. One definite problem centered in the large intestine, with a complete energy blockage in the forefront of her spine. Interesting.

Maddy didn't know what to do with this information yet, but she now had an idea of the severity of Felicia's condition. Complete blockages caused energy pathways to rework, regrow and reform. In Felicia's case, they spread out in tiny webs searching for other pathways to take care of the problem. Felicia's body was a spider web of tiny networks.

All illnesses and diseases affected the body's nervous systems and developed tension. As she had used one method to read the energy, Maddy used a companion method to soothe the ruffled energy of Felicia's aura, easing the tension rippling through the child's body into a smoothly flowing stream. Then Maddy went to work on one meridian, the one running up the front of Felicia's leg and chest where a minor blockage was forming.

The blockage disappeared under Maddy's ministration, surprising her with the speed of its disappearance. She knew better than to do too much at one time. Pulling back, she smiled as the clean meridian energy glowed brighter.

Maddy's energy levels dropped. She checked the hallway clock. Two hours already. No wonder, her reserves were long gone, her body dehydrated. Time to pull back.

The progress she'd made wasn't much, yet it was a start.

DREW WALKED INTO the pathology rooms at The Haven. Dr. Miko's odd tone of voice had made him drop everything to race over.

"Dr. Miko?" He scanned the gleaming stainless steel room. The joys of a private hospital – they got the best of everything. At the far end of the room, an assistant washed down an autopsy table, the hose forcing the bloody water down the gleaming drain.

"Over here." The strident voice came from behind him, to the left. He spun around. The tiny dynamo in green scrubs strode toward him, her close-cut peppered hair snug against her skull. A frown marred her face. "You didn't gown up," she snapped and led the way through to the offices. "I don't like people in my rooms."

Chastised, and with good reason, Drew remembered her rules too late. "Sorry, I couldn't find you and thought—"

"And thought I might be working and so you'd take a quick glance around. Like that changes anything." She pushed her thick-rimmed, black glasses up her nose and narrowed her gaze at him. "Do I know you?"

Drew hastily shoved his hand forward. "Detective Drew McNeil."

"McNeil? John McNeil's nephew?" She ignored his hand.

Drew tucked his hand back into his pocket. "Yes, that's correct."

"Right. He's a tough man. It must have been hard growing up with him. You don't have to be like him, you know."

Surprised at the personal comment, Drew stalled with a response, finally saying, "He's a good man."

"I didn't say he wasn't. What are you doing here?"

"You called me about a possible connection to an old case?"

Her face instantly sobered. "Right, no way to forget that nightmare." She took a deep breath before reciting, "I was new in the profession back then. That case is one I've never forgotten. Six children, all with no apparent cause of death. A small bruise was found at the base of their spines. No other marks, no DNA, no sign of violence – no proof of anything one way or another."

"What? You know the case?" Excitement jolted his gut. Did she have something helpful to offer? He'd love to make headway on this case. "It's one of our most mysterious cold cases."

Finely etched pain lined her face, and she nodded. "Those poor children. It was a terrible time back then – for all of us. I'd only been out of school a couple years and had seen nothing like it. I'm not sure if what I called you about today helps or hinders, or if it is even related to that investigation." Dr. Miko stared down at the floor, her brow creased in concentration.

When she raised her eyes she stared directly at him. "One of the recently deceased residents from Dr. Maddy's floor has a weird bruise at the base of his spine similar to those of the children who died years ago." Her gaze went to the double doors leading to the drawers holding the deceased. "I don't have any measurements to compare," she muttered in a soft voice to herself.

"Similar? How?"

"It's small, about the size of a quarter at the base of the spine. The bruising is different in appearance. I'm working from memory here. But from my recollection, it's not as tight or as neat a circle, and it's darker, I think. Maybe you can find the pictures so we can compare."

She showed him the photos she'd taken of Jansen Svaar's body, pointing to the second one. "See here. The edges are not clearly defined. The surface was not raised either. There was no rippling in the skin, as if a weapon had been forced against the skin. In fact, the bruising is light colored and soft, not harsh or deep. It doesn't penetrate the muscle layer below."

"Anything else?" Hope and fear kept his voice tight, controlled.

"Just that although he was sick, he was in remission. He just up and died. That's very common for his age and health group. This man *was* seventy-eight years old."

Drew sat back as she fired the facts at him. He sifted through what she'd said and what she hadn't. "I'm presuming you never found what caused the bruise?"

"No, I'm sorry. This may not be related at all since there's nothing else that's similar about them. If I remember correctly, those children were in their prime and healthy – very healthy." She leaned back, studying his face. "But that bruise...each had one...I just don't know."

Drew nodded, adding, "They all had families and were well-loved, all were found alone and there was no visible trauma to their bodies."

She stood up, giving her head a shake. "Until Dr. Maddy called, I hadn't thought about those kids for years. Then I found the one odd mark and she asked me to check for the second one – a matching, fainter bruise at the top of his head. It's hard to see because of the patient's full head of hair. However, it's there, nonetheless."

Drew didn't remember seeing anything about two bruises on these kids in the report. "And these kids, did they have the same bruising at the top of the head?" He held his breath. Waited for the answer.

"I don't know," she admitted softly. "If they did, I didn't see them. The bruise on this patient's spine is darker and more pronounced. The one on his head is softer and much harder to see. I wouldn't have noticed if Dr. Maddy hadn't asked me to search for it. The bruises on the kids' spines were already pale. If they had lighter, matching ones on the crowns of their heads, they would have been difficult, if not impossible to see."

"So it's possible that they did. Why did Dr. Maddy ask you about the second bruise?"

"I don't know." Dr. Miko's brow knitted in concentration. "She wasn't happy with my answer, either." She glanced at her phone. "Maybe she should come down so we can ask her."

MADDY STRODE DOWN the hallway toward Dr. Lenning. He lay huddled under his blankets. Maddy approached warily. He'd had two bad nights in a row. If he'd managed to go to sleep, she didn't want to wake him. The reno workers had been in and out but only to finish the little things. The area wasn't done, per se, however, it was coming along nicely.

Still, Dr. Lenning's area seemed lonely, lost in the bigger room without more patients to fill it with bustle and cheer. He was only fifteen-odd feet from the next patient, yet because of the open bareness, it appeared to be much farther.

As she approached his bed, he snuffled slightly. Maddy paused and shifted position to see if his eyes were open. No. He slept.

She frowned. He looked like hell. His color matched the white sheet he lay on; worse was the flaccidity of his face, as if he'd aged a decade overnight. Bad nights often made people appear older. Only in this case, he looked ancient. She'd have to check his file to see if Dr. Cunningham had changed his medications, but she didn't think he had. She decided to come back and visit with him later, when he was awake. See what, if anything, had changed in his life.

As much as she hadn't wanted it, he was here, and he needed care. It was her job to make him as comfortable as possible.

Checking her watch, she walked toward her next patient. Her cell phone went off. Dr. Miko.

Answering it, Maddy changed direction back to the privacy of her office.

"Hi, what's up?"

"Can you pop down for a moment?" Dr. Miko's voice, while always serious, had a stern overtone.

Maddy frowned. "I'll be there in a few minutes." Maddy walked back to the nurses' station, told them where she was heading then walked over to the stairwell. That's exactly what she needed – a run.

The stairwell was empty as usual. Maddy stood at the top and looked down, considering. Making a quick decision, Maddy slipped off her blue heels. As her bare feet hit the cement, chills of anticipation raced up her legs.

Grinning, and her heels hanging on two fingers, Maddy broke into a flat-out sprint and raced down the stairwell. The second floor landing, the first floor landing, all the way to the first of the lower levels. Hitting the brakes at the bottom, Maddy paused to gather her breath.

Exhilaration pulsed in her blood. Her shoulder-length bob swayed with her heaving breaths. It took another long moment of deep breathing before she slipped her heels back on.

The double doors opened easily as she walked toward Dr. Miko's office – a hoarder's paradise. Usually there was one chair available. Maddy turned toward it, then stopped. Her eyebrows rose in surprise and a swarm of butterflies took flight in her stomach. The detective she'd met in the stairwell several days ago stood in front of her. Again.

What was he doing here?

He smiled. "Hello, Dr. Maddy. How nice to see you again."

"Detective." Damn, that man had something. Her hormones started to do a hula dance. What was with that? Maddy shook her head to clear her mind. "What's going on?"

Roberta waved toward a chair. "Take a seat."

Maddy chuckled. "I'd love to. Where?"

Dr. Miko frowned, her gaze going from one piece of furniture to another. "Just move those." She pointed to one chair stacked high with books.

"Take mine." Drew stepped forward to clear off the spare chair.

Maddy smiled her thanks and sat down in his place as the detective emptied and pulled over his seat. "What's up?"

"I see you've already met Detective Drew McNeil."

Drew? So that was his name. Maddy sank back. She smiled inside. It suited him. "Yes, briefly."

Roberta reached for a folder and opened it. "I called him regarding a possible connection between Jansen's case and several old cases."

"What? Jansen? A criminal case?" Maddy leaned forward, her gaze going between the two. What on earth was Roberta talking about? "What did you find out?"

Dr. Miko frowned as she stared down at the papers in her hand. "I was working with the medical examiner at the time of the earlier cases." She glanced up at Maddy. "They're cases that have haunted me over the years. Six dead children who showed no apparent cause of death, no signs of violence and no explanations could be found for their deaths. They just, well…died. At the time, the politicians were saying a crime hadn't been committed because there was no evidence to support foul play." She grimaced. "Then again, nothing pointed to why the children died, either."

That was depressing, yet what did it have to do with her? Maddy waited for Roberta to continue. "And…?"

"The cases back then had one thing linking them together." Drew's gaze hardened as he looked from one woman to the other. "Each child had one small bruise at the base of their spines. Similar to the one found on Jansen."

Maddy's eyes opened wide. She stared at Drew in surprise before switching her gaze back to Dr. Miko. "That's…odd. What caused them?"

"No idea."

Fear rose in Maddy's chest. "I don't understand. Are you saying Jansen was murdered?"

"No, not at all. All I'm saying is that there are similarities with this body and with those from thirty-odd years ago. I'd love to understand what caused the bruising." Roberta folded her hands. "It may be nothing. However, if it turns out to be something, I wanted to make sure you were both in the know."

"What a horrible thought." Maddy's mind couldn't grasp the connection. She crossed her arms, holding them tight to her chest. Maybe her mind didn't *want* to see a connection. "Six kids? Boys or girls?"

Drew stepped in. "Both. No understandable reason for any of their deaths. It was a sad time – for everyone. No one knew how to handle it. Most people were divided as to whether a crime had even been committed. Like all cold cases, it's haunted many people."

"Can anything be found after all this time?"

Roberta looked at Drew, who tapped his fingers on the wooden arm of his chair. "Let's hope so."

Maddy stood, her knees a little shaky at the thought of a murderer operating at The Haven. The whole concept had a surreal overtone to it. "Well, thanks for letting me know." She smiled at Drew. "If there's anything I can do to help, call me."

He faced her. "I will need some information from you. Such as a list of all the visitors Jansen Svaar had while he was at The Haven."

"There's no formal list of visitors, but I'm sure we can come up with something for you. Give me your card, and I can email the names to you."

As Drew handed over his card Maddy couldn't help but notice the compelling energy he exuded so naturally. It was hard not to appreciate self-confidence and strength.

Maddy narrowly avoided knocking over a stack of books, and wound her way carefully out of the office. "Thanks, Dr. Miko. If you learn anything else, please let me know."

Drew held the door for her but stood in her way. "Dr. Miko forgot to ask something. Why did you ask her to check Jansen's crown for a matching bruise?"

Surprise lit her features. "Oh. That's because they're the two main energy entrances and exits from the body. The crown and the base of the spine."

He blinked and stepped back.

With a small smile, she walked to the stairwell, her mind full of implications from these new developments. As much as she'd like to discuss them further with Drew, she wasn't sure how much she should tell him. Her world was a touch unbelievable to those not involved in energy work. Striding down the hall quickly, she couldn't help a quick glance behind her.

He stood in the middle of the hallway, his hands fisted on his hips, staring at her. Maddy chuckled, gave him a small wave and entered the elevator, making good her escape. Her mind was more than a little overwhelmed, her emotions already somber. Already scared.

A murderer? At The Haven?

SATURDAY

MADDY STROLLED DOWN the street. Her mind consumed with the issues going on at work. She'd slept in on her day off, had lost herself in hours of research and then spent hours checking on her patients, even though it was her day off. It had been late by the time she'd gotten away.

Now, walking home, the evening sky was a cool gray and dry, not that there was any guarantee it would stay that way. Living in the greater Portland area, windy, wet and gray were the norm. One needed to appreciate nights like this.

Her favorite Italian restaurant was a couple of blocks past her apartment. She'd be a few minutes early, but would enjoy waiting by the fire at the restaurant with a glass of wine in hand. Family-owned and operated, Lugardo's offered good wholesome food for a decent price. Not that she cared about the price. Maddy had money. She worked hard, was paid well and spent little. Since she worked all the time, there was little opportunity to spend.

Her Visa bill popped into her mind. Right, nothing to spend it on except her lingerie. Bustiers, panties, thongs, garter belts, thigh-high stockings – it didn't matter, she loved them all. She smirked, her hand going instinctively to her waist where the purple thong with tiny white and gold flowers decorating the straps lay hidden beneath her clothing. The matching bustier was a treat. Maddy loved the sensuous feeling of wearing it – so delicate, feminine – and so hidden.

Reaching the front door of the tiny cafe, she pushed it open and entered another world. Momma Rose greeted her effusively and led her to an intimate table for two, covered with a red-checkered tablecloth, beside the fire.

"Oh my dear, you must be freezing. Come, sit. We will feed you, make you feel much better." As soon as Maddy sat down, Momma Rose took off. She returned within minutes with her tall portly husband. "Bill, Dr. Maddy is here. She's chilled."

Maddy chuckled at the eye-rolling look he gave her. "Good evening, Bill. As you can see, I'm fine. And hungry. Lunch was a long time ago." And it couldn't even be called lunch. She'd scarfed a yogurt cup along with her coffee around two o'clock as she'd waded through a stack of paperwork, a ritual that was becoming all too common in recent days.

Tonight was different. Stefan was joining her. Stefan, her mentor, best friend, fellow energy worker. As well, he was an incredibly talented psychic, with a physical beauty that was just plain unfair – he was a man after all.

"Ohhh no." Momma Rose, who carried a nice layer of padding around her full figure, sounded horrified. "That's not good. You need food. Good food."

Bill winked at her. "Maybe you should start with a glass of good wine. I've got a nice Merlot you should try."

Before she knew it, Maddy had a full glass of wine in her hand and a carafe sitting beside her. The wine had an earthy aroma and a hint of…was that…blackberry? Whatever it was, it made her taste buds sing. Maddy relaxed back into the deep cushioned chair and let the warmth of the fire roll over her.

The door opened. A murmur rose in the small room before dying off into a stunned silence. Maddy grinned. She didn't need to turn around to know that Stefan had arrived. Stunningly gorgeous, his presence caused a ruckus wherever he went. Maddy had known people's jaws to literally drop when he entered a room. And he's the nicest guy you'd ever meet.

Thank you.

So he'd been listening for her.

The voice floated through her head, a whisper of warmth and loving energy that made her heart lighten and her smile brighten.

She stared at the fire, enjoying the gold and orange flames doing their wild dance.

Stefan's shadow fell on the table.

"Sit, my dear. Your amazing beauty dwarfs the fire."

He snickered. "Only you talk to me that way." Stefan pulled out the other chair and sat. Reaching across the table, he picked up the carafe of wine, and inhaled the bouquet. "Good choice."

Maddy smiled at the blond Adonis as she took a sip. "Bill's choice."

"Good on Bill."

Momma Rose, continuing to chatter, rushed over to give Stefan a big hug. Finally, Stefan patted her shoulder and had a chance to answer. "I'm fine, Momma Rose. Life's good. Yes, I've been busy. And yes, I'm hungry."

Laughing, Momma Rose took off and returned with a second wine glass. She emptied the carafe into his glass before taking it away with her. She returned within minutes, a full carafe in one hand and a breadbasket piled high with hot buttered garlic bread.

Maddy reached for the steaming piece at the top, biting into it with a moan. "Lord, I'm hungry. It's been a hell of a day."

"It must have been. It takes a lot for you to call out for help."

The reminder that she'd called him and why, slowed her enjoyment of her treat. "I know. Didn't want to put you out. I did suggest that I drive up to your place."

"Not an issue. I've been in the city all day. I'm more than ready for a chance to sit and visit with an old friend." Stefan reached out, his long artist fingers hovering over the basket before making a selection. "Did you order?"

"No. Momma Rosa will bring us whatever she feels we need. Chances are my portion will be enough to feed three."

He grinned. "That's not a bad idea. You're dropping weight again, Maddy. Not good."

Maddy frowned at him. "Surely not. At least not enough to be noticeable."

"Only to someone who knows you well." Stefan studied her face intently. Maddy sipped her wine. She ignored him but couldn't stop the heat from rising up her face. Thankfully, Momma Rose arrived with two steaming plates. As she placed them down in front of them, Maddy giggled. Her plateful could feed a small army.

"Tut, tut." Momma Rose shook a finger at a grinning Stefan. "You make sure Dr. Maddy eats. She's too skinny. She needs a good man to take care of her."

Maddy's eyes widened in shocked amusement.

Stefan's grin deepened.

"You're right. She does need a good man."

Momma Rose beamed at him. "Yes, yes. She works too hard looking after everyone else. No one looks after her."

"We're working on it, Momma Rose. Not to worry. She'll be partnered soon."

Maddy, in the process of taking a sip of wine, choked, spitting wine everywhere as a beaming Mama Rose disappeared into the kitchen. Reaching for a napkin, Maddy gasped for breath then coughed until her eyes watered and her air passages cleared.

Reaching over, Stefan patted her on the back. "Are you okay?"

She glared, at him and gasped, "I was until you opened your mouth."

Stefan sat down, a gentle smirk turned her way. "Are you telling me that with all your energy work and healing ability, you have no idea that your single state is changing?"

Maddy put her napkin down on the table. Her astonishment turned to alarm. "Like you're one to talk. Why don't you have someone special in your life?" She glared at him. "Of course, I don't have any idea. There is one basic element missing here – it's called a man. The man."

A knowing grin swept across his face. "He's a relatively new addition to your life. However, he's there now. You know it, you feel it, and you're denying it." The smile dropped off. "And I do know what is happening in terms of my own private life, but there won't be any movement in that area for several months, or longer. Your time is now."

Maddy stared at one of the most powerful psychics in the modern world and didn't know what to say. Questions crowded her mind, but the biggest one demanded an answer. "Who?" she whispered, urgently, her gaze locked on his face. She needed to know. "Who?"

"I don't know."

Her spine straightened. "What? You can't tantalize me with tidbits. I need to know who." Outrage and disbelief swept through her, only to be replaced by the image of a tall linebacker-of-a-detective and that instinctive recognition she'd noticed when she'd first met him.

Ageless black eyes opened in front of her as Stefan slipped from reality to the seer he was. "He will save your life – at a price. Your healing abilities will be needed, at a level you rarely go."

The fire flared suddenly, then dimmed.

Shivers rippled down her spine. "What?" she whispered urgently. "When?"

"Soon. Too soon. Something in your world has gone wrong. Dangerously wrong." Stefan's voice echoed in an eerie whisper.

"Oh, God." Maddy watched, fascinated. She'd seen him do it time and time again: Stefan returned to himself, almost unaware of the shifting energies as he morphed through realities. Back to normal. With one eye cocked in her direction, Stefan lifted a fork piled high with spaghetti and a luscious meat sauce. "Problems?"

"No." Maddy smiled. "You shifted for a moment."

His fork stopped in midair. "I what?" His gaze turned inward. "Oh, so I did."

"A little unnerving message, too. Thanks for scaring the bejesus out of me." Maddy took a bite from her plate.

"Some of them are like that."

"Great," she murmured. "That adds to the reason I asked to meet with you."

Stefan ate heartily for a few moments before sitting back and lifting his glass of wine. He took a sip, studying her over the rim of his glass. "Speaking of which, what did you want to discuss?"

Casting a glance around the room to make sure no one else could hear, she leaned closer and said, "Something peculiar is going on." Quickly, she filled him in on the odd events on her floor, starting with the weird purple-black energy she'd found surrounding Eric and Jansen and then she told him about their subsequent deaths, the changes in the energy on the floor, and the new patients. "We both know black energy can be many things, including a toxic environment that over time can cause disease."

"And some people will hook their energy into another person to keep them connected. Look at husbands who are jealous of their wives or mothers that won't let their sons grow up. That can cause the toxic environment." Stefan took another bite of his dinner. "And people who hate each other or try to control others do the same thing."

"But usually unconsciously." It was important to recognize that people didn't know what they were doing to others – in most cases. But when people internalized these negative emotions, it squandered their energy and disease could be the result. She leaned back, her fingers gently rubbing her temples.

"Maintaining balance and conducting healing in this environment was always a challenge, but now…well, it's next to impossible."

Stefan's gaze narrowed on her face. "This energy, did it have any emotion attached to it?"

Maddy frowned and cast her mind back. "It happened so fast. I don't know. If I had to put a name to it, I'd have to say the energy had a feeling of 'need,' single-mindedness, almost a touch of desperation to it."

A grimace whispered across Stefan's face. "I was afraid you were going to say that."

"Why?" Maddy leaned forward. "What is it? I don't get it." Her barely touched plate of spaghetti sat forgotten. "What was it doing there?"

"I can't say for sure. There have been odd instances in history where people had the capability to take, for themselves, the life force of someone with diminished capacity."

A shocked gasp slid from Maddy's lips. "What?" Fearing someone might overhear, she twisted around to make sure no one was listening, then bent forward, whispering, "Do you know what you're saying? The implications?"

"Oh yes, I know exactly what I'm saying." He took another bite of his meal. He motioned for her to eat.

She stared blankly down at her full plate. "It really is possible to steal someone's energy?"

"Not just their energy, Maddy. Their life force."

"Good Lord. That means they actually, willfully kill another person?"

"Right. Theoretically, it's murder."

Maddy struggled to reconcile that the dark purple energy was something that belonged to a person and even worse, that that person murdered Jansen for his life force. "I've heard stories, of course, I hadn't put any credence to them."

"Nothing is impossible at this point. Have I personally seen a case like this? No. Given that you actually witnessed this in a place where you create a special healing energy, it makes me wonder if that healing energy is the attraction. Healing energy has a draw all its own. The Haven is full of dying and desperate people. It's not too far off to suppose that another patient might be doing this, one not lucky enough to be a recipient of your special skills. If they were receiving your healing energy, there'd be no need for them to steal it from someone else."

"No." Maddy shuddered. "Oh, no."

Stefan stared soberly at her. "It's a possibility."

Maddy shuddered violently and reached for her wine glass. Took a healthy drink. "That's terrible. Everyone there is dying."

"Exactly."

Maddy stared at him, confusion clouding her mind. "What? What do you mean?"

"Who would care? Death's expected there, isn't it? People die all the time. After all, that's why they go there. Think about it. Who would notice if a dying patient…died?"

Maddy's stomach roiled. The spaghetti searched for a quick exit. She pushed her chair back and leaned closer to the fire, gasping for calm and balance. Memories crowded her, starting with the crash team that had worked on Eric as she watched, followed by the creepy old woman from the hallway. She'd been so busy, so rushed off her feet, she hadn't had time to follow up on who she was.

Yet, hadn't she had an inkling? She stared at Stefan's calm, unaffected face.

"That's horrible." And unacceptable. Maddy worked with death and dying every day, but she'd never heard of anything so sick.

"Dying people don't have a strong life force, making them easy victims. They can't fight off predators. Add all that healing energy surrounding your patients…well…that's got to be attractive to someone who's desperately trying to heal." He stroked the back of her hand. "What better location for this type of murder to happen than a place full of people who won't be missed and where there are a number of people who are desperate to live – and will do so by any means possible?"

Silence surrounded them. Maddy straightened, staring into the flames, her mind racing in circles, trying to make sense of his words. "How close would this person have to be in order to accomplish such a feat?"

Stefan's brows furrowed. "If we're right and this is another sick person doing this, I don't think he could be very far away – like in another country or city – although if he's powerful and in good health that's possible. Ripples happen in energy levels but too much will actually cause a tear. I believe that's what's happening here. You remember those lessons, right? At a guess, I'd have to say the person either lives or works at The Haven…or is a regular visitor. Could even be someone who goes there on a regular basis for business purposes, like a delivery person." He paused. "Although if the person was connected to the victim in some way, like a family member or a lover, they could do this from further away."

"So." Maddy gulped, took a deep breath and blurted out, "Whoever this person is, he's using The Haven as a feeding ground?"

Stefan grimaced. "As much as I hate the way you put that, I'd have to say yes."

STEFAN WAITED UNTIL Maddy's lithe frame disappeared safely indoors before pulling away from the curb. She was a beautiful person inside and out. He felt honored to have her in his life. And he was more worried about her and the situation at The Haven than he'd dared let her see.

Several other powerful psychics and energy workers had already contacted him, wondering what had disturbed the energy field. He hadn't had much to give in the way of answers. It occurred to him, that without trying, he had collected a small group of powerful, aware individuals with unbelievable abilities of their own.

He'd helped several special women, like Sam and Kali, to develop their skills further. Helped them to stop hiding their lights and come out in a position of strength. Both had been blessed or cursed – depending on the viewpoint – with special talents. They'd each blossomed with a little training. He could see wonderful things in their futures. But they, along with several other people, still turned to him for answers.

Ripples in the energy field were normal – tears were not. He'd felt similar problems before, on a smaller scale. These tear-indicators had popped up over the last year at irregular intervals. Then about three months ago, something had changed, worsened. They became different, were off somehow. He wondered if something new, someone new was experimenting. He frowned, changing lanes to access the highway ramp. It almost seemed like the experimental stage was over and that whoever was doing this had put their newfound skills into practice.

Mastery would follow.

He had to find this person and stop them before more innocent people died.

People like Maddy.

He smiled fondly. She was a sweetheart. A giver, not a taker. A lover, even a fighter, but never a betrayer. Maddy's energy was pure and glorious. It had to be for the work she did. Anyone with less couldn't accomplish the good she did – their inner light wouldn't be strong enough.

He had always loved her – as a sister, as a soul-bound friend, as a partner on this journey through both sides of reality. People like Maddy made his life less lonely and more viable. He drew on her strength in times of his own need, as she did on his. She didn't recognize it yet, but the time of her awakening to yet another level of awareness was approaching.

It had to do with the tears in the energy levels. He didn't use the term evil often, not liking the misconceptions that arose immediately in people's minds. This was the first time in a long time that he felt driven to consider what that term meant for him – and for others.

He shifted lanes as he eased into mainstream traffic. The evening light had disappeared behind dark storm clouds. Stefan stared at the unfolding darkness, finding a matching soberness inside. Something nasty was brewing. The energies were stirring and gathering in a most unpleasant way.

The thought had no sooner formed in his mind when his world went black. His fingers convulsed on the steering wheel. The blackness ripped apart and his inner gaze fell on a horrific scene of bedridden people, twisting in agony, their silver cords stretched taut.

As Stefan watched, one silver cord snapped. The man's voice cried out, "Nooooo!" His panicked gaze locked onto Stefan for the briefest instant before the ghostlike entity winked out of existence.

Stefan's awareness slammed back into the vehicle, now crawling along in the wrong lane with traffic snarled around him. Panicked, he quickly pulled off onto the shoulder amid honking horns.

Trembling, Stefan hugged his arms around his chest and bowed his head. *Christ.* He hated receiving visions when he wasn't at home. A major reason he lived in hermit's isolation. Today, he had been forced to travel and had already experienced two of these.

Focused on his breathing, it still took several long moments before he could raise his head and let the tension drain calmly from his system.

He'd seen this type of energy before, when he was a kid. Too young to understand and too unimportant to make anyone else take notice.

Now they'd all get a second chance.

Hell was stopping by for another visit and it appeared its target was The Haven – this time.

SISSY DID FEEL so much better again today. Of course, the hot bubble bath with her favorite sea foam scent had helped. She did so love to indulge herself. Her healing improved every day. She laughed at the other old women in her room. They all whispered behind her back. She didn't care. She *was* getting better. She felt the improvement.

The other sick women weren't getting better. Look at them. They died a little more each day. Silly of them. They should be asking her how she was doing so much better than they were. Maybe they'd get healthier themselves if they practiced some of her tricks. She was here at The Haven, a long-term care facility. No one expected her to be discharged from the place.

So what if she'd been here for almost a year? She planned to walk out of here soon – healthy, happy and capable of dealing with the world outside.

Stupid doctors. What did they know?

MADDY, HER HAIR in a fluffy towel, slipped on a warm robe and stepped into her bedroom. The hot bath had been a relief after the chill she'd experienced since talking with Stefan.

Pulling a silk nightie from her closet, she tossed it on the bed then went to work drying her hair. She sneezed. Hopefully, she wasn't coming down with something. She really couldn't afford that right now.

She needed advice and who better than Janice Shiner? A powerful energy worker, Janice was one of the pioneers of the medical intuitive field. Not a medical doctor herself, she'd come into her abilities through the impending death of her only son. Janice's determination to save him had flung her into the world of colors, vibrations and transparencies. She'd managed to see inside her son's body to what the doctors had missed. Getting his doctor to listen to her had been a different story. Knowing the child was dying anyway, he'd changed the medication to treat the rapidly encroaching staph infection they'd missed the first time around.

Her son had lived through the experience, and both the doctor and Janice had been forever changed. She'd moved on to work with several other doctors, studying to understand and develop some kind of standardization of her work and to teach others. Out of those students, only a dozen were strong, practicing medical intuitives. Maddy was one of them. She'd been able, not only to see the human body in a unique way, but also manipulate the energy in such a way as to facilitate healing…occasionally with miraculous results.

She picked up the phone and made the call. "Janice, do you have a moment? I've got a possible situation developing and need your help."

"Tell me." Janice never wasted words or sugarcoated anything. Quickly, Maddy explained, adding in some of Stefan's concerns.

"I don't know about the tear stuff, I'm not much into that psychic business as you well know, and I don't buy into any evil stuff when I do energy work. As for this other business…" Janice's voice died off. "I've never seen it myself, although I remember Jimmy, one of my earlier students, telling me years ago, many years ago, about something similar."

"How long ago did this happen?"

"Oh, who knows? Twenty, maybe thirty years ago. It might even have been longer."

"What did he see?" Maddy walked over to her bed and sat down. With her spare hand, she continued to towel dry her hair.

"Something about a deep purple energy and blackness."

Maddy bolted to her feet. "That sounds like what I saw." She paced the small room. "Maybe he saw the same thing."

"Maybe, but who's to say? He didn't say much more. I think it kind of freaked him out, to tell you the truth. I know he wouldn't speak of it again."

"It freaked the hell out of me too." Maddy walked over to the big window, staring out at the blackness beyond her window. "I was hoping you'd say it wasn't anything to worry about or give me a solution to make it disappear. You know, that sort of thing."

Janice's voice took on its usual teacher tone. "Everything is energy. If what you are seeing is a person's energy, then it should be easy to see inside and find out exactly what they are doing. Then you might be able to find a way to stop it."

"And if I can see through it, I should be able to see the source of it." Maddy nodded. That made sense and matched her healing process.

"Right. Now if you don't have any other questions, I'll head to bed." Janice rang off, leaving Maddy feeling calmer and surer of herself. If something was afoot, she did have the skills to get to the bottom of it. That was the trick. She had to be there when it happened. Only she wasn't at The Haven during the night.

SUNDAY

On Sunday, Maddy woke late with more questions than answers.

She needed a better way to see what was happening on her floor. The floor had been deliberately set up with minimal video cameras. She needed to see the feeds from the ones that existed, and better yet, set up a few more. There were too many unsettling issues pulling her away from her work. She needed to focus on healing, on her patients, not all this other stuff. Surely that was for the police to sort out.

Now she was convinced that someone was killing her patients. All of this begged the question, could someone really kill another person by damaging, draining, and absorbing the person's energy, their life force, in some way? According to stories she'd heard, the answer was yes. Yet, why would they do this? What was their need? There was enough energy for every person, for every need. There was no shortage. Ever. The reason behind this was what she didn't understand. And who'd be targeted next.

And as much as she'd like to take the day off, she wanted to keep an eye on her floor. She didn't dare stop her vigilance with this mess going on.

Time to go to work and check on those video feeds.

Drew walked through the main floor of The Haven, heading for the stairs. As he pushed open the fire door to the stairs, he half-hoped he'd see the running wild woman again. Walking up slowly, he listened for any sound that might signal a door opening. No such luck. Then again, it was Sunday, and who knew if Dr. Maddy was on duty or not.

Taking the stairs two at a time, he arrived at his aunt's floor and strode over to speak to her. Doris had been at The Haven for over a year. In the beginning, she'd talked nonstop about coming home. Since her condition had started to deteriorate, she'd switched to speaking more about transferring to Dr. Maddy's floor. According to his uncle, the doctor had said her depression and declining mental state were concerns as well. Medication had helped improve her spirits.

He and John were her entire family, though Drew vaguely remembered talk about her having had a child long ago. He didn't know the whole story as his aunt had only come into his life to help out after his mother died from breast cancer when he was entering high school.

Drew had coped by going a little wild. His dad chased the bottle, or rather, a lot of bottles until his death a good ten years ago.

Walking into her room, Drew waved to a couple of his aunt's friends. He reached her bed and frowned. The bed was empty.

"She's gone to have her bath, she has."

Drew spun around to look at the patient across the floor. Her illness had reduced her frame almost to a rack of bones, but under a mop of pepper-gray hair her smile shone bright and true.

"Has she? Could you please tell her when she gets back that I'm just upstairs? I'll stop in and see her on my way out." Just about to turn away, he stopped and asked, "What kind of a day is she having?"

The heavily wrinkled neighbor grinned. "Not too good today. She was better yesterday."

Drew nodded. Everything was normal then.

Now to see if Dr. Maddy was in. In spite of his calm demeanor, his pulse raced. She fascinated him. He'd heard the rumors. Who hadn't? She'd had some phenomenal results and Drew knew his uncle had twisted someone's arm hard, to get in here. It would be interesting to see how he fared under Dr. Maddy's wing.

At the top floor, he pushed open the double doors and walked through onto Dr. Maddy's floor. Immediately the sensation of peace and love enveloped him. He stood still for a long moment. The tension in his shoulders eased as a long rippling sigh worked its way to freedom.

No wonder his aunt and uncle wanted in. He strode the first few feet into the main hallway, searching for the elusive doctor. The décor had an upbeat yet peaceful vibe to it.

Unlike the rest of The Haven, this floor plan laid out a series of sitting rooms and bedrooms, private yet social, open yet partially closed. Everything was designed for the comfort of a sleeping, healing patient versus the sterile, plastic look of the other floors of the home. Walking a few feet, he casually glanced in at the first bed on the left. He'd been right. There was real bedding and sheets on it. Not the standard issue hospital shit.

Impressed in spite of himself, he searched for the nurses' station.

"Excuse me. Is Dr. Maddy here?"

"I think she's with a patient, right now." The portly nurse wearing the nametag of Gerona, answered him. Her smile actually looked real.

He pulled out his badge to show her. "I do need to speak with her. Could you let her know I'm here, please?"

The smile beamed. "No problem. Take a seat in the waiting room."

"Thanks." He turned around. Waiting room?

"Down the hall and turn left."

He nodded his thanks, then followed the instructions and found himself at the entrance to a bright sunny sitting room that was more inviting than any room in his own house. He wandered over to the double French doors that opened out onto a large open balcony. It overlooked bright, cheerful gardens sprawled out behind The Haven. The seating area was more than generous and although there were a dozen or so straight-backed chairs, the space between the round tables was spacious enough for wheelchairs to maneuver.

He admired the view of the city park off in the distance. This was a nice place. He'd have to remember to congratulate his uncle for whatever devious moves he'd made to get in here. He just hoped those moves were legal.

"Hello, Detective. I understand you're waiting for me."

Drew spun around at the sound of her voice. He couldn't help it, his gaze slid to her feet. Three inch black stilettos. *Be still my beating heart.*

"Detective?"

Snapping his head up, he felt the heat climb his face. "Sorry. I wasn't sure you'd be in. Have you got a few moments?"

Maddy nodded. "I'm not normally in on Sundays. However, with new patients moving in there's a lot to do. Shall we go into my office or would you like to sit out here?"

"Out here would be great."

"Sure." She led the way and pulled out a chair at the farthest table. Turning to face the view, she sat down and crossed her legs.

Damn those long smooth legs. Drew had to forcibly pull his gaze away to stare out over the garden.

"As nice as this is, Detective, I'm assuming this isn't a social visit."

"No." Drew shifted toward her and pulled his notebook out of his pocket. "Thanks for sending the list of people that had visited Jansen Svaar. If you can think of anyone else he saw on a regular basis, please let me know." He narrowed his gaze, frowning at her. "I'm really here because I don't understand the significance of the bruise on the top of his head. You asked Dr. Miko to check for it, you gave me a quick explanation that made no sense, then you took off. So I also need to know if you have any idea how those bruises occurred?"

She was already shaking her head. "No, I don't. They are superficial, so it's not as if they were caused by a blow or from lying on something. Normal energy work doesn't leave marks of any kind. I just don't know."

"Have you ever done any procedure on Jansen that could have resulted on this type of bruising?"

"Absolutely not. Any procedures are well documented and there had been no need for any kind of intervention because he was doing so well. That's the thing, he was healing."

"So his death surprised you?" Drew jotted down a few notes but so far nothing helped.

"Yes and no."

He looked up in surprise.

"You have to realize that everyone here is expected to die sooner than later. Jansen's progress was remarkable yet he had a ways to go for a full recovery."

There was no arguing that.

She surprised him with her next comment. "I understand from Gerard that your uncle will be joining us soon." Her smile brightened. "That will be nice. We have several more beds we're filling over the next few days."

"How about extra staff to help with the extra work?"

Her smile dimmed. "Not going to happen. Budgets, economy and all that." She shrugged those slim shoulders and looked directly into his eyes. "It doesn't really matter. This floor operates separately from the rest of The Haven, so our budgetary needs are separate as well."

"Just how unusual is this floor?" Drew leaned in, his gaze narrowing on her face. Maybe now he could get real answers. "I hear rumors and conjecture, no actual facts. What exactly goes on up here?"

Her face assumed the professional polish of one about to give a prepared speech. He waved her quiet. "No. I don't want the sales pitch. I want to know what *you* do here." He pointed a finger at her. "This floor is named after you. As if you are in charge of something special. I agree it is special. I can see that. I can feel that. I walk through the doors to this floor and it's like coming home. It's warm, peaceful…loving. How? What are you doing to make it so different?"

Maddy sat back and studied him.

Drew stared back.

"It might be a little difficult to explain," she said, cautiously.

"Try me." He watched her huge chocolate eyes deepen as the expressions played across her face. He watched her carefully, hoping she wouldn't lie to him.

"This is off the record and has nothing to do with the case."

Drew pursed his lips and nodded. He snapped his notebook closed and dropped his pen on top. "Fine. Let's hear it."

Maddy leaned forward slightly, glanced toward the door to make sure they were alone, then back at his face. "It's not a deep mystery. However, due to the sensitive nature of the project, we keep it low key to avoid any paranoid backlash."

Interesting choice of words.

"I'm listening."

"I'm a medical intuitive as well as a licensed medical doctor."

Drew's gaze narrowed. Medical intuitive. Did he even know what that was?

She carried on. "As energy is so important to a person's health, we devised a system to maximize a person's healing by utilizing the energy of the person, his surroundings and of those he interacts with to help him to heal. It's like a city system where everything is interdependent and is only as good as the lowest element. In this case, the lowest element is the sick person.

"As each of these people start to heal, then the energy level around them and us becomes invigorated or energized. That then cycles back around for the patients to use for more healing. Most of these patients have been here for at least six months – an average time factor to clean their energy meridians and to open up their ability to utilize what's available so they can progress through their body's various health conditions and heal."

Drew blinked. *Say what?*

"That's why we can't accept just everyone here. And why the next six months will be tough on all of us with so many new patients coming in. The best scenario would be one new patient a month and even that can slow the healing progression for everyone. Adding a new person is adding a lower element every time. The other patients have to adjust to the shift in energy." She sat back. "I have to adjust, too," she admitted.

She spoke as if pondering the chances of having The Haven administrators change their plan. Fat chance. Drew knew 'money' people. If they managed to squeeze an extra dollar out of something, they'd try for two. Not that it would help here. He didn't understand exactly what she'd said and the only thing that had registered was that the people here were healing. *Healing?* These people were dying – weren't they?

The question refused to stay quiet. "When did your last patient die?"

Her mouth drooped. "Until Jansen, it had been just over eight months."

"That long? And how many patients do you have?"

"Over sixty."

"Over sixty and only one death. Holy crap. These people are in seriously bad condition before they come to you, aren't they?"

She nodded. "Yes, they're all terminal. They all need to have a life expectancy of at least six months to join the floor or it damages the energy. Even worse, a death will have a big impact on the other patients, particularly a bad death. Death can be a positive experience for those that have been ill for a long while or it can be a negative experience. Jansen's death affected everyone in a very negative way. We're still working through that."

Drew shook his head. "What's to figure out? Of course, everyone is upset. Someone who appeared to be getting better – something they were all hoping to do – died. And unexpectedly at that."

"It could be that. Or it could be something else." Maddy stared down at the frosted glass table, her finger tracing some invisible pattern. "I don't know."

"That sounds odd coming from a doctor."

She raised her face to the sunlight, a lopsided smile on her face. "Really? Well, I don't know that all doctors are black and white. Besides, like I said, I'm a medical intuitive and a doctor."

"What does that mean? I'm not sure that I've even heard that term before."

She didn't answer immediately. "The term can have a different meaning depending on the level of skill the medical intuitive possesses."

"I don't want to hear about anyone else. How does the term pertain to you?"

"I see the human body in terms of energy. By looking at different angles and layers, sometimes I can see inside the body and check what health issues exist and the possible contributing causes. More than that, I see the energy that flows through the body and where it's blocked."

"Sometimes?" It all sounded bizarre to him. He wasn't sure he liked the idea of someone being able to see under his skin.

"Most of the time."

Drew didn't know what to say. He searched her candid gaze. She was telling him the truth, as she knew it. "To do something like this on a small scale is hard enough, but on a large scale, like the scale of your floor, well…that has to be close to impossible."

"I hope not." She smiled gently. "Otherwise, I've wasted the last few years of my life. And as I plan to expand to help people before they become terminally ill…"

"Has everyone shown an improvement after arriving on your floor?"

"Yes."

"Yes?" He knew he sounded like a parrot repeating himself. He couldn't help it. Her success was unbelievable.

She nodded. "Everyone has improved since they've arrived. Although some have died eventually, we extended their lives and gave them a better quality of life. In the next phase, we'll work toward catching those diagnosed, but not so far along. The results should be faster. I'd be working on it now, but…money, the medical system, people's belief systems, you know. People do get better with good care to begin with and we can help that along."

The implications blew his mind. "You do realize the significance here, don't you? If people on your floor are healing, they could potentially go home again…as in cheat death. Right?"

Maddy pulled back and frowned. "Of course, although that's an odd way to look at it. Several people have gone home, younger ones. With our older ones, we really only expect to extend their lives for a bit."

He shook his head. "You're saying that some of your patients arrived with only six months left to live and walked out of here healthy?"

"On their way to being healthy, yes. We haven't seen instantaneous healing, except with a couple of children. For all the others, we've seen definite turns for the better with continued improvement."

"How many?" He had to know. He wondered if his uncle knew. Shit, of course the old bastard did. That's why he'd fought so hard to get in. And how the hell had he done that anyway? He'd been given less than six months, not more. According to Maddy, that should have made him ineligible.

"Twenty-one are continuing to improve at home."

"Out of sixty?"

"Roughly. We didn't have quite so many beds before." A confused frown settled on her face as she studied his face. "Why is that so shocking?"

"That's what – more than thirty percent? That's nuts."

"I'm quite proud of it." She flushed. "I know we can do better and we will as time moves on and I can pull the energy into better circulation. The results would also be more impressive if I had more children on my floor. They always seem to do well."

"Always?" Did she have any idea what she was suggesting here? If she did, why wasn't she working at the children's hospital? Oh yeah, because she'd heal everyone and shut down the center, putting hundreds of people out of work. Drew shook his head at his own sarcasm. But still, was she blind to the implications?

"Always – at least so far." Pride beamed from her face and her voice.

And she should be proud. He couldn't get his mind wrapped around the potential. No wonder Gerard worked to get as many patients under her care as possible. The patient-to-doctor ratio sucked, yet considering the doctor involved, not one patient would care.

A horrible thought crossed his mind. It had to be from too many years in law enforcement.

"You do realize what a premium bed space goes for on your floor."

"Actually, I don't. Gerard handles that stuff."

Drew nodded. It went along with what he'd heard from others about Maddy. She was all about her patients. "I wonder how hard it is to get a bed on your floor."

Maddy frowned and shook her head gently, sending her dark hair flipping around her shoulders. "Not hard. After all, it's just an application form."

"How many people know about the new wing on your floor?"

"We've tried to keep it quiet. There's already a huge waiting list. More beds means helping more people, but Gerard doesn't want the news to get out or he'll be inundated with new applications."

"Right. So the real question is – would someone kill off a patient in order to free up a bed so they *could* get on your floor?"

He knew she didn't understand. Confusion clouded her beautiful eyes. Then they widened in horror. "Oh, no."

DORIS SHIFTED UNCOMFORTABLY in her hospital bed and tried to adjust her covers to suit. She couldn't remember the last time she'd felt good enough to sit out on one of the many decks and enjoy the sunshine. She stared at her neighbor furtively. She was consumed with the mystery of her. How was she managing to look better every day? Turning to face forward, Doris studied the other two women in her room. They seemed the same as always. A little older, more worn, more tired. Not her neighbor though – she positively glowed.

Sniffing in the schoolteacher way she'd learned years ago, she tried to not care. Still it was hard. She wanted the same healing for herself. She tried so hard to do everything right. She used hand lotion, she drank lots of water, and tried to follow a beauty regime she'd gotten from a magazine years ago, but nothing made a difference. Then, for no apparent reason, her neighbor perked up and appeared better each day – as if she'd found the fountain of youth. And damn, she'd forgotten to ask her doctor about the woman's medications.

Getting on Maddy's Floor would help. At least then, she'd get a fighting chance to heal. She shifted again, pulling her blankets up higher. The weather had to be warmer outside than in this room.

With another surreptitious glance at her neighbor, she admitted it to herself. Fine, okay. Yes, she was jealous. She wanted to be as good as her neighbor. Surely there wasn't anything wrong with that?

THE TEMPERATURE IN Stefan's large home studio was normal, yet sweat rolled off his face. Stripping off a layer wasn't an option. Neither was slowing down. Grimly, he hung on as paint flew in all directions, globules of red splotched on his smock, the canvas before him and the linoleum beneath his feet where it joined puddles of black and blue that had gone before.

Stefan's arm ached. How long had he been painting? His shoulder said it had been hours. Chances were it was less than one.

If he was this exhausted after years of experience he could only imagine how Kali was doing with her psychic paintings. He'd been working with her to develop her skills, and as they were both artists, painting was a natural medium for them to use.

He swabbed the palette with his paintbrush, picking up more red before pounding down on the canvas. He moved to some silent demonic orders. Painting as demanded, refusing to stop – or maybe he was not able to stop – until the demon was exorcised from his mind.

Stefan didn't see what he was painting. Instead, he was gripped by one of the psychic visions that ruled his world. The canvas was there, but he didn't have the vision as a clear image in his mind.

When his arm lifted again, he groaned. He'd need a painkiller after this session. He closed his eyes, letting the energy flow through him. It would anyway. Resistance caused pain. If he relaxed, the pain would ease.

His arm dropped. The force gripping his body drained down to his feet and out through his toes. He shuddered. It was over – for now.

He bent forward, catching his breath from the fury so recently released from his soul. His hands rested on his knees. Finally, he straightened to study his paint-spattered fingers and pants. He frowned. He painted with only one hand. Why were both hands covered in color?

Stepping back, Stefan washed his hands, taking care to thoroughly scrub them. Now to look at the picture – not that he was eager to do so. The picture could be a geometric disaster or it could be a detailed masterpiece. Some of his paintings hung in galleries around the world.

Then there were the paintings that he instinctively knew this one was. Ones that revealed haunted visions that tormented the soul and terrified the mind forever. Mostly they were vicious outpourings of violence.

Gearing himself for what was to come, he turned to view his latest creation, and immediately closed his eyes again. Please not. Slowly, hoping he'd been wrong, he peeked from behind partially closed lids and groaned softly.

Death himself had created this painting.

Still, it gave him a good idea of how he might help Maddy.

DREW WAS WALKING down the stairs toward his aunt's ward when his cell phone rang. He frowned at the number. Memorial Hospital, the one attached to The Haven. Not good.

"Hello?"

"Detective Drew McNeil?"

"Yes, that's correct. What can I do for you?"

"We have a patient here who has been asking for you. A Scott Durnham."

Scott, the husband of the diary writer. "I know of him. What happened?"'

"He's suffering from a concussion due to a head injury inflicted as he tried to get in his car."

"Was he alone?" Drew frowned. "Was his vehicle stolen? His wallet? ID?"

"I don't have those details. You'd need to speak with Officer Dale Hansford. He's the one that called for the ambulance to pick up Mr. Durnham."

"Right. I'll do that. Was there a small diary or journal among his personal effects?" It would be too much to hope that Scott had the missing diary on him at the hospital. Not that they'd found anything of interest in the other diaries. But he'd be interested to read the diary written around the time of the boy's death.

He waited. There was a pause and a rustling of papers before she said, "No, only car keys and a mint."

So where was it? Scott had planned to drop it off at the station today. "Fine. I'll follow up with the officer. Is Mr. Durnham going to be okay?"

"He's with the doctor right now. So it's too early to say."

"Thanks, I'm at The Haven already. I'll walk over in a few minutes. I'd like to speak with him, if possible."

Hanging up, Drew called the precinct, looking for the officer.

"Dale Hansford here."

Drew identified himself. "Can you fill me in on the particulars of Scott Durnham's case?"

By the time Drew walked through the front doors of Memorial Hospital, he'd gotten as much information from the officer as was available. He stared at the gleaming corridors, the smell of disinfectant chasing him. Drew realized that regarding work and family, he spent way too many hours in medical centers of one kind or another. After getting directions, he strode down the hallway toward Scott's bed. Dinner was being served, people were eating and in some cases trays were already being collected.

Scott appeared to be sleeping, at peace except for the wrinkles across his forehead. Drew stopped at the foot of his bed. "Mr Durnham? I'm Detective Drew McNeil from the Cold Case Squad."

Scott's eyes flew open, his face creasing in a weak smile. "Detective."

"How are you feeling?"

"Like I had my head bashed in."

Drew grinned at the pissed-off tone. Anger was good. It kept one focused. Giving in was like giving up. Not so good for healing or for catching bad guys though. "Do you remember anything about what happened?"

"Not much. I was getting into my car when pain exploded at the side of my head."

"You didn't see your attacker?"

Scott wrinkled up his face. "Nope. I thought someone called me but when I started to turn around, the lights went out."

"What were you doing there?"

"Having a free breakfast at the seniors' center. Free, my ass. Had to stand in line for almost an hour, put up with shit from everyone else, then got into an argument. I should have stayed home."

"An argument?" Drew stepped closer, pulling up the single chair and sat. "What was that all about?"

"My wife's diary. I had it in my pocket, and that prick, Brent, made a comment about it. Then he followed it by a worse one about my dead son and I lost it. I thought I was done blowing up about all that mess, but apparently not." Scott moodily tugged at the sheets covering his chest.

"No one has seen a diary. It didn't come to the hospital with you, and the detective handling the case didn't see one at the scene."

Scott stared at him. "It was in my jacket pocket when I was in Emergency. I'm sure of that."

With Scott watching, Drew opened the locker beside the bathroom. He gathered up everything and dumped the lot on Scott's bed. Scott pushed himself back up against the pillows to watch.

Drew turned his attention to the jacket. He slipped his hands inside the pockets, first one then the other. "No diary." He laid the jacket within the injured man's reach.

Scott frowned and pulled it toward him, checking for himself.

Drew slowly went through the remaining items. There was no sign of the missing book. "Was it close in size to the others?"

"Exactly like the ones with the little lock on it. This one had blue sparkly things on it."

"Well, it's not here. Did it sit inside the pocket well or stick out? Could it have fallen out?"

"It fit in just fine. I kept my hand on it most of the time anyway." Scott dropped the jacket. "I suppose it's possible that it fell out somewhere. I've gotta find it. I need to ask the nurses." He threw back the bedding and swung his legs around the side. He groaned and grabbed his head.

"Whoa. I'll go. You stay here and rest up. You're no help if you don't get better." Drew helped him back under the covers. "I'll be right back."

"Thanks. I don't want that last one to go missing. I was telling the little Italian nurse about it. It's the one my wife wrote at the time of our son's death. I'd been looking for it for years. I'm finally going through the last of my wife's stuff. She's been gone so long now. I figured it's time I sell the old place." He stared at Drew as he leaned back. "I'd sure like to learn the truth before I die."

"I'm working on it, Scott. We'd all like to know what happened."

"Good to hear." With that, Scott leaned back and closed his eyes.

Drew took that as a good time to leave. He stopped in at the nurses' center first. After showing his identification, he asked about the diary.

"Sorry, I haven't seen it." The nurse pulled up Scott's information on the computer. "There's no notation of it here." She frowned. "He's sure he had it with him?"

"Yes, one of the nurses commented on it in Emergency."

"It didn't arrive here. You can check with them, maybe they're holding it over there." Her polite smile clearly said it wasn't her problem.

Not surprising. Stuff went missing all the time. "Thanks, I'll check there."

The nurse was already talking to someone else. He walked back toward Emergency, wondering if they had a lost and found here. He stopped to ask a nurse. They did, only the trip there proved fruitless.

Back at Emergency, he had to pull his badge in order to learn which nurses had attended Scott. Two nurses were still on shift. "I'd like to speak to them, please." The diary might or might not have important evidence in it but without it, he wouldn't know. He had to trust that Scott's memory hadn't played tricks on him and that he had indeed had the diary in his pocket while here.

A harried looking nurse approached from behind the counter. "You needed to see me?"

She frowned after hearing his problem. "I didn't see the diary myself. Sofie was there with me." She turned around, spotted the woman in question. "Sofie, can you come here for a second?"

The other woman, short and dark haired, walked over. "What's up?"

Drew quickly explained the problem. Sofie's face lit up. "That was such a pretty little book. I haven't seen those in decades. My mother used to write in one. And such a tragic story with it. That poor man."

"It's gone missing. Do you have any idea where it might have ended up?"

Sofie frowned. "No. I put it in the bag with his clothes. That's how I noticed it. We talked a little bit about it, and then I had to go. His personal effects should have traveled to his room with him."

It was Drew's turn to frown. "They did. Without the diary."

He asked a few more questions about who might have seen the diary and if someone had wanted to remove it, when it could have happened. He understood the women didn't like the line of questioning, but they answered readily enough.

The bag had stayed with Scott at all times. In theory, anyone who came by, treated him or moved him had access to the bag. It had no resale value. It might be considered a curiosity worth lifting though. However, as it was inside the closed bag, no one would know the diary was there. It was only important to Scott and of course himself.

MONDAY

GERARD OPENED THE door to the outer office as quietly as he could. Sandra was at the coffee maker, her back to him. Perfect. Maybe he'd be able to sneak past. His super efficient admin assistant was damn irritating sometimes.

"Good morning."

Gerard stiffened. Damn it. She'd heard him.

"Late, huh?" she said.

"Yeah, bad morning," he said, walking into his office and slammed the door shut.

Sandra opened it almost immediately. "Dr. Chandler called."

"What?" Gerard spun around, his back to the window. Not Chandler again. "What did he want?"

"He didn't say. He asked for Maddy's number." Sandra dropped several pieces of mail on his desk and turned to leave.

Instinctively, Gerard flung out his hand. "Wait. Did you give him her number?"

"Of course. Maddy's a big girl, but even she can't make a decision if she doesn't know the choices."

"Are you nuts?"

She turned and the door slammed behind her, leaving Gerard alone, sputtering in shock. Oh God, he didn't dare lose Maddy. The Haven would spin into a major crisis. Dr. Chandler wasn't allowed to steal her away. No way. "I need a new secretary, for Christ's sake, and maybe a new doctor. Damn it, Sandra, what have you done?" he cried.

From the other side of the door, she called back, "Nothing. Maddy's not likely to leave. As long as you treat her right."

Right. And he'd just added a patient she hated to her floor, cut her budget and increased her patient roster. He clenched the back of his chair. What should he do? Oh Lord, what should he do?

"By the way," Sandra's voice came through the door. "Maddy called. She wants to talk to you."

Oh shit.

His door shoved open and Sandra walked in again. Raising his gaze, anger and frustration warred inside him. He opened his mouth to blast Sandra when he saw the man behind her. Detective Drew McNeil. Damn it. He quickly schooled his features into a polite welcome while eyeing his visitor carefully. Why was he here? Personal or professional?

Gerard walked around his desk and shook hands with Drew. "Drew, nice to see you again. Please have a seat." Gerard sat down. His office phone beeped, and he pushed a button, cutting off the caller.

Catching the detective's questioning look, Gerard grinned sheepishly. "Some idiot did an article on the new wing opening up, now the phones won't quit ringing. People are trying to nab the unclaimed beds."

Focusing on the man across the desk from him, Gerard stretched out his arms and clasped his hands together. "What can I do for you?"

"I need to ask a few questions. It won't take a moment." Drew settled back into his chair and studied Gerard's face. "What do you know about Jansen Svaar's death?"

Raising an eyebrow in surprise, Gerard answered honestly, "Nothing. I only hear if there's a problem."

"And the bed placements?"

"The doctors arrange those to suit the needs of the patients. I have nothing to do with it." Gerard didn't know what the detective was getting at. His next question confused him even more, and started his stomach acids bubbling. It was about six dead kids from thirty years ago? He frowned. "I knew a couple of them. They went to my school. Everyone who lived here back then would remember those kids. I can't remember any details. Only that no one seemed to know what happened. Why are you asking?"

"Just following up a lead. Now, I understand from Dr. Maddy that, in order to get on her floor, there are stringent requirements in place – a prognosis of greater than six months to live, being one." Drew paused as he searched through his notes, then glanced up, sending Gerard a hard questioning look. "So how did my uncle's application get approved? Apparently, he's been given only three months to live."

Ice filled Gerard's veins. Managing a weak smile, he shuffled the mail on his desk. "Our criteria aren't always so cut and dry. Many elements are discussed before the administrators and medical teams involved determine who is approved." He looked directly at the detective. "Thankfully, it's not my decision alone, or any one person's determination. The waiting list is long and getting longer by the minute." He grimaced at the flashing lights on his phone. "Especially after today."

GERARD HAD FUSSED about purchasing more cameras. Maddy had talked him around. Two were being installed as she sat in her office – one to shine on the stairwell and one for the new area. She'd prefer more. This was a place to start though. With the weird energy invading her floor, she wanted to stay here all the time, to move right in so she could watch over everyone. Still, even if she did, she wouldn't be able to watch over everyone all at the same the time.

She'd love to discuss the black energy issue more with Drew. He needed time to adjust before she nailed him with this mess. Once the floor calmed for the night, she planned to do energy readings. She needed to know how far off balance the energy on her floor had shifted after Jansen's death and the arrival of three new patients.

Nancy popped her head in the door. "I'm heading home." She sighed. "Don't stay too late. You need your sleep. Especially with the extra workload."

"How's the newest patient…" Maddy wracked her brain. "John McNeil settling in?"

"The irascible soul is hell on wheels. He's in bed and is ecstatic about being here."

"Good. They make for the best patients." So this was the detective's uncle. That meant she could expect to see Drew soon. Hopefully not until tomorrow. He sent her energy flying, which made it hard to do neutral readings.

Nancy smirked. "This one will be a handful, no matter what."

"I'll go down and say 'hi' in a couple of minutes."

"Good luck. Too bad Dr. Cunningham isn't here… again." With that, she closed the door, leaving Maddy alone with her thoughts.

Dr. Cunningham had popped in briefly. In his early sixties, he spent most of his time working on the hospital side, his first love. She never complained about the workload because bringing another doctor onboard would affect the energy balance of the floor even more. Dr. Cunningham pulled his weight, and left her and her project alone the rest of the time. A perfect system until she became overwhelmed…

Maddy walked down the hallway to check on the cameras. She found the one in the stairway up and functioning. Good. That was one less thing to distract her. She strode down to where the new patient should be. The camera in that area should cover the new wing without affecting the privacy of the patients. Time to welcome John to her floor.

Arriving at his bedside, she smiled at the sight. He had a small, almost shriveled frame with a huge chest that puffed up at the sight of her.

"Good evening, John. Welcome to The Haven."

John's face lit up. For all his apparent joy at the move, it was evident he had found the excitement and the trip arduous. Any move was incredibly stressful on a patient of his age. But what she saw was so much more. Maddy immediately shifted her viewing so she could see his energy more clearly… and frowned. He wasn't just ill and looking for a place for his last year where he could enjoy some quality of life. John was dying – and would soon. Not today, not tomorrow, however, she doubted he'd last more than ten weeks. Her frown deepened. Her floor in The Haven was not a hospice unit, for all the misunderstandings in the public's view. For this floor she only accepted patients much healthier than John. Something had gone wrong in the selection process.

A second death on the floor wasn't going to be easy on the other patients. She pursed her lips. How had his application been accepted?

Frowning, she studied his chart. He was in death management stage. She glanced surreptitiously at his chest area, seeing the gray energy hovering. Yes, his chest was compromised. His shrunken frame wasted. There was some swelling of his hands.

"How's the swelling in your feet?"

She glanced at him as she lifted a corner of the blanket. At his nod, she flipped it back. Both ankles and feet had a tight, purple look to them.

"Is the pain manageable right now? Or do you need something stronger after the move?"

"No," he gasped, "It's okay. I don't know about sleeping tonight, though."

Maddy nodded. "We can give you something for that."

Stepping back, she studied him further. Should she ask or not? "Dr. Cunningham isn't here at this hour, but he'll stop by in the morning. Your transfer came late in the day. I'm sorry. I know that can be hard on individuals. We try to coordinate arrivals to coincide with the doctors' schedules."

"I wasn't going to wait another day. And I don't need a doctor. They can't even say what's wrong with me," he growled, frowning at her. "I need you."

Jolted, Maddy stared at him. "Pardon?"

"I need you and your magic. Don't you go denying it. You're the one responsible for the healing going on around here. I've heard all about it."

As she opened her mouth, he jumped right in. "Hell, half the world's heard about it."

"What?"

"Sure. It's all over the Internet. Checked it out myself." The growl in his voice deepened.

Maddy didn't know what to think. More to the point, did he really think that she was some kind of witch doctor, a miracle healer? That if he could trick his way onto her floor he would be miraculously healed? She had limited success here, helped by the stringent selection process – one that had obviously gone awry with him. There should have been several rounds of interviews, and medical checks, to start. There had been with Dr. Lenning and she'd actually done the testing and intake for Felicia herself.

"I'm not too sure what you've read or heard about me. I am a medical intuitive. That does allow me to see a different level, a different view of the body. Yes, I use energy to heal. And yes, we've had some phenomenal successes, where people have gone home because their condition had improved to that extent."

He nodded with satisfaction. "Right, then. Glad you're not going to give me all the denial bullshit." He settled back into his bed – the pain that had stiffened his face, easing.

"I'm not into denial, but you have a major misunderstanding going on. First off, the only people accepted into the program are those at a certain health level. Anything below that, the patient doesn't have the required strength or health for the healing required."

He blinked a couple of times. "What?" Fear slid across his features.

"I'm saying that your condition has advanced to the point that normally you wouldn't have been accepted here and I'm not sure how you were. Your application should have been declined. I'm sorry."

"How can you tell my condition?" he blustered, puffing his chest. "You haven't read my file."

Maddy's face softened. Just because patients had been told about their condition didn't mean they were ready to accept it. John should be managing his death right now. Instead, he was grasping at straws. He hadn't reached the point of acceptance.

Not unusual, as few people accepted a negative diagnosis easily. She suspected John had held off going to the doctor as long as he could, thereby minimizing treatment options. While Maddy dealt in death every day, she preferred to focus on life.

"I can see *you*. That's why I'm slightly different. I can't tell you when you'll die or any other hocus pocus stuff; however, I can see that your bones ache, your chest is compromised and you're having trouble breathing. Your body is suffering from major edema to the point you can't walk. There are energy blockages at several main intersections in your system that have been there for a long time."

Worry darkened his features. "What does all that mean?"

"It means getting here to my floor may not help you. I'm not sure there's anything I, or anyone, can do for you at this stage."

"But you're not sure?"

He latched onto the one straw she'd inadvertently offered. Maddy could understand the drowning man reaching for a life preserver. As much as she believed in the power of hope and positive thoughts, she also understood there had to be a level of acceptance, peace and belief. She didn't think he had much of those.

John looked to be rigid and grasping – not as if he were aware and accepting that he was close to the end of his life.

"No, I'm not a hundred percent sure."

John glared at her. "I've been to dozens of doctors. Each one says something different. No one can agree as to what's wrong with me because no one knows." He almost shouted the last words as his frustration rose to the boiling point. He coughed violently several times then collapsed back onto his bed, exhausted.

Using her most soothing voice, Maddy poured a glass of water for him from the carafe on his nightstand and said, "There are miracles in life. Still, you don't understand something here. This isn't just me working on your healing. You have to as well."

"How can I do anything? I'm sick. That's why I'm here. For you to work your magic."

He glared at her, using anger to hide the fear lurking in his eyes. Maddy stepped back ready to return to her office. "That's what I'm trying to say. This isn't a floor where you get to lie there and miracles happen. This is where people actively participate in their own healing. If you want to get better, you have to help make it happen."

She walked away, leaving him to think on that for a bit.

She wasn't trying to be cruel, but she needed to shake him out of the 'poor me' syndrome – to have him ask what he could do to help. Not that there was much in this case. He had weeks, maybe a few months, to live. The least she could do would be to make those as pain free and as enjoyable as possible.

On the other hand, she planned to roast Gerard alive – as soon as she found the damn weasel. He couldn't play with everyone's emotions like this. Damn that man. He shouldn't have let John in. Talk about setting up an important selection process, then failing to follow through.

Maddy walked past the nurses' station to the stairwell, pissed at Gerard, upset for John and disappointed in herself and her limited abilities. She needed to get away – even to another floor for a bit. To forget the machinations going on behind her back that threatened to sink her project, the bureaucratic bullshit that was all about money.

On the second floor, she walked through the wards, noting dinner had been delivered to most patients.

Dr. Susan Selsin, her carrot curls making her easily identifiable, stood talking with a colleague as Maddy approached. Her old friend's face lit up at the sight of Maddy. "Fancy that, Dr. Maddy's coming to visit."

Maddy grinned, feeling better already. "Hi, just thought I'd stop in and see how things are down here."

For the next hour, Maddy laughed and cheered everyone's progress. Susan concluded the tour when Maddy declared it was time to return to work.

It was time for her special energy work.

SISSY STRETCHED AND wiggled. She laughed at the odd sensation circulating through her body. It was as if she were adjusting to a new suit – a new birthday suit. She smirked at the other women in the ward. One glared at her, another shot her a disgusted look before turning away and reaching for her knitting.

"Don't know about you ladies, but I feel great." She giggled, like the fifteen-year-old she felt like inside.

"I need your drugs. Mine aren't doing anything for me," the old woman across the room said in disgust.

Murmurs and assenting groans answered.

Sissy's grin widened. Today, she felt great.

She looked over at the old woman beside her and couldn't prevent the pleased grin breaking out. That old biddy looked like she was one step away from death. Sad. Too bad for her.

Sissy knew that had been her future – once. Not now. She had a plan and it was finally working. Those damn doctors. You had to make it clear you weren't going to take their lack of care and progress lying down. If your doctor was no good, then get rid of him and get a new one. Like she'd done.

She didn't plan on living in bed 232 forever. Now she needed to work on the next stage of her healing. Everything was progressing, just like she'd planned.

She wiggled her toes. Perfect.

BACK UPSTAIRS, THE evening lights were on, dimming the fluorescent brightness to a mild soft light that was easier on everyone. Maddy let the nurses know where she was going before closing herself in her office. She turned off her phones, lowered the overhead lights and went to put on calming music. Standing in front of her music selection, she was hard pressed to decide between Zamfir and Yanni. Yanni won out. That man's piano skills were second to none.

Then she unbuttoned the top of her blouse, slipped off her jacket and kicked off her heels. Trying to relax, Maddy focused on her breathing and dropped into a deep meditative state. Having done this many times before, the routine was easy and comfortable. She sped through the process and expanded her consciousness out toward her patients. Moving easily, Maddy registered the energy levels on a grand scale. This was all about the big picture: looking for rents and tears in the fabric of the micro-ecosystem she was building. Like a giant pulsing bubble of warm, loving energy that worked to heal everyone on her floor – including the staff. Some of her nurses preferred nightshift because they experienced Maddy's work at its peak. Gerona had once suffered from terrible migraines, but no longer. Nancy used to suffer from ovarian cysts. They disappeared over a year ago.

Moving from the stairwell forward, she shifted the waves of energy, moving and adjusting as required to make a seamless blending of energy for the benefit of everyone there. It was slow work, and by the time Maddy made her way through the patient checks, she found herself tiring. Her forward movement stilled as she regrouped and assessed her progress.

Energy vibrated. How it vibrated said a lot about the type of energy, the health or strength of the energy and its purpose. It vibrated differently in an inanimate object, like the energy in a table, for example, versus the energy zipping around in a child.

It was the child, Felicia, she wanted to focus on.

Maddy planned to focus on the big picture for this trip, yet something about Felicia's aura disturbed her. Red swarmed her chest and lungs, not a pinkish red, but an angry blood red. Maddy frowned, drifting closer.

Felicia slept soundly.

Her body shimmered, active in sleep like that of everyone else. The red sat in the middle of her chest. It was pulsating, with mixed emotions, anger, love, pain – fear. Maddy pulled back slightly to look from a different angle. Yes, the energy was contained in Felicia's chest.

Just then, the bathroom door around the corner from Felicia's bed opened. It was Alexis, Felicia's mother, dressed all in black as if she already mourned the loss of her daughter. Only in her late thirties, her face had a reddish blush and her eyes were swollen. Her shoulders stooped in defeat though she put on a brave smile. Her emotions swarmed over Maddy. Maddy pulled back in an effort to distance herself from the pain, as the other woman's need and sorrow rushed at her.

Maddy struggled to detach from the mother's needy energy long enough to stay and complete her reading – except the woman's emotions were too strong. Maddy took one last look at Felicia. Now red energy filled the short distance between the mother and the daughter.

Disturbed, Maddy snapped back into her body and came out of the meditation. She grabbed her head with both hands as her temples resonated from the pounding energy shift that had created a massive headache. She rocked in place for several minutes until the pain eased. Gasping for breath, Maddy stretched out and groaned.

Alexis was hurting her daughter more than helping her. And she'd be horrified if she knew.

Somehow, Maddy had to help Alexis, before she killed her daughter – with fear and love.

Maddy walked quickly in the direction of Felicia's bed. This issue had to be dealt with now.

Felicia's mother sat in the same position as Maddy had seen her last, tears pouring down her face. Entering the small cheery area, Maddy quietly pulled up another visitor's chair and sat beside the grieving woman.

"Hello, Alexis."

The other woman gasped and spun around. "Oh my, I'm sorry. I never heard you."

Maddy placed one hand on the woman's arm. "You looked to be having a tough time right now. I hated to disturb you."

Alexis gave her a watery smile. "The feelings come and go. On the not so good days, they just live inside and leak all day."

"That's normal. Honor the feelings and honor the situation you're in. Let the tears pour when they need to and take time to do something nice for yourself." Maddy patted the painfully thin woman's hand. "You can't help her if you aren't doing so well yourself."

"I know that." She sniffled her tears back. "Honestly, I do. It's just so hard. She's all I have."

Sadness slipped into Maddy's heart. So much heartache for one person.

Felicia had a real opportunity here. Maddy had a good idea how she could help the child, except it was too early to tell the mother. It would be unethical to even mention a possibility of an improvement at this stage. Besides, the mother had to deal with the energy problems she was creating with her neediness. Loving energy was necessary, but it was destructive when delivered with the mother's negative emotions: anger, fear and sense of betrayal. In this case, it became suffocating like the red energy Maddy had seen earlier.

Speaking slowly, gently feeling her way, Maddy made a couple suggestions. "One of the things that is the hardest to deal with is the lack of control, the helplessness. That feeling of being powerless to the whims of fate, which in this case seem less than benevolent."

"Isn't that the truth? I wish there was something I could do to help."

The perfect opening Maddy had been hoping for. "There is. It's called spirit talking."

Alexis turned to her, frowning, hope flickering in her eyes. "What's that? Will it help her?"

"It's easy, and it will help both of you. You do it while she's resting. She can be asleep or not; it doesn't matter. What matters is the tone of voice you use. It must be positive. Not teary, not negative – and definitely not needy. What you're going to do is talk to her. You're talking to the Felicia you have always known and loved. You want to tell her how much her presence in your life means to you. Be sure to tell her you love her. Not in a grasping way, like 'don't leave me,' but in a positive way, with gratitude. 'Felicia, you're a wonderful blessing in my life.'"

Maddy studied Alexis's face. "Do you understand what I mean?"

"I think so. Will she hear me?" Alexis wiped her eyes and straightened in her seat.

"Absolutely. That's the joy of this. You're speaking to her spirit, not to her body or mind. It's like the coma patients who know that someone is there loving them, coaxing them back into awareness."

Alexis gazed down at her daughter in a new way. "Oh, I've heard of things like that."

"The biggest things to watch for are your tone of voice and making sure your intentions come from the heart. Don't just say the words – make sure you mean them. Be there in your heart for her." Peering closer, Maddy tried to see if Alexis understood the subtle difference.

Optimism shining in Alexis's eyes told Maddy she got it. "Right. So it's like, don't lie to her. If I'm going to do this, be honest."

"If you can't be honest, don't do it. You'll cause more hurt than healing. I'm sure there is a lot of the loving mother inside of you waiting for a chance to do something useful here. Felicia needs to have a reason to live and to know that she's loved. So give her something to fight for."

Alexis stared down at her daughter, such naked love on her face, Maddy's heart ached for her. To lose a child had to be the hardest loss.

Maddy smiled, adding one more caution. "Remember to think about helping her. Not what you're going to do if her condition worsens or the multitude of other 'what ifs.' This isn't about you – it's about her. Remember that and you'll be fine." Maddy stood, happy with the session. Alexis had a direction and it was one that would benefit everyone.

Alexis got to her feet and threw her arms around Maddy in a quick hug. "You have no idea how you've helped me tonight. I really appreciate it."

Maddy returned the hug and stepped back. "No problem. Now might be a good time to try it out. I'll be down with my other patients. Call if you need me."

"Thank you," Alexis called to her retreating back.

HE HADN'T MEANT to listen in. He'd had no choice. Their voices carried in the silence. The echo from the largely unfinished empty room bounced conversations of the closest patients his way, like the conversation with John earlier. Maddy hadn't pulled her punches on that one. However, he had to admit that she'd handled it very well.

Adam Lenning hated the thought of that poor child dying beside him. It was yet another unique factor to Maddy's Floor, mixing men and women and children in the same space. He'd had trouble with it when he found out. Now he understood. All the patients gelled into one big family. That understanding put everything in perspective. The strategy was quite smart, really.

Dr. Maddy was an enigma. He'd done her an injustice. Something he'd have to set right before his time came. He didn't know how yet. Maybe in a few weeks he'd work his way up to it. Apologies didn't come easy to him. They never had. It was hard to admit he'd been wrong – and in a big way. The more he saw of her active role here, the more he realized that Dr. Maddy had a gift. He didn't know much about the energy aspect of what she did, and because of his earlier criticism, chances were he wouldn't be included in the conversation for a while. They didn't trust him here. He didn't blame them.

One odd thing, though. As he learned more about her, understood her more and what she was trying to do, his sexual attraction had calmed. The fantasy relationship in his mind had changed to a more realistic goal, one of acceptance and friendship rather than romance.

Adam tucked himself deeper into his blankets. He'd yet to warm up from that lousy night and the obvious frailty of his body didn't help his mood. He knew he was dying. He didn't want to go quietly. He wanted to fight, kick and scream – rail at life's injustices. And he didn't have the energy to even start. His lips curled and damn him, he'd become a maudlin ass. How unforgivable.

"Dr. Lenning? How are you feeling today?"

Shit. Dr. Maddy.

Rolling over, he half-sat so he could see her. "Hello." He attempted a smile, unable to stop himself from drinking in the sight of her.

"The nurse said you didn't appear to be feeling well today."

The damn nurse hadn't said any such thing. Adam knew doctor speak as well as anyone. Better, in fact, because he had practiced it for over forty years. Being on the patient side, listening to it didn't feel very good, either. Still it was easier coming from her.

"I'm fine. A little tired maybe."

He followed Maddy's probing gaze as she checked him over. It was all he could do not to move restlessly under her perusal.

"You're still cold. I understand you didn't eat your breakfast this morning and only picked at your dinner last night."

Adam closed his eyes. Shit, he should be the one talking to the patients. Not her.

"Adam?"

Her soft voice was his undoing. Tears formed in the corners of his eyes. Christ, in a minute he was going to be bawling. Please, not in front of her. Never in front of her.

"I'm just having a tough day," he muttered under his breath. "Nothing to worry about."

"Maybe nothing to worry about but definitely something to talk about. Does your off day have to do with your pain level or your life level?"

His eyes open wider. "Life level? That's a new one for me."

"I use it to mean the stage of life you find yourself in. It wasn't too long ago you were in my shoes, handling a full roster of patients on your own. Now you find yourself on the other side. I can't imagine that being an easy shift to make."

He frowned, not expecting her warm, empathetic understanding. He didn't think he'd be so compassionate if their positions were reversed. "Maybe. I don't know. Can't say I like where I find myself today."

"Understandable. Still, for you, there are some treatment options. I'm sure you know them as well as I do. Plus, you have Dr. Cunningham on your side. That has to count for something."

"Not much. I've hardly seen him."

She laughed, her rich voice adding warmth and sparkle to the room. "He's not here tonight. He spends a lot of time in the hospital, as you know."

Not good. Dr. Maddy worked too hard. "He should be here, and you should be going home. You've been here since early this morning."

She stepped closer, smiling broadly. "And that's not unusual, either."

He smiled. True enough. Then he remembered what he'd planned to ask her. "Was someone in here recently?"

"In where?" She frowned at him. "We have visitors on the floor now, if that's what you mean."

"No. It felt like someone was looking in on me."

"Maybe someone did. They might have been lost or confused as to what bed their loved one was in."

"No. It was weirder than that. I thought I felt something similar a few nights ago. Tonight the sensation was much milder."

"Sensation?" she asked cautiously. He watched as she scanned his little corner of the world. He knew everything was in its place. He'd already checked.

"Before it was like a cold darkness washed over me. I know it sounds fanciful and undoctor-like, but I can't describe it any other way." He gave a helpless shrug. "It was different tonight – warmer, happier. It almost had a peacefulness to it."

She tilted her head, studying him. "Interesting. You felt this yet didn't see anything?"

"Right. Stupid, huh?" At least she didn't laugh.

"Not necessarily. I'll check with the nurses and see if anyone noticed anything out of the ordinary. Who knows, maybe a stranger wandered in here by accident."

He had to be content with that. He wanted to ask more. He

had a million questions. There were things going on here, undercurrents he didn't understand, and he wanted to. Sure that revealed a bit of hypocrisy on his part. However, he dared anyone to do things differently if the tables were turned.

He had no proof that Dr. Maddy would be able to help him. He did know that he felt better here on this floor than he had anywhere else. He didn't understand it, and that aspect no longer mattered. He wanted to be included in whatever was going on here.

Now if only he had the courage to ask her for that favor.

MADDY LEFT ADAM'S bedside, deep in thought. Was it possible he might have noticed her energy work from earlier? It wouldn't have been the first time a patient had felt her working, but she hadn't expected that level of sensitivity from him.

Maddy sighed in disgust at the judgmental thought. She wouldn't be able to help Adam if she didn't get rid of her own dislike for the man. If he shifted, warmed his energy – she glanced back at him – which he might be doing now, then the positive energy would move to encompass him on its own. That, in turn, would help to dissipate the remaining negativity he might be hanging onto.

Frowning, Maddy realized that having an old enemy in her bosom, so to speak, would have a profound effect on him. He might end up as a nice person.

And what about her? How would his presence here affect her? Maddy prided herself on being 'forward thinking' and 'in tune' with her own person. She didn't like to see herself as the one in the wrong. She needed to progress herself – in short, she needed to forgive him.

Yuck. Her stomach squeezed tight. He represented fear to her. Not so long ago, he had put her life's passion, her job, her beliefs and her reputation on the line. He'd raised her deepest, innermost fears, exposed them, forced her to see them. Maddy ran her fingers through her dark hair. She had a lot of work to do in that area of herself and not a whole lot of willingness to go there. Typical. Thankfully, energy work could be done in private.

For the sake of everyone on her floor, she needed to clear her own issues – regardless of how little she liked the idea.

TUESDAY

THE NEXT MORNING, Maddy yawned as she sat down at her office desk, staring at her espresso machine across from her. At this point, caffeine would need to be injected to do any good. She'd hardly slept.

"Dr. Maddy?"

Maddy glanced over to see one of the day nurses standing in her doorway. "What's the matter?"

"It's the new patient. He's unbelievable." Her cheeks bloomed with bright red flags of color.

New patient? "You mean John McNeil?"

"Yes. That guy's a madman."

Crap. Difficult patients were the norm for any hospital, but they couldn't stay that way here. Staff and patients alike either changed their attitude or were shipped downstairs. Not that it had happened before. Everyone was too grateful to be here to cause trouble. No one, including John, would be allowed to disturb the balance here.

"I'll go and speak with him."

Maddy marched toward John's bedside. She passed Felicia's mom, head bent over her daughter's hand, a soft smile on her face, and then by Adam's curled up body. Good, he slept.

Long before she made it to John's area, she heard John's voice, yelling at some hapless person.

"I said I don't want this. Get the hell away from me. Now!"

Maddy rounded the last curtain and stopped to observe the mess. Tina, one of the aides, had stripped his bed, trying to put on fresh sheets. A glance to the side showed the old ones had been soiled. Maddy checked John's energy and saw shame and anger radiating together. He'd had an accident, and because he needed help to fix the problem he was embarrassed. Anger was his weapon to hide his insecurities and the hatred he felt for his circumstances.

Maddy waited in silence for Tina to finish changing the bedding. She grinned at the woman, who rolled her eyes as she walked past, pushing the laundry cart.

John sat in a visitor's chair, oblivious to Maddy's presence. He dropped his head into his hands. Maddy gave him a minute longer. She approached him. "John. Bad night?"

He reared his head to glare at her. "A bad fucking life."

She had to cut through to the real problem. Patients had to come to terms with their situation before they could move forward. Their terminal conditions didn't give them the luxury of time to wallow. Sometimes she had to be hard in this business. "Only that's not quite true, is it? More like 'bad fucking end of life,' don't you think?"

He glared at her. "That's not funny."

"I wasn't trying to be funny. I deal in reality. The reality is you have a body that's in crisis. How that crisis is managed is up to you."

"I have no control over anything – not even my bowels, apparently." His growl held shame and embarrassment.

"Something that is to be expected, given your condition." She studied his face for a moment. "Or did you expect this not to happen after you achieved your transfer to The Haven?"

The pink on his face reddened. He stared down at the arm of his chair and refused to answer.

"If that's what your wish is, then you need to understand that such an improvement might happen, except healing is a process and tends to take time."

"I don't have any time."

"Hence the selection requirements to get on this floor."

He glared at her. "Gerard let me in, so I must have fit them."

"I'll discuss that with him soon. Why don't you take a nap? Rest will have a major impact on things, like making it to the bathroom on time. Let's get you back into bed."

"Sorry." He lumbered the few steps to the bed then clambered in. "I'm taking my temper out on you and I shouldn't be. I'm hoping with a little bit of time, you can help me."

Maddy walked forward and pulled the blankets up over his frail body. "And maybe I can. However, I need time. That means you need to give it to me. Avoid stress. Stop getting upset over the things you can't change and work on seeing something positive in your day. Find something to be grateful for every hour. Preferably every minute." She added the last bit as an afterthought.

"Why don't you ask me to do something easy, like pay off the national debt, or build a commune on the moon? I'm not much of a happy-vibe-type person," he grumped, pulling up his clean sheets.

Maddy laughed with real humor. Honest self-assessment was a great start. "Well, now is a good time to try. Your unhappy-vibe personality put you here, so what about trying something different to get you out of here?"

"Right. I'll let you know how that goes."

The wry look on his face made her laugh. "I'll see your progress, don't you worry. That's not exactly something you can hide."

"It doesn't appear that anything can be hidden from you anyway."

"True enough, so don't waste the energy. Just work on feeling better. Before you know it, you'll start thinking happier, healthier thoughts, and you'll manifest these in action."

"It's all gibberish, if you ask me."

For all his knocking of the process, John's eyes were brighter and he sat straighter.

"And if it works – who cares what you call it?" There was a hell of a lot more to it, but it gave John something concrete to focus on. Miracles did happen. She'd be the last one to shortchange his ability to create one.

He was the only one who could do that.

THE MORNING LIGHT shone brightly into Stefan's studio. He picked up the paintbrush and hesitated as he held it above the pallet of colors. He was wading neck-deep in dark, unchartered waters – ones he wasn't sure how to navigate.

He'd done many weird psychic things over the past decade and his talents had always grown, sometimes in ways that had scared the crap out of him. This was no different. Except he needed information on Maddy's Floor – and fast. He planned to use a technique like that used on his last painting. It had worked well then.

No time like the present to get started.

He dabbed his paintbrush into the black and started painting the newly renovated room at The Haven. Maddy's problem hadn't started there, but it was anchored there. Now he had to find a connection, something concrete so he could trace this energy to its source. She had emailed him several digital pictures of the room as a starting point.

The emailed pictures stood on the spare easel. He studied the details of the new wing then turned to his canvas.

Within minutes, he'd lost himself in the artistic process.

It took several hours for the image to take form. He switched colors several times as he layered in the details. When he came to adding the flooring around the finished bed, complete with patient, sheets and blankets, he switched to light browns. Placing the brush against the canvas, he tried to paint in the floor. The flooring laid down easily in the rest of the room, but the closer Stefan's brush went to the bed, the harder it was to force the brush to touch the canvas. Sweat filmed over his skin with the effort.

Breathing hard, he stopped to regroup. What the hell was going on? He tried to lift his arm again, but it suddenly felt as if it weighed two hundred pounds. He couldn't move it.

Stefan consciously relaxed his arm. Instantly the heavy sensation alleviated. Laying the brush on his palette, he shook his arm lightly. Next, he lifted his empty hand toward the painting.

That appeared to be fine.

The problem appeared to be in painting the floor around the bed, or rather, the color of the floor around the bed. Stefan quickly snatched up a fine brush and dabbed it in the white paint. He touched up the windowsill and accented the fold of a sheet. Then he moved to below the bed and tried to touch where the flooring should be.

His arm froze. It wouldn't allow his brush to connect with the canvas in that place.

Interesting.

Stefan stepped back and studied the picture. Only one color was going to be allowed there.

Stefan's inner senses strengthened as his 'knowing' kicked in: He was on the right path. He could feel the positive energy pulsing through his own veins. A sense of rightness. The recognition of another energy. An energy that wanted to be recognized.

And that would be this person's failing. Stefan knew the persona of this energy in some ways now. He couldn't recognize his signature yet, but he would. He had enough to search for him on the ethers. It might take a bit, but this painting would help.

With grim determination, Stefan picked up the black paint and finished the image, painting the blackness in where the brown hadn't been allowed to go.

This would be his starting point.

GERARD TRIED TO write the report explaining why he'd allowed John onto Maddy's Floor…without making it sound like he'd sold the bed to the highest bidder. That John was already in place helped, only not enough, as Maddy had reminded him. Gerard still had to justify his actions to the Board.

Shit.

Sandra walked in without warning. "That nice detective is on line one." She sauntered back out. "I told him you'd speak with him."

Picking up the phone, he used his most professional sales voice. "Drew? What can I do for you?"

"Sorry to bother you, but I'm looking for a diary that went missing in the ER while a patient was being worked on. He and several nurses swear it was there at the time. However, it didn't move with him and his personal effects when he was transferred to a room for the night."

Gerard frowned. Issues like this wouldn't normally make it to his desk, unless a patient threatened to file a lawsuit for loss of personal property. Insurance usually dealt with it. Was Drew asking about it personally or professionally?

"There is a lost and found department. Have you checked with them?"

"Several times. This diary relates to a cold case. I'm sure you can see that I need to follow up all leads to help me retrieve it."

"Hmmm." A cold case, so it was professional. Good luck with that. Time wasn't kind to evidence. "The only thing would be to ask everyone who was on shift that night—"

"Which I've done." Drew sighed, frustration and impatience obvious in his voice. "I don't know if it's stupidity, negligence or a criminal element at play here."

"I can ask the staff myself, see if that helps, but I can't imagine I'll get a different answer than you have."

"No, probably not. If you hear anything about it or if it turns up, please let me know. This is a police matter."

"I'll send out a staff-wide email and explain the importance of locating the diary. Maybe someone thought it was pretty and didn't realize its importance."

"Yes. That might be enough impetus to make someone do the right thing. Thanks."

After Drew hung up, Gerard shook his head. CEO of a major company and he was sending out emails about a missing diary. Who'd have thought? Shrugging at the comedy of his life, he brought up his email and starting writing.

DORIS STARED OUT the window. Embittered and diseased was not what she'd hoped for in this stage of her life. She hated her life. She felt out of control, on a train taking her somewhere she didn't want to go. Depression, they called it. She didn't care what name was given to it, it felt weird. Surely something was wrong.

She'd had enough to deal with over the last several decades. She didn't want to deal with anything else in this lifetime. Just the thought of reincarnation and repeating this process scared the crap out of her. Karma, yuck. She'd not been exactly a good girl this time around, and didn't have enough time to fix that, even if she had the inclination to do so.

No, she'd hang on as long as she could before going, kicking and screaming, through the final door. All that other New Age stuff fascinated her – as long as she was allowed to pick and choose what she wanted to believe.

Damn her brother, anyway. She wished her mind would shut up about it. Except the angry thoughts recycled endlessly.

The asshole was gloating. Well, maybe his move to Dr. Maddy's floor would come too late to save him. Damn if Doris wasn't going to have a party when his time came. A big one too, with everything he liked so he couldn't have any of it. And she'd use his damn money. Money that should have been hers. They'd been a family after all…at least some of the time. John had hated her mental instability, almost as much as he hated her constant boyfriends and her lifestyle. She shrugged. Too damn bad.

She groaned as she shifted on her bed. Everything hurt these days and nothing they gave her helped. Trapped inside a rotting body was not an experience for the lighthearted. She hoped her brother was suffering, too.

If he'd shared his wealth, she might have felt differently, particularly in light of their history. But he hadn't and now his actions had a direct negative impact on her life. He'd gotten in and she hadn't. She refused to let that be the end. Her pride wanted her to heal so badly. She wanted to parade in front of him before walking out the front doors of The Haven forever – preferably leaving him behind and suffering mightily.

She hadn't even heard about her transfer request yet. Surely, it had to be complete by now. It had been months. Damn it, she deserved Dr. Maddy's floor, not him.

MADDY WANTED TO go home. Her working day had once again extended well into the evening. She needed fresh air and a decent night's sleep. After shutting down and locking up her office, she pulled on her jacket and walked toward the stairwell. With a goodbye wave to the other nurses, she said, "I'm off."

The fresh air revived her somewhat. She stopped outside the hospital door and took several bracing gulps, appreciating the fresh air. Sometime during the day, it had rained, giving the air the feeling of renewal. Though she'd been eager to get some rest, walking toward her apartment, she realized she wasn't quite ready to go home and be cooped up inside again. That intimate little coffee bistro around the corner would be perfect. A bite to eat wouldn't hurt, either.

At the bistro, she chose a spot on the outdoor patio where the evening lanterns swayed in the warm breeze. Truly, it was a peaceful setting. The waitress brought her a latte with a beautiful heart design in the cream. With a happy sigh, Maddy settled back and sipped her coffee. Perfect. Too bad she was alone. A particular male would be a great addition to her evening.

"Excuse me, Dr. Maddy." A shadow fell across her table. "May I join you?"

Maddy looked up, startled, as her imagination manifested him beside her. "Detective? I didn't expect to see you here." Her heart bounced with joy.

"Please, call me Drew. And actually, I followed you in," he added with a sheepish grin.

She blinked. Did he have more questions or was there a more personal reason? Flustered, she said inanely, "Oh." Heat climbed her cheeks. "Please, sit down." Maddy's eyes widened as he folded his long frame onto the small bistro chair.

"It's okay. I won't break it." He laughed at her.

Her cheeks burned. "Sorry. It's always a concern, being tall myself. So much of the world appears a little fragile from up here."

"You wear your height well."

The heat on her cheeks deepened. "Thanks," she muttered, unsure what to say next. "So, why did you follow me in?"

Drew grimaced. "I wanted to double check on my uncle's condition after the transfer, I know it really isn't fair to ask, as you're off duty." His coffee arrived. He thanked the waitress. Maddy watched his interactions. Friendly, but not flirty. Nice. From the wattage on the waitress's face, she obviously thought so, too.

When he faced her, curiosity lit up his features. "What's that smile for?"

"I was thinking the waitress likes you."

"Who?" He turned around to see who she was talking about, then shrugged. "Really? I didn't notice."

"I know, that's why the smile. It's kind of nice."

His gaze narrowed and he took another hot sip of the brew. "Nice? Oh." He gulped, shrugging uncomfortably. "Uhm. So, is Uncle John settling in?"

"Yes, he is." Maddy studied the wrought iron table before looking straight into his eyes. "You know he's seriously ill."

Drew leaned forward. "Yes. He won't talk about it."

"No, he wouldn't. I have to admit, I'm troubled by his transfer." At Drew's frown, she explained, "His application shouldn't have been approved. He doesn't fit the strict protocols for the project."

"I wondered about that earlier when you explained the rules for your floor." Drew frowned. "I spoke to Gerard about it. He brushed me off with something like not everyone has to follow the same rules."

She didn't want to hear that. Stirrings of frustrated anger whipped through her. The viability of her research and the well-being of patients on her floor depended on everyone following the same strict entrance requirements. Damn Gerard. Everyone *had* to follow the same rules, or the medical community would dismiss the project. She eyed him curiously. "Do you know anything about how Gerard and John know each other?"

"Only that they've been acquainted for years."

"Well, I'm going to have a talk with Gerard in the morning. As for your uncle, his prognosis isn't good. You'll have to speak with his physician for the details."

"I have. Not that it's done much good. No one seems to be

able to pinpoint the root of the problem."

"There's not always an answer or a single cause. Several of your uncle's systems are crashing. Talk to Dr. Cunningham about him if you're concerned about his treatment."

Drew frowned. "I will. Did we put him at risk, moving him at this stage?" He paused and reconsidered. "I guess moving him couldn't do much more damage. He was adamant about getting onto your floor."

This time it was Maddy who winced. "That's because he seems to think I can work miracles. He wants me to heal him or seriously slow down the progression of his condition."

Drew blew out his breath and sat back to study her. "That doesn't sound like him. He's usually pretty grounded."

Maddy studied the caring in his face. That was kind of nice, too.

"We often find that people will grasp at any solution when facing imminent death." Hiding behind her own mug, Maddy studied him. His high cheekbones and squared off chin gave him a Nordic appearance. The dark hair with the slight curl to it added a youthfulness he probably wouldn't appreciate. There was dark stubble on his chin, an indication the detective had a long, hard day.

But then so had she.

They both had difficult jobs where they were in service to others. Another thing she liked about him.

He stretched out his legs, his shoulders relaxing. "You know, I have to say you're easy to be around."

Surprised, she answered lightly, "So are you."

Sipping her latte, she watched the surprised gleam in his eyes and chuckled. "I gather most people don't feel that way, do they?"

He shook his head and grinned. "The exact opposite, actually. Most women say I don't talk enough and that I'm too devoted to my job."

"Now, I've heard that one a time or two." Her candid answer drew a startled laugh from him, bringing out an endearing dimple in his cheek.

He leaned forward to study her face closer. "Do you think two workaholics might find time to go out for dinner together?"

"We do have to eat sometime." She pushed her coffee cup ahead of her on the table. "And if it means eating Chinese, absolutely, although I might consider something else as well. I've got an awful hankering for Almond Gai Ding."

"Tomorrow night? Would that work for you?"

Maddy grinned. "Tomorrow sounds great."

WEDNESDAY

A DEEP SENSE of unease woke Stefan from his restless sleep. *Now what?* He groaned and rolled over. What a horrible night. He hadn't slept more than a couple hours.

Lying flat on his back, he stared up at the ceiling, wondering about the dread pulsating through his veins. Something was stirring in the world. Something at The Haven. Again, he recognized it as something *evil.* He hated that term.

So many people gave it a religious connotation. He didn't. He defined the term as those who had no remorse, no conscious, no caring for the numerous people they hurt, tortured and killed. Evil wasn't a force from some horrible underworld. It was the force inside people that allowed them to act in horrible ways. He turned to his latest painting hanging on the wall opposite and talked to it.

"The Haven is the center of it all – why?" The painting and the empty room offered no answer, but it didn't stop him from thinking out loud.

"How can such negativity exist in such a warm, positive environment? The answer: It can't. Maddy's Floor should be a deterrent for this type of energy." Sitting, he pursed his lips. By the very laws of nature, that negativity would have to change and become more positive. Therefore, the negative energy isn't in the bubble – yet – but it's attracted to it, like a moth to a flame. The lovely healing energy Maddy is working hard to maintain for her patients is also a lure for this other energy.

Only how would anyone know unless they practiced energy work? Then they'd know, as the very energy would call to them. However, The Haven had stringent admission requirements for Maddy's Floor. It had to. Anything less would destroy the delicate balance.

Then again, he surmised this energy wasn't on the floor itself – or at least not inside the bubble.

He froze. The colors in the painting shifted ever so slightly.

Something here held a glimmer of truth. What if someone made it onto Maddy's Floor, someone who shouldn't have? What difference would that make? Would it shift the delicate balance between health and disease? Good and bad? Would it be enough to open a tear in the energy field? Or would it widen the rent that already existed?

He needed to talk to Maddy.

Throwing back the blankets, he swung his legs over the side and sat up.

And froze.

A vision snaked through his mind. Black curtains dropped before his eyes, taking him out of his reality into the world in-between. Then the curtain ripped back, showing him his new surroundings.

He blinked several times at the cheerfully bright, yet soothing walls staring back at him. The Haven. Blinking again, he found himself on Maddy's Floor. The vision showed him nothing unusual. Here, the energy had lightness, and a warmth he recognized as Maddy's signature.

He circled the floor, wondering what the vision was attempting to show him. The new wing sat outside the main bubble. There the energy was slightly less warm, less healing and definitely less energized. He frowned. There were several beds out there, only the people in them weren't included in the same healing bubble as the rest of the floor. The bubble wall between the two areas held strong and pulsated with a joyous blue radiance.

One bed touched the inside of the healing bubble. That would need to be fixed. It was a child. Stefan went there first. Maddy's heart would break if she weren't able to help the little one. The child's meridian pathways throbbed with power, and although thinner than he'd like to see, there was a determination that reassured him. She might be one of the lucky ones – brought to Maddy just in time.

Studying the energy layers, Stefan found two black spots sitting low on the first chakra. Both blended in together, easy to miss and big enough to cause problems. Maddy needed to start working on them right away.

He turned his attention to the two males in the new wing. Distracted by a sudden movement out of the corner of his eye, he noticed a small black thread under one of the beds. The strand, so black, so shiny, so full of life, its very presence throbbed. *What the hell?*

Stefan tried to move closer and couldn't. The vision froze him in place. The thread snaked out from under the bed, sliding maybe six inches before retreating until it completely disappeared. Stefan knew it sat underneath, waiting.

This is why he had been drawn here.

Just like his paintings, the black wispiness hid under the bed.

The thread slipped out again to wind around the metal leg of the bed.

It stopped. Then in a snake-like motion, it raised its head and appeared to stare in his direction.

Stefan shook his head. No. Not possible. No way could it see him. There's no way anyone had the strength, the skill to actually do that. God, he hoped not.

The snake's head never wavered.

Then it lunged.

Shocked, Stefan reared back and snapped through multiple dimensions, before finally slamming back into his body and his bedroom. The world wavered, distorted, and then finally sucked back into place with a loud pop. The last image he'd seen was the black snake-like thing heading toward the child's bed.

Stunned, Stefan barely moved. He focused on trying to catch a breath. His chest was so constricted he could barely gulp air. Everything in his room appeared the same, except for the goose bumps taking over his skin, and the chills racing down his spine.

Shaking, he reached for his cell phone.

MADDY'S PANICKED ARRIVAL at The Haven was less than stellar. Still shaken from the convoluted information Stefan had delivered over the phone – way too early for her brain to grasp – she took the elevator to the top floor. The place was deserted. It wasn't even six in the morning. Stefan had woken her from a deep sleep with his confusing message, sending her racing back to work.

Something about a black thread that had been as aware of Stefan's out of body journey as Stefan had been aware of it. Somehow, it connected to one of the two new arrivals in the renovated space. She hadn't had a chance to rebuild the energy on the floor to the levels that existed before Jansen's death. Felicia's arrival would have aggravated the balance as well. Extending the bubble to the new area wasn't something she'd complete overnight. At least not alone.

Maybe Stefan would help her widen the boundaries of the protected space, or create a secondary space. She didn't know the right way to move forward.

The current bubble had taken months to establish. The new area needed to vibrate at the same frequency as the older established area before both could be joined into one all-encompassing system. The process needed either more energy workers or more time.

Better yet, both.

The elevator crawled to a stop. She stepped onto her floor and stopped, assessing the energetic atmosphere and balance of the floor. Jansen's death had caused a ripple effect, though most others wouldn't recognize it. And it was to be expected. It wasn't like this was their first death on the floor.

Yet underneath all this energy, was a faint suggestion of something else. She leaned against the wall and closed her eyes. Something was wrong. How else could she describe the odd sensation? Stefan would help her, but only if he knew what they were dealing with. He'd told her to find out as much as possible this morning.

He'd ordered her to move Felicia's bed further into the protected area, and away from the bubble edge, no matter what.

"Dr. Maddy, are you all right?"

She opened her eyes. "I guess. At least I hope so." Walking toward the nurses' station, she delivered a reassuring smile to the two women watching her.

Gerona walked closer. "Bad night?"

Maddy shrugged off her jacket, hooking it over her shoulder. "Bad morning, actually."

"Well, for once, we had a good night. All the patients appear to have recovered their equilibrium and most everyone slept well."

Unlocking her office door, Maddy threw her a big cheery smile. "Now that's a good start to my day. No bad turns in the night? No calls for medics, nothing?"

"Nope. All calm."

"Great." Maddy strode over to the blinds, moved them aside and opened the windows, letting the fresh air filter through the small room. Then she made a quick dash to Felicia's room. Stopping at the entranceway, she saw Felicia, sound asleep on her left. Maddy shifted her vision. Carefully, going from side to side, she searched for any anomaly in the area.

Spinning around, she considered the position of Felicia's bed. It was in the protected healing bubble, only damn close to the edge. Too close. Maddy would take care of that as soon as possible, as Stefan suggested.

Everything seemed clear. Then she stepped into the new wing.

The air had an odd flatness to it. As if something weird had played out on the ethers. There was no discernible odor, not that she'd been expecting one. Still...something was off. She quietly checked on both sleeping patients. Their energy was clear, calm.

Striding back toward the nurses' center, she ordered the shifting of Felicia's bed and said, "I need to head down to security and check out that the new camera feeds are working. Hold my calls for a bit, will you?"

Once at the main office, she stepped into the security room, with its wall of monitors and counter of computers. She wanted to speak with Jean Paul, the man who headed the security department. He preferred the morning shift, but he rarely left on time. Most long-term care facilities had minimal security, but with the hospital attached and Maddy's project, it had been beefed up several years ago.

"Good morning, Dr. Maddy. Figures that you'd be in so early. I suppose you'd like to see how the new cameras are working upstairs, huh?" Jean Paul was small in stature with the charm of ten men. She liked him and his wife for the genuine people they were. That Jean Paul worked hard to keep The Haven secure and running smoothly was an added bonus.

"Yes, please. I presume they're functioning properly?"

"Of course. I always run a check on new equipment." He shrugged. "And as they were, I haven't checked since."

"I'd like to run through last night, if you don't mind."

"Sure enough." He motioned to a monitor on the wall. "I'll set up the digital feed here." He fiddled with a series of knobs and dials, punched in the date she wanted, then stopped and looked at her. "Is there one camera you'd like to see over another?"

"The one in the newly renovated section."

"Good." He made several adjustments before asking, "Any time frame in particular?"

Maddy pondered for a quick second. "If I don't have to watch in real time, then I'd like to go through the entire night." She turned to look at him. "But if it's like eight hours of sitting and watching, then no. I really would like to see around four to five am this morning."

"You can go as fast as you like." He reached forward and pointed out the controls for her. "Here is fast forward. You can slowly move forward or speed up until you reach a specific hour by watching this clock here. Then you can slow it back down or stop it altogether."

"That's perfect, thank you." Maddy pulled up an empty chair, waited until the digital feed started, then she sped it up slightly, watching as nurses went through their normal shifts. Maddy watched herself as she crossed in front of the camera lens on the way to speak with Felicia's mother, then Adam Lenning and John McNeil.

So far, all appeared normal.

She continued to watch, recognizing the hour when she'd gone home and left The Haven in the capable hands of the night shift. Hours passed by in a continuous, rarely disturbed mode. Adam got up and used the bathroom around three. She noticed how stiffly he moved. He made it back to bed without incident.

John shifted restlessly in his bed, for no apparent reason that she could see. He might not have taken a sleeping pill and that might account for his tossing and turning. She'd check when she went back upstairs. The video didn't allow much energy reading. In fact, she wasn't sure she'd be able to see much at all. The wee hours of the morning disappeared in a flash. Maddy thought she might have been wasting her time but then something odd flashed on screen.

She hit the stop button, backed up the feed and then went forward at a snail's pace. The area up by the ceiling showed a snowy fleck that hadn't been there before. She wondered if it represented Stefan's astral body. It wasn't obvious what it was. Most people wouldn't even recognize it was there unless it was pointed out. She'd been looking for it. Freezing the frame, she turned to ask Jean Paul about it, only to find he'd left the room.

She started the feed again. The snowy projection moved slightly, shifting, almost rippling as though floating on a breeze wafting through the room. Then it appeared to stop, freeze in place.

The camera didn't give a close-up of the snowy image or of the end of the bed in its view. There. She rewound the feed and bent close to the monitor. The picture was clear, except she couldn't make another item out.

What was at the foot of the bed? Something black popped up then slid back under. To Jean Paul, it would likely appear as a fault in the film or a dirt smudge, but to Maddy, it was something else entirely. That's what Stefan had seen in his vision.

She sat back. This black thread was under John McNeil's bed.

The snow flecks disappeared from one frame to the next, however, the black smudge stayed, inching out in the direction of Felicia's bed. Maddy stared in horror until it shrank back in itself, as if unable to go out further.

She rewound it once again and stared at the foot of the bed as the feed replayed the same few minutes. Checking the time, she realized this had taken place at 5:14 am this morning. Stefan had called her around half past five. She scanned the rest of the film but there wasn't much more to see. The camera couldn't capture the space under John's bed or the other side of the bed.

John was dying, from unknown causes. And his health was declining faster than expected. Now she just might know why.

Yet, he'd just arrived. So this black energy couldn't have come with him. She'd seen it or something similar hanging over Jansen's bed days ago. Jansen's bed *had* been partially out of the bubble due to the renovations. That's when he'd been attacked. Therefore the energy had been here first, had a connection to Jensen and theoretically, as it went after John, the person doing this knew him as well.

What were the odds of that?

Too much conjecture. It was giving her a headache.

All she knew for sure right now was that the black energy had anchored itself to John. He may have harbored this thread-connection a long time. In fact, it would feel like his energy after all this time. Not that John would have noticed. Few people did. That this energy didn't have a happy, healthy feel to it didn't mean it was evil or bad. Everyone wanted something and this energy was no different.

Now if only she knew what it was and what it wanted.

SISSY SAT UP slowly, testing her bones and her muscles. She felt like Sissy today, not an invalid. The pain had diminished slightly, but not enough to notice and not enough to count on. She frowned.

Surely, her new health program should have had a stronger or at least a longer-acting effect. As much as she was delighted with her obvious progress, it also pissed her off that she wasn't getting to the end of this road faster.

Every time she seemed to make a step forward, she slipped back several steps. She had to change that, and fast. Her patience was running out. Everyone else here was dying. It might be contagious.

She giggled. Her deathbed humor brightened her spirits.

"My, aren't we in a good mood today." The nurse bustled around, wrapped the blood pressure cuff on Sissy's arm and checked her temperature at the same time. Those tasks done, the nurse patted her arm and walked to the next bed.

Twenty minutes later, breakfast was served.

Sissy played with the food. Only ate because she needed the energy. She hadn't even finished before an aide, an older woman who looked like she should have retired years ago, showed up and began laying out clothes and makeup.

She sat and complied through the woman's hurried ministrations. Sissy wondered how the aides managed to keep up this pace all day. The staff was overworked and underpaid, the cliché of today's lifestyle. Everyone raced as if the world would end before nightfall. She didn't understand it.

Still, she was in a race too – a race against death.

MADDY STRODE TOWARD Gerard's office, her long gray tunic swishing from side to side. Endless questions streamed through her mind. The security tapes had added more of them. She had to do something. Her mind was ready to explode. Gerard was the target she'd chosen to vent some of her frustration. John was an issue – and he shouldn't be.

"He's on the phone, Dr. Maddy," Sandra said to her as she stormed to Gerard's door. "I don't think he wants to be disturbed."

She came to a dead stop and spun on her heels. Narrowing her gaze, she stared at Sandra. "Any idea how long he's going to be?"

"Not too long. He's arguing with someone again."

Maddy wrinkled her nose. Great, if he were already arguing, he'd be primed for a fight. She thought about that for a brief moment, only to realize she relished the idea. She'd been brooding over this since reading John's charts. Someone had bent the rules to get him onto her floor and in so doing, had jeopardized the project's integrity.

She smiled, showing her teeth. "No problem. I'll wait."

"Ohh. You want a piece of him too, huh? He's not having a good day." She perked up as a light on her phone console went out. "He's off. You can go in."

"Thanks." Maddy opened the door.

"I'm busy."

Maddy ignored his blustery yell.

"Too bad. I think you can find the time to see me." Maddy strode across the spacious office and took a seat in the chair facing Gerard's desk. She glared at him. "I've left several messages, so you should have expected me."

Gerard took one look at her and groaned. "Now what?"

"What kind of blackmail did John pull to make it onto my floor?" At the word blackmail, all the color disappeared from Gerard's face, making his pallor an almost perfect match to his white dress shirt. Maddy raised an eyebrow in surprise. Her off-the-cuff words had an effect that she hadn't expected. Interesting. As much as she'd said underhanded methods had been used, she hadn't really given serious thought to specifics.

"Sorry. What?" Gerard's gaze touched her face briefly before dropping down to his desk.

"I'm asking how and why John McNeil made it onto my floor?"

He glared at her, bravado written all over his face. "Maddy, you don't have ultimate control over who comes and who goes through The Haven."

She stared at him...hard. He dropped his gaze again, his fingers turning a pen over and over.

"What did you just say?" she asked softly, not sure what he was implying. The process was in place for many reasons. To say she didn't have ultimate control was true. Yet, if she didn't have the power to say who she could help and who she couldn't, why was she doing this project at all?

"Now, Maddy. Don't get upset. I didn't mean to imply that your vote isn't important. But sometimes there are extenuating circumstances..."

"Really." She crossed her legs and stared at him in disbelief. "That would make sense if we're talking about The Haven as a whole, but not for my floor. There were requirements for me starting this project, if you care to remember." Her voice rose as her anger flared. "John is more than welcome on any other floor. However, he does not fit on mine. He doesn't fit the health criteria in any way, and I'd like to know exactly why you decided to let him in."

His chin jutted out, his eyes narrowing in defiance "And I'm not going to tell you. I have to run this place based on many different factors, not just your criteria."

"Is that so?" Maddy stood up. "I guess we'll see about that. The success of this project, the extra money pouring into The Haven, is based on the results that I can produce. There are many reasons for the exacting criteria to get into the third-floor project, as you well know. I set the standards to make the program not only a success, but so it can be sustainable. And if you're not going to honor that..." She let the threat hang in the air.

Gerard bolted upright, alarm spreading across his face. He held his hands out as if he could stop her by that very motion. "Whoa, there's no need to become hostile here, Maddy. You don't want to do anything that might affect the long-term success of The Haven."

"Like you did? You've put my entire project – a project that paid for this new wing expansion, entirely by donations of these generous people, I might add – at risk. Do you know how many offers I've had to leave here and set up elsewhere? The inducements?" She gave him a hard look. "I refused the last one because I care about what I've built here. I care about my patients here. I care about what I can do here. However, if you are going to sell beds to the highest bidders and completely ignore what I can sustain – thereby destroying everything we've created – I'll go somewhere else where I can help patients without interference."

Gerard tugged at his shirt collar before finally loosening his tie and unbuttoning the top button of his shirt. "Dr. Chandler, by any chance?"

Watching Gerard sweat made her feel much better. About time. After what he'd done, he needed a reality check. "Dr. Chandler is very persuasive. I don't want to have to start all over again, but if you keep undermining my system, I will. If my energy is spread too thin to help my patients, the program is ruined."

Gerard gulped, then leaned forward earnestly. "Then leave John out of the project. Think of him as an isolated incident. He's on the same floor, only not on *your* floor," he wheedled. "And I'm sorry. It won't happen again."

She didn't believe it. How typical. Threaten the money and he crumbled. "It's not that easy. I can't exclude him. Energy is malleable to a certain extent so he'll benefit from being close."

"There's nothing wrong with it benefiting him, is there? The man's dying. If he gets a few extra weeks by being there, surely that's a good thing."

"A few extra weeks – the man's death will still be around the corner. Putting him into the program skews the result because he doesn't fit the criteria. Not to mention the effect his death will have on the other patients. You know that." She was frustrated and wanted him to know. "You did this on purpose, and I want to know why."

Goaded, Gerard snapped. "I didn't have any choice." He glared at her. "Our budgetary requirements are unbelievable right now. John offered to pay – and in a big way, I might add – for some necessary equipment. My hands were tied and we needed his money to help other patients. Okay?"

Maddy shifted back down into her chair. Gerard's face had blown into a cherry red color and the lines of his face had deepened with anger. She'd been right. John had bought his way in, an easy trick to play on the moneyman.

Maddy wasn't sure how she felt about everything now. That he'd sacrifice her trials was unacceptable. To lose necessary equipment due to a lack of funding? That didn't make sense either.

She stared at Gerard, who shifted like a truant child waiting for his punishment. What were the options? Could she keep John out of the project? He was in the renovated area with Adam Lenning. For the moment, that *was* outside the research floor's boundary.

And Felicia had been included in the trial. That was a good thing, as she had the potential for remarkable improvement – in fact, she'd shown wonderful stabilization, as of this morning. Maddy had high hopes she'd make a complete recovery.

Mentally, Maddy sorted the possibilities before she gave in. She didn't know what would be more debilitating to the other patients, to have John removed right now or to have him die within weeks of arriving. They wouldn't have much contact with each other. He wasn't in the same area, and not mobile enough to make use of the common areas.

Patients who died after being there for a while had a much

bigger impact on the others. They might just think John's illness had advanced too far when he arrived. Hell, that's exactly what she'd thought herself.

Now she wasn't so sure. The black energy hanging around him could be interfering with his health and recovery.

What the hell, she might as well include him in the energy. Besides, it would take a meaner doctor than she was to kick him out. Especially as she'd seen the possibility of a way to help him.

However, she also owed the people that had put their trust in her. She couldn't let the investors or her patients down. Her project was valuable and to lose the investors was to sideline the project. And that would slow the number of people she could help.

Maddy gave in and stood up. "I'll see what I can do. Don't do it again. This isn't what our investors want and I won't turn a blind eye again. I can understand the temptation to let patients buy their way in, but no more. They can damn well buy their way onto another floor."

She glared at him, not liking the gleam of hope in his eyes. If she let him get away with this, there'd be no end to his meddling in her affairs. "Do you understand? Don't get smug. That offer I refused won't go away for a long time."

Gerard bounded to his feet, relief washing over his face. He walked around the desk, his arm outstretched. "I promise, this one time only. Thank you." He clasped her hand with both of his, shaking it with fervent enthusiasm. "Thanks, Maddy. I really appreciate this."

"I mean what I said," she snapped, afraid he hadn't understood the severity of his actions. "No more going behind my back."

He grinned, the perfect salesman persona back in place. "I know, I know. I promise."

Pulling her hand free, she jabbed her finger at him, wanting him to understand how wrong he'd been and the severity of his actions. "And see that you don't forget it."

Maddy walked back out. Sandra smiled at her. "I see you know how to handle him, too."

"We'll see if my 'handling,' as you call it, is successful." She motioned to the closed door behind her. "He's definitely a wild card."

"Only if you give him rein. Hold tight and he's not bad. Give him too much rope and that boy will get into trouble every time…" Sandra's tone was light and airy, but with serious undercurrents.

Maddy's mood plummeted. Damn Gerard and his conniving ways. That he should put her project at risk for a bit of money was untenable. It had been unbelievably difficult to get this off the ground in the first place. To jeopardize it now... She tried to shrug off her mood.

Balance, peace and everything nice were what she needed as her focus. It was impossible to keep any type of healing energy flowing if there was a disturbance in her own mind – especially as she needed to do energy work right now.

Back in her office, she switched off her lights, switched on her music and took up a comfortable position on the floor.

Her mantra. Peace. Happiness. Joy.

Surprisingly, it only took a few minutes to go into a meditative state, where she consciously dropped the accumulated tension from her spine, unspoken words from her mind and the less-than-ideal emotions from her heart. She slowly deepened her state. Drifting down lower, she went even deeper until she slid out from this reality. Focusing on the people in her care, Maddy detached from her physical reality and moved out in her astral form. This was a common form of travel, usually done by people during their dream state. While in this state, and though generally involuntary, people often visited people and places they loved...and hated.

To do this consciously wasn't something one learned overnight.

For the first few seconds, she stretched, enjoying the sense of freedom. This reality left every opportunity open, the imagination unbelievable in its scope, the possibilities limitless. She knew from experience that she'd lose hours here, wallowing in this other existence. She also knew she wouldn't be able to stay here alone in her office without being disturbed for too long.

It was time to get to work.

JOHN DIDN'T FEEL too good. No. It was more like he didn't expect to ever feel good again. He'd achieved something he'd plotted, agonized over and had been striving for since he'd first fallen ill. For what? He'd bought his way in and had managed to piss off Dr. Maddy. Worse, she might not be able to help him. After all he'd done, defeat left a bitter taste in his mouth.

A specter of death hung over him. Sure, he might not die today or tomorrow, yet within a few months he'd be gone. His stomach almost heaved at the thought.

Darkness seemed to cover his world and his soul. He snorted, the sound so light as to be irrelevant if anyone else heard. That's how he felt these days, insignificant and unimportant, as if he had nothing left to offer.

A hot tear welled at the corner of his eye. John rolled his face into the pillow. He hated feeling so weak and helpless. He wasn't a goddamn wuss. He wasn't. And he wouldn't be. He refused.

Good, John. Don't give in. Don't give up.

John bolted upright, wincing at the pain as he did so. "Who's there? Who said that?"

His corner of the floor was empty except for that other doctor working on Adam over by the far wall. John sank back down. "Great, now I'm hearing things."

A light, tingling laughter filled the air. John's eyes narrowed. "Dr. Maddy?"

No answer.

Neither did she materialize around the corner. John searched around again. He didn't know what the hell was happening. The air warmed and lightened around him. A soothing heat slipped into his toes and worked its way slowly, inch by worn-out inch, up his legs. His knees throbbed when the heat reached them, making them feel good. Stronger. Something they hadn't felt like in years. He lay there, enjoying the healing power or whatever was going on. This had to be the secret of Dr. Maddy's floor.

Whatever it was, it felt real. It felt good.

The warmth reached his spine. He moaned in relief as the constant chaffing and brittleness in his bones eased. He didn't know what was happening, why or by whom but he was so damn grateful he didn't care. Prone and at peace, John lay in awe. So great was his joy, tears of wonder streamed down his cheeks. His poor body thrummed with healing effervescence.

As the heat slipped higher and higher, his heart calmed, his blood pulsed stronger, yet with serenity. The healing energy shifted, finally encompassing his face and head. His eyes closed. He rejoiced in the warmth bathing them from the inside. As the heat hit the top of his head, it seeped ever upward, as if squeezing through the very pores at the top of his head. He wanted the sensation to stay, the heat to turn around and slide down again, yet somehow he knew it wouldn't.

I will come again.

Tears streaked down the side of his face, only instead of feeling sad, John felt only grace and thankfulness.

Remember, find joy and acceptance in life and appreciate all that you have.

"Thank you," he whispered softly, afraid to dispel the magic of the moment.

Soft beautiful laughter tickled the air.

He felt a deep connection with the voice. Nothing lustful or lover-like. Instead, it was spiritual – something he never would have expected. He hadn't given the New Age crap any airtime in his world, and now all he could do was lie in his bed in amazement, wondering at the most beautiful experience of his life. He floated on that wave of wellness, until a sigh climbed his spine and escaped, taking with it years of toxic emotions, stress and negativity. He sank deeper and deeper into the feeling.

His last thought before succumbing to sleep was of Dr. Maddy.

What a class act.

WEDNESDAY EVENING

A HARD KNOCK sounded on the office door.

"Dr. Maddy? Are you in there? It's been over an hour."

Silence.

"Dr. Maddy?" The knock became a pounding. The doorknob twisted uselessly. The door was locked. "Maddy!" This time, the door rattled as the person on the other side tried to get in.

Maddy heard the noise, she understood the concern, but she hadn't returned to a functional enough state to answer Nancy.

"I'm here," she croaked out in a whisper, barely audible over the music still streaming throughout her room in soft muted tunes. She uncurled slowly from the yoga position she'd been twisted into for the last hour or so. Blood rushed through the veins in her legs and up her spine. She stretched, waited another quick moment, and tried her voice again.

"Nancy, I'm back. Everything's fine."

"Jesus, Maddy, don't do that to me. You promised you'd never lock this door again." She heard the sound of a heavy sigh, followed by a thunk as if Nancy dropped her forehead against the door. Or maybe it was her fist.

Maddy finished stretching and opened her eyes. After drawing a deep breath, she walked to the door and unlocked it.

As she opened the door, Nancy slumped against the doorjamb, staring at her grimly. "Jesus, you scared the crap out of me."

Smiling, Maddy tried to reassure her. "Sorry. This ended up being a pretty intense session."

Nancy huffed. "That's it. If you won't keep this room unlocked during your sessions, then I want a set of keys."

That was probably a good idea. Maddy's smile slipped. "I'll get you a set. I'm still feeling the effects of this session."

"Coffee. Your blood has peace, quiet and oxygen flowing through. It can't comprehend the lack of caffeine." Nancy eyed the counter area with its coffee maker. "I'll make you a fresh pot."

"You only want a cup for yourself." Maddy let Nancy propel her out to the small balcony. She took several deep breaths, feeling her blood pulse with life as it always did after a strong healing session. Basking in the sun, she waited another long moment to allow her awareness to fully return. When Nancy brought the coffee, she took a seat beside her in the shade to enjoy it.

"What happened this time that you went so deep?"

Maddy closed her eyes for a moment, letting the residual power flow through her body. "Nothing odd, just incredibly powerful. I haven't had a session like that for a while."

"Who were you working on this time?"

Opening her eyes, Maddy glanced at Nancy. "Several people. Felicia and John, the new patients, then some maintenance and tweaks on most of the others. I didn't make it through half of the patients though. I'll do another session this afternoon or tomorrow morning and see if I can touch the rest."

"Don't overdo it. You know how much this takes from you. Too bad management doesn't understand that."

"Hah, you wish." Maddy refused to rise to the bait. The two of them had been close friends for years. They often shared dinner, had coffee or rode bikes together on days off. Nancy was permanently watching her weight and Maddy was always eating – and getting skinnier – a contrast that drove Nancy nuts.

During the years of their friendship, Nancy had married and divorced and Maddy had gone through a couple of boyfriends. Through it all, they'd shared most things, especially their laughter and their tears.

"That's because they don't understand what goes on here." Maddy explained about the idea of blackmail. "John's arrival being the end result."

Nancy screwed up her face in exasperation, the words bursting out. "Unbelievable. If you don't get the results, then the donations dry up and not even the brass will have jobs. Yet, they let in the wrong people." Nancy sipped her coffee. "Good for John, I suppose, *if* you can help him. However, this shouldn't become healthcare available only to the rich and generous."

The coffee had cooled enough to drink. Maddy thought for a moment before answering. She took a long sip, reveling in the dark roasted flavor. "Gerard means well. But he likes the shine of gold." She refused to let the reminder of how John had arrived mar the peace and contentment coursing through her. "Anything going on while I was busy?"

"No, all's well." Nancy looked at Maddy over her cup. "That cute detective popped in, asking about you."

Startled, she almost spilled her coffee. "Drew?"

Nancy turned her full attention to Maddy's face. "Drew, is it? Interesting."

Heat rose on Maddy's cheeks. She hadn't meant to say Drew's name in quite that tone of voice. "We had coffee last night." And they were heading out for dinner tonight, only she didn't want to share that tidbit yet. "Did he leave a message?" she asked casually, shifting her legs. Perhaps a little too casually. She hoped Nancy wouldn't notice.

"Are you expecting one? Is there something going on here?" Nancy's grin widened. Her knowing gaze gave her a mischievous look.

Maddy didn't want to share her plans. She held the dinner date private, close to her heart. She couldn't imagine the relationship going anywhere, but there was nothing like the bloom of attraction in its initial stages.

"What was that look for?"

Maddy turned wide eyes to Nancy. "What?"

Nancy shifted so she could stare into Maddy's eyes. "Oh, wow." Nancy positively bounced. "You're really fascinated by the detective, aren't you?"

Maddy tried to appear interested in the garden. The sunlight danced on the bright white roses until they dominated the garden below. An unusual effect. She glanced at her friend. "I might be a little attracted. I mean, the guy's taller than me. You know how I feel about that."

"Yeah. For you, they're hot. For me, they're impossibly tall." Nancy stared down at her stubby legs. "You two can't get together. Your babies would be giraffes."

"Hah. Better than you and him. You'd have to use a stepladder to kiss him."

"Nah, I'd knock his knees out from under him. He's a good-looking hunk."

"Go find your own. He's mine."

"I knew it."

"Shit," Maddy groaned, caught by her own quick mouth. "Fine, okay. I'm interested." Maddy sipped her coffee, barely holding back her smirk.

"Yup, I thought so. So where are you going for dinner and are you taking him home afterwards?"

"Chinese. And I don't know." Maddy rolled her head back to study the sky. "Crap. Me and my big mouth."

Nancy howled. "You never were any good at keeping anything back."

Just then, the emergency alarms crashed through their peaceful idyll.

Cardiac arrest.

Both women raced down the hallway.

The nurses shouted out the bed number as they raced past. Number 364. Maddy's mind raced. Bed 364 was Adam Lenning. The code team converged ahead of Maddy, with two of her nurses already doing two-person CPR. Even as she joined them, the crash board went under him as the team efficiently went into action. Once monitors and IV were hooked up, Adam was bagged, and the first of the drugs administered. Maddy coordinated the resuscitation efforts, grateful that Gerard had followed through on her demands a couple years ago to updating the nurses' training – particularly on the AED units. For several frantic moments, they all worked on Adam.

Everyone watched for a heart rate. The irregular pulse was sweet. Now with any luck, they'd shock it into a regular beat. The defibrillator nurse stepped up. One shock. Nothing.

"Again."

A strong rhythmic pattern moved across the monitor. A sigh of relief swept the group.

"Okay, he's back." Maddy stepped back, surveying the organized chaos that always accompanied a code blue. Her document nurse was furiously writing everything up. She would need to contact Adam's family and let them know that he would be transferred to the hospital side for further tests. A warmed blanket was placed over his chilled flesh.

"I wonder what brought that on." Nancy stepped back over to Maddy's side. "How was he this morning?"

"He's one of the ones I didn't get to." And damned if she didn't feel guilty about that. There's no guarantee that she might have been able to hold off this attack even if she had reached him earlier. But that didn't stop her from her wondering.

"He doesn't have any history of heart problems."

Maddy looked up from the chart in her hand. "He does now." Glancing back, she examined Adam's energy level thoroughly. The orderlies had arrived and the cardiologist, who would order a battery of tests, had been notified. Adam was stabilized – for now.

Maddy wanted to know what had brought on the attack, and whether that black energy had anything to do with it.

It wasn't unusual for energy to build up to a critical point where the balance tipped in favor of mass development. There'd been no indication Maddy's Floor had reached that point. In fact, with the renovations disturbing everyone, the energy humming throughout the floor had actually thinned. But was it thin enough to allow someone through? She'd kept the energy wall thick and strong so the healing energy could resonate, but the expansion of the new wing had changed that and the new patients had also affected it. Heart attacks were an all too possible result. She'd have to do a session on Dr. Lenning tonight or tomorrow. Who knew what she might find.

Her energy work was going deeper now, faster, and even more smoothly. She'd been surprised at the sheer enjoyment John had felt during his session. Often, patients had no awareness while she was working on them – especially new ones. His awareness had increased her enjoyment, which had thereby increased the power of the session. It had been a pleasure this morning.

Another oddity slipped back into her mind.

What she hadn't felt was evidence of any debilitating disease racing throughout his body. She frowned. Every person reacted differently to illnesses and in John's case, there'd certainly been a lot going on. She'd expected that, except his pain level had hit her hard and she'd gone straight into healing mode to help him feel better instead of analyzing the problems – like she had with Felicia. But she needed to find out what his health issues were, or she'd never be able to sort out the best ways to help him. She had to go back in as soon as possible. And she needed to check for that black thread.

THE NEWS FILTERED downstairs. Gerard was speaking with the nutritionist when one of the staff approached them with the news. Adam had worked at The Haven for years. Staff and patients knew him, although not everyone liked him.

Shock socked him in the gut. *Shit.*

"He's pulled through, apparently. Dr. Maddy was on the spot."

"Good. He's a good man."

The nurse stared at him, one eyebrow raised. "I'm not one to speak ill of the dead and in his case, the almost dead; however, Dr. Lenning…a good man? That is debatable. He's damn lucky Dr. Maddy tried as hard as she did to revive him. Many in her position, with their history, wouldn't have."

And that's how the gossip would go. There'd be the critics that wondered why she'd brought him back after he'd been such a thorn in her side. Then there'd be others who knew that Maddy would do nothing but her best. And her best was pretty damn spectacular.

"Unless there's a no revive order, you know we have to try."

"And she did and it worked. I wonder how happy Adam will be when he wakes up."

Gerard listened quietly as various staff members discussed Adam Lenning's medical condition. Adam wasn't an easy person to begin with.

He excused himself from the now-raging discussion on life and death issues. In a place like The Haven, there was never an end to these discussions. They stormed one way, then the next, as fickle as the wind and the individuals that came and went.

Two hours later, he found Dr. Maddy at Adam's bedside. He appeared to be sleeping comfortably.

"Is he going to be okay?"

She nodded. "The cardiologist is running tests."

Just then, Adam's eyes opened, unfocused and with widened pupils. He stilled, and then searched for something that obviously disturbed him.

Maddy approached him, her hand on his shoulder. "Take it easy, Dr. Lenning. You've had a heart attack. Please stay calm."

His eyes locked on hers. "Where is it?" His voice trembled with the effort to speak. "I don't want it to get me."

Gerard exchanged glances with Maddy.

"What's after you, Adam?" Gerard stepped to the other side of the bed. "Did you see it? Can you describe it to me?"

"Yes." His voice dropped to a mere whisper. "It was a snake."

Dread filtered through Maddy. A snake. The black energy or a hallucination? Some drugs might cause hallucinations as side effect. She didn't see anything listed here that would do that. There'd been no change in his medication. Her frown deepened.

"When did you see the snake?"

Gerard frowned at her. "We don't have snakes loose in The Haven."

Maddy ignored him. "Adam, talk to me. Where and when did you see this snake?"

Calming down, as if realizing the snake must have been long gone or was no threat when they were there, Adam's eyes became less wild looking and more focused. He took a deep breath. "Gerard said it, didn't he? There are no snakes here."

"Still, I'd like to know what you saw." Maddy kept her voice gentle but firm.

He took another deep breath. "I thought I saw a black snake twisting around the end of my bed. It was thin and had no discernible markings. All I can say is I *seriously* thought it was there."

Gerard frowned, yet stayed quiet at Maddy's warning hand signal.

"How did the snake make you feel?" She ignored the questioning glance he sent her way. The answer was more important than either of them knew.

Adam's response was instantaneous. "Cold. Icy. Empty. As if it were the end. That snake represented death, I know it. I just never expected the grim reaper to be so small."

MADDY RACED INSIDE her front door, locked it behind her and started tugging her clothes off as fast as she could. Turning on her shower, she slipped off her underclothes and stepped into the hot spray. Her shoulders dropped three inches as the water washed away the tension and pressure she'd felt as she tried to get out of the office. She wanted to melt under this heat for hours.

Except she had less than an hour, probably half that now, before Drew arrived. She shut off the water and toweled dry. Clutching the towel to her chest, she scanned the walk-in closet for the perfect outfit.

Five minutes later, she stood on one foot, chewing her bottom lip, no further along in her decision process. In a fit of frustration, she snatched up black skin-tight slacks with a tiny path of butterflies flying up the outside of one leg. Dropping her towel, she slid into red lace bottoms and matching bra that had butterflies racing across the swell of her breast. Pulling on the pants, she topped it with a long red-hot sweater that hung to mid-thigh. After adding a black belt around her waist and black and red earrings for accessories, she stepped to the mirror to check her reflection. Yes, she was ready for anything – but her sopping hair wasn't.

Checking her watch, she grabbed the blow dryer and attacked her hair. With only minutes to spare, she slid her feet into four-inch red heels with tiny straps at the toes. She stood straight up and grinned. Now she felt more like herself.

The doorbell rang.

Opening the door, she watched Drew's face as he took in her outfit.

"Wow." He stopped in his tracks, blatant male appreciation obvious in his gaze.

Tingles rippled up and down her spine. Excited, nervous, she found herself attacked by shyness. To help cover up, she asked, "Is this appropriate? I didn't want to dress up too much."

He was wearing a suit. She didn't know whether it was an evening suit or he'd just come from work.

"You look great. Are you ready?"

She nodded. "Let me grab my purse." Leaving the door open, she walked into the living room where she'd tossed it in her mad dash to the shower earlier. "Okay, I'm ready."

She turned to find Drew wandering the room, stopping to look at the artifacts of her life. He studied a huge, complex oil painting on her wall, then stepped back a couple of feet and frowned. His head tilted.

Maddy suppressed a smirk. "Like it?"

He took another step back and shook his head. Finally, he turned to her, his brow furrowed. "What is it?"

Motioning with her hand, she said, "Step over here."

Drew frowned. "The view's different from there?" Backing up toward her, he studied the painting again. Maddy studied him. Would he see the different faces when viewed from this side?

It took about ten seconds. Then lightning struck. He glanced at her, wonder in his eye. "What the hell? Is this for real?" Puzzled delight lit his features as he walked around her living room, keeping an eye on the picture. "Who created this?"

"Stefan Kronos."

"Never heard of him." He walked to the other side, his gaze never leaving the painting. Stunned comprehension washed over his face.

"Most people haven't." Maddy smiled in delight at his reaction. She loved how Stefan, using copious amounts of paint in a three-dimensional way, had made different faces shine through, depending on where you stood to view the painting.

"That is the most striking piece of art I've ever seen."

"Stefan's a dear friend. I thought that perhaps you had heard of him because he's quite famous in the law enforcement world. As a psychic."

"As a *what*?" He slid her a sideways glance. "Did you say psychic?" He glanced back at the painting. "I don't know how good his psychic skills are, but he's one hell of a painter."

"I think his psychic skills are second to none. He works with law enforcement agencies across the country." She walked toward the front door. "Are we ready to go?"

"What?" Drew had turned back to the painting. "Yes, yes. Let's head out."

He led the way to his truck parked out front. "We're heading to a new classy Asian restaurant downtown." Turning on the engine, he pulled the truck out into the traffic. The evening light was bright with an almost-full moon riding high. Recognizing a capable driver, Maddy crossed her legs at the ankles and relaxed back into the seat.

She was game. All Chinese was good to her. "Have you been to this restaurant before?"

"Not for a few months." He glanced at her in the dim interior. "You did want Chinese food?"

"Thank you. I'm looking forward to it."

"There's fresh seafood on the buffet."

"Oh yummm." Maddy rested her head back and closed her eyes. She so needed this tonight, just to have a break from all the problems – to not have to think about anything for a while. Then Nancy's question about taking Drew home with her tonight flitted into her mind.

She shouldn't. Short-term affairs weren't her thing. They didn't know each other very well either…

None of that really mattered. She wanted him. The single question floating through her mind – what did she want him as – a friend or a lover?

"Tough day?"

"Hmmm."

"Not to worry. Tonight you'll forget all about it."

At the smug tone of voice, she rolled her head toward him.

"Yeah? How's that?"

"We're going dancing afterwards."

Maddy sat up. "Really?"

At his grin, her stomach started to bounce. She didn't remember the last time she'd really let loose on the dance floor. Her toes wiggled. They were so going to get a work out tonight.

JOHN ROLLED OVER for the umpteenth time. Another bad evening. What the hell was wrong now? Today, he'd had one of the best days in a long time, and if he could get some sleep for once, he might actually heal.

He pulled up the blankets, shivering in the night. The lights never went out here. There were night-lights along the hallways, and street lights giving a glow outside. Tonight, the moon aggravated the problem. He should ask for a sleeping pill.

"Or not," he muttered to himself.

Why did the sound of his voice not give him the same comforting feeling it usually did?

He hunkered deeper and sighed. He couldn't sleep. He was too freakin' scared.

Scared of dying. Afraid of death itself. Terrified of what came after – if anything.

Not that acknowledging his feelings would change them. Death was waiting for him.

One of the lights in the hallway flickered, throwing eerie shadows on the walls in his room, crawling on the ceiling, dancing through the emptiness. His back stiffened. His breathing rasped unevenly.

This was stupid. He was a grown man – a cop, for God's sake. Too old and experienced in the ways of the world to let flickering lights scare him. Yet, nothing would stop the pit in his stomach from sinking. Something was out there.

John stared in the direction of the light, nervous, his stomach clenching. Closing his eyes, he gasped for breath, desperate to control his anxiety level before it controlled him. A second light flickered. He whimpered as the darkness encroached, coming ever closer to his bed. He squeezed his eyes tightly closed. His heart pounded against his chest, screaming warnings at him. Please, not tonight. He didn't want to die tonight.

The blackness approached.

THURSDAY EARLY MORNING

MADDY ATE HER way through the phenomenal buffet, then danced the night away at The Pandosy. Drew moved with the best of them, and she loved the chance to toss her stress away. They danced and laughed their way into the wee hours of the morning.

They closed the club and Maddy still felt like rocking. However, by the time Drew pulled up outside her condo complex, her adrenaline had seeped out through her toes. Her feet were killing her and although her heart sang with happiness, her body's song slid toward slumber.

"I had a phenomenal night. Thank you so much for the dancing. I had forgotten what fun it was." She'd danced his socks off.

Drew switched off the ignition, leaning his head back against the headrest. "Come on, I'll walk you to the front door."

Maddy smiled and unlocked her door. "Not required." She motioned toward her building. "It's right there. You can watch me walk the twenty feet. You're tired, too. Go home to bed. I'll be fine."

She watched the argument rise on his face, but he bit his lip and stayed quiet. *Good on him.* He was a protector and that was nice.

His long fingers grasped her chin. "Thank you for spending the evening," he said, glancing at the clock on the dashboard, "or maybe I should say – the night – with me." He grinned.

She smirked back at him. "You wish."

"I do," he whispered. "Are you sure?"

She leaned across and gave him a kiss on the cheek. At the last moment, Drew turned his head and her lips stroked across his. He held the kiss a brief moment, letting her taste him, get a feel for him. His lips teased yet didn't force, tantalized yet didn't take over.

She knew she had to leave before he tempted her more. And

he did tempt her. The man was dynamite, on and off the dance floor. "I'm sure." She smiled wickedly. "Then again, I'm not against a second date tomorrow?"

A light fired in his eyes. "Tomorrow," he promised. "One kiss to hold me until then." A tiny smile crinkled the corner of his eyes and he lowered his head again. This was no gentle good-bye. No longer was he enticing or teasing. A small part of her brain dimly wondered if he was giving her a taste of what she'd be missing. Then her brain shut down.

He took her mouth in a possessive full-on promise, ravaging her lips with his heat. Their tongues danced and plunged, tasted then retreated. He gently stroked her swollen lips, his tongue soothing but promising more heat to come...and then he left Maddy gasping.

The man was magic.

Trembling, she barely managed to open her eyes to stare at him in wonder when he set her away from him. A tic pulsed at the side of his stern mouth. Deep blue velvet pulsed deep in his gaze. Good, she wasn't the only one affected.

"Get inside. I can't promise to be good any longer." He reached up to caress her bottom lip with his thumb, while his gaze hungrily devoured her. "You belong under lock and key."

Maddy was charmed.

A noise jarred her from the spell. "My phone. Someone's calling me. At this hour?"

"Then you'd better answer it," he whispered against her ear.

Maddy cleared her throat once, then again. "Hello."

"Dr Maddy? This is Amber on night shift. I wasn't sure if I should call you or not, as technically he's Dr. Cunningham's patient, but we can't reach him."

"What's the matter?"

"It's John. He's awake and incoherent."

"Meaning he can't speak clearly, his speech is slurring or he can't talk, period?"

"All of them."

"I'm coming in. Keep trying Dr. Cunningham as well. Did you call Emergency?"

"Yes, someone's on the way."

"They should be there by now. Emergency is in the same building, for heaven's sake. Who's on tonight?"

"I don't know. I put in two calls, except the hospital is crazy busy with some multiple car pileup on the freeway."

"Right. That's where Dr. Cunningham will be. Check with the hospital. I'll be there in ten. Stay on John. Make sure his breathing doesn't become impaired and hook him up to the heart machine. It sounds like he's heading for a stroke. And call Emergency again." Maddy slammed the phone closed and snatched up her handbag.

"Problems?"

Maddy stared at him, surprised by the question. She shook her head to clear it. "Your uncle has taken a turn for the worse. I need to go."

Eyebrows raised, he never said a word. He put the truck in drive, checked the traffic and pulled out onto the main road.

Maddy sighed with relief. "Thank you."

"He's my family."

"Let's hope he's okay. I can't do anything over a phone."

He shot her a sideways glance. "Can you do anything at all at this point?"

She glanced at him, unsure of what to say. "Maybe. I don't know." God, now she was babbling. Making a sudden decision, she said, "I'll try."

"Try what?" Confusion colored Drew's voice. "I don't understand what you do."

"And you won't understand this, either." She shifted into a more comfortable position. "Don't touch me. Tell me when you have parked so I can come back out."

With that, Maddy's consciousness jumped out of her body.

"Back out? Out of what?"

She recognized the shock and worry clouding Drew's face as he glanced from her to the road and back again. She didn't have time to soothe his nerves. John needed her help. Right now.

As fast as she thought his name, Maddy zipped to John's bedside in her astral form. Gerona was there, checking his vitals. Dr. Cunningham, his normal gray hair tousled, appeared to have just shown up. With a concerned frown on his face and tablet in hand he checked something on the minicomputer. She glanced at the machinery that registered John's heart rate. His color had faded, showing there had been some trauma to his system.

John's energy shuffled in a sluggish movement among the sheets. Below the bed, however, snug against the floor, were faint remnants of a black, darker energy. And not much of it, either.

Gazing at the matrix of different energy fields mixing and blending, Maddy deciphered several other energies besides Gerona's and Dr. Cunningham's that she assumed belonged to other nurses, aides and visitors. Taking her time, she followed each energy pathway as they entered and left the area.

The black energy never left.

Even as she watched, it faded, starting to disperse slightly. Moving closer, she saw the broken hazy energy beneath John's bed had an aged appearance, as if it had been there for a while. Could this be the same snake-like blur Stefan had seen earlier and that she'd noticed on the film? If so, there was nothing snake-like about it now. This energy had shattered into globules versus normal dark energy that resembled a black heavy cloud. Sometimes, she identified dark lines within the clouds, woven through the fog like a spider web, which showed her the level of damage in the body she was scanning.

Here though, instead of spider webs, the blackness wobbled, like shiny gobs of Jell-O. She approached them, wondering about the shimmer deep inside each piece. They were almost pretty. Except looking at them made her stomach heave at their alien sense of wrongness.

She wanted to touch them, yet wasn't sure how they would react. She wished she understood what they were and where they'd come from – not to mention their relationship to John.

Surrounding John with white light, she poured healing energy into stabilizing his heart rate. Seconds later, the machines beside John showed he'd stabilized.

Relief flooded her.

"What the hell?" Dr. Cunningham stood at the machine, hands on his hips. "That's bizarre. What's the chance he was only having a bad dream?"

"He wasn't talking properly." Gerona picked up the chart and wrote down the current vitals. "Maybe we should wake him up and check again."

"We tried waking him and it didn't work," Dr. Cunningham snapped.

John moaned and snuffled, shifting his thin legs in bed.

"John, wake up. Talk to me." Gerona prodded his shoulder gently.

Maddy watched as John opened his eyes and frowned.

"What's everyone doing here? Am I dying?"

Dr. Cunningham snorted. "Not today. The nurses overreacted, as usual."

Gerona's face thinned at the criticism. She stayed silent. Maddy frowned. Dr. Cunningham had never been anything other than respectful in her presence. Then again, he probably wasn't himself because he'd been swamped at the ER because of the accident. He also hated being bothered with trivial things.

However, Gerona was an experienced nurse. If she said there was something off, then Maddy would believe her. Amber had been the one who'd called her, but on Gerona's urging.

Maddy took another long assessing glance at John. The white energy would hold for a few hours, maybe a day or two. Somehow, they had to deal with this dark energy, fast and permanently. In the distance, she could hear Drew calling to her. She disconnected from John.

"Maddy? Maddy, we're here at the hospital. Come back, please."

After a heavy pause while she struggled to shift through realities, she sensed him lean over her. Maddy opened her eyes.

DREW REARED BACK in surprise. "Jesus." He closed his eyes in relief before reaching over and kissing her hard. "I don't know what you did. Just don't do it again *ever*, please. That's bloody scary." The cop in him had wanted to call 911; he'd been unsure enough to wait it out. Thank heavens she'd woken up when she had, if waking up was the right term for this.

She sat up slowly, and then closed her eyes as color washed over her face before quickly receding. "I'm fine," she whispered. "Thanks."

"Good," he retorted. "I'm not. How's my uncle?"

"Dying."

"What? Now?" *Jesus.* He looked up at the imposing structure outside the truck window.

"No." She chuckled lightly. "That's not what I meant. There's something weird going on with him that I can't figure out."

"Will he make it through the night?" Drew studied her face closely, as if the answers to the universe rested there.

Maybe they did. He knew his own beliefs in life and death, evidence and cold facts, were slowly eroding. Maddy had him questioning everything he thought he knew. He didn't know what the result would be – he hoped Maddy would be there at the end.

"As far as I can tell, yes. However, there are no guarantees here, remember that."

He tugged her into his arms. "Got it. You're not God. You're one of His angels."

Her snort was muffled by his shirt. She nestled in closer. Drew squeezed her gently, enjoying the rare comfort of holding her tight. Chances were good she didn't let this happen very often. He'd like nothing more than to take her home and hold her close for the rest of the night. "Do we need to go inside still?"

"No." She yawned and lifted her head. "I think he's fine now. Besides, his doctor is there with him, so I'm no longer needed."

He stroked a large hand over her face, smoothing the tousled locks back behind her ears. "And what do you need?" Leaning closer, he peered into her eyes. "This has obviously taken a toll on you."

"It has. It doesn't always, though. Tonight, I have to admit, I am tired."

"Let's get you home."

Tucking her up against his side, Drew started his truck. Maddy mumbled a slight protest as he removed his arm from around her shoulders. "It's all right. I'm not going anywhere. However you, my dear, are going to bed."

Maddy smiled up at him. "Sounds good to me," she whispered sleepily.

Sounded good to him too, only she was beyond anything more than crashing. True to his word, Drew had her back to her apartment within minutes. This time though, there was no suggestion of letting her walk up on her own. Drew came around and opened the passenger door and helped her to her feet.

Attempting to get out of the vehicle and walk up the sidewalk, Maddy stumbled. Drew held her close, clasped her around the waist with one arm and guided her through the front door to the elevator. At her apartment, she fumbled for her keys. Pulling them out, she handed them over to Drew.

Once inside, he shut the door behind them and gave her a gentle push toward her bedroom. "Bedtime."

"I'm going. I'm going," she muttered, stumbling through the doorway. "Good night."

"I'm not going anywhere. I want to make sure you're all right."

Holding onto the doorframe, she twisted around enough to face him. Surprise lit her features. "I'm fine, honest. I did do some energy work tonight, but it wasn't bad. The long night has just caught up with me."

"If you say so." Like hell. He'd seen how she'd looked in his car. A day-old corpse had more life.

"Honest. It's safe to leave me. I'll be in bed in like five minutes."

"Good, get going. I'm not leaving."

Exasperated, she turned around and kicked off her heels. "Then you might as well sleep in the spare room for the night. It's so late now, you're not going to get any sleep otherwise."

Not a bad idea. Drew swallowed hard as Maddy stripped off the red sweater as she went into her bedroom, leaving him with a stunning view of her slim back, ribs encased in a black and red bra, gentle curves heading down to the top of black pants.

So close and yet so far.

Resolutely, he walked toward the spare room and considered. Should he stay or go home? Home wasn't that far away, except leaving her might take more energy than he had. This way, he'd see her in the morning, even if only for an hour.

It would also give him a chance to take the relationship one step further.

Anything was worth that opportunity. He'd made a few discreet inquiries and everyone said the same thing. Maddy was known to be very selective when it came to male friends. Not a prude from what he'd learned – just careful.

He liked that. He didn't consider himself in the tomcat category, and it was nice to see she felt the same. Now if only he had some idea how she felt about him.

GERARD WALKED INTO the office very early, worn out from yet another sleepless night. For the first time since he'd been a young boy, he'd been plagued with nightmares. Endless hours remembering stuff he'd spent most of his lifetime forgetting. Just a horrible night.

These last few days had been hard. He hadn't realized how hard or how badly the stress had affected him. Jesus. What was he going to do down the road? But that wasn't fair. He was coming out of a long year of tight budget constraints, nonexistent wiggle room and staff shortages. Then there was John and that mess.

He wanted this stage of his life to be over and to move on to smoother times. He frowned. Since when had he ever had smoother times?

That brought him back to last night and his childhood nightmare. Demons had chased him. Blackness took over his mind and body. It controlled his hospital and the people in it. Sweat formed on his brow, even thinking about it.

Why were all those childhood memories he'd fought so long and so hard to forget coming back now? He'd walked away from his mother years ago. Begged to be taken away actually, and family services had honored his request. He'd had little contact in the intervening years. Good thing, too. The woman was nuts.

Gerard's secret fear was that it was genetic – that he'd end up as crazy as his mother.

He looked around. Sandra wasn't at her desk. Good. He didn't think he was up to speaking with her this morning. He shut and locked his door, hard pressed to not look around the darkened room. He hit the light switch, heaving a sigh of relief as the light washed away the darkness.

Maybe he needed to take a break. Take a holiday, if he still remembered what that was.

THURSDAY MORNING

IT WAS MORNING. And that had to be wrong. There was no reason in the world that Maddy could think of to explain why she was awake. After last night's dancing, followed by the panicked visit to The Haven, she should be sound asleep. Only she wasn't and that sucked.

Her cell phone rang as she slipped on her Egyptian cotton dress with the beautiful flowers winding down the left side and back.

It was Stefan. "Maddy, update on The Haven, please."

"John had an attack of some kind last night." Maddy walked out to the living room to slump down on the couch. "His symptoms mimicked a stroke. He's stable, and will need to be closely monitored." She sighed heavily. "I haven't contacted The Haven so I don't have an update yet." She went on to explain what she'd found.

Silence.

Maddy rubbed her temples. "These are psychic attacks, right?" This would be her first experience with something like this – but not for Stefan or other energy workers she knew. "I can't think of what else they could be. I know people are people. They always want something they don't have. And many are prepared to do some pretty horrible things to get it."

Stefan hesitated. "We have to assume this dangerous energy is anchored to John." His voice deepened. "It might have started with Jansen. We don't know enough at this point."

"True enough. From what I've seen, the energy slid around the base of the bed, moving and shifting. It always stayed close. Contained. Anchored." Closing her eyes, Maddy winced at the question even before she'd managed to ask it. "Stefan, is there any chance that John is doing this himself?"

"Unlikely, although with the little we know, we can't discount that."

"There has to be something more going on than what's related to John. The attack on Jansen happened prior to John's arrival." This was all so bizarre. "John's very pragmatic. He has no patience with any of this stuff. It's hard to imagine he has a hand in it."

Maddy didn't see it. She walked into her kitchen and pulled out the coffee grinder. She chose the setting she wanted before filling it with dark Costa Rican beans. She turned on the grinder, stepping away from the noise to continue talking. "We've both seen black energy causing problems in a person's energy system. It's the basis for all health problems, only the bigger blockages can cause personality changes, mental problems, diseases and, eventually…death."

"True, however, all we have to go on for the moment is the attack on John, regardless of whether he brought it or the energy latched onto him for some reason when he arrived."

"Right. I did a full session on him yesterday. I put the markers in place and ran some healing energy up and down his spine." The coffee grinder shut down. She walked back, filled the coffee carafe for two cups and poured the water into the back of the coffee maker.

"Did you notice anything wrong?"

She paused before placing the carafe on the maker. "Not at the time. This session went deeper and longer than I'd ever gone before. One of the nurses actually brought me out." Maddy measured the coffee and hit the start button. "It hit me afterwards that he didn't feel the same as my sick patients usually do. There wasn't the same sense of disease eating away at him or even the same sense of finality I get from terminal patients."

"This is new territory here. We don't know what might happen."

"Great." Maddy leaned against the counter, waiting for enough coffee to drip for her to steal a cup. "We've done so much work already in the main part that it could take months for the energy in the new section to match the level of the rest of the floor."

"Search for someone connected to him. In order to do this when they are not physically in the same room, they would have to be incredibly skilled and strong. Or desperate."

She said, "It has to be someone he knows and trusts. A lover, best friend or family member, most likely."

"Remember, this person might have been in John's life decades ago. Few people understand how much energy we get on a day-to-day basis from other people, much less how long we carry it once we do." Stefan paused, then added, "They could have placed hooks into his system years ago, an insignificant amount, initially, and then slowly increased it over time. And it's quite possible they didn't realize what they were doing."

"Then they've learned quickly," she retorted. "I've seen cords stretching from person to person, but these black clusters are new on me." And Maddy'd be fine if she never saw them again.

"Energy work is one of the greatest unknowns in our lifetime." Stefan sighed, as if the weight of the world rested on his shoulders. "Keep an eye on it. Anchor a field of your own to keep watch. Set it to trigger with any movement."

"How do we protect the other patients?"

"Set a stronger border. Strengthen the healing energy inside. You might want to set up a Kirlian camera too."

Maddy frowned. Kirlian photography took pictures of a person's energy. It would be interesting to see the images captured on her floor at night, but the cost would be horrific. "That's expensive. How can we minimize the cost?"

"Get a digital one?" He suggested. "I can lend you mine, only it's an older film model."

"Hmmm." The film would be used up an hour. It would have to be changed often and that cost would be prohibitive. "Digital would be better." She sighed. "There's no budget money for toys like this." Another thought occurred. "What if John dies? Would this clump of dark energy be able to transfer to a new host?"

"Anything's possible. We don't know enough. Make sure it doesn't shift to you. If you suddenly have a new person in your life, someone who's on your mind all the time, I'd be leery.

"Take a hard close look at them. The person tied to this black energy would need a way to get in somehow, but once he's there, this person appears to be able to do all kinds of things."

Maddy's mind sorted through Stefan's words. She leaned back against the counter and nearly dropped the phone.

"Oh my God!"

A very sleepy Drew raised an eyebrow at her. Dressed only in pants, Drew stood there, pinup perfect. Maddy gulped. How was it possible she'd forgotten him? He must think she'd lost it completely.

"Maddy!" Stefan's voice reverberated through the phone. "What's wrong?" A thick pause filled the phone. "Oh. That's what."

Heat rushed through her cheeks. Trust Stefan. He read her mind every time.

"I wouldn't if you didn't constantly advertise what you were thinking." There was a second heavy pause. "He's involved in a murder case, an old case and a new one." Stefan's voice took on an odd note, distant with an odd echo. Maddy sat back to listen as Stefan shifted into a different reality. She listened but kept her gaze locked on the virile male dominating her kitchen and her senses.

Drew reached into the open cupboard beside her, snagged two cups and poured coffee from the freshly made pot. He held one out for her.

Maddy nodded, struggling to stay focused on Stefan. A little hard to do with a half-naked man in her kitchen.

"He's got trouble. Dead kids, dead man. And that's not the end...this is just the beginning." Stefan spoke clearly but quietly.

"Can you help?" Maddy kept her voice calm and even. She needed Stefan's vision to continue and anything jarring or loud had the potential to snap him out of it.

Stefan's voice dropped, slurred. "Same energy."

Maddy leaned forward. "What? Stefan? Same energy as what?"

"The Haven. *Maddy's Floor.* Same energy."

Maddy ran her fingers through her hair. "Stefan," she whispered. "Talk to me, please. What about Maddy's Floor? Stefan, what does this killer have to do with my floor?"

"Wait..." His voice died. "Not...quite the same. Same, yet different." Stefan's voice had deteriorated to a deep slur. His words faded with his effort to maintain conscious awareness in both spheres.

"Can you see the person?"

"No. Energy."

"Can you trace it to the person?"

"Death. Drew is in danger."

"Drew?"

"Weird energy. Can't hold..." His voice warbled before draining away.

There was only blankness on the phone. A tinny sound gave her the sense he was still there, but not speaking. "Stefan." No answer. "Stefan, answer me."

Click.

DREW SIPPED THE coffee, enjoying the unusual sensation of being with someone first thing in the morning. He'd woken suddenly, reaching for a ringing phone. But it wasn't his, so he lay back and listened to the sound of Maddy's voice drifting to him from the kitchen.

He watched Maddy as she studied him. Then again, he was standing shirtless in her kitchen. Hopefully not a sight she was accustomed to seeing too often. And one she liked.

With one ear tuned to the conversation, he studied her face. Sleep had helped to restore the bloom of pink across her cheeks, and in that long cotton dress, she glowed. That woman wore her height well. She wasn't shy or self-conscious about it. That made all the difference in the world. Confidence was sexy.

He sighed. What an idiot. He was acting like a lovesick teenager.

MADDY WHIPPED UP breakfast while Drew got dressed. Even without much practice entertaining males early in the morning, making breakfast didn't take long. With her mind full of Stefan's disturbing words, she finished the job quickly and set two full plates of pancakes on the table. "Let's eat, then we'll talk."

Finishing first, Maddy sat back with a second cup of coffee and watched Drew polish off his plateful. Every bite went down with gusto. This man loved his food. He looked up.

"So what did you want to talk about?"

"Remember the painting you saw in the other room last night?" She raised her eyebrow in question. "That was the artist, Stefan, calling." Unsure how to continue, she sipped her coffee.

"What did he have to say?"

It wasn't that easy. If Drew didn't have working experience with psychics or knowledge of energy work, he wouldn't understand the gist of her answer. Even more complicated, he wouldn't understand the bits and pieces, the incompleteness of the information. "He's worked alongside the police for years and probably has names to give you as references."

He sipped his coffee and stared at her quizzically. "Why would

I care?"

"Because he's a powerful psychic and while talking to him, he slipped in and out of a vision. Your name came up. He said that you were busy with murder, an old case and a new one."

Drew's mouth opened, then closed before opening again. "He said *what*?"

She quickly went over the little bit that Stefan had picked up. When she mentioned dead kids, his cheeks sucked in and his eyes chilled. Black reached deep into his eyes. "I need to talk to him." Curt, sharp and no arguments allowed. She wasn't planning to argue, but knew Stefan usually avoided people.

"I'll have to call him."

"Do that." He took out his cell phone and tossed it at her.

She grimaced. "Now?"

"Now. Remember those dead kids? If he has any information that might help with that case, I need to know. The father of one of those children was attacked on Sunday, and with that bruise on Jansen's back that might link the old and new cases, well…"

Maddy sobered as she grasped the connection to his cold case. "I understand."

"Good. Thank you." Drew took a sip of coffee and motioned toward his cell.

Maddy slipped her own cell phone out instead. "He won't answer if he doesn't know who's calling. Even then, he doesn't always answer."

Stefan didn't answer her call. Reaching out mentally, she frowned. She couldn't sense him. A curl of unease unfurled deep in her stomach. "I think maybe we should go to his place. The phone went dead when I was talking to him earlier. I didn't worry at the time because I sensed he'd dropped into a deep sleep." She tilted her head. "Now I'm not getting a reading at all."

The decision made, she stood up abruptly. "I'm going."

Drew stared at his half-finished coffee. "Going? Now?"

"Now." Maddy snatched up her purse. "Sorry, but I mean *now*."

She hurried for the front door, not caring whether Drew was behind her or not.

When she arrived at the parking lot, she glanced back to see him rushing to catch up, shirt open and billowing behind him, his jacket hanging off two fingers over his shoulder. She paused. He looked like he'd enjoyed a hell of a wild night. Damn. She felt cheated.

"My truck or your car?" he asked.

"Your truck. And fast."

JOHN HUDDLED UNDER his covers. He'd barely closed his eyes all night. He'd been too scared. How many people were actually ready to meet their maker when the time came? He'd been sure he wouldn't see the dawn today. In his life, he'd done things he wasn't exactly proud of – getting onto Dr. Maddy's floor was just one more.

He hadn't done anywhere near enough for friends or family over the years. Drew would lose all respect for him if he knew. He'd do a lot to keep that from happening. He'd been hell on wheels throughout his years on the police force and he was proud of that, yet he'd not been easy on his family. He'd never married because he hadn't seen himself committing to one woman. But he could have helped his stepsister out when her son was so sick. The boy damn near died.

His stepsister hadn't done as well. Whether it was the scare of her son's close brush with death, her loose lifestyle or just an encroaching mental weakness, she'd slipped mentally. When Doris's mental state was first called into question, the boy had struggled – a lot, yet instead of stepping up and helping out, John had stayed in the background, not wanting to get involved.

He hadn't treated Drew much better, except he was his younger brother's boy and that made all the difference. Blood counted. He hadn't wanted kids and had regarded his nephew as his own. Drew would get everything when John was gone. He could help Doris now, if he wanted to. But some habits were too hard to break.

Tugging the blankets higher, John sank deeper into the mire he'd made for himself.

God, he'd never planned on *this* as his end.

What irony. What hell.

STEFAN, FOR THE first time, wondered at the sensibility of his actions. He thought he was lost, and in the etheric plane, no less. It wasn't the first time, but damn it, he hadn't expected it now.

During the call with Maddy, he'd thought about following the trace energy back to the source. Once the thought went out, the action had followed. He'd zipped out of his body to travel the energy field in search of who was doing this.

It was nice in theory but difficult in practice – at least like this. He'd wandered Maddy's Floor and probably scared the crap out of John, who couldn't see him. Instinctively John had still known something wasn't quite right.

Stefan found Maddy's dark faded *blob*, as she'd called it.

He'd tried several tricks. He'd tried to smother it, then to join with it, anything to get a handle on where it was coming from.

Nothing had worked. He didn't understand how or why, only it seemed the black globs were attached to, or maybe even originated from John. For the past ten minutes, he'd been trying to see through the dense material to see what and how and where it was attached. Was it to John or his bed?

Stefan hadn't been able to figure it out. That had pissed him off, and made him try harder.

And in the process, Stefan had burned up too much energy. He cast a cautious glance at the throbbing blackness that instinct said had helped drain his reserves faster than he'd expected. There was always enough energy available, but he required a certain level of power to access it. It was an easy mistake to make if you were inexperienced. He wasn't. Shit. He hadn't made a mistake like this in years, decades even.

He didn't have enough reserves to get back home.

MADDY'S SENSE OF urgency refused to abate on the trip to Stefan's. Her anxiousness even prevented her from reading his energy clearly. When she finally connected with him, it was faint at best. Maddy knew she was capable of connecting and scanning the energy of people around the world, but only when her emotional state was calm and balanced. If it were, then the physical distance *could* be crossed as fast as the thought was understood.

If her own energy were chaotic with worry, nothing would allow her to bridge even the shortest of distances.

The trip took close to twenty minutes, with Drew at the wheel. He drove up the long, winding gravel driveway and stopped outside Stefan's cedar house. As soon as the vehicle rolled to a stop Maddy hopped out.

She paid little attention to the oversized plants lining the driveway, noting only that Stefan's truck and car were both parked in front. She pounded on his door.

No answer.

She tested the knob and it turned easily under her hand. She pushed the door open and tossed a quick backward glance to make sure Drew was behind her, then stepped inside.

"Stefan, are you here?" She walked down the hallway. "It's Maddy. Stefan?"

"Any idea where he'd be?"

"Anywhere. He's very unconventional. He'll paint in a tuxedo if he feels like it, and as his days and nights are his, he abuses traditional constraints of time, does as he pleases."

The living room was empty. Maddy crossed the gleaming hardwood floor into the glass-enclosed sunroom that faced the wooded backyard. Stefan's special place. She walked in and almost missed him. He sat cross-legged in an oversized wicker chair.

"Stefan?" Maddy bent down to his level. His face was gray and lax. Switching her view, she searched his aura, finding it thin and discolored – dangerously so.

Drew crouched beside her. "He doesn't look so good." He flipped his cell phone open and dialed for emergency help.

Maddy slid a sideways glance his way, reached over and closed his phone.

Startled, he glanced at her. "What? I'm not supposed to call for an ambulance?"

Keeping her voice low, she murmured, "No medical professional can help with this."

Ignoring him, she studied Stefan's energy. Scanning him from his head to his toes, she saw no obvious cause for the energy drain. She knew he often took trips. Astral travel was one of his specialties. His silver cord appeared almost nonexistent, even fainter than his energy. She frowned. Crap, she was so worried about him she wasn't thinking straight.

Glancing at Drew, she found him staring at Stefan with a puzzled frown on his face.

"What?" Maddy struggled to understand his expression.

"If a doctor can't help him, and you're a doctor, how are you planning to do what others can't?"

"Well put." She grimaced. What should she tell him and how? He had very little understanding of energy work. He didn't even believe in psychics. She decided to take a chance. "I've told you about being a medical intuitive, and you've seen some weird stuff, like in the truck this morning. This is just a little more. I do energy work that's similar to what Stefan does."

"So you've said before. I don't know what that means."

"It means a lot of things. I don't have time to explain now." She motioned toward the comatose Stefan. "Not if I'm going to save him."

"Right. Later you and I are going to have a long talk." He stared at Stefan. "How do we help him?" Drew stood and studied the tasteful but minimalist style of the room. "Should we lay him down somewhere?"

"No, he can't be touched right now. Even the slightest disturbance of his energy can kill him."

"Shit. Are you serious?"

"Yes. His energy has dissipated. It's too fragile for much right now."

He shook his head. "Then what can you do?"

"Everything and nothing." She stepped back slightly and chose a spot directly beside Stefan.

"Can I help?"

"Pick a spot, sit down and don't talk." She waited until he sat. "I'm going in after him and bring him back. While I'm out, you can't touch either of us." She narrowed her eyes at him. "Do you understand? You can't touch me or him."

He grabbed her arm. "Whoa. And what am I to do if you end up looking like him?"

She frowned. "Then it's too late for both of us, but it won't happen. I'm not going to do the same thing he's doing. I'm not going to leave my body."

"What?" Drew turned his attention back to study Stefan. "What the hell does that mean? And is that what you did this morning?"

"It means he's walking around the planet consciously, in spirit form – without his body. He's very good at it. Many people are doing the same, you know. They just don't know they are doing it. And yes, that's similar to what I did…only not quite."

"Really," he murmured, disbelief caging his voice.

"Really."

"And you're not going to do that? So you won't end up looking dead like he does, right?"

"Right. Don't panic. I'll be back."

She closed her eyes and dropped her head forward. It took several precious minutes to calm her breathing and open her chakras to build the energy she needed for this. She was good, but Stefan was better. She could infuse his chakras with energy, both in physical form and etheric, but this was faster, safer.

Maddy sensed the lightness within her mind. She stretched toward it. She wasn't going to astral travel, she would astral project – follow his silver cord in her mind. Find him and figure out what was happening to him because he should have been able to get home by thought alone.

Lightness entered her heart, her spirit, her very soul. Maddy tilted her face skyward and smiled as her very blood sang with joy. Only by becoming one with the energy, to the emotion attached, could she free her mind to travel the etheric plane.

A heavy sigh worked up from deep inside. She slipped out on the warm breath and opened her eyes. The sensation gave everything a muted appearance, making the experience easier on her senses than if she'd truly left her body. This was like a foggy day in England. A bit eerie, a bit slower, but she could still get to where she needed to go.

Picking up Stefan's silver cord in a white haze was a little difficult. It wasn't possible to change the color of his cord, but she could change the color of the fog. All thoughts manifested immediately here. The hazy fog instantly changed to a lavender overtone, showing the silver cord as a glowing streak across the room. Maddy followed it out onto the etheric plane. The path twisted and turned, dipped and swerved, and through it all Maddy kept the silvery cord in sight.

Her focus stayed on Stefan, calling to him, sending him loving energy and a message that she was coming – to hold on until she arrived. The cord strengthened slightly. It brightened and pulsed. He had to be close.

She rounded several more corners and fell, literally, into a vast chamber of space. Stefan's cord lay crumpled, as did his astral body. Maddy saw her surroundings clearly, although they appeared as if on the other side of thick glass. She blinked once, and then blinked again as she recognized the location. Stefan had traveled here to her floor at The Haven – and here he'd fallen.

Moving around his prone astral body, Maddy studied his position. He was exhausted. With luck, that was the only problem.

Maddy moved closer. His cord pulsed. The thinness and fragile look of it, said he'd just gone too far, done too much. That was typical of him. Still, he shouldn't have run his system down to this level so fast.

She frowned.

He was lying within ten yards of John's bed.

Giving John a quick study, Maddy saw his silver cord, not as strong as she'd like to see it, but pulsing happily along. He appeared to be much better off than Stefan at the moment. Beneath the bed, the faded black patch now consisted of even smaller gobs of energy, as she'd come to think of them. They were softer looking, swollen, and they pulsed in an obscene gloating manner.

They gave her the creeps.

And she knew instinctively they were very dangerous – for everyone that came into contact with them.

Like Stefan had.

Glancing down, Maddy realized she needed to help him – now.

She leaned over Stefan. Being only energy, she stretched over him completely. Slowly, ever so slowly, soft as a feather, she let herself sink into him.

"Maddy?" Stefan's voice was as frail as that of someone over a hundred and twenty years old.

"Yes," she whispered into his mind. *"Stay calm. You need to absorb enough of my energy to get yourself back home where you belong."*

"Knew you'd come. Love you, kiddo."

Maddy smiled, her warmth and joy spreading deep into his astral body, blending and morphing into something else. She felt he'd revived sufficiently. *"Let's go."*

Instantly, they were flung back into their bodies like arrows from a bow.

Stefan's body jerked, collapsing him backward. For Maddy, who had only been energy on the outside, the homecoming wasn't so harsh. Still, she groaned as she fell backwards onto the hardwood floor and opened her eyes. Stefan's stained glass window stared down at her. Beautiful mermaids flaunted their bodies on the sunny rocks, as rain poured in a torrential downpour from above, making the window a more realistic portrait than she'd have thought possible.

"Maddy?"

Stefan's faint whisper galvanized her into action. She sat up and shuffled closer. "Stefan, how do you feel?"

"Like butter spread too thin on a slice of day-old bread."

Maddy related to his imagery. How many times had she felt the same way? "I still think you look good enough to eat."

The color slowly seeped into Stefan's face, chasing out the gray pallor. He smirked, bringing a rosy blush of color to his cheeks. "You're biased. You love me."

"True." Maddy reached out a gentle hand and pushed a fallen lock of hair back across his forehead. "What the hell happened?"

"That's something I'd sure as hell like to know, too."

Maddy spun around, surprised at the harshness of Drew's voice. Given the weird events he'd been thrown into, his reaction shouldn't have been unexpected.

He reached out and squeezed her shoulder. "You scared the crap out of me, you know that?"

Tossing him an intimate smile that eased the lines on his forehead, she nodded. For anyone who didn't know how this stuff worked, it would have been incredibly difficult to sit still and wait, not knowing if there'd be two gray bodies or none. "Thank you – for keeping your head and not panicking."

"And that was damn close, I'm telling you." Drew got up and paced the small room as Stefan and Maddy watched. "Don't ever leave me to watch over you two like that again."

After a couple of moments, Stefan pushed up from the chair to stand. He stretched and wiggled slightly, as if adjusting his body suit. Maddy grinned. He was the only person she knew who did that. Drew raised his eyebrow and shook his head in disbelief.

Stefan held out his hand. "I'm Stefan, by the way. Sorry for the initial introduction. It's not my usual style. You're Maddy's cop, I presume. Drew McNeil?"

Drew stepped forward and held out his hand. "Maddy's cop. I kinda like that. Yes, I'm Drew. She was worried after you disappeared during your phone conversation this morning. Although, if you two can do all of this…" He wafted his hand toward the papasan chair. "Then I don't understand why you'd bother with a phone. Can someone please explain what the hell just happened? And what's this you said earlier, about my murder cases?"

Maddy studied Drew's face, pale and drawn as he struggled to understand. He'd obviously had a difficult time when she'd left him alone, but he was handling it well. Secretly, she admitted liking Stefan's name for him, too. She wanted to see if Drew and her had a chance at a relationship. A real one, not a hot-affair-and-be-done-with-it sort of thing.

She'd done those; not anymore. They left a bad taste in her mouth. Although she wasn't exactly looking, she wasn't opposed to accepting what was before her. There was no denying the attraction between them. More than the heat they generated whenever their eyes met, was the energy that melded when they were together. Drew wouldn't be aware of it, yet his energy slid close to hers and snuggled at every opportune moment. She had to admit, she really liked that. She knew hers reached out and touched his energy often too.

They'd burn the sheets to hell and back when they finally got there.

And she, for one, couldn't wait.

STEFAN WATCHED THE two people now seated comfortably in his solarium. So this was the new man he'd seen in her life. Interesting. Close, yet not touching, their bodies had yet to match their minds. Their energies were way ahead of both. Snuggled up tight as they were, their auras blended naturally. He smiled. It wouldn't take them much longer. Danger and drama had a way of pushing people together and making them get over their differences faster. He was happy for them.

The best sound in the world had been Maddy's words when he'd been caught in no man's land.

"Stefan, are you all right?"

Startled, Stefan realized he'd been staring off for several minutes. "That black energy under John's bed did something to me, drained my energy faster than I've ever experienced before."

"I wondered about that when I found you. I've been watching those energy strands and clumps for a couple of days now. Today they were different."

"Different how?" Those fuller globules scared the hell out of him.

"Swollen, as if they'd just eaten."

"Nice." Stefan winced. "Thanks for that imagery, seeing as how I was probably the last meal."

"Today the globs were softer, almost happy, content. I don't know how to explain it."

"You're doing fine, and I think you're right. That energy is feeding on other, healthier, energy."

"For what purpose though?" Maddy stood up and wandered over to the front window. "Healing?"

Stefan studied Drew's face. He hadn't added much to the conversation, but he seemed to be trying to take everything in. "Has to be."

Drew interrupted. "Are you saying someone is stealing another person's energy from the new wing on Maddy's Floor?"

The disbelief in his voice reminded Stefan how odd this business would be to an onlooker. In Drew's case, he'd seen more than most. "Potentially, yes."

"And why are they still doing this? Wouldn't they have taken what they needed and stopped by now?" Drew stared hard at Stefan.

Stefan shook his head. "They can only access sick energy so they need so much more of it to be viable. That may be why this black energy is located where it is. I can't say for sure that it originated there. However, it's currently sitting under the bed of one of the patients on Maddy's Floor."

"There's only one patient in there now – John McNeil." Drew glanced over at Maddy.

Stefan could only guess at the discomfort sliding across her face.

Nodding slowly, she said, "That's correct."

"So, you're saying this is his energy. That's he's the one doing this?"

Stefan said, "It's possible, although that's the least likely scenario. It's more likely to be someone close to him, like a family member." A fine tremor slipped over Stefan's body. He needed recovery time. He glanced over, catching Maddy's grimace. He turned his attention to Drew, watching as his brows came together and his gaze narrowed on Maddy's face.

Drew asked, "A family member, like a stepsister? Or better yet, a blood relative, like a nephew?"

Stefan shrugged. "If they were close."

"Well, he has a nephew and they are close, but it's sure as hell is not him doing this."

"How do you know?"

"Because I'm that nephew."

THURSDAY AFTERNOON

DREW'S ANNOUNCEMENT THAT he was John's nephew raised Stefan's eyebrows. Maddy had forgotten to mention that fact to Stefan. Not that it had mattered. Drew wasn't the one causing the black energy. She'd seen his energy and knew he wasn't the one causing the trouble.

Besides, explanations would have to wait. Stefan desperately needed rest and Maddy needed to get back to work.

The trip back had been silent and uncomfortable. During the drive, Maddy made several important phone calls. The first was to request that the newly installed security cameras be checked to make sure they were working properly and that there was no unusual activity. Too bad there was no way to track visitors to Maddy's Floor, or The Haven in general. Maddy didn't know of one extended care home that had such a system in place. It would be helpful right now though.

In between these calls, a pulsating silence filled the truck. She knew Drew didn't understand what he'd seen today and that he had questions. Not knowing how or what to say, she hoped he'd give her a chance to sort it out before demanding an explanation.

In the back of her mind, she remembered the warning about Drew being in danger. She still hadn't figured that out either. And she needed to.

Maddy asked Drew to drop her off at The Haven. After the tense return journey, he pulled in front of The Haven and parked. She hopped out of his truck, gave him a hurried good-bye and practically ran to the front entrance.

"Maddy?" Drew asked.

Maddy turned around to face him. He'd hopped out but stood beside his truck.

"Where are you running to and why?"

She sighed. "To your uncle. Something's going on and I want

to see if I can figure it out. I need to know who else is in your uncle's life. People he knew really well in the past. And now. That includes those that he currently loves, who might love him, and those he may have loved at one time and definitely doesn't now."

"Do you have any idea how many people that could be?"

"People are getting sick, possibly dying, and you're a detective who's close to the victim," she said, exasperated. "Help us figure this out before someone else gets hurt."

He studied her, his eyes narrowed and assessing. "Say I do find these people, the ones who are still alive anyway, what can you do?"

"I'm not sure yet." She stared past him, considering. "It might narrow down the options. If I see these people, see their energies, I might be able to tell if they have anything to do with this. I can't guarantee it, of course. Energy is unique, like a fingerprint." She gazed at him. "Remember, Stefan thinks it's the same person who may have been involved with the deaths of all those kids. Cross reference the people from today with them and…"

"Right, I get it." He held up a hand. "Please keep me in the loop. When will it be safe to call Stefan to ask more questions?"

Maddy checked her watch. "Give him an hour, at least, if not twice that. He should have recovered enough by then."

"Good enough. Is my uncle safe?"

"I'm hoping so, at least for a little bit longer. We believe that whoever is doing this set their hooks into him a long time ago. And are acting on them now. I'm pretty sure that's the reason for his rapid physical decline recently. I don't know what they might do next."

"Can I put a guard on him? Move him to a safer place? What?"

Maddy's laugh was sad. "With energy work, they wouldn't need to be physically close to do this. Alibis are useless. I've scanned people in Egypt from my apartment. He's not safe anywhere. Consider The Haven one of the safest places for him to be right now because it's one of the few places where someone can see what's happening." She was adamant on that point.

Poor Drew, he was grappling with this new idea but he was getting it. The horrified understanding on his face said it all.

"Right. If someone wants to and has the skill to, they can cause the death of anyone, anywhere in the world," she said. "It wouldn't be easy and it would depend on the other person's health and mental state, but it's possible from any distance."

She kept talking as she reached for the front door. Drew followed. "I am suspicious this person had something to do with two other patients at the hospital, Dr. Lenning and Jansen Svaar – possibly for many more attacks and deaths over the years. Find a connection. Find your killer." She didn't want to bring up Eric Colgan as another potential victim at this point.

She'd follow up on him if this trail panned out. Pulling open the door, she glanced back over her shoulder. "And fast. Chances are this person will kill again, and soon."

DREW STARED AFTER her as she raced inside.

Could she and Stefan be right? If death were as simple as disconnecting someone's cord then, as impossible as it sounded, it would explain how those kids long ago had literally dropped dead on the spot. Like unplugging a lamp from a socket, they'd been unplugged from their cords.

Why those kids? Why no one else in the last thirty years? Were there other deaths that had gone unnoticed by law enforcement? Not that he'd blame them, with so little evidence and such a far-out cause of death – well, he was sure no one would have considered such a possibility. He wasn't sure he believed it himself. Getting other law enforcement to agree would be impossible. Obtaining a conviction based on conjecture – never.

Ice settled in his stomach. Perhaps it was something unrelated to his uncle – like the Internet had given this killer access to millions of potential victims?

No. Maddy said they had to have a personal connection. She also said with a connection, they didn't need to be close in order to do something like this. He couldn't imagine a world where killers chose victims by their ability to connect with the person, regardless of where they lived in the world. Civilization could degenerate into chaos.

In a smaller way, this could be happening right here and now, and might have been going on for decades. Uncle John wasn't doing this to himself – there was no way. Therefore, someone was doing it to him, and had been affecting his health for who knows how long. But who? He walked back to his truck. How many up-close-and-personal friends, lovers and enemies had his uncle collected over the years? Hundreds, if not thousands.

Drew pulled his car out of the lot and drove toward the office.

Wilson was working on his computer when Drew walked in. The man glanced up with a big smirk on his face. "About time you showed up. Figured I'd be working alone today. Hot date?"

Working with Wilson had to be one of the biggest blessings of the new job. Easy to work with, and open to ideas, he was like a gentle family dog – agreeable all the time.

Tossing him a glowering look, Drew booted up his computer and replied, "Yeah, hot date, followed by a panicked visit to hospital, then crashing in hot date's spare room, followed by a second panic visit to a different hot date's friend's home."

"Nice. What are you planning for a second date?" Wilson sat at his desk, leaning back comfortably. "Did the emergencies turn out to be okay?"

Drew plunked down in his chair, suddenly more tired than he cared to admit. He'd grabbed a few hours of sleep at Maddy's place but not enough. "They will be. A little scary for a while. My uncle took a turn for the worse, but he's expected to pull through, and the friend…well, I guess you might say he was unconscious for a while."

"Not quite the outing you'd planned, I presume?"

"No, not quite." Drew played with a pencil on the top of his desk, switching it end over end while he considered mentioning Stefan.

"Something wrong?"

"How do you feel about psychics?"

Wilson shrugged.

Encouraged, Drew continued. "Does the name Stefan Kronos mean anything to you?" He studied his partner's face carefully, looking for any scoffing.

Wilson's face registered surprise, not shock. "Ah." Wilson sat forward. "That must have been a hell of a date."

"You've heard of him?" Maddy had said he'd done work for the police. He hadn't expected Wilson to know him.

"Absolutely. He's one of the best in the business. A bit freaky, though. And the man is a genius artist, producing some of the most incredible paintings imaginable. It's a little too raw for the common folk. He's had phenomenal success working with law enforcement in this country and others. Scary dude for the stuff he knows. It's like he can look right through you – and apparently he can."

"So I've heard. So in your opinion, he's for real?"

"Solid gold."

"He's the one who had trouble this morning."

Wilson jumped to his feet. "What? How do you know him? He won't work with just anyone."

"Dr. Maddy is a good friend of his."

"Dr. Maddy? From The Haven? Wow, don't you move in high circles." Wilson reached the stack of folders on his desk. "I see transferring your uncle to The Haven moved you up in life, too."

"She was my hot date last night."

A long whistle of appreciation circled the room. "Wow. Wait…" Wilson paused, then a grin cracked his face.

Drew watched him put two and two together.

"So you spent last night in Dr. Maddy's spare room?" His smirk widened until he burst out laughing. "Talk about being so close…"

"And yet so far." Drew finished for him. "Right. You got it. So back to Stefan. Does his work stand up in court?"

"He hates courts. He tries to show you where to look so you can find the evidence to put these assholes away without him. It's his way of avoiding courts."

"Good enough." Drew refreshed the screen on his computer and while it did he reached for his notepad. Standing up, he walked to the wallboard holding the photos of the six dead kids. He tapped it gently with the notepad. "We may have caught a break on this case."

JOHN SANK DEEPER into his bedclothes, hating the chill that ran through his veins. Would he ever feel warm again? He shivered and pulled the covers up. He wanted to move to another area of the floor. One not so cold, empty and lonely. He had liked having Adam close by, only Adam was still in ICU. None of the medical team had been able to tell him when he would return. There was an eerie feeling, lying in a room full of gleaming empty beds. Definitely weird.

Then, his whole life was that way lately.

Maybe they'd changed his drugs. The doctor had gone over a bunch of stuff, but John hadn't paid too much attention. He didn't want to focus on the constant pain or the debilitating mess his body had become. Still, new medications would explain the hallucinations, the paranoid feelings, even the weird nightmares he'd been experiencing.

Feeling better with that realization, he shuffled his butt slightly until he was half-sitting.

This wasn't so bad. He smoothed the bedcovers down and reached for his remote. It lay at the end of his bed. Getting there was a little harder. Pulling his wasted legs over the edge of the bed, he shifted to a sitting position and reached again. He picked it up and wiggled back toward the head of his bed. As he swung his arm around to use the metal side for support, he dropped the television remote. It slid from the blankets against the metal frame and down to the floor.

"Shit."

He slid his feet to the floor. "Well, I had to go to the bathroom anyway." He tottered slowly in that direction, careful because of his unsteady gait. After washing his hands, he made his way back, painfully aware of every step. At the side of his bed, he bent slowly, hanging on to the metal frame for support. As his fingers reached for the remote, he twisted his head to look under the bed…and frowned.

What the hell was that?

He moved down the end of the bed and searched for something to poke underneath. An empty IV stand stood beside his bed.

Knowing he probably shouldn't try this and determined to give it a go, regardless, he bent down, lowering himself onto his knees and then he reached under the bed. He felt around. A weird tingling sensation started at his fingertips and slid up toward his elbow. John pulled his hand out and turned it this way and that, wondering what had changed.

The tingling slid up to his shoulder and across his chest.

Something was wrong, really wrong. Kneeling on the floor, he struggled to his feet only to collapse from the effort. He wasn't going to make it to his call button. Damn it.

The numbness carried down his chest, back, and deeper into his spine. The room spun. His vision blurred. He pitched head first to the floor.

MADDY WAS DELAYED on the main floor of The Haven. Two doctors had questions for her about their patients and her project. She couldn't exactly brush them off; neither could she get rid of the sense of wrongness building inside the place. It took a good fifteen minutes before the three of them reached the point of setting up a meeting.

By the time she managed to excuse herself, the feeling of being too late had her racing to the stairs.

Entering the stairwell, urgency slammed into her. Not understanding, but incapable of ignoring the energetic vibes, Maddy sprinted up the stairwell, her heels clacking with each step. The urgency built higher and grew stronger the closer she got to her floor. Her heart pounded as her stress levels topped out and a film of sweat covered her face. "Oh, God." She wrenched open the door and bolted down the corridor.

"Dr. Maddy?"

"What's wrong?"

The voices called out as she fled past the nurses' station. In the background, Maddy heard footsteps rushing in her wake.

She entered the new wing. John's bed was empty. Skidding to a stop, she spied his foot on the far side. Dropping to her knees beside him, she checked his vital signs while simultaneously shifting her vision to her inner eye. The black energy blob pulsed under the bed. It surrounded John's silver cord several feet away from his body, almost suffocating him. It was climbing ever so slowly up the length of the silvery lifeline. The energy of his arm closest to the silver cord had a gray tinge to it as the life force had weakened under the power of the draining blackness.

Two nurses dropped to their knees beside her.

Nancy asked. "What happened?"

"Don't know yet. Get him stabilized. Call for help, just don't move him yet."

Amelia raced off. Maddy glanced at Nancy. "I have to go under."

Nancy stared back, one eyebrow raised. "Can you do that here?"

She answered instinctively. "I have to. I don't have time to go to my office."

She lay down on the floor, took a deep breath and jumped free of her body.

Opening her astral eyes, Maddy studied the black threatening ooze surrounding John's cord. Releasing the tension in her chakras, she reached out to the region of John's cord the energy would envelope next. Mentally, she projected blue and lavender healing waves to that one spot. As if hit by a shock wave, the black energy rippled.

Like a war between titans, Maddy sized up the resistance immediately. There was a person attached to this mess. She sensed the intelligence, their surprise and their frustration. Force was no answer in working to change energy. It engaged the senses and fired up the mind and emotions. Energy, to work effectively, was all about stepping out of the way, sinking into the sensation while detaching from the ego. Maddy had learned to become one with the source of her being, the source of who she was inside, blanking out the issues of her life and awaking fresh from the experience – one with the world.

To work energy positively, she had to be full of grace and joy, content with herself – anything less and it would be too easy to leave a shadow, a tiny piece of herself, behind.

Maddy focused on the area of John's chest. She studied the shadowy energy carefully, needing to see how it reacted. Would it pull back in retreat? Or would it spread so thin as to disappear?

This energy tried to blend into John's energy.

Keeping her wall of healing energy in place, Maddy gently moved the blackness backwards. It thinned out, slinking tightly against John's aura. Her energy block held, maintained the pressure, forcing the apex of the slender layer of blackness to retreat. She sensed a building fury, the absolute blinding tension as the energy was thwarted. It vibrated in place for another moment, before receding down his arm.

Instantly, Maddy moved her energy forward, keeping a firm edge against the receding darkness. Keeping the block in place, she watched it detach from John's arm. The last final bit, infinitesimal in size, fell off, to sit on the floor quivering. She stretched out a finger, her hand full of warm lavender energy. And almost touched it. If the energy were a puppy, she'd be holding out her hand for it to sniff.

The blob wiggled.

Maddy frowned, pulling her hand back slightly. The blob followed. She stopped her retreat and waited to see what it would do. It came closer and closer. Her brows pulled together as realization struck. It was attracted to her energy, her healing energy. Only it wasn't strong enough to attach itself to her.

It wanted to be, though.

Stefan was right. It wasn't necessarily trying to kill anyone. It wanted the energy for itself.

It wanted energy it could use to heal. Healing, loving energy, like hers, would be at the top of the list. Old, sick energy had to be all this person had access to, meaning they were likely to be in the same physical health as those it victimized…feeding on those weaker than itself. A healthy person could repulse a weak attack without even being aware it was happening – unless the attacker had learned the art of killing instantly.

Who was doing this?

"Dr. Maddy?"

She blinked. Nancy was staring at her, or rather, at her body. Maddy gave the blob one last glance, settled two anchors in place for future use then realigned her energy to her physical body.

She closed her eyes for a long moment and when she reopened them, she was viewing the world with her physical eyes. Turning her head toward Nancy, her voice still slow and slurred, she said, "I'm here."

"Good." With a relieved voice, Nancy continued briskly, "John seems to be coming around. His color has improved and his vitals are picking up."

Moving slowly, Maddy sat up and studied John's face. His skin had taken on a more natural appearance, losing the dry, paper-thin look. Hearing footsteps approach, she stood slowly, using the bed for support. Nancy handed her the tablet.

She stepped out of the way as two brawny orderlies arrived and lifted John gently onto his bed. Nancy wrapped a warm blanket around his cool body and settled him in before checking his vitals. Maddy checked his file on her computer and perused his medications. She wrote a couple of quick notes and made a mental one to contact Dr. Cunningham.

John needed to have someone keep a close eye on him. The Kirlian cameras were a moot point. Maddy absolutely knew what was wrong on this floor now. She just didn't know how to stop it.

Most sick people wouldn't be able to save themselves. The attacks, as in John's case, would appear to be a natural decline in health. If energy were drained slowly but regularly, the process would also become familiar. Anything that becomes familiar then becomes harder to recognize or identify as wrong and therefore it would be almost impossible for someone to fight against its damaging effects. It would be viewed as chronic decline.

How would she combat something she couldn't see or recognize?

Walking back to her office, she massaged the back of her neck. Tension had collected there in a tightening pool of aches. She rotated her neck to loosen it.

"Is John okay?" Amelia raced to her side and walked beside her down the hall.

Maddy nodded. "Who attended him last?"

"I'll check. I haven't personally seen him since ten this morning. Candy should have seen him after lunch for his medications, and of course the staff served him lunch and picked up the dishes."

Maddy glanced at Nancy. "Find out names and when they were here, please."

Nancy nodded, but instead of leaving, she touched Maddy's arm. "Is something wrong? Some weird stuff's been going on lately."

"Yes. I don't have all the details. But I will." She refused to let anyone do this type of damage, to her patients or her project.

Maddy's Floor was for healing. It was hers to guard and to protect.

OCCUPANT OF BED 232 stretched out on her bed and pouted. She felt like a bedridden failure and therefore the nurses could damn well call her by her bed name today. Damn it, she hated to fail. She'd almost had it all. She'd wanted more, she'd needed more. She shouldn't have tried a second time today. Only this morning's session had been so brilliant, so wonderfully stimulating that like a crack addict, she had to try it again.

Damn that interfering upstart from the second session – whoever the hell they were. And she'd find out. Nudging up against her anger, fear threatened to settle in. She needed that energy. Without her daily healing injection, she wouldn't be able to function.

Her options were limited. John was the only one she had access to up there now, and his energy had sweetened. Had to be the influence of Dr. Maddy's floor. What the hell was that damn shield anyway? She'd sensed the power of it, she'd seen the loving energies inside of it, and she hadn't been able to enter – she'd tried, though.

She sighed. If she managed to figure out how to get to those people in that bubble, she wouldn't have to go after so many other people. And that child's energy, wow. Was she improving or what? Jealously twisted inside her. Just one smidgen of the child's energy and she would be free from pain for days, not to mention that would kick-start her healing and raise it to new levels.

It wasn't because she hadn't tried, because she had – many times. Somehow, Dr. Maddy had managed to create that bubble to block energy drainers like her. Wasn't that a sneaky thing to do? She stared at the ceiling tiles for a moment. She'd never been able to access Dr. Maddy's energy.

She'd have to consider that though. She needed to know more and do more. Damn doctors. Her skills would have blown this hospital apart if she'd been able to develop them as she should have.

Sinking deeper under the covers, she tugged fretfully at the bedding. She'd have to do without for now. But she had to find another source soon or the drought would send her physical condition spiraling downward. Best if her next donor were to carry Dr. Maddy's sweet, pure energy.

She'd have healed ten times over with that wonderful, positive energy. It was worth fifty of these dying old farts. Their life force was already dried out and decaying. Their energy helped sustain her, kept the worst of the pain away, but theirs would never heal her. She needed to access those patients under Dr. Maddy's care. Better yet, she needed to be under Dr. Maddy's care herself. Then she'd grab all the energy she needed.

Jansen. Now that had been a mistake. She'd gotten greedy. She'd been siphoning little bits off him for a long time, when all of a sudden she hadn't been able to access his energy. That damn bubble had kept her out and away from him, until his bed had been shifted. When she had access again, after so long, she'd lost control and gorged – had taken everything he had. She never experienced a healing quite like that before. It had felt so good she hadn't been able to stop. She might even have killed him. He'd certainly been dead the next day.

That had saddened her. They'd had good times years ago. Then he'd gotten back with his wife and had broken off the relationship. She hadn't meant to kill him.

But, oh Lord, it had felt good.

WHAT A DAY. Gerard dropped his head into his hands. The Board had called with more bad news, and he was on the firing line himself. He'd managed to duck – today. There was no doubt that his ass was being watched and his fingers had been slapped.

Gerard didn't like who he'd become. How had it happened? How had he become a person who sold beds to the highest bidder? Someone who held Maddy's Floor up as an enticement to desperate, dying people? Sure, Maddy was good, but as Jansen's death had proven, she wasn't perfect.

Although that blame might need to be placed at his feet, too. He'd forced her to take Adam on, snuck John in, and already had several fat checks in his hands for the next beds. Dr. Maddy had warned him that breaking away from protocols would change the project, and it had.

His pride had placed him in this position. When the budgets had gotten so bad, he'd wanted to show the others he could handle it. Prove that he could successfully run The Haven, despite the problems and the economy. God, what a fool he'd been then. His ego had won over his sense of right and wrong.

Dispirited, he crossed his arms on his desk and laid his head down.

MADDY CLOSED HER phone and placed it on her desk, confused and slightly disoriented. She stared down at it as if it might explain what had just happened. Gerard had actually apologized for the way he'd been bringing patients on board and disregarding the system specifically designed to maximize the healing abilities of The Haven. He'd agreed that there needed to be a solid rethink of their current policies and procedures, and was setting up a special meeting. Today he sounded more his old self, the strong-in-charge man who'd recruited her years earlier. His voice had surged with power, brimmed with resolution. What the hell had happened to him?

Her cell phone rang. This time it was Drew.

"How long has Nancy Colfax worked for you?"

Maddy started, her mind struggling to switch subjects so fast. "What? Nancy? Uhmmm, I don't know. Four, five years maybe? Why?"

"Did you know her mother had an affair with Uncle John? About six or seven years ago?"

Maddy glanced toward her closed office door. "No, although I can't say I'm surprised. I've heard John was quite a womanizer, and at his age, there might be any number of women connected in one way or other to my circle."

"So you didn't know?"

"No. I did not know." Maddy sighed, slumping back in her chair. "Then again, Nancy probably didn't, either."

"Oh?"

"She hasn't been close to her mother in a couple decades. They exchange the odd phone call. That's the extent of it. Why, are you checking up on her?"

"Not only her. I've extended the parameters to include everyone on the floor with a connection to John, no matter how tenuous. Another avenue to explore would be his caregivers."

Maddy rubbed the bridge of her nose. That would be a long list. "Talk to John. Let him know what's going on and see if he can narrow the list down. By the way, I went over the information Nancy compiled for me, but nothing pops."

"Right. I'll run a few more names, then come over."

She would get to see him again. She smiled "I think I know what caused the bruising," she said abruptly. "At least I might know. I had to think about whether this was possible or not." With a grimace, Maddy forged ahead. "I believe the bruises represent energy entering or exiting the body with extreme force. Normal energy movement wouldn't cause any damage."

A long silence filled the phone line. His voice, harsh and curt stepped in. "What kind of training does someone need to do this?"

"There's no formal training. However, several spiritual groups work with this energy. Some people can stumble on their own power without realizing it. There are people who hop out of their body on a daily basis and never realize it's an unusual skill."

"Can *you* access this energy?"

"Yes, but I wouldn't without the person's permission."

"Okay, I'll keep that in mind. I've got to go."

Her voice dropped to an intimate whisper. "See you later then."

After closing her phone, Maddy got to her feet. She grabbed her tablet and the large stack of paperwork on the side of her desk, strode down to the nurses' station and gratefully dumped the paperwork on the counter.

She greeted the two nurses who were busy working and continued down the hall to check on her patients. Belle slept, something she did most of the day now. Maddy gave her energy a cursory glance, checking for anything out of the ordinary. Everything appeared fine.

Feeling reassured, Maddy moved on from one to another, stopping to talk with those awake and to smile at those sleeping peacefully. With every patient, she searched their energy for any abnormalities, noting changes in blockages of their meridians and updating their files on her tablet.

As she moved toward Felicia, she was aware the energy of the space had changed – was becoming edgy, irritated.

Maddy frowned and picked up the pace.

A shriek split the air.

Maddy ran to Felicia's side.

Alexis sat on the other side of her daughter's bed. "Felicia, take it easy. It was just a nightmare. It's over now."

Felicia opened her eyes and gasped several times. A heavy sweat drenched her skin and sheets as she shuddered. "That wasn't much fun."

Maddy patted her hand as she noted the rapid vibration of the child's energy. Something had scared her badly. "Bad dreams can be like that."

Alexis thanked her. "I'm sure it was bad, baby. But it's all over. You're awake and the dream can't hurt you."

Felicia groaned. "I know, but I'm still scared."

Maddy checked her pulse, noting her heightened color and rapid breathing. Normal signs after a bad shock. "Do you want to tell me about it? The dream?"

Like a frightened rabbit, Felicia retreated deeper into the bedding, shaking her head rapidly. "No, I really don't."

Alexis patted her hand. "It's okay, sweetheart. You don't have to share if you don't want to."

"I don't want to," she whispered, wiping her eyes and face with the sheet.

Maddy settled on the edge of the bedside. Felicia might not want to tell her, yet it would help her a lot if she did. It would also give Maddy a good idea whether she had been affected by the aberrant energy, or something else.

From the box of tissues on the small side table, Alexis handed one to her daughter. "Use this, honey. Dry your tears then get some rest."

"I don't want to go back to sleep." Felicia struggled to shift herself upwards.

Maddy leaned over and gently helped the child sit up against the headboard. She gave a comical groan. "I'm not going to be able to do this much longer, you've gotten so big." She sat back down again. "You know, I think you've gained weight in the short time you've been here." And that was big news.

The two adults glanced at each other in pleased surprise. The fight, as always, was to stop the rapid weight decline. Weight gain was a dream rarely achieved with terminal patients.

Felicia grinned, hope a bright beacon shining on her face.

"Wow. What a smile, young lady." Maddy beamed back at her.

The blankets rippled as Felicia wiggled. "Thanks, I'm feeling lots better."

"That's what I want to hear. Now if we could only do something about those nightmares, huh?"

The smile slipped away from Felicia's face. She twisted the sheets around her fingers.

Reaching over, Maddy held Felicia's hand gently. "I know it's tough, but it would help me to stop them if I knew what they were about. Have you had these often?" Maddy watched the emotions cross her young charge's face. She loved working with children for that reason. They were so open so innocent so trusting. That's why they healed so beautifully.

Felicia shook her head. "No, I'm sleeping really well. It's just today when I had a nap. That's when it happened."

"What happened?"

"I don't know. I went to sleep while Mom read *Harry Potter* to me. The dream started fine, then it turned nasty."

That's the part Maddy needed to hear. Keeping her voice soft and gentle, she asked, "Nasty, how?"

When Felicia didn't answer and wouldn't raise her head, Maddy squeezed her hand gently, comforting her. "It's going to be okay, Felicia. Sometimes the medication we give people can make the mind do funny things."

In a faltering voice, Felicia tried to explain about the meadow and the black cloud that had started like rain and ended up chasing her. She'd fallen down and that's when the blackness tried to smother her. She'd sat up screaming, only to realize she was inside a bubble with the blackness clawing at the outside trying to get in.

Nice. Maddy gave her a bright smile. "Then it was a good dream, Felicia. You were protected inside this bubble. The darkness wasn't able to get you."

Felicia frowned, thinking hard, then her face cleared and she a huge grin split her face. "That's right. I was screaming because I was afraid it would get me, but it didn't. It couldn't because I was safe inside."

"And now you don't have to be scared anymore." Maddy's heart warmed. Felicia's spirit understood she was safe here. Not only safe, she was thriving. Since moving to The Haven, Felicia had shown steady improvement, and it was early. She slept better, mostly, and her arms and legs had strengthened a lot, giving her better mobility. Then there was her appetite. Maddy didn't have her prior record to go by, except the nurses had reported that Felicia was eating often and well. The food was probably better here, too. Maddy would strengthen the bubble around her even more. Felicia would stay safe. Now if only she could figure out how to keep John and Adam safe.

Grinning, Felicia reached her arms up. Maddy gave the child a big hug while her mother watched, tears in her eyes. Walking away, Maddy increased her pace as she moved toward John. Acid bubbled in her stomach. Worry chewed on her consciousness. Maddy needed to find the person doing this and fast. She skidded to a stop at the sound of voices.

Drew's.

"Maddy?"

Startled, Maddy found Drew standing beside his uncle's bed, eye to eye – concern all over his face.

She flushed. "Sorry. Lost in thought." She turned toward John, who lay on the bed. She noted a healthier tone to his skin. Odd to think that he might actually experience a miracle cure and walk out of here – if they could stop the person who was trying to kill him. Grinning at the two men, she said, "So what are you doing, shooting the breeze like two old women?"

John grunted. "Old women? Speak for yourself, young lady. You'll get old yourself one day."

The disgruntled look on his face matched the disgruntled tone of his voice. Maddy chuckled.

"You're perfect the way you are." Drew leaned forward and dropped a kiss on her cheek.

John whistled.

Maddy walked over to John, doing her best to ignore the heat washing over her cheeks and the even stronger heat pooling inside. John smiled at her.

"You dating my nephew?"

"Why?" Maddy kept her tone professional, her smile polite. Her doctor face.

John blustered. "What do you mean, why? Drew's family. What's his business is my business."

Maddy grinned. "Oh, good. So of course, you've given him a full list of all your lovers, haters and wannabes. Because what's your business is his business."

Drew laughed. "She's got you there, Uncle John."

John grumped. "That's private."

"Not anymore." Maddy kept her voice cheerful. She walked over and picked up John's wrist, automatically checking his pulse rate. She frowned. His rate was up.

John jerked his hand free. "I gave him the names already, damn it."

"Good." Maddy made a notation on the screen of her tablet. "This has to stop, Drew. I need to know my patients are safe."

"I'm working on it."

Maddy tapped her foot impatiently. "Not good enough."

John rose to Drew's defense. "Leave the detecting to him and focus on treating people. God knows I'm not cured yet."

Maddy gave him a hard gaze, her hands on her hips. He was right but still… "That's fine. I can transfer you back to your old ward, or Drew can help you to find another place you'd like more."

"Now wait." John struggled to sit up, his thin frame almost quivering with shock. "I'm sorry. I'm not wanting to get transferred."

"Well, maybe I'm wanting to transfer you. Especially after finding out you bribed your way in here."

John blustered, "So what if I did? Gerard needed some equipment and I needed a bed. It's called a trade." His face turned an indignant red.

Maddy glared at him.

John glared back. "You don't understand. They said I was dying and no one could give any answers as to why. I knew you were my only chance. Hell, I've been to every other damn doctor. Nothing. Being here has worked. I feel much better today. I don't know what you did, but it felt wonderful." Hope crossed his face. "I don't suppose I can get that every day?"

"Nope. So any method is fine as long as it works?" Maddy raised one eyebrow as she studied him. "And this from our old chief of police?"

He had the grace to look ashamed. His glance going one to the other and back again. "I admit to using underhanded methods to jump the list. I was desperate."

"Yeah, I got that. But what methods?"

"It's not pertinent." Spit formed at the corner of John's mouth. His gaze circled the room, avoiding hers.

Only it could be pertinent. Maddy's neck tingled. Whatever John was hiding had to come out. "Tell me. No more lies."

Drew held up a hand, except it had no effect.

"All right!" he yelled. "I did blackmail him into it. Okay?"

Maddy sniffed. "I figured that much out already. I want to know over what."

Drew walked over and placed a calming hand on her shoulder. "I understand that you're pissed about this." He turned to his uncle. "Now what did you blackmail Gerard about?"

"It's complicated." John glared at Drew. "And private."

"Too bad. Most things in life are. Give." Drew refused to back down.

"These are family secrets. Ours, too."

Drew reared back. "Ours? What are you talking about?"

"Gerard's sister."

Maddy scrunched up her face, confused. "What about her? I don't think I knew Gerard had a sister. He never mentions her." She shrugged. Her relationship with Gerard hadn't extended to personal conversations. She presumed he had a family like everyone else in the world.

"Well, he does, sort of… At least he's kept up the façade that she's his sister. Only she's not. She's his mother and she's on the second floor of The Haven. Has been for a while. She wants to transfer to your floor, but Gerard won't let her. She scared the hell out of him years ago." John grumped at her, distaste in his voice.

John glared at the two of them, before his shoulders sagged. The wrinkles on his face deepened with pain. "There's decades of family secrets here and I'm not going to tell you all of them. So don't ask. That's Gerard's personal hell – not for public knowledge. But his mother and I were close for a time, way back then. For all I know, Gerard is my son. And that relationship with his mother is not something I'm proud of and I'd just as soon not make it public knowledge."

He groaned and flopped backwards. "And just in case you didn't put two and two together, Gerard's mother is my stepsister, your aunt Doris."

"You're talking about Aunt Doris?" Shock sharpened Drew's voice.

"That means you're saying Gerard is my cousin? Why didn't I know?" He straightened and stared at Maddy. She raised one eyebrow and stared back. They both turned to frown at John.

He frowned back. "Yes, Doris. Damn it, don't look so shocked. It wasn't incest; she's not really your aunt and never was. There's no blood between us. I've told you that before. Why do you think her transfer to Maddy's Floor was never approved? Mental stability is one of the criteria to get here." His face puffed with outrage, the color darkening even more. "When things fell apart for him, Gerard and I worked to keep their relationship hidden."

Maddy stared at John. "And you blackmailed him with his own paternity?" Did nothing make any sense here?

Drew stared at him. "Blackmail? Really? Why would he care if anyone found out?"

John's face flushed a deeper red. He growled, "I didn't really blackmail him. I kinda threatened to. She's not all there, mentally. Been sliding in and out for years. He never wanted people to know about his parentage. It all goes back to a bad time when Gerard was about nine and he almost died in a car accident. He pulled through, obviously. Only his mother started to deteriorate around then and she hasn't been the same since.

"She knew a bunch of kids that died around the same time. Their deaths affected her weird like. The whole thing broke her up." John sat straighter, terrible memories clouding his expression. "She can't handle anyone even talking about it."

Maddy's antennae went up. She met Drew's gaze. *Dead kids.* "How long ago?"

The bluster was long gone from John's face. Weariness and shadows filled his eyes. "Almost thirty years ago. I tried to help her back then, only it was tough and I'm not much of a communicator. She wasn't easy to talk to. She'd spend hours at Gerard's bedside in marathon visits that exhausted her. She'd go home and sleep, then go back to the hospital again.

He gazed off in the distance. "Somewhere around the same time, these kids turned up dead. I remember the case well, because so many of us were undecided as to whether there'd been foul play involved or not. However, for her...hoping and praying so hard for

Gerard to live, when all around kids were dying around the community…well, she was so afraid that Gerard would be next. Needless to say, the stress damn near broke her."

"Had she known the kids? I mean the ones that died?" Drew asked.

"Several of them, if not all of them. It was a small, tightly knit community back then. I think we all knew them in one capacity or other. She'd done daycare for years and had gone on to teach piano, choir, and singing lessons." He shifted uncomfortably on the bed.

"That must have been hard for her." Twisting, Maddy tried to see how Drew was handling this. Confusion clouded his features.

"Well, it certainly did something to her. It seemed that the longer Gerard was in hospital, the more unstable she became."

"Has her mental state improved over the years?" Maddy frowned.

"She was really bad after Gerard recovered. It was a surprise because I thought she'd be fine then. Instead, she became worse. Kept talking about the dead kids as if they were still alive, as if through talking about them, she could make it so. Especially the first one that died, Sissy. She'd known her better than the others. Bad enough as it was, she was into that weird New Age stuff." His jaw clenched.

"Gerard asked to go into foster care, and he eventually changed his name. He said he didn't feel safe with her. I should have helped him then." He glared at both of them. "But I didn't and now he's still hiding the fact that she's his mother. Not sure she even recognizes him. Must be pretty hard… and I never helped."

His anger and guilt had caused him more than a few sleepless nights, Maddy could see. An inkling of an idea, a possibility grew in the back of her mind. She needed more information to see if it fit.

With a heavy sigh and a dark glare toward the window, John said, "Her doctor kept trying new medicine, hoping for improvements, and she did improve but had multiple setbacks as well. She was institutionalized at one time. Then after that doctor passed away, she got a new one and he seemed to be more knowledgeable. With this new medication, she's shown remarkable improvement. She's like a split personality. One day is good and the next she's a different person – even names herself differently at times." John shook his head. "I don't know. I used to visit every once in a while, then I got ill…and well, I haven't been able to. I call her often though."

Maddy stared at Drew. There it was. Her possibility grew into full-grown probability as her mind raced through the events with lightning speed. Could Gerard's sister, aka his mother, have something to do with the energy attacks going on here? Even worse, could she have done something to those kids thirty years ago? There was no motive more powerful than the love of a mother for her dying child, and if this woman felt she was losing Gerard, chances are she'd have done anything to save him.

Desperate people did desperate things, including killing other people's kids to save their own. Maddy had no idea if Doris's actions had saved Gerard. If she'd succeeded in killing these kids, and hadn't cleansed the children's energies from her own aura, then bits and pieces would have stayed with her – slowly poisoning her, and quite possibly manifesting as mental illness. The development of a personality disorder would be a given, and split personality disorder, a distinct possibility. A fascinating case.

Her medical training wanted to delve deeper. The medical intuitive side of her was stunned.

Drew stared at her. "Maddy? Is it possible she could be the person we're looking for?" he asked, his voice hard.

Doris was only one floor below, close enough to keep tabs on Maddy's Floor. Close enough to hear gossip about who was arriving and who was dying. Close enough for her weak, sick mind and body to access other sick people. Close enough to allow a small portion of her energy to float free and live attached to her lover, stepbrother and possibly…to the father of her child – the child being Gerard. That would explain John's ill health these last few years and the recent aggressive attacks on him since his arrival at the Haven.

What about Jansen though – had she known him? How many other deaths could she be responsible for on the floors below? Maybe Jansen – if there were a connection between them.

Yes, definitely possible.

"Yes," she whispered. "It might be." Maddy was stunned by the enormity of what this woman might have done, and what she would continue to do if she weren't stopped. "But you're never going to prove it. And if she's not in her right mind, she may not realize what she's been doing, either."

THURSDAY EVENING

STEFAN GLARED AT the phone. He glanced down at the paint on his hands, his smock, the floor. Damn it, even the phone had yellow on it. And it was Maddy calling. He pushed the speaker button.

"I'm fine. You don't need to keep checking up on me." He rolled his eyes at Maddy's musical laugh. God he loved that woman. She could switch his moods on a dime.

"Glad to hear it. And I'm still going to check up on you, the same as you'd do for me."

He grinned. "Fair enough." Pausing, he shifted energies. Something had changed. He heard it in her tone of voice. "What's wrong?"

Whatever it was involved The Haven. He scanned the markers Maddy had placed. All was normal.

"We think we finally understand some of what's going on, but we don't know how to proceed." Maddy explained how Doris played into the scenario, her relationship with the individuals and her mental state.

We? Oh, Drew was with her. Stefan frowned. "Her mental state makes sense if she's not protecting herself during her 'healing' sessions. We all know many people in psych wards are actually strong psychics that never learned control. What do you want me to do?"

"Drew doesn't have any way to prove what's happening. He's going to talk to his captain in the morning. Doris will have to undergo mental assessment. They will require legal advice as to how to proceed. The protective markers are still intact in John's aura. He appears fine. I've also placed markers on the edges of the bubble and Felicia's bed," she confessed.

She would. Stefan smiled. "That's unnecessary but understandable."

The smile in her voice made his widen. "I know, but she's a child." Her voice became brisk. "What do you think about Doris?"

Stefan finally spoke, slowly, carefully, as if working through a problem. "We know people accidentally bring away pieces of another person's energy with them for many reasons. Over time, Doris would have started disassociating with her reality and splintering off and connecting with these other people – even if they were dead. But..."

"But? Where are you going with all of this?"

Stefan rubbed his temple, only to stare at the smeared splotch of yellow on his fingers. Shit. Shaking his head, he returned to the conversation. "I'm not sure I'm convinced that in her condition she's strong enough to do everything that's been going on there."

"Energy work doesn't require physical strength..." she reminded him.

"No, but it does require some mental strength."

"True. And if she's shown this level of deterioration, then she might not be capable of such focus?" So how could she be stripping these people of their life force now? The answer was she shouldn't be able to. So if she wasn't, then who was?

"Unless one of her realities is strong enough to dominate – then we're dealing with a different person altogether, and that individual might be very capable."

"Exactly." With a heavy sigh, Maddy said, "I'm not sure what to do overnight. We need to keep her locked down, maybe sedated so she can't hurt anyone. Tomorrow, decisions can be made." Her voice thinned. "I really don't want to alert her. We won't know what to do until we know what our options are."

Stefan frowned. He could help. This painting wasn't going anywhere tonight. An emotional mess of bright oranges and yellows sat on the large square canvas. He'd come back to it. Besides, he wouldn't mind looking at this Doris person. See if she'd been the one who'd drained him so quickly. Or connect to another someone who did. "I'll keep an eye on them. I'm doing energy work myself this evening. I'll put in markers and check for any movement, while you *sleep*." Stefan chuckled at Maddy's gasp on the other end.

"Thanks," she said, her voice calm and steady. "Do the same for John, please, just in case. I need to know she's not going to be able to do any more damage tonight."

Snatching up a rag, Stefan tossed his paintbrush and cleaned his hands. "I'll keep an eye on her. If it's Doris, I might know when I check out her energy."

Hesitation tinged her voice. "You won't do anything foolish?"

Stefan groaned. "No. I won't. Everything will be fine. Go home, relax and for once – get some rest."

"Thanks," she said dryly.

His voice dropped the teasing tone, becoming distant and cool. "This isn't over, Maddy. All hell is going to break loose soon."

"What? Stefan, what did you say?"

Silence.

"Stefan?" she added sharply. "Are you there?"

Blinking hard, Stefan realized he'd drifted off somewhere. He cleared his throat. "I'm here. Sorry about that."

"Damn it Stefan…you did it again. You warned that things are going to get worse but gave no details."

He chuckled. "You know I have no control over that. If I get more information, I'll pass it on. In the meantime, say hello to Drew and tell him if he hurts you, he'll have me to deal with."

She laughed lightly. "I'm so not going to tell him that."

"Actually, I heard just fine," Drew spoke into the phone. "Hurting Maddy is not in my plans, Stefan. No worries there."

"Forewarned and all that." Stefan hung up, leaving Maddy gasping. Stefan shut off his phone and headed to his living room. He couldn't wait to see this woman.

Ten minutes later, he settled comfortably in his chair, and slipped free of his body. Stretching at the wonderful sense of freedom, he thought himself to The Haven. According to Maddy, this woman was a floor below hers, in bed 232. He found himself at her bedside instantly.

And stopped. Pink scalp showing through thinning hair, her skin translucent with age, she slept, the covers pulled tightly up to her chin.

This is the person who'd caused such havoc upstairs? He frowned. Surely not. Searching for her cord, he found her spirit inside her body, also resting. Not walking the ethers as he'd expected. Nothing about this scenario made sense. Still, asleep was good for him. He set a protective marker that would alert him if she left her space. There was no way she'd get out without him knowing.

Casting a final glance back at the old, frail-looking woman in the bed, he shook his head and left.

Surely not.

MADDY PROTESTED THE highhandedness of the males in her life, but accepted Drew's lead as he placed his hands on her shoulders and nudged her forward to the stairwell.

She stumbled in the hallway. "Okay, maybe I am tired."

"You need food and rest. Believe me, stress is more exhausting than anything else."

The stairwell was deserted as always. Maddy yawned. "Sounds good. Even better, a pepperoni pizza dripping with double cheese…but in a minute. I'm not going to rest until I check on your aunt's state myself."

Surprise lit his face. He followed willingly enough though, keeping a warm supportive hand on her back as they walked. She loved that protectiveness in him. The caring. That innate strength.

At the door to the landing he stepped forward and held it open. "Are you sure you're up for this?"

Striding through, her back straighter than it had been coming down the stairs, she nodded. "I won't sleep if I don't. Stefan will keep an eye on her, but if I can see her energy, scan her system, it will ease my mind."

By focusing on her destination, Maddy hoped to keep the fatigue at bay long enough to reach Doris's bedside. Drew called out, "Aunt Doris." He strolled closer. Doris was curled up in a ball, sleeping soundly.

Maddy stood at the end of the bed. It was so hard to see this tiny aged woman as a killer. That she was close enough in appearance to the woman she recalled seeing in the hallway outside Eric's ward only confirmed her suspicions and underlined her dismay.

Drew stood beside her.

There was no sign of the killer in her energy that lay close to her body, shimmering as in a deep sleep. Her cord was snuggled up peacefully inside her aura. She wasn't walking the ethers. She slept like a normal person.

Wrapping an arm around Maddy's shoulders, Drew tugged her closer. "Well?"

Maddy closed her eyes briefly. "She's calm, quiet. And she so doesn't look like a killer. Nor does her energy."

He squeezed her shoulders in a quick hug. "You're telling me."

He dropped a lingering kiss on her temple, before dropping his arm to turn her toward him. He searched her eyes. "Is it safe to leave? Are you ready to leave this here and go home to get some rest?"

She rubbed her eyes then glanced up at him with a quick smile. Warmth lit her gaze. "With the bubble strengthened, and Stefan looking after John and Doris, yes, it's safe. It's time to go home to that pizza." Her gaze deepened. "I have to admit to being very hungry."

Drew raised one brow at her. A hint of heat warming his gaze. "No problem," he whispered softly. "Shall I order it now, so it's there for us when we get to your place?"

"What, you have a pizza place on speed dial?" Maddy led the way to the elevators, their hands entwined.

Drew lifted her hand to press a kiss to the back of her wrist. "Of course. I'm a single male and a cop to boot. Pizza is a major food group."

She giggled. "Right, except don't forget, I'm a doctor, and I know what's good for you."

There was a pregnant pause.

Maddy caught his hesitation as she entered the elevator. She turned to face him, instantly caught by the possessive look in his eye. The air becoming still and hot. Her gaze caught. Her pulse raced. Her mind stalled at the look in his eyes.

Electricity flashed.

"I'm counting on that, Doctor… That you really do know what's good for me," he murmured, his voice deep and dark, "because I have high hopes of getting it."

Maddy gazed into Drew's eyes – they'd gone dark with emotion. Heat pooled in her lower belly, her breasts tingling in response. Her breath caught in her throat as heat arced between them.

Drew's jaw firmed and his cheeks hollowed out. "I suggest we go straight home."

Swallowing hard, Maddy didn't dare try for words. She just nodded.

The elevator dinged at the correct floor, opening its cage doors.

Maddy pulled herself together, threw off her lethargy and forced her gaze away from the promise in his. She didn't know how long it would take to get home, only that it would be too long. She shuddered and headed for the exit.

"My truck's over here."

Mutely, she fell into step beside him. Her entire being pulsed with tension. Christ, she couldn't believe how badly she wanted him. Here. Now.

Looking around the interior of his truck, she reached for control. She so didn't want to have their first time together as a mad grapple in the front seat like sex-starved teenagers.

The drive seemed interminable, yet probably lasted less than five minutes. Drew threw the vehicle into park and unlocked the doors. Maddy, still silent, gripped by a fever she'd never experienced before, exited the truck and ran to her front door.

Drew stayed close behind.

"Christ," she whispered as she pounded on the button to call the elevator.

"Here. Let's take this one," Drew said beside her. The doors opened and both bolted inside, careful not to touch.

Maddy shuddered. Drew held out a hand. She took a step back. "No, don't," she whispered. "Not here."

His jaw clenched and he closed his eyes briefly, his outstretched hand dropping to his side, closing into a tight fist.

If he touched her, she'd be lost. Here in an elevator, with her apartment only seconds away. This wasn't the time for that kind of sex. She wanted to make it home. She needed this heat – scorching, driving flames to spread throughout her body, setting fire to her nerve endings.

The elevator was taking too long.

She whimpered.

Drew sucked in his breath, tension radiating from his body. He whispered, like a prayer, "Almost there."

The elevator dinged and opened its doors.

They exploded from the interior and sped past the two doors to her apartment. Maddy fumbled for her keys, swearing under her breath as the lock refused to cooperate. Finally, she pushed the door open.

Drew gave her a gentle shove inside, following her in and slamming the door behind them. Locked it.

They both stopped to look at the other.

Drew opened his arms.

Maddy raced into them.

Their mouths met in a ravenous kiss that provided as much

relief as promise. She snuggled up tight and close, molding herself to the hard ridge between them. Maddy moaned again.

"Shhh." Drew took a deep breath and pulled back slightly, dropping his forehead against hers. "Take it easy. We have all night."

A broken laugh escaped, despite her best efforts. "Doesn't feel like it," she whispered. "It feels like it has to be now or I'm going to die."

A groan wrenched from deep in his chest, his gaze a gentle caress. "Me, too. Let's go to your bedroom."

Maddy blinked, and then glanced around, realizing they were jammed against the front closet. "Oh my God." Desperately trying to collect her thoughts, she said, "I can't believe this. I'm never like this."

"Oh?" The light in his eyes deepened and he bent his head once more.

Maddy evaded his touch. "Beat you there," she called behind her, leaving Drew standing startled in the hallway…but not for long. She'd barely reached her doorway when strong arms slid around her from behind, scooping her into his arms and moving forward in the same motion.

She shrieked and laughed as he tossed her onto her huge bed with such force the mound of comforter poofed up around her. He dropped on top of her.

Her laughter died as flames ignited inside. She kicked off her high heels, wrapped her silk-stockinged legs around his hips and levered tight against him.

Perfect.

His rigid penis rested against her pelvis.

She moaned.

He groaned.

She rocked her hips experimentally.

"Witch," he gasped against her lips as shudders wracked the long length of him. Frantic, he reared back and grabbed her shirt, tugging it up and over her head. Her arms were pulled up and back with the clothing when he stopped.

"What? What's wrong," she gasped, finally popping her head free.

Drew stared down at her, lust in every line of his face, his eyes filled with desire.

Maddy followed his gaze and smiled.

She arched her back, and winked at him. "Like that, do you?"

He flicked his gaze up to hers in disbelief before dropping back down again. "Christ, you are something else, you know that? There's got to be a law against that."

She giggled. "I guess that means you don't like it."

"I love it," he said reverently, "but what is it?"

"A bustier." And one of her favorites, with its black fishnet lacings across the front red lace panels that barely covered her ample breasts.

"Christ."

"I can take it off if you'd prefer," she whispered.

He reared back. "No! Never take it off. Good God." As if unable to contain himself, he bent over and traced the skin between the laces, tasting, teasing and touching.

Maddy cried out as pleasure screamed across her skin. Her nipples pressed hard against the fabric, almost popping free as she arched her back higher, begging and pleading for more. Drew slid his tongue across the lace edge of the bra and shuddered when he found the hardened points peeking out. Using his chin to drag the material lower, he took her left nipple into his mouth and sucked hard.

"Drew," she cried, her pelvis grinding up against him as tiny explosions began deep inside.

"Yes, let go. Fly, I'll be here when you come down."

Shudders rippled across her skin. She closed her eyes, arching higher.

"Let go," he whispered again, taking the right nipple deep inside his mouth and sucking hard.

Maddy cried out as the orgasm slammed through her.

Everything ceased to exist but this moment, this man and, oh God, that mouth. Only he didn't let her rest. He moved up to ravage her mouth, his own need rising to a frenzy.

"Yes," she whispered against his lips. "Oh, yes." Her fingers worked on his shirt buttons, popping the last one as she ripped it open, sliding the material partway down his arms. Taut muscles flexed and rippled under her questing hands as she found his belt buckle, loosening it before attacking the button on his pants.

"Shit." Drew shrugged out of his shirt. With an extraordinary effort, he rolled to the side. He brushed her hands away and stripped off his pants and underwear, even snagged his socks in the process. Within seconds, he peeled her skirt down and came to another sudden halt.

"Christ, woman, you're going to kill me."

He stroked her leg from one slim foot to the top of her thigh where the stockings ended. Her underwear? Only a tiny thong nestled at the top with thin ribbons rising high on her hips. He shuddered, dropped his head, and kissed her in the center of the thong.

Maddy cried out as her need for him once again picked up, threatening to consume her. She reached to slide her thong off, but he stopped her.

"I want you with me this time," she pleaded.

"Oh, I will be." He dropped one more kiss to the heart on the surface of the material and slid a finger under the edge, to stroke the plump moist skin underneath.

She moaned, twisting against him, crying when he removed his hand to slide the material off. Maddy surged up. She couldn't wait. She needed him now. She grabbed his head and tugged his mouth to hers, devouring his lips, nibbling at them, and then kissing them better.

Lowering himself until he rested over her, he held his weight on his forearms, his erection gently nudging against her. Maddy wrapped her legs around him, rubbing against him.

Drew plunged downward until he'd seated himself deep in her center. He dropped his head against her temple and swore.

She smoothed her hands down his back to the hollow at the base of his spine and teased the indent at the top of his muscled cheeks. Tremors rippled down her body. God, she needed this. She needed him.

He lifted his head, locked his gaze with hers and started to move. His hips thrust deeper and deeper. He slowed once, to reach under her backside to open her more, then plunged repeatedly. Increasing the tempo to a frenzied pace, Drew drove them back to the breaking point. Taking her mouth in a ravishing kiss, he withdrew almost all the way.

She cried out in protest.

Drew plunged deep, crushing his hips against hers.

Once again, Maddy's cries soared free as Drew sent her flying off the chasm. With a loud groan, he followed. Collapsing, he shifted his weight to his forearms again and rested his forehead against hers until his breath calmed. Shifting gently, he fell to the side and pulled her close.

Still trembling, Maddy curled into his arms and closed her eyes. With the rapid beat of his heart pounding under her ear, she smiled. Exhausted and exultant, she let the night take her under and she slept.

FRIDAY

WHEN MADDY OPENED her eyes the next morning, early rays of sunshine were already peeking through her curtains. She lay there for a long moment, enjoying the sensation of being held as if she were the most precious thing in the world.

"I wondered when you'd wake up." Tucked behind her, Drew's warm breath bathed the side of her face. "I wasn't sure what time you needed to go to work."

From the circle of his arms, she saw the clock register seven in the morning. "This is fine." She murmured. "This is better than fine. This is wonderful."

He cuddled her closer. Maddy snuggled in, loving the full naked-body embrace. She closed her eyes for a brief second.

"Maddy?" Her shoulders were being gently shaken.

She moaned, and tried to burrow deeper into the blankets.

"Come on, sweetheart. We fell back asleep. It's 8:30 am. Time to get moving."

Her eyes blinked open and she sat upright in shock. "What?" She stared at the clock. "Okay, now I'm late."

She threw back the covers and stood, wincing at the unaccustomed achiness. She'd been well loved last night. After making love for the first time, they'd followed with a second, gentler session that had ended up with the rest of her clothing taken off. After that, they decided other hungers needed to be appeased and they'd ordered pizza. That and a bottle of wine had led to yet another session of wild lovemaking lasting well into the night. No wonder they'd slept in.

Ten minutes later, showered and wrapped in a towel, she stood in front of her bedroom closet.

Drew, bare-chested with his shirt in his hand, walked over to her. He dropped a kiss on her temple. "Are you okay?" Warm, loving concern followed his gaze from her to the tossed room.

She smiled. "Yes. I'm more than okay, but I do have to get moving." Bending down, she collected the lingerie and one stocking on the floor at her feet, and dropped them in the hamper.

"I hope I didn't destroy those last night."

She turned with a silk stocking draped across her arm. "What, these?" She added the stocking to the rest of the items. "They are hardy. Besides," she said with a wicked grin, "I have more."

"Be still my beating heart."

She smirked. She placed one hand on either side of his face and kissed him, long, lovingly and with enough heat to send her pulse skyrocketing. Pulling back, she stared at his flushed skin and the glazed look in his eyes. "Now it's a good morning."

He shuddered and closed his eyes. "That was not fair."

Her laughter filled the room as she dressed quickly, heat still pulsing through her veins. "Tonight, I'll make it up to you."

"Oh, God."

Slipping into navy slacks, she asked, "Did you make coffee?"

"Couldn't find any to make," he replied. He shrugged into his shirt and started to do up the buttons, pausing to study the spot where the last one should have been.

"Do you have time to stop and pick up something on the way?" he said, tucking his shirt in.

She checked the clock and made a face. "No, I'll go straight in and make coffee at my office."

"Great, that gets you coffee. What about breakfast?"

With a cheeky grin, she ran to the kitchen, where she grabbed her purse and keys. She opened the breadbox. "Good thing I remembered these blueberry muffins from Nancy. You take two and I'll take two." She bagged them quickly and handed him his.

"I'm going to see my uncle, so I'll drive you there."

"Perfect, thanks."

At The Haven, he parked in 'visitor parking' and walked in together. While they waited for the elevator, Drew cocked an eyebrow at her. "No sign of the wild woman running up the stairs today?"

She laughed, stepping into the elevator in front of him. Thankfully, they were alone. She punched the buttons for her floor. "No. Wild woman was in full swing last night. She's going to rest up today." A smile played at the corner of her lips.

He eyed her intently. "Rest up for what?"

Just as the doors were about to open, she reached over, kissed him on the corner of the lips and whispered into his ear, "For tonight!"

And walked out of the elevator and into her world.

DR. LENNING SHIFTED slowly into a sitting position in his bed and looked around. He'd been in more than his fair share of hospitals, but he didn't recognize this room. Where was he?

A frown settled between his brows as he stared at the white curtains and standard issue sheets. He smoothed the material between his fingers and made a face. Maddy's Floor had much nicer bedding, not to mention the surroundings. This was regular hospital issue.

"Hey, nice to see you awake." A strange nurse walked into his cubicle and pulled the curtains around his bed. She looked down at him, automatically reaching for the blood pressure cuff hanging on the side.

"How long have I been asleep?" he asked, settling back against his pillows. "What happened?"

"You had a heart attack. You're in the hospital side of The Haven." She gave him a bright professional smile that told him nothing. Typical.

"Where's Dr. Maddy?"

The nurse pursed her lips. "She's on her floor. I thought Dr. Cunningham was your physician?"

"I suppose he is." He turned away, staring at the rolling curtain at his side. So it was over. His one and only chance to save his life through Dr. Maddy was gone. The feelings of lost opportunity and sadness inside almost overwhelmed him. He was going to die soon. He'd played the last trump card and now he was out of options. Dr. Maddy hadn't wanted him there. He'd paid to get there in the first place and now, God – if there were a God – was punishing him. Whether it was because of his errant attraction or his attempt to hurt one of His angels, it no longer mattered. The hope of survival that had dangled in front of him these long months had been snatched away, leaving him bereft, lost and alone.

To his horror, tears heated the corners of his eyes. He squeezed them shut, not wanting the nurse to see. He was the doctor; he shouldn't ever be in this position. What was that saying? *Physician, heal thyself?* Well, he'd tried, and look where he was now.

He'd wagered everything on being saved by the one woman

he'd tried to destroy – and he'd lost.

"How's the pain level?" A note of concern had entered the nurse's voice.

Shit. She was still there. "It's not too bad. I'm just tired."

"Then rest. You'll be feeling better in no time." With a motherly pat on his shoulder that made his skin crawl with disgust, she left. No nurse would have dared do that to him before.

He hadn't been a broken-down, useless man when he practiced medicine. He'd been a commander at the leading edge of technology. Now he was a lump for nurses to practice their skills with thermometers and blood pressure cuffs.

God, how the mighty had fallen.

Dr. Cunningham came around the still-closed curtains, his tablet in his hand. Adam waited while the doctor tapped away on his tablet. Times had certainly changed in the medical world. He loved technology, and didn't miss paper files or charts, either. Computers and tablets made a doctor's life so much easier.

"So, how's the patient this morning?" He peered over at Adam, his gaze assessing and clear.

"Waiting to die, like yesterday and the day before."

"Well, I don't know where you thought you were yesterday; however, out cold here in ICU is where I found you – not that you're going to stay here. You've stabilized and if this continues overnight, we'll make arrangements to transfer you back."

Back? Adam opened his eyes and cleared his throat, almost afraid to ask the burning question. "Am I going back to Maddy's Floor?"

"I believe so, although we are having some issues with the new wing, so that may take another day or two. If that's the case, we'll put you on a different floor until your room is ready."

Dr. Cunningham starting to write down something on the tablet while Adam watched.

He was afraid to hope, afraid to believe. Desperation and fear warred together. In that moment, he saw the scales of justice as they balanced or didn't balance, regarding his life. He'd been a good doctor, a loyal partner, a fair man. Only he'd been hell on wheels to his colleagues. He'd been toughest on Dr. Maddy.

If he was clearing his chest, then he needed to come clean and tell Maddy the truth. Why he'd done what he'd done and how he'd changed. He needed to apologize, to ask her forgiveness and ask for her help. He'd been given a second chance and he'd do his damnedest to make the most of it.

Reaching out a shaky hand, he motioned to Dr. Cunningham just as a one of the many nurses came in to speak with him. Adam waited until they were finished. Dr. Cunningham walking closer. "What can I do for you, Adam?"

"Please tell Dr. Maddy that I need to speak with her. I have something I need to tell her. Something urgent."

The nurse bustled around getting the blood pressure cuff ready. Adam shooed her away. He might die today and that would be a shame. Maddy needed to hear what he had to say. "Just a minute – this is important."

She snagged the cuff around his arm regardless and pumped it up. Adam ignored her like she ignored him.

Dr. Cunningham raised his eyebrow. "Sure, no problem. I'll call her down in a minute."

Adam relaxed. Just another few minutes and she'd come to him. "Thank you. Just another moment, then I can tell her," he whispered to himself.

Then he could bare his soul.

And find his salvation.

MADDY LEANED BACK in her high-backed office chair and sighed blissfully. At least her wonderful night had given her the energy to tackle anything. Good thing, as her day had been full of minor emergencies and it was only half over. Stefan had checked in to say both Doris and John had peacefully slept the night away in their own beds.

She'd heard nothing from Drew or John all morning, and Nancy had delivered a message that Dr. Lenning wanted to speak with her *now*. Nancy hadn't said it quite that way, but Maddy had gotten the gist of it.

Checking her watch, she considered when to fit in five more minutes. Blowing out a gust of breath, she decided there was no time like the present. Besides, going for a walk would help clear her head.

Maddy stood, straightened her tunic and ran down the stairs. She needed the exercise, only one floor was hardly worth the trouble. Still, the joy she felt at the endorphins rushing through her system told her just how bad her stress levels had been lately.

At the double doors, she put on her polished face, walked into the second-floor ward that led to the attached hospital unit. At the front desk, she asked for directions to Dr. Lenning's location. She frowned as she followed the corridor to a ward. She'd expected him to have a private room, not that there was any guarantee one was available. The hospital was as busy and as overcrowded as the rest of The Haven. Chances are Dr. Lenning was lucky to have any bed.

The ward was busy with nurses and visitors. The privacy curtains were pulled closed around Dr. Lenning's bed.

Standing at the outside edge, she called out, "Dr. Lenning, may I come in?"

No answer. Maddy frowned. Perhaps he'd gone back to sleep. She walked toward his bed, catching a glimpse of the window around the corner. At least he'd be able to see outside. Wards were notorious for lack of privacy and freshness.

There was still no sound. A nurse walked toward her, pushing a medication cart and holding a medication cup in the other. Maddy stepped forward to open the curtain for her. The nurse said, "Thanks, Dr. Maddy. We don't get to see you here—" Complete horror washed over her face and she screamed.

Maddy jumped forward. Dr. Lenning lay on his back, blood pouring from a knife stuck high on his chest.

"Shit."

DREW PULLED INTO the parking lot of The Haven. After everything that had happened, he sure as hell hadn't seen this one coming. Maddy had been calm when he'd answered the call and damn near hysterical by the end. His stomach knotted. If she'd been minutes earlier, she might have been the one impaled with a fucking blade.

His hands sweated at the thought. Showing his badge, he swept through the front doors. It was easy to follow the chaos to the group of uniforms clustered outside one room. Noting the detective off to one side, he held up his own badge and motioned toward Maddy. At the detective's nod, Drew walked toward her.

Maddy sat in the hallway on a straight-backed chair, looking like a wilted celery stalk. Her face, pale, shocked. Her eyes round and glistening. His heart went out to her. "Hey, how are you holding up?"

"I've been better." Her smile wobbled. He pulled her into his arms for a comforting hug. He wasn't sure who needed the hug the most. His heart was still pounding, even though he saw she was safe.

"I'm taking you upstairs, then I have to speak with the detectives." He squeezed her gently, ending with a lingering kiss. "I don't want whoever did this to wonder if you'd had an opportunity to speak with Dr. Lenning before he went unconscious."

She shivered. "Nice thought."

Nancy waited for them at the nurses' center. "Maddy, is it true what they're saying? That Dr. Lenning was attacked?"

"Yes, he's in surgery right now. Nancy, who called you to pass on the message?"

"My friend Susie. I've known her for a while. She said Dr. Lenning had asked his doctor to send for you, but she figured he'd be too busy so she contacted me." Nancy shrugged. "She was trying to save the doctor another task and Dr. Lenning had said it was urgent."

"She didn't know what this was about?" Drew stepped in.

With a quick shake of her head, Nancy said, "She didn't say and I didn't ask."

"I'll check with her." Drew smiled, placing a hand in the small of Maddy's back and nudging her toward her office. "Maddy is going to be in her office for a while, keeping a low profile while the police try to sort out this mess."

"Good. I'm glad they're here. The floor's on lockdown, so we'll be fine up here."

Drew nodded. "Then let me out and I'll go see what I can find."

Nancy walked him to the stairwell and unlocked it.

"Make sure you lock up tight," he said.

"We will. You won't be able to get back in without someone's help. And with this mess going on, you'll only be able to go out on the first floor."

The door shut and was locked as he watched. The alarm was reset before he turned to go down the steps to what waited for him there.

GERARD HUNG UP the phone, still in shock. "Dr. Lenning has been stabbed while in ICU. Unbelievable." He repeated it several times aloud, not sure when it would register. The police were all over

The Haven, searching for the suspect and questioning the staff, patients and visitors. *God, what a PR mess.* This was a busy place. Surely, someone had seen something. The attacker had to be nuts. There's no way they'd get away with this.

He'd needed to call the Board. Containment was a priority.

A horrible suspicion preyed on his mind. He knew one person who was crazy. Could she have done this? No, not possible. His mother was neither mentally nor physically capable.

It made him think though. He'd hidden for so long. If there were even the slightest possibility that she was a danger to anyone – well, the new Gerard wanted to make sure he told someone so they could decide if she was dangerous or not.

Drew was the most likely person. Although finding out they were family would be a shock. Not that he thought of either John or Drew in that light. He'd removed himself as far from that family line as he could. He knew it was to time to clear the air and start fresh, without secrets.

Sandra walked into his office. "Gerard, did I hear correctly? Adam was attacked in his hospital room?"

"Stabbed in bed."

Her hands automatically covered her mouth in shock. "Oh no! That's unbelievable. Is he going to be all right?"

Gerard stood up. "He's in surgery now." He walked to the window then turned back to face her. "I have to go speak with the detective downstairs. I should have done something about this a long time ago."

She stared at him. "About what?"

"I don't have time to go into it now. I want you to stay here. Lock yourself in after I leave. I'll call when this is over."

He walked back to his desk, picked up the phone and punched in the numbers. "Hey, are you downstairs? Good, I need to speak with you. I'll be there in five minutes."

Gerard hung up. "I'll be back as soon as I can."

"You can explain afterwards. Please be careful."

"I will." A man had to stop running sometime. He walked out to face his past.

MADDY WAITED UNTIL Nancy completed the lockdown procedure. She couldn't get her mind wrapped around the attack on Adam. She desperately wanted to believe he'd survive. The knife had been high, but…

"All I can think about is what Dr. Lenning might have wanted to tell me."

"And there's no answer to that question for the moment. That's why you need to stay busy. Get at that paperwork on your desk. I'll head back to the nurses' station, get some of my work done, and we'll see how we're both doing in an hour or so." Nancy smiled at Maddy as she stood up. "This will work out; you'll see."

"I hope so." Maddy watched the door shut behind her friend. She hoped the police were efficient. That type of energy swirling around down there would be destructive if it made its way up here. As it was, she was certainly going to need Stefan's help to restore the balance once this was over.

Ignoring the confusion in her mind, she reached for the stack of work. An hour later, she'd worked her way through a good half of it. The stack continued to dwindle until she reached the last piece of paper. It was information that needed to be added to Jansen's file. She brought up the file on her computer. Sadness swept through her. This wasn't an easy thing to do on a day like this one. At least she wouldn't have Dr. Lenning's file to deal with. That would be Dr. Cunningham's job.

Maddy sifted through every bit of information there was. She'd had Jansen as a patient for over a year and the information was vast. Starting at the back, and slowly moving forward she read the notations, went over lab results and charts, wondering if she'd missed something.

It took an hour before she came to the night of his death. In a somber mood, Maddy realized guilt still plagued her, even though she had no idea what else she could have done.

A piece of something out of place niggled the back of her mind. Something didn't jibe. What? She wandered through the pages, looking to confirm a simple piece of information. There. In one conversation, she'd noted that Jansen had admitted to having had several affairs and quietly requested tests for STD because he hadn't wanted his wife to know. The tests had proved negative.

Except he'd had affairs. He'd been particularly worried because an old flame was on another floor and she hadn't been concerned about keeping her affairs private. Had Doris and Jansen been involved at one point? When sexual intercourse took place, energy, as well as body fluids, was exchanged. It would have been easy enough for her to recognize that energy and follow the pathway upstairs to Jansen. And with his bed shifted due to the renovations, Doris might well have had something to do with Jansen's death.

However, she wasn't getting out of her bed to walk the hallways and stab people, certainly not without someone noticing. So, just because Dr. Lenning had been on the same floor as Doris's room when he was stabbed, that didn't mean his attack had anything to do with her.

Adam had made plenty of enemies on his own over the years. She frowned. However, if he died, that did free up another bed on her floor. According to Drew and Gerard, the competition for beds could lead some people to commit murder, which meant everyone in The Haven was suspect. How many patients had applied for a transfer, and how many staff members knew someone who had put in an application form?

That included Doris again. She apparently wanted the transfer very badly. If she weren't capable of doing something like that herself, did she have someone who'd have done this for her?

Either the two crimes weren't connected and there were two perpetrators, or they were connected and Doris had someone helping her.

Yet, nothing explained why Dr. Lenning had been attacked. There'd been no attempt to suck his life force. That knife stabbed into his chest had panic written all over it.

So, why him?

How could she find out? She picked up her cell phone and called one of the nurses she knew well downstairs. "Jenny, this is Dr. Maddy. I have an unusual question. Your patient Doris – does she ever talk about her past relationships?"

Jenny laughed. "Are you kidding? I think it's those memories that are keeping her alive, maybe even healing her. She's something, that one. Now, of course, she's a bit touched in her head, so I wouldn't be listening to everything she said. Still, she apparently has a taste for men in uniform. You know, doctors, police officers, and firefighters. Men like that."

Maddy frowned. Jansen had been a shipyard worker.

"Oh, and that sailor man, apparently he'd been a hot number, too."

"She never mentioned any names, did she?"

"Well, a lot depended on her mental state on any given day. I can tell you that she's been passing around quite freely that there are several of her old flames here in the hospital with her right now."

"Really? That might be a lot of people, considering the population of The Haven."

"True enough. I can't remember any other names, though."

Maddy smiled. "Right, thanks. You've been a big help." Maddy intended to ring off, but remembered something else at the last minute. "Are the police still crawling all around the place?"

"The hallways are blue with them."

Maddy rang off and quickly called Drew. "I'm in the process of closing Jansen Svaar's file and it started me thinking. I think Doris might have been one of Jansen's lovers. And now I'm wondering if Dr. Lenning might have been one as well."

"Not likely. Adam is gay. He had a thirty-year relationship until his partner passed away five years ago. Besides, she's not up to getting out of her bed and stabbing Adam. She's just not capable of that."

Maddy blinked. *Adam was gay?* She shrugged. "So maybe not." She paused. "Not without help anyway," Maddy added as an afterthought.

"Help? As in a partner?" Drew's voice took on a brisk tone. "Let me check a couple things and call you back."

The phone went dead.

Her door opened. She looked up. "Hey, stranger. Good to see you."

FRIDAY EVENING

DREW PUT AWAY his cell phone. He'd considered the concept of a partner, only hadn't been able to put one in the right place to make sense. Nothing about this case made sense.

"Damn it." Now he had to contend with Gerard. He spotted him weaving through the crowded hallway. Once Gerard saw Drew, his gaze locked on him as he made his way over.

As he approached, Drew studied him for family features. Was this man part of his family? Gerard strode determinedly forward...on a mission, a little bit like himself.

"Drew, thanks for waiting." Gerard came to a stop, his eyes a little wild and his hair presenting the opposite of his usual CEO-slick appearance.

"No problem. What did you want to talk about?" Drew crossed his arms and leaned against the wall, waiting. He'd learned a long time ago to make others speak first. Gerard took a deep breath, opened his mouth as if to speak, and then closed it again.

"I'm sorry. This is a little hard."

Drew pursed his lips. "Go ahead when you're ready."

Gerard stared past his shoulder, his eyes unfocused as if looking inward. "Well. It's just...I mean...I don't know if this is relevant or not."

"You let me decide that."

Gerard slipped his hands into his pants pocket and leaned against the wall facing Drew. "The thing is, my mom is a patient here on the second floor, and she's a little touched in the head."

"Right, my aunt Doris."

Astonishment swept across Gerard's face. "Oh, you know already?"

Drew snorted. "I know she's your mother and my uncle John's stepsister, making us cousins of a sort, and that there's a possibility that my uncle might even be your father." Drew watched as the information filtered through Gerard's mind.

Gerard's mouth opened. No sound came out.

"What?"

Interesting. Drew grinned. "Oh, you didn't know that part? How typical of Uncle John."

Raising his brows, Gerard calmly said, "As far as I knew, my dad was Roger Lionel, and he died before I was born."

"And that may be."

Drew tossed off the information as if it were of no importance.

"I didn't know my real father, so another unknown father hardly makes any difference." Gerard stared off in the distance before continuing. "My childhood was tough. I almost died when I was nine or ten, and I spent months, even years, getting back to normal health. The thing is, back then…." He took a deep breath. "Back then, my mother kept saying some pretty creepy stuff."

Gerard searched the area to make sure no one was listening. He bent his head closer. "She kept saying that she'd sacrifice anyone and everyone if it meant I'd live."

Drew straightened, disappointed. "That's not uncommon when a parent is faced with a dying child."

"True. She used to rock back and forth, sitting cross-legged at the end of my bed and whisper stuff like that all the time. She tried everything from healers to meditation to all different kinds of weird New Age stuff. At first, I was too sick to care, but as I improved, I realized the more I healed, the worse she seemed to get. The only way I could cope was to ignore her, block out everything she said. Some of it was beyond creepy." He shuddered once before appearing to get a grip on his emotions. He continued, "Since then, she's been in and out, stable and unstable. Certain medications seemed to help her stabilize for several years. Then they'd stop working and she'd deteriorate."

He slumped against the wall and stared at Drew glumly. "I'm not proud of it, but back then I didn't want anything to do with her and her freaky statements. One phrase in particular stuck in my mind. She kept repeating in this eerie monotone voice, 'Sissy had to go' and then Sissy, a school friend of mine, died along with those other five kids."

Drew stiffened. "Sissy? She actually said that name?"

Gerard's face shadowed with the memory. "Yes. Sissy used to come to the house for piano lessons twice a week. Then I heard

Sissy had died. I tell you, it freaked me out. Hell, I don't even know if all these bits are just the twisted memories of the scared, sick kid I was back then." He rubbed a hand over his face.

"Six kids died within a few months. We knew them all. At the time, I couldn't believe she'd had anything to do with their deaths. I wouldn't believe. Then I couldn't get the possibility out of my mind. I went into foster care not long after I got out of the hospital. I was terrified I'd be next." Gerard stared moodily down the hallway. "Then Dr. Miko said there was something odd recently, about Jansen's death that sounded all too familiar. Unexplained bruises at the base of the spine." Gerard came to an abrupt stop, pain crinkling his features.

That made sense. Gerard was the CEO of The Haven, so it was likely he would be in touch with Dr. Miko over this. "Okay. As an adult looking back, can you see what, if anything, your mother might have had to do with those deaths?"

"I don't know that she had anything to do with them. Just little things she said at the time made me think she had. I don't even remember exactly what she said. But…" He stopped again. "She used to say that no one would know what she'd done. That the tiny mark told no tales and soon with a little more practice, she wouldn't even leave that." He rubbed the bridge of his nose. "I don't know if that makes any sense. It certainly didn't to me."

Comprehension hit Drew. He stared down the hallway, trying to work through the information. People were coming and going with purpose all around them. As unbelievable as it sounded, Gerard had just confirmed what he and Maddy had already worked out. He just couldn't get his mind wrapped around it. Was it possible, that Gerard's mother, his aunt Doris, could have caused all this?

"I hate to think that she hurt others to save me." Gerard stared past Drew's head toward the other end of the hall. "I don't even understand what she might have done. But then, I didn't believe in Maddy's skills before either, and look at some of the things she's achieved."

"If your mother did this and saved you back then, why wouldn't she have healed herself before now?"

A puzzled frown settled on Gerard's face. "I'm not sure. Her new medication may have been a factor. She's been much more alert this last year."

"That makes sense. And you're right, I've noticed some improvement too." Drew shrugged. "It's not easy visiting with people who don't always recognize you." He pulled out his notebook. "Who is her doctor? How long has she been in his care?"

"Dr. Cunningham is now. He's helped her a lot."

Drew wrote the name down in his booklet. "Why did she change doctors?"

"Her old doctor died…about two years ago, I think."

Drew raised his eyebrows. Another death? "There're a lot of deaths strewn around in this mess."

"This one died naturally in his sleep."

A natural death in this mess? Not likely. "I'll look into it. What was his name?"

"Dr. Michaels."

"How old was he?"

"Somewhere in his early sixties, I think. He retired. She was moved to Dr. Cunningham's care and Dr. Michaels passed on a few months later, I believe." Gerard's face twisted, as if finally comprehending Drew's train of thought. "Oh, no. She wouldn't have had anything to do with that."

"Depending on her mental state now, we may never know the answer to that question." Drew leaned back against the wall, realizing his cousin had to be a good eight or nine years older than he was. "It's so hard to contemplate this stuff. It's like the *Twilight Zone* meets the *Ghost Whisperer*."

The two men stood in silence.

"Is there anyone close enough to her they'd help her do this stuff?" Drew had a hard time seeing his aunt as Gerard's mother, let alone a murderess. When Doris entered his own life in his late teen years, he'd had a hard time calling her aunt, to begin with. He'd only done it for her sake. Since his graduation they'd gone their own ways, touching base occasionally. It's only after his uncle had fallen so sick that Drew realized he was in danger of losing both of them and had tried to reconnect with her. It had been a little too late, considering her mental state.

Gerard shook his head. "I don't think so. She doesn't have many people in her life." He half-laughed, a dry bitterness to his tone. "That's not quite true." He fisted his hands on his hips. "She's had so many men that I didn't bother to keep track of them.

"Of course, Dr. Cunningham's been there most of my life. He's been the stable uncle in the background. It's one of the reasons I offered him the job here. Then there's John. He's been even more of a background shadow."

Drew narrowed his gaze on Gerard's face. Along with an awful lot of deaths, Dr. Cunningham's name kept coming up in the conversation. "Do you know how long Dr. Cunningham has been in *her* life?"

"Oh, easily decades. If you'd told me he was my father, I would have believed you in a heartbeat. He's been around forever."

"Would he know about what she might have done for you?"

"Probably. He's been into this New Age stuff for as long as I remember. They used to get into these weird conversations and I'd walk away. It was easier not to know. Of course, that's also what made him perfect for the Maddy's Floor Project."

Drew straightened slowly. That clinched it. Of course he was. He had to have some special qualifications or interests to be part of the project with Maddy. Drew wasn't sure he'd ever seen the man. "You know, I think I'd like to speak with Dr. Cunningham."

"He spoke to the police a while ago. He's probably gone home by now."

Drew started walking toward the police who were still talking to the staff. "Why did the police want to talk to Dr. Cunningham?"

Hurrying to catch up, Gerard said, "Procedure. He was the last one to see Dr. Lenning before the attack."

"He was Dr. Lenning's doctor?"

"Sure, that was Dr. Maddy's way of getting around having Adam on her floor. Talk to Cunningham. I doubt he has anything to hide."

Drew walked up to the first uniformed officer he saw. Pulling out his own badge, he asked the officer if Dr. Cunningham had been questioned.

"Briefly. He's gone upstairs to deal with an emergency."

"You aren't looking at him for this?"

"Him? No. He had every right to be there. Besides, why would he kill anyone that way? Easier to slip them an overdose or an air bubble, and no one would ever know."

Drew thanked him and stepped back out of the way. Dr. Cunningham wouldn't stab anyone, unless he didn't want anyone to suspect him. Turning back to Gerard, he muttered. "Let's go and speak with your mother." It was easier to call his aunt Gerard's mother – it helped him dissociate from his own relationship with her. The thought of Gerard being his cousin was still something he'd have to wrap his mind around.

Gerard led the way down one of the hallways on the left. Drew had never approached his aunt's room from this direction. It was a bright, happy area, although not anywhere near as nice as on Maddy's Floor.

They stopped at the bed number 232. The curtains were closed, giving her some privacy. Drawing it back, the men stepped forward. Drew's lips twitched at the knickknacks his aunt had on the night table and hanging on the wall. The full-length mirror stood as it always had, by the side of her bed. His aunt loved that mirror. It had gone everywhere with her.

"Doris, it's Gerard. How are you?"

Doris beamed at them, her face full of rosy health…and vacant eyes.

"Hi. How nice of you to visit."

Drew studied her face. There were no signs of recognition at all. She didn't know Gerard. She didn't appear to recognize him, either.

"Aunt Doris?"

His aunt's face wrinkled in confusion, her gaze going from Gerard to Drew and back again.

Gerard sighed heavily. "I'm your son, Mom, and this is your nephew, Drew. We both visit you regularly."

She beamed at him. "Such nice boys." She reached out a hand to the side. "Have you met Sissy? She's a lovely lady, isn't she?" She leaned forward and whispered. "She's getting so much better here. It's not fair." Then Doris leaned back, shot her friend a smile and turned back to face them.

It took a moment to sink in.

Then Drew didn't believe what he was seeing.

Aunt Doris was speaking to the woman in the mirror.

She was speaking to her reflection.

Sissy was her reflection.

This was one of her bad days. She'd have recognized him for sure if it had been a good day. He'd heard her say Sissy a few times over these last months, only hadn't connected the name to the first dead girl in his cold case files. Who would? Even now, it didn't make any sense.

Drew changed course. "I'm going to find Dr. Cunningham. Maybe I'll have better luck there."

They wished her a good day and closed the curtain again.

Walking away, Gerard said, "Sorry, sometimes she's fine and the next, well, she's Sissy. It's like a complete split personality. I never know what to expect."

The two men walked toward the stairwell. "I haven't seen her this bad in a while myself. I stopped in to visit several times this last week, but never managed to connect for one reason or another. Is she failing or has her medication been changed?"

"I'll come up with you and we can ask Paul. He'll be more comfortable speaking if I'm around." Gerard disarmed the doors to the stairs, arming them again once they were through, then repeated the process once they stood outside Maddy's Floor. The main hallway had the overhead lights turned down as if it were sleep time for patients.

Gerard walked over to the light switch and flipped it back on. Nothing happened. He frowned.

"Now this is weird."

"Nothing weird about it. Something's wrong." Drew pulled his weapon. "There are no nurses at the station, and there's nothing but silence here." He scouted the long hallway and the open patient areas. His eyes adjusted to the nighttime light settings. The small lights along the hallway at knee height were still on.

"Gerard, what's around the corner?"

"There's a nurses' supply station, lunchroom, a conference room and several clinical rooms."

"So if there's a problem here and someone has taken over the floor, where would the staff be locked up?"

Gerard blinked. "Chances are in the lunchroom or the conference room. Depends on how many staff are still on. It's not that late, so there might be visitors on the floor too. With the lockdown in effect, no one is allowed to leave."

Walking stealthily down the hallway past the nurse's station, Drew peered around the corner. Empty. He frowned. With Gerard on his heels, he walked through the main areas. Patients were in their beds. No one appeared to be bothered. Televisions were playing, radios on – only there were no nurses, orderlies, or aides. All the staff on duty for this shift were missing.

Drew considered that. Maddy's office was at one end of the floor. His uncle was at the other. Undecided, he searched from one end to the other. Then he motioned in the direction of his uncle. "Let's try the new wing."

Closer to John's bed, he heard voices. He held up a hand to

stop Gerard's forward movement. "Shh."

A muffled murmur.

He moved another couple of feet and slid along the side wall. He could almost make out the words.

"You didn't think I was going to walk away from all this, did you?" The deep masculine voice destroyed the hope in Drew's heart.

HER WORLD HAD taken a left into chaos. Dr. Cunningham held that damn gun as capably as he held a surgeon's knife. There wasn't even a tremor to indicate nervousness. He'd walked into her office and had taken control of the floor. He'd forced her staff into her office and locked it, then with the gun at her back, he'd walked through the floor checking to make sure there was no one else.

Where the hell was Drew? And Stefan? She'd sent him several messages mentally, but outside of an acknowledgement from him a few seconds ago, there'd been nothing. At least, she knew the cops would be alerted.

In the meantime, she had to deal with one of the worst betrayals possible. The other person, who'd invested so much time and effort into her healing project, was…a killer. It did explain so much though. Like why she'd never noticed any sense of 'alien' energy at work. It hadn't been a stranger. Paul Cunningham had been working here since her project had started. His energy belonged here.

Somehow, she needed to buy them all more time so Drew could come rescue them. And she needed John to continue to stay calm and quiet. Not to mention her other patients. Damn Paul, anyway. How dare he put these people in danger like this?

Maddy strove to keep her voice calm and neutral. "I don't suppose so. Still, it's not as if anyone would be able to find you if you disappeared. Not with what you know how to do."

"You would."

She stalled. Of course, she would, but he didn't need to know that. "Possibly. Still that doesn't mean I'd do anything about it. You know the patients and this project mean everything to me. I'd hardly jeopardize them."

"You wouldn't be able to help yourself. You're a sanctimonious do-gooder."

She tried for a light laugh. "I won't be able to prove anything.

Just walk away." She hoped she'd injected the right amount of reasonable eagerness. She was no actress, and she'd always been a terrible poker player.

"I plan on it. Just like I plan on getting younger – no lying around waiting to die for me." Dr. Cunningham laughed. "How's that for a goal?"

"Not bad, if you can do it." She winced. Doubting him wasn't the best way to keep him amiable.

"Oh, I can, and you know it. It took me years to figure out what Doris had done, and then years of befriending that whore to figure how to get her to teach me. It took years of practicing to get to the point where I could siphon off a person's energy like she could. What wasn't fun was getting her stable enough to teach."

"I don't understand; what exactly *are* you doing? Like, what was the point of the black energy under John's bed? Why would you need that there?"

"You don't understand anything. John and Doris have been playing one-upmanship forever. Why do you think he's been sick for so long? Doris has had her hooks into John for years. It's only since we managed to get the right drugs into her and she realized how much time she'd lost that she wanted to make John pay. The hooks were already in place. The dark energy was her way of feeding off him. But it's made her crazier, too. She's getting worse. I've had to increase her medication again. Rather gross, actually."

He shrugged. "If she remains drugged, then the energy will only stay if I choose to continue to feed it. If I don't, then it will wither away. I know enough to continue my training on my own." He stared at her curiously. "She's gotten away with it for a long time."

"So she really killed this way?" Shock and pain at the terrible betrayal twisted her insides. Her brain was stuck on the fact that the man who was supposed to be making a success of Maddy's Floor had been using it as a feeding ground for his evil purposes.

"Well, I can't kill anyone that way yet, but I can make them really sick while I take their energy and use it for myself."

"So was it you or Doris who killed Jansen?" Maddy couldn't believe what she was hearing. Or reconcile the woman downstairs with the killer who'd taken Jansen's life – and who knew how many others?

"That was the demonstration that went a little too far. Man, she's smooth like that. Years of practice, she said. That's how she saved her son from sure death when he was just a kid. Once he'd healed, she had to do it every few months or more, almost like a junkie needing a fix, except that engaging in that process changed her. Her mental state deteriorated. Eventually, she had trouble remembering what to do and how to do it.

"That's where I came in. I finally stabilized her medications, and when I explained to her that her old doctor was to blame, she killed him out of revenge."

He laughed, a macabre sound that made Maddy cringe inside. If Cunningham got away with the knowledge he had...well there'd be no stopping him. "She's something. She also knew things about energy that most of us would never imagine. The combination was deadly."

Maddy said, "Except for one slight problem. She's a mental case from hell due to that knowledge...that's all." Her sarcasm was lost on him. The things these two people had done made her want to vomit.

He shrugged. "She was on the delicate side to begin with."

"Do you know who she killed years ago to save her son?"

"Ask that detective friend of yours. He'd be able to look it up. She picked on children back then because they were so innocent and open. That made it easier for her. Besides, children's energy is healthier and stronger than adult energy. She wasted much of it because she didn't really know what she was doing.

"She believed that children's energy was better to heal a child. Something about being a better match, like blood types. Once her mental state started to slide, she wasn't capable of doing that anymore. She said it had something to do with a healthy person's energy being able to block hers. The healthy energy would see her energy as abnormal – parasitic. For those here on Maddy's Floor, their energy systems are compromised already, making them easier targets." He laughed. "Thanks for giving us this wonderful opportunity."

So it wasn't a feeding ground, at least not for him. Instead, her floor had been his training field.

He walked around Maddy, keeping the gun trained on her and John, who'd stayed still.

He slipped his hand in his pocket. He pulled a small blue book out of his pocket and waved it around. "Talk about coincidence. I had an old guy come into the ER. He'd gotten into an argument with another old fart about this diary. Seems his kid was murdered years ago and this is the diary his wife kept at the time. She listed all the people and places the kid had been in contact with – to help the police find his killer. All these years, the diary had been lost in the house.

"I grabbed it out of curiosity, thinking to accidentally 'find' it and return it later. Only it actually lists Doris in here several times, so I couldn't hand it over." His face twisted with satisfaction. "After all these years, she was finally going to be caught. I wasn't going to hang around to wait for that. Who knows what she'd end up saying."

Like a crazy man who'd pulled off something everyone else said couldn't be done, he was proud of himself. His work.

Maddy stood in shocked disbelief.

"Doris might still say something." Maddy didn't want to put Doris in any danger, yet she needed to keep Dr. Cunningham talking.

"No, she won't. I've changed her medication. She'll be a blathering idiot by now."

Nice. Use her mental illness to make her a non-suspect. Maddy tossed her head. "So much for being a doctor and caring about your patients."

"I've been a great doctor. When have I ever done a patient wrong? And no, Doris doesn't come into this. She's a bloody murderer. You should be thanking me for taking care of the problem. She won't be able to kill any more people now. Too bad you didn't realize she was hurting and killing people right under your nose." His voice changed to mimic a woman's high voice, his hand wafting in front of him. "Oh no, not Dr. Maddy – she's so perfect."

Maddy winced. That sounded horrible coming from him. "I've never professed to be perfect."

"Maybe not, but you've been blind to her murderous tricks. She's killed at least two men that I know of, one young and one old, and that's just in the last two weeks. She told me about them. She'd known the one since forever and the young one since he was a kid. Said she couldn't resist. Even then, her grasp on reality wasn't very good. The more she did, the worse she got. She hadn't gone after those two with the intent to kill, but hadn't been able to stop herself. She's losing control. I had to stop her. I couldn't trust her anymore." Something about the look on his face – it had turned analytical – gave Maddy the impression he wanted to experience the same sensations Doris had.

Maddy shuddered. Two? Eric and Jansen? One young and one old. And maybe more that she didn't know about. They'd have to go back to the date of Doris's arrival and check. She'd heard a whisper in her mind during her mad flight to Eric's bed that day. Could that have been Doris?

Paul continued to talk. "Adam told me how much he needed to see you, to tell you the truth. I had no idea what he'd planned to tell you, although the odds were good that it wasn't in my favor. He'd overheard me on the phone one day when I thought he'd been sleeping. I'd been confirming my travel plans to the Canary Islands. I didn't dare let him tell anyone.

"I panicked actually. With Doris done and out of the picture, I'd planned to leave this weekend anyway." He snorted. "But how the hell you got the message I don't know. No one was supposed to find him that fast. Had to have been that nurse. Because there you were…again." He glared at her. "Made me move my schedule up."

Maddy's jaw dropped. "You stabbed Adam just because he *might* have overheard a phone call of yours? A call that in no way connected you to any murders or attacks…yet you stabbed him for that?" The more she studied his face and his aura, the more she realized how unstable *he* was. "You've been practicing the techniques Doris has shown you, haven't you?"

"Of course." He glared at her. "I'm over sixty, Maddy. I have no intention of waiting until I'm dying before I start availing myself of all that glorious energy. That would be stupid."

"Stupid or not, you've made the same mistake she did. You've been collecting bits and pieces of other people around you. See Doris, the way she is? That's your future."

He rolled his eyes. "Nonsense. I've perfected her technique. She's the nutcase. I'm careful. I have a beautiful future ahead of me. No one is going to mess that up." His head cocked to one side. A calculating look came over his face.

"Don't make a sound," he whispered, his gaze sweeping over John huddled under his covers and the rest of the empty room.

Maddy had been harboring a snake in her own space and hadn't known it. He'd used her and her project. Unforgivable. She thought he'd been such a stalwart supporter, a hard worker and a good friend. Instead, that shell harbored a hardened, callous animal.

An odd sound whispered from behind her.

Dr. Cunningham motioned to something behind Maddy. "Welcome to the party. But throw your gun to the ground."

Maddy spun around.

Drew and Gerard walked into the open.

Drew glared, steely eyed at Dr. Cunningham, the gun steady in his hand.

"Do it. Or Maddy gets the first bullet."

The gun dropped from Drew's hand. Drew kicked it off to the side. A muscle in his jaw pulsed, but he never dropped his gaze from Dr. Cunningham.

Crap. The right man was here to help her – the wrong man was holding the gun.

Drew's face bolstered her courage. Pissed, his eyes held a cold, hard edge. Damn, the man looked good. And damn, she had it bad, if she could stand here with a crazed killer and think how wonderful Drew looked.

"Maddy, are you okay?" Drew's eyes were still trained on the gun.

"Why don't you ask me how I'm doing?" John's querulous voice quavered from the direction of the bed. His small, shrunken frame hard to see under the blankets. "I'm fine, thank you. Almost dead because of him and his damn mother. I could hardly believe all he was saying." He pointed at Drew. "Now, what the hell are you going to do about this mess?"

Dr. Cunningham snorted. "As if he's in a position to do anything."

"He's my nephew and he's a cop, so he'd damn well better do something."

Maddy winced. Just what she needed – a fight between a patient and a killer. "Everything is going to be fine, John."

"Sorry, Maddy, you're not going to be able to fix everything this time," Dr. Cunningham said, moving the gun between the four of them. "So who wants to go first?"

Without warning, Drew jumped him. The gun went off as Drew kicked it out of Dr. Cunningham's hands. The two men went down in a flurry of arms and legs. Gerard rushed in to help. Maddy snagged up the gun as it skidded across the floor, then waded into the fight to hold the gun to her colleague's head.

"Stop right there, or I'll shoot."

The men froze, their chests heaving. Dr. Cunningham laughed and snatched at the gun. In the fight to keep it, somehow the gun was fired again. She couldn't see if it did any damage as Dr. Cunningham wrenched it from her hands. "You won't kill me. You're too damn soft."

A third gunshot sounded.

Maddy jumped back. The first gun dropped to the floor as Dr. Cunningham fell, groaning. Everyone turned to John, who held himself up on one elbow, shaky but defiant, a small revolver in his hand.

"Like I'm going to let some asshole like him kill me."

Drew walked over and plucked that gun from his John's hand. "You don't need that anymore."

Maddy dropped to the floor, her instincts taking over. John had shot true. Dr. Cunningham was dead.

With his cell phone Gerard called for security and emergency assistance.

Maddy looked at Drew. "I can't believe it was him. He was actually using my project to hurt people." The whole concept bewildered her. "He stabbed Adam. I passed him in the hallway on my way to Adam's room. I didn't think anything of it at the time." She shivered. "He had such an odd look on his face."

"Maddy, where are the staff?"

The color drained from her face. "Oh my God, I forgot about them. They're locked in my office."

"I'll go get them." Gerard ran down the hallway as security opened the locked doors. Police flooded the area. She was so going to need Stefan's help to rid the floor of these negative energies, to restore the healing balance here – but not tonight.

Maddy stepped back, turning to look at Drew and gasped in shock. "Damn it, Drew, why didn't you tell me you'd been hurt?" Maddy reached his side, her hand slapping down on his chest.

He tried to brush her hands away. "No, I'm fine."

Only he wasn't. Maddy gaped at her hand. Fresh blood dripped from her fingers. As Maddy watched, the color drained from his face and he leaned on her slightly before collapsing. She slid her arms around him and tried to support his weight as two officers raced over to help.

Maddy dropped to her knees by his side. "Oh, God." She slid her hand underneath. There was no exit hole. "Call emergency, he's been shot in the chest." A nurse ran toward her. Maddy snapped, "Get a stretcher. We have to get him downstairs. Now!"

Organized chaos ensued when Maddy's training and the training of those around her kicked in.

MADDY HAD TROUBLE remembering the sequence of events or the people involved after that. The next thing she knew, she was staring at the closed surgery doors. She'd been stopped from entering as Drew was rushed inside.

Firmly, the surgical nurse turned her around and pushed her in the direction of the waiting room.

Maddy paced for the first hour, then sat for the next. She'd been pouring energy into the operating room since she'd been kicked out. She'd tried to direct it into him, but there'd been so many people clogging the path, she hadn't been able to do that. She should have left her body and gone in to help heal him, but she'd been so distraught she couldn't function on that level now. Stefan was in there funneling energy, but he wasn't the healer – she was.

What was taking them so long? When no one came out after a reasonable time, she knew in her heart it was bad. Why hadn't she checked Drew first? Because she hadn't known he'd been hurt. He'd acted so normal and she'd been so numbed by the shooting of Dr. Cunningham, and what she'd learned…she hadn't realized exactly what had happened.

He'd been in there a long time. Too long. Nancy had even come to check on her, handing her a hot coffee. Maddy had phoned John to update him. Now everyone had to wait. Currently, Gerard sat beside her. The CEO had never looked so haggard.

Maddy sympathized. Her world centered on what was going on in the surgical room. She was locked in by her fear. In a place of no return. She should be helping them. She had skills that could help – if she were calm enough.

She needed to find her center of balance. He needed her. She shuddered. He had the best team possible working on him. They'd save him. They had to.

Maddy. Stefan's voice in her mind stopped her in her tracks. *Stop and calm down. He needs your help. Our help. It's bad. You have to pull back. You're needed but you can't help him like this.*

Just then, the door opened and Dr. Samson, a physician she knew slightly, came out. The blood drained from her face at the look on his.

Drew hadn't made it.

He didn't want to meet her gaze. She ran up to him. "Dr. Maddy, we tried. Honest. He'd lost too much blood. The tears on the inside..." Dr. Samson shook his head. "I'm sorry, but the bullet nicked an artery—"

Maddy was no longer listening. She bolted through the double doors and into the OR. Drew was still on the operating table, a sheet over his head, blood coating – well, everything. They'd tried. She got that. Only they didn't know what she did.

She might be able to save him. There was one more thing she could do. She'd never tried on someone this far gone, but...

Once she saw his cord, threadlike and wispy and still attached, she knew for sure. She flipped the sheet back to see his face. As Maddy pulled up a high stool from against the wall, the operating nurses withdrew, leaving her alone.

Stefan... Help.

Maddy closed her eyes and slipped out of her body.

And slipped into Drew's.

It took a long scary minute to find his consciousness.

Maddy? What the hell?

Hush. You're hurt. I have to heal you. Don't waste your energy. Think about life, living and loving. Especially about loving. And Maddy had to do the same. To take her abilities to this level, with this deadly level of damage, she had to let go. Of her fears, her doubts, her emotions. She had to be one with him, no walls, no hesitation, no holding back – *she had to be him.*

Maddy poured her energy into his damaged body, filling his heart with life, his veins with the blood and his body with healing energy. She knitted the artery closed, repaired torn tissues and damaged muscle.

The whole time she sensed Stefan's protective energy around her, funneling love, caring and energy her way. To heal like this took strength. It took acceptance. It took surrender. To herself. To Drew. To what could have been. To what could be.

She didn't know how long she was in there. She didn't care. She wouldn't leave until it was done. Seconds ticked by, then minutes. Vaguely, she heard noises going on behind her. She knew the OR staff watched her. She thought someone wanted to move her, but heard Nancy stopped them before making the attempt. She didn't worry. Stefan would take care of them. Right now, she was caught in an energy frenzy that filled the room with heavy pulsing vibrations.

Static buzzed and the air moved on its own. No one there could misunderstand that something major was stirring in the ethers.

Maddy's space. That was her domain.

The OR belonged to the medical world. The ethers belonged to her. She intensified her efforts. She had to save Drew. He'd become too important to let go. She wasn't even sure if she could anymore. If he died, he might take her with him at this point.

Dimly, she heard a series of beeps, followed by yelling and the sound of rushing footsteps. Maddy shoved everything out of her mind. The waves pulsed from her fingers, her heart and her soul.

More. Stronger energy, whiter energy. Everything she had, everything she'd been, everything she was – poured into his soul.

"Maddy?"

"Maddy. Stop. We can take it from here."

Let go, Maddy. He's back. Stefan's warm, loving voice slipped deeper into her subconscious, pulling her back, helping her return home. Finally, other voices penetrated the fog she'd buried herself in. Maddy slowly sensed other people in the room. She saw the matrix of other energies working at her side, working to save Drew.

"He's back. We've got him. It's okay. Let go now before you collapse."

"Dr. Maddy, stop!"

Maddy heard something else too. *Maddy, I love you. Let go, sweetheart. I'm fine.*

Love you, too. Sorry, I couldn't let you go. Then she did let go and crumpled to the floor, unconscious.

SATURDAY

DREW WOKE UP feeling like shit. He groaned and tried to roll over. Pain stabbed at his chest and radiated outward. A cry wrenched free. Christ, he hurt.

"Don't move, you've been shot and you've had surgery. You're going to be fine. However, you're going to feel terrible for a while."

Duh.

He opened his eyes. A very tired looking, breathtakingly lovely Maddy sat on the edge of his hospital bed, smiling at him. His first attempt to speak was a little weak, a little thin. "Does this mean I get to move to Maddy's Floor?"

"Hell no. You won't be here for longer than a day or two at the most. Just long enough to regain your strength. And if you behave, they might release you early for good behavior." When she smiled down at him Drew thought he'd never seen anything so beautiful as his beloved Maddy.

Memories filtered back into his mind. A sporadic image. The odd word.

"Did you have a hand in my recovery?" Drew studied the weariness on her face. Had she slept at all? He glanced over at the chair beside his bed. Sure enough, her purse and what looked to be several discarded coffee cups sat on the floor beside it.

The room around him came into clearer view. His surroundings were nowhere near as nice as Maddy's Floor. Still, like she said, he wouldn't be here long enough to care. As a matter of fact, he wasn't feeling too bad at all.

"Maybe. How are you feeling?"

"I feel good. How about you? Did you sit in that chair all night? Have you no sense at all?" he teased.

"I'm fine." She snickered. "I'm not the one who walked into a bullet."

He closed his eyes at the reminder. "Right. I'm willing to forget that part. It couldn't have been that bad. I'm here, aren't I?"

Dr. Samson walked into the room in time to hear that last part. "And that part is a miracle. I'm going to tell you, young man, you shouldn't be here at all. You took a bullet to the chest that nicked a main artery of your heart. You bled out on us and for all our best efforts, we lost you. We gave up." He tapped on his stylus for a moment then looked up to run a professional eye over Drew.

Drew started. What? "I died?" His gaze encompassed Dr. Samson and Maddy, her lips quirking at his question.

Dr. Samson nodded. His years of medical experience showed in the pure white hair and wrinkles, but his face was animated. "Not only died, but we couldn't revive you. And we tried hard." He walked over to where Maddy sat. "I went out, told this young lady, and she bolted into the operating room and refused to let you go."

Maddy patted Drew's hand, her warm eyes smiling down at him.

The doctor studied her, a light in his eyes, wonder in his voice. "I've got to tell you, I've seen a lot of things in my life, including many miracles, but I've never ever seen anything like what I saw her do to you. She healed the hole in your artery, made your heart beat again, filled your veins with blood, and did too many other things to mention. I stood in the back of that room with my colleagues and watched in awe while the room pulsed and glowed as she put you back together."

He shoved his hands in his pockets and rocked back on his heels. "Somehow, she did what shouldn't have been possible to do – she brought you back to life." With an apologetic glance at Maddy, he explained, "I only stepped in to help because she appeared to be on the point of collapse. We stitched you closed and that's about it."

He patted Maddy's shoulder. "Now that I have some idea of what goes on in the special project of yours, young lady, I've got to admit, I'd like to learn a whole lot more."

Maddy looked up at him, a small smile playing at the corner of her lips. "Anytime."

"It obviously takes a toll on you, and I can see why you don't want to advertise your abilities. So make sure you rest for a couple of days yourself. Okay?"

"I will," she promised and watched him leave the room.

Turning back to face Drew, she found him studying her speculatively. "What's that look for?"

"You can do that? Bring people back from the dead?"

She frowned, shook her head, stared down at the sheets, her hands instinctively smoothing the wrinkles away. "You mean the others I've helped? There are a lot of factors that go into it, and then sometimes, if everything goes well, I might stop some of them from dying. Not always and not everyone, but sometimes…I can save one."

"And that makes it all worthwhile," he said, instinctively knowing the answer to his question. Because he had died. And she had brought him back.

She gazed down at him, her eyes so warm and loving.

He knew he was blessed.

"And that makes it all worthwhile."

"Speaking of people dying, how are Dr. Lenning and my uncle?"

"Your uncle is raising hell on my floor, and soon Dr. Lenning will be returning to help him." She grinned in delight. "Those two are going to get along wonderfully. Stefan says 'hi' and to stop doing things like catching bullets or you'll give *him* a heart attack."

"Well, you can tell him that I don't plan on ever going through that again."

She laughed. "I'm sure he knows already."

Drew studied her face. "I also remember something else while I was under."

Maddy gazed at him quizzically. "Really? What was that?"

"I remember a certain doctor telling me that she loved me."

A rosy flush rolled across her cheeks. She gave him a knowing smile. "That's okay – you said it first."

"Did not," he protested.

"Did too." They grinned at each other.

"Mean it?" he asked, studying her face intently.

She studied his features, her insides melting. "Absolutely. Did you?"

"Oh yes." He tugged her toward him, and kissed her thoroughly. So thoroughly, she didn't think he'd be in the hospital for more than a day – if that. "I feel great. It must be that extra dose of Maddy energy."

She grimaced. "There might be a few side effects of that, by the way."

"Like a more intimate knowledge of what you're thinking and

feeling?" he murmured, tugging her back down to nestle against his good side. "Yes, I'm healing very rapidly, thank you."

She chuckled. "Yes, something like that. Of course, it works both ways, and just to inform you, the hospital bed is not the place to make love – you're not that healthy."

Surprise lit the depths of his eyes and he chuckled. "This will take some getting used to. We have a fun journey ahead of us."

"That it will be," she whispered against his lips. "Scared yet?"

"No way. Interested. Intrigued. In love. And looking forward to seeing how well this works out for both of us." Laughter colored his voice.

Sounds good to me, she whispered in her mind.

And to me, too. Did I tell you I love you, Dr. Maddy?

Not recently.

Well, I do. Now and forever.

Author's Note

Thank you for reading Psychic Visions Books 1–3! If you enjoyed my book, I'd appreciate it if you'd leave a review.

Dear reader,

I love to hear from readers, and you can contact me at my website: www.dalemayer.com or at my Facebook author page. To be informed of new releases and special offers, sign up for my newsletter. And if you are interested in joining Dale Mayer's Fan Club, here is the Facebook sign up page.

Cheers,
Dale Mayer

Thank you for reading *Psychic Visions Books 1–3*. The series continues with Garden of Sorrow.

Garden of Sorrow

Book 4 of Psychic Visions Series

Buy this book at your favorite vendor.

Her world is in chaos. His world is in order. She wants to help the innocent. He wants to catch the guilty. But someone is trying to make sure that neither gets what they want.

Alexis Gordon has spent the last year trying to get over the loss of her sister. Then she goes to work on a normal day…and reality as she knows it…disappears.

Detective Kevin Sutherland, armed with his own psychic abilities, recognizes her gift and calls in his friend Stefan Kronos, a psychic artist and law enforcement consultant, to help her develop her skills. But Kevin has never seen anything like this case – a killer with a personal vendetta to stop Alexis from finding out more about him…and his long dead victims.

The killer can be stopped. He must be stopped. But he's planning on surviving…even after death.

Psychic Vision Series

Tuesday's Child

Hide'n Go Seek

Maddy's Floor

Garden of Sorrow

Knock, Knock...

Rare Find

Eyes to the Soul

Now You See Her

Shattered

Into the Night...

Psychic Visions 3in1

Psychic Visions Set 4–6

Psychic Visions Set 7–9

Your Free Book Awaits!

KILL OR BE KILLED

Part of an elite SEAL team, Mason takes on the dangerous jobs no one else wants to do – or can do. When he's on a mission, he's focused and dedicated. When he's not, he plays as hard as he fights.

Until he meets a woman he can't have but can't forget. Software developer, Tesla lost her brother in combat and has no intention of getting close to someone else in the military. Determined to save other US soldiers from a similar fate, she's created a program that could save lives. But other countries know about the program, and they won't stop until they get it – and get her.

Time is running out … For her … For him … For them …

DOWNLOAD a ***complimentary*** copy of MASON? Just tell me where to send it!

Second Chances

Go ahead. Take Charge of your life. Move forward...if you can...

Changing her future means letting go of her past. Karina heads to a weekend seminar and discovers the speaker is the person she needs to move on from. But she soon realizes bigger issues are facing her...

Brian has moved on, at least he'd believed he had... until he sees Karina in his audience...and realizes he's been lying to himself.

Passion pulls them together, love binds them together, but a revengeful enemy determines to keep the two apart...and destroy them both.

Touched by Death

adult RS/thriller

Death had touched anthropologist Jade Hansen in Haiti once before, costing her an unborn child and perhaps her very sanity.

A year later, determined to face her own issues, she returns to Haiti with a mortuary team to recover the bodies of an American family from a mass grave. Visiting his brother after the quake, independent contractor Dane Carter puts his life on hold to help the sleepy town of Jacmel rebuild. But he finds it hard to like his brother's pregnant wife or her family. He wants to go home, until he meets Jade – and realizes what's missing in his own life. When the mortuary team begins work, it's as if malevolence has been released from the earth. Instead of laying her ghosts to rest, Jade finds herself confronting death and terror again.

And the man who unexpectedly awakens her heart – is right in the middle of it all.

About the Author

Dale Mayer is a USA Today bestselling author best known for her Psychic Visions and Family Blood Ties series. Her contemporary romances are raw and full of passion and emotion (Second Chances, SKIN), her thrillers will keep you guessing (By Death series), and her romantic comedies will keep you giggling (It's a Dog's Life and Charmin Marvin Romantic Comedy series).

She honors the stories that come to her – and some of them are crazy and break all the rules and cross multiple genres!

To go with her fiction, she also writes nonfiction in many different fields with books available on resume writing, companion gardening and the US mortgage system. She has recently published her Career Essentials Series. All her books are available in print and ebook format.

Connect with Dale Mayer Online

Dale's Website – www.dalemayer.com

Twitter – @DaleMayer

Facebook – facebook.com/DaleMayer.author

Also by Dale Mayer

Published Adult Books:

Psychic Vision Series

Tuesday's Child

Hide'n Go Seek

Maddy's Floor

Garden of Sorrow

Knock, Knock...

Rare Find

Eyes to the Soul

Now You See Her

Shattered

Into the Night...

Psychic Visions 3in1

Psychic Visions Set 4–6

Psychic Visions Set 7–9

By Death Series

Touched by Death – Part 1

Touched by Death – Part 2

Touched by Death – Parts 1&2

Haunted by Death

Chilled by Death

Second Chances...at Love Series

Second Chances – Part 1

Second Chances – Part 2

Second Chances – complete book (Parts 1 & 2)

Charmin Marvin Romantic Comedy Series

Broken Protocols

Broken Protocols 2

Broken Protocols 3

Broken Protocols 3.5

Broken Protocols 1-3

Broken and... Mending

Skin

Scars

Scales (of Justice)

Glory

Genesis

Tori

Celeste

Glory Trilogy

Biker Blues

Biker Blues: Morgan, Part 1

Biker Blues: Morgan, Part 2

Biker Blues: Morgan, Part 3

Biker Baby Blues: Morgan, Part 4

Biker Blues: Morgan, Full Set

Biker Blues: Salvation, Part 1

Biker Blues: Salvation, Part 2

Biker Blues: Salvation, Part 3

Biker Blues: Salvation, Full Set

SEALs of Honor

Mason: SEALs of Honor, Book 1

Hawk: SEALs of Honor, Book 2

Dane: SEALs of Honor, Book 3

Swede: SEALs of Honor, Book 4

Shadow: SEALs of Honor, Book 5

Cooper: SEALs of Honor, Book 6

Markus: SEALs of Honor, Book 7

Evan: SEALs of Honor, Book 8

Chase: SEALs of Honor, Book 9

Brett: SEALs of Honor, Book 10

SEALs of Honor, Books 1–3

Collections

Dare to Be You…

Dare to Love…

Dare to be Strong…

RomanceX3

Standalone Novellas

It's a Dog's Life

Riana's Revenge

Published Young Adult Books:

Family Blood Ties Series

Vampire in Denial

Vampire in Distress

Vampire in Design

Vampire in Deceit

Vampire in Defiance

Vampire in Conflict

Vampire in Chaos

Vampire in Crisis

Vampire in Control

Vampire in Charge

Family Blood Ties 3in1

Family Blood Ties set 4–6

Family Blood Ties set 7–9

Sian's Solution – A Family Blood Ties Short Story

Design series

Dangerous Designs

Deadly Designs

Darkest Designs

Design Series Trilogy

Standalone

In Cassie's Corner

Gem Stone (a Gemma Stone Mystery)

Time Thieves

Published Non-Fiction Books:

Career Essentials

Career Essentials: The Résumé

Career Essentials: The Cover Letter

Career Essentials: The Interview

Career Essentials: 3 in 1

Printed in Great Britain
by Amazon